THE
LIVING DEAD

Other books edited by John Joseph Adams

Wastelands: Stories of the Apocalypse
Seeds of Change

THE
LIVING DEAD

edited by John Joseph Adams

NIGHT SHADE BOOKS
SAN FRANCISCO

First Edition

ISBN 978-1-59780-143-0

Night Shade Books
Please visit us on the web at
http://www.nightshadebooks.com

CONTENTS

"You know Macumba? Voodoo. My granddad was a priest in Trinidad. He used to tell us, 'When there's no more room in hell, the dead will walk the earth.'"

—Ken Foree as "Peter" in George A. Romero's *Dawn of the Dead*

INTRODUCTION
by John Joseph Adams

When I first started assembling this anthology, I thought to myself: *This is not going to be the sort of book that begins with an origin of the word* zombie. Because that's not the point, is it? Zombie fiction is about the unburied dead returning to life and seeking human victims. It's about battling a frightening, implacable foe and imagining what it would be like to survive the end of the world and trying to figure out what to do when the dead won't stay dead.

Regardless of where the word actually comes from, today the word "zombie" generally refers to the sort of shambling reanimated corpses as depicted in George A. Romero's landmark film *Night of the Living Dead*. In his short fiction collection *Zombie Jam*, author David J. Schow explains the influence of Romero: "The plain fact is that the aptly-christened 'Romero zombies' have infiltrated the culture to the extent that even people who have never experienced the movies 'know' what zombies are in shortform: They're dead, they walk, they want to eat you, and they usually outnumber you."

Most of the stories in this book are either inspired by Romero's "unholy trilogy"—*Night of the Living Dead, Dawn of the Dead*, and *Day of the Dead*—or are a reaction to it. That influence is obvious in much of the fiction contained herein, and authors frequently cite seeing Romero's films as pivotal moments in their youth (and, indeed, their lives).

So why are we so drawn to zombie fiction? What's so appealing about the idea of the living dead?

John Langan, author of "How the Day Runs Down" (pg. 457), says that zombies—the post-Romero zombie that has defined our current concept of the beast—have the virtue of simplicity. "While you can trace aspects of their behavior to a host of monsters that have come before (like vampires, they rise from the dead; like ghouls and werewolves, they eat our flesh; like Frankenstein's monster, they're reanimated corpses; like most monsters, they have a particular weakness that will kill them immediately), they boil all that down to the basics: they're back from the dead, they want to eat us, they can be killed with a shot to the head," he says. "I suspect that part of their effectiveness lies in the way they present us to ourselves, by which I mean, if you think about a monster like the vampire or

1

the werewolf, you can see them as aspects of human behavior magnified and embodied; i.e. the vampire's connection to various kinds of (taboo) eroticism has been explored ad infinitum, while the werewolf's link to animal violence has also been recognized. With the zombie, what you get is *us*, pretty much as we are, maybe with a little damage, and we consume one another. No eroticism, no animal violence, just a single, overwhelming appetite. That's simultaneously very straightforward and very disturbing."

David Barr Kirtley, author of "The Skull-Faced Boy" (pg. 321), says that there are two reasons we find zombies appealing. "One, I think there's an enormous segment of our brain that's evolved for running away from packs of predators, and zombie stories give us a rare opportunity to take this primal part of our psyches out for a spin," he says. "And, two, zombies are a great metaphor. The great mass of humanity often comes across to us as unreasoningly hostile and driven to consumption, and the image of the zombie captures this perfectly."

The popularity of zombies comes from the fact that the vampire that we all loved got lost, says "The Age of Sorrow" (pg. 332) author Nancy Kilpatrick. "A lot of us miss the old resuscitated corpse, the ugly vampire, the mindless one that can't be reasoned with," she says. "I think zombies were there already and evolved from the Haitian Voodoo zombie to the Romero zombie that evolved further over the course of his film series so that the cause of zombification became different and rather than being bland slaves, they turned into full-blown predators, en masse. Most of us miss the predatory vampire. Zombies I think have ascended in popularity because they not only fill that archetypal void, but they also reflect society's fear of something overtaking us, making us less-than-human, or the victim of that less-than-human. It's especially traumatizing when less-than-human is family, friends and neighbors, but hey, strangers, in numbers, will do it for most of us—I think there's an inherent fear of mindless mobs in all of us. It's the hordes that swarm over you. Add to that our unconscious horror of our rampant consumption in the first world and it's like a hundred-thousand inhuman Pac-Men, eating everything in sight. There's not much in the horror field that terrifies me, but zombies do. Their driven, single-minded quality is both terrifying and awe-inspiring. I think it's what all sane people fear, being confronted by something/someone that has your destruction at heart and which/who can't be stopped."

And now a note about the stories that are in this book and the ones that aren't.

In the process of assembling this anthology, I read more zombie stories than you could possibly imagine, and I found more good ones than could possibly fit in one volume, even a mammoth tome like this one. So, in order to help narrow down my selections, I created a few loose guidelines for myself.

First, I wanted to avoid taking too many stories from any one source.

Second, I wanted to avoid taking too many stories from other zombie anthologies. I discovered a lot of great zombie fiction elsewhere and thought that this book would be more valuable to zombie fans if it were to collect that material. Many hardcore zombie aficionados will have already read John Skipp and Craig Spector's zombie anthologies (*Book of the Dead*, *Still Dead*, and *Mondo Zombie*) or James Lowder's Eden Studios zombie anthologies (*The Book of All Flesh*, *The Book of More Flesh*, and *The Book of Final Flesh*), so rather than reprint a large number of stories from those books, I reprinted a few from those volumes, but focused my efforts elsewhere. (And for those of you who haven't read any of those other zombie anthologies, well, go dig them up.)

Third, I deliberately didn't always choose the "obvious" story from an author. (Assuming, of course, that the stories I included instead were just as good.) For instance, I didn't reprint Joe R. Lansdale's "On the Far Side of the Cadillac Desert with Dead Folks" or David J. Schow's "Jerry's Kids Meet Wormboy" because they each have written other great zombie stories as well, and I figured if you've read one story by either of them, it would have been that one.

Fourth, I didn't want to use anything that felt like an excerpt of a larger work, so, for example, that meant omitting anything from Max Brooks's excellent zombie novel *World War Z*. (Although the novel is episodic, reading the episodes separately robs them of some of their power, I thought; instead, I'll just urge you to go buy it *right now*. Well, after you've bought *this* book.)

And finally, I wanted the anthology to include a wide range of zombie fiction, incorporating all types of zombies, from the Romero-style zombie to the techno-zombie and everything in between. So herein you will find the dead mysteriously returned to life hungering for human flesh, corpses reanimated by necromancers, corpses reanimated by technology and/or science, voodoo zombies, revenants, and other, less easily categorized zombies.

But getting back to the appeal of zombies… So what about it? Why do *you* enjoy zombie fiction? Well, whatever your reason for liking zombie stories, there are enough great zombie stories in the pages that follow to please even the most discerning zombie aficionado. So dive in and consume these stories as if they were the brains of the last human left on Earth. *Bon appétit!*

THIS YEAR'S CLASS PICTURE

by Dan Simmons

Dan Simmons is the best-selling, award-winning author of the Hyperion Cantos, the first book of which won the Hugo Award for best novel. He is also the author of many other novels including *The Terror*, the *Ilium/Olympos* duology, the World Fantasy Award-winning *Song of Kali*, and the Stoker Award-winning *Carrion Comfort*. His short fiction has also achieved great acclaim, most of which has been collected in the volumes *Prayers to Broken Stones*, *Lovedeath*, and *Worlds Enough & Time*.

"This Year's Class Picture" was the winner of three major awards: the Stoker, World Fantasy, and Theodore Sturgeon Memorial Award; its translation into Japanese also won the Seiun Award. Another translation—into French—saw the story adapted for the stage; it was produced as a play—"La Jour de la Photo de Classe"—in Paris in 2007.

This story originally appeared in the anthology *Still Dead* edited by John Skipp and Craig Spector, the second of their seminal zombie anthologies (following *Book of the Dead*). It concerns a school teacher, in a zombie-ravaged world, who deals with the return of the living dead by doing what she's always done, but with more manacles and shotguns.

Ms. Geiss watched her new student coming across the first-graders' playground from her vantage point on the balcony of the old school's belfry. She lowered the barrel of the Remington .30-06 until the child was centered in the crosshairs of the telescopic sight. The image was quite clear in the early morning light. It was a boy, not one she knew, and he looked to have been about nine or ten when he died. His green *Teenage Mutant Ninja Turtles* t-shirt had been slashed down the center and there was a spattering of dried blood along the ragged cleft. Ms. Geiss could see the white gleam of an exposed rib.

She hesitated, lifting her eye from the sight to watch the small figure lurch and stumble his way through the swing sets and around the jungle gym. His age was right, but she already had twenty-two students. More than that, she knew, and the class became difficult to manage. And today was class picture day and she did not need the extra aggravation. Plus, the child's appearance was on the borderline

4

of what she would accept in her fourth grade... especially on class picture day.

You never had that luxury before *the Tribulations,* she chided herself. She put her eye back against the plastic sunhood of the sight and grimaced slightly as she thought of the children who had been "mainstreamed" into her elementary classes over the years: deaf children, blind children, borderline autistic children, children suffering from epilepsy and Down's syndrome and hyperactivity and sexual abuse and abandonment and dyslexia and *petit mal* seizures... children dying of cancer and children dying of AIDS...

The dead child had crossed the shallow moat and was approaching the razor wire barriers that Ms. Geiss had strung around the school just where the first-graders' gravel playground adjoined the fourth-graders' paved basketball and four-square courts. She knew that the boy would keep coming and negotiate the wire no matter how many slices of flesh were torn from his body.

Sighing, already feeling tired even before the school day had formally begun, Ms. Geiss lowered the Remington, clicked on the safety, and started down the belfry ladder to go and greet her new student.

She peered in her classroom door on the way to the supply closet on the second floor. The class was restless, daylight and hunger stirring them to tug against the chains and iron collars. Little Samantha Stewart, technically too young for fourth grade, had torn her dress almost off in her nighttime struggles. Sara and Sarah J. were tangled in each other's chains. Todd, the biggest of the bunch and the former class bully, had chewed away the rubber lining of his collar again. Ms. Geiss could see flecks of black rubber around Todd's white lips and knew that the metal collar had worn away the flesh of his neck almost to the bone. She would have to make a decision about Todd soon.

On the long bulletin board behind her desk, she could see the thirty-eight class pictures she had mounted there. Thirty-eight years. Thirty-eight class pictures, all taken in this school. Starting with the thirty-second year, the photographs became much smaller as they had gone from the large format cameras the photo studio had used to the school Polaroid that Ms. Geiss had rigged to continue the tradition. The classes were also smaller. In her thirty-fifth year there had been only five students in her fourth grade. Sarah J. and Todd had been in that class—alive, pink-skinned, thin and frightened looking, but healthy. In the thirty-sixth year there were no living children... but seven students. In the next-to-last photograph, there were sixteen faces. This year, today, she would have to set the camera to get all twenty-two children in the frame. *No,* she thought, *twenty-three with the new boy.*

Ms. Geiss shook her head and walked on to the supply closet. She had fifteen minutes before the school bell was programmed to ring.

Carrying the capture pole, pliers, police handcuffs, heavy gloves, and the rubber apron from the supply closet, Ms. Geiss hurried down the broad stairway to the first floor. At the front door she checked the video monitors to make sure that the outer courtyard, walkway, and fourth-grade playground were empty except for the new boy, tied on the apron, slung the Remington over her shoulder, pulled on the gloves, unbolted the steel-reinforced door, made sure the pliers and handcuffs were reachable in the big apron pocket, lifted the capture pole, and stepped out to meet her new student.

The boy's t-shirt and jeans had been slashed even more by the razor wire. Tatters of bloodless flesh hung from his forearms. As Ms. Geiss moved out into the sunlight, he raised his dead face and dulled eyes in her direction. His teeth were yellow.

Ms. Geiss held her breath as the boy lurched and scrabbled in her direction. It was not because of his smell; she was used to the roadkill scent of the children. This new boy was a bit worse than most of her students, not quite as bad as Todd. His trousers were soaked with gasoline from wading the moat at the edge of the school ground and the gasoline smell drove away some of his stench. She found herself holding her breath because even after all these months… *years*, she realized… there was still a certain tension in meeting a new student.

The boy lurched the last fifteen feet toward her across the courtyard cement. Ms. Geiss steadied herself and raised the capture pole.

At one time the capture pole had been a seven-foot wood-and-brass rod for raising and lowering the tall upper windows in the old school. Ms. Geiss had modified it by mounting a heavy fishing reel wound about with heavy-duty baling wire, adding eyelets to guide the wire, and jury-rigging a device on the end to lock off the double-thick loop. She'd gotten the idea from watching old videos of *Mutual of Omaha's Wild Kingdom*. Whatshisname, the big, handsome fellow who'd done all of the work… Jim… had used a similar device to catch rattlesnakes.

This poor child is more deadly than any rattlesnake, thought Ms. Geiss. And then she concentrated totally on the capture.

There were no problems. The child lunged. Ms. Geiss dropped the double loop of wire over his head, released the catch to tighten the noose, and locked it in. The wire sank deep into the boy's throat but was too thick to slice flesh. If he had been breathing, the noose would have strangled him, but that was no longer a concern.

Ms. Geiss took a step forward and the boy lurched, staggered, swung his arms, and went over backward, his head striking concrete with a sickening, soft-melon sound. The teacher checked over her shoulder to make sure the courtyard and playground were still clear, and then she pinned the flailing child, first with the extended capture pole, and then with her foot. The boy's fingernails scrabbled against the thick leather of her high boot.

With a practiced motion, Ms. Geiss dropped the pole, secured the child's wrists with one gloved hand, handcuffed him with her free hand, and sat on his chest, tucking her print dress in as she did so. Ms. Geiss weighed one hundred and ninety-five pounds, and there was no question of the child escaping. With a critical eye she assessed his wounds: the chest wound had been the fatal one and it looked as if it had been administered by a meat cleaver or long knife; the other gashes, tears, bites, and a single bullet wound high on the child's shoulder had all been added after he was dead.

Ms. Geiss nodded as if satisfied, pried back the wriggling child's lips as if inspecting a horse, and pulled his teeth with the pair of pliers. The boy made no outcry. She noticed that flies had lain eggs in the corner of his eyes and she made a mental note to take care of that during cleanup.

Shifting her weight only slightly, the teacher reversed position on the boy's chest, lifted his bound wrists, and efficiently pulled his fingernails off with the pliers. The only blood was in the dried and matted substance under his nails.

The child was snapping at her like an angry turtle, but his gums would never have penetrated skin, much less Ms. Geiss's rubber Wellingtons and the corduroy trousers she wore under the dress.

She glanced over her shoulder again. Months ago she had been surprised by five of them—all adults—who had come soundlessly through the wire while she had been watching the children at recess, and there had been only six cartridges in the Remington. One of the head shots had been a near miss; she had corrected her aim when the lurching man was only four feet from her, and the adrenaline of that encounter kept her vigilant.

The playground was empty. Ms. Geiss grunted, pulled the new boy to his feet with the wire noose, opened the door with one hand, and shoved him in ahead of her with the pole. There would be just enough time for cleanup before the first bell rang.

The first thing on the morning's agenda was writing the schedule on the chalkboard. Ms. Geiss had always done that to show the children what they would be doing and learning that day.

The first thing on the written schedule was the Pledge of Allegiance. Ms. Geiss decided that she would go ahead with that and introduce the new boy after it. He sat now in the third from the last desk in the row closest to the windows. Ms. Geiss had taken the handcuffs off, clipped on the leg manacles that were bolted to the floor, run the waist chain around him, attached it to the long chain that ran the length of the desks, and set his iron collar in place. The boy had flailed at her, his dead eyes glimmering for a second with something that might have been hunger, but a child's arms were simply too short to do damage to an adult.

Even before the Tribulations, Ms. Geiss had smiled when she watched movies or television shows where children used judo or karate to flip adults around the room. From her many years' experience, she knew that simple laws of mechanics meant that a child's punch was usually harmless. They simply didn't have the mass, arm length, and leverage to do much damage. With the new boy's teeth and claws pulled, Ms. Geiss could handle him without the capture pole or chains if she wished.

She did not so wish. She treated the children with the distance and respect for contamination she had shown her one HIV-positive child back before the Tribulations.

Pledge of Allegiance time. She looked at her class of twenty-three children. A few were standing and straining toward her, clanking their chains, but most were sprawled across the desks or leaning from their seats as if they could escape by crawling across the floor. Ms. Geiss shook her head and threw the large switch on her desk. The six twelve-volt batteries were arranged in series, their cable leads connected to the gang chain which ran from desk to desk. She actually saw sparks and smelled the ozone.

The electricity did not hurt them, of course. Nothing could hurt these children. But something in the voltage did galvanize them, much as Galvani's original experiments had activated frog legs into kicking even though the legs were separated from the frogs' bodies.

The students spasmed, twitched, and lurched upright with a great clanking of chains. They rose to their toes as if trying to rise above the voltage flowing into their lower bodies. Their hands splayed and curled spasmodically in front of their chests. Some opened their mouths as if screaming silently.

Ms. Geiss put her hand over her heart and faced the flag above the doorway. "I pledge allegiance to the flag," she began, "of the United States of America…"

She introduced the new boy as Michael. He had no identification on him, of course, and Ms. Geiss was sure that he had not attended this school before the Tribulations, but there were no other Michaels in the class and the boy looked as if he might have been a Michael. The class paid no attention to the introduction. Neither did Michael.

Mathematics was the first class after the Pledge. Ms. Geiss left the class alone long enough to go downstairs, check the row of video monitors, and get the learning rewards from the long row of open freezers in the downstairs hall. She had scavenged the freezers from the Safeway last year. Donnie had helped. Ms. Geiss blinked twice when she thought of Donnie, her friend and the former custodian. Donnie had helped with so many things… without him she could never have managed the work of processing the learning rewards out at the chicken nugget plant on the edge of town… or wiring the Radio Shack video cameras and monitors. If only Donnie hadn't stopped to help that truck filled with refugees that had broken down just off the Interstate…

Ms. Geiss shook off her reverie, adjusted the sling of the Remington, and carried the box of learning rewards to the teachers' lounge. She set the microwave for three minutes.

The smell of the heated nuggets set the students into clanking, lurching agitation when she entered the classroom. Ms. Geiss set the reward box on the table near her desk and went to the chalkboard to start the math lesson.

Thank God Donnie knew how to handle the chicken nugget processing equipment out at the plant, she thought as she wrote numerals from 0 to 10.

The children, of course, would not have eaten chicken nuggets. The children, as with all of those who had returned during the Tribulations, had a taste for only one thing.

Ms. Geiss glanced at the tray of heated nuggets. Against her will, the smell made her own mouth water. Somewhere in one of those freezer boxes, she knew, were the deep-fried and nugget-processed remains of Mister Delmonico, the former principal, as well as at least half the former staff of the elementary school. It had been Donnie who had realized that the spate of suicides in the small town should not go to waste; it had been Donnie who remembered the chicken nugget plant and the large freezers there. It had been Donnie who had seen how useful it would be to have some nuggets with one when encountering a wandering pack of the hungry undead. Donnie had said that it was like the way burglars brought a rare steak along to distract guard dogs.

But it had been Ms. Geiss who saw the potential of the nuggets as learning rewards. And in her humble opinion, the overbearing Mr. Delmonico and the other lazy staff members had never served the cause of education as well as they were doing now.

"One," said Ms. Geiss, pointing to the large numeral she had drawn on the board. She raised one finger. "Say 'one.'"

Todd chewed at the new rubber ring Ms. Geiss had set in his collar. Kirsten tripped over her chain and went facedown on the desk. Little Samantha clawed at her own clothes. Justin, still chubby ten months after his death, gummed the plastic back of the seat in front of him. Megan lurched against the chains. Michael had twisted himself around until he was staring at the back of the room.

"One," repeated Ms. Geiss, still pointing to the numeral on the chalkboard. "If you can't say it, hold up *one* hand. One. One."

John snapped his toothless gums in a wet, regular rhythm. Behind him, Abigail sat entirely motionless except for the slow in-and-out of her dry tongue. David batted his face over and over against the lid of his desk. Sara chewed on the white tips of bones protruding from her fingers while behind her, Sarah J. suddenly thrust her hand up, one finger striking her eye and staying there.

Ms. Geiss did not hesitate. "Very *good*, Sarah," she said and hurried down the row between groping hands and smacking mouths. She popped the nugget in Sarah J.'s slack mouth and stepped back quickly.

"One!" said Ms. Geiss. "Sarah raised *one* finger."

All the students were straining toward the nugget tray. Sarah J.'s finger was still embedded in her eye.

Ms. Geiss stepped back to the chalkboard. In her heart, she knew that the child's spasmodic reaction had been random. It did not matter, she told herself. Given enough time and positive reinforcement, the connections will be made. Look at Helen Keller and her teacher, Annie Sullivan. And that was with a totally blind and deaf child who had had only a few months of language before the darkness descended on her. That one baby word—*wa-wa*—had allowed Helen, years later, to learn everything.

And these children had possessed *years* of language and thought before…

Before they died, completed Ms. Geiss. *Before their minds and memories and personalities unraveled like a skein of rotten thread.*

Ms. Geiss sighed and touched the next numeral. "Two," she said cheerily. "Anyone show me… show me any way you can… show me *two*."

After her own lunch and while the students were resting after their feeding time, Ms. Geiss continued with the bulldozing of houses.

At first she thought that isolating the school grounds with the moat and razor wire, lighting it with the searchlights at night, and installing the video monitors had been enough. But *they* still got through.

Luckily, the town was small—fewer than three thousand—and it was almost forty miles to a real city. Now that the Tribulations had separated the quick and the dead, there were almost none of the former and few of the latter left in the area. A few cars filled with terrified living refugees roared through town, but most never left the Interstate and in recent months the sound of passing vehicles had all but stopped. A few of *them* filtered in—from the countryside, from the distant city, from their graves—and they were drawn to the generator-powered searchlights like moths to a flame, but the school's thick walls, steel-mesh screens, and warning devices always kept them out until morning. And in the morning, the Remington solved the problem.

Still, Ms. Geiss wanted a clearer field of fire—what Donnie had once called an "uncompromised killing zone." She had reminded Donnie that the term "killing zone" was a misnomer, since they were not killing anything, merely returning the things to their natural state.

And so Ms. Geiss had driven out to the line shack near the unfinished section of the Interstate and come back with the dynamite, blasting caps, detonators, priming cord, and a Caterpillar D-7 bulldozer. Ms. Geiss had never driven a bulldozer, never exploded dynamite, but there were manuals at the line shack, and books in the Carnegie Library. Ms. Geiss had always been amazed at people's ignorance of how much knowledge and useful information there was in books.

Now, with a half hour left in her lunch break, she entered the bulldozer's open-sided shelter, climbed up onto the wide seat of the D-7, disengaged the clutch lever, set the speed selector to neutral, pushed the governor control to the firewall, stood on the right steering wheel and locked it in position with a clamp, made sure that the gears were in neutral, and reached for the starter controls. She paused to make sure that the Remington .30-06 was secure in the clamp that had once held a fire extinguisher near her right hand. Visibility was better with the houses in a three-block radius of the school blown apart this way, but there were still too many foundations and heaps of rubble that the things could hide behind. She could see nothing moving.

Ms. Geiss set the transmission and compression levers to their correct settings, pushed the starting-engine clutch in, opened a fuel valve, set the choke, dropped the idling latch, clicked on the ignition switch, and pulled the lever that engaged the electric starter.

The D-7 roared into life, black diesel smoke blowing from the vertical exhaust pipe. Ms. Geiss adjusted the throttle, let the clutch out, and gave traction to just the right tread so that the massive 'dozer spun to its left and headed for the largest pile of rubble.

An adult corpse scrabbled out of a collapsed basement on her right and clawed across bricks toward her. The thing's hair was matted back with white dust, its teeth broken but sharp. One eye was gone. Ms. Geiss thought that she recognized it as Todd's stepfather—the drunkard who used to beat the boy every Friday night.

It raised its arms and came at her.

Ms. Geiss glanced at the Remington, decided against it. She gave traction to the left treads, swung the bulldozer smartly to the right, and lowered the big blade just as she opened the throttle up. The lower edge of the blade caught the staggering corpse just above its beltline. Ms. Geiss dropped the blade once, twice, stopping the third time only when the corpse was cut in half. The legs spasmed uselessly, but fingers clawed at steel and began pulling the upper half of the thing onto the blade.

Ms. Geiss pulled levers, got the machine in reverse, put it back in low gear, lowered the blade, and bulldozed half a ton of rubble over both halves of the twitching corpse as she shoved the mass of debris back into the basement. It took less than a minute to move another ton of rubble over the hole. Then she backed up, checked to make sure that no other things were around, and began filling in the basement in earnest.

When she was done, she stepped down and walked across the area; it was flat and smooth as a gravel parking lot. Todd's stepfather might still be twitching and clawing down there, at least his upper half, but with twelve tons of rubble packed and compacted over him, he wasn't going anywhere.

Ms. Geiss only wished that she could have done this to all the drunk and abusive fathers and stepfathers she'd known over the decades.

She mopped her face with a handkerchief and checked her watch. Three minutes until reading class began. Ms. Geiss surveyed the flattened city blocks, interrupted by only a few remaining piles of rubble or collapsed foundations. Another week and her field of fire would be uninterrupted. Stopping to catch her breath, feeling her sixty-plus years in the arthritic creak of her joints, Ms. Geiss climbed back aboard the D-7 to fire it up and park it in its shelter for the night.

Ms. Geiss read aloud to her class. Each afternoon in the lull after her lunch and the students' feeding time, she read from books she knew that they had either read in their short lifetimes or had had read to them. She read from *Goodnight Moon, Pat the Bunny, Gorilla, Heidi, Bunnicula, Superfudge, Black Beauty, Richard Scarry's ABC Book, Green Eggs and Ham, Tom Sawyer, Animal Sounds, Harold and the Purple Crayon, Peter Rabbit, Polar Express, Where the Wild Things Are,* and *Tales of a Fourth Grade Nothing.* And while Ms. Geiss read she watched for the slightest flicker of recognition, of interest… of life in those dead eyes.

And saw nothing.

As the weeks and months passed, Ms. Geiss read from the children's favorite series: *Curious George* books, and *Madeleine* books, and the *Black Stallion* series, *Ramona* books, the *Berenstain Bears,* and *Clifford* books, and—despite the fact that priggish, politically correct librarians had tried to remove them from the children's public library shelves not long before the Tribulations began—*The Bobbsey Twins* and *The Hardy Boys* and *Nancy Drew.*

And the students did not respond.

On rainy days, days when the clouds hung low and Ms. Geiss's spirits hung lower, she would sometimes read to them from the Bible, or from her favorite Shakespeare plays—usually the comedies but occasionally *Romeo and Juliet* or *Hamlet*—and sometimes she would read from her favorite poet, John Keats. But after the dance of words, after the last echo of beauty had faded, Ms. Geiss would look up and no intelligent gaze would be looking back. There would be only the dead eyes, the slack faces, the open mouths, the aimless, mindless stirrings, and the soft stench of rank flesh.

It was not too dissimilar from her years of teaching live children.

This afternoon Ms. Geiss read what she always thought of as their favorite, *Goodnight Moon,* enjoying as she went the lilt and litany of the small ceremony of the young rabbit's endless goodnights to everything in his room as he attempted to put off the inevitable moment of sleep. Ms. Geiss finished the little book and looked up quickly, trying, as always, to catch the flicker in the eye, the animation in the muscles around mouth or eye.

Slackness. Vacuity. They had ears but did not hear.

Ms. Geiss sighed softly. "We'll do geography before recess," she said.

The projected slides were brilliant in the darkened room. The Capitol dome in Washington. The St. Louis Arch. The Space Needle in Seattle. The World Trade Center.

"Hold up your hand when you see a city you know," said Ms. Geiss over the whirring of the projector's fan. "Make a motion when you see something familiar."

The Chicago Lakefront. Denver with mountains rising in the background. Bourbon Street and Mardi Gras time. The Golden Gate Bridge.

The slides clicked past in Kodachrome splendor. The children stirred sluggishly, just beginning to respond to the first stirrings of renewed hunger. No one raised a hand. No one seemed to notice the bright image of the Brooklyn Bridge on the screen.

New York, thought Ms. Geiss, remembering the September day twenty-seven years earlier when she had taken the photograph. The first invigorating breezes of autumn had made them wear sweaters as she and Mr. Farnham, the science coordinator she had met at the NEA convention, had walked across the pedestrian deck of the Brooklyn Bridge. They had gone to the Metropolitan Museum of Art and then walked in Central Park. The rustle of every leaf had seemed audible and separate to Ms. Geiss's heightened senses on that perfect afternoon. They had almost kissed when he dropped her at the Hotel Barbizon that evening after dinner at the River Cafe. He had promised to call her. It was only months later that Ms. Geiss had heard from a teacher friend from Connecticut that Mr. Farnham was married, had been married for twenty years.

The children rustled their chains.

"Raise an arm if you recognize New York City from the pictures," said Ms. Geiss tiredly. No arm was raised into the bright beam of the projection lamp. Ms. Geiss tried to imagine New York City now, years after the onset of the Tribulations. Any survivors there would be food for the hundreds of thousands, the *millions* of flesh-hungry, unclean creatures that had inherited those filthy streets...

Ms. Geiss advanced rapidly through the remaining slides: San Diego, the Statue of Liberty, a bright curve of Hawaiian beach, Monhegan Island in the morning fog, Las Vegas at night... all places she had seen in her wonderful summers, all places she would never see again.

"That's all the geography for today," said Ms. Geiss and switched off the projector. The students seemed agitated in the darkness. "Recess time," said their teacher.

Ms. Geiss knew that they did not need exercise. Their dead muscles would not atrophy if they were not used. The brilliant spring daylight only made the children seem more obscene in their various stages of decomposition.

But Ms. Geiss could not imagine keeping fourth graders in class all day without a recess.

She led them outside, still attached to their four gang chains, and secured the ends of the chains to the iron rods she had driven into the gravel and asphalt playgrounds. The children lurched this way and that, finally coming to a stop, straining at the end of their tethers like small, scabrous, child-shaped balloons waiting for the Macy's parade to begin. No child paid attention to another. A few leaned in Ms. Geiss's direction, toothless gums smacking as if in anticipation, but the sight and sound of that was so common that Ms. Geiss felt neither threat nor alarm.

She wandered farther out across the fourth-graders' playground, threaded her way through the winding exit maze she had left in the razor wire, crossed the gravel expanse of the first-graders' playground, and stopped only when she reached the moat she had dug around the small city block the old school and its playgrounds occupied. Ms. Geiss called it a moat; the military-engineering manuals she had found in the stacks of the Carnegie Library called it a tank trap. But the specifications for a tank trap called for a ditch at least eight feet deep and thirty feet wide, with berms rising at an angle of 45 degrees. Ms. Geiss had used the D-7 to dig a moat half that deep and wide, with the slowly eroding banks no greater than twenty degrees. However the dead would come at her, she thought, it was improbable that they would be driving tanks.

The gasoline was a touch she garnered from an old article on Iraqi defenses during the Gulf War. Finding the gasoline was no problem—Donnie had commandeered a large tanker truck to borrow gas from the underground Texaco tanks to power the generator he and she had set up in the school—but keeping the fuel in the moat from soaking into the soil had been a puzzler until Ms. Geiss had thought of the huge sheets of black poly left out at the highway department depot.

She looked down at the tepid moat of gasoline now, thinking how silly this self-defense measure had been… like the spotlights on the school, or the video cameras.

But it had kept her busy.

Like pretending to teach these poor lost souls? Ms. Geiss shook away the thought and walked back to the playground, raising her whistle to her lips to signify the end of recess. None of the students reacted to the whistle, but Ms. Geiss blew it anyway. It was tradition.

She took them to the art room to shoot the pictures. She did not know why the studio used to take the pictures there—the color would have been infinitely better if they had posed the children outside—but the photo had been taken in the art room for as long as anyone could remember, the students lined up—shortest in the front rows even though the front rows were kneeling—everyone posed under the huge ceramic map of the United States, each state made of fired, brown clay and set in place by some art class half a century or more ago. The corners of the ceramic states had curled up and out of alignment as if some seismic event was tearing the nation apart. Texas had fallen out eight or nine years ago and the pieces were glued in without great care, making the state look like a federation of smaller states.

Ms. Geiss had never liked Texas. She had been a girl when President Kennedy was killed in Texas, and in her opinion things had gone to hell in the country ever since then.

She led the children in by rows, slipped the end of their gang chains over the radiator, set a warmed pan of learning rewards on the floor between the camera and the class, checked to make sure the film pack she had put in that morning was advanced properly, set the timer, moved quickly to stand next to Todd—straining, as the other students were straining, to get at the nuggets—and tried to smile as the timer hissed and the shutter clicked.

She shot two more Polaroid pictures and only glanced at them before setting them in the pocket of her apron. Most of the children were facing front. That was good enough.

There were ten minutes left in the school day by the time she had the class tethered in their seats again, but Ms. Geiss could not bring herself to do a spelling list or to read aloud again or even to force crayons in their hands and set the butcher paper out. She sat and stared at them, feeling the fatigue and sense of uselessness as a heavy weight on her shoulders.

The students stared in her direction… or at least in the direction of the pan of cooling nuggets.

At three P.M. the dismissal bell rang, Ms. Geiss went up the wide aisles tossing nuggets to the children, and then she turned out the lights, bolted the door shut, and left the classroom for the day.

It is morning and there is a richness of light Ms. Geiss has not noticed for years. As she moves to the chalkboard to write the class's assignments next to the schedule chalked there, she notices that she is much younger. She is wearing the dress she had worn the morning she and Mr. Farnham walked across the Brooklyn Bridge.

"Please get your reading books out," she says softly. "*Green Salad Seasons* group, bring your books and comprehension quiz sheets up front. *Mystery Sneaker,* I'll take a look at your vocabulary words when we're finished here. *Sprint,* please copy the Skillsbook assignment and be ready to come up front at ten-fifteen to answer questions. Anyone who finishes early may get a Challenge Pack from the interest center."

The children scatter quietly to their assigned tasks. The group at the front table read with Ms. Geiss and answer questions quietly while the other children work with that soft, almost subliminal hum that is the universal background noise of a good classroom.

While the *Green Salad Seasons* group writes answers to questions at the end of the story, Ms. Geiss walks among the other children.

Sara wears a kerchief in the form of a cap. The knots protrude like tiny rabbit ears. Normally Ms. Geiss does not allow caps or kerchiefs to be worn in the classroom, but Sara has undergone chemotherapy and has lost her hair. The class does not tease her about it, not even Todd.

Now Sara leans over her Skillsbook and squints at the questions there. Occasionally she chews at the eraser on the end of her pencil. She is nine years old. Her eyes are blue and her complexion is as milkily translucent as a shard of expensive porcelain. Her cheeks seem touched with a healthy blush, and it is only upon closer inspection that one can see that this is a soft pass of makeup that her mother has applied, that Sara is still pale and wan from her illness.

Ms. Geiss stops by the child's desk. "Problem, Sara?"

"I don't understand this." Sara stabs a finger at a line of instructions. Her fingernails are as chewed as the eraser on her pencil.

"It says to find the proper prefix and put it before the word," whispers Ms. Geiss. Up front, Kirsten is sharpening a pencil with a loud grinding. The class looks up as Kirsten blows shavings off into the waste basket, carefully inspects the point, and begins the grinding again.

"What's a prefix?" Sara whispers back.

Ms. Geiss leans closer. The two are temporarily joined in a bond of conspiracy produced by their proximity and the hypnotic background hum of classroom activity. Ms. Geiss can feel the warmth from the girl's cheek near hers.

"You remember what a prefix is," says Ms. Geiss and proceeds to show the girl.

She returns to the front table just as *Green Salad Seasons,* her top group, leaves for their desks and *Sprint,* her small remedial group, comes forward. There are only six students in *Sprint* and four of them are boys.

"David," she says, "can you tell me how the dolphin both helped and hurt the boy?"

David frowns as if in deep thought and chews on the wood of his pencil. His Skillsbook page is blank.

"Todd," says Ms. Geiss, "can you tell us?"

Todd turns fierce eyes in her direction. The boy always seems distracted, involved in some angry internal argument. "Tell you what?"

"Tell us how the dolphin both helped and hurt the boy?"

Todd begins to shrug but avoids the motion at the last moment. Ms. Geiss has broken him of that habit by patient and positive reinforcement—praise, extra classroom duties if he can get through the day without shrugging, a Good Scholar Certificate to take home at the end of the week. "It saved him," says Todd.

"Very good," says Ms. Geiss with a smile. "Saved him from what?"

"From the shark," says Todd. His hair is uncombed and unwashed, his neck grubby, but his eyes are bright blue and angrily alive.

"And how did it almost hurt the boy?" asks Ms. Geiss, looking around the small group to see who should participate next.

"They're coming, Ms. Geiss," Todd says loudly.

She glances back at her biggest student, preparing to warn him about interrupting, but what she sees freezes her before she can speak.

Todd's eyes are suddenly vacuous, sunken, and clouded white. His skin has become the color and texture of a dead fish's belly. His teeth are gone and his gums are a desiccated blue. Todd opens his mouth wider and suddenly it is not a mouth at all, but just a hole excavated into a dead thing's face. The voice that emerges rises out of the thing's belly like a tinny recording echoing in some obscene doll.

"Quick, Ms. Geiss, they're coming to hurt us. Wake up!"

Ms. Geiss sat up in bed, heart racing, gasping for breath. She found her glasses on her nightstand, set them in place, and peered around the room.

Everything was in order. Bright light from the external spotlights came through the blinds in the tall window and painted white rectangles on the floor of the upstairs classroom she had modified as her bed-and-living room. Ms. Geiss listened hard over the pounding of her pulse but heard nothing unusual from the classroom below her. There were no noises from outside. The silent row of video monitors near her couch showed the empty hallways, the light-bathed courtyard, the empty playgrounds. The closest monitor showed the dark classroom: the students stood or sprawled or leaned or strained at chains. They were all accounted for.

Just a dream, Ms. Geiss told herself. *Go back to sleep.*

Instead she rose, pulled her quilted robe on over her flannel nightgown, tied her rubber apron on over that, stepped into her boots, lifted the Remington, found the bulky pair of night-vision goggles that Donnie had brought from the city surplus store, and went out to climb the wide ladder to the belfry.

Ms. Geiss stepped out onto the narrow platform that ran around the belfry. She could see in all four directions and only a bit of the east yard of the school was blocked by the front gable. The spotlights reached across the playgrounds and moat and illuminated the first rows of bulldozed rubble where surrounding houses had been. Nothing moved.

The teacher yawned and shook her head. The night air was chill; she could see her breath. *I'm getting too old to spook myself like this. There's more threat from the bands of refugees than from the adult dead things.*

She turned to go down the ladder, but at the last second paused by the junction box she and Donnie had rigged there. Sighing softly, she threw the switch that doused the spotlights and then fumbled with the night vision goggles. They were bulky, clumsy to fit on her head, and she could not wear her glasses under them. Also, she always felt like she looked like an idiot with the things on her head. Still, Donnie had risked a trip to the city to get them. She moved her glasses up on her forehead and tugged the goggles down.

She turned and froze. Things moved to the west, just beyond where the blaze of spotlights had reached. Pale blobs moved through the rubble there, rising out of basements and spider holes in the rubble-strewn lots. Ms. Geiss could tell that they were dead by the way they stumbled and rose again, faltering at obstacles but never failing to come on again. There were twenty… no, at least thirty tall forms moving toward the school.

She turned to the north. Another thirty or more figures moving there, almost to the street. To the east, more figures moving, already within a stone's throw of the moat. Still more to the south.

There were more than a hundred of the dead approaching the school.

Ms. Geiss tugged off the goggles and sat on the edge of the ladder, lowering her head almost to her knees so that the black spots in her vision receded and she could breathe again.

They've never organized like this. Never come all at once.

She felt her heart lurch, shudder, and then commence pounding again.

I didn't think there were that many of the things left around here. How…

Part of her mind was screaming at her to quit theorizing and do something. *They're coming for the children!*

It made no sense. The dead ate only living flesh… or the flesh of things recently living. It should be *her* they were after. But the terrible conviction remained: *They want the children.*

Ms. Geiss had protected her children for thirty-eight years. She had protected them from the worst of life's sharp edges, allowing them to have the safest and most productive year she could provide. She had protected her children from each other, from the bullies and mean-spirited amongst themselves; she had protected them from callous, stupid administrators; she had shielded them from the vagaries of ill-formed curriculum and faddish district philosophies. Ms. Geiss had, as well as she was able, protected her fourth graders from the tyrannies of too-early adulthood and the vulgarities of a society all too content with the vulgar.

She had protected them—with all her faculties and force of will—from being beaten, kidnapped, emotionally abused or sexually molested by the monsters who had hidden in the form of parents, step-parents, uncles, and friendly strangers.

And now these dead things were coming for her children.

Ms. Geiss went down the ladder with her apron and quilted robe flapping.

Ms. Geiss did not have any idea why there had been a flare pistol in the highway storage depot in the room next to where she had found the blasting caps, but she had appropriated the pistol. There had been only three flares, heavy things that looked like oversized shotgun shells. She had never fired one.

Now she hurried back to the belfry with the flare pistol in her hand and the three flares in her apron pocket. She had also grabbed four boxes of .30-06 cartridges.

Some of the dead things were still a hundred yards away from the playground, but others were already wading the moat.

Ms. Geiss extracted a flare from the apron, opened the pistol, and fumbled to set the cartridge in. She forced herself to stop and take a breath. The night goggles were hanging around her neck, heavy as an albatross. *Where are my glasses? What did I do with my glasses?*

She reached up into her hair, pulled her bifocals down, took another breath, and dropped the flare cartridge into the pistol. She clicked the breech shut and threw the spotlight switch, flooding the playgrounds with white light.

A dozen or more of the things were across the moat. Scores more were almost to the street on each side.

Ms. Geiss raised the flare gun in both hands, shut her eyes, and squeezed the trigger. The flare arched too high and fell a dozen yards short of the moat. It burned redly on gravel. A naked corpse with exposed shinbones gleaming stepped over the flare and continued lurching toward the school. Ms. Geiss reloaded, lowered her aim, and fired toward the west.

This time the flare struck the banked mud on the far side of the moat and dropped out of sight. The red glare sizzled for a second and then faded. A dozen more pale forms waded the shallow barrier.

Ms. Geiss loaded the final flare. Suddenly there was a *wooosh* like a wind from nowhere and a stretch of the western moat went up in flames. There was a lull and then the flames leaped north and south, turning the corner like a clever display of falling dominoes. Ms. Geiss moved to the east side of the belfry catwalk and watched as the fire leaped along the moat until the school was in the center of a giant rectangle of thirty-foot flames. Even from fifty yards away she could feel the heat against her face. She dropped the flare gun into her large apron pocket.

The two dozen or so figures that had already crossed the moat lumbered across the playground. Several went down in the razor wire, but then ripped their way free and continued on.

Ms. Geiss looked at her hands. They were no longer shaking. Carefully she loaded the Remington until the magazine was full. Then she rigged the rifle's sling the way the books had shown, set her elbows firmly on the railing, took a deep breath, and set her eye to the telescopic sight. With the flames still burning, she would not have needed the searchlights. She found the first moving figure, set the crosshairs on its temple, and slowly squeezed the trigger. Then she moved her aim to the next form.

At the edge of the playground, the other things were crossing the moat despite the flames. It appeared that none had turned back. Incredibly, a few came through charred but intact; most emerged burning like fuel-primed torches, the flames shimmering around their forms in parallel waves of orange and black. They continued forward long after rotted clothes and rotted flesh had burned away almost to the bone. Even half-deafened by the report of the Remington, Ms. Geiss could hear the distant *pops* as cerebral fluid, superheated into steam by the burning corpse beneath it, exploded skulls like fragmentation grenades. Then the figure collapsed and added its pyre to the illumination.

Ms. Geiss shifted her aim, fired, checked over the sight to make sure the thing had gone down and stayed down, found another target, aimed, and fired again. After three shots she would shift along the balcony to a different quadrant, brace herself, and choose her targets. She reloaded five times.

When she was finished, there were over a hundred forms lying on the playground. Some were still burning. All were still.

But she could hear the crashing and rattling of steel mesh where more of the things had gotten through, especially on the east side of the school. The gable there had blocked her line of fire. Thirty or more of the things had gotten to the school and were tearing at window screens and the reinforced doors.

Ms. Geiss raised the collar of her robe and wiped her face. There was soot there from the smoke and she was surprised to see that her eyes were watering. Slinging the Remington, Ms. Geiss went down the ladder and went to her room. Donnie's 9mm Browning automatic pistol was in the drawer where she had put it on the day she had cremated him. It was loaded. There were two additional magazines and a yellow box of additional cartridges in the drawer.

Ms. Geiss put the box and magazines in her apron pocket, hefted the pistol, and went down the wide stairway to the first floor.

In the end, it was exhaustion that almost killed her.

She had fired all three of the magazines, reloaded once, and was sure that none of the things were left when she sat down on the front walk to rest.

The last corpse had been a tall man with a long beard. She had aimed the Browning from five feet away and put the last round through the thing's left eye. The thing had gone down as if its strings had been cut. Ms. Geiss collapsed herself, sitting heavily on the sidewalk, too exhausted and disgusted even to go back through the front door.

The flames in the moat had burned down below ground level. Smaller heaps added their smoke and glow to air already filled with a dark haze. A score of sprawled forms littered the front steps and sidewalk. Ms. Geiss wanted to weep but was too tired to do anything but lower her head and take deep, slow breaths, trying to filter out the stench of cooked carrion.

The bearded corpse in front of her lunged up and scrabbled across the six feet of sidewalk to her, fingers clawing.

Ms. Geiss had time to think *The bullet struck bone, missed the brain* and the thing had batted away the Browning and forced her backward, pinning the slung rifle under her. Her glasses were knocked off her face as the thing's cold fingers ripped at her. Its mouth began to descend, as if offering her a lipless, open-mouthed kiss.

Ms. Geiss's right hand was pinned but her left was free; she scrabbled in her apron pocket, scattering loose bullets, finding and discarding the pliers, finally emerging with something heavy in her grip.

The dead thing lunged to bite off her face, to chew its way through to her brain. Ms. Geiss set the cartoon-wide muzzle of the flare pistol in its maw, thumbed the hammer back, and squeezed the trigger.

Most of the fires were out by sunrise, but the air smelled of smoke and corruption. Ms. Geiss shuffled her way down the hall, unbolted the classroom, and stood looking at the class.

The students were uncharacteristically quiet, as if they had somehow been aware of the night's events.

Ms. Geiss did not notice. Feeling exhaustion breaking over her like a wave, she fumbled with clasps, undid their neck and waist restraints, and led them outside by the gang chains. She pulled them through the gaps in the razor wire as if she were walking a pack of blind and awkward dogs.

At the edge of the playground she unlocked their iron collars, unclasped them from the gang chains, and dropped the chains in the gravel. The small forms stumbled about as if seeking the balance of the end of their tethers.

"School is out," Ms. Geiss said tiredly. The rising sun threw long shadows and hurt her eyes. "Go away," she whispered. "Go home."

She did not look back as she trudged through the wire and into the school.

For what seemed like a long while the teacher sat at her desk, too tired to move, too tired to go upstairs to sleep. The classroom seemed empty in a way that only empty classrooms could.

After a while, when the sunlight had crawled across the varnished wood floors almost to her desk, Ms. Geiss started to rise but her bulky apron got in her way. She took off the apron and emptied the pockets onto her desktop: pliers, a yellow cartridge box, the 9mm Browning she had retrieved, the handcuffs she had taken off Michael yesterday, more loose bullets, three Polaroid snapshots. Ms. Geiss glanced at the first snapshot and then sat down suddenly.

She raised the photograph into the light, inspected it carefully, and then did the same with the next two.

Todd was smiling at the camera. There was no doubt. It was not a grimace or a spasm or a random twitch of dead lips. Todd was staring right at the camera and smiling—showing only gums, it was true—but smiling.

Ms. Geiss looked more carefully and realized that Sara was also looking at the camera. In the first snapshot she had been looking at the food nuggets, but in the second photograph…

There was a sliding, scraping sound in the hallway.

My God, I forgot to close the west door. Ms. Geiss carefully set the photographs down and lifted the Browning. The magazine was loaded, a round was racked in the chamber.

The scraping and sliding continued. Ms. Geiss set the pistol on her lap and waited.

Todd entered first. His face was as slack as ever, but his eyes held… something. Sara came in next. Kirsten and David came through a second later. One after the other, they shuffled into the room.

Ms. Geiss felt too tired to lift her arms. She knew that despite her musings on the ineffectuality of children's hands and arms as weapons, twenty-three of them would simply overwhelm her like an incoming tide. She did not have twenty-three cartridges left.

It did not matter. Ms. Geiss knew that she would never hurt these children. She set the pistol on the desk.

The children continued to struggle into the room. Sarah J. came through after Justin. Michael brought up the rear. All twenty-three were here. They milled and stumbled and jostled. There were no chains.

Ms. Geiss waited.

Todd found his seat first. He collapsed into it, then pulled himself upright. Other children tripped and bumped against one another, but eventually found their places. Their eyes rolled, their gazes wandered, but all of them were looking approximately forward, more or less at Ms. Geiss.

Their teacher sat there for another long moment, saying nothing, thinking nothing, daring barely to breathe lest she shatter the moment and find it all illusion.

The moment did not shatter, but the morning bell did ring, echoing down the long halls of the school. The last teacher sat there one moment longer, gathering her strength and resisting the urge to cry.

Then Ms. Geiss rose, walked to the chalkboard, and in her best cursive script, began writing the schedule to show them what they would be doing and learning in the day ahead.

SOME ZOMBIE CONTINGENCY PLANS

by Kelly Link

Kelly Link is the author of many wonderful short stories, which have been collected in two volumes—*Stranger Things Happen* and *Magic for Beginners*—with
a third, *Pretty Monsters*, due out shortly. Her short fiction has appeared in *The
Magazine of Fantasy & Science Fiction, Realms of Fantasy, Asimov's Science Fiction, Conjunctions,* and in anthologies such as *McSweeney's Mammoth Treasury
of Thrilling Tales, The Dark, The Faery Reel,* and *Best American Short Stories.* With
her husband, Gavin J. Grant, Link runs Small Beer Press and edits the zine *Lady
Churchill's Rosebud Wristlet.* Grant and Link also co-edit (with Ellen Datlow)
The Year's Best Fantasy and Horror annual. Her fiction has earned her an NEA
Literature Fellowship and won a variety of awards, including the Hugo, Nebula,
World Fantasy, Stoker, Tiptree, and Locus awards.

"Some Zombie Contingency Plans" first appeared in Link's collection, *Magic
for Beginners* (which, incidentally, also includes another great zombie story
called "The Hortlak"). As this story illustrates, a zombie contingency plan is an
important thing to have, so before we progress any further in this anthology,
you should have a look at this tale so that you can stop and consider a plan of
your own. In fact, you may want to think about that now; although this book is
a rather weighty tome it probably wouldn't make a very effective weapon against
the living dead.

This is a story about being lost in the woods.

This guy Soap is at a party out in the suburbs. The thing you need to know
about Soap is that he keeps a small framed oil painting in the trunk of his car.
The painting is about the size of a paperback novel. Wherever Soap goes, this
oil painting goes with him. But he leaves the painting in the trunk of his car,
because you don't walk around a party carrying a painting. People will think
you're weird.

Soap doesn't know anyone here. He's crashed the party, which is what he
does now, when he feels lonely. On weekends, he just drives around the suburbs
until he finds one of those summer twilight parties that are so big that they

spill out onto the yard.

Kids are out on the lawn of a two-story house, lying on the damp grass and drinking beer out of plastic cups. Soap has brought along a six-pack. It's the least he can do. He walks through the house, past four black guys sitting all over a couch. They're watching a football game and there's some music on the stereo. The television is on mute. Over by the TV, a white girl is dancing by herself. When she gets too close to it, the guys on the couch start complaining.

Soap finds the kitchen. There's one of those big professional ovens and a lot of expensive-looking knives stuck to a magnetic strip on the wall. It's funny, Soap thinks, how expensive stuff always looks more dangerous, and also safer, both of these things at the same time. He pokes around in the fridge and finds some pre-sliced cheese and English muffins. He grabs three slices of cheese, the muffins, and puts the beer in the fridge. There's also a couple of steaks, and so he takes one out, heats up the broiler.

A girl wanders into the kitchen. She's black and her hair goes up and up and on top are these sturdy, springy curls like little waves. Toe to top of her architectural haircut, she's as tall as Soap. She has eyes the color of iceberg lettuce. There's a heart-shaped rhinestone under one green eye. The rhinestone winks at Soap like it knows him. She's gorgeous, but Soap knows better than to fool around with girls who aren't out of high school yet, maybe. "What are you doing?" she says.

"Cooking a steak," Soap says. "Want one?"

"No," she says. "I already ate."

She sits up on the counter beside the sink and swings her legs. She's wearing a bikini top, pink shorts, and no shoes. "Who are you?" she says.

"Will," Soap says, although Will isn't his name. Soap isn't his real name, either.

"I'm Carly," she says. "You want a beer?"

"There's beer in the fridge," Will says, and Carly says, "I know there is."

Will opens and closes drawers and cabinet doors until he's found a plate, a fork and a knife, and garlic salt. He takes his steak out of the oven.

"You go to State?" Carly says. She pops off the beer top against the lip of the kitchen counter, and Will knows she's showing off.

"No," Will says. He sits down at the kitchen table and cuts off a piece of steak. He's been lonely ever since he and his friend Mike got out of prison and Mike went out to Seattle. It's nice to sit in a kitchen and talk to a girl.

"So what do you do?" Carly says. She sits down at the table, across from him. She lifts her arms up and stretches until her back cracks. She's got nice tits.

"Telemarketing," Will says, and Carly makes a face.

"That sucks," she says.

"Yeah," Will says. "No, it isn't too bad. I like talking to people. I just got out of prison." He takes another big bite of steak.

"No way," Carly says. "What did you do?"

Will chews. He swallows. "I don't want to talk about it right now."

"Okay," Carly says.

"Do you like museums?" Will says. She looks like a girl who goes to museums.

Some drunk white kid wanders into the kitchen. He says hey to Will and then he lies down on the floor with his head under Carly's chair. "Carly, Carly, Carly," he says. "I am so in love with you right now. You're the most beautiful girl in the world. And you don't even know my name. That's hurtful."

"Museums are okay," Carly says. "I like concerts. Jazz. Improvisational comedy. I like stuff that isn't the same every time you look at it."

"How about zombies?" Will says. No more steak. He mops up meat juice with one of the muffins. Maybe he could eat another one of those steaks. The kid with his head under Carly's chair says, "Carly? Carly? Carly? I like it when you sit on my face, Carly."

"You mean like horror movies?" Carly says.

"The living dead," says the kid under the chair. "The walking dead. Why do the dead walk everywhere? Why don't they just catch the bus?"

"You still hungry?" Carly says to Will. "I could make you some cinnamon toast. Or some soup."

"They could carpool," the kid under the chair says. "Hey y'all, I don't know why they call carpools *carpools*. It's not like there are cars with swimming pools in them. Because people might drown on their way to school. What a weird word. Carpool. Carpool. Carly's pool. There are naked people in Carly's pool, but Carly isn't naked in Carly's pool."

"Is there a phone around here?" Will says. "I was thinking I should call my dad. He's having open-heart surgery tomorrow."

It's not his name, but let's call him Soap. That's what they called him in prison, although not for the reasons you're thinking. When he was a kid, he'd read a book about a boy named Soap. So he didn't mind the nickname. It was better than Oatmeal, which is what one guy ended up getting called. You don't want to know why Oatmeal got called Oatmeal. It would put you off oatmeal.

Soap was in prison for six months. In some ways, six months isn't a long time. You spend longer inside your mother. But six months in prison is enough time to think about things and all around you, everyone else is thinking too. It can make you go crazy, wondering what other people are thinking about. Some guys thought about their families, and other guys thought about revenge, or how they were going to get rich. Some guys took correspondence courses or fell in love because of what one of the volunteer art instructors said about one of their watercolors. Soap didn't take an art course, but he thought about art. Art was why Soap was in prison. This sounded romantic, but really, it was just stupid.

Even before Soap and his friend Mike went to prison, Soap was sure that he'd had opinions about art, even though he hadn't known much about art. It was the same with prison. Art and prison were the kind of things that you had opinions about, even if you didn't know anything about them. Soap still didn't know much about art. These were some of the things that he had known about art before prison:

> He knew what he liked when he saw it. As it had turned out, he knew what he liked, even when he couldn't see it.

> Museums gave him hiccups. He had hiccups a lot of the time while he was in prison too.

These were some of the things Soap figured out about art while he was in prison:

> Great art came out of great suffering. Soap had gone through a lot of shit because of art.

> There was a difference between art, which you just looked at, and things like soap, which you used. Even if the soap smelled so good that you didn't want to use it, only smell it. This was why people got so pissed off about art. Because you didn't eat it, and you didn't sleep on it, and you couldn't put it up your nose. A lot of people said things like "That's not art" when whatever they were talking about could clearly not have been anything else, except art.

When Soap got tired of thinking about art, he thought about zombies. He worked on his zombie contingency plan. Thinking about zombies was less tiring than thinking about art. Here's what Soap knew about zombies:

> Zombies were not about sex.

> Zombies were not interested in art.

> Zombies weren't complicated. It wasn't like werewolves or ghosts or vampires. Vampires, for example, were the middle/upper-middle management of the supernatural world. Some people thought of vampires as rock stars, but really they were more like Martha Stewart. Vampires were prissy. They had to follow rules. They had to look good. Zombies weren't like that. You couldn't exorcise zombies. You didn't need luxury items like silver bullets or crucifixes or holy water. You just shot zombies in the head, or set fire to them, or hit them over the head really hard. There were some guys in the prison who knew about that. There were guys in the prison who knew about anything you might want to know about. There were guys who knew things that you didn't want to know. It was like a library, except it wasn't.

Zombies didn't discriminate. Everyone tasted equally good as far as zombies were concerned. And anyone could *be* a zombie. You didn't have to be special, or good at sports, or good-looking. You didn't have to smell good, or wear the right kind of clothes, or listen to the right kind of music. You just had to be slow.

Soap liked this about zombies.

There is never just one zombie.

There was something about clowns that was worse than zombies. (Or maybe something that was the same. When you see a zombie, you want to laugh at first. When you see a clown, most people get a little nervous. There's the pallor and the cakey mortician-style makeup, the shuffling and the untidy hair. But clowns were probably malicious, and they moved fast on those little bicycles and in those little, crammed cars. Zombies weren't much of anything. They didn't carry musical instruments and they didn't care whether or not you laughed at them. You always knew what zombies wanted.) Given a choice, Soap would take zombies over clowns any day. There was a white guy in the prison who had been a clown. Nobody was sure why he was in prison.

It turned out that everyone in the prison had a zombie contingency plan, once you asked them, just like everyone in prison had a prison escape plan, only nobody talked about those. Soap tried not to dwell on escape plans, although sometimes he dreamed that he was escaping. Then the zombies would show up. They always showed up in his escape dreams. You could escape prison, but you couldn't escape zombies. This was true in Soap's dreams, just the way it was true in the movies. You couldn't get any more true than that.

According to Soap's friend Mike, who was also in prison, people worried too much about zombies and not enough about icebergs. Even though icebergs were real. Mike pointed out that icebergs were slow, like zombies. Maybe you could adapt zombie contingency plans to cope with icebergs. Mike asked Soap to start thinking about icebergs. No one else was. Somebody had to plan for icebergs, according to Mike.

Even after Soap got out of prison, when it was much too late, he still dreamed about escaping from prison.

"So whose house is this, anyway?" Will asks Carly. She's walking up the stairs in front of him. If he reached out just one hand, he could untie her bikini top. It would just fall off.

"This girl," Carly says, and proceeds to relate a long, sad story. "A friend of mine. Her parents took her to France for this bicycle tour. They're into Amway.

This trip is some kind of bonus. Like, her father sold a bunch of water filters and so now everyone has to go to France and build their own bicycles. In Marseilles. Isn't that lame? She can't even speak French. She's a Francophilophobe. She's a klutz. Her parents don't even like her. If they could have, they would have left her at home. Or maybe they'll leave her somewhere in France. Shit, would I love to see her try and ride a bike in France. She'll probably fall right over the Alps. I hate her. We were going to have this party and then she said I should go ahead and have it without her. She's really pissed off at her parents."

"Is this a bathroom?" Will says. "Hold on a minute."

He goes in and takes a piss. He flushes and when he goes to wash his hands, he sees that the people who own this house have put some chunk of fancy soap beside the sink. He sniffs the soap. Then he opens up the door. Carly is standing there talking to some Asian girl wearing a strapless dress with little shiny fake plastic flowers all over it. It's too big for her in the bust, so she's holding the front out like she's waiting for someone to come along and drop a weasel in it. Will wonders who the dress belongs to, and why this girl would want to wear an ugly dress like that, anyway.

He holds out the soap. "Smell this," he says to Carly and she does. "What does it smell like?"

"I don't know," she says. "Marmalade?"

"Lemongrass," Will says. He marches back into the bathroom and opens up the window. There's a swimming pool down there with people in it. He throws the soap out the window and some guy in the pool yells, "Hey!"

"Why'd he do that?" the girl in the hall says. Carly starts laughing.

Soap's friend Mike had a girlfriend named Jenny. Jenny never came to see Mike in prison. Soap felt bad about this.

Soap's dad was living in New Zealand and every once in a while Soap got a postcard.

Soap's mom, who lived in California out near Manhattan Beach, was too busy and too pissed off with Soap to visit him in prison. Soap's mom didn't tolerate stupidity or bad luck.

Soap's older sister, Becka, was the only family member who ever came to visit him in prison. Becka was an actress-waitress who had once been in a low-budget zombie movie. Soap had watched it once and wasn't sure which was stranger: seeing your sister naked, or seeing your naked sister get eaten by zombies. Becka was almost good looking enough to be on a reality dating show, but not funny looking or sad enough to be on one of the makeover shows. Becka was always giving notice. So then their mom would buy Becka a round-trip ticket to go visit Soap. Soap figured he was supposed to be an example to Becka: find a good job and keep it, or you'll end up in prison like your brother.

Becka might have been average in L.A., but average in L.A. is Queen of Mars in the visiting room of a federal penitentiary in North Carolina. Guys kept asking Soap when they were going to see his sister on TV.

Soap's mom owned a boutique right on Manhattan Beach. It was called Float. Becka and Soap called it Wash Your Mouth. The boutique sold soaps and shampoos, nothing else. The soaps and shampoos were supposed to smell like food. What the soaps really smelled like were those candles that were supposed to smell like food, but which smelled instead like those air fresheners which hang from the rearview mirrors in taxis or stolen cars. Like looking behind you smells like strawberries. Like making a clean getaway smells the same as the room freshener Soap and Becka used to spray when they'd been smoking their mother's pot, before she got home.

Once when they were in high school, Soap and Becka had bought a urinal cake. It smelled like peppermint. They'd taken the urinal cake out of its packaging and put it in a fancy box with some tissue paper and a ribbon. Soap had wrapped it up and given it to their mother for Mother's Day. Told her it was a pumice soap for exfoliating feet. Soap liked soap that smelled like soap. His mom was always sending care packages of soaps that smelled like olive oil and neroli and peppermint and brown sugar and cucumber and martinis and toasted marshmallow.

You weren't supposed to have bars of soap in prison. If you put a bar of soap in a sock, you could hit somebody over the head with it. You could clobber somebody. But Becka made an arrangement with the guards in the visiting room, and the guards in the visiting room made an arrangement with the guards in charge of the mailroom. Soap gave out his mother's soaps to everyone in prison. Whoever wanted them. It turned out everyone wanted soap that smelled like food: social workers and prison guards and drug dealers and murderers and even people who hadn't been able to afford good lawyers. No wonder his mom's boutique did so well.

While Soap was in prison, Becka kept Soap's painting for him. Sometimes he asked and she brought it with her when she came to visit. He made her promise not to give it to their mother, not to pawn it for rent money, to keep it under her bed where it would be safe as long as her roommate's cat didn't sneak in. Becka promised that if there were a fire or an earthquake, she'd rescue the painting first. Even before she rescued her roommate or her roommate's cat.

Carly takes Will into a bedroom. There's a big painting of a flower garden, and under the painting is a king-sized bed with dresses lying all over it. There are dresses on the floor. "Go ahead and call your dad," Carly says. "I'll come back in a while with some more beer. You want another beer?"

"Why not?" Will says. He waits until she leaves the room and then he calls his dad. When his dad picks up the phone, he says, "Hey, Dad, how's it going?"

"Junior!" his dad says. "How's it going?"

"Did I wake you up? What time is it there?" Junior says.

"Doesn't matter," his dad says. "I was working on a jigsaw puzzle. No picture on the box. I think it's lemurs. Or maybe binturongs."

"Not much," Junior says. "Staying out of trouble."

"Super," his dad says. "That's super."

"I was thinking about that thing we talked about. About how I could come visit you sometime?" Junior says.

"Sure," his dad says. His dad is always enthusiastic about Junior's ideas. "Hey, that would be great. Get out of that fucking country while you still can. Come visit your old dad. We could do father-son stuff. Go bungee jumping."

The girl in the plastic flower dress marches into the bedroom. She takes the dress off and drops it on the bed. She goes into the closet and comes out again holding a dress made out of black and purple feathers. It looks like something a dancer in Las Vegas might wear when she got off work.

"Some girl just came in and took off all her clothes," Junior says to his dad.

"Well you give her my best," his dad says, and hangs up.

"My dad says hello," Junior says to the naked girl. Then he says, "My dad and I have a question for you. Do you ever worry about zombies? Do you have a zombie contingency plan?"

The girl just smiles like she thinks that's a good question. She puts the new dress on. She walks out. Will calls his sister, but Becka isn't answering her cell phone. So Will picks up all the dresses and goes into the closet. He hangs them up. People clean up after themselves. Zombies don't.

In Will's opinion, zombies are attracted to suburbs the way that tornadoes are attracted to trailer parks. Maybe it's all the windows. Maybe houses in suburbs have too many windows and that's what drives zombies nuts.

If the zombies showed up tonight, Will would barricade the bedroom door with the heavy oak dresser. Will will let the naked girl come in first. Carly too. The three of them will make a rope by tying all those dresses together and escape through the window. Maybe they could make wings out of that feather dress and fly away. Will could be the Bird Man of Suburbitraz.

Will looks under the bed, just to make sure there are no zombies or suitcases or that drunk guy from downstairs under there.

There's a little black kid in Superman pajamas curled up asleep under the bed.

When Becka was a kid, she kept a suitcase under the bed. The suitcase was full of things that were to be rescued in case of an earthquake or a fire or murderers. The suitcase's secondary function was using up some of the dangerous, dark space under the bed which might otherwise have been inhabited by monsters or dead people. Here be suitcases. In the suitcase, Becka kept a candle shaped like a dragon, which she'd bought at the mall with some birthday money and then couldn't bear to use as a candle; a little ceramic dog; some favorite stuffed animals; their mother's charm bracelet; a photo album; *Black Beauty* and a whole lot of other horse books. Every once in a while Becka and her little brother would drag the suitcase back out from under the bed and sort through it. Becka would take things out and put other things in. Her little brother always felt happy and safe when he helped Becka do this. When things got bad, you would rescue what you could.

Modern art is a waste of time. When the zombies show up, you can't worry about art. Art is for people who aren't worried about zombies. Besides zombies and icebergs, there are other things that Soap has been thinking about. Tsunamis, earthquakes, Nazi dentists, killer bees, army ants, black plague, old people, divorce lawyers, sorority girls, Jimmy Carter, giant squids, rabid foxes, strange dogs, news anchors, child actors, fascists, narcissists, psychologists, ax murderers, unrequited love, footnotes, zeppelins, the Holy Ghost, Catholic priests, John Lennon, chemistry teachers, redheaded men with British accents, librarians, spiders, nature books with photographs of spiders in them, darkness, teachers, swimming pools, smart girls, pretty girls, rich girls, angry girls, tall girls, nice girls, girls with superpowers, giant lizards, blind dates who turn out to have narcolepsy, angry monkeys, feminine hygiene commercials, sitcoms about aliens, things under the bed, contact lenses, ninjas, performance artists, mummies, spontaneous combustion. Soap has been afraid of all of these things at one time or another. Ever since he went to prison, he's realized that he doesn't have to be afraid. All he has to do is come up with a plan. Be prepared. It's just like the Boy Scouts, except you have to be even more prepared. You have to prepare for everything that the Boy Scouts didn't prepare you for, which is pretty much everything.

Soap is a waste of time too. What good is soap in a zombie situation? Soap sometimes imagines himself trapped in his mother's soap boutique. Zombies are coming out of the surf, dripping wet, hellishly hungry, always so fucking slow, shuffling hopelessly up through the sand of Manhattan Beach. Soap has barricaded himself in Float with his mother and some blond Japanese tourists with surfboards. "Do something, sweetheart!" his mother implores. So Sweetheart throws water all over the floor. There's the surfboards, a baseball bat under the counter, some rolls of quarters, and a swordfish mounted up on the wall, but Sweetheart decides the cash register is best for bashing. He tells the Japanese tourists to get down on their hands and knees and rub soap all over the floor. When the zombies finally find a way into Float, his mother and the tourists can hide behind the counter. The zombies will slip all over the floor and Sweetheart will bash them in the head with the cash register. It will be just like a Busby Berkeley zombie musical.

"What's going on?" Carly says. "How's your father doing?"

"He's fine," Will says. "Except for the open-heart surgery thing. Except for that, he's good. I was just looking under the bed. There's a little kid under there."

"Oh," Carly says. "Him. That's the little brother. Of my friend. *Le bro de mon ami.* I'm taking care of him. He likes to sleep under the bed."

"What's his name?" Will says.

"Leo," Carly says. She hands Will a beer and sits down on the bed beside him. "So tell me about this prison thing. What did you do? Should I be afraid of you?"

"Probably not," Will says. "It doesn't do much good to be afraid of things."

"So tell me what you did," Carly says. She burps so loud that Will is amazed that the kid under the bed doesn't wake up. Leo.

"This is a great party," Will says. "Thanks for hanging out with me."

"Somebody just puked out of a window in the living room. Someone else almost threw up in the swimming pool, but I got them out in time. If someone throws up on the piano, I'm in big trouble. You can't get puke out from between piano keys."

Will thinks Carly says this like she knows what she's talking about. There are girls who have had years of piano lessons, and then there are girls who have taken piano lessons who also know how to throw a party and how to clean throw-up out of a piano. There's something sexy about a girl who knows how to play the piano, and keys that stick for no apparent reason. Will doesn't have any zombie contingency plans that involve pianos, and it makes him sick. How could he have forgotten pianos?

"I'll help you clean up," Will says. "If you want."

"You don't have to try so hard, you know," Carly says. She stares right at him, like there's a spider on his face or an interesting tattoo, some word spelled upside down in a foreign language that she wants to understand. Will doesn't have any tattoos. As far as he's concerned, tattoos are like art, only worse.

Will stares right back. He says, "When I was at this party outside Kansas City, I heard this story about a kid who threw a lot of parties while his parents were on vacation. Right before they got home, he realized how fucked up the house was, and so he burned it down." This story always makes Will laugh. What a dumb kid.

"You want to help me burn down my friend's house?" Carly says. She smiles, like, what a good joke. What a nice guy he is. "What time is it? Two? If it's two in the morning, then you have to tell me why you went to prison. It's like a rule. We've known each other for at least an hour, and it's late at night and I still don't know why you were in prison, even though I can tell you want to tell me or otherwise you wouldn't have told me you were in prison in the first place. Was what you did that bad?"

"No," Will says. "It was just really stupid."

"Stupid is good," Carly says. "Come on. Pretty please."

She pulls back the cover on the bed and crawls under it, pulls the sheets up to her chin. Good night, Carly. Good night, Carly's gorgeous tits.

It was so small and it was so far away, even when you looked at it up close. Soap said it was trees. A wood. Mike said it was a painting of an iceberg.

When Soap thinks about the zombies, he thinks about how there's nowhere you can go that the zombies won't find you. Even the fairy tales that Becka used to read to him. Ali Baba and the Forty Zombies. Open Zombie. Snow White and the Seven Tiny Zombies.

Any place Will thinks of, the zombies will eventually get there too. He pictures all of these places as paintings in a gallery, because as long as a place is just a painting, it's a safe place. Landscapes with frames around them, to keep the landscapes from leaking out. To keep the zombies from getting in. A ski resort in summer, all those lonely gondolas. An oil rig on a sea at night. The Museum of Natural History. The Playboy mansion. The Eiffel Tower. The Matterhorn. David Letterman's house. Buckingham Palace. A bowling alley. A Laundromat. He puts himself in the painting of the flower garden that's hanging above the bed where he and Carly are sitting, and it's sunny and warm and safe and beautiful. But once he puts himself into the painting, the zombies show up just like they always do. The space station. New Zealand. He bets his dad thinks he's safe from zombies in New Zealand, because it's an island. His dad is an idiot.

People paint trees all the time. All kinds of trees. Art is supposed to be about things like trees. Or icebergs, although there are more paintings of trees than there are paintings of icebergs, so Mike doesn't know what he's talking about.

"I wasn't in prison for very long," Soap says. "What Mike and I did wasn't really that bad. We didn't hurt anybody."

"You don't look like a bad guy," Carly says. And when Soap looks at Carly, she looks like a nice kid. A nice girl with nice tits. But Soap knows you can't tell by looking.

Soap and Mike were going to be rich once they got out of college. The two of them had it all figured out. They were going to have an excellent website, just as soon as they figured out what it was going to be about, and what to call it. While they were in prison, they decided this website would have been about zombies. That would have been fucking awesome.

Hungryzombie.com, lonelyzombie.com, nakedzombie.com, soyoumarriedazombie.com, zombiecontingencyplan.com, dotcomofthewalkingdead.com were just a few of the names they came up with. In Will's opinion, people will go anywhere if there's a zombie involved.

Cool people would have gone to the site and hooked up. People would have talked about old horror movies, or about their horrible temp jobs. There would have been comics and concerts. There would have been advertising, sponsors, movie deals. Soap would have been able to afford art. He would have bought Picassos and Vermeers and original comic book art. He would have bought drinks for women. Beautiful, bisexual, bionic women with unpronounceable names and weird habits in bed.

Only by the time Soap and Mike and the rest of their friends got out of school, all of that was already over. Nobody cared if you had a website. Everybody already had websites. No one was going to give you money.

There were lots of guys who knew how to do what Soap and Mike knew how to do. It turned out that Mike's and Soap's parents had paid a lot of money for them to learn how to do things that everyone could already do.

Mike had a girlfriend named Jenny. Soap liked Jenny because she teased him, but Jenny really isn't important to this story. She wasn't ever going to fall in love with Soap, and Soap knew it. What matters is that Jenny worked in a museum, and so Soap and Mike started going to museum events, because you got Brie on crackers and wine and martinis. Free food. All you had to do was wear a suit and listen to people talk about art and mortgages and their children. There would be a lot of older women who reminded Soap of his mother, and it was clear that Soap reminded these women of their sons. What was never clear was whether these women were flirting with him, or whether they wanted his advice about something that even they couldn't put their finger on.

One morning, in prison, Soap woke up and realized that the opportunity had been there and he'd never even seen it. He and Mike, they could have started a website for older upper-middle-class women with strong work ethics and confused, resentful grown-up children with bachelor degrees and no jobs. That was better than zombies. They could even have done some good.

"Okay," Will says. "I'll tell you why I went to prison. But first you have to tell me what you'd do if zombies showed up at your party. Tonight. I ask everyone this. Everyone has a zombie contingency plan."

"You mean like with colleges, just in case you don't get into your first choice?" Carly says. She holds an eyelid open, puts her finger to her eyeball, and pops out a contact lens. She puts it on the table beside the bed. She doesn't take the other lens out. Maybe that eye isn't scratchy. "So my eyes aren't actually green. The breasts are real, by the way. I don't watch a lot of horror movies. They give me nightmares. Leo likes that stuff."

Will sits on the other side of the bed and watches her. She's thinking about it. Maybe she likes how the world looks through one green contact lens. "My parents keep a gun in the fridge. I guess I'd go get it and shoot the zombies? Or maybe I'd hide in my mom's closet? Behind all her shoes and stuff? I'd cry a lot. I'd scream for help. I'd call the police."

"Okay," Will says. "I was just wondering. What about your brother? How would you protect him?"

Carly yawns like she isn't impressed at all, but Will can see she's impressed. It's just that she's sleepy, too. "Smart Will. You knew this was my house all along. You knew Leo was my brother. Am I such a bad liar?"

"Yeah," Will says. "There's a picture of you and Leo over on your parents' dresser."

"Okay," Carly says. "This is my parents' bedroom. They're in France building bicycles, and they left me and they left Leo here. So I threw a party. Serves them right if someone burns their house down."

"I feel like we've known each other for a long time," Will says. "Even though we just met. For example, I knew your eyes weren't really green."

"We don't really know each other very well," Carly says. But she says it in a friendly way. "I keep trying to get to know you better. I bet you didn't know that I want to be president someday."

"I bet you didn't know that I think about icebergs a lot, although not as much as I think about zombies," Will says.

"I'd like to go live on an iceberg," Carly says. "And I'd like to be president too. Maybe I could do both. I could be the first black woman president who lives on an iceberg."

"I'd vote for you," Will says.

"Will," Carly says. "Don't you want to get under the covers with me? Are you intimidated by the fact that I'm going to be president someday? Are you intimidated by competent, successful women?"

Will says, "Do you want to fool around or do you want me to tell how I ended up in prison? Door A or Door B. I'm a really good kisser, but Leo is asleep under the bed. Your brother." Jenny and Mike used to go off and kiss in the museum where Jenny worked, but Soap never kissed Jenny. Once, in college, Soap kissed Mike. They were both drunk. Men kissed men in prison. White men made out with black men. Becka used to make out with her boyfriends out on the beach while her brother hid in the dunes and watched. In the zombie movie, a zombie ate Becka's lips. You don't ever want to kiss a zombie.

"He's a heavy sleeper," Carly says. "Maybe you should just tell me what you did and we can go from there."

Soap and Mike and a couple of their friends were at one of the parties at the little private museum where Jenny worked. They drank a lot of wine and they didn't eat much except some olives. Jenny was busy and so Soap and Mike and their friends left the gallery where the wine and cheese were laid out, where the docents and the rich people were getting to know each other, and wandered out into the rest of the museum. They got farther and farther away from Jenny's event, but nobody told them to come back and nobody showed up and asked them what they were doing. The other galleries were dark and so somebody dared Mike to go in one of them. They wanted to see if an alarm would go off. Mike did and the alarm didn't.

Next Soap went into the gallery. His name wasn't Soap then. His name was Arthur, but everybody called him Art. Ha ha. You couldn't see anything in the gallery. Art felt stupid just standing there, so he put his hands straight out in front of him in the darkness and walked forward until his fingers touched a wall. He kept his fingers on the wall and walked around the room. Every now and then his fingers would touch a frame and he'd move his hand up and down and along the frame to see how big the painting was. He walked all the way around the room until he was at the door again.

Then somebody else went in, it was Markson who went in, and when Markson came out, he was holding a painting in his arms. It was about three feet by three feet. A painting of a ship with a lot of masts and sails. Lots of little dabs of blue. Little people on the deck of the ship, looking busy.

"Holy shit," Mike said. "Markson, what did you just do?"

You have to understand that Markson was an idiot. Everyone knew that. Right then he was a drunk idiot, but everyone else was drunk too.

"I just wanted to see what it looked like," Markson said. "I didn't think it would be so heavy." He put the painting down against the wall.

No alarms were going off. The gallery on the other side of the hall was dark too. So they made it a game. Everyone went into one of the galleries and walked around and chose a painting. Then you came out again and saw what you had. Someone got a Seurat. Someone had a Mary Cassatt. Someone else had a Winslow Homer. There were a lot of paintings by artists whom none of them knew. So those didn't count. Art went back into the first gallery. This time he was slow. There were already some gaps on the gallery wall. He put his ear up against some of the paintings. He felt that he was listening for something, only he didn't know what.

He chose a very small painting. When he got it out into the hall, he saw it was an oil painting. A blobby blue-green mass that might have been water or a person or it might have been trees. Woods from very far away. Something slow and far away. He couldn't read the artist's signature.

Mike was in the other gallery. When he came out with a painting, the painting turned out to be a Picasso. Some sad-looking freaky woman and her sad-looking freaky dog. Everyone agreed that Mike had won. Then that idiot Markson said, "I bet you can't walk out of here with that Picasso."

Sometimes when he's in houses that don't belong to him, Soap feels bad. He shouldn't be where he is. He doesn't belong anywhere. Nobody really knows him. If they did, they wouldn't like him. Everyone always seems happier than Soap, and as if they know something that Soap doesn't. He tells himself that things will be different when the zombies show up.

"You guys stole a Picasso?" Carly says.

"It was a minor Picasso. Hardly a Picasso at all. We weren't really stealing it," Will says. "We just thought it would be funny to smuggle it out of Jenny's museum and see how far we got with it. We just walked out of the museum and nobody stopped us. We put the Picasso in the car and drove back to our apartment. I took that little painting too, just so the Picasso would have company. And because I wanted to spend some more time looking at it. I put it under my coat, under one arm, while the other guys were helping Mike get past the party without being seen. We hung the Picasso in the living room when we got back and I put the little painting in my bedroom. We were still drunk when the police showed up. Jenny lost her job. We went to prison. Markson and the other guys had to do community service."

He stops talking. Carly takes his hand. She squeezes it. She says, "That's the weirdest story I've ever heard. Why is it that everything is so much sadder and funnier and so much more true when you're drunk?"

"I haven't told you the weird part yet," Will says. He can't tell her the weirdest part of the story, although maybe he can try to show her.

"Did I tell you that I used to be on my school's debate team?" Carly says. "That's the weirdest thing about me. I like getting in arguments. The boy with his head under my chair, I kicked his ass in a debate about marijuana. I humiliated him all over the map."

Will doesn't use drugs anymore. It's too much like being in a museum. It makes everything look like art, and makes everything feel like just before the zombies show up. He says, "The museum said that I hadn't stolen the little painting from them. They said it wasn't theirs, even when I explained the whole thing. I told the truth and everyone thought I was lying. The police asked around, just in case Mike and I had done the same thing somewhere else, at some other museum, and nobody came forward. Nobody knew the artist's name. So finally they just gave the painting back to me. They thought I was trying to pull some scam."

"So what happened to it?" Carly says.

"I've still got it. My sister kept it for me while I was in prison," Will says. "For two years. Since I got out, I've been trying to find a place to ditch it. I've left it a couple of places, but then it turns out that I haven't. I can't leave it behind. No matter how hard I try. It doesn't belong to me, but I can't get rid of it."

"My friend Jessica does this thing she calls shopleaving," Carly says. "When someone gives her a hideous shirt for her birthday or if she buys a book and it's not any good, she goes into a store and leaves the shirt on a hanger. She leaves the book on the shelf. Once she took this crazy, mean parakeet to a shoe store and put him in a shoebox. What happened to your friend? Mike?"

"He went to Seattle. He started up a website for ex-cons. He got a lot of funding. There are a lot of people out there who have been in prison. They need websites."

"That's nice," Carly says. "That's like a happy ending."

"I've got the painting in the car," Will says. "Do you want it?"

"I like van Gogh," Carly says. "And Georgia O'Keeffe."

"Let me go get it," Will says. He goes downstairs before she can stop him. The guys on the couch are watching somebody's wedding video now. He wonders what they would think if they knew Carly was upstairs in bed, waiting for him. The dancing girl is in the kitchen with the boy under the table. The girl in the dress is out on the lawn. She isn't doing anything except maybe looking at stars. She watches Will go to his car, open the trunk, and take out the little painting. Out behind the house, Will can hear people in the pool. Will hasn't felt this peaceful in a long time. It's like that first slow part in a horror movie, before the bad thing happens. Will knows that sometimes you shouldn't try to anticipate the bad thing. Sometimes you are supposed to just listen to swimmers fooling around in a pool. People you can't see. The night and the moon and the girl in the dress. Will stands on the lawn for a while, holding the painting, wishing that Becka was here with him. Or Mike.

Will takes the painting back upstairs and into the master bedroom. He turns the lights off and wakes Carly up. She's been crying in her sleep. "Here it is," he says.

"Will?" Carly says. "You turned off the light. Is it the ocean? It looks like the ocean. I can't really see anything."

"Sure you can," Will says. "There's moonlight."

"I only have one contact lens in," Carly says.

Will stands on the bed and lifts the painting of the garden off its picture hook. How can a painting of some flowers be so heavy? He leans it against the bed and hangs up the painting from the car. Iceberg, zombie, a bunch of trees. Some obscured and unknowable thing. How are you supposed to tell what it is? It makes him want to die, sometimes. "There you go," he says. "It's yours."

"It's beautiful," Carly says. Will thinks maybe she's crying again. She says, "Will? Will you just lie down with me? For a little while?"

Sometimes Soap has this dream. He isn't sure whether it's a prison dream or a dream about art or a dream about zombies. Maybe it isn't about any of those things. He dreams that he's in a dark room. Sometimes it's an enormous room, very long and narrow. Sometimes there are people in it, leaning silently up against the walls. He can only figure out if there are people or how big the room is when he stretches out his arms and walks forward. He has no idea what they're doing in the room with him. He has no idea what he's supposed to do, either. Sometimes it's a very small room. It's dark. It's dark.

"Hey, kid. Hey, Leo. Wake up, Leo. We gotta go." Soap is lying on the floor beside the bed, holding up the dust ruffle. He has to whisper. Carly is asleep on the too-big bed, under the covers.

Leo uncurls. He wriggles forward, towards Will. Then he wiggles back again, away from Will. He's maybe six or seven years old. "Who are you?" Leo says. "Where's Carly?"

"Carly sent me to get you, Leo," Soap says. "You have to be very, very quiet and do exactly what I say. There are zombies in the house. There are brain-eating zombies in the house. We have to get to a safe place. We have to go get Carly. She needs us." Leo stretches out his hand. Soap takes it and pulls him out from under the bed. He picks Leo up. Leo holds on to Will tightly. He doesn't weigh a lot, but he's so warm. Little kids have fast metabolisms.

"The zombies are chasing Carly?" Leo says.

"That's right," Soap says. "We have to go save her."

"Can I bring my robot?" Leo says.

"I've already put your robot in the car," Will says. "And your dinosaur T-shirt and your basketball."

"Are you Wolverine?" Leo says.

"That's right," Wolverine says. "I'm Wolverine. Let's get out of here."

Leo says, "Can I see your claws?"

"Not now," Wolverine says.

"I have to go to the bathroom before we go," Leo says.

"Okay," Wolverine says. "That's a great idea. I'm proud of you for telling me that."

Some things that you could try with zombies, but which won't work:

Panic.

Don't panic. Remain calm.

Call the police.

Take them out to dinner. Get them drunk.

Ask them to come back later.

Ignore them.

Take them home.

Tell them jokes. Play board games with them.

Tell them you love them.

Rescue them.

Wolverine and Leo have a backpack. They put a box of Cheerios and some bananas and Leo and Carly's parents' gun and a Game Boy and some batteries and a Ziploc bag full of twenty-dollar bills from the closet in the master bedroom in the backpack. There's a late-night horror movie on TV, but no one is there to watch it. The girl in the dress on the lawn is gone. If there's someone in the pool, they're keeping quiet.

Wolverine and Leo get in Wolverine's car and drive away.

Carly is dreaming that she's the President of the United States of America. She's living in the White House—it turns out that the White House is built out of ice. It's more like the Whitish Greenish Bluish House. Everybody wears big fur coats and when President Carly gives presidential addresses, she can see her breath. All her words hanging there. She's hanging out with rock stars and Nobel Prize winners. It's a wonderful dream. Carly's going to save the world. Everyone loves her, even her parents. Her parents are so proud of her. When she wakes up, the first thing she sees—before she sees all the other things that are missing besides the oil painting of the woods that nobody lives in, nobody painted, and nobody stole—is the empty space on the wall in the bedroom above her parents' bed.

DEATH AND SUFFRAGE

by Dale Bailey

Dale Bailey is the author of the novels *The Fallen, House of Bones,* and *Sleeping Policemen* (with Jack Slay, Jr.). His short stories have appeared in *The Magazine of Fantasy & Science Fiction, Amazing Stories,* and *SCI FICTION.* He has also written a non-fiction book, *American Nightmares: The Haunted House Formula in American Popular Fiction.* This story won the International Horror Guild Award, and was adapted into an episode of the television series *Masters of Horror.* Bailey has also twice been nominated for the Nebula Award.

In his collection, *The Resurrection Man's Legacy,* Bailey says that due to the real-world events that mirrored the events of this story, "Death and Suffrage" seems to confirm the dictum that the writer of fiction can no longer compete with the strangeness of contemporary reality. "It's also an example of how completely a writer's intentions can go awry. In keeping with the pun in the title, I intended this one to be short and light," Bailey says. "But somewhere along the way it turned long and very dark indeed."

It's funny how things happen, Burton used to tell me. The very moment you're engaged in some task of mind-numbing insignificance—cutting your toenails, maybe, or fishing in the sofa for the remote—the world is being refashioned around you. You stand before a mirror to brush your teeth, and halfway around the planet flood waters are on the rise. Every minute of every day, the world transforms itself in ways you can hardly imagine, and there you are, sitting in traffic or wondering what's for lunch or just staring blithely out a window. History happens while you're making other plans, Burton always says.

I guess I know that now. I guess we all know that.

Me, I was in a sixth-floor Chicago office suite working on my résumé when it started. The usual chaos swirled around me—phones braying, people scurrying about, the televisions singing exit poll data over the din—but it all had a forced artificial quality. The campaign was over. Our numbers people had told us everything we needed to know: when the polls opened that morning, Stoddard was up seventeen points. So there I sat, dejected and soon to be unemployed, with my feet on a rented desk and my lap-top propped against my knees, mulling over synonyms for *directed.* As in *directed a staff of fifteen.*

39

As in *directed public relations for the Democratic National Committee.* As in *directed a national political campaign straight into the toilet.*

Then CNN started emitting the little overture that means somewhere in the world history is happening, just like Burton always says.

I looked up as Lewis turned off the television.

"What'd you do that for?"

Lewis leaned over to shut my computer down. "I'll show you," he said.

I followed him through the suite, past clumps of people huddled around televisions. Nobody looked my way. Nobody had looked me in the eye since Sunday. I tried to listen, but over the shocked buzz in the room I couldn't catch much more than snatches of unscripted anchor-speak. I didn't see Burton, and I supposed he was off drafting his concession speech. "No sense delaying the inevitable," he had told me that morning.

"What gives?" I said to Lewis in the hall, but he only shook his head.

Lewis is a big man, fifty, with the drooping posture and hangdog expression of an adolescent. He stood in the elevator and watched the numbers cycle, rubbing idly at an acne scar. He had lots of them, a whole face pitted from what had to be among the worst teenage years in human history. I had never liked him much, and I liked him even less right then, but you couldn't help admiring the intelligence in his eyes. If Burton had been elected, Lewis would have served him well. Now he'd be looking for work instead.

The doors slid apart, and Lewis steered me through the lobby into a typical November morning in Chicago: a diamond-tipped wind boring in from the lake, a bruised sky spitting something that couldn't decide whether it wanted to be rain or snow. I grew up in Southern California—my grandparents raised me—and there's not much I hate more than Chicago weather; but that morning I stood there with my shirt-sleeves rolled to the elbow and my tie whipping over my shoulder, and I didn't feel a thing.

"My God," I said, and for a moment, my mind just locked up. All I could think was that not two hours ago I had stood in this very spot watching Burton work the crowd, and then the world had still been sane. Afterwards, Burton had walked down the street to cast his ballot. When he stepped out of the booth, the press had been waiting. Burton charmed them, the consummate politician even in defeat. We could have done great things.

And even then the world had still been sane.

No longer.

It took me a moment to sort it all out—the pedestrians shouldering by with wild eyes, the bell-hop standing dumbfounded before the hotel on the corner, his chin bobbing at half-mast. Three taxis had tangled up in the street, bleeding steam, and farther up the block loomed an overturned bus the size of a beached plesiosaur. Somewhere a woman was screaming atonally, over and over and over, with staccato hitches for breath. Sirens wailed in the distance. A t.v. crew was getting it all on tape, and for the first time since I blew Burton's chance to hold the highest office in the land, I stood in the presence of a journalist who wasn't shoving a mike in my face to ask me what had come over me.

I was too stunned even to enjoy it.

Instead, like Lewis beside me, I just stared across the street at the polling place. Dead people had gathered there, fifteen or twenty of them, and more arriving. Even then, there was never any question in my mind that they were dead. You could see it in the way they held their bodies, stiff as marionettes; in their shuffling gaits and the bright haunted glaze of their eyes. You could see it in the lacerations yawning open on the ropy coils of their guts, in their random nakedness, their haphazard clothes—hospital gowns and blood-stained blue jeans and immaculate suits fresh from unsealed caskets. You could see it in the dark patches of decay that blossomed on their flesh. You could just see that they were dead. It was every zombie movie you ever saw, and then some.

Gooseflesh erupted along my arms, and it had nothing to do with the wind off Lake Michigan.

"My God," I said again, when I finally managed to unlock my brain. "What do they want?"

"They want to vote," said Lewis.

The dead have been voting in Chicago elections since long before Richard J. Daley took office, one wag wrote in the next morning's *Tribune, but yesterday's events bring a whole new meaning to the tradition.*

I'll say.

The dead had voted, all right, and not just in Chicago. They had risen from hospital gurneys and autopsy slabs, from open coffins and embalming tables in every precinct in the nation, and they had cast their ballots largely without interference. Who was going to stop them? More than half the poll-workers had abandoned ship when the zombies started shambling through the doors, and even workers who stayed at their posts had usually permitted them to do as they pleased. The dead didn't threaten anyone—they didn't do much of anything you'd expect zombies to do, in fact. But most people found that inscrutable gaze unnerving. Better to let them cast their ballots than bear for long the knowing light in those strange eyes.

And when the ballots were counted, we learned something else as well: They voted for Burton. Every last one of them voted for Burton.

"It's your fault," Lewis said at breakfast the next day.

Everyone else agreed with him, I could tell, the entire senior staff, harried and sleep-deprived. They studied their food as he ranted, or scrutinized the conference table or scribbled frantic notes in their day-planners. Anything to avoid looking me in the eye. Even Burton, alone at the head of the table, just munched on a bagel and stared at CNN, the muted screen aflicker with footage of zombies staggering along on their unfathomable errands. Toward dawn, as the final tallies rolled in from the western districts, they had started to gravitate toward cemeteries. No one yet knew why.

"*My* fault?" I said, but my indignation was manufactured. About five that morning, waking from nightmare in my darkened hotel room, I had arrived at the same conclusion as everyone else.

"The goddamn talk show," Lewis said, as if that explained everything.

And maybe it did.

The goddamn talk show in question was none other than *Crossfire* and the Sunday before the polls opened I got caught in it. I had broken the first commandment of political life, a commandment I had flogged relentlessly for the last year. Stay on message, stick to the talking points.

Thou shalt not speak from the heart.

The occasion of this amateurish mistake was a six-year-old girl named Dana Maguire. Three days before I went on the air, a five-year-old boy gunned Dana down in her after-school program. The kid had found the pistol in his father's nightstand, and just as Dana's mother was coming in to pick her up, he tugged it from his insulated lunch sack and shot Dana in the neck. She died in her mother's arms while the five-year-old looked on in tears.

Just your typical day in America, except the first time I saw Dana's photo in the news, I felt something kick a hole in my chest. I can remember the moment to this day: October light slanting through hotel windows, the television on low while I talked to my grandmother in California. I don't have much in the way of family. There had been an uncle on my father's side, but he had drifted out of my life after my folks died, leaving my mother's parents to raise me. There's just the two of us since my grandfather passed on five years ago, and even in the heat of a campaign, I try to check on Gran every day. Mostly she rattles on about old folks in the home, a litany of names and ailments I can barely keep straight at the best of times. And that afternoon, half-watching some glib CNN hardbody do a stand-up in front of Little Tykes Academy, I lost the thread of her words altogether.

Next thing I know, she's saying, "Robert, Robert—" in this troubled voice, and me, I'm sitting on a hotel bed in Dayton, Ohio, weeping for a little girl I never heard of. Grief, shock, you name it—ten years in public life, nothing like that had ever happened to me before. But after that, I couldn't think of it in political terms. After that, Dana Maguire was personal.

Predictably, the whole thing came up on *Crossfire*. Joe Stern, Stoddard's campaign director and a man I've known for years, leaned into the camera and espoused the usual line—you know, the one about the constitutional right to bear arms, as if Jefferson had personally foreseen the rapid-fire semi-automatic with a sixteen-round clip. Coming from the mouth of Joe Stern, a smug fleshy ideologue who ought to have known better, this line enraged me.

Even so, I hardly recognized the voice that responded to him. I felt as though something else was speaking through me—as though a voice had possessed me, a speaker from that broken hole in the center of my chest.

What it said, that voice, was: "If Grant Burton is elected, he'll see that every handgun in the United States is melted into pig iron. He'll do everything in his power to save the Dana Maguires of this nation."

Joe Stern puffed up like a toad. "This isn't about Dana Maguire—"

The voice interrupted him. "If there's any justice in the universe, Dana Maguire will rise up from her grave to haunt you," the voice said. It said, "If it's not about Dana Maguire, then what on Earth is it about?"

Stoddard had new ads in saturation before the day was out: Burton's face, my words in voice-over. *If Grant Burton is elected, he'll see that every handgun in the United States is melted into pig iron.* By Monday afternoon, we had plummeted six points and Lewis wasn't speaking to me.

I couldn't seem to shut him up now, though.

He leaned across the table and jabbed a thick finger at me, overturning a styrofoam cup of coffee. I watched the black pool spread as he shouted. "We were up five points, we had it won before you opened your goddamn—"

Angela Dey, our chief pollster, interrupted him. "Look!" she said, pointing at the television.

Burton touched the volume button on the remote, but the image on the screen was clear enough: a cemetery in upstate New York, one of the new ones where the stones are set flush to the earth to make mowing easier. Three or four zombies had fallen to their knees by a fresh grave.

"Good God," Dey whispered. "What are they doing?"

No one gave her an answer and I suppose she hadn't expected one. She could see as well as the rest of us what was happening. The dead were scrabbling at the earth with their bare hands.

A line from some old poem I had read in college—

—*ahh, who's digging on my grave*—

—lodged in my head, rattling around like angry candy, and for the first time I had a taste of the hysteria that would possess us all by the time this was done. Graves had opened, the dead walked the earth. All humanity trembled.

Ahh, who's digging on my grave?

Lewis flung himself back against his chair and glared at me balefully. "This is all your fault."

"At least they voted for us," I said.

Not that we swept into the White House at the head of a triumphal procession of zombies. Anything but, actually. The voting rights of the dead turned out to be a serious constitutional question, and Stoddard lodged a complaint with the Federal Election Commission. Dead people had no say in the affairs of the living, he argued, and besides, none of them were legally registered anyway. Sensing defeat, the Democratic National Committee counter-sued, claiming that the sheer *presence* of the dead may have kept legitimate voters from the polls.

While the courts pondered these issues in silence, the world convulsed. Church attendance soared. The president impaneled experts and blue-ribbon commissions, the Senate held hearings. The CDC convened a task force to search for biological agents. At the UN, the Security Council debated a quarantine against the United States; the stock market lost fifteen percent on the news.

Meanwhile, the dead went unheeding about their business. They never spoke or otherwise attempted to communicate, yet you could sense an intelligence, inhuman and remote, behind their mass resurrection. They spent the next weeks opening fresh graves, releasing the recently buried from entombment. With bare hands, they clawed away the dirt; through sheer numbers, they battered apart the concrete vaults and sealed caskets. You would see them in the streets, stinking of formaldehyde and putrefaction, their hands torn and ragged, the rich earth of the grave impacted under their fingernails.

Their numbers swelled.

People died, but they didn't *stay* dead; the newly resurrected kept busy at their graves.

A week after the balloting, the Supreme Court handed down a decision over-turning the election. Congress, meeting in emergency session, set a new date for the first week of January. If nothing else, the year 2000 debacle in Florida had taught us the virtue of speed.

Lewis came to my hotel room at dusk to tell me.

"We're in business," he said.

When I didn't answer, he took a chair across from me. We stared over the fog-shrouded city in silence. Far out above the lake, threads of rain seamed the sky. Good news for the dead. The digging would go easier.

Lewis turned the bottle on the table so he could read the label. I knew what it was: Glenfiddich, a good single malt. I'd been sipping it from a hotel tumbler most of the afternoon.

"Why'nt you turn on some lights in here?" Lewis said.

"I'm fine in the dark."

Lewis grunted. After a moment, he fetched the other glass. He wiped it out with his handkerchief and poured.

"So tell me."

Lewis tilted his glass, grimaced. "January fourth. The president signed the bill twenty minutes ago. Protective cordons fifty yards from polling stations. Only the living can vote. Jesus. I can't believe I'm even saying that." He cradled his long face in his hands. "So you in?"

"Does he want me?"

"Yes."

"What about you, Lewis? Do you want me?"

Lewis said nothing. We just sat there, breathing in the woodsy aroma of the scotch, watching night bleed into the sky.

"You screwed me at staff meeting the other day," I said. "You hung me out to dry in front of everyone. It won't work if you keep cutting the ground out from under my feet."

"Goddamnit, I was *right*. In ten seconds, you destroyed everything we've worked for. We had it won."

"Oh come on, Lewis. If *Crossfire* never happened, it could have gone either way. Five points, that's nothing. We were barely outside the plus and minus, you know that."

"Still. Why'd you have to say that?"

I thought about that strange sense I'd had at the time: another voice speaking through me. Mouthpiece of the dead.

"You ever think about that little girl, Lewis?"

He sighed. "Yeah. Yeah, I do." He lifted his glass. "Look. If you're angling for some kind of apology—"

"I don't want an apology."

"Good," he said. Then, grudgingly: "We need you on this one, Rob. You know that."

"January," I said. "That gives us almost two months."

"We're way up right now."

"Stoddard will make a run. Wait and see."

"Yeah." Lewis touched his face. It was dark, but I could sense the gesture. He'd be fingering his acne scars, I'd spent enough time with him to know that. "I don't know, though," he said. "I think the right might sit this one out. They think it's the fuckin' Rapture, who's got time for politics?"

"We'll see."

He took the rest of his scotch in a gulp and stood. "Yeah. We'll see."

I didn't move as he showed himself out, just watched his reflection in the big plate glass window. He opened the door and turned to look back, a tall man framed in light from the hall, his face lost in shadow.

"Rob?"

"Yeah?"

"You all right?"

I drained my glass and swished the scotch around in my mouth. I'm having a little trouble sleeping these days, I wanted to say. I'm having these dreams.

But all I said was, "I'm fine, Lewis. I'm just fine."

I wasn't, though, not really.

None of us were, I guess, but even now—maybe *especially* now—the thing I remember most about those first weeks is how little the resurrection of the dead altered our everyday lives. Isolated incidents made the news—I remember a serial killer being arrested as his victims heaved themselves bodily from their shallow backyard graves—but mostly people just carried on. After the initial shock, markets stabilized. Stores filled up with Thanksgiving turkeys; radio stations began counting the shopping days until Christmas.

Yet I think the hysteria must have been there all along, like a swift current just beneath the surface of a placid lake. An undertow, the kind of current that'll kill you if you're not careful. Most people looked okay, but scratch the surface and we were all going nuts in a thousand quiet ways.

Ahh, who's digging on my grave, and all that.

Me, I couldn't sleep. The stress of the campaign had been mounting steadily even before my meltdown on *Crossfire*, and in those closing days, with the polls in California—and all those lovely delegates—a hair too close to call, I'd been waking grainy-eyed and yawning every morning. I was feeling guilty, too. Three years ago, Gran broke her hip and landed in a Long Beach nursing home. And while I talked to her daily, I could never manage to steal a day or two to see her, despite all the time we spent campaigning in California.

But the resurrection of the dead marked a new era in my insomnia. Stumbling to bed late on election night, my mind blistered with images of zombies in the streets, I fell into a fevered dream. I found myself wandering through an abandoned city. Everything burned with the tenebrous significance of dreams—every brick and stone, the scraps of newsprint tumbling down highrise canyons, the darkness pooling in the mouths of desolate subways. But the worst thing of all was the sound, the lone sound in all that sea of silence: the obscurely terrible cadence of a faraway clock, impossibly magnified, echoing down empty alleys and forsaken avenues.

The air rang with it, haunting me, drawing me on at last into a district where the buildings loomed over steep, close streets, admitting only a narrow wedge of sky. An open door beckoned, a black slot in a high, thin house. I pushed open the gate, climbed the broken stairs, paused in the threshold. A colossal grandfather clock towered within, its hands poised a minute short of midnight. Transfixed, I watched the heavy pendulum sweep through its arc, driving home the hour.

The massive hands stood upright.

The air shattered around me. The very stones shook as the clock began to toll. Clapping my hands over my ears, I turned to flee, but there was nowhere to go. In the yard, in the street—as far as I could see—the dead had gathered. They stood there while the clock stroked out the hours, staring up at me with those haunted eyes, and I knew suddenly and absolutely—the way you know things in dreams—that they had come for me at last, that they had always been coming for me, for all of us, if only we had known it.

I woke then, coldly afraid.

The first gray light of morning slit the drapes, but I had a premonition that no dawn was coming, or at least a very different dawn from any I had ever dared imagine.

Stoddard made his run with two weeks to go.

December fourteenth, we're 37,000 feet over the Midwest in a leased Boeing 737, and Angela Dey drops the new numbers on us.

"Gentleman," she says, "we've hit a little turbulence."

It was a turning point, I can see that now. At the time, though, none of us much appreciated her little joke.

The resurrection of the dead had shaken things up—it had put us on top for a month or so—but Stoddard had been clawing his way back for a couple of weeks, crucifying us in the farm belt on a couple of ag bills where Burton cast deciding votes, hammering us in the south on vouchers. We knew that, of course, but I don't think any of us had foreseen just how close things were becoming.

"We're up seven points in California," Dey said. "The gay vote's keeping our heads above water, but the numbers are soft. Stoddard's got momentum."

"Christ," Lewis said, but Dey was already passing around another sheet.

"It gets worse," she said. "Florida, we're up two points. A statistical dead heat. We've got the minorities, Stoddard has the seniors. Everything's riding on turnout."

Libby Dixon, Burton's press secretary, cleared her throat. "We've got a pretty solid network among Hispanics—"

Dey shook her head. "Seniors win that one every time."

"Hispanics *never* vote," Lewis said. "We might as well wrap Florida up with a little bow and send it to Stoddard."

Dey handed around another sheet. She'd orchestrated the moment for maximum impact, doling it out one sheet at a time like that. Lewis slumped in his seat, probing his scars as she worked her way through the list: Michigan, New York, Ohio, all three delegate rich, all three of them neck-and-neck races. Three almost physical blows, too, you could see them in the faces ranged around the table.

"What the hell's going on here?" Lewis muttered as Dey passed out another sheet, and then the news out of Texas rendered even him speechless. Stoddard had us by six points. I ran through a couple of Alamo analogies before deciding that discretion was the better part of wisdom. "I thought we were gaining there," Lewis said.

Dey shrugged. I just read the numbers, I don't make them up.

"Things could be worse," Libby Dixon said.

"Yeah, but Rob's not allowed to do *Crossfire* any more," Lewis said, and a titter ran around the table. Lewis is good, I'll give him that. You could feel the tension ease.

"Suggestions?" Burton said.

Dey said, "I've got some focus group stuff on education. I was thinking maybe some ads clarifying our—"

"Hell with the ads," someone else said, "we've gotta spend more time in Florida. We've got to engage Stoddard on his ground."

"Maybe a series of town meetings?" Lewis said, and they went around like that for a while. I tried to listen, but Lewis's little icebreaker had reminded me of the dreams. I knew where I was—37,000 feet of dead air below me, winging my way toward a rally in Virginia—but inside my head I hadn't gone anywhere at all. Inside my head, I was stuck in the threshold of that dream house, staring out into the eyes of the dead.

The world had changed irrevocably, I thought abruptly.

That seems self-evident, I suppose, but at the time it had the quality of genuine revelation. The fact is, we had all—and I mean everyone by that, the entire culture, not just the campaign—we had all been pretending that nothing much had changed. Sure, we had UN debates and a CNN feed right out of a George Romero movie, but the implications of mass resurrection—the spiritual implications—had yet to bear down upon us. We were in denial. In that moment, with the plane rolling underneath me and someone—Tyler O'Neill I think it was, Libby Dixon's mousy assistant—droning on about going negative, I thought of something I'd heard a professor mention back at Northwestern: Copernicus formulated the heliocentric model of the solar system in the mid-1500s, but the Church didn't get around to punishing anyone for it until they threw Galileo in jail nearly a hundred years later. They spent the better part of a century trying to ignore the fact that the fundamental geography of the universe had been altered with a single stroke.

And so it had again.

The dead walked.

Three simple words, but everything else paled beside them—social security, campaign finance reform, education vouchers. *Everything.*

I wadded Dey's sheet into a noisy ball and flung it across the table. Tyler O'Neill stuttered and choked, and for a moment everyone just stared in silence at that wad of paper. You'd have thought I'd hurled a hand grenade, not a two-paragraph summary of voter idiocy in the Lone Star State.

Libby Dixon cleared her throat. "I hardly thin—"

"Shut up, Libby," I said. "Listen to yourselves for Christ's sake. We got zombies in the street and you guys are worried about going negative?"

"The whole…" Dey flapped her hand. ". . . zombie thing, it's not even on the radar. My numbers—"

"People *lie*, Angela."

Libby Dixon swallowed audibly.

"When it comes to death, sex, and money, everybody lies. A total stranger calls up on the telephone, and you expect some soccer mom to share her feelings about the fact that grandpa's rotten corpse is staggering around in the street?"

I had their attention all right.

For a minute the plane filled up with the muted roar of the engines. No human sound at all. And then Burton—Burton smiled.

"What are you thinking, Rob?"

"A great presidency is a marriage between a man and a moment," I said. "You told me that. Remember?"

"I remember."

"This is your moment, sir. You have to stop running away from it."

"What do you have in mind?" Lewis asked.

I answered the question, but I never even looked Lewis's way as I did it. I just held Grant Burton's gaze. It was like no one else was there at all, like it was just the two of us, and despite everything that's happened since, that's the closest I've ever come to making history.

"I want to find Dana Maguire," I said.

I'd been in politics since my second year at Northwestern. It was nothing I ever intended—who goes off to college hoping to be a senate aide?—but I was idealistic, and I liked the things Grant Burton stood for, so I found myself working the phones that fall as an unpaid volunteer. One thing led to another—an internship on the Hill, a post-graduate job as a research assistant—and somehow I wound up inside the beltway.

I used to wonder how my life might have turned out had I chosen another path. My senior year at Northwestern, I went out with a girl named Gwen, a junior, freckled and streaky blonde, with the kind of sturdy good looks that fall a hair short of beauty. Partnered in some forgettable lab exercise, we found we had grown up within a half hour of one another. Simple geographic coincidence, two Californians stranded in the frozen north, sustained us throughout the winter and into the spring. But we drifted in the weeks after graduation, and the last I had heard of her was a Christmas card five or six years back. I remember opening it and watching a scrap of paper slip to the floor. Her address and phone number, back home in Laguna Beach, with a little note. *Call me sometime*, it said, but I never did.

So there it was.

I was thirty-two years old, I lived alone, I'd never held a relationship together longer than eight months. Gran was my closest friend, and I saw her three times a year if I was lucky. I went to my ten year class reunion in Evanston, and everybody there was in a different life-place than I was. They all had kids and homes and churches.

Me, I had my job. Twelve hour days, five days a week. Saturdays I spent three or four hours at the office catching up. Sundays I watched the talk shows and then it was time to start all over again. That had been my routine for nearly a decade, and in all those years I never bothered to ask myself how I came to be there. It never even struck me as the kind of thing a person ought to ask.

Four years ago, during Burton's re-election campaign for the Senate, Lewis said a funny thing to me. We're sitting in a hotel bar, drinking Miller Lite and eating peanuts, when he turns to me and says, "You got anyone, Rob?"

"Got anyone?"

"You know, a girlfriend, a fiancée, somebody you care about."

Gwen flickered at the edge of my consciousness, but that was all. A flicker, nothing more.

I said, "No."

"That's good," Lewis said.

It was just the kind of thing he always said, sarcastic, a little mean-hearted. Usually I let it pass, but that night I had just enough alcohol zipping through my veins to call him on it.

"What's that supposed to mean?"

Lewis turned to look at me.

"I was going to say, you have someone you really care about—somebody you want to spend your life with—you might want to walk away from all this."

"Why's that?"

"This job doesn't leave enough room for relationships."

He finished his beer and pushed the bottle away, his gaze steady and clear. In the dim light his scars were invisible, and I saw him then as he could have been in a better world. For maybe a moment, Lewis was one step short of handsome.

And then the moment broke.

"Good night," he said, and turned away.

A few months after that—not long before Burton won his second six-year Senate term—Libby Dixon told me Lewis was getting a divorce. I suppose he must have known the marriage was coming apart around him.

But at the time nothing like that even occurred to me.

After Lewis left, I just sat at the bar running those words over in my mind. *This job doesn't leave enough room for relationships*, he had said, and I knew he had intended it as a warning. But what I felt instead was a bottomless sense of relief. I was perfectly content to be alone.

Burton was doing an event in St. Louis when the nursing home called to say that Gran had fallen again. Eighty-one-year-old bones are fragile, and the last time I had been out there—just after the convention—Gran's case manager had privately informed me that another fall would probably do it.

"Do what?" I had asked.

The case manager looked away. She shuffled papers on her desk while her meaning bore in on me: another fall would kill her.

I suppose I must have known this at some level, but to hear it articulated so baldly shook me. From the time I was four, Gran had been the single stable institution in my life. I had been visiting in Long Beach, half a continent from home, when my family—my parents and sister—died in the car crash. It took the state police back in Pennsylvania nearly a day to track me down. I still remember the moment: Gran's mask-like expression as she hung up the phone, her hands cold against my face as she knelt before me.

She made no sound as she wept. Tears spilled down her cheeks, leaving muddy tracks in her make-up, but she made no sound at all. "I love you, Robert," she said. She said, "You must be strong."

That's my first true memory.

Of my parents, my sister, I remember nothing at all. I have a snapshot of them at a beach somewhere, maybe six months before I was born: my father lean and smoking, my mother smiling, her abdomen just beginning to swell. In the picture, Alice—she would have been four then—stands just in front of them, a happy blonde child cradling a plastic shovel. When I was a kid I used to stare at that photo, wondering how you can miss people you never even knew. I did though, an almost physical ache way down inside me, the kind of phantom pain amputees must feel.

A ghost of that old pain squeezed my heart as the case manager told me about Gran's fall. "We got lucky," she said. "She's going to be in a wheelchair a month or two, but she's going to be okay."

Afterwards, I talked to Gran herself, her voice thin and querulous, addled with pain killers. "Robert," she said, "I want you to come out here. I want to see you."

"I want to see you, too," I said, "but I can't get away right now. As soon as the election's over—"

"I'm an old woman," she told me crossly. "I may not be here after the election."

I managed a laugh at that, but the laugh sounded hollow even in my own ears. The words had started a grim little movie unreeling in my head—a snippet of Gran's cold body staggering to its feet, that somehow inhuman tomb light shining out from behind its eyes. I suppose most of us must have imagined something like that during those weeks, but it unnerved me all the same. It reminded me too much of the dreams. It felt like I was there again, gazing out into the faces of the implacable dead, that enormous clock banging out the hours.

"Robert—" Gran was saying, and I could hear the Demerol singing in her voice. "Are you there, Ro—"

And for no reason at all, I said:

"Did my parents have a clock, Gran?"

"A clock?"

"A grandfather clock."

She was silent so long I thought maybe *she* had hung up.

"That was your uncle's clock," she said finally, her voice thick and distant.

"My uncle?"

"Don," she said. "On your father's side."

"What happened to the clock?"

"Robert, I want you to come out he—"

"*What happened to the clock, Gran?*"

"Well, how would I know?" she said. "He couldn't keep it, could he? I suppose he must have sold it."

"What do you mean?"

But she didn't answer.

I listened to the swell and fall of Demerol sleep for a moment, and then the voice of the case manager filled my ear. "She's drifted off. If you want, I can call back later—"

I looked up as a shadow fell across me. Lewis stood in the doorway.

"No, that's okay. I'll call her in the morning."

I hung up the phone and stared over the desk at him. He had a strange expression on his face.

"What?" I said.

"It's Dana Maguire."

"What about her?"

"They've found her."

Eight hours later, I touched down at Logan under a cloudy midnight sky. We had hired a private security firm to find her, and one of their agents—an expressionless man with the build of an ex-athlete—met me at the gate.

"You hook up with the ad people all right?" I asked in the car, and from the way he answered, a monosyllabic "Fine," you could tell what he thought of ad people.

"The crew's in place?"

"They're already rigging the lights."

"How'd you find her?"

He glanced at me, streetlight shadow rippling across his face like water. "Dead people ain't got much imagination. Soon's we get the fresh ones in the ground, they're out there digging." He laughed humorlessly. "You'd think people'd stop burying 'em."

"It's the ritual, I guess."

"Maybe." He paused. Then: "Finding her, we put some guys on the cemeteries and kept our eyes open, that's all."

"Why'd it take so long?"

For a moment there was no sound in the car but the hum of tires on pavement and somewhere far away a siren railing against the night. The agent rolled down his window and spat emphatically into the slipstream. "City the size of Boston," he said, "it has a lot of fucking cemeteries."

The cemetery in question turned out to be everything I could have hoped for: remote and unkempt, with weathered gothic tombstones right off a Hollywood back lot. And wouldn't it be comforting to think so, I remember thinking as I got out of the car—the ring of lights atop the hill nothing more than stage dressing, the old world as it had been always. But it wasn't, of course, and the ragged figures digging at the grave weren't actors, either. You could smell them for one, the stomach-wrenching stench of decay. A light rain had begun to fall, too, and it had the feel of a genuine Boston drizzle, cold and steady toward the bleak fag end of December.

Andy, the director, turned when he heard me.

"Any trouble?" I asked.

"No. They don't care much what we're about, long as we don't interfere."

"Good."

Andy pointed. "There she is, see?"

"Yeah, I see her."

She was on her knees in the grass, still wearing the dress she had been buried in. She dug with single-minded intensity, her arms caked with mud to the elbow, her face empty of anything remotely human. I stood and stared at her for a while, trying to decide what it was I was feeling.

"You all right?" Andy said.

"What?"

"I said, are you all right? For a second there, I thought you were crying."

"No," I said. "I'm fine. It's the rain, that's all."

"Right."

So I stood there and half-listened while he filled me in. He had several cameras running, multiple filters and angles, he was playing with the lights. He told me all this and none of it meant anything at all to me. None of it mattered as long as I got the footage I wanted. Until then, there was nothing for me here.

He must have been thinking along the same lines, for when I turned to go, he called after me: "Say, Rob, you needn't have come out tonight, you know."

I looked back at him, the rain pasting my hair against my forehead and running down into my eyes. I shivered. "I know," I said. A moment later, I added: "I just—I wanted to see her somehow."

But Andy had already turned away.

I still remember the campaign ad, my own private nightmare dressed up in cinematic finery. Andy and I cobbled it together on Christmas Eve, and just after midnight in a darkened Boston studio, we cracked open a bottle of bourbon in celebration and sat back to view the final cut. I felt a wave of nausea roll over me as the first images flickered across the monitor. Andy had shot the whole thing from distorted angles in grainy black and white, the film just a hair overexposed to sharpen the contrast. Sixty seconds of derivative expressionism, some media critic dismissed it, but even he conceded it possessed a certain power.

You've seen it, too, I suppose. Who hasn't?

She will rise from her grave to haunt you, the opening title card reads, and the image holds in utter silence for maybe half a second too long. Long enough to be unsettling, Andy said, and you could imagine distracted viewers all across the heartland perking up, wondering what the hell was wrong with the sound.

The words dissolve into an image of hands, bloodless and pale, gouging at moist black earth. The hands of a child, battered and raw and smeared with the filth and corruption of the grave, digging, digging. There's something remorseless about them, something relentless and terrible. They could dig forever, and they might, you can see that. And now, gradually, you awaken to sound: rain hissing from a midnight sky, the steady slither of wet earth underhand, and something else, a sound so perfectly lacking that it's almost palpable in its absence, the unearthly silence of the dead. Freeze frame on a tableau out of Goya or Bosch: seven or eight zombies, half-dressed and rotting, laboring tirelessly over a fresh grave.

Fade to black, another slug line, another slow dissolve.

Dana Maguire came back.

The words melt into a long shot of the child, on her knees in the poison muck of the grave. Her dress clings to her thighs, and it's a dress someone has taken some care about—white and lacy, the kind of dress you'd bury your little girl in if you had to do it—and it's ruined. All the care and heartache that went into that dress, utterly ruined. Torn and fouled and sopping. Rain slicks her blonde hair black against her skull. And as the camera glides in upon Dana Maguire's face, half-shadowed and filling three-quarters of the screen, you can glimpse the wound at her throat, flushed clean and pale. Dark roses of rot bloom along the high ridge of her cheekbone. Her eyes burn with the cold hard light of vistas you never want to see, not even in your dreams.

The image holds for an instant, a mute imperative, and then, mercifully, fades. Words appear and deliquesce on an ebon screen, three phrases, one by one:

The dead have spoken.

Now it's your turn.

Burton for president.

Andy touched a button. A reel caught and reversed itself. The screen went gray, and I realized I had forgotten to breathe. I sipped at my drink.

The whiskey burned in my throat, it made me feel alive.

"What do you think?" Andy said.

"I don't know. I don't know what to think."

Grinning, he ejected the tape and tossed it in my lap. "Merry Christmas," he said, raising his glass. "To our savior born."

And so we drank again.

Dizzy with exhaustion, I made my way back to my hotel and slept for eleven hours straight. I woke around noon on Christmas day. An hour later, I was on a plane.

By the time I caught up to the campaign in Richmond, Lewis was in a rage, pale and apoplectic, his acne scars flaring an angry red. "You seen these?" he said, thrusting a sheaf of papers at me.

I glanced through them quickly—more bad news from Angela Dey, Burton slipping further in the polls—and then I set them aside. "Maybe this'll help," I said, holding up the tape Andy and I had cobbled together.

We watched it together, all of us, Lewis and I, the entire senior staff, Burton himself, his face grim as the first images flickered across the screen. Even now, viewing it for the second time, I could feel its impact. And I could see it in the faces of the others as well—Dey's jaw dropping open, Lewis snorting in disbelief. As the screen froze on the penultimate image—Dana Maguire's decay-ravaged face—Libby Dixon turned away.

"There's no way we can run that," she said.

"We've got—" I began, but Dey interrupted me.

"She's right, Rob. It's not a campaign ad, it's a horror movie." She turned to Burton, drumming his fingers quietly at the head of the table. "You put this out there, you'll drop ten points, I guarantee it."

"Lewis?" Burton asked.

Lewis pondered the issue for a moment, rubbing his pitted cheek with one crooked finger. "I agree," he said finally. "The ad's a frigging nightmare. It's not the answer."

"The ad's revolting," Libby said. "The media will eat us alive for politicizing the kid's death."

"We *ought* to be politicizing it," I said. "We ought to make it mean something."

"You run that ad, Rob," Lewis said, "every redneck in America is going to remember you threatening to take away their guns. You want to make that mistake twice?"

"Is it a mistake? For Christ's sake, the dead are walking, Lewis. The old rules don't apply." I turned to Libby. "What's Stoddard say, Libby, can you tell me that?"

"He hasn't touched it since election day."

"Exactly. He hasn't said a thing, not about Dana Maguire, not about the dead people staggering around in the street. Ever since the FEC overturned the election, he's been dodging the issue—"

"Because it's political suicide," Dey said. "He's been dodging it because it's the right thing to do."

"Bullshit," I snapped. "It's *not* the right thing to do. It's pandering and it's cowardice—it's moral cowardice—and if we do it we deserve to lose."

You could hear everything in the long silence that ensued—cars passing in the street, a local staffer talking on the phone in the next room, the faint tattoo of Burton's fingers against the formica table top. I studied him for a moment, and once again I had that sense of something else speaking through me, as though I were merely a conduit for another voice.

"What do you think about guns, sir?" I asked. "What do you really think?"

Burton didn't answer for a long moment. When he did, I think he surprised everyone at the table. "The death rate by handguns in this country is triple that for every other industrialized nation on the planet," he said. "They ought to be melted into pig iron, just like Rob said. Let's go with the ad."

"Sir—" Dey was standing.

"I've made up my mind," Burton said. He picked up the sheaf of papers at his elbow and shuffled through them. "We're down in Texas and California, we're slipping in Michigan and Ohio." He tossed the papers down in disgust. "Stoddard looks good in the south, Angela. What do we got to lose?"

We couldn't have timed it better.

The new ad went into national saturation on December 30th, in the shadow of a strange new year. I was watching a bowl game in my hotel room the first time I saw it on the air. It chilled me all over, as though I'd never seen it before. Afterwards, the room filled with the sound of the ball game, but now it all seemed hollow. The cheers of the fans rang with a labored gaiety, the crack of pads had the crisp sharpness of movie sound effects. A barb of loneliness pierced me. I would have called someone, but I had no one to call.

Snapping off the television, I pocketed my key-card.

Downstairs, the same football game was playing, but at least there was liquor and a ring of conversation in the air. A few media folks from Burton's entourage clustered around the bar, but I begged off when they invited me to join them. I sat at a table in the corner instead, staring blindly at the television and drinking scotch without any hurry, but without any effort to keep track either. I don't know how much I drank that night, but I was a little unsteady when I stood to go.

I had a bad moment on the way back to my room. When the elevator doors slid apart, I found I couldn't remember my room number. I couldn't say for sure I had even chosen the right floor. The hotel corridor stretched away before me, bland and anonymous, a hallway of locked doors behind which only strangers slept. The endless weary grind of the campaign swept over me, and suddenly I was sick of it all—the long midnight flights and the hotel laundries, the relentless blur of cities and smiling faces. I wanted more than anything else in the world to go home. Not my cramped apartment in the District either.

Home. Wherever that was.

Independent of my brain, my fingers had found my key-card. I tugged it from my pocket and studied it grimly. I had chosen the right floor after all.

Still in my clothes, I collapsed across my bed and fell asleep. I don't remember any dreams, but sometime in the long cold hour before dawn, the phone yanked me awake. "Turn on CNN," Lewis said. I listened to him breathe as I fumbled for the remote and cycled through the channels.

I punched up the volume.

"—unsubstantiated reports out of China concerning newly awakened dead in remote regions of the Tibetan Plateau—"

I was awake now, fully awake. My head pounded. I had to work up some spit before I could speak.

"Anyone got anything solid?" I asked.

"I'm working with a guy in State for confirmation. So far we got nothing but rumor."

"If it's true—"

"If it's true," Lewis said, "you're gonna look like a fucking genius."

Our numbers were soft in the morning, but things were looking up by mid-afternoon. The Chinese weren't talking and no one yet had footage of the Tibetan dead—but rumors were trickling in from around the globe. Unconfirmed reports from UN Peacekeepers in Kosovo told of women and children clawing their way free from previously unknown mass graves.

By New Year's Day, rumors gave way to established fact. The television flickered with grainy images from Groznyy and Addis Ababa. The dead were arising in scattered locales around the world. And here at home, the polls were shifting. Burton's crowds grew larger and more enthusiastic at every rally, and as our jet winged down through the night towards Pittsburgh, I watched Stoddard answering questions about the crisis on a satellite feed from C-SPAN. He looked gray and tired, his long face brimming with uncertainty. He was too late, we owned the issue now, and watching him, I could see he knew it, too. He was going through the motions, that's all.

There was a celebratory hum in the air as the plane settled to the tarmac. Burton spoke for a few minutes at the airport, and then the Secret Service people tightened the bubble, moving us en masse toward the motorcade. Just before he ducked into the limo, Burton dismissed his entourage. His hand closed about my shoulder. "You're with me," he said.

He was silent as the limo slid away into the night, but as the downtown towers loomed up before us he turned to look at me. "I wanted to thank you," he said.

"There's no—"

He held up his hand. "I wouldn't have had the courage to run that ad, not without you pushing me. I've wondered about that, you know. It was like you knew something, like you knew the story was getting ready to break again."

I could sense the question behind his words—*Did you know, Rob? Did you?*—but I didn't have any answers. Just that impression of a voice speaking through me from beyond, from somewhere else, and that didn't make any sense, or none that I was able to share.

"When I first got started in this business," Burton was saying, "there was a local pol back in Chicago, kind of a mentor. He told me once you could tell what kind of man you were dealing with by the people he chose to surround himself with. When I think about that, I feel good, Rob." He sighed. "The world's gone crazy, that's for sure, but with people like you on our side, I think we'll be all right. I just wanted to tell you that."

"Thank you, sir."

He nodded. I could feel him studying me as I gazed out the window, but suddenly I could find nothing to say. I just sat there and watched the city slide by, the past welling up inside me. Unpleasant truths lurked like rocks just beneath the visible surface. I could sense them somehow.

"You all right, Rob?"

"Just thinking," I said. "Being in Pittsburgh, it brings back memories."

"I thought you grew up in California."

"I did. I was born here, though. I lived here until my parents died."

"How old were you?"

"Four. I was four years old."

We were at the hotel by then. As the motorcade swung across two empty lanes into the driveway, Gran's words—

—*that was your uncle's clock, he couldn't keep it*—

—sounded in my head. The limo eased to the curb. Doors slammed. Agents slid past outside, putting a protective cordon around the car. The door opened, and cold January air swept in. Burton was gathering his things.

"Sir—"

He paused, looking back.

"Tomorrow morning, could I have some time alone?"

He frowned. "I don't know, Rob, the schedule's pretty tight—"

"No, sir. I mean—I mean a few hours off."

"Something wrong?"

"There's a couple of things I'd like to look into. My parents and all that. Just an hour or two if you can spare me."

He held my gaze a moment longer.

Then: "That's fine, Rob." He reached out and squeezed my shoulder. "Just be at the airport by two."

That night I dreamed of a place that wasn't quite Dana Maguire's daycare. It *looked* like a daycare—half a dozen squealing kids, big plastic toys, an indestructible grade of carpet—but certain details didn't fit: the massive grandfather clock, my uncle's clock, standing in one corner; my parents, dancing to big band music that seemed to emanate from nowhere.

I was trying to puzzle this through when I saw the kid clutching the lunch sack. There was an odd expression on his face, a haunted heartbroken expression, and too late I understood what was about to happen. I was trying to move, to scream, anything, as he dragged the pistol out of the bag. But my lips were sealed, I couldn't speak. Glancing down, I saw that I was rooted to the floor. Literally *rooted*. My bare feet had grown these long knotted tendrils. The carpet was twisted and raveled where they had driven themselves into the floor.

My parents whirled about in an athletic fox-trot, their faces manic with laughter. The music was building to an awful crescendo, percussives bleeding seamlessly together, the snap of the snare drums, the terrible booming tones of the clock, the quick sharp report of the gun.

I saw the girl go over backwards, her hands clawing at her throat as she convulsed. Blood drenched me, a spurting arterial fountain—I could feel it hot against my skin—and in the same moment this five-year-old kid turned to stare at me. Tears streamed down his cheeks, and this kid—this child really, and that's all I could seem to think—

—*he's just a child he's only a child*—

—he had my face.

I woke then, stifling a scream. Silence gripped the room and the corridor beyond it, and beyond that the city. I felt as if the world itself were drowning, sunk fathoms deep in the fine and private silence of the grave.

I stood, brushing the curtains aside. An anonymous grid of lights burned beyond the glass, an alien hieroglyph pulsing with enigmatic significance. Staring out at it, I was seized by an impression of how fragile everything is, how thin the barrier that separates us from the abyss. I shrank from the window, terrified by a sense that the world was far larger—and immeasurably stranger—than the world I'd known before, a sense of vast and formless energies churning out there in the dark.

I spent the next morning in the Carnegie Library in Oakland, reeling through back issues of the *Post-Gazette*. It didn't take long to dig up the article about the accident—I knew the date well enough—but I wasn't quite prepared for what I found there. Gran had always been reticent about the wreck—about everything to do with my life in Pittsburgh, actually—but I'd never really paused to give that much thought. She'd lost her family, too, after all—a grand-daughter, a son-in-law, her only child—and even as a kid, I could see why she might not want to talk about it.

The headline flickering on the microfilm reader rocked me, though. *Two die in fiery collision*, it read, and before I could properly formulate the question in my mind—

—*there were three of them*—

—I was scanning the paragraphs below. Disconnected phrases seemed to hover above the cramped columns—bridge abutment, high speed, alcohol-related—and halfway through the article, the following words leapt out at me:

> Friends speculate that the accident may have been   the product of a suicide pact. The couple were said to be grief-stricken following the death of their daughter, Alice, nine, in a bizarre shooting accident three weeks ago.

I stood, abruptly nauseated, afraid to read any further. A docent approached—

"Sir, are you all—"

—but I thrust her away.

Outside, traffic lumbered by, stirring the slush on Forbes Avenue. I sat on a bench and fought the nausea for a long time, cradling my face in my hands while I waited for it to pass. A storm was drifting in, and when I felt better I lifted my face to the sky, anxious for the icy burn of snow against my cheeks. Somewhere in the city, Grant Burton was speaking. Somewhere, reanimated corpses scrabbled at frozen graves.

The world lurched on.

I stood, belting my coat. I had a plane to catch.

I held myself together for two days, during our final campaign swing through the Midwest on January 3 and the election that followed, but I think I had already arrived at a decision. Most of the senior staff sensed it, as well, I think. They congratulated me on persuading Burton to run the ad, but they didn't come to me for advice much in those final hours. I seemed set-apart somehow, isolated, contagious.

Lewis clapped me on the back as we watched the returns roll in. "Jesus, Rob," he said, "you're supposed to be happy right now."

"Are you, Lewis?"

I looked up at him, his tall figure slumped, his face a fiery map of scars.

"What did you give up to get us here?" I asked, but he didn't answer. I hadn't expected him to.

The election unfolded without a hitch. Leaving off their work in the grave-yards, the dead gathered about the polling stations, but even they seemed to sense that the rules had changed this time around. They made no attempt to cast their ballots. They just stood behind the cordons the National Guard had set up, still and silent, regarding the proceedings with flat remorseless eyes. Voters scurried past them with bowed heads, their faces pinched against the stench of decay. On *Nightline*, Ted Koppel noted that the balloting had drawn the highest turnout in American history, something like ninety-three percent.

"Any idea why so many voters came out today?" he asked the panel.

"Maybe they were afraid not to," Cokie Roberts replied, and I felt an answer-ing chord vibrate within me. Trust Cokie to get it right.

Stoddard conceded soon after the polls closed in the west. It was obvious by then. In his victory speech, Burton talked about a mandate for change. "The people have spoken," he said, and they had, but I couldn't help wondering what might be speaking through them, and what it might be trying to say. Some commentators speculated that it was over now. The dead would return to the graves, the world would be the old world we had known.

But that's not the way it happened.

On January 5, the dead were digging once again, their numbers always swell-ing. CNN was carrying the story when I handed Burton my resignation. He read it slowly and then he lifted his gaze to my face.

"I can't accept this, Rob," he said. "We need you now. The hard work's just getting underway."

"I'm sorry, sir. I haven't any choice."

"Surely we can work something out."

"I wish we could."

We went through several iterations of this exchange before he nodded. "We'll miss you," he said. "You'll always have a place here, whenever you're ready to get back in the game."

I was at the door when he called to me again.

"Is there anything I can do to help, Rob?"

"No, sir," I said. "I have to take care of this myself."

I spent a week in Pittsburgh, walking the precipitous streets of neighbor-hoods I remembered only in my dreams. I passed a morning hunting up the house where my parents had lived, and one bright, cold afternoon I drove out 76 and pulled my rental to the side of the interstate, a hundred yards short of the bridge where they died. Eighteen wheelers thundered past, throwing up glittering arcs of spray, and the smell of the highway enveloped me, diesel and iron. It was pretty much what I had expected, a slab of faceless concrete, nothing more.

We leave no mark.

Evenings, I took solitary meals in diners and talked to Gran on the telephone—tranquil gossip about the old folks in the home mostly, empty of anything real. Afterwards, I drank Iron City and watched cable movies until I got drunk enough to sleep. I ignored the news as best I could, but I couldn't help catching glimpses as I buzzed through the channels. All around the world, the dead were walking.

They walked in my dreams, as well, stirring memories better left forgotten. Mornings, I woke with a sense of dread, thinking of Galileo, thinking of the Church. I had urged Burton to engage this brave new world, yet the thought of embracing such a fundamental transformation of my own history—of following through on the article in the *Post-Gazette*, the portents within my dreams—paralyzed me utterly. I suppose it was by then a matter mostly of verifying my own fears and suspicions—suppose I already knew, at some level, what I had yet to confirm. But the lingering possibility of doubt was precious, safe, and I clung to it for a few days longer, unwilling to surrender.

Finally, I could put it off no longer.

I drove down to the Old Public Safety Building on Grant Street. Upstairs, a grizzled receptionist brought out the file I requested. It was all there in untutored bureaucratic prose. There was a sheaf of official photos, too, glossy black and white prints. I didn't want to look at them, but I did anyway. I felt it was something I ought to do.

A little while later, someone touched my shoulder. It was the receptionist, her broad face creased with concern. Her spectacles swung at the end of a little silver chain as she bent over me. "You all right?" she asked.

"Yes, ma'am, I'm fine."

I stood, closing the file, and thanked her for her time.

I left Pittsburgh the next day, shedding the cold as the plane nosed above a lid of cloud. From LAX, I caught the 405 South to Long Beach. I drove with the window down, grateful for the warmth upon my arm, the spike of palm fronds against the sky. The slipstream carried the scent of a world blossoming and fresh, a future yet unmade, a landscape less scarred by history than the blighted industrial streets I'd left behind.

Yet even here the past lingered. It was the past that had brought me here, after all.

The nursing home was a sprawl of landscaped grounds and low-slung stucco buildings, faintly Spanish in design. I found Gran in a garden overlooking the Pacific, and I paused, studying her, before she noticed me in the doorway. She held a paperback in her lap, but she had left off reading to stare out across the water. A salt-laden breeze lifted her gray hair in wisps, and for a moment, looking at her, her eyes clear in her distinctly boned face, I could find my way back to the woman I had known as a boy.

But the years intervened, the way they always do. In the end, I couldn't help noticing her wasted body, or the glittering geometry of the wheelchair that enclosed her. Her injured leg jutted before her.

I must have sighed, for she looked up, adjusting the angle of the chair. "Robert!"

"Gran."

I sat by her, on a concrete bench. The morning overcast was breaking, and the sun struck sparks from the wave-tops.

"I'd have thought you were too busy to visit," she said, "now that your man has won the election."

"I'm not so busy these days. I don't work for him anymore."

"What do you mean—"

"I mean I quit my job."

"*Why?*" she said.

"I spent some time in Pittsburgh. I've been looking into things."

"Looking into things? Whatever on Earth is there to look *into*, Robert?" She smoothed the afghan covering her thighs, her fingers trembling.

I laid my hand across them, but she pulled away. "Gran, we need to talk."

"Talk?" She laughed, a bark of forced gaiety. "We talk every day."

"Look at me," I said, and after a long moment, she did. I could see the fear in her eyes, then. I wondered how long it had been there, and why I'd never noticed it before. "We need to talk about the past."

"The past is dead, Robert."

Now it was my turn to laugh. "Nothing's dead, Gran. Turn on the television sometime. Nothing stays dead anymore. *Nothing.*"

"I don't want to talk about that."

"Then what do you want to talk about?" I waved an arm at the building behind us, the ammonia-scented corridors and the endless numbered rooms inhabited by faded old people, already ghosts of the dead they would become. "You want to talk about Cora in 203 and the way her son never visits her or Jerry in 147 whose emphysema has been giving him trouble or all the—"

"All the what?" she snapped, suddenly fierce.

"All the fucking minutia we always talk about!"

"I won't have you speak to me like that! I raised you, I made you what you are today!"

"I know," I said. And then, more quietly, I said it again. "I know."

Her hands twisted in her lap. "The doctors told me you'd forget, it happens that way sometimes with trauma. You were so *young*. It seemed best somehow to just… let it go."

"But you lied."

"I didn't choose any of this," she said. "After it happened, your parents sent you out to me. Just for a little while, they said. They needed time to think things through."

She fell silent, squinting at the surf foaming on the rocks below. The sun bore down upon us, a heartbreaking disk of white in the faraway sky.

"I never thought they'd do what they did," she said, "and then it was too late. After that… how could I tell you?" She clenched my hand. "You seemed okay, Robert. You seemed like you were fine."

I stood, pulling away. "How could you know?"

"Robert—"

I turned at the door. She'd wheeled the chair around to face me. Her leg thrust toward me in its cast, like the prow of a ship. She was in tears. "Why, Robert? Why couldn't you just leave everything alone?"

"I don't know," I said, but even then I was thinking of Lewis, that habit he has of probing at his face where the acne left it pitted—as if someday he'll find his flesh smooth and handsome once again, and it's through his hands he'll know it. I guess that's it, you know: we've all been wounded, every one of us.

And we just can't keep our hands off the scars.

I drifted for the next day or two, living out of hotel rooms and haunting the places I'd known growing up. They'd changed like everything changes, the world always hurrying us along, but I didn't know what else to do, where else to go. I couldn't leave Long Beach, not till I made things up with Gran, but something held me back.

I felt ill at ease, restless. And then, as I fished through my wallet in a bar one afternoon, I saw a tiny slip of paper eddy to the floor. I knew what it was, of course, but I picked it up anyway. My fingers shook as I opened it up and stared at the message written there, *Call me sometime*, with the address and phone number printed neatly below.

I made it to Laguna Beach in fifty minutes. The address was a mile or so east of the water, a manicured duplex on a corner lot. She had moved no doubt—five years had passed—and if she hadn't moved she had married at the very least. But I left my car at the curb and walked up the sidewalk all the same. I could hear the bell through an open window, footsteps approaching, soft music lilting from the back of the house. Then the door opened and she was there, wiping her hands on a towel.

"Gwen," I said.

She didn't smile, but she didn't close the door either.

It was a start.

The house was small, but light, with wide windows in the kitchen overlooking a lush back lawn. A breeze slipped past the screens, infusing the kitchen with the scent of fresh-cut grass and the faraway smell of ocean.

"This isn't a bad time, is it?" I asked.

"Well, it's unexpected to say the least," she told me, lifting one eyebrow doubtfully, and in the gesture I caught a glimpse of the girl I'd known at Northwestern, rueful and wry and always faintly amused.

As she made coffee, I studied her, still freckled and faintly gamine, but not unchanged. Her eyes had a wary light in them, and fresh lines caged her thin upper lip. When she sat across from me at the table, toying with her coffee cup, I noticed a faint pale circle around her finger where a ring might have been.

Maybe I looked older too, for Gwen glanced up at me from beneath a fringe of streaky blonde bangs, her mouth arcing in a crooked smile. "You look younger on television," she said, and it was enough to get us started.

Gwen knew a fair bit of my story—my role in Burton's presidential campaign had bought me that much notoriety at least—and hers had a familiar ring to it. Law school at UCLA, five or six years billing hours in one of the big LA firms before the cutthroat culture got to her and she threw it over for a job with the ACLU, trading long days and a handsome wage for still longer ones and almost no wage at all. Her marriage had come apart around the same time. "Not out of any real animosity," she said. "More like a mutual lack of interest."

"And now? Are you seeing anyone?"

The question came out with a weight I hadn't intended.

She hesitated. "No one special." She lifted the eyebrow once again. "A habit I picked up as a litigator. Risk aversion."

By this time, the sky beyond the windows had softened into twilight and our coffee had grown cold. As shadows lengthened in the little kitchen, I caught Gwen glancing at the clock.

She had plans.

I stood. "I should go."

"Right."

She took my hand at the door, a simple handshake, that's all, but I felt something pass between us, an old connection close with a kind of electric spark. Maybe it wasn't there at all, maybe I only wanted to feel it—Gwen certainly seemed willing to let me walk out of her life once again—but a kind of desperation seized me.

Call it nostalgia or loneliness. Call it whatever you want. But suddenly the image of her wry glance from beneath the slant of hair leaped into mind.

I wanted to see her again.

"Listen," I said, "I know this is kind of out of the blue, but you wouldn't be free for dinner would you?"

She paused a moment. The shadow of the door had fallen across her face. She laughed uncertainly, and when she spoke, her voice was husky and uncertain. "I don't know, Rob. That was a long time ago. Like I said, I'm a little risk aversive these days."

"Right. Well, then, listen—it was really great seeing you."

I nodded and started across the lawn. I had the door of the rental open when she spoke again.

"What the hell," she said. "Let me make a call. It's only dinner, right?"

I went back to Washington for the inauguration.

Lewis and I stood together as we waited for the ceremony to begin, looking out at the dead. They had been on the move for days, legions of them, gathering on the Mall as far as the eye could see. A cluster of the living, maybe a couple hundred strong, had been herded onto the lawn before the bandstand—a token crowd of warm bodies for the television cameras—but I couldn't help thinking that Burton's true constituency waited beyond the cordons, still and silent and unutterably patient, the melting pot made flesh: folk of every color, race, creed, and age, in every stage of decay that would allow them to stand upright. Dana Maguire might be out there somewhere. She probably was.

The smell was palpable.

Privately, Lewis had told me that the dead had begun gathering elsewhere in the world, as well. Our satellites had confirmed it. In Cuba and North Korea, in Yugoslavia and Rwanda, the dead were on the move, implacable and slow, their purposes unknown and maybe unknowable.

"We need you, Rob," he had said. "Worse than ever."

"I'm not ready yet," I replied.

He had turned to me then, his long pitted face sagging. "What happened to you?" he asked.

And so I told him.

It was the first time I had spoken of it aloud, and I felt a burden sliding from my shoulders as the words slipped out. I told him all of it: Gran's evasions and my reaction to Dana Maguire that day on CNN and the sense I'd had on *Crossfire* that something else, something vast and remote and impersonal, was speaking through me, calling them back from the grave. I told him about the police report, too, how the memories had come crashing back upon me as I sat at the scarred table, staring into a file nearly three decades old.

"It was a party," I said. "My uncle was throwing a party and Mom and Dad's babysitter had canceled at the last minute, so Don told them just to bring us along. He lived alone, you know. He didn't have kids and he never thought about kids in the house."

"So the gun wasn't locked up?"

"No. It was late. It must have been close to midnight by then. People were getting drunk and the music was loud and Alice didn't seem to want much to do with me. I was in my uncle's bedroom, just fooling around the way kids do, and the gun was in the drawer of his nightstand."

I paused, memory surging through me, and suddenly I was there again, a child in my uncle's upstairs bedroom. Music thumped downstairs, jazzy big band music. I knew the grown-ups would be dancing and my dad would be nuzzling Mom's neck, and that night when he kissed me good night, I'd be able to smell him, the exotic aromas of bourbon and tobacco, shot through with the faint floral essence of Mom's perfume. Then my eyes fell upon the gun in the drawer. The light from the hall summoned unsuspected depths from the blued barrel.

I picked it up, heavy and cold.

All I wanted to do was show Alice. I just wanted to show her. I never meant to hurt anyone. I never meant to hurt Alice.

I said it to Lewis—"I never meant to hurt her"—and he looked away, unable to meet my eyes.

I remember carrying the gun downstairs to the foyer, Mom and Dad dancing beyond the frame of the doorway, Alice standing there watching. "I remember everything," I said to Lewis. "Everything but pulling the trigger. I remember the music screeching to a halt, somebody dragging the needle across the record, my mother screaming. I remember Alice lying on the floor and the blood and the weight of the gun in my hand. But the weird thing is, the thing I remember best is the way I felt at that moment."

"The way you felt," Lewis said.

"Yeah. A bullet had smashed the face of the clock, this big grandfather clock my uncle had in the foyer. It was chiming over and over, as though the bullet had wrecked the mechanism. That's what I remember most. The clock. I was afraid my uncle was going to be mad about the clock."

Lewis did something odd then. Reaching out, he clasped my shoulder—the first time he'd ever touched me, really *touched* me, I mean—and I realized how strange it was that this man, this scarred, bitter man, had somehow become the only friend I have. I realized something else, too: how rarely I'd known the touch of another human hand, how much I hungered for it.

"You were a kid, Rob."

"I know. It's not my fault."

"It's no reason for you to leave, not now, not when we need you. Burton would have you back in a minute. He owes this election to you, he knows that. Come back."

"Not yet," I said, "I'm not ready."

But now, staring out across the upturned faces of the dead as a cold January wind whipped across the Mall, I felt the lure and pull of the old life, sure as gravity. The game, Burton had called it, and it was a game, politics, the biggest Monopoly set in the world and I loved it and for the first time I understood *why* I loved it. For the first time I understood something else, too: why I had waited years to ring Gwen's doorbell, why even then it had taken an active effort of will not to turn away. It was the same reason: *Because* it was a game, a game with clear winners and losers, with rules as complex and arcane as a cotillion, and most of all because it partook so little of the messy turmoil of real life. The stakes seemed high, but they weren't. It was ritual, that's all—movement without action, a dance of spin and strategy designed to preserve the status quo. I fell in love with politics because it was safe. You get so involved in pushing your token around the board that you forget the ideals that brought you to the table in the first place. You forget to speak from the heart. Someday maybe, for the right reasons, I'd come back. But not yet.

I must have said it aloud for Lewis suddenly looked over at me. "What?" he asked.

I just shook my head and gazed out over the handful of living people, stirring as the ceremony got underway. The dead waited beyond them, rank upon rank of them with the earth of the grave under their nails and that cold shining in their eyes.

And then I *did* turn to Lewis. "What do you think they want?" I asked.

Lewis sighed. "Justice, I suppose," he said.

"And when they have it?"

"Maybe they'll rest."

A year has passed, and those words—*justice, I suppose*—still haunt me. I returned to D.C. in the fall, just as the leaves began turning along the Potomac. Gwen came with me, and sometimes, as I lie wakeful in the shelter of her warmth, my mind turns to the past.

It was Gran that brought me back. The cast had come off in February, and one afternoon in March, Gwen and I stopped by, surprised to see her on her feet. She looked frail, but her eyes glinted with determination as she toiled along the corridors behind her walker.

"Let's sit down and rest," I said when she got winded, but she merely shook her head and kept moving.

"Bones knit, Rob," she told me. "Wounds heal, if you let them."

Those words haunt me, too.

By the time she died in August, she'd moved from the walker to a cane. Another month, her case manager told me with admiration, and she might have relinquished even that. We buried her in the plot where we laid my grandfather to rest, but I never went back after the interment. I know what I would find.

The dead do not sleep.

They shamble in silence through the cities of our world, their bodies slack and stinking of the grave, their eyes coldly ablaze. Baghdad fell in September, vanquished by battalions of revolutionaries, rallying behind a vanguard of the dead. State teems with similar rumors, and CNN is on the story. Unrest in Pyongyang, turmoil in Belgrade.

In some views, Burton's has been the most successful administration in history. All around the world, our enemies are falling. Yet more and more these days, I catch the president staring uneasily into the streets of Washington, aswarm with zombies. "Our conscience," he's taken to calling them, but I'm not sure I agree. They demand nothing of us, after all. They seek no end we can perceive or understand. Perhaps they are nothing more than what we make of them, or what they enable us to make of ourselves. And so we go on, mere lodgers in a world of unpeopled graves, subject ever to the remorseless scrutiny of the dead.

GHOST DANCE

by Sherman Alexie

Sherman Alexie is the author of many books, including *The Absolutely True Diary of a Part-Time Indian*, which won the National Book Award and made several best of the year lists, including being named a *New York Times* notable book. Other books include *Flight*, *Ten Little Indians*, *Indian Killer*, and *Reservation Blues*. A collection of interconnected stories, *The Lone Ranger and Tonto Fistfight in Heaven*, served as the basis for a screenplay called *Smoke Signals*, which was made into a film in 1998. Alexie's short work has appeared in a number of anthologies, including *Best American Short Stories*, *The Year's Best Fantasy and Horror*, and *O. Henry Prize Stories*. In addition to being an accomplished author and screenwriter, Alexie is also world-renowned for his poetry, for which he was awarded an NEA Fellowship.

This story originally appeared in *McSweeney's Mammoth Treasury of Thrilling Tales*. Like much of Alexie's other work, this story draws on his Native American heritage. (Unlike most of his work, it features the dead returning to life hungering for human flesh.) It explores themes of racism and the lingering resentment over The Battle of Little Bighorn—Custer's Last Stand—more than 130 years after the fact.

Two cops, one big and the other little, traveled through the dark. The big cop hated Indians. Born and raised in a Montana that was home to eleven different reservations and over 47,000 Indians, the big cop's hatred had grown vast. Over a twenty-two-year law enforcement career he'd spent in service to one faded Montana town or another, the big cop had arrested 1,217 Indians for offenses ranging from shoplifting to assault, from bank robbery to homicide, all of the crimes committed while under the influence of one chemical or another.

"Damn redskins would drink each other's piss if they thought there was enough booze left in it," the big cop said to the little cop, a nervous little snakeboy just a few years out of Anaconda High School.

"Sure," said the little cop. He was a rookie and wasn't supposed to say much at all.

It was June 25th, three in the morning, and still over 100 degrees. Sweating through his polyester uniform, the big cop drove the patrol car east along

Interstate 90, heading for the Custer Memorial Battlefield on the banks of the Little Big Horn River.

"But you want to know the worst thing I ever saw?" asked the big cop. He drove with one hand on the wheel and the other in his crotch. He felt safer that way.

"Sure," said the little cop.

"Out on the Crow rez, I caught these Indian boys," the big cop said. "There were five or six of them scalp-hunters, all of them pulling a train on this pretty little squaw-bitch."

"That's bad."

"Shoot, that ain't the bad part. Gang rape is, like, a sacred tradition on some of these rez ghettoes. Hell, the bad part ain't the rape. The bad part is the boys were feeding this girl some Lysol sandwiches."

"What's a Lysol sandwich?"

"You just take two slices of bread, spray them hard with Lysol, slam them together, and eat it all up."

"That'll kill you, won't it?"

"Sure, it will kill you, but slow. Make you a retard first, make you run around in a diaper for about a year, and then it will kill you."

"That's bad."

"About the worst thing there is," said the big cop.

The little cop stared out the window and marveled again at the number of visible stars in the Montana sky. The little cop knew he lived in the most beautiful place in the world.

The big cop took the Little Big Horn exit off I-90, drove the short distance to the visitors' center, and then down a bumpy road to the surprisingly simple gates of the Custer Memorial Cemetery.

"This is it," said the big cop. "This is the place where it all went to shit."

"Sure," said the little cop.

"Two hundred and fifty-six good soldiers, good men, were murdered here on that horrible June day in 1876," said the big cop. He'd said the same thing many times before. It was part of a speech he was always rehearsing.

"I know it," said the little cop. He wondered if he should say a prayer.

"If it wasn't for these damn Indians," said the big cop, "Custer would've been the president of these United States."

"Right."

"We'd be living in a better country right now, let me tell you what."

"Yes, we would."

The big cop shook his head at all of the injustice of the world. He knew he was a man with wisdom and felt burdened by the weight of that powerful intelligence.

"Well," said the big cop. "We've got some work to do."

"Sure," said the little cop.

The cops stepped outside, both cursing the ridiculous heat, and walked to the back of the car. The big cop opened the trunk and stared down at the two Indian men lying there awake, silent, bloodied, and terrified. The cops had picked them up hitchhiking on the Flathead Reservation and driven them for hours through the limitless dark.

"Come on out of there, boys," said the big cop with a smile.

The Indians, one a young man with braids and the other an older man with a crew cut, crawled out of the trunk and stood on unsteady legs. Even with already-closing eyes and broken noses, with shit and piss running down their legs, and with nightstick bruises covering their stomachs and backs, the Indians tried to stand tall.

"You know where you are?" the big cop asked the Indians.

"Yes," said the older one.

"Tell me."

"Little Big Horn."

"You know what happened here?"

The older Indian remained silent.

"You better talk to me, boy," said the big cop. "Or I'm going to hurt you piece by piece."

The older Indian knew he was supposed to be pleading and begging for mercy, for his life, as he'd had to beg for his life from other uniformed white men. But the older Indian was suddenly tired of being afraid. He felt brave and stupid. The younger Indian knew how defiant his older friend could be. He wanted to run.

"Hey, chief," said the big cop. "I asked you a question. Do you know what happened here?"

The older Indian refused to talk. He lifted his chin and glared at the big cop.

"Fuck it," said the big cop as he pulled his revolver and shot the older Indian in the face, then shot him twice more in the chest after he crashed to the ground. Though the big cop had lived and worked violently, this was his first murder, and he was surprised by how easy it was.

After a moment of stunned silence, the younger Indian ran, clumsily zigzagging between gravestones, and made it thirty feet before the big cop shot him in the spine, and dropped him into the dirt.

"Oh, Jesus, Jesus, Jesus," said the younger cop, terrified. He knew he had to make a decision: Be a good man and die there in the cemetery with the Indians or be an evil man and help disappear two dead bodies.

"What do you think of that?" the big cop asked the little cop.

"I think it was good shooting."

Decision made, the little cop jogged over to the younger Indian lying there alive and half-paralyzed. His spine was shattered, and he'd die soon, but the Indian reached out with bloodied hands, grabbed handfuls of dirt, rock, and grass, tearing his nails off in the process, and pulled himself away in one last stupid and primal effort to survive. With his useless legs dragging behind him, the Indian looked like a squashed bug. Like a cockroach in blue jeans, thought the little cop and laughed a little, then retched his truck stop dinner all over the back of the dying Indian.

There and here, everywhere, Indian blood spilled onto the ground, and seeped down into the cemetery dirt.

The big cop kneeled beside the body of the old Indian and pushed his right index finger into the facial entrance wound and wondered why he was doing such a terrible thing. With his damn finger in this dead man's brain, the big cop felt himself split in two and become twins, one brother a killer and the other an eyewitness to murder.

Away, the little cop was down on all fours, dry heaving and moaning like a lonely coyote.

"What's going on over there?" asked the big cop.

"This one is still alive," said the little cop.

"Well, then, finish him off."

The little cop struggled to his feet, pulled his revolver, and pressed it against the back of the Indian's head. Maybe he would have found enough cowardice and courage to pull the trigger, but he never got the chance. All around him, awakened and enraptured by Indian blood, the white soldiers in tattered uniforms exploded from their graves and came for the little cop. As he spun in circles, surrounded, he saw how many of these soldiers were little more than skeletons with pieces of dried meat clinging to their bones. Some of the soldiers still had stomachs and lungs leaking blood through jagged wounds, and other soldiers picked at their own brains through arrow holes punched into their skulls, and a few dumb, clumsy ones tripped over their intestines and ropy veins spilling onto the ground. Dead for over a century and now alive and dead at the same time, these soldiers rushed the little cop. Backpedaling, stepping side to side, the little cop dodged arms and tongueless mouths as he fired his revolver fifteen times. Even while panicked and shooting at moving targets, he was still a good marksman. He blasted the skull off one soldier, shot the arms off two others and the leg off a third, had six bullets pass through the ribs of a few officers and one zip through the empty eye socket of a sergeant. But even without arms, legs, and heads, the soldiers came for him and knocked him to the ground, where they pulled off his skin in long strips, exposed his sweet meats, and feasted on him. Just before two privates pulled out his heart and tore it into halves, the little cop watched a lieutenant, with a half-decayed face framing one blue eye, feed the big cop's cock and balls to a horse whose throat, esophagus, and stomach were clearly visible through its ribs.

That night, as the Seventh Cavalry rose from their graves in Montana, Edgar Smith slept in his bed in Washington, D.C., and dreamed for the first time about the death of George Armstrong Custer.

Inside the dream, it was June 1876 all over again, and Custer was the last survivor of his own foolish ambitions. On a grassy hill overlooking the Little

Big Horn River, Custer crawled over the bodies of many dead soldiers and a few dead Indians. Seriously wounded, but strong enough to stand and stagger, then walk on broken legs, Custer was followed by a dozen quiet warriors, any one of them prestigious enough to be given the honor of killing this famous Indian Killer, this Long Hair, this Son of the Morning Star. Crazy Horse and Sitting Bull walked behind Custer, as did Gall, Crow King, Red Horse, Low Dog, Foolish Elk, and others close and far. But it was a quiet Cheyenne woman, a warrior whose name has never been spoken aloud since that day, who stepped forward with an arrow in her hand and stabbed it through Custer's heart. After Custer fell and died, the Cheyenne woman stood over his body and sang for two hours. She sang while her baby son slept in the cradleboard on her back. She sang an honor song for the brave Custer, for the great white warrior, and when she ended her song, she kneeled and kissed the general. But Custer was no longer Custer. The quiet Cheyenne woman kissed Edgar Smith lying dead in the greasy grass of his dream.

A ringing telephone pulled Edgar from sleep. Reflexively and professionally, he answered, heard the details of his mission, grabbed a bag that was always packed, and hurried for the airport. Brown-eyed, brown-haired, pale of skin, and just over six feet tall, he was completely unremarkable in appearance, a blank Caucasian slate. Measured by his surface, Edgar could have been a short-stop for the New York Yankees, a dentist from Sacramento, or the night shift manager at a supermarket. This mutability made him the ideal FBI agent.

Two hours after the phone call, after his Custer dream, Edgar sat in a window seat of the FBI jet flying toward the massacre site in Montana. All around him, other anonymous field agents busied themselves with police reports and history texts, with biographies and data on Native American radicals, white separatists, domestic terrorists, religious cultists, and the other assorted crazies who lived within a five-hundred-mile radius of the Custer Memorial Battlefield.

"Can you imagine the number of men it took to pull this off?" asked one agent. "Over two hundred graves looted and sacked. How big a truck do you need to haul off two hundred bodies? You'd need a well-trained army. I'm thinking militia."

"But it's two hundred dead bodies buried for a hundred years, so that's about two million pieces of dead bodies," said another agent. "Hell, you'd be haul-ing loose teeth, ribs, some hair, a fingernail or two, and just plain dust. You'd need a vacuum for all this. It's not the size of the job; it's the ritual nature of it. You have to be crazy to do this, and you have to be even crazier to convince a bunch of other people to do it with you. We're looking for the King of the Crazy People."

"You want my opinion?" asked the third agent. "I'm thinking these two dead Indians, along with a bunch of other radical Indians, were desecrating these graves. I mean, it is the anniversary of Custer's Last Stand, right? They were trying to get back at Custer."

"But Custer isn't even buried there," said a fourth agent. "He's buried at

West Point."

"So maybe these were stupid Indians," said yet another agent. "These Indians were pissing and shitting the graves, digging them up, and piling the bones and shit into some old pickup. And along come our local boys, Mr. Fat Cop and Mr. Skinny Cop, who shoot a couple of renegades before the rest of the tribe rises up and massacres them."

"That's well and good," said the last agent, "but damn, the local coroner says our cops were chewed on. Human bite marks all over their bones and what's left of their bodies. Are you saying a cannibalistic army of Indian radicals ate the cops?"

All of the agents, hard-core veterans of domestic wars, laughed long and hard. They'd all seen the evil that men do, and it was usually simple and concise, and always the result of the twisted desire for more power, money, or sex. Perhaps the killers in this case were new and unusual. The FBI agents thrilled at the possibility of discovering an original kind of sin and capturing an original group of sinners. The local cops had described the massacre scene as the worst thing they'd ever seen, but each FBI agent was quite confident he'd already seen the worst death he would ever see. One more death, no matter how ugly, was just one more death.

In his seat apart from the other agents, Edgar wondered why he had dreamed about Custer on the same night, at the very same moment, these horrible murders were happening on the battlefield that bore Custer's name. He didn't believe in ESP or psychics, in haunted houses or afterlife experiences, or in any of that paranormal bullshit. Edgar believed in science, in cause and effect, in the here and now, in facts. But no matter how rational he pretended to be, he knew the world had always contained more possibilities than he could imagine, and now, here he was, confronted by the very fact of a dream killing so closely tied with real killings. Edgar Smith was scared.

He was even more scared after he and the other agents walked over a rise and stood before the Little Big Horn massacre site. Three of the agents immediately vomited and could only work the perimeter of the scene. Another agent, who was the first rescuer at the bombing of the U.S. military barracks in Beirut and had searched the rubble for bodies and pieces of body, turned back at the cemetery gate and retired on half-pension. Everybody else ran back to their cars and donned thick yellow hazmat suits with oxygen tanks. Trembling with terror and nausea, the agents worked hard. They had a job to do, and they performed it with their customary grace and skill, but all along, the agents doubted they had enough strength to face an enemy capable of such destruction.

Edgar counted two hundred and fifty-six open graves, all of them filled with blood, pieces of skin, and unidentifiable body parts. Witches' cauldrons, thought Edgar as he stared down into the worst of them. The dirt and grass were so soaked with blood and viscera that it felt like walking through mud. And then there was the dead. One of the state cops, or what was left of him, was smeared all over his cruiser. He was now a pulp-filled uniform and one thumb dark with fingerprint powder. The other cop was spread over a twenty-foot circle, his blood and bones mixing with the blood and bones of one Indian. The other Indian, older, maybe fifty years old, was largely untouched, except for twenty or thirty tentative bite marks, as if his attackers had tasted him and found him too sour. One tooth, a human molar, was broken off at the root and imbedded in the old Indian's chin. This was all madness, madness, madness, and Edgar knew that a weaker person could have easily fallen apart here and run screaming into the distance. A weaker person might have looked for escape, but Edgar knew he would never truly leave this nightmare.

And yet, Edgar could only know the true extent of this nightmare after he followed the blood trails. There were two hundred and fifty-six blood trails, one for each grave, and they led away from the cemetery in all directions. Occasionally, five or ten or fifteen blood trails would merge into one, until there were only forty or fifty blood trails in total, all of them leading away in different directions. Eventually all of these trails faded into the grass and dirt, and became only a stray drop of blood, a strip of shed skin, or small chip of bone, then a series of footprints or single hoofprint before they disappeared altogether. Edgar had no idea what humans, animals, or things had left these blood trails, but they were gone now, traveling in a pattern that suggested they were either randomly fleeing from the murder scene or beginning a carefully planned hunt.

Early the next morning, in Billings, Montana, Junior Estes sat on the front counter of the Town Pump convenience store, where he'd worked graveyard shift for two years. He worked alone that night because his usual partner, Harry Quakenbrush, had called in sick at the last moment.

"Jesus," Junior had cursed. "You know I can't get nobody to work graveyard at the last sec. Come on, Harry, if you ain't got cancer of the balls, then you better get your ass in here."

"It is cancer of the nuts, and you should feel sorry for bringing it up," Harry had said as he'd hung up the phone and crawled back into bed with his new girlfriend.

So Junior was all by himself in the middle of the night, and knew he couldn't cashier, stock the coolers, and disinfect the place all at the same time, so he decided to do nothing. He might get fired when the boss man showed up at 6 a.m., but he knew Harry would get fired, too, and that would be all right enough. Most nights, twenty or thirty insomniacs, other night shift workers, and the just plain crazy would wander into the store, but only two hookers had been in that night and had pointedly ignored Junior. Poor Junior wasn't ugly, but he was lonely, and that made him stink.

At 3:17 a.m., according to the time stamped on the surveillance tape, Junior noticed a man staggering in slow circles around the gas pump. Junior grabbed a baseball bat from beneath the counter and dashed outside. The external cameras were too blurry and dark to pick up much detail as he confronted the drunken man. A few years earlier, up north in Poplar, a drunk Indian had set a gas pump on fire and burned down half a city block, so Junior must have remembered that as he pushed the man away from the store. Then, at the very edge of the video frame, the drunken man grabbed Junior by the head and bit out his throat. As the video rolled, the drunken man fell on Junior and ate him. Later examination of the videotape revealed that the drunken man was horribly scarred and that he was wearing a Seventh Cavalry uniform, circa 1876.

Edgar and another agent were on the scene twenty minutes after Junior was killed. In the parking lot, as Edgar knelt over Junior's mutilated body, he felt like he was falling; then he did fall. In a seizure, with lightning arcing from one part of his brain to another, Edgar saw a series of mental images, as clear as photographs, as vivid as film. He saw death.

On Sheep Mountain, near the Montana-Wyoming border, six members of the Aryan Way Militia were pulled out of an SUV and dismembered.

Edgar saw this and somehow knew that Richard Usher, the leader of the Aryan Way, was the great-grandson of a black coal miner named Jefferson Usher.

On an isolated farm near Jordan, Montana, a widowed farmer and his three adult sons fought an epic battle against unknown intruders. Local police would gather five hundred and twelve spent bullet shells, five shotguns with barrels twisted from overheating, two illegal automatic rifles with jammed firing mechanisms, and six pistols scattered around the farm and grounds. The bodies of the farmer and his sons were missing.

But Edgar saw their stripped skeletons buried in a shallow grave atop the much deeper grave of a one-thousand-year-old buffalo jump near the Canadian border. Edgar saw this and somehow knew the exact latitude and longitude of that particular buffalo jump. He knew the color of the grass and dirt.

Outside Killdeer, North Dakota, a few miles from the Fort Berthold Indian Reservation, five Hidatsa Indians were found nailed to the four walls and ceiling of an abandoned hunting cabin.

Edgar saw these bodies and suddenly knew these men's names and the names of all of their children, but he also knew their secret names, the tribal names that had been given to them in secret ceremonies and were never said aloud outside of the immediate family.

All told, sixty-seven people were murdered that night and Edgar saw all of their deaths. Somehow, he knew their histories and most personal secrets. He saw their first cars, marriages, sex, and fights. He suddenly knew them and mourned their butchery as if he'd given birth to them.

And then, while still inside his seizure and fever-dream, and just when Edgar didn't know if his heart could withstand one more murder, he saw survival.

At a highway rest stop off Interstate 94, a trucker changing a flat tire was attacked and bitten by a soldier, but he fought him off with the tire iron. He jumped into his truck and ran over twelve other soldiers as he escaped. Throwing sparks by riding on one steel rim and seventeen good tires, he drove twenty miles down the freeway and nearly ran down the Montana State Patrolman who finally stopped him.

Edgar saw an obese white trucker weep in the arms of the only black cop within a one-thousand-mile radius.

In the Pryor Forest, Michael X, a gold-medal winner in downhill bicycling at the last ESPN X Games, escaped five soldiers on horseback by riding his bike off a cliff and dropping two hundred feet into Big Horn Lake. With a broken leg and punctured lung, Michael swam and waded north for ten miles before a local fisherman pulled him out of the river.

Edgar could taste the salt in the boy's tears.

At Crow Agency, a seven-year-old Indian girl was using the family outhouse when she was attacked. While the soldiers tore off the door, she sneaked out the moon-shaped window and crawled onto the outhouse roof. On the roof, she saw she was closer to a tall poplar tree than to her family's trailer, and there was nobody else home anyway, so she jumped to the ground and outran two soldiers to the base of the tree. She climbed for her life to the top and balanced on a branch barely strong enough to hold her weight. Again and again, the two soldiers climbed after her, but their decayed bones could not support the weight of their bodies, and so they broke apart, hands and arms hanging like strange fruit high in the tree, while their bodies kicked and screamed on the ground below.

Here, Edgar pushed himself into his vision, into the white-hot center of his fever, and attacked those two soldiers with his mind.

"Go away," he screamed as he seized in the convenience store parking lot. The other agents thought Edgar was hallucinating and screaming at ghosts. But Edgar's voice traveled through the dark and echoed in the soldiers' ears. The little Indian girl heard Edgar's disembodied voice and wondered if God was trying to save her. But the soldiers were not afraid of God or his voice. Edgar watched helplessly as the soldiers leaned against the tree, pushed it back and forth, and swung the girl at the top in an ever-widening arc. Edgar knew they were trying to break the tree at the base.

"Leave her alone," he screamed.

But the soldiers ignored him and worked against the tree. Up high, the Indian girl cried for her mother and father, who had gone to a movie and were unaware that the babysitter had left their daughter alone in the house.

"Stop, stop, stop," Edgar screamed. He was desperate. He knew the girl would die unless he stopped the soldiers, and then he knew, without knowing why he knew, exactly how to stop them.

"Attention," he screamed.

The two soldiers, obedient and well trained, immediately stood at full attention.

"Right face," Edgar screamed.

With perfect form, the two soldiers faced right, away from the tree.

"Forward march," Edgar screamed.

Stunned, the little Indian girl watched the two soldiers marching away from her. They marched into the darkness. Edgar knew the soldiers would keep marching until they fell into a canyon or lake, or until they crossed an old road where a fast-moving logging truck might smash them into small pieces. Edgar knew these two soldiers would never stop. He knew all of these soldiers, all two hundred and fifty-six of them, would never quit, not until they had found whatever it was they were searching for.

Sixty miles away from that little girl, Edgar burned with vision-fever as he saw the world with such terrible clarity. In that filthy Town Pump parking lot, illuminated by cheap neon, his fellow agents kneeled over him, held his arms and legs, and shoved a spoon into his mouth so he wouldn't swallow his tongue. Edgar pushed and pulled with supernatural strength. Six other men could barely hold him down. Then it was over. Edgar quickly awoke from his seizure, stood on strong legs, rushed to a dispatch radio transmitter, and told his story. On open channels, Edgar told dozens of police officers and FBI agents exactly where to find dead bodies and survivors. And once those doubtful police officers and agents traveled all over Montana, Wyoming, North and South Dakota, and across the border into Canada, and found exactly what Edgar had said would be found, he was quickly escorted to a hospital room, where he was first examined and found healthy, and then asked again and again how he had come to know what he knew. He told the truth, and they did not believe him, and he didn't blame them because he knew that it sounded crazy. He'd interviewed hundreds of people who claimed to see visions of the past and future. He'd made fun of them all, and now he wondered how many of them had been telling the truth. How many of those schizophrenics had really been talking to God? How many of those serial killers had really been possessed by the Devil? How many murdered children had returned to haunt their surviving parents?

"I don't know what else to say; it's the truth," Edgar said to his fellow agents, who were so sad to see a good man falling apart, and so they left him alone in his hospital room. In the dark, Edgar listened hard for the voices he was sure would soon be speaking to him, and he wondered what those voices would ask him to do and if he would honor their requests. Edgar felt hunted and haunted, and when he closed his eyes, he smelled blood and he didn't know how much of it would be spilled before all of this was over.

BLOSSOM

by David J. Schow

David J. Schow is a bit of a legend in zombie circles. He's the author of the notorious story "Jerry's Kids Meet Wormboy," as well as several others, which have been collected in *Zombie Jam*. He's also the author of the novels *The Kill Riff*, *The Shaft*, *Bullets of Rain*, and *Rock Breaks Scissors Cut*. His most recent novel is *Gun Work*, a hard-boiled crime novel due out in November. Schow co-wrote (with John Shirley) the screenplay for *The Crow*, and has written teleplays for TV shows such as Showtime's *Masters of Horror*. As for non-fiction, Schow has authored *The Outer Limits: The Official Companion*, and a collection of essays called *Wild Hairs*. He's also generally considered to be the originator of the term "splatterpunk."

In *Zombie Jam*, Schow says: "'Blossom' is a simple story, written in a single day, the process beginning with the image of a beautiful nude woman eating flowers, working backward from that image. Along the way it was decided that the incidental background of the story would address the notion of what it was like in the big cities two nights before the spread of the zombie virus made survival the overriding issue."

"Each of us has a moment," Quinn told her. "The moment when we shine; that instant when we are at our absolute best. Just as each of us has an aberration, a hidden secret. Some might call it a perversion, though that's rather a rough word. Crude. Nonspecific. Is it a perversion to do that thing you're best at, to enjoy your individual moment?"

Amelia nodded vaguely, watching the older man through her glass of Sauvignon Blanc. He was going to answer his own obtuse question, and the answer he had already decided upon was no. It was the puffery that preceded the crunch—was she going to fuck him tonight, or not? She was positive he had already answered that one in his head as well. Dinner had run to ninety-five bucks, not counting the wine or the tip. Dessert had been high-priced, higher-caloried, chocolate, elegant. Cabs had been taken and token gifts dispensed.

She had worked in loan approvals at Columbia Savings for nine months, riding the receptionist's desk. Older men frequently asked her out. When Quinn invited her to dinner, a weekend date, she had pulled his file, consulted his figures, and said yes. All the girls in the office did it. He drove a Jaguar XJS and was into condo development.

The dinner part had been completed two hours ago. Now it was his *place*. When your income hit the high six figures there was no such animal as date rape. Amelia had herpes. It was inactive tonight. Best to stay mum; it was like compensation. To her certain knowledge she had never bedded bisexuals or intravenous-drug users, and in truth she feared contracting AIDS in the same unfocused way she feared getting flattened in a crosswalk by a bus. It could happen. But probably not. There was no way in the world either of them could fit a condom over their mouths, so it was academic. Right?

Quinn's watery gray eyes glinted as he rattled on about aberrations and special moments. Probably the wine. It had gotten to Amelia half an hour ago, a fuzzy vino cloud that put her afloat and permitted her to tune out Quinn's voice while staring past him, to nod and generate tiny noises of acknowledgment on a schedule that allowed him to believe she was actually listening. She had disconnected and felt just fine. She took a deep, languorous breath keeping him on the far side of her wine glass, and stifled the giggle that welled within her. Oh my yes, she felt nice, adrift on a cumulus pillow of gasified brain cells. She would look past him, through him, in just this way when he was on top of her, grunting and sweating and believing he had seduced her... just as he now believed she was paying attention.

She rewound back to the last utterance she cared to remember and acted upon it. "I have an aberration," she said. She added a glowing smile and toyed with a long curl of her copper hair. Just adorable.

His interest came full blast, too eager. "Yes? Yes?" He replaced his wine glass on the clear acrylic tabletop and leaned forward to entreat her elucidation.

She played him like a catfish on a hook. "No. It's silly, really." *Look at my legs,* she commanded.

Through the tabletop he watched her legs recross. The whisper of her stockings flushed his face with blood. His brain was giddy, already jumping forward in time, to the clinch. "Please," he said. His voice was so cultured, his tone so paternal. He was losing control and she could smell it.

She kept a childlike killer smile precisely targeted. "Well. Okay." She rose, a slim and gracile woman of thirty-four, one who fought hard to keep what she had and had nothing to show for her effort except a stupid airhead bimbo job at Columbia Savings. So much bitterness, there beneath the manner and cosmetics.

There was a tall vase of irises on an antique end table near the fireplace. Firelight mellowed all the glass and Scandinavian chrome in the room and danced in the floor-to-ceiling wraparound windows of Quinn's eighth-floor eyrie. He kept his gaze on her. The fire was in his eyes as well.

Every inch the coquette, Amelia bit off the delicate chiffon of the iris. Chewed. Swallowed. And smiled.

Quinn's face grew robust with pleasure. His old man's eyes cleared.

"Ever since I was a little girl," she said. "Perhaps because I saw my cat, Sterling, eating grass. I like the flavor. I don't know. I used to think the flower's life added to mine."

"And this is your…" Quinn had to clear his throat. "Aberration. Ah." He left his chair to close up the distance between them. It became evident that his erection was making him blunder.

Amelia's eyes dipped to notice, bemused, and she ate another flower. She had made a point of telling Quinn she liked lots of flowers, and he and his Gold Card had come through in rainbow colors. All over the penthouse were long-stemmed roses, carnation bouquets, spring bunches, mums, more.

Quinn found the sight of Amelia chewing the flowers throat-closingly erotic. His voice grew husky and repeated her name. It was time for him to lunge. "Let me show you my specialty. Dear Amelia. My aberration."

She had been tied up before. So far, no big deal. Quinn used silk scarves to secure her wrists and ankles to the mahogany poles of the four-poster bed. With a long, curved, ebony-handled knife he halved the front of her dress. Into the vanilla highlands of her breasts he mumbled promises of more expensive replacement garments. His hands lost their sophistication and became thick-fingered, in a big masculine hurry, shredding her hose to the knees and groping to see if she was as moist as his fantasies. Then he was thrusting. Amelia rocked and pretended to orgasm. This would be done in a hurry. No big deal.

He withdrew, still hard, saying, "Don't be afraid." She had been falling asleep.

She expected him to go for the knife again, to stroke her nipples with its razor edge or tease her nerve endings with mock danger. Instead, he reached into a headboard compartment and brought out a rubber mask festooned with sewn leather and buckles and shiny gold zippers. It almost made her laugh. She protested. The contraption engulfed her head like a thick, too-tight glove. She thought of getting stuck in a pullover sweater, only this material was definitely nonporous. Her lungs felt brief panic until the thing was fully seated and she could gulp air through the nose and mouth slits.

Then Quinn resumed pushing himself into her, his prodding more urgent now. He broke rhythm only to zip the holes in the mask shut.

Fear blossomed loud in her chest, becoming a fireball. She pulled in a final huge draught of air before he zipped the nose shut, and wasted breath making incomprehensible mewling noises against the already-sealed mouth hole. She could not tell him now of her congenital lung problems, that respiration was sometimes a chore. When the weather was wrong, she had to resort to prescription medication just to breathe. It had never come up, all through dinner. They had been too busy with aberrations and prime moments and eating flowers….

All she could feel now was a slow explosion in her chest and the steady pounding down below, in and out. She began to buck and heave, thrashing. Quinn loved every second of it, battering her lustily despite her abrupt lack of lubrication. The friction vanished when he came inside her.

Panting, he lumbered immediately to the bathroom. When he returned, Amelia had not changed position, and he finally noticed she was no longer breathing.

Sometimes it went down this way, he thought. The price of true passion, however aberrant. But she was still moist and poised at the ready, so he opted to have one more go.

He huffed with surprise when she began to squirm beneath him again. He went *aahhh* and started stroking rigid and slippery in a fast tempo. That was it—she had fainted. Sometimes it went down that way as well—orgasm put them in the Zone for a while. She would awaken on high-burn and come her teeny secretary brains right out.

Her jaw wrenched around at a ridiculous angle and bit into the leather muzzle of the mask from within, shredding a hole. A drop of Quinn's sweat flew to mix with the blood staining her teeth and the vomit clogging her throat, and before Quinn could make sense out of what he thought he saw, Amelia bit his nose off.

In the brief second before the pain hit, Quinn thought of that crazy shit on the news. Cannibal attacks on the eastern seaboard. Some whackpot scientist had claimed that dead people were reviving and eating live people. It was all Big Apple ratshit. Yet it flashed through Quinn's mind right now because Amelia had bitten his nose off *and was chewing it up and swallowing the pieces.*

His throat flooded with the foaming pink backwash of inhaled blood. He made a liquid gargling noise as he tried to recoil, to back out of her, to get the hell away from this fucking lunatic, but she had a deathgrip on him below-decks, as well.

Then Quinn was able to yell, and he did because he could feel the ring of vaginal muscle increasing pressure, locking up beyond the circumference of his cock. The more he tried to pull out, the harder he got. He'd heard of men getting stuck in wine bottles the same way. You can't compress a liquid. Blood was a liquid. His panic erection was vised with no options. He shoved wildly against the bed, blood pumping from the cavern in his face. He began hitting her with both fists, but she was beyond feeling a thing.

When he felt the muscle sever his penis like a wire cutter, he began to scream hoarsely. None of his neighbors would pay any mind. Weird games, aberrations, were the standard menu at Quinn's. Suddenly freed, he sprawled backward. Blood gushed, ruining the carpet and sputtering from his crotch. He watched the stump of his still-stiff manhood vanish into the slick red chasm between Amelia's legs, overwhelmed by the sight of it being swallowed whole by the orifice that had bitten it off.

Quinn hit the floor and kept screaming until catatonia blanketed him.

It took Amelia about half an hour to gnaw through her bonds. She spent another hour and a half eating Quinn. During her meal the life left his body, and the queer radiations mentioned on the news did their alien work. By then there was not enough left of his corpse to rise, or walk, or eat anyone else. The pieces lolled around on the floor, feeling the first pangs of a new hunger, unearthly and unsatisfiable.

Her savaged dress dropped away. Swaying side-to-side she found her way into the room where they had dined when they were alive. Sparks of remembered behavior capered through her dead brain matter, evaporating for the last time. She began eating the flowers in their vases, in no hurry to begin her nightwalk. The flowers were alive, but dying every moment. Their life might become hers. When she stopped, all the bouquets had been stripped.

Eventually Amelia found her way to a door, and moved into the world to seek others of her newborn kind. Never again would she be as beautiful. It was her moment, just as Quinn had said. She blended with the shadows, a striking, cream-skinned nude with flower petals drifting down from her mouth, ocher, mauve, bright red.

THE THIRD DEAD BODY

by Nina Kiriki Hoffman

Nina Kiriki Hoffman is the author of several novels, including the Bram Stoker Award-winning *The Thread That Binds the Bones*, *A Fistful of Sky*, *A Stir of Bones*, *Spirits That Walk in Shadow*, and *Catalyst*, which was a finalist for the Philip K. Dick Award.

Her short fiction has appeared in such magazines as *Weird Tales*, *Realms of Fantasy*, and *The Magazine of Fantasy & Science Fiction*, and in numerous anthologies, such as *Firebirds*, *The Coyote Road*, and *Redshift*. Her work has been nominated for the World Fantasy Award and the Nebula Award four times each.

In the nineties, Hoffman went through a summer where she read one serial killer biography after another. "I was in the grip of some monstrous curiosity about how far humans will go," she says. "My favorite book that summer was about a case that wasn't even solved at the time, *The Search for the Green River Killer*, by Carlton Smith and Thomas Guillen. Part of my thinking in 'The Third Dead Body' was to give the victim a voice. There were so many victims. In this case, where the serial killer was the celebrity—as so often happens—I wanted to focus elsewhere."

I didn't even know Richie. I surely didn't want to love him. After he killed me, though, I found him irresistible.

I opened my eyes and dirt fell into them. Having things fall into my eyes was one of my secret terrors, but now I blinked and shook my head and most of the dirt fell away and I felt all right. So I knew something major had happened to me.

With my eyes closed, I shoved dirt away from my face. While I was doing this I realized that the inside of my mouth felt different. I probed with my tongue, my trained and talented tongue, and soon discovered that where smooth teeth had been before there were only broken stumps. What puzzled me about this and about the dirt in my eyes was that these things didn't hurt. They bothered me, but not on a pain level.

I frowned and tried to figure out what I was feeling. Not a lot. Not scared or mad, not hot or cold. This was different too. I usually felt scared, standing on street corners waiting for strangers to pick me up, and cold, working evenings in skimpy clothes that showed off my best features. Right now, I felt nothing.

I sat up, dirt falling away from me, and bumped into branches that gridded my view of the sky. Some of them slid off me. The branches were loose and wilting, not attached to a bush or tree. I used my hands to push them out of the way and noticed that the backs of my fingers were blackened beyond my natural cocoa color. I looked at them, trying to remember what had happened before I fell asleep or whatever—had I dipped my fingers in ink? But no; the skin was scorched. My fingerprints were gone. They would have told police that my name was Tawanda Foote, which was my street name.

My teeth would have led police to call me Mary Jefferson, a name I hadn't used since two years before, when I moved out of my parents' house at fifteen.

In my own mind, I was Sheila, a power name I had given myself no one could have discovered from any evidence about me.

No teeth, no fingerprints; Richie really didn't want anybody to know who I was, not that anybody ever had.

Richie.

With my scorched fingers I tried to take my pulse, though it was hard to find a vein among the rope burns at my wrists. With my eyes I watched my own naked chest. There were charred spots on my breasts where Richie had touched me with a burning cigarette. No pulse, but maybe that was because the nerves in my fingertips were dead. No breathing. No easy answer to that, so I chose the hard answer:

Dead.

I was dead.

After I pushed aside the branches so I could see trees and sky, I sat in my own grave dirt and thought about this.

My grannie would call this dirt goofer dust; any soil that's been piled on a corpse, whether the body's in a box or just loose like me, turns into goofer dust. Dirt next to dead folk gets a power in it, she used to say.

She used to tell me all kinds of things. She told me about the walking dead; but mostly she said they were just big scary dummies who obeyed orders. When I stayed up too late at night reading library books under my covers with a flashlight, she would say, "Maybe you know somebody who could give those nightwalkers orders. Maybe she can order 'em to come in here and turn off your light."

She had started to train me in recognizing herbs and collecting conjo ingredients, but that was before I told the preacher what really happened when I sat in Grand-père's lap, and Grand-père got in trouble with the church and then with other people in the Parish. I had a lot of cousins, and some of the others started talking up about Grand-père, but I was the first. After the police took Grand-père away, Grannie laid a curse on me: "May you love the thing that hurts you, even after it kills you." She underlined it with virgin blood, the wax of black candles, and the three of spades.

I thought maybe if I left Louisiana I could get the curse off, but nobody I knew could uncross me and the curse followed me to Seattle.

In the midst of what was now goofer dust, I was sitting next to something. I reached out and touched it. It was another dead body. "Wake up," I said to the woman in the shallow grave beside me. But she refused to move.

So: no fingerprints, no teeth. I was dead, next to someone even deader, and off in some woods. I checked in with my body, an act I saved for special times when I could come out of the numb state I spent most of my life in, and found I wasn't hungry or thirsty. All the parts of me that had been hurting just before Richie, my last trick, took a final twist around my neck with the nylon cord he was so fond of, all those parts were quiet, not bothering me at all; but there was a burning desire in my crotch, and a pinprick of fire behind my eyes that whispered to me, "Get up and move. We know where to go."

I looked around. At my back the slope led upward toward a place where sun broke through trees. At my feet it led down into darker woods. To either side, more woods and bushes, plants Grannie had never named for me, foreign as another language.

I moved my legs, bringing them up out of the goofer dust. All of me was naked; dirt caught in my curly hair below. I pulled myself to my feet and something fell out of my money pit, as my pimp Blake liked to call my pussy. I looked down at what had fallen from me. It was a rock flaked and shaped into a blade about the size of a flat hand, and it glistened in the dulled sunlight, wet and dark with what had come from inside me, and maybe with some of his juices too.

The fire in my belly flared up, but it wasn't a feeling like pain; it felt like desire.

I put my hands to my neck and felt the deep grooves the rope had left there. Heat blossomed in my head and in my heart. I wanted to find the hands that had tightened the rope around my neck, wrists, and ankles. I wanted to find the eyes that had watched my skin sizzle under the kiss of the burning cigarette. I wanted to find the mind that had decided to plunge a crude blade into me like that. The compulsion set in along my bones, jetted into my muscles like adrenaline. I straightened, looked around. I had to find Richie. I knew which direction to look: something in my head was teasing me, nudging me—a fire behind my eyes, urging me back to the city.

I fought the urge and lifted more branches off the place where I had lain. If I was going to get to Seattle from here, wherever here was, I needed some clothes. I couldn't imagine anybody stopping to pick me up with me looking the way I did. I knew Richie had worked hard to get rid of all clues to who I was, but I thought maybe my companion in the grave might not be so naked of identity, so I brushed dirt off her, and found she was not alone. There were two bodies in the dirt, with no sign of afterlife in them except maggots, and no trace of clothes. One was darker than me, with fewer marks on her but the same rope burns around her neck. The other one was very light, maybe white. She was really falling apart. They looked like they must smell pretty bad, but

I couldn't smell them. I couldn't smell anything. I could see and hear, and my muscles did what I told them, but I didn't feel much except the gathering fire inside me that cried for Richie.

I brushed dirt back over the other women and moved the branches to cover their resting place again.

Downslope the trees waited, making their own low-level night. Upslope, open sun: a road, probably. I scrambled up toward the light.

The heat in my head and heart and belly burned hotter, and I churned up the hillside and stepped into the sun.

A two-lane highway lay before me, its yellow dotted center stripe bright in the sun. Its edges tailed into the gravel I stood on. Crushed snack bags and Coke and beer cans lay scattered in the bushes beside the road; cellophane glinted. I crossed the road and looked at the wooded hill on its far side, then down in the ditch. No clothes. Not even a plastic bag big enough to make into a bikini bottom.

The heat inside me was like some big fat drunk who will not shut up, yelling for a beer. I started walking, knowing which direction would take me toward town without knowing how I knew.

After a while a car came from behind me. Behind was probably my best side; my microbraids hung down to hide the marks on my neck, and Richie hadn't done any cigarette graffiti on my back that I could remember. A lot of tricks had told me I had a nice ass and good legs; even my pimp had said it, and he never said anything nice unless he thought it was true or it would get him what he wanted. And he had everything he wanted from me.

I could hear the car slowing, but I was afraid to look back. I knew my mouth must look funny because of the missing teeth, and I wasn't sure what the rest of my face looked like. Since I couldn't feel pain, anything could have happened. I bent my head so the sun wasn't shining in my face.

"Miss? Oh, miss?" Either a woman's deep voice came from the car behind me, or a man's high one; it sounded like an older person. The engine idled low as the car pulled up beside me. It was a red Volkswagen Rabbit.

I crossed my arms over my chest, hiding the burn marks and tucking my rope-mark bracelets into the crooks of my elbows.

"Miss?"

"Ya?" I said, trying to make my voice friendly, not sure I had a voice at all.

"Miss, are you in trouble?"

I nodded, my braids slapping my shoulders and veiling my face.

"May I help you, miss?"

I cleared my throat, drew in breath. "Ya-you goin' do down?" I managed to say.

"What?"

"Down," I said, pointing along the road. "Seaddle."

"Oh. Yes. Would you like a ride?"

"Mm-hmm," I said. "Cloze?" I glanced up this time, wondering if the car's driver was man or woman. A man might shed his shirt for me, but a woman, unless she was carrying a suitcase or something, might not have anything to offer.

"Oh, you poor thing, what happened to you?" The car pulled up onto the shoulder ahead of me and the driver got out. It was a big beefy white woman in jeans and a plaid flannel shirt. She came toward me with a no-nonsense stride. She had short dark hair. She was wearing a man's khaki cloth hat with fishing flies stuck in the band, all different feathery colors. "What ha—"

I put one hand over my face, covering my mouth with my palm.

"What happened—" she whispered, stopping while there was still a lot of space between us.

"My boyfriend dreeded me preddy bad," I said behind my hand. My tongue kept trying to touch the backs of teeth no longer there. It frustrated me that my speech was so messy. I thought maybe I could talk more normally if I touched my tongue to the roof of my mouth. "My boyfriend," I said again, then, "treated me pretty bad."

"Poor thing, poor thing," she whispered, then turned back to the car and rummaged in a back seat, came up with a short-waisted Levi's jacket and held it out to me.

I ducked my head and took the jacket. She gasped when I dropped my arms from my chest. I wrapped up in the jacket, which was roomy, but not long enough to cover my crotch. Then again, from the outside, my crotch didn't look so bad. I turned the collar up to cover my neck and the lower part of my face. "Thank you," I said.

Her eyes were wide, her broad face pale under her tan. "You need help," she said. "Hospital? Police?"

"Seattle," I said.

"Medical attention!"

"Won't help me now." I shrugged.

"You could get infections, die from septicemia or something. I have a first aid kit in the car. At least let me—"

"What would help me," I said, "is a mirror."

She sighed, her shoulders lowering. She walked around the car and opened the passenger side door, and I followed her. I looked at the seat. It was so clean, and I was still goofer dusted. "Gonna get it dirty," I said.

"Lord, that's the last thing on my mind right now," she said. "Get in. Mirror's on the back of the visor."

I slid in and folded down the visor, sighed with relief when I saw my face. Nothing really wrong with it, except my chin was nearer to my nose than it should be, and my lips looked too dark and puffy. My eyes weren't blackened and my nose wasn't broken. I could pass. I gapped the collar just a little and winced at the angry dark rope marks around my neck, then clutched the collar closed.

The woman climbed into the driver's seat. "My name's Marti," she said, holding out a hand. Still keeping the coat closed with my left hand, I extended my right, and she shook it.

"Sheila," I said. It was the first time I'd ever said it out loud. She. La. Two words for woman put together. I smiled, then glanced quickly at the mirror, and saw that a smile was as bad as I'd thought. My mouth was a graveyard of broken teeth, brown with old blood. I hid my mouth with my hand again.

"Christ!" said Marti. "What's your boyfriend's name?"

"Don't worry about it," I said.

"If he did that to you, he could do it to others. My daughter lives in Renton. This has to be reported to the police. Who is he? Where does he live?"

"Near Sea-Tac. The airport."

She took a deep breath, let it out. "You understand, don't you, this is a matter for the authorities?"

I shook my head. The heat in my chest was scorching, urging me on. "I have to go to town now," I said, gripping the door handle.

"Put your seat belt on," she said, slammed her door, and started the car.

Once she got started, she was some ball-of-fire driver. Scared me—even though there wasn't anything I could think of that could hurt me.

"Where were we, anyway?" I asked after I got used to her tire-squealing cornering on curves.

"Well, I was coming down from Kanaskat. I'm on my way in to Renton to see my daughter. She's got a belly-dance recital tonight, and—" She stared at me, then shook her head and focused on the road.

The land was leveling a little. We hit a main road, Highway 169, and she turned north on it.

The burning in my chest raged up into my throat. "No," I said, reaching for her hand on the steering wheel.

"What?"

"No. That way." I pointed back to the other road we had been on. Actually the urge inside me was pulling from some direction between the two roads, but the smaller road aimed closer to where I had to go.

"Maple Valley's this way," she said, not turning, "and we can talk to the police there, and a doctor."

"No," I said.

She looked at me. "You're in no state to make rational decisions," she said.

I closed my hand around her wrist and squeezed. She cried out. She let go of the steering wheel and tried to shake off my grip. I stared at her and held on, remembering my grand-mère's tales of the strength of the dead.

"Stop," I said. I felt strange, totally strange, ordering a woman around the way a pimp would. I knew I was hurting her, too. I knew I could squeeze harder, break the bones in her arm, and I was ready to, but she pulled the car over to the shoulder and stamped on the brake.

"I got to go to Sea-Tac," I said. I released her arm and climbed out of the car. "Thanks for ride. You want the jacket back?" I fingered the denim.

"My Lord," she said, "you keep it, child." She was rubbing her hand over the wrist I had gripped. She heaved a huge sigh. "Get in. I'll take you where you want to go. I can't just leave you here."

"Your daughter's show?" I said.

"I'll phone. We're going someplace with phones, aren't we?"

I wasn't sure exactly where we would end up. I would know when we arrived.... I remembered the inside of Richie's apartment. But that was later. First he had pulled up next to where I was standing by the highway, rolled down the passenger window of his big gold four-door Buick, said he'd like to party and that he knew a good place. Standard lines, except I usually told johns the place, down one of the side streets and in the driveway behind an abandoned house. I had asked him how high he was willing to go. My pimp had been offering me coke off and on but I'd managed not to get hooked, so I was still a little picky about who I went with; but Richie looked clean-cut and just plain clean, and his car was a couple years old but expensive; I thought he might have money.

"I want it all," Richie had said. "I'll give you a hundred bucks."

I climbed into his car.

He took me down off the ridge where the Sea-Tac Strip is to a place like the one where I usually took my tricks, behind one of the abandoned houses near the airport that are due to be razed someday. There's two or three neighborhoods of them handy. I asked him for money and he handed me a hundred, so I got in back with him, but then things went seriously wrong. That was the first time I saw and felt his rope, the first time I heard his voice cursing me, the first time I tasted one of his sweaty socks, not the worst thing I'd ever tasted, but close.

When he had me gagged and tied up and shoved down on the back seat floor, he drove somewhere else. I couldn't tell how long the drive was; it felt like two hours but was probably only fifteen or twenty minutes. I could tell when the car drove into a parking garage because the sounds changed. He put a shopping bag over my head and carried me into an elevator, again something I could tell by feel, and then along a hall to his apartment. That was where I learned more about him than I had ever wanted to know about anybody.

I didn't know his apartment's address, but I knew where Richie was. If he was at the apartment, I would direct Marti there even without a map. The fire inside me reached for Richie like a magnet lusting for a hammer.

Shaping words carefully, I told Marti, "Going to the Strip. Plenty of phones."

"Right," she said.

"On the other road." I pointed behind us.

She sighed. "Get in."

I climbed into the car, and she waited for an RV to pass, then pulled out and turned around.

As soon as we were heading the way I wanted to go, the fire inside me cooled a little. I sat back and relaxed.

"Why are we going to the—to the Strip?" she asked. "What are you going to do when we get there?"

"Don't know," I said. We were driving toward the sun, which was going down. Glare had bothered me before my death, but now it was like dirt in my eyes, a minor annoyance. I blinked and considered this, then shrugged it off.

"Can't you even tell me your boyfriend's name?" she asked.

"Richie."

"Richie what?"

"Don't know."

"Are you going back to him?"

Fire rose in my throat like vomit. I felt like I could breathe it out and it would feel good. It felt good inside my belly already. I was drunk with it. "Oh, yes," I said.

"How can you?" she cried. She shook her head. "I can't take you back to someone who hurt you so much." But she didn't stop driving.

"I have to go back," I said.

"You don't. You can choose something else. There are shelters for battered women. The government should offer you some protection. The police...."

"You don't understand," I said.

"I do," she said. Her voice got quieter. "I know what it's like to live with someone who doesn't respect you. I know how hard it is to get away. But you *are* away, Sheila. You can start over."

"No," I said, "I can't."

"You can. I'll help you. You can live in Kanaskat with me and he'll never find you. Or if you just want a bus ticket someplace—back home, wherever that is—I can do that for you, too."

"You don't understand," I said.

She was quiet for a long stretch of road. Then she said, "Help me understand."

I shook my braids back and opened the collar of the jacket, pulled down the lapels to bare my neck. I stared at her until she looked back.

She screamed and drove across the center lane. Fortunately there was no other traffic. Still screaming, she fought with the steering wheel until she straightened out the car. Then she pulled over to the shoulder and jumped out of the car and ran away.

I shut off the car's engine, then climbed out. "Marti," I yelled. "Okay, I'm walking away now. The car's all yours. I'm leaving. It's safe. Thanks for the jacket. Bye." I buttoned up the jacket, put the collar up, buried my hands in the pockets, and started walking along the road toward Richie.

I had gone about a quarter mile when she caught up with me again. The sun had set and twilight was deepening into night. Six cars had passed going my way, but I didn't hold out my thumb, and though some kid had yelled out a window at me, and somebody else had honked and swerved, nobody stopped.

It had been so easy to hitch before I met Richie. Somehow now I just couldn't do it.

I heard the Rabbit's sputter behind me and kept walking, not turning to look at her. But she slowed and kept pace with me. "Sheila?" she said in a hoarse voice. "Sheila?"

I stopped and looked toward her. I knew she was scared of me. I felt strong and strange, hearing her call me by a name I had given myself, as if I might once have had a chance to make up who I was instead of being shaped by what had happened to me. I couldn't see it being possible now, though, when I was only alive to do what the fire in me wanted.

Marti blinked, turned away, then turned back. "Get in," she said.

"You don't have to take me," I said. "I'll get there sooner or later. Doesn't matter when."

"Get in."

I got back into her car.

For half an hour we drove in silence. She crossed Interstate 5, paused when we hit 99, the Strip. "Which way?"

I pointed right. The fire was so hot in me now I felt like my fingertips might start smoking any second.

She turned the car and we cruised north toward the Sea-Tac Airport, my old stomping grounds. We passed expensive hotels and cheap motels, convenience stores and fancy restaurants. Lighted buildings alternated with dark gaps. The roar of planes taking off and landing, lights rising and descending in the sky ahead of us, turned rapidly into background. We drove past the Goldilocks Motel, where Blake and I had a room we rented by the week, and I didn't feel anything. But as we passed the intersection where the Red Lion sprawls on the corner of 188th Street and the Pacific Highway, fire flared under my skin. "Slowly," I said to Marti. She stared at me and slowed the car. A mile further, past the airport, one of the little roads led down off the ridge to the left. I pointed.

Marti got in the left-turn lane and made the turn, then pulled into a gas station on the corner and parked by the rest rooms. "Now wait," she said. "What are we doing, here?"

"Richie," I whispered. I could feel his presence in the near distance; all my wounds were resonating with his nearness now, all the places he had pressed himself into me with his rope and his cigarette and his sock and his flaked stone knife and his penis, imprinting me as his possession. Surely as a knife slicing into a tree's bark, he had branded me with his heart.

"Yes," said Marti. "Richie. You have any plans for what you're going to do once you find him?"

I held my hands out, open, palms up. The heat was so strong I felt like anything I touched would burst into flame.

"What are you going to do, strangle him? Have you got something to do it with?" She sounded sarcastic.

I was having a hard time listening to her. All my attention was focused down the road. I knew Richie's car was there, and Richie in it. It was the place he had taken me to tie me up. He might be driving this way any second, and I didn't want to wait any longer for our reunion, though I knew there was no place he could hide where I couldn't find him. My love for him was what animated me now.

"Strangle," I said, and shook my head. I climbed out of the car.

"Sheila!" said Marti.

I let the sound of my self-given name fill me with what power it could, and stood still for a moment, fighting the fire inside. Then I walked into the street, stood in the center so a car coming up out of the dark would have to stop. I strode down into darkness, away from the lights and noise of the Strip. My feet felt like match-heads, as if a scrape could strike fire from them.

Presently the asphalt gave way to potholes and gravel; I could tell by the sound of pebbles sliding under my feet. I walked past the first three dark houses to the right and left, looming shapes in a darkness pierced by the flight lights of airplanes, but without stars. I turned left at the fourth house, dark like the others, but with a glow behind it I couldn't see with my eyes but could feel in my bones. Heat pulsed and danced inside me.

I pushed past an overgrown lilac bush at the side of the house and stepped into the broad drive in back. The car was there, as I had known it would be. Dark and quiet. Its doors were closed.

I heard a brief cry, and then the dome light went on in the car. Richie was sitting up in back, facing away from me.

Richie.

I walked across the crunching gravel, looking at his dark head. He wore a white shirt. He was staring down, focused, his arms moving. As I neared the car, I could see he was sitting on a woman. She still had her clothes on. (Richie hadn't taken my clothes off until he got me in his apartment.) Tape was across her mouth, and her head thrashed from side to side, her upper arms jerking as Richie bound his thin nylon rope around her wrists, her legs kicking. I stood a moment looking in the window. She saw me and her eyes widened. She made a gurgling swallowed sound behind the sock, the tape.

I thought: he doesn't need her. He has me.

I remembered the way my mind had struggled while my body struggled, screaming silently: no, oh no, Blake, where are you? No one will help me, the way no one has ever helped me, and I can't help myself. That hurts, that hurts. Maybe he'll play with me and let me go if I'm very, very good. Oh, God! What do you want? Just tell me, I can do it. You don't have to hurt me! Okay, rip me off, it's not like you're the first, but you don't have to hurt me.

Hurt me.

I love you. I love you so much.

I stared at him through the glass. The woman beneath him had stilled, and she was staring at me. Richie finally noticed, and whirled.

For a moment we stared at each other. Then I smiled, showing him the stumps of my teeth, and his blue eyes widened.

I reached for the door handle, opened it before he could lock it.

"Richie," I said.

"Don't!" he said. He shook his head, hard, as though he were a dog with wet fur. Slowly, he lifted one hand and rubbed his eye. He had a big bread knife in the other hand, had used it to cut the rope, then flicked it across the woman's cheek, leaving a streak of darkness. He looked at me again. His jaw worked.

"Richie."

"Don't! Don't. . . interrupt."

I held out my arms, my fingertips scorched black as if dyed or tattooed, made special, the wrists dark beyond the ends of my sleeves. "Richie," I said tenderly, the fire in me rising up like a firework, a burst of stars. "I'm yours."

"No," he said.

"You made me yours." I looked at him. He had made Tawanda his, and then he had erased her. He had made Mary his, and then erased her. Even though he had erased Tawanda and Mary, these feelings inside me were Tawanda's: *whoever hurts me controls me*; and Mary's: *I spoke up once and I got a curse on me I can't get rid of. If I'm quiet maybe I'll be okay.*

But Sheila? Richie hadn't erased Sheila; he had never even met her.

It was Tawanda who was talking. "You killed me and you made me yours," she said. My fingers went to the jacket, unbuttoned it, dropped it behind me. "What I am I owe to you."

"I—" he said, and coughed. "No," he said.

I heard the purr of car engines in the near distance, not the constant traffic of the Strip, but something closer.

I reached into the car and gripped Richie's arm. I pulled him out, even though he grabbed at the door handle with his free hand. I could feel the bone in his upper arm as my fingers pressed his muscles. "Richie," I whispered, and put my arms around him and laid my head on his shoulder.

For a while he was stiff, tense in my embrace. Then a shudder went through him and he loosened up. His arms came around me. "You're mine?" he said.

"Yours," said Tawanda.

"Does that mean you'll do what I say?" His voice sounded like a little boy's.

"Whatever you say," she said.

"Put your arms down," he said.

I lowered my arms.

"Stand real still." He backed away from me, then stood and studied me. He walked around, looking at me from all sides. "Wait a sec, I gotta get my flashlight." He went around to the trunk and opened it, pulled out a flashlight as long as his forearm, turned it on. He trained the beam on my breasts, my neck. "I did you," he said, nodding. "I did you. You were good. Almost as good as the first one. Show me your hands again."

I held them out and he stared at my blackened fingers. Slowly he smiled, then looked up and met my eyes.

"I was going to visit you," he said. "When I finished with this one. I was coming back to see you.

"I couldn't wait," said Tawanda.

"Don't talk," Richie said gently.

Don't talk! Tawanda and Mary accepted that without a problem, but I, Sheila, was tired of people telling me not to talk. What did I have to lose?

On the other hand, what did I have to say? I didn't even know what I wanted. Tawanda's love for Richie was hard to fight. It was the burning inside me, the sizzling under my skin, all I had left of life.

"Will you scream if I say so?" said Richie in his little boy's voice.

"Yes," said Tawanda; but suddenly lights went on around us, and bullhorn voices came out of the dark.

"Hold it right there, buddy! Put your hands up!"

Blinking in the sudden flood of light, Richie slowly lifted his hand, the knife glinting in the left one, the flashlight in the other.

"Step away from him, miss," said someone else. I looked around too, not blinking; glare didn't bother me. I couldn't see through it, though. I didn't know who was talking. "Miss, move away from him," said another voice from outside the light.

"Come here," Richie whispered, and I went to him. Releasing the flashlight, he dropped his arms around me, held the knife to my neck, and yelled, "Stay back!"

"Sheila!" It was Marti's voice this time, not amplified.

I looked toward her.

"Sheila, get away from him!" Marti yelled. "Do you want him to escape?"

Tawanda did. Mary did. They, after all, had found the place where they belonged. In the circle of his arms, my body glowed, the fire banked but burning steady.

He put the blade closer to my twisted throat. I could almost feel it. I laid my head back on his shoulder, looking at his profile out of the corner of my eye. The light glare brought out the blue in his eye. His mouth was slightly open, the inside of his lower lip glistening. He turned to look down into my face, and a slight smile curved the corner of his mouth. "Okay," he whispered, "we're going to get into the car now." He raised his voice. "Do what I say and don't struggle." Keeping me between him and the lights, he kicked the back door closed and edged us around the car to the driver's side. Moving in tandem, with his arm still around my neck, we slid in behind the wheel, me going first. "Keep close," he said to me. "Slide down a little so I can use my arm to shift with, but keep close."

"Sheila!" screamed Marti. The driver's side window was open.

Richie started the car.

"Sheila! There's a live woman in the back of that car!"

Tawanda didn't care, and Mary didn't care, and I wasn't even sure I cared. Richie shifted from park into drive and eased his foot off the brake and onto the gas pedal; I could feel his legs moving against my left shoulder. From the back seat I heard a muffled groan. I looked up at Richie's face. He was smiling.

Just as he gunned the engine, I reached up and grappled the steering-wheel-mounted gear shift into park. Then I broke the shift handle off.

"You said you'd obey me," he said, staring down into my face. He looked betrayed, his eyes wide, his brow furrowed, his mouth soft. The car's engine continued to snarl without effect.

Fire blossomed inside me, hurting me this time because I'd hurt him. Pain came alive. I coughed, choking on my own tongue, my throat swollen and burning, my wrists and ankles burning, my breasts burning, between my legs a column of flame raging up inside me. I tried to apologize, but I no longer had a voice.

"You promised," said Richie in his little boy's voice, looking down at me.

I coughed. I could feel the power leaving me; my arms and legs were stiffening the way a body is supposed to do after death. I lifted my crippling hands as high as I could, palms up, pleading, but by that point only my elbows could bend. It was Tawanda's last gesture.

"Don't make a move," said a voice. "Keep your hands on the wheel."

We looked. A man stood just outside the car, aiming a gun at Richie through the open window.

Richie edged a hand down the wheel toward me.

"Make a move for her and I'll shoot," said the man. Someone else came up beside him, and he moved back, keeping his gun aimed at Richie's head, while the other man leaned in and put handcuffs on Richie.

"That's it," said the first man, and he and the second man heaved huge sighs.

I lay curled on the seat, my arms bent at the elbows, my legs bent at the knees. When they pulled Richie out of the car I slipped off his lap and lay stiff, my neck bent at an angle so my head stuck up sideways. "This woman needs medical attention," someone yelled. I listened to them freeing the woman in the back seat, and thought about the death of Tawanda and Mary.

Tawanda had lifted me out of my grave and carried me for miles. Mary had probably mostly died when Grannie cursed me and drove me out of the house. But Sheila? In a way, I had been pregnant with Sheila for years, and she was born in the grave. She was still looking out of my eyes and listening with my ears even though the rest of me was dead. Even as the pain of death faded, leaving me with clear memories of how Richie had treated me before he took that final twist around my neck, the Sheila in me was awake and feeling things.

"She's in an advanced state of rigor," someone said. I felt a dim pressure around one of my arms. My body slid along the seat toward the door.

"Wait," said someone else. "I got to take pictures."

"What are you talking about?" said another. "Ten minutes ago she was walking and talking."

Lights flashed, but I didn't blink.

"Are you crazy?" said the first person. "Even rapid-onset rigor doesn't come on this fast."

"Ask anybody, Tony. We all saw her."

"Try feeling for a pulse. Are you sure he wasn't just propping her up and moving her around like a puppet? But that wouldn't explain…."

"You done with the pictures yet, Crane?" said one of the cops. Then, to me, in a light voice, "Honey, come on out of there. Don't just lie there and let him photograph you like a corpse. You don't know what he does with the pictures."

"Wait till the civilians are out of here before you start making jokes," said someone else. "Maybe she's just in shock."

"Sheila?" said Marti from the passenger side.

"Marti," I whispered.

Gasps.

"Sheila, you did it. You did it."

Did what? Let him kill me, then kill me again? Suddenly I was so angry I couldn't rest. Anger was like the fire that had filled me before, only a lower, slower heat. I shuddered and sat up.

Another gasp from one of the men at the driver's side door. "See?" said the one with the shock theory. One of them had a flashlight and shone it on me. I lifted my chin and stared at him, my microbraids brushing my shoulders.

"Kee-rist!"

"Oh, God!"

They fell back a step.

I sucked breath in past the swelling in my throat and said, "I need a ride. And feeling for a pulse? I think you'll be happier if you don't."

Marti gave me back her jacket. I rode in her Rabbit; the cop cars and the van from the medical examiner's office tailed us. Marti had a better idea of where she had found me than I did.

"What's your full name?" she said when we were driving. "Is there anybody I can get in touch with for you?"

"No. I've been dead to them for a couple years already."

"Are you sure? Did you ever call to check with them?"

I waited for a while, then said, "If your daughter was a hooker and dead, would you want to know?"

"Yes," she said immediately. "Real information is much better than not knowing."

I kept silent for another while, then told her my parents' names and phone number. Ultimately, I didn't care if the information upset them or not.

She handed me a little notebook and asked me to write it down, turning on the dome light so I could see what I was doing. The pain of scorching had left my fingers again. Holding the pen was awkward, but I managed to write out what Marti wanted. When I finished, I slipped the notebook back into her purse and turned off the light.

"It was somewhere along here," she said half an hour later. "You have any feeling for it?"

"No." I didn't have a sense of my grave the way I had had a feeling for Richie. Marti's headlights flashed on three Coke cans lying together by the road, though, and I remembered seeing a cluster like that soon after I had climbed up the slope. "Here," I said.

She pulled over, and so did the three cars following us. Someone gave me a flashlight and I went to the edge of the slope and walked along, looking for my own footprints or anything else familiar. A broken bramble, a crushed fern, a tree with a hooked branch—I remembered them all from the afternoon. "Here," I said, pointing down the mountainside.

"Okay. Don't disturb anything," said the cop named Joe. One of the others started stringing up yellow tape along the road in both directions.

"But—" I was having a feeling now, a feeling that Sheila had lived as long as she wanted. All I needed was my blanket of goofer dust, and I could go back to sleep. When Joe went back to his car to get something, I slipped over the edge and headed home.

I pushed the branches off the other two women and lay down beside their bodies, thinking about my brief life. I had helped somebody and I had hurt somebody, which I figured was as much as I'd done in my first two lives.

I pulled dirt up over me, even over my face, not blinking when it fell into my eyes; but then I thought, Marti's going to see me sooner or later, and she'd probably like it better if my eyes were closed. So I closed my eyes.

THE DEAD

by Michael Swanwick

Michael Swanwick is the author of the novels *Bones of the Earth*, *Griffin's Egg*, *In the Drift*, *The Iron Dragon's Daughter*, *Jack Faust*, *Stations of the Tide*, *Vacuum Flowers*, and *The Dragons of Babel*. His short fiction has appeared in *Asimov's Science Fiction*, *Analog*, *The Magazine of Fantasy & Science Fiction*, and in numerous anthologies, and has been collected in *Cigar-Box Faust*, *A Geography of Unknown Lands*, *Gravity's Angels*, *Moon Dogs*, *Puck Aleshire's Abecedary*, *Tales of Old Earth*, and *The Dog Said Bow-Wow*. He is the winner of numerous awards, including the Hugo, Nebula, Sturgeon, Locus, and World Fantasy awards.

This story, which was a finalist for both the Hugo and Nebula awards, first appeared in *Starlight 1*. Here, the zombies are not a menace but a commodity: luxury goods to be bought and sold on the free market. Besides zombies, it also features cold-blooded businessmen; it's hard to say which is more frightening.

Three boy zombies in matching red jackets bussed our table, bringing water, lighting candles, brushing away the crumbs between courses. Their eyes were dark, attentive, lifeless; their hands and faces so white as to be faintly luminous in the hushed light. I thought it in bad taste, but "This is Manhattan," Courtney said. "A certain studied offensiveness is fashionable here."

The blond brought menus and waited for our order.

We both ordered pheasant. "An excellent choice," the boy said in a clear, emotionless voice. He went away and came back a minute later with the freshly strangled birds, holding them up for our approval. He couldn't have been more than eleven when he died and his skin was of that sort connoisseurs call "milk glass," smooth, without blemish, and all but translucent. He must have cost a fortune.

As the boy was turning away, I impulsively touched his shoulder. He turned back. "What's your name, son?" I asked.

"Timothy." He might have been telling me the *spécialité de maison*. The boy waited a breath to see if more was expected of him, then left.

Courtney gazed after him. "How lovely he would look," she murmured, "nude. Standing in the moonlight by a cliff. Definitely a cliff. Perhaps the very one where he met his death."

"He wouldn't look very lovely if he'd fallen off a cliff."

"Oh, don't be unpleasant."

The wine steward brought our bottle. "Chateau La Tour '17." I raised an eyebrow. The steward had the sort of old and complex face that Rembrandt would have enjoyed painting. He poured with pulseless ease and then dissolved into the gloom. "Good lord, Courtney, you *seduced* me on cheaper."

She flushed, not happily. Courtney had a better career going than I. She outpowered me. We both knew who was smarter, better connected, more likely to end up in a corner office with the historically significant antique desk. The only edge I had was that I was a male in a seller's market. It was enough.

"This is a business dinner, Donald," she said, "nothing more."

I favored her with an expression of polite disbelief I knew from experience she'd find infuriating. And, digging into my pheasant, murmured, "Of course." We didn't say much of consequence until dessert, when I finally asked, "So what's Loeb-Soffner up to these days?"

"Structuring a corporate expansion. Jim's putting together the financial side of the package, and I'm doing personnel. You're being headhunted, Donald." She favored me with that feral little flash of teeth she made when she saw something she wanted. Courtney wasn't a beautiful woman, far from it. But there was that fierceness to her, that sense of something primal being held under tight and precarious control that made her hot as hot to me. "You're talented, you're thuggish, and you're not too tightly nailed to your present position. Those are all qualities we're looking for."

She dumped her purse on the table, took out a single folded sheet of paper. "These are the terms I'm offering." She placed it by my plate, attacked her torte with gusto.

I unfolded the paper. "This is a lateral transfer."

"Unlimited opportunity for advancement," she said with her mouth full, "if you've got the stuff."

"Mmm." I did a line-by-line of the benefits, all comparable to what I was getting now. My current salary to the dollar—Ms. Soffner was showing off. And the stock options. "This can't be right. Not for a lateral."

There was that grin again, like a glimpse of shark in murky waters. "I knew you'd like it. We're going over the top with the options because we need your answer right away—tonight preferably. Tomorrow at the latest. No negotiations. We have to put the package together fast. There's going to be a shitstorm of publicity when this comes out. We want to have everything nailed down, present the fundies and bleeding hearts with a *fait accompli*."

"My God, Courtney, what kind of monster do you have hold of now?"

"The biggest one in the world. Bigger than Apple. Bigger than Home Virtual. Bigger than HIVac-IV," she said with relish. "Have you ever heard of Koestler Biological?"

I put my fork down.

"Koestler? You're peddling corpses now?"

"Please. Postanthropic biological resources." She said it lightly, with just the right touch of irony. Still, I thought I detected a certain discomfort with the nature of her client's product.

"There's no money in it." I waved a hand toward our attentive waitstaff. "These guys must be—what?—maybe two percent of the annual turnover? Zombies are luxury goods: servants, reactor cleanups, Hollywood stunt deaths, exotic services"—we both knew what I meant—"a few hundred a year, maybe, tops. There's not the demand. The revulsion factor is too great."

"There's been a technological breakthrough." Courtney leaned forward. "They can install the infrasystem and controllers and offer the product for the factory-floor cost of a new subcompact. That's way below the economic threshold for blue-collar labor.

"Look at it from the viewpoint of a typical factory owner. He's already down-sized to the bone and labor costs are bleeding him dry. How can he compete in a dwindling consumer market? Now let's imagine he buys into the program." She took out her Mont Blanc and began scribbling figures on the tablecloth. "No benefits. No liability suits. No sick pay. No pilferage. We're talking about cutting labor costs by at least two-thirds. Minimum! That's irresistible, I don't care how big your revulsion factor is. We project we can move five hundred thousand units in the first year."

"Five hundred thousand," I said. "That's crazy. Where the hell are you going to get the raw material for—?"

"Africa."

"Oh, God, Courtney." I was struck wordless by the cynicism it took to even consider turning the sub-Saharan tragedy to a profit, by the sheer, raw evil of channeling hard currency to the pocket Hitlers who ran the camps. Courtney only smiled and gave that quick little flip of her head that meant she was accessing the time on an optic chip.

"I think you're ready," she said, "to talk with Koestler."

At her gesture, the zombie boys erected projector lamps about us, fussed with the settings, turned them on. Interference patterns moiréd, clashed, meshed. Walls of darkness erected themselves about us. Courtney took out her flat and set it up on the table. Three taps of her nailed fingers and the round and hairless face of Marvin Koestler appeared on the screen. "Ah, Courtney!" he said in a pleased voice. "You're in—New York, yes? The San Moritz. With Donald." The slightest pause with each accessed bit of information. "Did you have the antelope medallions?" When we shook our heads, he kissed his fingertips. "Magnificent! They're ever so lightly braised and then smothered in buffalo mozzarella. Nobody makes them better. I had the same dish in Florence the other day, and there was simply no comparison."

I cleared my throat. "Is that where you are? Italy?"

"Let's leave out where I am." He made a dismissive gesture, as if it were a trifle. But Courtney's face darkened. Corporate kidnapping being the growth industry it is, I'd gaffed badly. "The question is—what do you think of my offer?"

"It's… interesting. For a lateral."

"It's the start-up costs. We're leveraged up to our asses as it is. You'll make out better this way in the long run." He favored me with a sudden grin that went mean around the edges. Very much the financial buccaneer. Then he leaned forward, lowered his voice, maintained firm eye contact. Classic people-handling techniques. "You're not sold. You know you can trust Courtney to have checked out the finances. Still, you think: It won't work. To work, the product has to be irresistible, and it's not. It can't be."

"Yes, sir," I said. "Succinctly put."

He nodded to Courtney. "Let's sell this young man." And to me, "My stretch is downstairs."

He winked out.

Koestler was waiting for us in the limo, a ghostly pink presence. His holo, rather, a genial if somewhat coarse-grained ghost afloat in golden light. He waved an expansive and insubstantial arm to take in the interior of the car and said, "Make yourselves at home."

The chauffeur wore combat-grade photomultipliers. They gave him a buggish, inhuman look. I wasn't sure if he was dead or not. "Take us to Heaven," Koestler said.

The doorman stepped out into the street, looked both ways, nodded to the chauffeur. Robot guns tracked our progress down the block.

"Courtney tells me you're getting the raw materials from Africa."

"Distasteful, but necessary. To begin with. We have to sell the idea first—no reason to make things rough on ourselves. Down the line, though, I don't see why we can't go domestic. Something along the lines of a reverse mortgage, perhaps, life insurance that pays off while you're still alive. It'd be a step towards getting the poor off our backs at last. Fuck 'em. They've been getting a goddamn free ride for too long; the least they can do is to die and provide us with servants."

I was pretty sure Koestler was joking. But I smiled and ducked my head, so I'd be covered in either case. "What's Heaven?" I asked, to move the conversation onto safer territory.

"A proving ground," Koestler said with great satisfaction, "for the future. Have you ever witnessed bare-knuckles fisticuffs?"

"No."

"Ah, now there's a sport for gentlemen! The sweet science at its sweetest. No rounds, no rules, no holds barred. It gives you the real measure of a man—not just of his strength but his character. How he handles himself, whether he keeps cool under pressure—how he stands up to pain. Security won't let me go to the clubs in person, but I've made arrangements."

Heaven was a converted movie theater in a rundown neighborhood in Queens. The chauffeur got out, disappeared briefly around the back, and returned with two zombie bodyguards. It was like a conjurer's trick. "You had these guys stashed in the *trunk?*" I asked as he opened the door for us.

"It's a new world," Courtney said. "Get used to it."

The place was mobbed. Two, maybe three hundred seats, standing room only. A mixed crowd, blacks and Irish and Koreans mostly, but with a smattering of uptown customers as well. You didn't have to be poor to need the occasional taste of vicarious potency. Nobody paid us any particular notice. We'd come in just as the fighters were being presented.

"Weighing two-five-oh, in black trunks with a red stripe," the ref was bawling, "tha gang-bang *gang*sta, tha bare-knuckle *brawla,* tha man with tha—"

Courtney and I went up a scummy set of back stairs. Bodyguard-us-body-guard, as if we were a combat patrol out of some twentieth-century jungle war. A scrawny, potbellied old geezer with a damp cigar in his mouth unlocked the door to our box. Sticky floor, bad seats, a good view down on the ring. Gray plastic matting, billowing smoke.

Koestler was there, in a shiny new hologram shell. It reminded me of those plaster Madonnas in painted bathtubs that Catholics set out in their yards. "Your permanent box?" I asked.

"All of this is for your sake, Donald—you and a few others. We're pitting our product one-on-one against some of the local talent. By arrangement with the management. What you're going to see will settle your doubts once and for all."

"You'll like this," Courtney said. "I've been here five nights straight. Counting tonight." The bell rang, starting the fight. She leaned forward avidly, hooking her elbows on the railing.

The zombie was gray-skinned and modestly muscled, for a fighter. But it held up its hands alertly, was light on its feet, and had strangely calm and knowing eyes.

Its opponent was a real bruiser, a big black guy with classic African features twisted slightly out of true so that his mouth curled up in a kind of sneer on one side. He had gang scars on his chest and even uglier marks on his back that didn't look deliberate but like something he'd earned on the streets. His eyes burned with an intensity just this side of madness.

He came forward cautiously but not fearfully, and made a couple of quick jabs to get the measure of his opponent. They were blocked and countered.

They circled each other, looking for an opening.

For a minute or so, nothing much happened. Then the gangster feinted at the zombie's head, drawing up its guard. He drove through that opening with a slam to the zombie's nuts that made me wince.

No reaction.

The dead fighter responded with a flurry of punches, and got in a glancing blow to its opponent's cheek. They separated, engaged, circled around.

Then the big guy exploded in a combination of killer blows, connecting so solidly it seemed they would splinter every rib in the dead fighter's body. It brought the crowd to their feet, roaring their approval.

The zombie didn't even stagger.

A strange look came into the gangster's eyes, then, as the zombie counterattacked, driving him back into the ropes. I could only imagine what it must be like for a man who had always lived by his strength and his ability to absorb punishment to realize that he was facing an opponent to whom pain meant nothing. Fights were lost and won by flinches and hesitations. You won by keeping your head. You lost by getting rattled.

Despite his best blows, the zombie stayed methodical, serene, calm, relentless. That was its nature.

It must have been devastating.

The fight went on and on. It was a strange and alienating experience for me. After a while I couldn't stay focused on it. My thoughts kept slipping into a zone where I found myself studying the line of Courtney's jaw, thinking about later tonight. She liked her sex just a little bit sick. There was always a feeling, fucking her, that there was something truly repulsive that she *really* wanted to do but lacked the courage to bring up on her own.

So there was always this urge to get her to do something she didn't like. She was resistant; I never dared try more than one new thing per date. But I could always talk her into that one thing. Because when she was aroused, she got pliant. She could be talked into anything. She could be made to beg for it.

Courtney would've been amazed to learn that I was not proud of what I did with her—quite the opposite, in fact. But I was as obsessed with her as she was with whatever it was that obsessed her.

Suddenly Courtney was on her feet, yelling. The hologram showed Koestler on his feet as well. The big guy was on the ropes, being pummeled. Blood and spittle flew from his face with each blow. Then he was down; he'd never even had a chance. He must've known early on that it was hopeless, that he wasn't going to win, but he'd refused to take a fall. He had to be pounded into the ground. He went down raging, proud and uncomplaining. I had to admire that.

But he lost anyway.

That, I realized, was the message I was meant to take away from this. Not just that the product was robust. But that only those who backed it were going to win. I could see, even if the audience couldn't, that it was the end of an era. A man's body wasn't worth a damn anymore. There wasn't anything it could do that technology couldn't handle better. The number of losers in the world had just doubled, tripled, reached maximum. What the fools below were cheering for was the death of their futures.

I got up and cheered too.

In the stretch afterwards, Koestler said, "You've seen the light. You're a believer now."

"I haven't necessarily decided yet."

"Don't bullshit me," Koestler said. "I've done my homework, Mr. Nichols. Your current position is not exactly secure. Morton-Western is going down the tubes. The entire service sector is going down the tubes. Face it, the old economic order is as good as fucking gone. Of course you're going to take my offer. You don't have any other choice."

The fax outed sets of contracts. "A Certain Product," it said here and there. Corpses were never mentioned.

But when I opened my jacket to get a pen, Koestler said, "Wait. I've got a factory. Three thousand positions under me. I've got a motivated workforce. They'd walk through fire to keep their jobs. Pilferage is at zero. Sick time practically the same. Give me one advantage your product has over my current workforce. Sell me on it. I'll give you thirty seconds."

I wasn't in sales and the job had been explicitly promised me already. But by reaching for the pen, I had admitted I wanted the position. And we all knew whose hand carried the whip.

"They can be catheterized," I said—"no toilet breaks."

For a long instant Koestler just stared at me blankly. Then he exploded with laughter. "By God, that's a new one! You have a great future ahead of you, Donald. Welcome aboard."

He winked out.

We drove on in silence for a while, aimless, directionless. At last Courtney leaned forward and touched the chauffeur's shoulder.

"Take me home," she said.

Riding through Manhattan I suffered from a waking hallucination that we were driving through a city of corpses. Gray faces, listless motions. Everyone looked dead in the headlights and sodium vapor streetlamps. Passing by the Children's Museum I saw a mother with a stroller through the glass doors. Two small children by her side. They all three stood motionless, gazing forward at nothing. We passed by a stop-and-go where zombies stood out on the sidewalk drinking forties in paper bags. Through upper-story windows I could see the sad rainbow trace of virtuals playing to empty eyes. There were zombies in the park, zombies smoking blunts, zombies driving taxies, zombies sitting on stoops and hanging out on street corners, all of them waiting for the years to pass and the flesh to fall from their bones.

I felt like the last man alive.

Courtney was still wired and sweaty from the fight. The pheromones came off her in great waves as I followed her down the hall to her apartment. She stank of lust. I found myself thinking of how she got just before orgasm, so desperate, so desirable. It was different after she came, she would fall into a state of calm assurance; the same sort of calm assurance she showed in her business life, the aplomb she sought so wildly during the act itself.

And when that desperation left her, so would I. Because even I could recognize that it was her desperation that drew me to her, that made me do the things she needed me to do. In all the years I'd known her, we'd never once had breakfast together.

I wished there was some way I could deal her out of the equation. I wished that her desperation were a liquid that I could drink down to the dregs. I wished I could drop her in a wine press and squeeze her dry.

At her apartment, Courtney unlocked her door and in one complicated movement twisted through and stood facing me from the inside. "Well," she said. "All in all, a productive evening. Good night, Donald."

"Good night? Aren't you going to invite me inside?"

"No."

"What do you mean, no?" She was beginning to piss me off. A blind man could've told she was in heat from across the street. A chimpanzee could've talked his way into her pants. "What kind of idiot game are you playing now?"

"You know what no means, Donald. You're not stupid."

"No I'm not, and neither are you. We both know the score. Now let me in, goddamnit."

"Enjoy your present," she said, and closed the door.

I found Courtney's present back in my suite. I was still seething from her treatment of me and stalked into the room, letting the door slam behind me. So that I was standing in near-total darkness. The only light was what little seeped through the draped windows at the far end of the room. I was just reaching for the light switch when there was a motion in the darkness.

'Jackers! I thought, and all in a panic lurched for the light switch, hoping to achieve I don't know what. Credit-jackers always work in trios, one to torture the security codes out of you, one to phone the numbers out of your accounts and into a fiscal trapdoor, a third to stand guard. Was turning the lights on supposed to make them scurry for darkness, like roaches? Nevertheless, I almost tripped over my own feet in my haste to reach the switch. But of course it was nothing like what I'd feared.

It was a woman.

She stood by the window in a white silk dress that could neither compete with nor distract from her ethereal beauty, her porcelain skin. When the lights came on, she turned toward me, eyes widening, lips parting slightly. Her breasts swayed ever so slightly as she gracefully raised a bare arm to offer me a lily. "Hello, Donald," she said huskily. "I'm yours for the night." She was absolutely beautiful.

And dead, of course.

Not twenty minutes later I was hammering on Courtney's door. She came to the door in a Pierre Cardin dressing gown and from the way she was still cinching the sash and the disarray of her hair I gathered she hadn't been expecting me.

"I'm not alone," she said.

"I didn't come here for the dubious pleasures of your fair white body." I pushed my way into the room. But couldn't help remembering that beautiful body of hers, not so exquisite as the dead whore's, and now the thoughts were inextricably mingled in my head, death and Courtney, sex and corpses, a Gordian knot I might never be able to untangle.

"You didn't like my surprise?" She was smiling openly now, amused.

"No, I fucking did not!"

I took a step toward her. I was shaking. I couldn't stop fisting and unfisting my hands.

She fell back a step. But that confident, oddly expectant look didn't leave her face. "Bruno," she said lightly. "Would you come in here?"

A motion at the periphery of vision. Bruno stepped out of the shadows of her bedroom. He was a muscular brute, pumped, ripped, and as black as the fighter I'd seen go down earlier that night. He stood behind Courtney, totally naked, with slim hips and wide shoulders and the finest skin I'd ever seen.

And dead.

I saw it all in a flash.

"Oh, for God's sake, Courtney!" I said, disgusted. "I can't believe you. That you'd actually… That thing's just an obedient body. There's nothing there—no passion, no connection, just… physical presence."

Courtney made a kind of chewing motion through her smile, weighing the implications of what she was about to say. Nastiness won.

"We have equity now," she said.

I lost it then. I stepped forward, raising a hand, and I swear to God I intended to bounce the bitch's head off the back wall. But she didn't flinch—she didn't even look afraid. She merely moved aside, saying, "In the body, Bruno. He has to look good in a business suit."

A dead fist smashed into my ribs so hard I thought for an instant my heart had stopped. Then Bruno punched me in my stomach. I doubled over, gasping. Two, three, four more blows. I was on the ground now, rolling over, helpless and weeping with rage.

"That's enough, baby. Now put out the trash."

Bruno dumped me in the hallway.

I glared up at Courtney through my tears. She was not at all beautiful now. Not in the least. You're getting older, I wanted to tell her. But instead I heard my voice, angry and astonished, saying, "You… you goddamn, fucking necrophile!"

"Cultivate a taste for it," Courtney said. Oh, she was purring! I doubted she'd ever find life quite this good again. "Half a million Brunos are about to come on the market. You're going to find it a lot more difficult to pick up *living* women in not so very long."

I sent away the dead whore. Then I took a long shower that didn't really make me feel any better. Naked, I walked into my unlit suite and opened the curtains. For a long time I stared out over the glory and darkness that was Manhattan.

I was afraid, more afraid than I'd ever been in my life.

The slums below me stretched to infinity. They were a vast necropolis, a nev-erending city of the dead. I thought of the millions out there who were never going to hold down a job again. I thought of how they must hate me—me and my kind—and how helpless they were before us. And yet. There were so many of them and so few of us. If they were to all rise up at once, they'd be like a tsunami, irresistible. And if there was so much as a spark of life left in them, then that was exactly what they would do.

That was one possibility. There was one other, and that was that nothing would happen. Nothing at all.

God help me, but I didn't know which one scared me more.

THE DEAD KID

by Darrell Schweitzer

Darrell Schweitzer is the author of the novels *The Shattered Goddess* and *The Mask of the Sorcerer*, as well as numerous short stories, which have been collected in *Transients, Nightscapes, Refugees from an Imaginary Country*, and *Necromancies and Netherworlds*. Well-known as an editor and critic, he co-edited the magazine *Weird Tales* for several years, and is currently co-editing anthologies with Martin H. Greenberg for DAW Books, such as *The Secret History of Vampires*.

Schweitzer says one of the inspirations for "The Dead Kid" was the true story of the "Boy in the Box," whose corpse was found in a woods in northeast Philadelphia in 1957. The case remains unsolved, and there are police detectives who have obsessed over it throughout their entire careers and into their retirement. "They don't even know his name," Schweitzer says. "He is a complete mystery."

Schweitzer joked that given the mystery surrounding this case, the zombie tale he imagined is as good an explanation as any. Turns out that an informant—who is deeply unreliable—said that the boy's name was Jonathan… just like in this story.

So perhaps he has the real answer after all.

I

It's been a lot of years, but I think I'm still afraid of Luke Bradley, because of what he showed me.

I knew him in the first grade, and he was a tough guy even then, the sort of kid who would sit on a tack and insist it didn't hurt, and then make *you* sit on the same tack (which definitely *did* hurt) because you were afraid of what he'd do if you didn't. Once he found a bald-faced hornet nest on tree branch, broke it off, and ran yelling down the street, waving the branch around and around until finally the nest fell off and the hornets came out like a *cloud*. Nobody knew what happened after that because the rest of us had run away.

We didn't see Luke in school for a couple days afterwards, so I suppose he got stung rather badly. When he did show up he was his old self and beat up three other boys in one afternoon. Two of them needed stitches.

When I was about eight, the word went around the neighborhood that Luke Bradley had been eaten by a werewolf. "Come on," said Tommy Hitchens, Luke's current sidekick. "I'll show you what's left of him. Up in a tree."

I didn't believe any werewolf would have been a match for Luke Bradley, but I went. When Tommy pointed out the alleged remains of the corpse up in the tree, I could tell even from a distance that I was looking at a t-shirt and a pair of blue-jeans stuffed with newspapers.

I said so and Tommy flattened me with a deft right hook, which broke my nose, and my glasses.

The next day, Luke was in school as usual, though I had a splint on my nose. When he saw me, he called me a "pussy" and kicked me in the balls.

Already he was huge, probably a couple of years older than the rest of the class. Though he never admitted it, everybody knew he'd been held back in every grade at least once, even kindergarten.

But he wasn't stupid. He was *crazy.* That was the fascination of hanging out with him, even if you could get hurt in his company. He did *wild* things that no one else dared even think about. There was the stunt with the hornet nest, or the time he picked up fresh dogshit in both his bare hands and claimed he was going to *eat* it right in front of us before everybody got grossed out and ran because we were afraid he was going to make *us* eat it. Maybe he really did. He was just someone for whom the rules, *all* the rules, simply did not apply. That he was usually in detention, and had been picked up by the police several times only added to his mystique.

And in the summer when I was twelve, Luke Bradley showed me the dead kid.

Things had progressed quite a bit since then. No one quite believed all the stories of Luke's exploits, though he would beat the crap out of you if you questioned them to his face. Had he really stolen a car? Did he really hang onto the outside of a P&W light-rail train and ride all the way into Philadelphia without getting caught?

Nobody knew, but when he said to me and to my ten-year-old brother Albert, "Hey you two scuzzes"—*scuzz* being his favorite word of the moment—"there's a *dead kid* in Cabbage Creek Woods. Wanna see?" it wasn't really a question.

Albert tried to turn away, and said, "David, I don't think we should," but I knew what was good for us.

"Yeah," I said. "Sure we want to see."

Luke was already more than a head taller than either of us and fifty pounds heavier. He was cultivating the "hood" image from some hand-me-down memory of James Dean or Elvis, with his hair up in a greasy swirl and a black leather jacket worn even on hot days when he kept his shirt unbuttoned so he could show off that he already had chest hair.

A cigarette dangled from his lips. He blew smoke in my face. I strained not to cough.

"Well come on, then," he said. "It's really cool."

So we followed him, along with a kid called Animal, and another called Spike—the beginnings of Luke's "gang," with which he said he was going to make himself famous one day. My little brother tagged after us, reluctantly at first, but then as fascinated as I was to be initiated into this innermost, forbidden secret of the older, badder set.

Luke had quite a sense of showmanship. He led us under bushes, crawling through natural tunnels under vines and dead trees where, when we were smaller, we'd had our own secret hideouts, as, I suppose, all children do. Luke and his crowd were getting too big for that sort of thing, but they went crashing through the underbrush like bears. I was small and skinny enough. David was young enough. In fact it was all we could do to keep up.

With a great flourish, Luke raised a vine curtain and we emerged into the now half-abandoned Radnor Golf Course. It was an early Saturday morning. Mist was still rising from the poorly tended greens. I saw one golfer, far away. Otherwise we had the world to ourselves.

We ran across the golf course, then across Lancaster Pike, then up the hill and back into the woods on the other side.

I only thought for a minute, *Hey wait a minute, we're going to see a corpse, a kid like us, only dead…* but, as I said, for Luke Bradley or even with him, all rules were suspended, and I knew better than try to ask what the kid died of, because we'd see soon enough.

In the woods again, by secret and hidden ways, we came to the old "fort," which had probably been occupied by generations of boys by then, though of course right now it "belonged" to the Luke Bradley Gang.

I don't know who built the fort or why. It was a rectangle of raised earth and piled stone, with logs laid across for a roof, and vines growing thickly over the whole thing so that from a distance it just looked like a hillock or knoll. That was part of its secret. You had to know it was there.

And only Luke could let you in.

He raised another curtain of vines, and with a sweep of his hand and a bow said, "Welcome to my house, you assholes."

Spike and Animal laughed while Albert and I got down on our hands and knees and crawled inside.

Immediately I almost gagged on the awful smell, like rotten garbage and worse. Albert started to cough. I thought he was going to throw up. But before I could say or do anything, Luke and his two henchmen had come in after us, and we all crowded around a pit in the middle of the dirt floor which didn't used to be there. Now there was a four-foot drop, a roughly square cavity, and in the middle of that, a cardboard box which was clearly the source of the unbelievable stench.

Luke got out a flashlight, then reached down and opened the box.

"It's a dead kid. I found him in the woods in this box. He's mine."

I couldn't help but look. It was indeed a dead kid, an emaciated, pale thing, naked but for what might have been the remains of filthy underpants, lying on its side in a fetal position, little clawlike hands bunched up under its chin.

"A dead kid," said Luke. "Really cool."

Then Albert really was throwing up and screaming at the same time, and scrambling to get *out* of there, only Animal and then Spike had him by the back of his shirt the way you pick up a kitten by the scruff of its neck, and they passed him back to Luke, who held his head in his hands and forced him down into that pit, saying, "Now look at it you fucking pussy faggot, this because it's really cool."

Albert was sobbing and sniffling when Luke let him go, but he didn't try to run, nor did I, even when Luke got a stick and poked the dead kid with it.

"This is the best part," he said.

We didn't run away then because we *had* to watch just to convince ourselves that we weren't crazy, because of what we were seeing.

Luke poked and the dead kid *moved,* spasming at first, then grabbing at the stick feebly, and finally crawling around inside the box like a slow, clumsy animal, just barely able to turn, scratching at the cardboard with bony fingertips.

"What *is* he?" I had to ask.

"A *zombie,*" said Luke.

"Aren't zombies supposed to be black?"

"You mean like a nigger?" That was another of Luke's favorite words this year. He called everybody "nigger" no matter what color they were.

"Well, you know. Voodoo. In Haiti and all that."

As we spoke the dead kid reared up and almost got out of the box. Luke poked him in the forehead with his stick and knocked him down.

"I suppose if we let him *rot* long enough he'll be black enough even for *you.*"

The dead kid stared up at us and made a bleating sound. The worst thing of all was that he didn't have any eyes, only huge sockets and an oozy mess inside them.

Albert was sobbing for his mommy by then, and after a while of poking and prodding the dead kid, Luke and his friends got tired of this sport. Luke turned to me and said, "You can go now, but you know if you or your pisspants brother tell about this, I'll kill you both and put you in there for the dead kid to *eat.*"

II

I can't remember much of what Albert and I did for the rest of that day. We ran through the woods, tripped, fell flat on our faces in a stream. Then later we were walking along the old railroad embankment turning over ties to look for snakes, and all the while Albert was babbling on about the dead kid and how we had to do something. I just let him talk until he got it all out of him, and when we went home for dinner and were very quiet when Mom and our stepdad Steve tried to find out what we had been doing all day.

"Just playing," I said. "In the woods."

"It's good for them to be outdoors," Steve said to Mom. "Too many kids spent all their time in front of the TV watching *unwholesome* junk these days. I'm glad our kids are *normal*."

But Albert ended up screaming in his sleep for weeks and wetting his bed, and things were anything but normal that summer. He was the one with the obvious problems. He was the one who ended up going to a "specialist," and whatever he said in therapy must not have been believed, because the police didn't go tearing up Cabbage Creek Woods, Luke Bradley and his neanderthals were not arrested, and I was more or less left alone.

In fact, I had more unsupervised time than usual. And I used it to work out problems of my own, like I hated school and I hated Stepdad Steve for the sanctimonious prig he was. I decided, with the full wisdom of my twelve years and some months, that if I was to survive in this rough, tough, evil world, I was going to have to become tough myself, *bad,* and very likely evil.

I decided that Luke Bradley had the answers.

So I sought him out. It wasn't hard. He had a knack for being in the right place at the right time when you're ready to sell your soul, just like the Devil.

I met him in town, in front of the Wayne Toy Town, where I used to go to buy model kits and stuff. I still liked building models, and doing scientific puzzles, though I would never admit it to Luke Bradley.

So I just froze when I saw him there.

"Well, well," he said. "If it ain't the little pussy scuzz." He blew smoke from the perennial cigarette.

"Hello, Luke," I said. I nodded to his companions, who included Spike, Animal, and a virtually hairless, pale gorilla who went by the unlikely name of Corky. As I spoke, I slipped my latest purchase into my shoulder bag and hoped he didn't notice.

Corky grabbed me by the back of the neck and said, "Whaddaya want me to do with him?"

But before Luke could respond, I said, "Hey, have you still got the dead kid at the fort?"

They all hesitated. They weren't expecting that.

"Well he's *cool,*" I said. "I want to see him again."

"Okay," said Luke.

We didn't have any other way to get there, so we walked, about an hour, to Cabbage Creek Woods. Luke dispensed with ceremony. We just crawled into the fort and gathered around the pit.

The smell, if anything, was worse.

This time, the dead kid was already moving around inside the box. When Luke opened the cardboard flaps, the dead kid stood up, with his horrible, pus-filled eye-sockets staring. He made that bleating, groaning sound again. He clawed at the edge of the box.

"Really cool," I forced myself to say, swallowing hard.

"I can make him do tricks," said Luke. "Watch this."

I watched as he shoved his finger *through* the skin under the dead kid's chin and lifted him up like a hooked fish out of the pit. The dead kid scrambled over the edge of the box, then crouched down on the dirt floor at the edge of the pit, staring into space.

Luke passed his hand slowly in front of the dead kid's face. He snapped his fingers. The dead kid didn't respond. Luke smacked him on the side of the head. The dead kid whimpered a little, and made that bleating sound.

"Everybody outside," Luke said.

So we all crawled out, and then Luke reached back inside with a stick and touched the dead kid, who came out too, clinging to the stick, trying to chew on it, but not quite coordinated enough, so that he just snapped his teeth in the air and rubbed the side of his face along the stick.

I could see him clearly now. He really *was* rotten, with bone sticking out at his knees and elbows, only scraggly patches of dark hair left on his head, every rib showing in hideous relief on his bare back, and *holes* through his skin between some of them.

"Look!" said Luke. "Look at him dance!" He swirled the stick around and around, and the dead kid clung to it, staggering around in a circle.

Corky spoke up. "Ya think if'n he gets dizzy he'll puke?"

Luke yanked the stick out of the dead kid's hands, then hit him hard with it across the back with a *thwack!* The dead kid dropped to all fours and just stayed there, his head hanging down.

"Can't puke. Got no guts left!" They all laughed at that. I didn't quite get the joke.

But despite everything, I *tried* to get the joke, despite even the incongruity that I really was, like it or not, a more or less "normal" kid and right now I had a model kit for a plastic Fokker Triplane in my schoolbag. I still wanted to measure up to Luke Bradley, for all I was more afraid of him than I had ever been. I figured you had to be afraid of what you did and who you hung out with if you were going to be really *bad*. You did what Luke did. That was what transgression was all about.

So I unzipped my fly and pissed on the dead kid. He made that bleating sound. The others chuckled nervously. Luke grinned.

"Pretty cool, Davey, my boy. Pretty cool."

Then Luke started to play the role of wise elder brother. He put his arm around my shoulders. He took me a little ways apart from the others and said, "I like you. I think you got something special in there." He rapped on my head with his knuckles, hard, but I didn't flinch away.

Then he led me back to the others and said, "I think we're gonna make David here a member of the gang."

So we all sat down in the clearing with the dead kid in our circle, as if he were one of the gang too. Luke got out an old briefcase from inside the fort and produced some very crumpled nudie magazines and passed them around and we all looked at the pictures. He even made a big, funny show of opening out a foldout for the dead kid to admire.

He smoked and passed cigarettes out to all of us. I'd never had one before and it made me feel sick, but Luke told me to hold the smoke in, then breathe it out slowly.

I was amazed and appalled when, right in front of everyone, he unzipped his pants and started to jerk off. The others did it too, making a point of trying to squirt on the dead kid.

Luke looked at me. "Come on, join in with the other gentlemen." The other "gentlemen" brayed like jackasses.

I couldn't move then. I really wanted to be like them, but I knew I wasn't going to measure up. All I could hope for now was to put up a good front so maybe they'd decide I wasn't a pussy after all and maybe let me go after they beat me up a little bit. I could hope for that much.

But Luke had other ideas. He put his hand on the back of my neck. It could have been a friendly gesture, or if he squeezed, he could have snapped my head off for all I could have done anything about it.

"Now David," he said, "I don't care if you've even *got* a dick, any more than I care if *he* does." He jerked his thumb at the dead kid. "But if you want to join our gang, if you want to be cool, you have to meet certain standards."

He flicked a switchblade open right in front of my face. I thought he was going to cut my nose with it, but with a sudden motion he slashed the dead kid's nose right off. It flew into the air. Corky caught it, then threw it away in mindless disgust.

The dead kid whimpered. His face was a black, oozing mess.

Then Luke took hold of my right hand and slashed the back of it. I let out a yell, and tried to stop the bleeding with my other hand.

"No," Luke said. "Let him lick it. He needs a little blood now and then to keep him healthy."

I screamed then, and sobbed, and whimpered the way Albert had that first time, but Luke held onto me with a grip so strong that *I* was the one who wriggled like a fish on a line, and he held my cut hand out to the dead kid.

I couldn't look, but something soft and wet touched my hand, and I could only think, Oh God, what kind of infection or disease am I going to get from this?

"Okay David," Luke said then. "You're doing just fine, but there is one more test. You have to *spend the whole night* in the fort with the dead kid. We've all done it. Now it's your turn."

They didn't wait for my answer, but, laughing, hauled me back inside the fort. Then Luke had the dead kid hooked under the chin again, and lowered him down into his box in the pit.

The others crawled back outside. Before he left, Luke turned to me, "You have to stay here until tomorrow morning. You know what I'll do to you if you pussy out."

So I spent the rest of the afternoon, and the evening, inside that fort with the dead kid scratching around in his box. It was already dark in the fort. I couldn't tell what time it was. I couldn't think very clearly at all. I wondered if anyone was looking for me. I lay very still. I didn't want to be found, especially not by the dead kid, who, for all I knew, could crawl out of the box and the pit if he really wanted to and maybe rip my throat out and drink my blood.

My hand hurt horribly. It seemed to be swelling. I was sure it was already rotten. The air was thick and foul.

But I stayed where I was, because I was afraid, because I was weak with nausea, but also, incredibly, because somehow, somewhere, deep down inside myself I still wanted to show how *tough* I was, to be like Luke Bradley, to be as amazing and crazy as he was. I knew that I *wasn't* cut out for this, and that's why I wanted it—to be *bad,* so no one would ever beat me up again and if I hated my stepdad or my teachers I could just tell them to go fuck off, as Luke would do.

Hours passed, and still the dead kid circled around and around inside his cardboard box, sliding against the sides. He made that bleating, coughing sound, as if he were trying to talk and didn't have any tongue left. For a time I thought there was almost some sense in it, some pattern. He was *clicking* like a cricket. This went on for hours. Maybe I even slept for a while, and fell into a kind of dream in which I was sinking slowly down into incredibly foul-smelling muck and there were thousands of bald-faced hornets swarming over me, all of them with little Luke Bradley faces saying, "Cool… really cool…" until their voices blended together and became a buzzing, then became wind in the trees, then the roar of a P&W light-rail train rushing off toward Philadelphia; and the dead kid and I were hanging onto the outside of the car, swinging wildly. My arm hit a pole and snapped right off, and black ooze was pouring out of my shoulder, and the hornets swarmed over me, eating me up bit by bit.

Once, I am certain, the dead kid *did* reach up and touch me, very gently, running his dry, sharp fingertip down the side of my cheek, cutting me, then withdrawing with a little bit of blood and tears on his fingertip, to drink.

But, strangest of all, I wasn't afraid of him then. It came to me, then, that we too had more in common than not. We were both afraid and in pain and lost in the dark.

III

Then somehow it was morning. The sunlight blinded me when Luke opened the vine curtain over the door.

"Hey. You were really brave. I'm impressed, Davey."

I let him lead me out of the fort, taking comfort in his chum/big-brother manner. But I was too much in shock to say anything.

"You passed the test. You're one of us," he said. "Welcome to the gang. Now there is one last thing for you to do. Not a test. You've passed all the tests. It's just something we do to celebrate."

His goons had gathered once more in the clearing outside the fort.

One of them was holding a can of gasoline.

I stood there, swaying, about to faint, unable to figure out what the gasoline was for.

Luke brought the dead kid outside.

Corky poured gasoline over the dead kid, who just bleated a little and waved his hands in the air.

Luke handed me a cigarette lighter. He flicked it until there was a flame.

"Go on," he said. "It'll be cool."

But I couldn't. I was too scared, too sick. I just dropped to my knees, then onto all fours and started puking.

So Luke lit the dead kid on fire and the others hooted and clapped as the dead kid went up like a torch, staggering and dancing around the clearing, trailing black, oily smoke. Then he fell down and seemed to shrivel up into a pile of blackened, smoldering sticks.

Luke forced me over to where the dead kid had fallen and made me touch what was left with my swollen hand.

And the dead kid *moved.* He made that bleating sound. He whimpered.

"You see? You can't kill him because he's already dead."

They were all laughing, but I just puked again, and finally Luke hauled me to my feet by both shoulders, turned me around, and shoved me away staggering into the woods.

"Come back when you stop throwing up," he said.

IV

Somehow I found my way home, and when I did, Mom just stared at me in horror and said, "My God, what's that awful smell?" But Stepdad Steve shook me and demanded to know where I had been and what I'd been doing? Did I know the police were looking for me? Did I care? (No, and no.) He took me into the bathroom, washed and bandaged my hand, then held me so I couldn't turn away and said, "Have you been taking drugs?"

That was so stupid I started to laugh, and he *smacked* me across the face, something he rarely did, but this time, I think, he was determined to beat the truth out of me, and Mommy, dearest Mommy didn't raise a finger to stop him as he laid on with his hand, then his belt, and I was shrieking my head off.

All they got out of me was the admission that I had been with Luke Bradley and his friends.

"I *don't* want you to associate with *those* boys any further. They're unwholesome."

He didn't know a tenth of it, and I started to laugh again, like I was drunk or something, and he was about to hit me again when Mom finally made him stop.

She told me to change my clothes and take a bath and then go to my room. I wasn't allowed out except for meals and to go to the bathroom.

That was fine with me. I didn't *want* to come out. I wanted to bury myself in there, to be quiet and dead, like the dead kid in his box.

But when I fell asleep, I was screaming in a dream, and I woke up screaming, in the dark, because it was night again.

Mom looked in briefly, but didn't say anything. The expression on her face was more of disgust than concern, as if she really wanted to say, *Serves him damn right but, Oh God, another crazy kid we'll have to send to the so, so expensive psychiatrist and I'd rather spend the money on a new mink coat or a car or something.*

It was my kid brother Albert who snuck over to my bed and whispered, "It's the dead kid, isn't it?"

"Huh?"

"The dead kid. He talks to me in my dreams. He's told me all about himself. He's lost. His father's a magician, who is still trying to find him. There was a war between magicians, or something, and that's how he got lost."

"Huh? Is this something you read in a comic book?"

"*No!* It's the dead kid. You know what we have to do, David. We have to go save him."

I have to give my brother credit for bringing about my moral redemption as surely as if he'd handed me my sanity back on a silver platter and said, *Go on, don't be a pussy. Take it.*

Because he was right. We had to save the dead kid.

Maybe the dead kid talked to Albert in his dreams, but he didn't tell me anything. Why should he?

Still, I'd gotten the message.

So, that night, very late, Albert and I got dressed and slipped out the window of our room, dropping onto the lawn. *He wasn't afraid,* not a little bit. He led me, by the ritual route, under the arching bushes, through the tunnels of vines to all our secret places, as if we had to be *there* first to gain some special strength for the task at hand.

Under the bushes, in the darkness, we paused to scratch secret signs in the dirt.

Then we scurried across the golf course, across the highway, into Cabbage Creek Woods.

We came to the fort by the light of a full moon now flickering through swaying branches. It was a windy night. The woods were alive with sounds of wood creaking and snapping, of animals calling back and forth, and night-birds cawing. Somewhere, very close at hand, an owl cried out.

Albert got down on all fours in the doorway of the fort, poked his head in, and said, "Hey, dead kid! Are you in there?"

He backed out, and waited. There was a rustling sound, but the dead kid didn't come out. So we both crawled in and saw why. There wasn't much left of him. He was just a bundle of black sticks, his head like a charred pumpkin balanced precariously on top. All he could do was sit up weakly and peer over the side of the box.

So we had to lift him out of the pit, box and all.

"Come on," Albert said to him. "We want to show you some stuff."

We carried the dead kid between us. We took him back across the golf course, under the bushes, to our special places. We showed him the secret signs. Then we took him into town. We showed him the storefronts, Wayne Toy Town where I bought models, where there were always neat displays of miniature battlefields or of monsters in the windows. We showed him where the pet store was and the ice cream store, and where you got comic books.

Albert sat down on the merry-go-round in the playground, holding the dead kid's box securely beside him. I pushed them around slowly. Metal creaked.

We stood in front of our school for a while, and Albert and the dead kid were *holding hands,* but it seemed natural and right.

Then we went away in the bright moonlight, through the empty streets. No one said anything, because whatever the dead kid could say or hear wasn't in words anyway. I couldn't hear it. I think Albert could.

In the end the dead kid scrambled out of his box. Somehow he had regained enough strength to walk. Somehow, he was beginning to heal. In the end, he wanted to show *us* something.

He led us back across the golf course but away from Cabbage Creek Woods. We crossed the football field at Radnor High School, then went across the street, up in back of Wyeth Labs and across the high bridge over the P&W tracks. I was afraid the dead kid would slip on the metal stairs and fall, but he went more steadily than we did. (Albert and I were both a little afraid of heights.)

He led us across another field, into woods again, then through an opening where a stream flowed beneath the Pennsylvania Railroad embankment. We waded ankle-deep in the chilly water and came, at last, to the old Grant Estate, a huge ruin of a Victorian house which every kid knew was haunted, which our parents told us to stay away from because it was dangerous. (There were so many stories about kids murdered by tramps or falling through floors.) But now it wasn't a ruin at all, no broken windows, no holes in the roof. Every window blazed with light.

From a high window in a tower, a man in black gazed down at us.

The dead kid looked up at him, then began to run.

I hurried after him. Now it was Albert (who had better sense) who hung back. I caught hold of the dead kid's arm, as if to stop him, and I felt possessive for a moment, as if I *owned* him the way Luke Bradley had owned him.

"Hey dead kid," I said. "Where are you going?"

He turned to me, and by some trick of the moonlight he seemed to have a face, pale, round, with dark eyes; and he said to me in that bleating, croaking voice of his, actually forming words for once, "My name is Jonathan."

That was the only thing he ever said to me. He never talked to me in dreams.

He went to the front of the house. The door opened. The light within seemed to swallow him. He turned back, briefly, and looked at us. I don't think he was just a bundle of sticks anymore.

Then he was gone and all the lights blinked out, and it was dawn. My brother and I stood before a ruined mansion in the morning twilight. Birds were singing raucously.

"We'd better get home," Albert said, "or we'll get in trouble."

"Yeah," I said.

V

That autumn, I began junior high school. Because I hadn't been very successful as a bad boy, and my grades were still a lot higher, I wasn't in any of Luke Bradley's classes. But he caught up with me in the locker room after school, several weeks into the term. All he said was, "I know what you did," and beat me so badly that he broke several of my ribs and one arm, and smashed in the whole side of my face, and cracked the socket around my right eye. He stuffed me into a locker and left me there to die, and I spent the whole night in the darkness, in great pain, amid horrible smells, calling out for the dead kid to come and save me as I'd saved him. I made bleating, clicking sounds.

But he didn't come. The janitor found me in the morning. The smell was merely that I'd crapped in my pants.

I spent several weeks in the hospital, and afterwards Stepdad Steve and Mom decided to move out of the state. They put both me and Albert in a prep school.

It was only after I got out of college that I went back to Radnor Township in Pennsylvania, where I'd grown up. Everything was changed. There was a Sears headquarters where the golf course used to be. Our old house had vanished beneath an apartment parking lot. Most of Cabbage Creek Woods had been cut down to make room for an Altman's department store, and the Grant Estate was gone too, to make room for an office complex.

I didn't go into the remaining woods to see if the fort was still there.

I imagine it is. I imagine other kids own it now.

Later someone told me that Luke Bradley (who turned out to have really been three years older than me) had been expelled from high school, committed several robberies in the company of his three goons, and then all of them were killed in a shootout with the police.

What Luke Bradley inadvertently showed me was that I could have been with the gang all the way to their violent and pointless end, if Albert and the dead kid, whose name was Jonathan, hadn't saved me.

MALTHUSIAN'S ZOMBIE

by Jeffrey Ford

Jeffrey Ford is the author of several novels, including *The Physiognomy*, *The Portrait of Mrs. Charbuque*, *The Girl in the Glass*, and *The Shadow Year*. He is a four-time winner of the World Fantasy Award, and has also won the Nebula and Edgar awards. He is a prolific author of short fiction, whose work has appeared in *The Magazine of Fantasy & Science Fiction*, *SCI FICTION*, and in numerous anthologies. Two collections of his short work have been published: *The Fantasy Writer's Assistant and Other Stories* and *The Empire of Ice Cream*, with a third—*The Drowned Life*—on the way.

The idea for this story came from Ford's reading of Julian Jaynes's *The Origin of Consciousness in the Breakdown of the Bicameral Mind*. "The book posits that the voice of god in ancient cultures was in fact one side of the brain communicating with the other across the corpus callosum, through the Wernicke's Area," Ford says.

Add to this the fact that at the time, as now, Ford was teaching Poe. He says the setup of the story is sort of like what Poe would do: "take some speculative aspect of science, a theory that has not been corroborated, an idea not many know the extent of, and extrapolate a bizarre, fanciful tale from it."

1

I'm not sure what nationality Malthusian was, but he spoke with a strange accent; a stuttering lilt of mumblement it took weeks to fully comprehend as English. He had more wrinkles than a witch and a shock of hair whiter and fuller than a Samoyed's ruff. I can still see him standing at the curb in front of my house, slightly bent, clutching a cane whose ivory woman's head wore a blindfold. His suit was a size and a half too large, as were his eyes, peering from behind lenses cast at a thickness that must have made his world enormous. The two details that halted my raking and caused me to give him more than a neighborly wave were his string tie and a mischievous grin I had only ever seen before on my six-year-old daughter when she was drawing one of her monsters.

"Malthusian," he said from the curb.

I greeted him and spoke my name.

He mumbled something and I leaned closer to him and begged his pardon. At this, he turned and pointed back at the house down on the corner. I knew it had recently changed hands, and I surmised he had just moved in.

"Welcome to the neighborhood," I said.

He put his hand out and I shook it. His grip was very strong, and he was in no hurry to let go. Just as I realized he was aware of my discomfort, his grin turned into a wide smile and he released me. Then he slowly began to walk away.

"Nice to meet you," I said to his back.

He turned, waved, and let loose an utterance that had the cadence of poetry. There was something about leaves and fruit and it all came together in a rhyme. Only when he had disappeared into the woods at the end of the block did I realize he had been quoting Pope. " 'Words are like leaves, where they most abound, beneath, little fruit or sense is found.' " As a professor of literature, this amused me, and I decided to try to find out more about Malthusian.

I was on sabbatical that year, supposedly writing a book concerning the structure of Poe's stories, which I saw as lacking the energetic ascent of the Fichtian curve and being comprised solely of denouement. Like houses of Usher, the reader comes to them, as in a nightmare, with no prior knowledge, at the very moment they begin to crumble. What I was really doing was dogging it in high fashion. I'd kiss my wife goodbye as she left for work, take my daughter to school, and then return home to watch reruns of those shows my brother and I had devoted much of our childhood to. Malthusian's daily constitutional was an opportunity to kill some time, and so, when I would see him passing in front of the house, I'd come out and engage him in conversation.

Our relationship grew slowly at first, until I began to learn the cues for his odd rendering of the language. By Thanksgiving I could have a normal conversation with him, and we began to have lengthy discussions about literature. Oddly enough, his interests were far more contemporary than mine. He expressed a devotion to Pynchon, and the West African writer Amos Tutuola. I realized I had spent too long teaching the canon of Early American works and began to delve into some of the novels he mentioned. One day I asked him what he had done before his retirement. He smiled and said something that sounded like *mind-fucker*.

I was sure I had misunderstood him. I laughed and said, "What was that?"

"Mind-fucker," he said. "Psychologist."

"Interesting description of the profession," I said.

He shrugged and his grin dissipated. When he spoke again, he changed the subject to politics.

Through the winter, no matter the weather, Malthusian walked. I remember watching him struggle along through a snowstorm one afternoon, dressed in a black overcoat and black Tyrolean hat, bent more from some invisible weight than a failure of his frame. It struck me then that I had never seen him on his return journey. The trails through the woods went on for miles, and I was unaware of one that might bring him around to his house from the other end of the block.

I introduced him to Susan, my wife, and to my daughter, Lyda. There, at the curb, he kissed both their hands, or tried to. When Lyda pulled her hand back at his approach, he laughed so I thought he would explode. Susan found him charming, but asked me later, "What the hell was he saying?"

The next day, he brought a bouquet of violets for her; and for Lyda, because she had shown him her drawing pad, he left with me a drawing he had done rolled up and tied with a green ribbon. After dinner, she opened it and smiled. "A monster," she said. It was a beautifully rendered charcoal portrait of an otherwise normal middle-aged man, wearing an unnerving look of total blankness. The eyes were heavy lidded and so realistically glassy, the attitude of the body so slack, that the figure exuded a palpable sense of emptiness. At the bottom of the page in a fine calligraphic style were written the words *Malthusian's Zombie.*

"I told him I liked monsters," said Lyda.

"Why is that a monster?" asked Susan, who I could tell was a little put off by the eerie nature of the drawing. "It looks more like a college professor on sabbatical."

"He thinks nothing," said Lyda, and with her pinky finger pointed to the zombie's head. She had me tack it to the back of her door, so that it faced the wall unless she wanted to look at it. For the next few weeks, she drew zombies of her own. Some wore little hats, some bow ties, but all of them, no matter how huge and vacant the eyes, wore mischievous grins.

In early spring, Malthusian invited me to come to his house one evening to play a game of chess. The evening air was still quite cool, but the scent of the breeze carried the promise of things green. His house, which sat on the corner lot, was enormous, by far the largest in the neighborhood. It had three acres of woods appended to it and at the very back touched upon a lake that belonged to the adjacent town.

Malthusian was obviously not much for yard work or home repair; the very measure of a man in this part of the world. A tree had cracked and fallen through the winter and it still lay partially obstructing the driveway. The three-story structure and its four tall columns in front needed paint; certain porch planks had succumbed to dry rot and its many windows were streaked and smudged. The fact that he took no initiative to rectify these problems made him yet more likable to me.

He met me at the door and ushered me into his home. I had visions of the place being like a dim, candle-lit museum of artifacts as odd as their owner, and had hoped to decipher Malthusian's true character from them as if they were clues in a mystery novel. There was nothing of the sort. The place was well lit and tastefully, though modestly, decorated.

"I hope you like merlot," he said as he led me down an oak paneled hallway toward the kitchen.

"Yes," I said.

"It's good for the heart," he said and laughed.

The walls I passed were lined with photographs of Malthusian with different people. He moved quickly and I did not linger out of politeness, but I thought I saw one of him as a child, and more than one of him posing with various military personnel. If I wasn't mistaken, I could have sworn I had caught the face of an ex-president in one of them.

The kitchen was old linoleum in black-and-white checkerboard design, brightly lit by overhead fluorescent lights. Sitting on a table in the center of the large expanse was a chessboard, a magnum of dark wine, two fine crystal goblets, and a thin silver box. He took a seat on one side of the table and extended his hand to indicate I was to sit across from him. He methodically poured wine for both of us, opened the box, retrieved a cigarette, lit it, puffed once, and then led with his knight.

"I'm not very good," I said as I countered with my opposite knight.

He waved his hand in the air, flicked ash onto the floor, and said, "Let's not let it ruin our game."

We played in silence for some time and then I asked him something that had been on my mind since he had first disclosed his profession to me. "And what type of psychologist were you? Jungian? Freudian?"

"Neither," he said. "Those are for children. I was a rat shocker. I made dogs drool."

"Behaviorist?" I asked.

"Sorry to disappoint," he said with a laugh.

"I teach the Puritans with the same method," I said and this made him laugh louder. He loosened his ever-present string tie and cocked his glasses up before plunging through my pitiful pawn defense with his bishop.

"I couldn't help but notice those photos in the hall," I said. "Were you in the army?"

"Please, no insults," he said. "I worked for the U.S. government."

"What branch?" I asked.

"One of the more shadowed entities," he said. "It was necessary in order to bring my mother and father and sister to this country."

"From where?" I asked.

"The old country."

"Which one is that?"

"It no longer exists. You know, like in a fairy tale, it has disappeared through geopolitical enchantment." With this he checked me by way of a pawn/castle combination.

"Your sister?" I asked.

"She was much like your girl, Lyda. Beautiful and brilliant and what an artist."

As with the game, he took control of the conversation from here on out, directing me to divulge the history of my schooling, my marriage, the birth of my daughter, the nature of our household.

It was a gentle interrogation, the wine making me nostalgic. I told him everything and he seemed to take the greatest pleasure in it, nodding his head at my declaration of love for my wife, laughing at all of Lyda's antics I could remember, and I remembered all of them. Before I knew it, we had played three games, and I was as lit as a stick of kindling. He led me down the hallway to the front door.

As if from thin air, he produced a box of chocolates for my wife. "For the lady," he said. Then he placed in my hand another larger box. Through bleary eyes, I looked down and saw the image of Rat Fink, the pot-bellied, deviant rodent who had been a drag racing mascot in the late sixties.

"It's a model," he told me. "Help the girl make it, she will enjoy this monster."

I smiled in recognition of the figure I had not seen since my teens.

"Big Daddy Roth," he said, and with this eased me out the door and gently closed it behind me.

Although I had as my mission to uncover the mystery of Malthusian, my visit had made him more of an enigma. I visited him twice more to play chess, and on each of the occasions, the scenario was much the same. The only incident that verged on revelation was when Lyda and I constructed the model and painted it. "Rat shocker," I remembered him telling me. I had a momentary episode in which I envisioned myself salivating at the sound of a bell.

On the day that Lyda brought me spring's first crocus, a pale violet specimen with an orange mouth, Malthusian was taken away in an ambulance. I was very worried about him and enlisted Susan, since she was a nurse practitioner, to use her connections in the hospitals to find out where he was. She spent the better part of her Friday evening making calls but came up with nothing.

2

Days passed, and I began to think that Malthusian might have died. Then, a week to the day after the ambulance had come for him, I found a note in my mailbox. All it said was *Chess Tonight*.

I waited for the appointed hour, and after Susan had given me a list of things to ask about the old man's condition and Lyda a get-well drawing of a dancing zombie, I set out for the house on the corner.

He did not answer the door, so I opened it and called inside, "Hello?"

"Come," he called from back in the kitchen.

I took the hallway and found him sitting at the chess table. The wine was there, and the cigarette case, but there was no board.

"What happened?" I said when I saw him.

Malthusian looked yet more wrinkled and stooped, sitting in his chair like a sack of old clothes. His white hair had thinned considerably and turned a pale shade of yellow. In his hands he clutched his cane, which I had never seen him use before while in his house, and that childish grin, between malevolence and innocence, had been replaced by the ill, forced smile of Rat Fink.

"No chess?" I asked as a way of masking my concern.

"A game of a different order tonight," he said and sighed.

I was about to ask again what had happened, but he said, "Drink a glass of wine and then you will listen."

We sat in silence as I poured and drank. I had never noticed before but the blindfold on the ivory woman's head did not completely cover her left eye. She half stared at me as I did what I was told. When the glass was empty and I had poured another, he looked up and said, "Now, you must listen carefully. I give you my confession and the last wish of a dying man."

I wanted to object but he brought the cane to his lips in order to silence me.

"In 1969, September, I was attending a conference of the American Psychological Association in Washington, D.C. A professor from Princeton, one Julian Jaynes, gave a lecture there. Have you heard of him?" he asked.

I shook my head.

"Now you will," he said. "The outrageous title of his address was 'The Origin of Consciousness in the Breakdown of the Bicameral Mind.' Just the name of it led many to think it was pure snake oil. When Mr. Jaynes began to explain his theory, they were sure of it. Individual consciousness as we know it today, he said, is a very recent development in the history of mankind. Before that, like schizophrenics, human beings listened to a voice that came from within their own heads and from this took their cues. These were post-ice age hunter-gatherers for whom it was important to think with a single mind. They heard the voice of some venerable elder of their tribe who had since, perhaps, passed on. This was the much-touted 'voice of God.' Individual ego was virtually nonexistent."

"You mean," I said, "when the ancients refer to the word of the Lord, they were not speaking figuratively?"

"Yes, you follow," he said and smiled, lifting the wine glass to his lips with a trembling hand. "I could tell you that this phenomenon had to do with the right hemispherical language center of the brain and a particular zone called Wernicke's area. When this area was stimulated in modern laboratory experiments, the subjects very often heard authoritarian voices that either admonished or commanded. But they were very distant voices. The reason, Jaynes believed, was that these auditory hallucinations were travelling from the right hemisphere to the left, not through the corpus callosum—the, shall we call it, bridge that joins the hemispheres—but rather through another passageway, the anterior commissure."

"I'm hanging on by a thread, now," I said.

Malthusian did not acknowledge my joke, but closed his eyes momentarily and pressed on as if it would all soon become clear.

"Whereas Jaynes gives many explanations for the growing faintness of the voice of God—genocide, natural upheavals, parental selection, environmental demands requiring the wonderful plasticity of the human brain to enact these changes—my fellow researchers and I believed that the muting of the voice was a result of the rapid shrinking of the anterior commissure to its present state of no more than one-eighth of an inch across. This, we believed, was the physiological change that fractured the group mind into individual consciousness. 'Father, why have you forsaken me?' You see? There is much more, but that is the crux."

"The survival of human beings depended upon this change?" I asked.

"The complexity of civilization required diversification."

"Interesting," was all I could manage.

"As I said," Malthusian went on, "very few took Jaynes seriously, but I did. His ideas were revolutionary, but they were not unfounded." Here, he took a cigarette from the silver case and lit it.

"Is that smart," I asked, nodding at the cigarette, "considering your health?"

"I have been conditioned by Philip Morris," he said with a smile.

"This theory is only the beginning, I can tell," I said.

"Very good, professor," he whispered. "As Farid ud-Din Attar might have written—if this tale I am about to tell you were inscribed with needles upon the corner of the eye, it would still serve as a lesson to the circumspect."

He lifted the bottle of wine and poured me another glass. "To begin with, if you tell anyone what I am about to tell you, you will be putting your family and yourself in great jeopardy. Understood?"

I thought momentarily of Malthusian's photos with all those military personnel and his telling me that he had been employed by one of the more shadowed entities of the government. A grim silence filled the room as those huge eyes of his focused on mine. I thought of leaving, but instead I slowly nodded.

"I was part of a secret government project called Dumbwaiter. The title might have been humorous if not for the heinous nature of the work we were doing. As psychologists, we were assigned the task of creating dedicated assassins, men devoid of personal volition, who would do anything—*anything*—that they were ordered to do. Mind control, it is sometimes called. The CIA had, for a short period, thought that the drug LSD might be useful in this pursuit, but instead of creating drones they spread cosmic consciousness. Once this failed, the Behaviorists were called in.

"My lab was situated in a large, old Victorian house out in the woods. No one would have suspected that some bizarre Cold War experiment was taking place in its basement. I had two partners and, working off Jaynes's theory, through surgery and the implanting of pig arteries and chimpanzee neurons, we widened and filled the anterior commissure in a test subject's brain in order to increase the volume of the auditory hallucination. Through conditioning, my voice became the voice of God for our subject. I was always in his head. One verbal command from me and my order would remain with him, inside his mind, until the task was completed."

What else was I to think but that Malthusian was pulling my leg. "Do I look that gullible?" I said and laughed so hard I spilled a drop of my wine on the table.

The old man did not so much as smile. "We had created a zombie," he said. "You laugh, but you should be laughing at yourself. You do not realize how, without any of our work, the human mind is so perfectly suggestible. The words 'obedience' and 'to listen' share the same root in more than half a dozen languages. With our experiment, this man would do whatever he was told. The results even surprised us. I instructed him to learn fluent French in a week. He did. I instructed him to play a Chopin nocturne on the piano after only hearing it once. He did. I instructed him to develop a photographic memory. I commanded him to stop aging. At times, for the purpose of a particular assignment, I might instruct him to become fatter, thinner, even shorter."

"Impossible," I said.

"Nonsense," said Malthusian. "It has been known for some time now that the mere act of deep thought can change the physiological structure of the brain. If only my colleagues and I could publish our findings, others would also know that prolonged, highly focused thought is capable of transforming the physiological structure of more than just the brain."

It was obvious to me at this time that Malthusian's illness had affected his mind. I put on a serious face and pretended to follow along, exhibiting a mixed sense of wonder and gravity.

"Why are you telling me all of this?" I asked.

"Why, yes, why," he said, and, more astonishing than his tale, tears began to form at the corners of his eyes. "The zombie had been useful. Please don't ask me specifically how, but let us just say that his work resulted in the diminution of agitators against democracy. But then, with the end of the Cold War, our project was disbanded. We were ordered to eliminate the zombie and set fire to the facility, and were given large sums of cash to resume normal life—with the threat that if we were to breathe a word about Dumbwaiter to anyone, we would be killed."

"Eliminate the zombie?" I said.

He nodded. "But I had pangs of conscience. My own God was talking to me. This man, whom we had hollowed out and filled with my commands, had been kidnapped. Just an average healthy citizen with a wife and a small child had been taken off the street one day by men in a long dark car. His loved ones never knew what had become of him. Likewise, I had made a deal to never see my own family again when I promised to work on Dumbwaiter. I disappeared after my parents and sister were brought to this country. For me to contact them in any way would mean their demise. I have missed them terribly through the years, especially my sister, with whom I had a strong bond after surviving the horrors of the old country. For this reason, I could not dispose of the zombie."

"That would be murder," I said, and instantly regretted it.

"It would have been murder either way," said Malthusian. "Either I killed the subject or they killed us *and* our subject. Instead, I took a chance and left to the ravages of the fire a cadaver we had on ice there for many years. We hoped that no one was aware of it, that if a body was found in the ashes that would be enough to suffice. Remember, this is the government we are talking about. We had worked for them long enough to know that their main priority was silence." Malthusian went silent himself, nodding his head upon his chest. I thought for a second that he had fallen asleep. When I cleared my throat, he reached for the wine but stopped. He did the same with the cigarette case. Then he looked up at me.

"I'm dying," he said.

"This very moment?" I asked.

"Soon, very soon."

"Did they tell you that at the hospital?"

"I'm a doctor. I know."

"Is there something you need me to do? Do you want me to contact your sister?" I asked.

"No, you must not mention any of this. But there is something I want you to do," he said.

"Call the ambulance?"

"I want you to take care of the zombie until the transformation is complete."

"What are you talking about?" I said, and smiled.

"He's here with me, in the house. He has been with me all along since we burned the lab." Malthusian dropped the cane on the floor, leaned forward on the table and reached for me with his left hand. I pushed the chair back and stood away from the table to avoid his grasp.

"I've been working with him, trying to reverse the effects of the experiment. The change has begun, but it will take a little longer than I have left to complete it. You must help me to return this poor man to his family so that he can enjoy what is left of his life. He is beginning to remember a thing or two and the aging process is slowly starting to return him to his rightful maturity. If I should die, I require you to merely house him until he remembers where he is from. It won't take very long now."

"Dr. Malthusian," I said. "I think you need to rest. You are not making any sense."

The old man slowly stood up. "You will wait!" he yelled at me, holding his arm up and pointing with one finger. "I will get him."

I said nothing more, but watched as Malthusian precariously leaned over to retrieve his cane. Then he hobbled out of the room, mumbling something to himself. When I heard him mounting the stairs to the second floor, I tiptoed out of the kitchen, down the hall, and out the front door. I reached the street and started running like I was ten years old.

Later, in bed, after locking all the doors and windows, I woke Susan up and told her everything that Malthusian had said. When I got to the part about the zombie, she started laughing.

"He wants you to baby-sit his zombie?" she asked.

"It's not funny," I said. "He worked for some secret branch of the government."

"That's the one all the kooks work for," she said. "You're a man with way too much time on his hands."

"He was pretty convincing," I said, now grinning myself.

"What if I told you they were putting Frankenstein together in the basement of the hospital? If he's not crazy, he's probably playing with your mind. He seems to have a healthy measure of mischief about him. That string tie is a good indicator."

I wasn't completely convinced, but Susan allayed my fears enough to allow me to get to sleep. My dreams were punctuated by wide-eyed stares and piano music.

I forced myself to believe that Susan was right, and that I had better ignore Malthusian and get to work on my book. The summer was quickly approaching and soon the autumn would send me back to teaching. It would be a great embarrassment to return to work in September empty-handed. I picked up where I had left off months earlier on the manuscript—a chapter concerning "The Facts in the Case of M. Valdemar." The return to work was what I needed to anchor me against the tide of Malthusian's weirdness, but that particular story by the great American hoaxer, second only to P. T. Barnum, had *zombie* written all over it.

One afternoon, when I was about to leave the house to go to the local bookstore, I looked out the front window and saw the old man slowly shuffling up the street. I had neither seen nor heard from Malthusian since the night I had abandoned him in his fit of madness two weeks prior. It would have been a simple thing to leave the living room and hide in the kitchen, but instead I quickly ducked down beneath the sill. As I crouched there, I wondered at the fear I had developed for my neighbor.

Five minutes went by, and when I thought he should have passed on to where the woods began at the end of the block, I raised my head above the windowsill. There he was, standing at the curb, hunched over, staring directly at me like some grim and ghastly bird of yore. I uttered a brief, startled gasp, and as if he could hear me, he brought the top of his cane up and tapped it lightly against the brim of his Tyrolean hat. Then he turned and moved off. This little scene threw me into a panic. I never went to the bookstore, and when it was time for Lyda to get out of school, I drove over and picked her up instead of letting her take the bus, which would have left her off at the corner. My panic was short-lived, for that evening, at dinner, as I was about to describe the event to Susan, we heard the ambulance.

It is sad to say, but Malthusian's death was a relief to me. Lyda and I watched from a distance as they brought him out on the wheeled stretcher. Susan, who was afraid of nothing, least of all death, went all the way to his house and spoke to the EMTs. She was not there long when we saw her begin walking back.

"Massive heart attack," she said as she approached, shaking her head.

"That's a shame," I said.

Lyda put her arm around my leg and hugged me.

The next morning, while I was wandering around the house looking for inspiration to begin working on Poe again, I discovered that Lyda had draped a silk purple flower, plucked from Susan's dining-room table arrangement, around the neck of Rat Fink. The sight of this made me smile, and as I reached out to touch the smooth illusion of the blossom, I was interrupted by a knocking at the door. I left my daughter's room and went downstairs. Upon opening the front door, I discovered that there was no one there. As I stood, looking out, I heard the knocking sound again. It took me a few long seconds to adjust to the fact that the sound was coming from the back of the house.

"Who knocks at the back door?" I said to myself as I made my way through the kitchen.

3

His eyes were the oval disks of Japanese cartoon characters, glassy and brimming with nothing. Like the whiteness of Melville's whale, you could read anything into them, and while Lyda and I sat staring at him staring at the wall, I projected my desires and frustrations into those mirrors with a will I doubt Ahab could have mustered.

"A blown Easter egg," said Lyda, breaking the silence.

And in the end, she was right. There was an exquisite emptiness about him. His face was drawn, his limbs thin but wiry with real muscle. He looked like a fellow who might at one time have worked as a car mechanic or a UPS delivery man. I guessed his age to be somewhere in the late thirties but knew, from what Malthusian had suggested, that his youth was merely compliance to a command. I wondered how old he would become when the spell was broken. *Perhaps, like Valdemar in Poe's story,* I thought, *he will eventually be reduced to a pool of putrescence.*

We had been sitting with the zombie for over an hour when Susan finally arrived home from work. Lyda got up from her seat and ran into the living room to tell her mother that we had a visitor.

"Guess who?" I heard her ask. She led Susan by the hand into the kitchen.

Upon discovering our guest, the first word out of her mouth was, "No." It wasn't like the shriek of a heroine being accosted by a creature in the horror movies. This was the *no* of derailed late-night amorous advances, a response to Lyda's pleading to stay up till eleven on a school night.

"Let's be sensible about this," I said. "What are we going to do?"

"Call the police," said Susan.

"Are you crazy?" I said. "The very fact that he is here proves that what Malthusian told me was all true. We'd be putting our lives in danger."

"Go play," Susan said to Lyda.

"Can the zombie play?" she asked.

"The zombie has to stay here," I said and pointed toward the kitchen entrance.

When Lyda was gone, Susan sat down at the table and she and I stared at him some more. His breathing was very shallow, and with the exception of this subtle movement of his chest he sat perfectly still. There was something very relaxing about his presence.

"This is crazy," she said to me. "What are we going to do with him?"

"Malthusian said he would soon remember where he was from, and that we should take him to his home whenever the memory of it became clear to him."

"Can't we just drive him somewhere and let him out of the car?" asked Susan. "We'll leave him off in the parking lot at the mall."

"You wouldn't do that with a cat, but you would abandon a human being?" I said.

She shook her head in exasperation. "Well, what does he do? It doesn't look like much is becoming clear to him," she said.

I turned to the zombie and said, "What is your name?"

He didn't move.

Susan reached over and snapped her fingers in front of his face. "Hey, Mister Zombie, what should we call you?"

"Wait a second," I said. "He doesn't answer questions, he responds to commands."

"Tell me your name," Susan said to him.

The zombie turned his head slightly toward her and began to slowly move his lips. "Tom," he said and the word sort of fell out of his mouth, flat and dull as an old coin.

Susan brought her hand up to cover a giggle. "Tommy the zombie," she said.

"Pathetic," I said and couldn't suppress my own laughter even though there were shadowed entities at large in the world who might engineer our demise.

We had never had so unassuming a house guest. Tom was like that broom standing in the kitchen closet until you need it. The novelty of performance upon command soon wore off. Sure, we got a little mileage out of the stage hypnotist antics—"Bark like a dog." "Act like a chicken." I know it sounds a bit unfeeling, but we did it, I suppose, simply because we could, similar in spirit to the whim of the government that originally engineered the poor man's circumstance. Lyda put an end to this foolishness. She lectured to us about how we should respect him. We were embarrassed by her words, but at the same time pleased that we had raised such a caring individual. As it turned out, she had a real affection for the zombie. He was, for Lyda, the puppy we would not let her have.

It was not difficult remembering to command him to go to the bathroom twice a day, or to eat, or shower. What was truly hard was keeping him a secret. We all swore to each other that we would tell no one. Susan and I were afraid that Lyda, so completely carried away by her new friend, might not be able to contain herself at school. Think of the status one would reap in the third grade if it was known you had your own zombie at home. Throughout the ordeal, she proved to be the most practical, the most caring, the most insightful of all of us.

The utter strangeness of the affair did not strike me until the next night when I woke from a bad dream with a dry mouth. Half in a daze, I got out of bed and went to the kitchen for a glass of water. I took my drink and, going into the living room, sat down on the couch. For some reason, I was thinking about Poe's "The Fall of the House of Usher," and how D. H. Lawrence had described it as a story of vampirism. I followed a thread of thought that looped in and out of that loopy story and ended with an image of the previously airy and lethargic Madeline bursting out of her tomb to jump on old Roderick. Then I happened to look to the left, and jumped, myself, realizing that the zombie had been sitting next to me the entire time.

Tom could make a great pot of coffee. He vacuumed like a veteran chambermaid. Susan showed him how to do hospital corners when making the beds. When he was not busy, he would simply sit on the couch in the living room and stare directly across at the face of the grandfather clock. It was clear that he had a conception of time, because it was possible to set him like a VCR. If we were going out, we could tell him, "Make and eat a bologna sandwich at one P.M." "Go to the bathroom at three."

Somewhere in the second week of his asylum with us, I got the notion to become more expansive in my commands. I recalled Malthusian telling me that he was capable of playing Chopin after only listening to a piece once. It became clear that the requests I had been making of him were penny ante. I upped the stakes and instructed him to begin typing my handwritten notes for the Poe book. He flawlessly copied exactly what I had on the paper. Excited by this new breakthrough, I then told him to read a grammar book and correct the text. *Voilà!*

It became rapidly evident that we would have to get Tom some new clothes, since he continued to wear the same short-sleeved gray Sears workshirt and pants day in and day out. There was no question he would have worn them until they were reduced to shreds. Susan went to the store on her way home from work one night and bought him a few things. The next day, as an experiment, we told him to get dressed, choosing items from the pile of garments we laid before him. He came out of the spare bedroom, wearing a pair of loose-fitting khakis and a black T-shirt that had written in white block letters across it *I'm with Stupid.* We all got a charge out of this.

"Laugh, Tom," said Lyda.

The zombie opened wide his mouth, and from way back in his throat came a high-pitched "Ha… ha."

The horror of it melted my smile, and I began to wonder about his choice of shirts. That is when I noticed that a distinct five o'clock shadow had sprouted across his chin and sunken cheeks. "My God," I thought, without telling Susan or Lyda, "the aging process has begun."

When Tom wasn't pulling his weight around the house, Lyda usually had him engaged in some game. They played catch, cards, Barbies, and with those activities that were competitions, Lyda would tell him when it was his turn to win—and he would. For the most part, though, they drew pictures. Sitting at the kitchen table, each with a pencil and a few sheets of paper, they would create monsters. Lyda would have to tell Tom what to draw.

"Now do the werewolf with a dress and a hat. Mrs. Werewolf," she said.

That zombie could draw. When he was done there was a startlingly well-rendered, perfectly shadowed and shaded portrait of Lon Chaney in drag, a veritable hirsute Minnie Pearl. Susan hung it with magnets on the refrigerator.

"Take a bow," Lyda told him and he bent gracefully at the waist in a perfect forty-five degree angle.

My wife and daughter didn't notice that Tom was changing, but I did. Slowly, over the course of mere days, his hair had begun to thin out, and crow's feet formed at the corners of his eyes. This transformation I was seeing the first signs of was astounding to me. I wondered what it was that Malthusian had done to offset the effects of the original surgery that had been performed on him. Perhaps it was a series of commands; some kind of rigid behavioristic training. I hated to think of the old man poking around in Tom's head in that checkerboard kitchen under the fluorescent lights. What also puzzled me was how Malthusian had transferred command of the zombie to myself and my family. I began paying much closer attention to him, waiting for a sign that he had begun to recollect himself.

4

I held the drawing out to Lyda and asked her, "Who did this?"

She took it from me and upon seeing it smiled. "Tom," she said. "Yesterday I told him to draw whatever he wanted."

"It's good, don't you think?" I asked.

"Pretty good," she said and turned back to the television show she had been watching.

The portrait I held in my hand was of a young woman with long, dark hair. This was no monster. She was rendered with the same attention to detail as had been given to Mrs. Werewolf, but this girl, whoever she was, was beautiful. I was especially drawn to the eyes, which were luminous, so full of warmth. She wore an expression of amusement—a very subtle grin and a self-consciously dramatic arching of the eyebrows. I went to the kitchen and called for Tom to come in from the living room.

I told him to take his usual drawing seat, and then I handed him the picture. "You will tell me who this is," I commanded.

He stared for a moment at the portrait, and then it happened, a fleeting expression of pain crossed his face. His hand trembled slightly for a moment.

"You must tell me," I said.

"Marta," he said, and although it was only a word, I could have sworn there was a hint of emotion behind it.

"You must tell me if this is your wife," I said.

He slowly brought his left hand to his mouth, like a robot programmed to enact the human response of awe.

"Tell me," I said.

From behind his fingers, he whispered, "My love."

It was a foolish thing to do, but I applauded. As if the sound of my clapping suddenly severed his cognizance, he dropped his hand to his side and returned to the zombie state.

I sat down and studied him. His hair had begun to go gray at the edges, and his beard was now very noticeable. Those wrinkles I had detected the first sign of a few days earlier were now more prominent, as was the loosening of the skin along his chin line. Invading his blank affect was a vague aura of weariness. As impossible as it might sound, he appeared to me as if he had shrunken a centimeter or two.

"My love," I said out loud. These words were the most exciting shred of humanity to have surfaced, not so much for their dramatic weight, but more because he had failed to follow my instruction and definitively answer the question.

I left him alone for the time being, seeing as how he seemed quite saddened by the experience of remembering; but later, when Susan had returned home, we cleared the kitchen table after dinner and tried to advance the experiment. We conscripted Lyda into the plot, since it was when he was with her that he had created the portrait of Marta.

"Tell him to draw a picture of his house," I whispered to her. She nodded and then Susan and I left the kitchen and went into the living room to wait.

"He looks terrible," Susan said to me.

"The spell is slowly dissolving," I said. "He is becoming what he should be."

"The human mind is frightening," she said.

"The Haunted Palace," I told her.

Twenty minutes later, Lyda came in to us, smiling, carrying a picture.

"Look what he drew," she said, laughing.

He had created a self-portrait. Beneath the full-length picture were the scrawled words *Tommy the Zombie.*

I pointed to the words and said, "Well, that didn't work as I had planned, but this is rather interesting."

"A sense of humor?" said Susan.

"No," said Lyda. "He is sad."

"Maybe we shouldn't push him," I said.

"Wait," said Susan and sat forward suddenly. "Tell him now to draw his home."

Lyda nodded and was gone.

An hour passed and Susan and I waited in silence for the results. We could hear Lyda, in the kitchen, talking to him as they worked. She was telling him about this boy in her class in school who always bites the skin on his fingers.

"When Mrs. Brown asked Harry why he bites his skin, you know what he said?" asked Lyda.

There was a moment of silence and then we heard the deep, flat response, "What?"

Susan and I looked at each other.

"Harry told her," said Lyda, "he bites it because that way his father, who is very old, won't die."

A few minutes passed and then came a most disturbing sound, like a moan from out of a nightmare. Susan and I leaped up and ran into the kitchen. Lyda was sitting there, gaping at Tom, who was pressing on the pencil with a shaking hand, writing as if trying to carve initials into a tree trunk. There was sweat on his brow and tears in his eyes. I went over behind him and looked over his shoulder. There was a picture of a ranch-style house with an old carport on its left side. In the front window, I could make out the figures of a black cat and a woman's face. He was scrawling numbers and letters across the bottom of the picture.

"Twenty-four Griswold Place," I said aloud. And when he finished and slumped back into his seat, I saw the name of the town and spoke it. "Falls Park."

"That's only an hour north of here," said Susan.

I patted Tom on the back and told him, "You're going home," but by then his consciousness had again receded.

The next morning I got up well before sunrise and ordered Tom down the hall to the guest bedroom to change. He set to the task, a reluctant zombie, his rapid aging causing him to shuffle along, slightly bent over. Literally overnight, his hair had lost more of its color and there was a new, alarming sense of frailty about him. While he was dressing, I went in and kissed Susan good-bye and told her I was taking him as we had planned.

"Good luck," she said.

"Do you want to see him?" I asked.

"No, I'm going to go back to sleep, so that when I wake up I will be able to discount the entire thing as a bad dream."

"I hope I get him there before he croaks," I told her. "He's older than ever today."

I settled Tom in the backseat of the car and told him to buckle the belt. Then I got in and started driving. It was still dark as I turned onto the road out of town. Of course, I was taking a big chance by hoping that he might still know someone at the address he had written down. Decades had passed since he had been abducted, but I didn't care. Think ill of me if you like, but as with the lawyer in Melville's "Bartleby, the Scrivener," who ends up finally abandoning the scribe, which of you would have done as much as we did? Shadowed entities be damned, it had to come to an end.

"You're going home," I said over my shoulder to him as I drove.

"Home, yes," he said, and I took this for a good sign.

I looked into the rearview mirror, and could only see the top of his head. He seemed to have shrunk even more. To prepare myself for a worst-case scenario, I wondered what the bill would be to have a pool of putrescence steam-cleaned from my backseat.

About halfway into the journey, he started making some very odd sounds—coughing and hushed choking. This gave way to a kind of grumbling language that he carried on with for miles. I couldn't make out what he was saying, and to block it out, I eventually turned on the radio.

Even with the map, the address, and the drawing, it took me an hour and forty-five minutes to find the place. The sun was just beginning to show itself on the horizon when I pulled up in front of 24 Griswold Place. It was remarkable how perfect his drawing had been.

"Go now and knock on that door," I said pointing.

I was going to get out of the car and help him, but before I could get my belt off, I heard the back door open and close. Turning, I saw his figure moving away from the car. He was truly an old man now, moving beneath the weight of those years that, in the brief time of our trip, had caught up and overtaken him. I hoped that his metamorphosis had finally ended.

A great wave of sorrow passed through me, and I couldn't let him go without saying good-bye. I pressed the button for the window on his side. When it had rolled down, I called out, "Good luck."

He stopped walking, turned slowly to face me, and then I knew that the transformation was complete. His hair had gone completely white, and his face was webbed with wrinkles. It was Malthusian. He stood there staring at me, and his eyes were no smaller because he did not wear glasses.

I shook with the anger of betrayal. "You bastard," I yelled.

"Let's not let it ruin our game," he said with a thick accent, and then turned and went up the front steps.

I was so stunned, I couldn't move. He knocked on the door. After a few moments, a woman, as old as he, answered. I heard her give a short scream and then she threw her arms around him. "You've returned," she said in that same accent. She ushered him into the house and then the door slammed closed.

"Marta Malthusian, the sister," I said to myself and slammed the steering wheel. I don't know how long I sat there, staring blankly, trying to sort out the tangled treachery and love of a mad man turning a zombie into a zombie of himself. Eventually, I put the car in gear, wiped the drool from my chin, and started home.

BEAUTIFUL STUFF

by Susan Palwick

Susan Palwick is the author the novels *Flying in Place, The Necessary Beggar,* and *Shelter.* Much of her short fiction—which has appeared in *Asimov's Science Fiction, Amazing Stories, The Magazine of Fantasy & Science Fiction,* and elsewhere—was recently collected in the volume *The Fate of Mice.* Her work has been a finalist for the World Fantasy, Locus, and Mythopoeic awards, and *Flying in Place* won the Crawford Award for best first fantasy novel. She is Associate Professor of English at the University of Nevada, Reno, and lives in the foothills of the Sierra Nevada with her husband and three cats.

This story came from Palwick's rage at various political figures trying to use the victims of 9/11 as campaign fodder or as a fuel for war. "I found myself wondering, 'If all those dead people could come back, what would they want us to do?'" she says. This story would seem to indicate that she doesn't think the dead would have the same agendas as the living.

Rusty Kerfuffle stood on a plastic tarp in an elegant downtown office. The tarp had been spread over fine woolen carpet, the walls were papered in soothing monochrome linen, and the desk in front of Rusty was gleaming hardwood. There was a paperweight on the desk. The paperweight was a crystal globe with a purple flower inside it. In the sunlight from the window, the crystal sparkled and the flower glowed. Rusty desired that paperweight with a love like starvation, but the man sitting behind the desk wouldn't give it to him.

The man sitting behind the desk wore an expensive suit and a tense expression; next to him, an aide vomited into a bucket. "Sir," the aide said, raising his head from the bucket long enough to gasp out a comment. "Sir, I think this is going to be a public-relations disaster."

"Shut up," said the man behind the desk, and the aide resumed vomiting. "You. Do you understand what I'm asking for?"

"Sure," Rusty said, trying not to stare at the paperweight. He knew how smooth and heavy it would feel in his hands; he yearned to caress it. It contained light and life in a precious sphere: a little world.

Rusty's outfit had been a suit once. Now it was a rotting tangle of fibers. His ear itched, but if he scratched it, it might fall off. He'd been dead for three months. If his ear fell off in this fancy office, the man behind the desk might not let him touch the paperweight.

The man behind the desk exhaled, a sharp sound like the snort of a horse. "Good. You do what I need you to do, and you get to walk around again for a day. Understand?"

"Sure," said Rusty. He also understood that the walking part came first. The man behind the desk would have to re-revive Rusty, and all the others, before they could do what had been asked of them. Once they'd been revived, they got their day of walking whether they followed orders or not. "Can I hold the paperweight now?"

The man behind the desk smiled. It wasn't a friendly smile. "No, not yet. You weren't a very nice man when you were alive, Rusty."

"That's true," Rusty said, trying to ignore his itching ear. His fingers itched too, yearning for the paperweight. "I wasn't."

"I know all about you. I know you were cheating on your wife. I know about the insider trading. You were a morally bankrupt shithead, Rusty. But you're a hero now, aren't you? Because you're dead. Your wife thinks you were a saint."

This was, Rusty reflected, highly unlikely. Linda was as adept at running scams as he'd ever been, maybe more so. If she was capitalizing on his death, he couldn't blame her. He'd have done the same thing if she'd been the one who had died. He was glad to be past that. The living were far too complicated.

He stared impassively at the man behind the desk, whose tie was speckled with reflections from the paperweight. The aide was still vomiting. The man behind the desk gave another mean smile and said, "This is your chance to be a hero for real, Rusty. Do you understand that?"

"Sure," Rusty said, because that was what the man wanted to hear. The sun had gone behind a cloud: the paperweight shone less brightly now. It was just as tantalizing as it had been before, but in a more subdued way.

"Good. Because if you don't come through, if you say the wrong thing, I'll tell your wife what you were really doing, Rusty. I'll tell her what a pathetic slimebag you were. You won't be a hero anymore."

The aide had raised his head again. He looked astonished. He opened his mouth, as if he wanted to say something, but then he closed it. Rusty smiled at him. I may have been a pathetic slimebag, he thought, but I never tried to blackmail a corpse. Even your cringing assistant can see how morally bankrupt that is. The sun came out again, and the paperweight resumed its sparkling. "Got it," Rusty said happily.

The man behind the desk finally relaxed a little. He sat back in his chair. He became indulgent and expansive. "Good, Rusty. That's excellent. You're going to do the right thing for once, aren't you? You're going to help me convince all those cowards out there to stop sitting on their butts."

"Yes," Rusty said. "I'm going to do the right thing. Thank you for the opportunity, sir." This time, he wasn't being ironic.

"You're welcome, Rusty."

Rusty felt himself about to wiggle, like a puppy. "Now can I hold the paperweight? Please?"

"Okay, Rusty. Come and get it."

Rusty stepped forward, careful to stay on the tarp, and picked up the paperweight. It was as smooth and heavy and wonderful as he had known it would be. He cradled it to his chest, the glass pleasantly cool against his fingers, and began swaying back and forth.

Rusty had never understood the science behind corpse revival, but he supposed it didn't matter. Here he was, revived. He did know that the technique was hideously expensive. When it was first invented, mourning families had forked over life savings, taken out second mortgages, gone into staggering debt simply to have another day with their lost loved ones.

That trend didn't last long. The dead weren't attractive. The technique only worked on those who hadn't been embalmed or cremated, because there had to be a more-or-less intact, more-or-less chemically unaltered body to revive. That meant it got used most often on accident and suicide victims: the sudden dead, the unexpected dead, the dead who had gone without farewells. The unlovely dead, mangled and wounded.

The dead smelled, and they were visibly decayed, depending on the gap between when they had died and when they had been revived. They shed fingers and noses. They left behind pieces of themselves as mementos. And they had very little interest in the machinations of the living. Other things drew them. They loved flowers and animals. They loved to play with food. Running faucets enchanted them. The first dead person to be revived, a Mr. Otis Magruder, who had killed himself running into a tree while skiing, spent his twenty-four hours of second life sitting in his driveway making mud pies while his wife and children told him how much they loved him. Each time one of his relations delivered another impassioned statement of devotion, Otis nodded and said, "Uh-huh." And then he ran his fingers through more mud, and smiled. At hour eighteen, when his wife, despairing, asked if there was anything she could tell him, anything she could give him, he cocked his head and said, "Do you have a plastic pail?"

Six hours later, when Otis was mercifully dead again, his wife told reporters, "Well, Otis was always kind of spacey. That's why he ran into that tree, I guess." But it turned out that the other revived dead—tycoons, scientists, gangsters—were spacey too. The dead didn't care about the same things the living did.

These days, the dead were revived only rarely, usually to testify in criminal cases involving their death or civil cases involving the financial details of their estates. They made bad witnesses. They became distracted by brightly colored neckties, by the reflection of the courtroom lights in the polished wood of the witness box, by the gentle clicking of the clerk's recording instrument. It was very difficult to keep them on track, to remind them what they were supposed to be thinking about. On the other hand, they had amazingly accurate memories once they could be cajoled into paying attention to the subject at hand. Bribes of balloons and small, brightly colored toys worked well; jurors became used to watching the dead weep in frustration while scolding lawyers held matchbox cars and neon-hued stuffed animals just out of reach. But once the dead gave the information the living sought, they always told the truth. No one had ever caught one of the dead lying, no matter how dishonest the corpse might have been while it was still alive.

It had been very difficult for the man behind the desk to break through Rusty's fascination with the paperweight. It had taken a lot to get Rusty's attention. Dirt about Rusty's affairs and insider deals hadn't done it. None of that mattered anymore. It was a set of extraneous details, as distant as the moon and as abstract as ethics, which also had no hold on Rusty.

Rusty's passions and loyalties were much more basic now.

He stood in the elegant office, rocking the paperweight as if it were a baby, crooning to it, sometimes holding it at arm's length to admire it before bringing it back safely to his chest again. He had another two hours of revival left this time; the man behind the desk would revive him and the others again in a month, for another twenty-four hours. Rusty fully intended to spend every minute of his current two hours in contemplation of the paperweight. When he was revived again in a month, he'd fall in love with something else.

"You *idiot*," said the man who had been sitting behind the desk. He wasn't behind a desk now; he was in a refrigerated warehouse, a month after that meeting with Rusty. He was yelling at his aide. Around him were the revived dead, waiting to climb into refrigerated trucks to be taken to the rally site. It was a lovely, warm spring day, and they'd smell less if they were kept cool for as long as possible. "I don't want *them*." He waved at two of the dead, more mangled than any of the others, charred and lacerated and nearly unrecognizable as human bodies. One was playing with a paperclip that had been lying on the floor; the other opened and closed its hand, trying to catch the dust motes that floated in the shafts of light from the window.

The aide was sweating, despite the chill of the warehouse. "Sir, you said—"

"I know what I said, you moron!"

"Everyone who was there, you said—"

"Idiot." The voice was very quiet now, very dangerous. "Idiot. Do you know why we're doing this? Have you been paying *attention*?"

"Sir," the aide stuttered. "Yes sir."

"Oh, really? Because if you'd been paying *attention, they* wouldn't be here!"

"But—"

"Prove to me that you understand," said the dangerously quiet voice. "Tell me why we're doing this."

The aide gulped. "To remind people where their loyalties lie. Sir."

"Yes. And where *do* their loyalties lie? Or where *should* their loyalties lie?"

"With innocent victims. Sir."

"Yes. Exactly. And are those, those *things* over there"—an impassioned hand waved at the two mangled corpses—"are they innocent victims?"

"No. Sir."

"No. They aren't. They're the monsters who were responsible for all these *other* innocent victims! They're the *guilty* ones, aren't they?"

"Yes sir."

"They *deserve* to be dead, don't they?"

"Yes sir." The aide stood miserably twisting his hands.

"The entire point of this rally is to demonstrate that some people *deserve* to be dead, isn't it?"

"Yes sir!"

"Right. So why in the name of everything that's holy were those *monsters* revived?"

The aide coughed. "We were using the new technique. Sir. The blanket-revival technique. It works over a given geographical area. They were mixed in with the others. We couldn't be that precise."

"Fuck that," said the quiet voice, succinctly.

"It would have been far too expensive to revive all of them individually," the aide said. "The new technique saved us—"

"Yes, I know how much it saved us! And I know how much we're going to lose if this doesn't work! Get rid of them! I don't want them on the truck! I don't want them at the rally!"

"Sir! Yes sir!"

The aide, once his boss had left, set about correcting the situation. He told the two unwanted corpses that they weren't needed. He tried to be polite about it. It was difficult to get their attention away from the paperclip and the dust motes; he had to distract them with a penlight and a Koosh ball, and that worked well enough, except that some of the other corpses got distracted too and began crowding around the aide, cooing and reaching for the Koosh ball. There were maybe twenty of them, the ones who had been closest; the others, thank God, were still off in their own little worlds. But these twenty all wanted that Koosh ball. The aide felt like he was in a preschool in hell, or possibly in a dovecote of extremely deformed and demented pigeons.

"Listen to me!" he said, raising his voice over the cooing. "Listen! You two! You with the paperclip and you with the dust motes! We don't want you, okay? We just want everyone else! You two, do *not* get on the trucks! Have you got that? Yes? Is that a nod? Is that a yes?"

"Yesh," said the corpse with the paperclip, and the one who'd been entranced by the dust motes nodded.

"All right then," said the aide, and tossed the Koosh ball over their heads into a corner of the warehouse. There was a chorus of happy shrieks and a stampede of corpses. The aide took the opportunity to get out of there, into fresh air. His Dramamine was wearing off. He didn't know if the message had really gotten through or not, but fuck it: this whole thing was going to be a public-relations disaster, no matter who got on the trucks. He no longer cared if he kept his job. In fact, he hoped he got fired, because that way he could collect unemployment. As soon as the rally was over, he'd go home and start working on his resumé.

Back in the warehouse, Rusty had a firm grip on the Koosh ball. He had purposefully stayed at the back of the crowd. He knew what he had to do, and he had been concentrating very hard on staying focused, although it was difficult not to be distracted by all the wonderful things around him: the aide's tie, a piece of torn newspaper on the floor, the gleaming hubcaps of the trucks. His mind wasn't working as well as it had been during his first revival, and it took all his energy to concentrate. He stayed at the back of the crowd and kept his eyes on the Koosh ball, and when the aide tossed it into the corner, Rusty was the first one there. He had it. He picked it up, thrilling at its texture, and did the hardest thing he had ever done: he sacrificed the pleasure of the Koosh ball. He forced himself to let go of it for the greater good. He tossed it into the back of the nearest truck and watched his twenty fellows rush in joy up the loading ramp. Were the two unwanted corpses there? Yes, they were. In the excitement, they had forgotten their promise to the aide.

Rusty ran to the truck. He climbed inside with the others, fighting his longing to join the exuberant scramble for the Koosh ball. But instead, Rusty Kerfuffle, who was not a hero and had not been a very nice man, pulled something from his pocket. He had a pocket because the man with the quiet voice had given him a new blue blazer to wear, so he'd be more presentable, and inside the pocket was a glass paperweight with a purple flower inside. Rusty had been allowed to keep the paperweight last time, because no one else wanted to touch it now. "It has fucking corpse germs all over it," the man with the quiet voice had told him, and Rusty had trembled with joy. He wouldn't have to fall in love with something else after all; he could stay in love with this.

Rusty used the paperweight now to distract the two unwanted corpses, and several of the others closest to him, from the Koosh ball. And then he started talking to them—although it was very, very hard for him to stay on track, because all he wanted to do was fondle the paperweight—and waited for the truck doors to be closed.

Outside the warehouse, it was spring: a balmy, fragrant season. The refrigerated trucks rolled past medians filled with cheerful flowers, past sidewalks where pedestrians strolled, their faces lifted to the sun, past parks where children on swings pumped themselves into the air in ecstasies of flight. At last the convoy of trucks pulled into a larger park, the park at the center of the city, and along tree-lined roads to a bandstand in the very center of that park. The man with the quiet voice stood at the bandstand podium, his aide beside him. One side of the audience consisted of people waving signs in support of the man with the quiet voice. The other side consisted of people waving signs denouncing him. Both sides were peppered with reporters, with cameras and microphones. The man with the quiet voice stared stonily down the center aisle and read the speech prepared by his aide.

"Four months ago," he said, "this city suffered a devastating attack. Hundreds of innocent people were killed. Those people were your husbands and wives, your children, your brothers and sisters, your friends. They were cut down in the prime of their lives by enemies to whom they had done no harm, who wanted nothing more than to destroy them, to destroy all of us. They were cut down by pure evil."

The man with the quiet voice paused, waiting for the crowd to stir. It didn't. The crowd waited, watching him. The only thing that stirred was the balmy spring wind, moving the leaves. The man at the podium cleared his throat. "As a result of that outrageous act of destruction, the brave leaders of our great nation determined that we had to strike back. We could not let this horror go unanswered. And so we sent our courageous troops to address the evil, to destroy the evil, to stamp out the powers that had cut down our loved ones in their prime."

Again he paused. The audience stirred now, a little bit. Someone on one side waved a sign that said, "We Will Never Forget!" Someone on the other side waved a sign that said, "An Eye for An Eye Makes the Whole World Blind." The cameras whirred. The birds twittered. The refrigerated trucks rolled up to the edge of the band shell, and the man at the podium smiled.

"I supported the courageous decision of our brave leaders," he said. His voice was less quiet now. "There was only one way to respond to this devastating grief, this hideous loss, this violation of all that we hold dear and sacred. This was the principled stance taken by millions of people in our great nation. But certain others among us, among you"—here he glared at the person who had waved the second sign—"have claimed that this makes me unworthy to continue to hold office, unworthy to continue to be your leader. If that is true, then many of the leaders of this country are also unworthy."

His voice had risen to something like a crescendo. The woman standing next to the man who had waved the second sign cupped her hands around her mouth and called out cheerfully, "No argument there, boss!" A few people laughed; a few people booed; the cameras whirred. The man at the podium glared, and spoke again, now not quietly at all.

"But it is *not* true! The leaders of this city, of this state, of this nation must be brave! Must be principled! Must be ready to fight wrong wherever they find it!"

"Must be ready to send innocent young people to kill other innocent young people," the same woman called back. The booing was louder now. The man at the podium smiled, grimly.

"Let us remember who is truly innocent. Let us remember who was truly innocent four months ago. If they could speak to us, what would they say? Well, you are about to find out. I have brought them here today, our beloved dead, to speak to us, to tell us what they would have us do."

He gave a signal. The truck doors were opened. The corpses shambled out, blinking in the glorious sunshine, gaping at trees and flowers and folding chairs and whirring cameras. The crowd gave a gratifying gasp, and several people began to sob. Others began to retch. Additional aides in the audience, well prepared for all eventualities, began handing out packets of tissues and barf bags, both imprinted with campaign slogans.

Rusty Kerfuffle, doggedly ignoring the trees and flowers and folding chairs and cameras, doggedly ignoring the knowledge that his beloved paperweight was in his pocket, moved toward the podium, dragging the unwanted corpses with him. In the van, he had accomplished the very difficult task of removing certain items of clothing from other corpses and outfitting these two, so maybe the man with the quiet voice wouldn't realize what he was doing and try to stop him. At least for the moment, it seemed to be working.

The man with the quiet voice was saying something about love and loss and outrage. His aides were trying to corral wandering corpses. More people in the audience were retching. Rusty, holding an unwanted corpse's hand in each of his—the three of them like small children crossing a street together—squinted his eyes almost shut, so he wouldn't see all the distracting things around him. Stay focused, Rusty. Get to the podium.

He got to the podium. Three steps up and he was on the podium, the unwanted corpses beside him. The man with the quiet voice turned and smiled at him. "And now, ladies and gentlemen, I give you Rusty Kerfuffle, the heroic husband of Linda Kerfuffle, whom you've all seen on television. Linda, are you here?"

"Darling!" gasped a woman in the crowd. She ran toward the podium but was overtaken by retching halfway there. Rusty wondered how much she was being paid.

An aide patted Linda on the back and handed her a barf bag. The aide on the platform murmured "public-relations disaster" too softly for the microphones. The quiet man coughed and cleared his throat and poked Rusty in the back.

Rusty understood that this was his cue to do something. "Hi, Linda," said Rusty. He couldn't tell if the microphones had picked that up, so he waved. Linda waved back, took a few steps closer to the podium, and was overcome with retching again.

The aide on the platform groaned, and the man with the quiet voice forged grimly ahead. "I have brought back Rusty and these other brave citizens and patriots, your lost loved ones, to tell you how important it is to fight evil, to tell you about the waste and horror of their deaths, to implore you to do the right thing, since some of you have become misled by propaganda."

Rusty had just caught a glimpse of a butterfly, and it took every ounce of his will not to turn to run after it, to walk up to the microphone instead. But he did his duty. He walked up to the microphone, pulling his two companions.

"Hi," he said. "I'm Rusty. Wait, you know that."

The crowd stared at him, some still retching. Linda was wiping her mouth. Some people were walking away. "Wait," Rusty called after them. "It's really important. It really is." A few stopped and turned, standing with their arms folded; others kept walking. Rusty had to say something to make them stop. "Wait," he said. "This guy's wrong. I wasn't brave. I wasn't patriotic. I cheated on my wife. Linda, I cheated on you, but I think you knew that. I think you were cheating on me too. It's okay; it doesn't matter now. I cheated on other stuff too. I cheated on my taxes. I was guilty of insider trading. I was a morally bankrupt shithead." He pointed at the man with the quiet voice. "That's his phrase, not mine, but it fits." There: now he couldn't be blackmailed.

Most of the people who'd been walking away had stopped now: good. The man with the quiet voice was hissing. "Rusty, what are you doing?"

"I'm doing what he wants me to do," Rusty said into the microphone. "I'm, what was that word, imploring you to do the right thing."

He stopped, out of words, and concentrated very hard on what he was going to say next. He caught a flash of purple out of the corner of his left eye. Was that another butterfly? He turned. No: it was a splendid purple bandana. The aide on the platform was waving it at Rusty. Rusty's heart melted. He fell in love with the bandana. The bandana was the most exquisite thing he had ever seen. Who wouldn't covet the bandana? And indeed, one of his companions, the one on the left, was snatching at it.

Rusty took a step toward the bandana and then forced himself to stop. No. The aide was trying to distract him. The aide was cheating. The bandana was a trick. Rusty still had his paperweight. He didn't need the bandana.

Heartsick, nearly sobbing, Rusty turned back to the podium, dragging the other corpse with him. The other corpse whimpered, but Rusty prevailed. He knew that this was very important. It was as important as the paperweight in his pocket. He could no longer remember why, but he remembered that he had known once.

"Darling!" Linda said, running toward him. "Darling! I forgive you! I love you! Dear Rusty!"

She was wearing a shiny barrette. She never wore barrettes. It was another trick. Rusty began to tremble. "Linda," he said into the microphone. "Shut up. Shut up and go away, Linda. I have to say something."

Rusty's other companion, the one on his right, let out a small squeal and tried to lurch toward Linda, towards the barrette. "No," Rusty said, keeping desperate hold. "You stay here. Linda, take that shiny thing off! Hide it, Linda!"

"Darling!" she said, and the right-hand corpse broke away from Rusty and hopped off the podium, toward Linda. Linda screamed and ran, the corpse trotting after her. Rusty sighed; the aide groaned again; the quiet man cursed, softly.

"Okay," Rusty said, "so here's what I have to tell you." Some of the people in the crowd who'd turned to watch Linda and her pursuer turned back toward Rusty now, but others didn't. Well, he couldn't do anything about that. He had to say this thing. He could remember what he had to say, but he couldn't remember why. That was all right. He'd say it, and then maybe he'd remember.

"What I have to tell you is, dying hurts," Rusty said. The crowd murmured. "Dying hurts a lot. It hurts—everybody hurts." Rusty struggled to remember why this mattered. He dimly remembered dying, remembered other people dying around him. "It hurts everybody. It makes everybody the same. This guy, and that other one who ran away, they hurt too. This is Ari. That was Ahmed. They were the ones who planted the bomb. They didn't get out in time. They died too." Gasps, some louder murmurs, louder cursing from the man with the quiet voice. Rusty definitely had everyone's attention now.

He prodded Ari. "It hurt," Ari said.

"And?" said Rusty.

"We're sorry," said Ari.

"Ahmed's sorry too," said Rusty. "He told me. He'd have told you, if he weren't chasing Linda's shiny hair thing."

"If we'd known, we wouldn't have done it," Ari said.

"Because?" Rusty said patiently.

"We did it for the wrong reasons," Ari said. "We expected things to happen that didn't happen. Paradise, and, like, virgins." Ari looked shyly down at his decaying feet. "I'm sorry."

"More," Rusty said. "Tell them more."

"Dying hurts," said Ari. "It won't make you happy. It won't make anybody happy."

"So please do the right thing," said Rusty. "Don't kill anybody else."

The man with the quiet voice let out a howl and leaped toward Rusty. He grabbed Rusty's free arm, the right one, and pulled; the arm came off, and the man with the quiet voice started hitting Rusty over the head with it. "You fucking incompetent! You traitor! You said you'd tell them—"

"I said I'd do the right thing," Rusty said. "I never said my version of the right thing was the same as yours."

"You lied!"

"No, I didn't. I misled you, but I told the truth. What are you going to do, kill me?" He looked out at the crowd and said, "We're the dead. You loved some of us. You hated others. We're the dead. We're here to tell you: please don't kill anybody else. Everybody will be dead soon enough, whether you kill them or not. It hurts."

The crowd stared; the cameras whirred. None of the living there that day had ever heard such long speeches from the dead. It was truly a historic occasion. A group of aides had managed to drag away the man with the quiet voice, who was still brandishing Rusty's arm; Rusty, with his one arm, stood at the podium with Ari.

"Look," Rusty said. He let go of Ari's hand and reached around to pull the paperweight out of his pocket. He held it up in front of the crowd. Ari cooed and reached for it, entranced, but Rusty held it above his head. "Look at this! Look at the shiny glass. Look at the flower. It's beautiful. You have all this stuff in your life, all this beautiful stuff. Sunshine and grass and butterflies. Barrettes. Bandanas. You don't have that when you're dead. That's why dying hurts."

And Rusty shivered, and remembered: he remembered dying, knowing he'd never see trees again, never drink coffee, never smell flowers or see buildings reflected in windows. He remembered that pain, the pain of knowing what he was losing only when it was too late. And he knew that the living wouldn't understand, couldn't understand. Or maybe some of them did, but the others would only make fun of them. He finished his speech lamely, miserably, knowing that everyone would say it was just a cliché. "Enjoy the beautiful stuff while you have it."

The woman who had heckled the man with the quiet voice was frowning. "You're advocating greed! That's what gets people killed. People murder each other for stuff!"

"No," Rusty said. He was exhausted. She didn't understand. She'd probably never understand unless she died and got revived. "Just enjoy it. Look at it. Don't fight. You don't get it, do you?"

"No," she said. "I don't."

Rusty shrugged. He was too tired; he couldn't keep his focus anymore. He no longer cared if the woman got it or not. The man with the quiet voice had been taken away, and Rusty had done what he had wanted to do, although it seemed much less important now than it had even a month ago, when he was first revived. He remembered, dimly, that no one had ever managed to teach the living anything much. Some of them might get it. He'd done what he could. He'd told them what mattered.

His attention wandered away from the woman, away from the crowd. He brought the paperweight back down to chest level, and then he sat down on the edge of the platform, and Ari sat with him, and they both stared at the paperweight, touching it, humming in happiness there in the sunshine.

The crowd watched them for a while, and then it wandered away, too. The other corpses had already wandered. The dead meandered through the beautiful budding park, all of them in love: one with a sparrow on the walk, one with a silk scarf a woman in the audience had given him, one with an empty, semicrushed milk carton she had plucked out of a trash can. The dead fell in love, and they walked or they sat, carrying what they loved or letting it hold them in place. They loved their beautiful stuff for the rest of the day, until the sun went down; and then they lay down too, their treasures beside them, and slept again, and this time did not wake.

SEX, DEATH AND STARSHINE

by Clive Barker

Clive Barker is probably best known as the writer and director of the *Hellraiser* saga, which was based on his novella "The Hellbound Heart." He has written and directed other films as well, such as *Lord of Illusions* and *Nightbreed*. Other works of his have been adapted to film by others, such as his short story "The Forbidden," which was made into the film *Candyman*.

In addition to his work in Hollywood, he is the best-selling, award-winning author of many novels, such as *The Damnation Game*, *Weaveworld*, *Imajica*, *The Thief of Always*, and *Sacrament*. His most recent is *Mister B. Gone*. His landmark short story collections, the *Books of Blood*, won him a World Fantasy Award and established his reputation as a master of horror.

In *The Mammoth Book of Zombies*, Barker is quoted as saying, "Zombies are the ideal late-twentieth-century monsters. A zombie is the one thing you can't deal with. It survives anything. Frankenstein and Dracula could be sent down in many ways. Zombies, though, fall outside all this. You can't argue with them. They just keep coming at you."

The zombies in the story that follows aren't quite the killing machines that Barker's quote suggests, but the relentlessness he implies with "They just keep coming at you" is certainly present.

Diane ran her scented fingers through the two days' growth of ginger stubble on Terry's chin.

"I love it," she said, "even the grey bits."

She loved everything about him, or at least that's what she claimed.

When he kissed her: I love it.

When he undressed her: I love it.

When he slid his briefs off: I love it, I love it, I love it.

She'd go down on him with such unalloyed enthusiasm, all he could do was watch the top of her ash-blonde head bobbing at his groin, and hope to God nobody chanced to walk into the dressing-room. She was a married woman, after all, even if she was an actress. He had a wife himself, somewhere. This tête-à-tête would make some juicy copy for one of the local rags, and here he was trying to garner a reputation as a serious-minded director; no gimmicks, no gossip; just art.

Then, even thoughts of ambition would be dissolved on her tongue, as she played havoc with his nerve-endings. She wasn't much of an actress, but by God she was quite a performer. Faultless technique; immaculate timing: she knew either by instinct or by rehearsal just when to pick up the rhythm and bring the whole scene to a satisfying conclusion.

When she'd finished milking the moment dry, he almost wanted to applaud.

The whole cast of Calloway's production of *Twelfth Night* knew about the affair, of course. There'd be the occasional snide comment passed if actress and director were both late for rehearsals, or if she arrived looking full, and he flushed. He tried to persuade her to control the cat-with-the-cream look that crept over her face, but she just wasn't that good a deceiver. Which was rich, considering her profession.

But then La Duvall, as Edward insisted on calling her, didn't need to be a great player, she was famous. So what if she spoke Shakespeare like it was Hiawatha, dum de dum de dum de dum? So what if her grasp of psychology was dubious, her logic faulty, her projection inadequate? So what if she had as much sense of poetry as she did propriety? She was a star, and that meant business.

There was no taking that away from her: her name was money. The Elysium Theatre publicity announced her claim to fame in three-inch Roman Bold, black on yellow:

"Diane Duvall: star of *The Love Child*."

The Love Child. Possibly the worst soap opera to cavort across the screens of the nation in the history of that genre, two solid hours a week of under-written characters and mind-numbing dialogue, as a result of which it consistently drew high ratings, and its performers became, almost overnight, brilliant stars in television's rhinestone heaven. Glittering there, the brightest of the bright, was Diane Duvall.

Maybe she wasn't born to play the classics, but Jesus was she good box-office. And in this day and age, with theatres deserted, all that mattered was the number of punters on seats.

Calloway had resigned himself to the fact that this would not be the definitive *Twelfth Night*, but if the production were successful, and with Diane in the role of Viola, it had every chance, it might open a few doors to him in the West End. Besides, working with the ever-adoring, ever-demanding Miss D. Duvall had its compensations.

Calloway pulled up his serge trousers, and looked down at her. She was giving him that winsome smile of hers, the one she used in the letter scene. Expression Five in the Duvall repertoire, somewhere between Virginal and Motherly.

He acknowledged the smile with one from his own stock, a small, loving look that passed for genuine at a yard's distance. Then he consulted his watch.

"God, we're late, sweetie."

She licked her lips. Did she really like the taste that much?

"I'd better fix my hair," she said, standing up and glancing in the long mirror beside the shower.

"Yes."

"Are you OK?"

"Couldn't be better," he replied. He kissed her lightly on the nose and left her to her teasing.

On his way to the stage he ducked into the Men's Dressing Room to adjust his clothing, and dowse his burning cheeks with cold water. Sex always induced a giveaway mottling on his face and upper chest. Bending to splash water on himself Calloway studied his features critically in the mirror over the sink. After thirty-six years of holding the signs of age at bay, he was beginning to look the part. He was no more the juvenile lead. There was an indisputable puffiness beneath his eyes, which was nothing to do with sleeplessness, and there were lines too, on his forehead, and round his mouth. He didn't look the *wunderkind* any longer; the secrets of his debauchery were written all over his face. The excess of sex, booze and ambition, the frustration of aspiring and just missing the main chance so many times. What would he look like now, he thought bitterly, if he'd been content to be some unenterprising nobody working in a minor rep, guaranteed a house of ten aficionados every night, and devoted to Brecht? Face as smooth as a baby's bottom probably, most of the people in the socially committed theatre had that look. Vacant and content, poor cows.

"Well, you pays your money and you takes your choice," he told himself. He took one last look at the haggard cherub in the mirror, reflecting that, crow's feet or not, women still couldn't resist him, and went out to face the trials and tribulations of Act III.

On stage there was a heated debate in progress. The carpenter, his name was Jake, had built two hedges for Olivia's garden. They still had to be covered with leaves, but they looked quite impressive, running the depth of the stage to the cyclorama, where the rest of the garden would be painted. None of this symbolic stuff. A garden was a garden: green grass, blue sky. That's the way the audience liked it North of Birmingham, and Terry had some sympathy for their plain tastes.

"Terry, love."

Eddie Cunningham had him by the hand and elbow, escorting him into the fray.

"What's the problem?"

"Terry, love, you cannot be serious about these fucking (it came trippingly off the tongue: fuck-ing) hedges. Tell Uncle Eddie you're not serious before I throw a fit." Eddie pointed towards the offending hedges. "I mean look at them." As he spoke a thin plume of spittle fizzed in the air.

"What's the problem?" Terry asked again.

"Problem? Blocking, love, blocking. *Think* about it. We've rehearsed this whole scene with me bobbing up and down like a March hare. Up right, down left—but it doesn't work if I haven't got access round the back. And look! These fucking things are flush with the backdrop."

"Well they have to be, for the illusion, Eddie."

"I can't get round though, Terry. You must see my point."

He appealed to the few others on stage: the carpenters, two technicians, three actors.

"I mean—there's just not enough time."

"Eddie, we'll re-block."

"Oh."

That took the wind out of his sails.

"No?"

"Um."

"I mean it seems easiest, doesn't it?"

"Yes… I just liked…"

"I know."

"Well. Needs must. What about the croquet?"

"We'll cut that too."

"All that business with the croquet mallets? The bawdy stuff?"

"It'll all have to go. I'm sorry, I haven't thought this through. I wasn't thinking straight."

Eddie flounced.

"That's all you ever do, love, think straight…"

Titters. Terry let it pass. Eddie had a genuine point of criticism; he had failed to consider the problems of the hedge-design.

"I'm sorry about the business; but there's no way we can accommodate it."

"You won't be cutting anybody else's business, I'm sure," said Eddie. He threw a glance over Calloway's shoulder at Diane, then headed for the dressing-room. Exit enraged actor, stage left. Calloway made no attempt to stop him. It would have worsened the situation considerably to spoil his departure. He just breathed out a quiet "oh Jesus," and dragged a wide hand down over his face. That was the fatal flaw of this profession: actors. "Will somebody fetch him back?" he said. Silence.

"Where's Ryan?"

The Stage Manager showed his bespectacled face over the offending hedge.

"Sorry?"

"Ryan, love—will you please take a cup of coffee to Eddie and coax him back into the bosom of the family?"

Ryan pulled a face that said: you offended him, you fetch him. But Calloway had passed this particular buck before: he was a past master at it. He just stared at Ryan, defying him to contradict his request, until the other man dropped his eyes and nodded his acquiescence.

"Sure," he said glumly.

"Good man."

Ryan cast him an accusatory look, and disappeared in pursuit of Ed Cunningham.

"No show without Belch," said Calloway, trying to warm up the atmosphere a little. Someone grunted: and the small half-circle of onlookers began to disperse. Show over.

"OK, OK," said Calloway, picking up the pieces, "let's get to work. We'll run through from the top of the scene. Diane, are you ready?"

"Yes."

"OK. Shall we run it?"

He turned away from Olivia's garden and the waiting actors just to gather his thoughts. Only the stage working lights were on, the auditorium was in darkness. It yawned at him insolently, row upon row of empty seats, defying him to entertain them. Ah, the loneliness of the long-distance director. There were days in this business when the thought of life as an accountant seemed a consummation devoutly to be wished, to paraphrase the Prince of Denmark.

In the Gods of the Elysium, somebody moved. Calloway looked up from his doubts and stared through the swarthy air. Had Eddie taken residence on the very back row? No, surely not. For one thing, he hadn't had time to get all the way up there.

"Eddie?" Calloway ventured, capping his hand over his eyes. "Is that you?"

He could just make the figure out. No, not a figure, figures. Two people, edging their way along the back row, making for the exit. Whoever it was, it certainly wasn't Eddie.

"That isn't Eddie, is it?" said Calloway, turning back into the fake garden.

"No," someone replied.

It was Eddie speaking. He was back on stage, leaning on one of the hedges, cigarette clamped between his lips. "Eddie…"

"It's all right," said the actor good-humouredly, "don't grovel; I can't bear to see a pretty man grovel."

"We'll see if we can slot the mallet-business in somewhere," said Calloway, eager to be conciliatory.

Eddie shook his head, and flicked ash off his cigarette.

"No need."

"Really—"

"It didn't work too well anyhow."

The Grand Circle door creaked a little as it closed behind the visitors. Calloway didn't bother to look round. They'd gone, whoever they were.

"There was somebody in the house this afternoon."

Hammersmith looked up from the sheets of figures he was poring over.

"Oh?" His eyebrows were eruptions of wire-thick hair that seemed ambitious beyond their calling. They were raised high above Hammersmith's tiny eyes in patently fake surprise. He plucked at his bottom lip with nicotine-stained fingers.

"Any idea who it was?"

He plucked on, still staring up at the younger man; undisguised contempt on his face.

"Is it a problem?"

"I just want to know who was in looking at the rehearsal that's all. I think I've got a perfect right to ask."

"Perfect right," said Hammersmith, nodding slightly and making his lips into a pale bow.

"There was talk of somebody coming up from the National," said Calloway. "My agents were arranging something. I just don't want somebody coming in without me knowing about it. Especially if they're important."

Hammersmith was already studying the figures again. His voice was tired.

"Terry: if there's someone in from the South Bank to look your opus over, I promise you, you'll be the first to be informed. All right?"

The inflexion was so bloody rude. So run-along-little-boy. Calloway itched to hit him.

"I don't want people watching rehearsals unless I authorize it, Hammersmith. Hear me? And I want to know who was in today."

The Manager sighed heavily.

"Believe me, Terry," he said, "I don't know myself. I suggest you ask Tallulah—she was front of house this afternoon. If somebody came in, presumably she saw them."

He sighed again.

"All right… Terry?"

Calloway left it at that. He had his suspicions about Hammersmith. The man couldn't give a shit about theatre, he never failed to make that absolutely plain; he affected an exhausted tone whenever anything but money was mentioned, as though matters of aesthetics were beneath his notice. And he had a word, loudly administered, for actors and directors alike: butterflies. One-day wonders. In Hammersmith's world only money was forever, and the Elysium Theatre stood on prime land, land a wise man could turn a tidy profit on if he played his cards right.

Calloway was certain he'd sell off the place tomorrow if he could maneuver it. A satellite town like Redditch, growing as Birmingham grew, didn't need theatres, it needed offices, hypermarkets, warehouses: it needed, to quote the councilors, growth through investment in new industry. It also needed prime sites to build that industry upon. No mere art could survive such pragmatism.

Tallulah was not in the box, nor in the foyer, nor in the Green Room.

Irritated both by Hammersmith's incivility and Tallulah's disappearance, Calloway went back into the auditorium to pick up his jacket and go to get drunk. The rehearsal was over and the actors long gone. The bare hedges looked somewhat small from the back row of the stalls. Maybe they needed an extra few inches. He made a note on the back of a show bill he found in his pocket: Hedges, bigger?

A footfall made him look up, and a figure had appeared on stage. A smooth entrance, up-stage centre, where the hedges converged. Calloway didn't recognize the man.

"Mr. Calloway? Mr. Terence Calloway?"

"Yes?"

The visitor walked down stage to where, in an earlier age, the footlights would have been, and stood looking out into the auditorium.

"My apologies for interrupting your train of thought."

"No problem."

"I wanted a word."

"With me?"

"If you would."

Calloway wandered down to the front of the stalls, appraising the stranger.

He was dressed in shades of grey from head to foot. A grey worsted suit, grey shoes, a grey cravat. Piss-elegant, was Calloway's first, uncharitable summation. But the man cut an impressive figure nevertheless. His face beneath the shadow of his brim was difficult to discern.

"Allow me to introduce myself."

The voice was persuasive, cultured. Ideal for advertisement voice-overs: soap commercials, maybe. After Hammersmith's bad manners, the voice came as a breath of good breeding.

"My name is Lichfield. Not that I expect that means much to a man of your tender years."

Tender years: well, well. Maybe there was still something of the *wunderkind* in his face.

"Are you a critic?" Calloway inquired.

The laugh that emanated from beneath the immaculately swept brim was ripely ironical.

"In the name of Jesus, no," Lichfield replied.

"I'm sorry, then, you have me at a loss."

"No need for an apology."

"Were you in the house this afternoon?"

Lichfield ignored the question. "I realize you're a busy man, Mr. Calloway, and I don't want to waste your time. The theatre is my business, as it is yours. I think we must consider ourselves allies, though we have never met."

Ah, the great brotherhood. It made Calloway want to spit, the familiar claims of sentiment. When he thought of the number of so-called allies that had cheerfully stabbed him in the back; and in return the playwrights whose work he'd smilingly slanged, the actors he'd crushed with a casual quip. Brotherhood be damned, it was dog-eat-dog, same as any over-subscribed profession.

"I have," Lichfield was saying, "an abiding interest in the Elysium." There was a curious emphasis on the word abiding. It sounded positively funereal from Lichfield's lips. Abide with me.

"Oh?"

"Yes, I've spent many happy hours in this theatre, down the years, and frankly it pains me to carry this burden of news."

"What news?"

"Mr. Calloway, I have to inform you that your *Twelfth Night* will be the last production the Elysium will see."

The statement didn't come as much of a surprise, but it still hurt, and the internal wince must have registered on Calloway's face.

"Ah… so you didn't know. I thought not. They always keep the artists in ignorance don't they? It's a satisfaction the Apollonians will never relinquish. The accountant's revenge."

"Hammersmith," said Calloway.

"Hammersmith."

"Bastard."

"His clan are never to be trusted, but then I hardly need to tell you that."

"Are you sure about the closure?"

"Certainly. He'd do it tomorrow if he could."

"But why? I've done Stoppard here, Tennessee Williams—always played to good houses. It doesn't make sense."

"It makes admirable financial sense, I'm afraid, and if you think in figures, as Hammersmith does, there's no riposte to simple arithmetic. The Elysium's getting old. We're *all* getting old. We creak. We feel our age in our joints: our instinct is to lie down and be gone away."

Gone away: the voice became melodramatically thin, a whisper of longing.

"How do you know about this?"

"I was, for many years, a trustee of the theatre, and since my retirement I've made it my business to—what's the phrase?—keep my ear to the ground. It's difficult, in this day and age, to evoke the triumph this stage has seen…"

His voice trailed away, in a reverie. It seemed true, not an effect.

Then, business-like once more: "This theatre is about to die, Mr. Calloway. You will be present at the last rites, through no fault of your own. I felt you ought to be… warned."

"Thank you. I appreciate that. Tell me, were you ever an actor yourself?"

"What makes you think that?"

"The voice."

"Too rhetorical by half, I know. My curse, I'm afraid. I can scarcely ask for a cup of coffee without sounding like Lear in the storm."

He laughed, heartily, at his own expense. Calloway began to warm to the fellow. Maybe he was a little archaic-looking, perhaps even slightly absurd, but there was a full-bloodedness about his manner that caught Calloway's imagination. Lichfield wasn't apologetic about his love of theatre, like so many in the profession, people who trod the boards as a second-best, their souls sold to the movies.

"I have, I will confess, dabbled in the craft a little," Lichfield confided, "but I just don't have the stamina for it, I'm afraid. Now my wife—"

Wife? Calloway was surprised Lichfield had a heterosexual bone in his body.

"—My wife Constantia has played here on a number of occasions, and I may say very successfully. Before the war of course."

"It's a pity to close the place."

"Indeed. But there are no last-act miracles to be performed, I'm afraid. The Elysium will be rubble in six weeks' time, and there's an end to it. I just wanted you to know that interests other than the crassly commercial are watching over this closing production. Think of us as guardian angels. We wish you well, Terence, we all wish you well."

It was a genuine sentiment, simply stated. Calloway was touched by this man's concern, and a little chastened by it. It put his own stepping-stone ambitions in an unflattering perspective. Lichfield went on: "We care to see this theatre end its days in suitable style, then die a good death."

"Damn shame."

"Too late for regrets by a long chalk. We should never have given up Dionysus for Apollo."

"What?"

"Sold ourselves to the accountants, to legitimacy, to the likes of Mr. Hammersmith, whose soul, if he has one, must be the size of my fingernail, and grey as a louse's back. We should have had the courage of our depictions, I think. Served poetry and lived under the stars."

Calloway didn't quite follow the allusions, but he got the general drift, and respected the viewpoint.

Off stage left, Diane's voice cut the solemn atmosphere like a plastic knife.

"Terry? Are you there?"

The spell was broken: Calloway hadn't been aware how hypnotic Lichfield's presence was until that other voice came between them. Listening to him was like being rocked in familiar arms. Lichfield stepped to the edge of the stage, lowering his voice to a conspiratorial rasp.

"One last thing, Terence—"

"Yes?"

"Your Viola. She lacks, if you'll forgive my pointing it out, the special qualities required for the role."

Calloway hung fire.

"I know," Lichfield continued, "personal loyalties prevent honesty in these matters."

"No," Calloway replied, "you're right. But she's popular."

"So was bear-baiting, Terence."

A luminous smile spread beneath the brim, hanging in the shadow like the grin of the Cheshire Cat.

"I'm only joking," said Lichfield, his rasp a chuckle now. "Bears can be charming."

"Terry, there you are."

Diane appeared, over-dressed as usual, from behind the tabs. There was surely an embarrassing confrontation in the air. But Lichfield was walking away down the false perspective of the hedges towards the backdrop.

"Here I am," said Terry.

"Who are you talking to?"

But Lichfield had exited, as smoothly and as quietly as he had entered. Diane hadn't even seen him go.

"Oh, just an angel," said Calloway.

The first Dress Rehearsal wasn't, all things considered, as bad as Calloway had anticipated: it was immeasurably worse. Cues were lost, props mislaid, entrances missed; the comic business seemed ill-contrived and laborious; the performances either hopelessly overwrought or trifling. This was a *Twelfth Night* that seemed to last a year. Halfway through the third act Calloway glanced at his watch, and realized an uncut performance of *Macbeth* (with interval) would now be over.

He sat in the stalls with his head buried in his hands, contemplating the work that he still had to do if he was to bring this production up to scratch. Not for the first time on this show he felt helpless in the face of the casting problems. Cues could be tightened, props rehearsed with, entrances practised until they were engraved on the memory. But a bad actor is a bad actor is a bad actor. He could labour till doomsday neatening and sharpening, but he could not make a silk purse of the sow's ear that was Diane Duvall.

With all the skill of an acrobat she contrived to skirt every significance, to ignore every opportunity to move the audience, to avoid every nuance the playwright would insist on putting in her way. It was a performance heroic in its ineptitude, reducing the delicate characterization Calloway had been at pains to create to a single-note whine. This Viola was soap-opera pap, less human than the hedges, and about as green.

The critics would slaughter her.

Worse than that, Lichfield would be disappointed. To his considerable surprise the impact of Lichfield's appearance hadn't dwindled; Calloway couldn't forget his actorly projection, his posing, his rhetoric. It had moved him more deeply than he was prepared to admit, and the thought of this *Twelfth Night*, with this Viola, becoming the swan-song of Lichfield's beloved Elysium perturbed and embarrassed him. It seemed somehow ungrateful.

He'd been warned often enough about a director's burdens, long before he became seriously embroiled in the profession. His dear departed guru at the Actors' Centre, Wellbeloved (he of the glass eye), had told Calloway from the beginning:

"A director is the loneliest creature on God's earth. He knows what's good and bad in a show, or he should if he's worth his salt, and he has to carry that information around with him and keep smiling."

It hadn't seemed so difficult at the time.

"This job isn't about succeeding," Wellbeloved used to say, "it's about learning not to fall on your sodding face."

Good advice as it turned out. He could still see Wellbeloved handing out that wisdom on a plate, his bald head shiny, his living eye glittering with cynical delight. No man on earth, Calloway had thought, loved theatre with more passion than Wellbeloved, and surely no man could have been more scathing about its pretensions.

It was almost one in the morning by the time they'd finished the wretched run-through, gone through the notes, and separated, glum and mutually resentful, into the night. Calloway wanted none of their company tonight: no late drinking in one or others' digs, no mutual ego-massage. He had a cloud of gloom all to himself, and neither wine, women nor song would disperse it. He could barely bring himself to look Diane in the face. His notes to her, broadcast in front of the rest of the cast, had been acidic. Not that it would do much good.

In the foyer, he met Tallulah, still spry though it was long after an old lady's bedtime.

"Are you locking up tonight?" he asked her, more for something to say than because he was actually curious.

"I always lock up," she said. She was well over seventy: too old for her job in the box office, and too tenacious to be easily removed. But then that was all academic now, wasn't it? He wondered what her response would be when she heard the news of the closure. It would probably break her brittle heart. Hadn't Hammersmith once told him Tallulah had been at the theatre since she was a girl of fifteen?

"Well, goodnight Tallulah."

She gave him a tiny nod, as always. Then she reached out and took Calloway's arm.

"Yes?"

"Mr. Lichfield…" she began.

"What about Mr. Lichfield?"

"He didn't like the rehearsal."

"He was in tonight?"

"Oh yes," she replied, as though Calloway was an imbecile for thinking otherwise, "of course he was in."

"I didn't see him."

"Well… no matter. He wasn't very pleased."

Calloway tried to sound indifferent.

"It can't be helped."

"Your show is very close to his heart."

"I realize that," said Calloway, avoiding Tallulah's accusing looks. He had quite enough to keep him awake tonight, without her disappointed tones ringing in his ears.

He loosed his arm, and made for the door. Tallulah made no attempt to stop him. She just said: "You should have seen Constantia."

Constantia? Where had he heard that name? Of course, Lichfield's wife.

"She was a wonderful Viola."

He was too tired for this mooning over dead actresses; she was dead wasn't she? He had said she was dead, hadn't he?

"Wonderful," said Tallulah again.

"Goodnight, Tallulah. I'll see you tomorrow."

The old crone didn't answer. If she was offended by his brusque manner, then so be it. He left her to her complaints and faced the street.

It was late November, and chilly. No balm in the night-air, just the smell of tar from a freshly laid road, and grit in the wind. Calloway pulled his jacket collar up around the back of his neck, and hurried off to the questionable refuge of Murphy's Bed and Breakfast.

In the foyer Tallulah turned her back on the cold and dark of the outside world, and shuffled back into the temple of dreams. It smelt so weary now: stale with use and age, like her own body. It was time to let natural processes take their toll; there was no point in letting things run beyond their allotted span. That was as true of buildings as of people. But the Elysium had to die as it had lived, in glory.

Respectfully, she drew back the red curtains that covered the portraits in the corridor that led from foyer to stalls. Barrymore, Irving: great names and great actors. Stained and faded pictures perhaps, but the memories were as sharp and as refreshing as spring water. And in pride of place, the last of the line to be unveiled, a portrait of Constantia Lichfield. A face of transcendent beauty; a bone structure to make an anatomist weep.

She had been far too young for Lichfield of course, and that had been part of the tragedy of it. Lichfield the Svengali, a man twice her age, had been capable of giving his brilliant beauty everything she desired; fame, money, companionship. Everything but the gift she most required: life itself.

She'd died before she was yet twenty, a cancer in the breast. Taken so suddenly it was still difficult to believe she'd gone.

Tears brimmed in Tallulah's eyes as she remembered that lost and wasted genius. So many parts Constantia would have illuminated had she been spared. Cleopatra, Hedda, Rosalind, Electra…

But it wasn't to be. She'd gone, extinguished like a candle in a hurricane, and for those who were left behind life was a slow and joyless march through a cold land. There were mornings now, stirring to another dawn, when she would turn over and pray to die in her sleep.

The tears were quite blinding her now, she was awash. And oh dear, there was somebody behind her, probably Mr. Calloway back for something, and here was she, sobbing fit to burst, behaving like the silly old woman she knew he thought her to be. A young man like him, what did he understand about the pain of the years, the deep ache of irretrievable loss? That wouldn't come to him for a while yet. Sooner than he thought, but a while nevertheless.

"Tallie," somebody said.

She knew who it was. Richard Walden Lichfield. She turned round and he was standing no more than six feet from her, as fine a figure of a man as ever she remembered him to be. He must be twenty years older than she was, but age didn't seem to bow him. She felt ashamed of her tears.

"Tallie," he said kindly, "I know it's a little late, but I felt you'd surely want to say hello."

"Hello?"

The tears were clearing, and now she saw Lichfield's companion, standing a respectful foot or two behind him, partially obscured. The figure stepped out of Lichfield's shadow and there was a luminous, fine-boned beauty Tallulah recognized as easily as her own reflection. Time broke in pieces, and reason deserted the world. Longed-for faces were suddenly back to fill the empty nights, and offer fresh hope to a life grown weary. Why should she argue with the evidence of her eyes?

It was Constantia, the radiant Constantia, who was looping her arm through Lichfield's and nodding gravely at Tallulah in greeting.

Dear, dead Constantia.

The rehearsal was called for nine-thirty the following morning. Diane Duvall made an entrance her customary half hour late. She looked as though she hadn't slept all night.

"Sorry I'm late," she said, her open vowels oozing down the aisle towards the stage.

Calloway was in no mood for foot-kissing.

"We've got an opening tomorrow," he snapped, "and everybody's been kept waiting by you."

"Oh really?" she fluttered, trying to be devastating. It was too early in the morning, and the effect fell on stony ground.

"OK, we're going from the top," Calloway announced, "and everybody please have your copies and a pen. I've got a list of cuts here and I want them rehearsed in by lunchtime. Ryan, have you got the prompt copy?"

There was a hurried exchange with the ASM and an apologetic negative from Ryan.

"Well get it. And I don't want any complaints from anyone, it's too late in the day. Last night's run was a wake, not a performance. The cues took forever; the business was ragged. I'm going to cut, and it's not going to be very palatable."

It wasn't. The complaints came, warning or no, the arguments, the compromises, the sour faces and muttered insults. Calloway would have rather been hanging by his toes from a trapeze than maneuvering fourteen highly strung people through a play two-thirds of them scarcely understood, and the other third couldn't give a monkey's about. It was nerve-wracking.

It was made worse because all the time he had the prickly sense of being watched, though the auditorium was empty from Gods to front stalls. Maybe Lichfield had a spyhole somewhere, he thought, then condemned the idea as the first signs of budding paranoia.

At last, lunch.

Calloway knew where he'd find Diane, and he was prepared for the scene he had to play with her. Accusations, tears, reassurance, tears again, reconciliation. Standard format.

He knocked on the Star's door.

"Who is it?"

Was she crying already, or talking through a glass of something comforting?

"It's me."

"Oh."

"Can I come in?"

"Yes."

She had a bottle of vodka, good vodka, and a glass. No tears as yet.

"I'm useless, aren't I?" she said, almost as soon as he'd closed the door. Her eyes begged for contradiction.

"Don't be silly," he hedged.

"I could never get the hang of Shakespeare," she pouted, as though it were the Bard's fault. "All those bloody words." The squall was on the horizon, he could see it mustering.

"It's all right," he lied, putting his arm around her. "You just need a little time."

Her face clouded.

"We open tomorrow," she said flatly. The point was difficult to refute.

"They'll tear me apart, won't they?"

He wanted to say no, but his tongue had a fit of honesty.

"Yes. Unless—"

"I'll never work again, will I? Harry talked me into this, that damn half-witted Jew: good for my reputation, he said. Bound to give me a bit more clout, he said. What does he know? Takes his ten bloody per cent and leaves me holding the baby. I'm the one who looks the damn fool aren't I?"

At the thought of looking a fool, the storm broke. No light shower this: it was a cloudburst or nothing. He did what he could, but it was difficult. She was sobbing so loudly his pearls of wisdom were drowned out. So he kissed her a little, as any decent director was bound to do, and (miracle upon miracle) that seemed to do the trick. He applied the technique with a little more gusto, his hands straying to her breasts, ferreting under her blouse for her nipples and teasing them between thumb and forefinger.

It worked wonders. There were hints of sun between the clouds now; she sniffed and unbuckled his belt, letting his heat dry out the last of the rain. His fingers were finding the lacy edge of her panties, and she was sighing as he investigated her, gently but not too gently, insistent but never too insistent. Somewhere along the line she knocked over the vodka bottle but neither of them cared to stop and right it, so it sloshed on to the floor off the edge of the table, counterpointing her instructions, his gasps.

Then the bloody door opened, and a draught blew up between them, cooling the point at issue.

Calloway almost turned round, then realized he was unbuckled, and stared instead into the mirror behind Diane to see the intruder's face. It was Lichfield. He was looking straight at Calloway, his face impassive.

"I'm sorry, I should have knocked."

His voice was as smooth as whipped cream, betraying nary a tremor of embarrassment. Calloway wedged himself away, buckled up his belt and turned to Lichfield, silently cursing his burning cheeks.

"Yes… it would have been polite," he said.

"Again, my apologies. I wanted a word with—" his eyes, so deep-set they were unfathomable, were on Diane "—your star," he said.

Calloway could practically feel Diane's ego expand at the word. The approach confounded him: had Lichfield undergone a volte-face? Was he coming here, the repentant admirer, to kneel at the feet of greatness?

"I would appreciate a word with the lady in private, if that were possible," the mellow voice went on.

"Well, we were just—"

"Of course," Diane interrupted. "Just allow me a moment, would you?"

She was immediately on top of the situation, tears forgotten.

"I'll be just outside," said Lichfield, already taking his leave.

Before he had closed the door behind him Diane was in front of the mirror, tissue-wrapped finger skirting her eye to divert a rivulet of mascara.

"Well," she was cooing, "how lovely to have a well-wisher. Do you know who he is?"

"His name's Lichfield," Calloway told her. "He used to be a trustee of the theatre."

"Maybe he wants to offer me something."

"I doubt it."

"Oh don't be such a drag, Terence," she snarled. "You just can't bear to have anyone else get any attention, can you?"

"My mistake."

She peered at her eyes.

"How do I look?" she asked.

"Fine."

"I'm sorry about before."

"Before?"

"You know."

"Oh… yes."

"I'll see you in the pub, eh?"

He was summarily dismissed apparently, his function as lover or confidant no longer required.

In the chilly corridor outside the dressing room Lichfield was waiting patiently. Though the lights were better here than on the ill-lit stage, and he was closer now than he'd been the night before, Calloway could still not quite make out the face under the wide brim. There was something—what was the idea buzzing in his head?—something artificial about Lichfield's features. The flesh of his face didn't move as interlocking system of muscle and tendon, it was too stiff, too pink, almost like scar-tissue.

"She's not quite ready," Calloway told him.

"She's a lovely woman," Lichfield purred.

"Yes."

"I don't blame you…"

"Um."

"She's no actress though."

"You're not going to interfere are you, Lichfield? I won't let you."

"Perish the thought."

The voyeuristic pleasure Lichfield had plainly taken in his embarrassment made Calloway less respectful than he'd been.

"I won't have you upsetting her—"

"My interests are your interests, Terence. All I want to do is see this production prosper, believe me. Am I likely, under those circumstances, to alarm your Leading Lady? I'll be as meek as a lamb, Terence."

"Whatever you are," came the testy reply, "you're no lamb."

The smile appeared again on Lichfield's face, the tissue round his mouth barely stretching to accommodate his expression.

Calloway retired to the pub with that predatory sickle of teeth fixed in his mind, anxious for no reason he could focus upon.

In the mirrored cell of her dressing-room Diane Duvall was just about ready to play her scene.

"You may come in now, Mr. Lichfield," she announced.

He was in the doorway before the last syllable of his name had died on her lips.

"Miss Duvall," he bowed slightly in deference to her. She smiled; so courteous. "Will you please forgive my blundering in earlier on?"

She looked coy; it always melted men.

"Mr. Calloway—" she began.

"A very insistent young man, I think."

"Yes."

"Not above pressing his attentions on his Leading Lady, perhaps?"

She frowned a little, a dancing pucker where the plucked arches of her brows converged.

"I'm afraid so."

"Most unprofessional of him," Lichfield said. "But forgive me—an understandable ardor."

She moved upstage of him, towards the lights of her mirror, and turned, knowing they would back-light her hair more flatteringly.

"Well, Mr. Lichfield, what can I do for you?"

"This is frankly a delicate matter," said Lichfield. "The bitter fact is—how shall I put this?—your talents are not ideally suited to this production. Your style lacks delicacy."

There was a silence for two beats. She sniffed, thought about the inference of the remark, and then moved out of centre-stage towards the door. She didn't like the way this scene had begun. She was expecting an admirer, and instead she had a critic on her hands.

"Get out!" she said, her voice like slate.

"Miss Duvall—"

"You heard me."

"You're not comfortable as Viola, are you?" Lichfield continued, as though the star had said nothing.

"None of your bloody business," she spat back.

"But it is. I saw the rehearsals. You were bland, unpersuasive. The comedy is flat, the reunion scene—it should break our hearts—is leaden."

"I don't need your opinion, thank you."

"You have no style—"

"Piss off."

"No presence and no style. I'm sure on the television you are radiance itself, but the stage requires a special truth, a soulfulness you, frankly, lack."

The scene was hotting up. She wanted to hit him, but she couldn't find the proper motivation. She couldn't take this faded poseur seriously. He was more musical comedy than melodrama, with his neat grey gloves, and his neat grey cravat. Stupid, waspish queen, what did he know about acting?

"Get out before I call the Stage Manager," she said, but he stepped between her and the door.

A rape scene? Was that what they were playing? Had he got the hots for her? God forbid.

"My wife," he was saying, "has played Viola—"

"Good for her."

"—and she feels she could breathe a little more life into the role than you."

"We open tomorrow," she found herself replying, as though defending her presence. Why the hell was she trying to reason with him; barging in here and making these terrible remarks. Maybe because she was just a little afraid. His breath, close to her now, smelt of expensive chocolate.

"She knows the role by heart."

"The part's mine. And I'm doing it. I'm doing it even if I'm the worst Viola in theatrical history, all right?"

She was trying to keep her composure, but it was difficult. Something about him made her nervous. It wasn't violence she feared from him: but she feared something.

"I'm afraid I have already promised the part to my wife."

"What?" she goggled at his arrogance.

"And Constantia will play the role."

She laughed at the name. Maybe this was high comedy after all. Something from Sheridan or Wilde, arch, catty stuff. But he spoke with such absolute certainty. *Constantia will play the role;* as if it was all cut and dried.

"I'm not discussing this any longer, Buster, so if your wife wants to play Viola she'll have to do it in the fucking street. All right?"

"She opens tomorrow."

"Are you deaf, or stupid, or both?"

Control, an inner voice told her, you're overplaying, losing your grip on the scene. Whatever scene this is.

He stepped towards her, and the mirror lights caught the face beneath the brim full on. She hadn't looked carefully enough when he first made his appearance: now she saw the deeply etched lines, the gougings around his eyes and his mouth. It wasn't flesh, she was sure of it. He was wearing latex appliances, and they were badly glued in place. Her hand all but twitched with the desire to snatch at it and uncover his real face.

Of course. That was it. The scene she was playing: the Unmasking.

"Let's see what you look like," she said, and her hand was at his cheek before he could stop her, his smile spreading wider as she attacked. This is what he wants, she thought, but it was too late for regrets or apologies. Her fingertips had found the line of the mask at the edge of his eye-socket, and curled round to take a better hold. She yanked.

The thin veil of latex came away, and his true physiognomy was exposed for the world to see. Diane tried to back away, but his hand was in her hair. All she could do was look up into that all-but fleshless face. A few withered strands of muscle curled here and there, and a hint of a beard hung from a leathery flap at his throat, but all living tissue had long since decayed. Most of his face was simply bone: stained and worn.

"I was not," said the skull, "embalmed. Unlike Constantia."

The explanation escaped Diane. She made no sound of protest, which the scene would surely have justified. All she could summon was a whimper as his hand-hold tightened, and he hauled her head back.

"We must make a choice, sooner or later," said Lichfield, his breath smelling less like chocolate than profound putrescence, "between serving ourselves and serving our art."

She didn't quite understand.

"The dead must choose more carefully than the living. We cannot waste our breath, if you'll excuse the phrase, on less than the purest delights. You don't want art, I think. Do you?"

She shook her head, hoping to God that was the expected response.

"You want the life of the body, not the life of the imagination. And you may have it."

"Thank... you."

"If you want it enough, you may have it."

Suddenly his hand, which had been pulling on her hair so painfully, was cupped behind her head, and bringing her lips up to meet his. She would have screamed then, as his rotting mouth fastened itself on to hers, but his greeting was so insistent it quite took her breath away.

Ryan found Diane on the floor of her dressing-room a few minutes before two. It was difficult to work out what had happened. There was no sign of a wound of any kind on her head or body, nor was she quite dead. She seemed to be in a coma of some kind. She had perhaps slipped, and struck her head as she fell. Whatever the cause, she was out for the count.

They were hours away from a Final Dress Rehearsal and Viola was in an ambulance, being taken into Intensive Care.

"The sooner they knock this place down, the better," said Hammersmith. He'd been drinking during office hours, something Calloway had never seen him do before. The whisky bottle stood on his desk beside a half-full glass. There were glass-marks ringing his accounts, and his hand had a bad dose of the shakes.

"What's the news from the hospital?"

"She's a beautiful woman," he said, staring at the glass. Calloway could have sworn he was on the verge of tears.

"Hammersmith? How is she?"

"She's in a coma. But her condition is stable."

"That's something, I suppose."

Hammersmith stared up at Calloway, his erupting brows knitted in anger.

"You runt," he said, "you were screwing her, weren't you? Fancy yourself like that, don't you? Well, let me tell you something, Diane Duvall is worth a dozen of you. A dozen!"

"Is that why you let this last production go on, Hammersmith? Because you'd seen her, and you wanted to get your hot little hands on her?"

"You wouldn't understand. You've got your brain in your pants." He seemed genuinely offended by the interpretation Calloway had put on his admiration for Miss Duvall.

"All right, have it your way. We still have no Viola."

"That's why I'm canceling," said Hammersmith, slowing down to savor the moment.

It had to come. Without Diane Duvall, there would be no *Twelfth Night*; and maybe it was better that way.

A knock on the door.

"Who the fuck's that?" said Hammersmith softly. "Come."

It was Lichfield. Calloway was almost glad to see that strange, scarred face. Though he had a lot of questions to ask of Lichfield, about the state he'd left Diane in, about their conversation together, it wasn't an interview he was willing to conduct in front of Hammersmith. Besides, any half-formed accusations he might have had were countered by the man's presence here. If Lichfield had attempted violence on Diane, for whatever reason, was it likely that he would come back so soon, so smilingly?

"Who are you?" Hammersmith demanded.

"Richard Walden Lichfield."

"I'm none the wiser."

"I used to be a trustee of the Elysium."

"Oh."

"I make it my business—"

"What do you want?" Hammersmith broke in, irritated by Lichfield's poise.

"I hear the production is in jeopardy," Lichfield replied, unruffled.

"No jeopardy," said Hammersmith, allowing himself a twitch at the corner of his mouth. "No jeopardy at all, because there's no show. It's been cancelled."

"Oh?" Lichfield looked at Calloway.

"Is this with your consent?" he asked.

"He has no say in the matter; I have sole right of cancellation if circumstances dictate it; it's in his contract. The theatre is closed as of today: it will not reopen."

"Yes it will," said Lichfield.

"What?" Hammersmith stood up behind his desk, and Calloway realized he'd never seen the man standing before. He was very short.

"We will play *Twelfth Night* as advertised," Lichfield purred. "My wife has kindly agreed to understudy the part of Viola in place of Miss Duvall."

Hammersmith laughed, a coarse, butcher's laugh. It died on his lips however, as the office was suffused with lavender, and Constantia Lichfield made her entrance, shimmering in silk and fur. She looked as perfect as the day she died: even Hammersmith held his breath and his silence at the sight of her.

"Our new Viola," Lichfield announced.

After a moment Hammersmith found his voice. "This woman can't step in at half a day's notice."

"Why not?" said Calloway, not taking his eyes off the woman. Lichfield was a lucky man; Constantia was an extraordinary beauty. He scarcely dared draw breath in her presence for fear she'd vanish.

Then she spoke. The lines were from Act V, Scene I:
"If nothing lets to make us happy both
But this my masculine usurp'd attire,
Do not embrace me till each circumstance
Of place, time, fortune, do cohere and jump
That I am Viola."
The voice was light and musical, but it seemed to resound in her body, filling each phrase with an undercurrent of suppressed passion.

And that face. It was wonderfully alive, the features playing the story of her speech with delicate economy.

She was enchanting.

"I'm sorry," said Hammersmith, "but there are rules and regulations about this sort of thing. Is she Equity?"

"No," said Lichfield.

"Well you see, it's impossible. The union strictly precludes this kind of thing. They'd flay us alive."

"What's it to you, Hammersmith?" said Calloway. "What the fuck do you care? You'll never need set foot in a theatre again once this place is demolished."

"My wife has watched the rehearsals. She is word perfect."

"It could be magic," said Calloway, his enthusiasm firing up with every moment he looked at Constantia.

"You're risking the Union, Calloway," Hammersmith chided.

"I'll take that risk."

"As you say, it's nothing to me. But if a little bird was to tell them, you'd have egg on your face."

"Hammersmith: give her a chance. Give all of us a chance. If Equity blacks me, that's my look-out." Hammersmith sat down again.

"Nobody'll come, you know that, don't you? Diane Duvall was a star; they would have sat through your turgid production to see her, Calloway. But an unknown…? Well, it's your funeral. Go ahead and do it, I wash my hands of the whole thing. It's on your head, Calloway, remember that. I hope they flay you for it."

"Thank you," said Lichfield. "Most kind."

Hammersmith began to rearrange his desk, to give more prominence to the bottle and the glass. The interview was over: he wasn't interested in these butterflies any longer.

"Go away," he said. "Just go away."

"I have one or two requests to make," Lichfield told Calloway as they left the office. "Alterations to the production which would enhance my wife's performance."

"What are they?"

"For Constantia's comfort, I would ask that the lighting levels be taken down substantially. She's simply not accustomed to performing under such hot, bright lights."

"Very well."

"I'd also request that we install a row of footlights."

"Footlights?"

"An odd requirement, I realize, but she feels much happier with foot-lights."

"They tend to dazzle the actors," said Calloway. "It becomes difficult to see the audience."

"Nevertheless... I have to stipulate their installation."

"OK."

"Thirdly—I would ask that all scenes involving kissing, embracing or other-wise touching Constantia be re-directed to remove every instance of physical contact whatsoever."

"Everything?"

"Everything."

"For God's sake why?"

"My wife needs no business to dramatize the working of the heart, Ter-ence."

That curious intonation on the word "heart." Working of the *heart*.

Calloway caught Constantia's eye for the merest of moments. It was like being blessed.

"Shall we introduce our new Viola to the company?" Lichfield suggested.

"Why not?"

The trio went into the theatre.

The re-arranging of the blocking and the business to exclude any physical contact was simple. And though the rest of the cast were initially wary of their new colleague, her unaffected manner and her natural grace soon had them at her feet. Besides, her presence meant that the show would go on.

At six, Calloway called a break, announcing that they'd begin the Dress at eight, and telling them to go out and enjoy themselves for an hour or so. The company went their ways, buzzing with a new-found enthusiasm for the pro-duction. What had looked like a shambles half a day earlier now seemed to be shaping up quite well. There were a thousand things to be sniped at, of course: technical shortcomings, costumes that fitted badly, directorial foibles. All par for the course. In fact, the actors were happier than they'd been in a good while. Even Ed Cunningham was not above passing a compliment or two.

Lichfield found Tallulah in the Green Room, tidying.

"Tonight..."

"Yes, sir."

"You must not be afraid."

"I'm not afraid," Tallulah replied. "What a thought. As if—"

"There may be some pain, which I regret. For you, indeed for all of us."

"I understand."

"Of course you do. You love the theatre as I love it: you know the paradox of this profession. To play life... ah, Tallulah, to play life... what a curious thing it is. Sometimes I wonder, you know, how long I can keep up the illusion."

"It's a wonderful performance," she said.

"Do you think so? Do you really think so?" He was encouraged by her favorable review. It was so galling, to have to pretend all the time; to fake the flesh, the breath, the look of life. Grateful for Tallulah's opinion, he reached for her.

"Would you like to die, Tallulah?"

"Does it hurt?"

"Scarcely at all."

"It would make me very happy."

"And so it should."

His mouth covered her mouth, and she was dead in less than a minute, conceding happily to his inquiring tongue. He laid her out on the threadbare couch and locked the door of the Green Room with her own key. She'd cool easily in the chill of the room, and be up and about again by the time the audience arrived.

At six-fifteen Diane Duvall got out of a taxi at the front of the Elysium. It was well dark, a windy November night, but she felt fine; nothing could depress tonight. Not the dark, not the cold.

Unseen, she made her way past the posters that bore her face and name, and through the empty auditorium to her dressing-room. There, smoking his way through a pack of cigarettes, she found the object of her affection.

"Terry."

She posed in the doorway for a moment, letting the fact of her reappearance sink in. He went quite white at the sight of her, so she pouted a little. It wasn't easy to pout. There was a stiffness in the muscles of her face but she carried off the effect to her satisfaction.

Calloway was lost for words. Diane looked ill, no two ways about it, and if she'd left the hospital to take up her part in the Dress Rehearsal he was going to have to convince her otherwise. She was wearing no make-up, and her ash-blonde hair needed a wash.

"What are you doing here?" he asked, as she closed the door behind her.

"Unfinished business," she said.

"Listen... I've got something to tell you..."

God, this was going to be messy. "We've found a replacement, in the show." She looked at him blankly. He hurried on, tripping over his own words, "We thought you were out of commission, I mean, not permanently, but, you know, for the opening at least..."

"Don't worry," she said.

His jaw dropped a little.

"Don't worry?"

"What's it to me?"

"You said you came back to finish—"

He stopped. She was unbuttoning the top of her dress. She's not serious, he thought, she can't be serious. Sex? Now?

"I've done a lot of thinking in the last few hours," she said as she shimmied the crumpled dress over her hips, let it fall, and stepped out of it. She was wearing a white bra, which she tried, unsuccessfully, to unhook. "I've decided I don't care about the theatre. Help me, will you?"

She turned round and presented her back to him. Automatically he unhooked the bra, not really analyzing whether he wanted this or not. It seemed to be a *fait accompli*. She'd come back to finish what they'd been interrupted doing, simple as that. And despite the bizarre noises she was making in the back of her throat, and the glassy look in her eyes, she was still an attractive woman. She turned again, and Calloway stared at the fullness of her breasts, paler than he'd remembered them, but lovely. His trousers were becoming uncomfortably tight, and her performance was only worsening his situation, the way she was grinding her hips like the rawest of Soho strippers, running her hands between her legs.

"Don't worry about me," she said. "I've made up my mind. All I really want…"

She put her hands, so recently at her groin, on his face. They were icy cold.

"All I really want is you. I can't have sex *and* the stage… There comes a time in everyone's life when decisions have to be made."

She licked her lips. There was no film of moisture left on her mouth when her tongue had passed over it.

"The accident made me think, made me analyze what it is I really care about. And frankly—" She was unbuckling his belt. "—I don't give a shit—"

Now the zip.

"—about this, or any other fucking play."

His trousers fell down.

"—I'll show you what I care about."

She reached into his briefs, and clasped him. Her cold hand somehow made the touch sexier. He laughed, closing his eyes as she pulled his briefs down to the middle of his thigh and knelt at his feet.

She was as expert as ever, her throat open like a drain. Her mouth was somewhat drier than usual, her tongue scouring him, but the sensations drove him wild. It was so good, he scarcely noticed the ease with which she devoured him, taking him deeper than she'd ever managed previously, using every trick she knew to goad him higher and higher. Slow and deep, then picking up speed until he almost came, then slowing again until the need passed. He was completely at her mercy.

He opened his eyes to watch her at work. She was skewering herself upon him, face in rapture.

"God," he gasped, "that is *so* good. Oh yes, oh yes."

Her face didn't even flicker in response to his words, she just continued to work at him soundlessly. She wasn't making her usual noises, the small grunts of satisfaction, the heavy breathing through the nose. She just ate his flesh in absolute silence.

He held his breath a moment, while an idea was born in his belly. The bobbing head bobbed on, eyes closed, lips clamped around his member, utterly engrossed. Half a minute passed; a minute; a minute and a half. And now his belly was full of terrors.

She wasn't breathing. She was giving this matchless blow-job because she wasn't stopping, even for a moment, to inhale or exhale.

Calloway felt his body go rigid, while his erection wilted in her throat. She didn't falter in her labor; the relentless pumping continued at his groin even as his mind formed the unthinkable thought:

She's dead.

She has me in her mouth, in her cold mouth, and she's dead. That's why she'd come back, got up off her mortuary slab and come back. She was eager to finish what she'd started, no longer caring about the play, or her usurper. It was this act she valued, this act alone. She'd chosen to perform it for eternity.

Calloway could do nothing with the realization but stare down like a damn fool while this corpse gave him head.

Then it seemed she sensed his horror. She opened her eyes and looked up at him. How could he ever have mistaken that dead stare for life? Gently, she withdrew his shrunken manhood from between her lips.

"What is it?" she asked, her fluting voice still affecting life.

"You… you're not… breathing."

Her face fell. She let him go.

"Oh darling," she said, letting all pretence to life disappear, "I'm not so good at playing the part, am I?"

Her voice was a ghost's voice: thin, forlorn. Her skin, which he had thought so flatteringly pale was, on second view, a waxen white.

"You are dead?" he said.

"I'm afraid so. Two hours ago: in my sleep. But I had to come, Terry; so much unfinished business. I made my choice. You should be flattered. You are flattered, aren't you?"

She stood up and reached into her handbag, which she'd left beside the mirror. Calloway looked at the door, trying to make his limbs work, but they were inert. Besides, he had his trousers round his ankles. Two steps and he'd fall flat on his face.

She turned back on him, with something silver and sharp in her hand. Try as he might, he couldn't get a focus on it. But whatever it was, she meant it for him.

Since the building of the new Crematorium in 1934, one humiliation had come after another for the cemetery. The tombs had been raided for lead coffin-linings, the stones overturned and smashed; it was fouled by dogs and graffiti. Very few mourners now came to tend the graves. The generations had dwindled, and the small number of people who might still have had a loved one buried there were too infirm to risk the throttled walkways, or too tender to bear looking at such vandalism.

It had not always been so. There were illustrious and influential families interred behind the marble facades of the Victorian mausoleums. Founder fathers, local industrialists and dignitaries, any and all who had done the town proud by their efforts. The body of the actress Constantia Lichfield had been buried here ("Until the Day Break and the Shadows Flee Away"), though her grave was almost unique in the attention some secret admirer still paid to it.

Nobody was watching that night, it was too bitter for lovers. Nobody saw Charlotte Hancock open the door of her sepulchre, with the beating wings of pigeons applauding her vigour as she shambled out to meet the moon. Her husband Gerard was with her, he less fresh than she, having been dead thirteen years longer. Joseph Jardine, *en famille,* was not far behind the Hancocks, as was Marriott Fletcher, and Anne Snell, and the Peacock Brothers; the list went on and on. In one corner, Alfred Crawshaw (Captain in the 17th Lancers) was helping his lovely wife Emma from the rot of their bed. Everywhere faces pressed at the cracks of the tomblids—was that not Kezia Reynolds with her child, who'd lived just a day, in her arms? and Martin van de Linde (the Memory of the Just is Blessed) whose wife had never been found; Rosa and Selina Goldfinch: upstanding women both; and Thomas Jerrey, and—

Too many names to mention. Too many states of decay to describe. Sufficient to say they rose: their burial finery flyborn, their faces stripped of all but the foundation of beauty. Still they came, swinging open the back gate of the cemetery and threading their way across the wasteland towards the Elysium. In the distance, the sound of traffic. Above, a jet roared in to land. One of the Peacock brothers, staring up at the winking giant as it passed over, missed his footing and fell on his face, shattering his jaw. They picked him up fondly, and escorted him on his way. There was no harm done; and what would a Resurrection be without a few laughs?

So the show went on.
"If music be the food of love, play on,
Give me excess of it; that, surfeiting,
The appetite may sicken and so die—"
Calloway could not be found at Curtain; but Ryan had instructions from Hammersmith (through the ubiquitous Mr. Lichfield) to take the show up with or without the Director.

"He'll be upstairs, in the Gods," said Lichfield. "In fact, I think I can see him from here."

"Is he smiling?" asked Eddie.

"Grinning from ear to ear."

"Then he's pissed."

The actors laughed. There was a good deal of laughter that night. The show was running smoothly, and though they couldn't see the audience over the glare of the newly installed footlights they could feel the waves of love and delight pouring out of the auditorium. The actors were coming off stage elated.

"They're all sitting in the Gods," said Eddie, "but your friends, Mr. Lichfield, do an old ham good. They're quiet of course, but such big smiles on their faces."

Act I, Scene II; and the first entrance of Constantia Lichfield as Viola was met with spontaneous applause. Such applause. Like the hollow roll of snare drums, like the brittle beating of a thousand sticks on a thousand stretched skins. Lavish, wanton applause.

And, my God, she rose to the occasion. She began the play as she meant to go on, giving her whole heart to the role, not needing physicality to communicate the depth of her feelings, but speaking the poetry with such intelligence and passion the merest flutter of her hand was worth more than a hundred grander gestures. After that first scene her every entrance was met with the same applause from the audience, followed by almost reverential silence.

Backstage, a kind of buoyant confidence had set in. The whole company sniffed the success; a success which had been snatched miraculously from the jaws of disaster.

There again! Applause! Applause!

In his office, Hammersmith dimly registered the brittle din of adulation through a haze of booze.

He was in the act of pouring his eighth drink when the door opened. He glanced up for a moment and registered that the visitor was that upstart Calloway. Come to gloat I daresay, Hammersmith thought, come to tell me how wrong I was.

"What do you want?"

The punk didn't answer. From the corner of his eye Hammersmith had an impression of a broad, bright smile on Calloway's face. Self-satisfied half-wit, coming in here when a man was in mourning.

"I suppose you've heard?"

The other grunted.

"She died," said Hammersmith, beginning to cry. "She died a few hours ago, without regaining consciousness. I haven't told the actors. Didn't seem worth it."

Calloway said nothing in reply to this news. Didn't the bastard care? Couldn't he see that this was the end of the world? The woman was dead. She'd died in the bowels of the Elysium. There'd be official enquiries made, the insurance would be examined, a post-mortem, an inquest: it would reveal too much.

He drank deeply from his glass, not bothering to look at Calloway again.

"Your career'll take a dive after this, son. It won't just be me: oh dear no."

Still Calloway kept his silence.

"Don't you care?" Hammersmith demanded.

There was silence for a moment, then Calloway responded. "I don't give a shit."

"Jumped up little stage-manager, that's all you are. That's all *any* of you fucking directors are! One good review and you're God's gift to art. Well let me set you straight about that—"

He looked at Calloway, his eyes, swimming in alcohol, having difficulty focusing. But he got there eventually.

Calloway, the dirty bugger, was naked from the waist down. He was wearing his shoes and his socks, but no trousers or briefs. His self-exposure would have been comical, but for the expression on his face. The man had gone mad: his eyes were rolling around uncontrollably, saliva and snot ran from mouth and nose, his tongue hung out like the tongue of a panting dog.

Hammersmith put his glass down on his blotting pad, and looked at the worst part. There was blood on Calloway's shirt, a trail of it which led up his neck to his left ear, from which protruded the end of Diane Duval's nail-file. It had been driven deep into Calloway's brain. The man was surely dead.

But he stood, spoke, walked.

From the theatre, there rose another round of applause, muted by distance. It wasn't a real sound somehow; it came from another world, a place where emotions ruled. It was a world Hammersmith had always felt excluded from. He'd never been much of an actor, though God knows he'd tried, and the two plays he'd penned were, he knew, execrable. Book-keeping was his forte, and he'd used it to stay as close to the stage as he could, hating his own lack of art as much as he resented that skill in others.

The applause died, and as if taking a cue from an unseen prompter, Calloway came at him. The mask he wore was neither comic nor tragic, it was blood and laughter together. Cowering, Hammersmith was cornered behind his desk. Calloway leapt on to it (he looked so ridiculous, shirt-tails and balls flip-flapping) and seized Hammersmith by the tie.

"Philistine," said Calloway, never now to know Hammersmith's heart, and broke the man's neck—snap!—while below the applause began again.

"Do not embrace me till each circumstance
Of place, time, fortune, do cohere and jump
That I am Viola."

From Constantia's mouth the lines were a revelation. It was almost as though this *Twelfth Night* were a new play, and the part of Viola had been written for Constantia Lichfield alone. The actors who shared the stage with her felt their egos shriveling in the face of such a gift.

The last act continued to its bitter-sweet conclusion, the audience as enthralled as ever to judge by their breathless attention.

The Duke spoke: "Give me thy hand;

And let me see thee in thy woman's weeds."

In the rehearsal the invitation in the line had been ignored: no-one was to touch this Viola, much less take her hand. But in the heat of the performance such taboos were forgotten. Possessed by the passion of the moment the actor reached for Constantia. She, forgetting the taboo in her turn, reached to answer his touch.

In the wings Lichfield breathed "no" under his breath, but his order wasn't heard. The Duke grasped Viola's hand in his, life and death holding court together under this painted sky.

It was a chilly hand, a hand without blood in its veins, or a blush in its skin.

But here it was as good as alive.

They were equals, the living and the dead, and nobody could find just cause to part them.

In the wings, Lichfield sighed, and allowed himself a smile. He'd feared that touch, feared it would break the spell. But Dionysus was with them tonight. All would be well; he felt it in his bones.

The act drew to a close, and Malvolio, still trumpeting his threats, even in defeat, was carted off. One by one the company exited, leaving the clown to wrap up the play.

"A great while ago the world began,

With hey, ho, the wind and the rain,

But that's all one, our play is done

And we'll strive to please you every day."

The scene darkened to blackout, and the curtain descended. From the Gods rapturous applause erupted, that same rattling, hollow applause. The company, their faces shining with the success of the Dress Rehearsal, formed behind the curtain for the bow. The curtain rose: the applause mounted.

In the wings, Calloway joined Lichfield. He was dressed now: and he'd washed the blood off his neck.

"Well, we have a brilliant success," said the skull. "It does seem a pity that this company should be dissolved so soon."

"It does," said the corpse.

The actors were shouting into the wings now, calling for Calloway to join them. They were applauding him, encouraging him to show his face.

He put a hand on Lichfield's shoulder.

"We'll go together, sir," he said.

"No, no, I couldn't."

"You must. It's your triumph as much as mine." Lichfield nodded, and they went out together to take their bows beside the company.

In the wings Tallulah was at work. She felt restored after her sleep in the Green Room. So much unpleasantness had gone, taken with her life. She no longer suffered the aches in her hip, or the creeping neuralgia in her scalp.

There was no longer the necessity to draw breath through pipes encrusted with seventy years' muck, or to rub the backs of her hands to get the circulation going; not even the need to blink. She laid the fires with a new strength, pressing the detritus of past productions into use: old backdrops, props, costuming. When she had enough combustibles heaped, she struck a match and set the flame to them. The Elysium began to burn.

Over the applause, somebody was shouting:

"Marvelous, sweethearts, marvelous."

It was Diane's voice, they all recognized it even though they couldn't quite see her. She was staggering down the centre aisle towards the stage, making quite a fool of herself.

"Silly bitch," said Eddie.

"Whoops," said Calloway.

She was at the edge of the stage now, haranguing him.

"Got all you wanted now, have you? This your new lady-love is it? Is it?"

She was trying to clamber up, her hands gripping the hot metal hoods of the footlights. Her skin began to singe: the fat was well and truly in the fire.

"For God's sake, somebody stop her," said Eddie. But she didn't seem to feel the searing of her hands; she just laughed in his face. The smell of burning flesh wafted up from the footlights. The company broke rank, triumph forgotten.

Somebody yelled: "Kill the lights!"

A beat, and then the stage lights were extinguished. Diane fell back, her hands smoking. One of the cast fainted, another ran into the wings to be sick. Somewhere behind them, they could hear the faint crackle of flames, but they had other calls on their attention.

With the footlights gone, they could see the auditorium more clearly. The stalls were empty, but the Balcony and the Gods were full to bursting with eager admirers. Every row was packed, and every available inch of aisle space thronged with audience. Somebody up there started clapping again, alone for a few moments before the wave of applause began afresh. But now few of the company took pride in it.

Even from the stage, even with exhausted and light-dazzled eyes, it was obvious that no man, woman or child in that adoring crowd was alive. They waved fine silk handkerchiefs at the players in rotted fists, some of them beat a tattoo on the seats in front of them, most just clapped, bone on bone.

Calloway smiled, bowed deeply, and received their admiration with gratitude. In all his fifteen years of work in the theatre he had never found an audience so appreciative.

Bathing in the love of their admirers, Constantia and Richard Lichfield joined hands and walked down-stage to take another bow, while the living actors retreated in horror.

They began to yell and pray, they let out howls, they ran about like discovered adulterers in a farce. But, like the farce, there was no way out of the situation.

There were bright flames tickling the roof-joists, and billows of canvas cascaded down to right and left as the flies caught fire. In front, the dead: behind, death. Smoke was beginning to thicken the air, it was impossible to see where one was going. Somebody was wearing a toga of burning canvas, and reciting screams. Someone else was wielding a fire extinguisher against the inferno. All useless: all tired business, badly managed. As the roof began to give, lethal falls of timber and girder silenced most.

In the Gods, the audience had more or less departed. They were ambling back to their graves long before the fire department appeared, their cerements and their faces lit by the glow of the fire as they glanced over their shoulders to watch the Elysium perish. It had been a fine show, and they were happy to go home, content for another while to gossip in the dark.

The fire burned through the night, despite the never less than gallant efforts of the fire department to put it out. By four in the morning the fight was given up as lost, and the conflagration allowed its head. It had done with the Elysium by dawn.

In the ruins the remains of several persons were discovered, most of the bodies in states that defied easy identification. Dental records were consulted, and one corpse was found to be that of Giles Hammersmith (Administrator), another that of Ryan Xavier (Stage Manager) and, most shockingly, a third that of Diane Duvall. "Star of *The Love Child* burned to death," read the tabloids. She was forgotten in a week.

There were no survivors. Several bodies were simply never found.

They stood at the side of the motorway, and watched the cars careering through the night. Lichfield was there of course, and Constantia, radiant as ever.

Calloway had chosen to go with them, so had Eddie, and Tallulah. Three or four others had also joined the troupe.

It was the first night of their freedom, and here they were on the open road, traveling players. The smoke alone had killed Eddie, but there were a few more serious injuries amongst their number, sustained in the fire. Burned bodies, broken limbs. But the audience they would play for in the future would forgive them their petty mutilations.

"There are lives lived for love," said Lichfield to his new company, "and lives lived for art. We happy band have chosen the latter persuasion."

"There was a ripple of applause amongst the actors.

"To you, who have never died, may I say: welcome to the world!"

Laughter: further applause.

The lights of the cars racing north along the motorway threw the company into silhouette. They looked, to all intents and purposes, like living men and women. But then wasn't that the trick of their craft? To imitate life so well the illusion was indistinguishable from the real thing? And their new public, awaiting them in mortuaries, churchyards and chapels of rest, would appreciate the skill more than most. Who better to applaud the sham of passion and pain they would perform than the dead, who had experienced such feelings, and thrown them off at last?

The dead. They needed entertainment no less than the living; and they were a sorely neglected market.

Not that this company would perform for money, they would play for the love of their art, Lichfield had made that clear from the outset. No more service would be done to Apollo.

"Now," he said, "which road shall we take, north or south?"

"North," said Eddie. "My mother's buried in Glasgow, she died before I ever played professionally. I'd like her to see me."

"North it is, then," said Lichfield. "Shall we go and find ourselves some transport?"

He led the way towards the motorway restaurant, its neon flickering fitfully, keeping the night at light's length. The colors were theatrically bright: scarlet, lime, cobalt, and a wash of white that splashed out of the windows on to the car park where they stood. The automatic doors hissed as a traveler emerged, bearing gifts of hamburgers and cake to the child in the back of his car.

"Surely some friendly driver will find a niche for us," said Lichfield.

"All of us?" said Calloway.

"A truck will do; beggars can't be too demanding," said Lichfield. "And we are beggars now: subject to the whim of our patrons."

"We can always steal a car," said Tallulah.

"No need for theft, except in extremity," Lichfield said. "Constantia and I will go ahead and find a chauffeur."

He took his wife's hand.

"Nobody refuses beauty," he said.

"What do we do if anyone asks us what we're doing here?" asked Eddie nervously. He wasn't used to this role; he needed reassurance.

Lichfield turned towards the company, his voice booming in the night:

"What do you do?" he said, "Play life, of course! And smile!"

STOCKHOLM SYNDROME

by David Tallerman

David Tallerman's stories have appeared in a variety of publications, such as *Flash Fiction Online*, *Andromeda Spaceways Inflight Magazine*, and *Pseudopod*. He's also sold work to *Aoife's Kiss*, the anthology *Barren Worlds*, and the British comic *Futurequake*. He is a graduate of York University, where he specialized in the literary history of witchcraft.

"Stockholm Syndrome" follows an unnamed protagonist who has survived the beginning of the zombie apocalypse, but at the cost of his family, his home, his whole way of life. "While he's not a bad guy, he's not really a good guy either," Tallerman says. "Stuck on his own with no one to talk to and not much to do, he has to confront that for maybe the first time in his life. He sees some uncomfortable similarities between himself and the walking corpses out in the streets, which has to be a harsh awakening for anybody."

Tallerman argues that facing a single zombie is usually just funny, but if you get a hundred of them, or a thousand, then suddenly they don't seem so funny anymore. On the other hand: "It's easy to forget the threat of a lone zombie," he says. "At least until he's chomping on your guts."

One of them, I called him Billy—he was more, what'd you call it? More *animated* than the rest. Mostly they just wander about. Occasionally they'll pick things up and then get bored and put them down and go back to wandering again. They don't make much noise. I guess they know that there're people around, for a few days at the start they bashed at the boards up over the windows and tried to push against the doors. They can't climb and they ain't got much in the way of strength, so eventually they gave that up. And after that they just shambled about, or sometimes just lay there.

It's funny how sometimes they look like people and sometimes they don't. The first ones, the ones who came up out of the ground or wherever they were, guess what you'd call the first generation—some of them are pretty normal looking. But the way they walk, that lumbering, slowly like they're taking baby-steps and watching their feet all the time, that's what makes them so different. 'Course, the other ones, the ones that the first generation got to, some of those are real messed up: bits hanging off and big messy wounds, sometimes their faces are half off. They're just like dead people who're up and walking about. They're easier to deal with I guess, even though it's pretty crazy to see them like that. But at least you know where you stand.

So anyway, I was talking about Billy. Billy, he was first generation through and through. I don't know what his story was, but when he turned up about two weeks ago he was wearing a suit, a real nice suit, he even still had a carnation in his buttonhole. I don't know, maybe they was burying him when it happened. You've got to wonder what they'd have thought, when they was burying him and he got up like that.

Anyway, he cut quite a figure when he walked up of Main Street in that suit. Well, not walked, y'know, I guess he shambled as much as the rest of them, but somehow he seemed kind of smarter than the others—more alert. And in that suit, he reminded me of my kid, when we buried him. That's why I named him Billy.

Billy made himself at home pretty quick. It didn't take him long to figure that there were just two houses with people in, mine and the place over the road. Both of us had boarded ourselves in pretty good. Actually, I shouldn't go taking the credit for that—when I got here, after my car came off the freeway a couple of miles up, I found this place pretty much like it is now. They'd got in through a window and it was still left open—a couple of them had got in and then I figure the other two must've been the ones whose house it was. Four's about as many as you could handle, up close like that—I had my old revolver still on me. I guess I was lucky though, getting them before they got me. Guess it could have easily gone the other way.

I hauled the bodies out the window and boarded it up again before the others figured out what'd gone on. All in all, I was real lucky—there was a rifle here with one of those telescopic sights, and a whole load of tins, all sorts of things. They was all set to wait it out, and then they just must have got careless. It can happen. It ain't easy to keep concentrating all the time, not with things the way they are. I've tried not to mess with their property too much—it wouldn't be decent. That gun and the food's all I really need.

But I'm getting off the subject again—this is Billy's story, it ain't mine. And the thing was, as soon as he'd walked into town like that, you could see that something was different. I guess I should have known that he meant trouble, but you get bored, with nothing to do all day and the radio and TV giving out nothing but static. I should have just shot him right then. At first, y'know, you take every shot you can get—but after a while you get to realizing that there's always gonna be more of them than you got bullets. However many bullets you got there'll always be more of them.

So, maybe that's what I was thinking when I didn't take my shot on Billy. Or maybe it was because he'd looked so much like my kid when he was walking up Main Street. Or maybe it was just that I was bored and here was something happening. I suppose it don't matter much.

Either way, you could see that he was a bit smarter, that he wasn't just gonna settle down to blundering about with the rest of them. First off, he walked all round the house across the road, and every so often he'd bang on a board or something, like he was testing the place. Then, when he got done with that, he came and did the same to mine—I could hear him scratching on that window where I'd got in. I got to say, I was impressed. You get sick of the stupid way they act, they're like dumb, lazy children, and it starts to grate on your nerves after a while. It was nice to see one of them showing a bit of initiative; even if it did look like it was gonna spell trouble.

I wasn't too worried for myself—I checked the boards every morning, and every so often I'd hammer up another couple, more for something to do than anything, 'cause like I said they'd pretty much given up on trying to get in. But I didn't know about the family across the road; I didn't know whether they were taking precautions or not. The place looked okay from the outside. Sounds kind of stupid now, but I didn't like to pry too much. I knew that there were four of them, I figured they were a husband and wife and two kids, but that was as far as I'd got. It's a wide street, I couldn't see much without the sight, and that just felt too much like—I don't know—like I was some kind of pervert. Even with everything all screwed up like this, people have got to have some right to privacy, haven't they?

There wasn't any way we could talk to each other, if the phones had been working then I could have just looked them up in the book I guess. Or maybe I could've put a sign up, but I didn't know if they'd have any way to read it. So, I just tried to leave them alone as much as I could.

Billy obviously got it into his head that they were a better bet, because after the first day he didn't bother with me too much. But I kept my eye on him, 'cause he was interesting—least he was compared with the others, and because they were everywhere, as far as you could see, they were about all there was to look at. It was the same for them, they were curious, as much as they could be—who was this, walking around like he had some kind of an agenda or something?

In the meanwhile, Billy had taken a project on himself—the second day after he walked into town, he picked himself out a particular window, round on the right-hand side of the family's house, just after where the porch ended. Even with the scope, I could barely make him out there. There was the porch, and a big old tree in the way, and I could just about see him moving around but that was it. 'Course, I could guess what he'd be up to—he must have decided that there was a weak spot, he thought maybe if he kept going at it he'd be able to get in sooner or later. I didn't give much for his chances. There was no way they wouldn't have heard him there, and if they thought there was any chance of him getting through they'd be hammering up two new boards for every one he managed to get off—least, that was what I'd of been doing.

Probably he'd get bored after a day or two, and go to sitting and wandering like the rest of them. That thought made me kind of sad, somehow. I mean

God knows it wasn't like I wanted him to succeed or nothing—I just didn't want to have to watch him give up either. Shit, I don't know, maybe it was like I wanted to see him make something of himself; I didn't want him to wind up like my Billy did. Yeah, it sounds pretty stupid, I know that. I guess I don't know what I was thinking—just seemed like it would of been a shame is all.

When I got up the next day, he was still at it. But it wasn't just that—he'd gathered himself an audience as well. A lot of the others—maybe there was a hundred, maybe even more—had gathered about on the lawn. Some of them were standing but a lot were just sitting around, like he was putting on a performance for them or something. I still couldn't make out exactly what Billy himself was up to. It got to be frustrating—what could he be doing to get all of their attentions like that? After a while I started hunting around for a better view, and then I remembered there was a ladder to the attic, and sure enough once I got up there, there was a big window looking out over the street. The room had been converted, looked like it was a kid's room but then the kid had left and the parents hadn't wanted to change it any.

The window was so big that I could sit up on the ledge. And from there, sure enough, I could see Billy pretty clear. It was quite a shock. I ain't ever seen one of them go at anything the way he was at those planks—tearing at them with his hands, over and over. His fingers were all bloody; with the sight I reckoned I could make out bits of bone where he'd torn the ends clean off. He was a mess, but that wasn't slowing him any—I guess he wasn't even feeling it. He just kept tearing at the planks, not paying any attention to anything else. He'd got a couple down already; they were lying on the grass next to him. I didn't figure it was gonna do him any good though—the family would put up more on the inside, and if he started on those they'd just have to put up some more. Even if he was a bit stronger and a bit smarter than the rest, he still wasn't about to keep up.

Still, the way he was going at it, it was hard to take your eyes off. Apart from a break at lunchtime I watched Billy all day, 'til it started to get too dark. The last I saw, he was about halfway there on the outside planks. He was still at it when I left him—I suppose the dark didn't bother him too much.

I got up early the next day, and shifted all my supplies up into the attic room, along with a gas stove I'd found. It was like he'd become the center of my life all of a sudden—I remember thinking how I was just like those other dumb bastards who were sitting out there on the lawn with him, watching him like he was the star attraction in a freak show.

Only, when I got up to my perch on the sill, they weren't sitting anymore. They were in a big mass now, with Billy right there in the center in that nice suit of his, and every single one of them was after getting into that window. Maybe twenty of them were clawing at the planks, all together, and I could tell straight away that whatever the family was doing on the inside there wasn't anything that could stop that—the sheer weight of all those bodies all together.

Sure enough, it was only about a minute after I got up there that the whole thing caved in, planks and bodies all falling in together—I remember some crazy part of my brain thinking, it was like Billy had been waiting for me, as if he liked that he'd got an audience.

I didn't do anything, what would've been the point? If the family had been on the other side, and I figured they must've been, then they'd have been dead about the moment those planks gave up. I wasn't feeling much either—like maybe I was in shock. They kept on climbing through the window, all of them, fighting each other to get in like it was the only thing that'd ever mattered to them. Even once the room was full they kept on going, 'til there were just a few left on the lawn, and even they were still pushing and shoving.

It was quiet, a weird kind of quiet considering what'd just happened, but I didn't even notice it until the screaming started. And then it seemed strange there being a noise, 'cause I'd gotten so used to it being quiet all the time. I had to put down the rifle for a second, just so I could look to see where it was coming from. It was up on the second floor, on the far side from where they'd got in—the little daughter, maybe she was about twelve years old. They must've locked her in there, thinking she'd be safer maybe. She was hanging half out of the window, and she was screaming—she wasn't looking at me, I don't know if she knew I was there, if she was screaming for somebody to help her or just screaming. There wasn't a thing that I could've done for her. If she'd gotten out onto the porch and down to the road, maybe then I could've done something, but there was no way to tell her that. I picked up the rifle again, I don't know why, whether I was thinking to get some of them before they got to her, or whether I thought I'd make it easier on her. That's what I should've done, I guess—I don't know if I even thought of it then, it's a hard thing to think.

And, y'know, I think I'd guessed that it was going to be Billy that got to her first, least I wasn't a bit surprised when he appeared. The girl didn't even realize he was there she was so caught up with her screaming. It was a long double window, and there were a couple of feet between them still. Billy was shuffling up like he had all the time in the world, and I had a good clean shot, would have taken his head right off.

I squeezed on the trigger—and then I stopped. All I could think about was how I'd been happier since Billy had walked up of Main Street, about how much he'd looked like my kid. Maybe he was one of them but he was smart, and did I have the right to kill him? And somewhere, there was a voice in my head saying, you can't get them all, there just ain't the bullets, one of them's going to get her and why shouldn't it be Billy? I knew that I was wrong—if I could buy her a bit more time then maybe she'd wake up and get out onto the porch.

I went to take the shot again. But by then, it was too late.

Billy lurched forward, and he got hold of her head with those bloody stumps of hands that he had left, and he bit down hard into her cheek. Then he just stayed like that, with his mouth covering half of her face—almost like he was kissing her except for the blood streaming down between them, pouring out all over his nice suit. I could see his jaw moving through the sight. Suddenly, he didn't look like my kid no more; he just looked like a monster. I pulled the trigger—and for a couple of seconds his head was just a red cloud, with the blood raining down over everything. When it cleared he was still standing there, and even though there wasn't anything to hold it up, his face was still clamped over hers. I pulled the trigger again, and then they both crumpled down. I knew she was dead any way, but that didn't make it feel any better.

So, that's the end of Billy's story. And I guess it's the end of mine as well. Yesterday, I found this old tape recorder, and I just wanted to talk it all through I suppose, get it out in the open. Probably no one's ever going to hear it. But maybe there'll be a day when this is all over, and maybe there's something we could learn from it. Maybe everyone will try to forget as quick as they can when they'd be better off remembering. 'Cause, what I've been thinking is, the worst thing that they've done to us, it ain't killing us. It's making us like them—making us so we can't feel anything. Whether they get to you or not, you start to getting a little less human every day, you get deader inside.

Or, I don't know, maybe I was always like this. I haven't ever cried for Barbara and my little girl, not once, even though I miss them so bad it hurts—something in me just can't do it. But then, I didn't cry for Billy either—seeing them put him in the ground I was just angry, and wondering why he had to do a stupid, selfish thing like that. Shit, I know I wasn't a good father to him, but if he'd just talked to me then there's got to have been something I could've said.

But I guess that I understand Billy a little better now—I wish he was here and I could tell him that, instead of talking to this dumb machine. One of the policemen said to me, Billy didn't really know what he was doing, 'cause nobody shoots themselves in the chest—in the mouth he said, with the barrel facing upwards, that's the best way.

It'd be hell to do with that rifle, but I was lucky, there're a couple of bullets left in the revolver—and I'll only need the one.

I guess what I was trying to say before, what they've taught us—it's that being alive ain't the same thing as living. And me, I figure that I'm already dead.

At least now I'll get to stay that way.

BOBBY CONROY COMES BACK FROM THE DEAD

by Joe Hill

Joe Hill is the best-selling author of the novel *Heart-Shaped Box* and the short story collection *20ᵗʰ Century Ghosts*, both of which won the Bram Stoker Award. He's also won the World Fantasy Award for his novella "Voluntary Committal," and his story "Best New Horror" won both the British Fantasy Award and the Stoker. Hill is currently working on a comic book miniseries with artist Gabriel Rodriguez called *Locke & Key*. Right around the time this anthology sees print, a hardcover collecting all of the comics should be available.

On his website, www.joehillfiction.com, Hill describes this story as a tale of two ex-lovers who have a chance meeting one day in 1977 on the set of *Dawn of the Dead*, where both have found work as extras. "Theoretically, 'Bobby Conroy' is a romance," he says. "The real romance on display here, though, is my twenty-year love affair with the zombie movies of George Romero."

Bobby didn't know her at first. She was wounded, like him. The first thirty to arrive all got wounds. Tom Savini put them on himself.

Her face was a silvery blue, her eyes sunken into darkened hollows, and where her right ear had been was a ragged-edged hole, a gaping place that revealed a lump of wet red bone. They sat a yard apart on the stone wall around the fountain, which was switched off. She had her pages balanced on one knee—three pages in all, stapled together—and was looking them over, frowning with concentration. Bobby had read his while he was waiting in line to go into makeup.

Her jeans reminded him of Harriet Rutherford. There were patches all over them, patches that looked as if they had been made out of kerchiefs; squares of red and dark blue, with paisley patterns printed on them. Harriet was always wearing jeans like that. Patches sewn into the butt of a girl's Levi's still turned Bobby on.

His gaze followed the bend of her legs down to where her blue jeans flared at the ankle, then on to her bare feet. She had kicked her sandals off, and was twisting the toes of one foot into the toes of the other. When he saw this he felt his heart lunge with a kind of painful-sweet shock.

"Harriet?" he said. "Is that little Harriet Rutherford who I used to write love poems to?"

She peered at him sideways, over her shoulder. She didn't need to answer, he knew it was her. She stared for a long, measuring time, and then her eyes opened a little wider. They were a vivid, very undead green, and for an instant he saw them brighten with recognition and unmistakable excitement. But she turned her head away, went back to perusing her pages.

"No one ever wrote me love poems in high school," she said. "I'd remember. I would've died of happiness."

"In detention. Remember we got two weeks after the cooking show skit? You had a cucumber carved like a dick. You said it needed to stew for an hour and stuck it in your pants. It was the finest moment in the history of the Die Laughing Comedy Collective."

"No. I have a good memory and I don't recall this comedy troupe." She looked back down at the pages balanced on her knee. "Do you remember any details about these supposed poems?"

"How do you mean?"

"A line. Maybe if you could remember something about one of these poems—one line of heart-rending verse—it would all come flooding back to me."

He didn't know if he could at first; stared at her blankly, his tongue pressed to his lower lip, trying to call something back and his mind stubbornly blank.

Then he opened his mouth and began to speak, remembering as he went along: "*I love to watch you in the shower, I hope that's not obscene.*"

"*But when I see you soap your boobs, I get sticky in my jeans!*" Harriet cried, turning her body towards him. "Bobby Conroy, *goddamn*, come here and hug me without screwing up my makeup."

He leaned into her and put his arms around her narrow back. He shut his eyes and squeezed, feeling absurdly happy, maybe the happiest he had felt since moving back in with his parents. He had not spent a day in Monroeville when he didn't think about seeing her. He was depressed, he daydreamed about her, stories that began with exactly this moment—or not exactly *this* moment, he had not imagined them both made-up like partially decomposed corpses, but close enough.

When he woke every morning, in his bedroom over his parents' garage, he felt flat and listless. He'd lie on his lumpy mattress and stare at the skylights overhead. The skylights were milky with dust, and through them every sky appeared the same, a bland, formless white. Nothing in him wanted to get up. What made it worse was he still remembered what it felt like to wake in that same bed with a teenager's sense of his own limitless possibilities, to wake charged with enthusiasm for the day. If he daydreamed about meeting Harriet again, and falling into their old friendship—and if these early morning daydreams sometimes turned explicitly sexual, if he remembered being with her in her father's shed, her back on the stained cement, her too-skinny legs pulled open, her socks still on—then at least it was something to stir his blood a little, get him going. All his other daydreams had thorns on them. Handling them always threatened a sudden sharp prick of pain.

They were still holding each other when a boy spoke, close by. "Mom, who are you hugging?"

Bobby Conroy opened his eyes, shifted his gaze to the right. A little blue-faced dead boy with limp black hair was staring at them. He wore a hooded sweatshirt, the hood pulled up.

Harriet's grip on Bobby relaxed. Then, slowly, her arms slid away. Bobby regarded the boy for an instant longer—the kid was no older than six—and then dropped to Harriet's hand, the wedding band on her ring finger.

Bobby looked back at the kid, forced a smile. Bobby had been to more than seven hundred auditions during his years in New York City, and he had a whole catalog of phony smiles.

"Hey chumley," Bobby said. "I'm Bobby Conroy. Your mom and me are old buddies from way back when Mastodons walked the earth."

"Bobby is my name too," the boy said. "Do you know a lot about dinosaurs? I'm a big dinosaur guy myself."

Bobby felt a sick pang that seemed to go right through the middle of him. He glanced at her face—didn't want to, couldn't help himself—and found Harriet watching him. Her smile was anxious and compressed.

"My husband picked it," she said. She was, for some reason, patting his leg. "After a Yankee. He's from Albany originally."

"I know about Mastodons," Bobby said to the boy, surprised to find his voice sounded just the same as it ever did. "Big hairy elephants the size of school buses. They once roamed the entire Pennsylvanian plateau, and left mountainous Mastodon poops everywhere, one of which later became Pittsburgh."

The kid grinned, and threw a quick glance at his mother, perhaps to appraise what she made of this off-hand reference to poop. She smiled indulgently.

Bobby saw the kid's hand and recoiled. "Ugh! Wow, that's the best wound I've seen all day. What is that, a fake hand?"

Three fingers were missing from the boy's left hand. Bobby grabbed it and yanked on it, expecting it to come off. But it was warm and fleshy under the blue makeup, and the kid pulled it out of Bobby's grip.

"No," he said. "It's just my hand. That's the way it is."

Bobby blushed so intensely his ears stung, and was grateful for his makeup. Harriet touched Bobby's wrist.

"He really doesn't have those fingers," she said.

Bobby looked at her, struggling to frame an apology. Her smile was a little fretful now, but she wasn't visibly angry with him, and the hand on his arm was a good sign.

"I stuck them into the table-saw but I don't remember because I was so little," the boy explained.

"Dean is in lumber," Harriet said.

"Is Dean staggering around here somewhere?" Bobby asked, craning his head and making a show of looking around, although of course he had no idea what Harriet's Dean might look like. Both floors of the atrium at the center of the mall were crowded with other people like them, made-up to look like the recent dead. They sat together on benches, or stood together in groups, chatting, laughing at each other's wounds, or looking over the mimeographed pages they had been given of the screenplay. The mall was closed—steel gates pulled down in front of the entrances to the stores—no one in the place but the film crew and the undead.

"No, he dropped us off and went in to work."

"On a Sunday?"

"He owns his own yard."

It was as good a set-up for a punch line as he had ever heard, and he paused, searching for just the right one… and then it came to him that making wisecracks about Dean's choice of work to Dean's wife in front of Dean's five-year-old might be ill-advised, and never mind that he and Harriet had once been best friends and the royal couple of the Die Laughing Comedy Collective their senior year in high school. Bobby said, "He does? Good for him."

"I like the big gross tear in your face," the little kid said, pointing at Bobby's brow. Bobby had a nasty scalp wound, the skin laid open to the lumpy bone. "Didn't you think the guy who made us into dead people was cool?"

Bobby had actually been a little creeped out by Tom Savini, who kept referring to an open book of autopsy photographs while applying Bobby's makeup. The people in those pictures, with their maimed flesh and slack unhappy faces, were really dead, not getting up later to have a cup of coffee at the craft services table. Savini studied their wounds with a quiet appreciation, the same as any painter surveying the subject of his art.

But Bobby could see what the kid meant about how he was cool. With his black leather jacket, motorcycle boots, black beard, and memorable eyebrows—thick black eyebrows that arched sharply upward, like Dr. Spock or Bela Lugosi—he looked like a death metal rock god.

Someone was clapping their hands. Bobby glanced around. The director, George Romero, stood close to the bottom of the escalators, a bearish man well over six feet tall, with a thick brown beard. Bobby had noticed that many of the men working on the crew had beards. A lot of them had shoulder length hair too, and wore army-navy castoffs and motorcycle boots like Savini, so that they resembled a band of counterculture revolutionaries.

Bobby and Harriet and little Bob gathered with the other extras to hear what Romero had to say. He had a booming confident voice and when he grinned his cheeks dimpled, visible in spite of the beard. He asked if anyone present knew anything about making movies. A few people, Bobby included, raised their hands. Romero said thank God someone in this place does, and everyone laughed. He said he wanted to welcome them all to the world of big-budget Hollywood film-making, and everyone laughed at that too, because George Romero only made pictures in Pennsylvania, and everyone knew *Dawn of the Dead* was lower than low budget, it was a half-step above no-budget. He said he was grateful to them all for coming out today, and that for ten hours of grueling work, which would test them body and soul, they would be paid *in cash*, a sum so colossal he dare not say the number aloud, he could only show it. He held aloft a dollar bill, and there was more laughter. Then Tom Savini, up on the second floor, leaned over the railing, and shouted, "Don't laugh, that's more than most of us are getting paid to work on this turkey."

"Lots of people are in this film as a labor of love," George Romero said. "Tom is in it because he likes squirting pus on people." Some in the crowd moaned. "Fake pus! Fake pus!" Romero cried.

"You *hope* it was fake pus," Savini intoned from somewhere above, but he was already moving away from the railing, out of sight.

More laughter. Bobby knew a thing or two about comic patter, and had a suspicion that this bit of the speech was rehearsed, and had been issued just this way, more than once.

Romero talked for a while about the plot. The recently dead were coming back to life; they liked to eat people; in the face of the crisis the government had collapsed; four young heroes had sought shelter in this mall. Bobby's attention wandered, and he found himself looking down at the other Bobby, at Harriet's boy. Little Bob had a long, solemn face, dark chocolate eyes and lots of thick black hair, limp and disheveled. In fact, the kid bore a passing resemblance to Bobby himself, who also had brown eyes, a slim face, and a thick untidy mass of black hair on his head.

Bobby wondered if Dean looked like him. The thought made his blood race strangely. What if Dean dropped in to see how Harriet and little Bobby were doing, and the man turned out to be his exact twin? The thought was so alarming it made him feel briefly weak—but then he remembered he was made-up like a corpse, blue-face, scalp wound. Even if they looked exactly alike they wouldn't look anything alike.

Romero delivered some final instructions on how to walk like a zombie—he demonstrated by allowing his eyes to roll back in his head and his face to go slack—and then promised they'd be ready to roll on the first shot in a few minutes.

Harriet pivoted on her heel, turned to face him, her fist on her hip, eyelids fluttering theatrically. He turned at the same time, and they almost bumped into each other. She opened her mouth to speak but nothing came out. They were standing too close to each other, and the unexpected physical proximity seemed to throw her. He didn't know what to say either, all thought suddenly wiped from his mind. She laughed, and shook her head, a reaction that struck him as artificial, an expression of anxiety, not happiness.

"Let's set, pardner," she said. He remembered that when a skit wasn't going well, and she got rattled, she sometimes slipped into a big drawling John Wayne impersonation on stage, a nervous habit he had hated then and that he found, in this moment, endearing.

"Are we going to have something to do soon?" little Bob asked.

"Soon," she said. "Why don't you practice being a zombie? Go on, lurch around for a while."

Bobby and Harriet sat down at the edge of the fountain again. Her hands were small, bony fists on her thighs. She stared into her lap, her eyes blank, gaze directed inward. She was digging the toes of one bare foot into the toes of the other again.

He spoke. One of them had to say something.

"I can't believe you're married and you have a kid!" he said, in the same tone of happy astonishment he reserved for friends who had just told him they had been cast in a part he himself had auditioned for. "I love this kid you're dragging around with you. He's so cute. But then, who can resist a little kid who looks half-rotted?"

She seemed to come back from wherever she had been, smiled at him—almost shyly.

He went on, "And you better be ready to tell me everything about this Dean guy."

"He's coming by later. He's going to take us out to lunch. You should come."

"That could be fun!" Bobby cried, and made a mental note to take his enthusiasm down a notch.

"He can be really shy the first time he meets someone, so don't expect too much."

Bobby waved a hand in the air: *pish-posh.* "It's going to be great. We'll have lots to talk about. I've always been fascinated with lumber yards and—plywood."

This was taking a chance, joshing her about the husband he didn't know. But she smirked and said:

"Everything you ever wanted to know about two-by-fours but were afraid to ask."

And for a moment they were both smiling, a little foolishly, knees almost touching. They had never really figured out how to talk to each other. They were always half-on-stage, trying to use whatever the other person said to set up the next punch-line. That much, anyway, hadn't changed.

"God I can't believe running into you here," she said. "I've wondered about you. I've thought about you a lot."

"You have?"

"I figured you'd be famous by now," she said.

"Hey, that makes two of us," Bobby said, and winked. Immediately he wished he could take the wink back. It was fake and he didn't want to be fake with her. He hurried on, answering a question she hadn't asked. "I'm settling in. Been back for three months. I'm staying with my parents for a while, kind of readapting to Monroeville."

She nodded, still regarding him steadily, with a seriousness that made him uncomfortable. "How's it going?"

"I'm making a life," Bobby lied.

In between set-ups, Bobby and Harriet and little Bob told stories about how they had died.

"I was a comedian in New York City," Bobby said, fingering his scalp wound. "Something tragic happened when I went on stage."

"Yeah," Harriet said. "Your act."

"Something that had never happened before."

"What, people laughed?"

"I was my usual brilliant self. People were rolling on the floor."

"Convulsions of agony."

"And then as I was taking my final bow—a terrible accident. A stagehand up in the rafters dropped a forty pound sandbag right on my head. But at least I died to the sound of applause."

"They were applauding the stagehand," Harriet said.

The little boy looked seriously up into Bobby's face, and took his hand. "I'm sorry you got hit in the head." His lips grazed Bobby's knuckles with a dry kiss.

Bobby stared down at him. His hand tingled where little Bob's mouth had touched it.

"He's always been the kissiest, huggiest kid you ever met," Harriet said. "He's got all this pent-up affection. At the slightest sign of weakness he's ready to slobber on you." As she said this she ruffled little Bobby's hair. "What killed you, squirt?"

He held up his hand, waggled his stumps. "My fingers got cut off on Dad's table-saw and I bled to death."

Harriet went on smiling but her eyes seemed to film over slightly. She fished around in her pocket and found a quarter. "Go get a gumball, bud."

He snatched it and ran.

"People must think we're the most careless parents," she said, staring expressionlessly after her son. "But it was no one's fault about his fingers."

"I'm sure."

"The table saw was unplugged and he wasn't even two. He never plugged anything in before. We didn't know he knew how. Dean was right there with him. It just happened so fast. Do you know how many things had to go wrong, all at the same time for that to happen? Dean thinks the sound of the saw coming on scared him and he reached up to try and shut it off. He thought he'd be in trouble." She was briefly silent, watching her son work the gumball machine, then said, "I always thought about my kid—this is the one part of my life I'm going to get right. No indiscriminate fuck-ups about this. I was planning how when he was fifteen he'd make love to the most beautiful girl in school. How'd he be able to play five instruments and he'd blow everyone away with all his talent. How'd he be the funny kid who seems to know everyone." She paused again, and then added, "He'll be the funny kid now. The funny kid always has something wrong with him. That's why he's funny—to shift people's attention to something else."

In the silence that followed this statement, Bobby had several thoughts in rapid succession. The first was that *he* had been the funny kid when he was in school; did Harriet think there had been something wrong with *him* he had been covering for? Then he remembered they were *both* the funny kids, and thought: *what was wrong with us?*

It had to be something, otherwise they'd be together now and the boy at the gumball machine would be theirs. The thought which crossed his mind next was that, if little Bobby was *their* little Bobby, he'd still have ten fingers. He felt a seething dislike of Dean the lumber man, an ignorant squarehead whose idea of spending together-time with his kid probably meant taking him to the fair to watch a truck-pull.

An assistant director started clapping her hands and hollering down for the undead to get into their positions. Little Bob trotted back to them.

"Mom," he said, the gumball in his cheek. "You didn't say how you died." He was looking at her torn-off ear.

"I know," Bobby said. "She ran into this old friend at the mall and they got talking. You know, and I mean they *really* got talking. *Hours* of blab. Finally her old friend said, hey, I don't want to chew your ear off here. And your mom said, aw, don't worry about it…"

"A great man once said, lend me your ears," Harriet said. She smacked the palm of her hand hard against her forehead. "Why did I listen to him?"

Except for the dark hair, Dean didn't look anything like him. Dean was *short*. Bobby wasn't prepared for how short. He was shorter than Harriet, who was herself not much over five and a half feet tall. When they kissed, Dean had to stretch his neck. He was compact, and solidly built, broad at the shoulders, deep through the chest, narrow at the hips. He wore thick glasses with gray plastic frames, the eyes behind them the color of unpolished pewter. They were shy eyes—his gaze met Bobby's when Harriet introduced them, darted away, returned and darted away again—not to mention old; at the corners of them the skin was creased in a web of finely etched laugh lines. He was older than Harriet, maybe by as much as ten years.

They had only just been introduced when Dean cried suddenly, "Oh you're *that* Bobby! You're *funny* Bobby. You know we almost didn't name our *kid* Bobby because of you. I've had it drilled into me, if I ever run into you, I'm supposed to reassure you that naming him Bobby was my idea. Cause of Bobby Murcer. Ever since I was old enough to imagine having kids of my own I always thought—"

"I'm funny!" Harriet's son interrupted.

Dean caught him under the armpits and lofted him into the air. "You sure are!"

Bobby wasn't positive he wanted to have lunch with them, but Harriet looped her arm through his and marched him toward the doors out to the parking lot, and her shoulder—warm and bare—was leaning against his, so there was really no choice.

Bobby didn't notice the other people in the diner staring at them, and forgot they were in makeup until the waitress approached. She was hardly out of her teens, with a head of frizzy yellow hair that bounced as she walked.

"We're dead," little Bobby announced.

"Gotcha," the girl said, nodding and pointing her ball-point pen at them. "I'm guessing you either all work on the horror movie, or you already tried the special, which is it?"

Dean laughed, dry, bawling laughter. Dean was as easy a laugh as Bobby had ever met. Dean laughed at almost everything Harriet said, and most of what Bobby himself said. Sometimes he laughed so hard, the people at the next table started in alarm. Once he had control of himself, he would apologize with unmistakable earnestness, his face flushed a delicate shade of rose, eyes gleaming and wet. That was when Bobby began to see at least one possible answer to the question that had been on his mind ever since learning she was married to Dean who-owned-his-own-lumber-yard: *why him?* Well—he was a willing audience, there was that.

"So I thought you were acting in New York City," Dean said, at last. "What brings you back?"

"Failure," Bobby said.

"Oh—I'm sorry to hear that. What are you up to now? Are you doing some comedy locally?"

"You could say that. Only around here they call it substitute teaching."

"Oh! You're teaching! How do you like it?"

"It's great. I always planned to work either in film or television or junior high. That I should finally make it so big subbing eighth grade gym—it's a dream come true."

Dean laughed, and chunks of pulverized chicken-fried steak flew out of his mouth.

"I'm sorry. This is awful," he said. "Food everywhere. You must think I'm a total pig."

"No, it's okay. Can I have the waitress bring you something? A glass of water? A trough?"

Dean bent so his forehead was almost touching his plate, his laughter wheezy, asthmatic. "Stop. Really."

Bobby stopped, but not because Dean said. For the first time he had noticed Harriet's knee was knocking his under the table. He wondered if this was intentional, and the first chance he got he leaned back and looked. No, not intentional. She had kicked her sandals off and was digging the toes of one foot into the other, so fiercely that sometimes her right knee swung out and banged his.

"Wow, I would've loved to have a teacher like you. Someone who can make kids laugh." Dean said.

Bobby chewed and chewed, but couldn't tell what he was eating. It didn't have any taste.

Dean let out a shaky sigh, wiped the corners of his eyes again. "Of course, I'm not funny. I can't even remember knock-knock jokes. I'm not good for much else except working. And Harriet is *so* funny. Sometimes she puts on shows for Bobby and me, with these dirty socks on her hands, we get laughing so hard we can't breathe. She calls it the trailer park muppet show. Sponsored by Pabst Blue Ribbon." He started laughing and thumping the table again. Harriet stared intently into her lap. Dean said, "I'd love to see her do that on Carson. This is—what do you call them, routines?—this could be a classic routine."

"Sure sounds it." Bobby said. "I'm surprised Ed McMahon hasn't already called to see if she's available."

When Dean dropped them back at the mall and left for the lumber yard, the mood was different. Harriet seemed distant, it was hard to draw her into any kind of conversation—not that Bobby felt like trying very hard. He was suddenly irritable. All the fun seemed to have gone out of playing a dead person for the day. It was mostly waiting—waiting for the gaffers to get the lights just so, for Tom Savini to touch up a wound that was starting to look a little too much like Latex, not enough like ragged flesh—and Bobby was sick of it. The sight of other people having a good time annoyed him. Several zombies stood in a group, playing hacky-sack with a quivering red spleen, and laughing. It made a juicy splat every time it hit the floor. Bobby wanted to snarl at them for being so merry. Hadn't any of them heard of method acting, Stanislavsky? They should all be sitting apart from one another, moaning unhappily and fondling giblets. He heard *himself* moan aloud, an angry frustrated sound, and little Bobby asked what was wrong. He said he was just practicing. Little Bob went to watch the hacky-sack game.

Harriet said, without looking at him, "That was a good lunch, wasn't it?"

"*Sen*-sational," Bobby said, thinking *better be careful*. He was restless, charged with an energy he didn't know how to displace. "I feel like I really hit it off with Dean. He reminds me of my grandfather. I had this great grandfather who could wiggle his ears and who thought my name was Evan. He'd give me a quarter to stack wood for him, fifty cents if I'd do it with my shirt off. Say, how old *is* Dean?"

They had been walking together. Now Harriet stiffened, stopped. Her head swiveled in his direction, but her hair was in front of her eyes, making it hard to read the expression in them. "He's nine years older than me. So what?"

"So nothing. I'm just glad you're happy."

"I *am* happy," Harriet said, her voice a half-octave too high.

"Did he get down on one knee when he proposed?"

Harriet nodded, her mouth crimped, suspicious.

"Did you have to help him up afterwards?" Bobby asked. His own voice was sounding a little off-key, too, and he thought *stop now*. It was like a cartoon, he saw Wile E. Coyote strapped to the front of a steam engine, jamming his feet down on the rails to try to brake the train, smoke boiling up from his heels, feet swelling, glowing red.

"Oh you prick," she said.

"I'm sorry!" he grinned, holding his hands palms-up in front of him. "Kidding, kidding. Funny Bobby, you know. I can't help myself." She hesitated—had been about to turn away—not sure whether she should believe him or not. Bobby wiped his mouth with the palm of his hand. "So we know what you do to make Dean laugh. What's he do to make you laugh? Oh that's right, he isn't *funny*. Well what's he do to make your heart race? Besides kiss you with his dentures out?"

"Leave me alone, Bobby," she said. She turned away, but he came around to get back in front of her, keep her from walking off.

"No."

"Stop."

"Can't," he said, and suddenly he understood he was angry with her. "If he isn't funny he must be something. I need to know what."

"*Patient*," she said.

"Patient," Bobby repeated. It stunned him—that this could be her answer.

"With me."

"With you," he said.

"With Robert."

"Patient," Bobby said. Then he couldn't say anything more for a moment because he was out-of-breath. He felt suddenly that his makeup was itching on his face. He wished that when he started to press she had just walked away from him, or told him to fuck off, or hit him even, wished she had responded with anything but *patient*. He swallowed. "That's not good enough." Knowing he couldn't stop now, the train was going into the canyon, Wile E. Coyote's eyes bugging three feet out of his head in terror. "I wanted to meet whoever you were with and feel sick with jealousy, but instead I just feel sick. I wanted you to fall in love with someone good-looking and creative and brilliant, a novelist, a playwright, someone with a sense of humor and a fourteen-inch dong. Not a guy with a buzz cut and a lumber yard, who thinks erotic massage involves a tube of Ben Gay."

She smeared at the tears dribbling down her face with the backs of her hands. "I knew you'd hate him, but I didn't think you'd be mean."

"It's not that I hate him. What's to hate? He's not doing anything any other guy in his position wouldn't do. If I was two feet tall and geriatric, I'd *leap* at the chance to have a piece of ass like you. You bet he's patient. He better be. He ought to be down on his fucking knees every night, bathing your feet in sacramental oils, that you'd give him the time of day."

"You had your chance," she said. She was struggling not to let her crying slip out of control. The muscles in her face quivered with the effort, pulling her expression into a grimace.

"It's not about what chances I had. It's about what chances you had."

This time when she pivoted away from him, he let her go. She put her hands over her face. Her shoulders were jerking and she was making choked little sounds as she went. He watched her walk to the wall around the fountain where they had met earlier in the day. Then he remembered the boy and turned to look, his heart drumming hard, wondering what little Bobby might've seen or heard. But the kid was running down the broad concourse, kicking the spleen in front of him, which had now collected a mass of dust bunnies around it. Two other dead children were trying to kick it away from him.

Bobby watched them play for a while. A pass went wide, and the spleen skidded past him. He put a foot on it to stop it. It flexed unpleasantly beneath the sole of his shoe. The boys stopped three yards off, stood there breathing hard, awaiting him. He scooped it up.

"Go out," he said, and lobbed it to little Bobby, who made a basket catch and hauled away with his head down and the other kids in pursuit.

When he turned to peek at Harriet he saw her watching him, her palms pressed hard against her knees. He waited for her to look away, but she didn't, and finally he took her steady gaze as an invitation to approach.

He crossed to the fountain, sat down beside her. He was still working out how to begin his apology, when she spoke.

"I wrote you. You stopped writing back," she said. Her bare feet were wrestling with each other again.

"I hate how overbearing your right foot is," he said. "Why can't it give the left foot a little space?" But she wasn't listening to him.

"It didn't matter," she said. Her voice was congested and hoarse. The makeup was oil-based, and in spite of her tears, hadn't streaked. "I wasn't mad. I knew we couldn't have a relationship, just seeing each other when you came home for Christmas." She swallowed thickly. "I really thought someone would put you in their sitcom. Every time I thought about that—about seeing you on TV, and hearing people laugh when you said things—I'd get this big stupid smile on my face. I could float through a whole afternoon thinking about it. I don't understand what in the world could've made you come back to Monroeville."

But he had already said what in the world drew him back to his parents and his bedroom over the garage. Dean had asked in the diner, and Bobby had answered him truthfully.

One Thursday night, only last spring, he had gone on early in a club in the Village. He did his twenty minutes, earned a steady if-not-precisely-overwhelming murmur of laughter, and a spatter of applause when he came off. He found a place at the bar to hear some of the other acts. He was just about to slide off his stool and go home when Robin Williams leaped on stage. He was in town for SNL, cruising the clubs, testing material. Bobby quickly shifted his weight back onto his stool and sat listening, his pulse thudding heavily in his throat.

He couldn't explain to Harriet the import of what he had seen then. Bobby saw a man clutching the edge of a table with one hand, his date's thigh with the other, grabbing both so hard his knuckles were drained of all color. He was bent over with tears dripping off his face, and his laughter was high and shrill and convulsive, more animal than human, the sound of a dingo or something. He was shaking his head from side to side and waving a hand in the air, *stop, please, don't do this to me*. It was hilarity to the point of distress.

Robin Williams saw the desperate man, broke away from a discourse on jerking off, pointed at him and shouted, "*You!* Yes, *you*, frantic hyena-man! You get a free pass to every show I do for the rest of my motherfucking life!" And then there was a sound rising in the crowd, more than laughter or applause, although it included both. It was a low, thunderous rumble of uncontained delight, a sound so immense it was felt as much as heard, a thing that caused the bones in Bobby's chest to hum.

Bobby himself didn't laugh once, and when he left his stomach was churning. His feet fell strangely, heavily against the sidewalk, and for some time he did not know his way home. When at last he was in his apartment, he sat on the edge of his bed, his suspenders pulled off, and his shirt unbuttoned, and for the first time felt things were hopeless.

He saw something flash in Harriet's hand. She was jiggling some quarters.

"Going to call someone?" he asked.

"Dean," she said. "For a ride."

"Don't."

"I'm not staying. I can't stay."

He watched her tormented feet, toes struggling together, and finally nodded. They stood at the same time. They were, once again, standing uncomfortably close.

"See you then," she said.

"See you," he said. He wanted to reach for her hand, but didn't, wanted to say something, but couldn't think what.

"Are there a couple people around here who want to volunteer to get shot?" George Romero asked, from less than three feet away. "It's a guaranteed close-up in the finished film."

Bobby and Harriet put their hands up at the same time.

"Me," Bobby said.

"Me," said Harriet, stepping on Bobby's foot as she moved forward to get George Romero's attention. "Me!"

"It's going to be a great picture, Mr. Romero," Bobby said. They were standing shoulder to shoulder, making small talk, waiting for Savini to finish wiring Harriet with her squib—a condom partially filled with cane syrup and food coloring that would explode to look like a bullet hit. Bobby was already wired… in more than one sense of the word. "Someday everyone in Pittsburgh is going to claim they walked dead in this movie."

"You kiss ass like a pro," Romero said. "Do you have a show-biz background?"

"Six years off-Broadway," Bobby said. "Plus I played most of the comedy clubs."

"Ah, but now you're back in greater Pittsburgh. Good career move, kid. Stick around here, you'll be a star in no time."

Harriet skipped over to Bobby, her hair flouncing. "I'm going to get my tit blown off!"

"Magnificent," Bobby said. "People just have to keep on going, because you never know when something wonderful is going to happen."

George Romero led them to their marks, and walked them through what he wanted from them. Lights pointed into silver spangly umbrellas, casting an even white glow, and a dry heat, over a ten-foot stretch of floor. A lumpy striped mattress rested on the tiles, just to one side of a square pillar.

Harriet would get hit first, in the chest. She was supposed to jerk back, then keep coming forward, showing as little reaction to the shot as she could muster. Bobby would take the next bullet in the head and it would bring him down. The squib was hidden under one Latex fold of his scalp wound. The wires that would cause the Trojan to explode were threaded through his hair.

"You can slump first, and slide down and to the side," George Romero said. "Drop to one knee if you want, and then spill yourself out of the frame. If you're feeling a bit more acrobatic you can fall straight back, just be sure you hit the mattress. No one needs to get hurt."

It was just Bobby and Harriet in the shot, which would picture them from the waist up. The other extras lined the walls of the shopping mall corridor, watching them. Their stares, their steady murmuring, induced in Bobby a pleasurable burst of adrenaline. Tom Savini knelt on the floor, just outside the framed shot, with a hand-held metal box in hand, wires snaking across the floor toward Bobby and Harriet. Little Bob sat next to him, his hands cupped under his chin, squeezing the spleen, his eyes shiny with anticipation. Savini had told little Bob all about what was going to happen, preparing the kid for the sight of blood bursting from his mother's chest, but little Bob wasn't worried. "I've been seeing gross stuff all day. It isn't scary. I like it." Savini was letting him keep the spleen as a souvenir.

"Roll," Romero said. Bobby twitched—what, they were rolling? Already? He only just gave them their marks! Christ, Romero was still standing in front of the camera!—and for an instant Bobby grabbed Harriet's hand. She squeezed his fingers, let go. Romero eased himself out of the shot. "Action."

Bobby rolled his eyes back in his head, rolled them back so far he couldn't see where he was going. He let his face hang slack. He took a plodding step forward.

"Shoot the girl," Romero said.

Bobby didn't see her squib go off, because he was a step ahead of her. But he heard it, a loud, ringing crack that echoed; and he smelled it, a sudden pungent whiff of gunpowder. Harriet grunted softly.

"Annnd," Romero said. "Now the other one."

It was like a gunshot going off next to his head. The bang of the blasting cap was so loud, it immediately deafened his eardrums. He snapped backward, spinning on his heel. His shoulder slammed into something just behind him, he didn't see what. He caught a blurred glimpse of the square pillar next to the mattress, and in that instant was seized with a jolt of inspiration. He smashed his forehead into it on his way down, and as he reeled away, saw he had left a crimson flower on the white plaster.

He hit the mattress, the cushion springy enough to provide a little bounce. He blinked. His eyes were watering, creating a visual distortion, a subtle warping of things. The air above him was filled with blue smoke. The center of his head stung. His face was splattered with cool, sticky fluid. As the ringing in his ears faded, he simultaneously became aware of two things. The first was the sound, a low, subterranean bellow, a distant, steady rumble of applause. The sound filled him like breath. George Romero was moving toward them, also clapping, smiling in that way that made dimples in his beard. The second thing he noticed was Harriet curled against him, her hand on his chest.

"Did I knock you down?" he asked.

"'Fraid so," she said.

"I knew it was only a matter of time before I got you in bed with me," he said.

Harried smiled, an easy contented smile like he hadn't seen at any other time, the whole day. Her blood-drenched bosom rose and fell against his side.

Little Bob ran to the edge of the mattress and leaped onto it with them. Harriet got an arm underneath him, scooped him up, and rolled him into the narrow space between her and Bobby. Little Bob grinned and put his thumb in his mouth. His face was close to the boy's head, and suddenly he was aware of the smell of little Bob's shampoo, a melon-flavored scent.

Harriet watched him steadily across her son, still with that same smile on her face. His gaze drifted toward the ceiling, the banks of skylights, the crisp, blue sky beyond. Nothing in him wanted to get up, wanted to move past the next few moments. He wondered what Harriet did with herself when Dean was at work and little Bobby was at school. Tomorrow was a Monday; he didn't know if he would be teaching or free. He hoped free. The work week stretched ahead of him, empty of responsibilities or concerns, limitless in its possibilities. The three of them, Bobby, and the boy, and Harriet, lay on the mattress, their bodies pressed close together and there was no movement but for their breathing.

George Romero turned back to them, shaking his head. "That was great, when you hit the pillar, and you left that big streak of gore. We should do it again, just the same way. This time you could leave some brains behind. What do you two kids say? Either one of you feel like a do-over?"

"Me," Bobby said.

"Me," said Harriet. "Me."

"Yes please," said little Bobby, around the thumb in his mouth.

"I guess it's unanimous," Bobby said. "Everyone wants a do-over."

THOSE WHO SEEK FORGIVENESS

by Laurell K. Hamilton

Laurell K. Hamilton is the best-selling author of the Anita Blake: Vampire Hunter series, which began with *Guilty Pleasures* and was continued most recently with *Blood Noir*. Another popular series of Hamilton's is the Meredith Gentry series, which began with *A Kiss of Shadows* and will continue with *Swallowing Darkness* later this year. Hamilton has written a number of other novels as well, such as her first, *Nightseer*, an epic fantasy, as well as the media tie-in novels *Ravenloft: Death of a Darklord* and *Star Trek: The Next Generation: Nightshade*. Her short work has appeared in magazines such as *Dragon* and *Marion Zimmer Bradley's Fantasy Magazine*, and in the *Sword and Sorceress* series of anthologies.

"Those Who Seek Forgiveness" is the first story Hamilton wrote about her iconic character Anita Blake. In her collection, *Strange Candy*, Hamilton says that the cemetery in this story is based on the cemetery where her mother is buried. "It was a place I knew very well, because my grandmother, who raised me, took me often," she says. "I guess it was inevitable that I would write about the dead; my childhood was haunted by death. Not real ghosts, but the ghosts of memory and loss."

"Death is a very serious matter, Mrs. Fiske. People who go through it are never the same."

The woman leaned forward, cradling her face in her hands. Her slim shoulders shook quietly for a few minutes. I passed another box of tissues her way. She groped for them blindly and then looked up. "I know you can't bring him back, exactly."

She wiped at two tears, which escaped and rolled down flawless cheekbones. The purse she clutched so tightly was reptile, at least two hundred dollars. Her accessories—lapel pin, high heels, hat, and gloves—were all black as her purse. Her suit was gray. Neither color suited her, but they emphasized her pale skin and hollow eyes. She was the sort of woman that made me feel too short, too dark, and gave me the strange desire to lose ten more pounds. If she hadn't been so genuinely grief-stricken, I could have disliked her.

"I have to talk to Arthur. That's my husband… was my husband." She took a deep breath and tried again. "Arthur died suddenly. A massive coronary." She blew delicately into a tissue. "His family did have a history of heart disease, but he always took such good care of himself." She finished with a watery hiccup. "I want to say good-bye to him, Miss Blake."

I smiled reassuringly. "We all have things left unsaid when death comes suddenly. But it isn't always best to raise the dead and say it."

Her blue eyes stared intently through a film of tears. I was going to discourage her as I discourage every one of my clients, but this one would do it. There was a certain set to the eyes that said *serious.*

"There are certain limitations to the process." My boss didn't allow us to show slides or pictures or give graphic descriptions, but we were supposed to tell the truth. One good picture of a decaying zombie would have sent most of my clients screaming.

"Limitations?"

"Yes, we can bring him back. You came to us promptly. That helps. He's been buried only three days. But as a zombie your husband will only have limited use of his body and mind. And as the days go by, that will grow worse, not better."

She stood up very straight, tears drying on her face. "I was hoping you could bring him back as a vampire."

I kept my face carefully blank. "Vampires are illegal, Mrs. Fiske."

"A friend told me that…you could get that done here." She finished in a rush, searching my face.

I smiled my best professional smile. "We do not do vampires. And even if we did, you can't make an ordinary corpse into a vampire."

"Ordinary?"

Very few people who came to us had even a remote idea of how rare vampires were, or why. "The deceased would have to have been bitten by a werewolf, vampire, or other supernatural creature, while alive. Being buried in unconsecrated ground would help. Your husband, Arthur, was never bitten by a vampire while alive, was he?"

"No," she half laughed, "he was bitten by my Yorkshire terrier once."

I smiled, encouraging her turn of spirits. "That won't quite do it. Your husband can come back as a zombie or not at all."

"I'll take it," she said quietly, all serious and very still.

"I will warn you that most families find it advisable to lay the zombie to rest after a time."

"Why?"

Why? I saw the happy family embracing their lost loved one. I saw the family sick, horrified, bringing the decaying corpse to be put down. The smiling relative reduced to a shambling horror.

"What exactly do you want Arthur to do when he arises?"

She looked down and shredded another tissue. "I want to say good-bye to him."

"Yes, Mrs. Fiske, but what do you want him to do?"

She was silent for several minutes. I decided to prompt her. "For instance, a woman came in wanting her husband raised so he could take out life insurance. I told her most insurance companies won't insure the walking dead." She grinned at that. "And that is what Arthur will come back as—the walking dead."

Her smile faltered, and tears came again. "I want Arthur to forgive me." She hid her face in her hands and sobbed. "I had an affair for several months. He found out, had a heart attack, and died." She seemed to gain strength from the words, and the tears slowed. "You see that I have to talk to him one last time. I have to tell him I love him, only him. I want Arthur to forgive me. Can he do that as a… zombie?"

"I've found that the dead are very forgiving of the living, when they die of natural causes. Your husband will have ample brainpower to speak. He will be himself at first. As the days progress, he will lose memory. He will begin to decay, first mentally, then physically."

"Decay?"

"Yes, slowly, but after all, he is dead."

The relatives didn't really believe that a fresh zombie wasn't alive. Knowing intellectually that someone smiling and talking is the walking dead is one thing. Emotionally, it is very different. But they believed as time passed and as he or she began to look like a walking corpse.

"It's temporary then?"

"Not exactly." I came from behind the desk and sat next to her. "He could stay a zombie possibly forever. But his physical and mental state would deteriorate until he was not much better than an automaton in tattered flesh."

"Tattered… flesh," she whispered.

I touched her hand. "I know it's a hard choice, but that is the reality." *Tattered flesh* didn't really touch the white sheen of bone through rotting flesh, but it was a term our boss allowed.

She gripped my hand and smiled. "Thank you for telling me the truth. I still want to bring Arthur back. Even if it's just long enough to say a few words."

So she was going to do it, as I had known she would. "So you don't want him for weeks, or days, only long enough to talk."

"I think so."

"I don't mean to rush you, Mrs. Fiske, but I need to know before we set up an appointment. You see, it takes more time and energy to raise and then lay to rest, one right after another." If she laid and raised quickly enough, Mrs. Fiske might be able to remember Arthur at his best.

"Oh, of course. If possible I would like to talk for several hours."

"Then it's best if you take him home for at least the evening. We can schedule putting him back for tomorrow night." I would push for a quick laying to rest. I didn't think Mrs. Fiske could take watching her husband rot before her eyes.

"That sounds good." She took a deep breath. I knew what she was going to say. She looked so brave and resolute. "I want to be there when you bring him back."

"Your presence is required, Mrs. Fiske. You see, a zombie has no real will of its own. Your husband should be able to think on his own at first, but as time wears on, the zombie finds it very difficult to decide things. The person, or persons, who raised it will have control over it."

"You and I?"

"Yes."

She paled even more, her grip tightening.

"Mrs. Fiske?" I got her a glass of water. "Sip it slowly." When she seemed better, I asked, "Are you sure you're up to this tonight?"

"Is there anything I need to bring?"

"A suit of your husband's clothes would be nice. Maybe a favorite object, hat, trophy, to help him orient himself. The rest I'll supply." I hesitated, because some of the color had crept into her face, but she needed to be prepared. "There will be blood at the ceremony."

"Blood." Her voice was a breathy whisper.

"Chicken, I'll bring it. There will also be some ointment to spread over our faces and hands. It glows faintly and smells fairly strange, but not unpleasant." Her next question would be the usual.

"What do we do with the blood?"

I gave the usual answer. "We sprinkle some on the grave and some on us."

She swallowed very carefully, looking slightly gray.

"You can back out now but not later. Once you've paid your deposit, it can't be refunded. And once the ceremony begins, to break the circle is very dangerous."

She looked down, thinking. I liked that. Most who agreed right away were afraid later. The brave ones took time to answer. "Yes." She sounded very convinced. "To make peace with Arthur, I can do it."

"Good for you. How is tonight?"

"About midnight," she added hopefully.

I smiled. Everyone thought midnight was the perfect time for raising the dead. All that was required was darkness. Some people did put a great deal of stock in certain phases of the moon, but I had never found it necessary. "No, how about nine o'clock?"

"Nine?"

"If that will be all right. I have two other appointments tonight, and nine was left open."

She smiled. "That will be fine." Her hand shook as she signed the check for half the fee, the other half to be delivered after the raising.

We shook hands, and she said, "Call me Carla."

"I'm Anita."

"I'll see you at nine tonight at Wellington Cemetery."

I continued for her, "Between two large trees and across from the only hill."

"Yes, thank you." She flashed a watery smile and was gone.

I buzzed our receptionist area. "Mary, I'm booked up for this week and won't be seeing any more clients, until at least next Tuesday."

"I'll see to it, Anita."

I leaned back in my chair and soaked up the silence. Three animations a night was my limit. Tonight they were all routine, or almost. I was bringing back my first research scientist. His three colleagues couldn't figure out his notes, and their deadline, or rather grant, was running close. So dear Dr. Richard Norris was coming back from the dead to help them out. They were scheduled for midnight.

At three this next morning I would meet the widowed Mrs. Stiener. She wanted her husband to clear up some nasty details with his will.

Being an animator meant very little nightlife, no pun intended. Afternoons were spent interviewing clients and evenings raising the dead. Though we few were very popular at a certain kind of party—the sort where the host likes to brag about how many celebrities he knows, or worse yet, the kind who simply want to stare. I don't like being on display and refuse to go to parties unless forced. Our boss likes to keep us in the public eye to dispel rumors that we are witches or hobgoblins.

It's pretty pitiful at parties. All the animators huddled, talking shop like a bunch of doctors. But doctors don't get called *witch, monster, zombie queen*. Very few people remember to call us animators. For most, we are a dark joke. "This is Anita. She makes zombies, and I don't mean the drink." Then there would be laughter all around, and I would smile politely and know I'd be going home early.

Tonight there was no party to worry over, just work. Work was power, magic, a strange dark impulse to raise more than what you were paid for. Tonight would be cloudless, moonlit, and starred; I could feel it. We were different, drawn to the night, unafraid of death and its many forms, because we had a sympathy for it.

Tonight I would raise the dead.

Wellington Cemetery was new. All the tombstones were nearly the same size, square or rectangle, and set off into the night in near-perfect rows. Young trees and perfectly clipped evergreen shrubs lined the gravel driveway. The moon rode strong and high, bathing the scene clearly, if mysteriously, in silver and black. A handful of huge trees dotted the grounds. They looked out of place among all this newness. As Carla had said, only two of them grew close together.

The drive spilled into the open and encircled the hill. The mound of grass-covered earth was obviously man-made, so round, short, and domed. Three other drives centered on it. A short way down the west drive stood two large trees. As my car crunched over gravel, I could see someone dressed in white. A flare of orange was a match, and the reddish pinpoint of a cigarette sprang to life.

I stopped the car, blocking the drive, but few people on honest business visit cemeteries at night. Carla had beaten me here, very unusual. Most clients want to spend as little time as possible near the grave after dark. I walked over to her before unloading equipment.

There was a litter of burned-out cigarettes like stubby white bugs about her feet. She must have been here in the dark for hours waiting to raise a zombie. She either was punishing herself or enjoyed the idea. There was no way of knowing which.

Her dress, shoes, even hose, were white. Earrings of silver flashed in the moonlight as she turned to me. She was leaning against one of the trees, and its black trunk emphasized her whiteness. She only turned her head as I came up to her.

Her eyes looked silver-gray in the light. I couldn't decipher the look on her face. It wasn't grief.

"It's a beautiful night, isn't it?"

I agreed that it was.

"Carla, are you all right?" She stared at me terribly calm. "I'm feeling much better than I did this afternoon."

"I'm very glad to hear that. Did you remember to bring his clothes and a memento?"

She motioned to a dark bundle by the tree.

"Good, I'll unload the car." She didn't offer to help, which was not unusual. Most of the time it was fear that prevented it. I realized my Omega was the only car in sight.

I called softly, but sound carries on summer nights. "How did you get here? I don't see a car."

"I hired a cab, it's waiting at the gate."

A cab. I would love to have seen the driver's face when he dropped her off at the cemetery gates. The three black chickens clucked from their cage in the backseat. They didn't have to be black, but it was the only color I could get for tonight. I was beginning to think our poultry supplier had a sense of humor.

Arthur Fiske was only recently dead, so from the box in the trunk I took only a jar of homemade ointment and a machete. The ointment was pale off-white with flecks of greenish light in it. The glowing flecks were graveyard mold. You wouldn't find it in this cemetery. It only grew in graveyards that had stood for at least a hundred years. The ointment also contained the obligatory spider webs and other noisome things, plus herbs and spices to hide the smell and aid the magic. If it was magic.

I smeared the tombstone with it and called Carla over. "It's your turn now, Carla." She stubbed out her cigarette and came to stand before me. I smeared her face and hands and told her, "You stand just behind the tombstone throughout the raising."

She took her place without a word while I placed ointment on myself. The pine scent of rosemary for memory, cinnamon and cloves for preservation, sage for wisdom, and lemon thyme to bind it all together seemed to soak through the skin itself.

I picked the largest chicken and tucked it under my arm. Carla stood where I had left her, staring down at the grave. There was an art to beheading a chicken with only two hands.

I stood at the foot of the grave to kill the chicken. Its first artery blood splashed onto the grave. It splattered over the fading chrysanthemums, roses, and carnations. A spire of white gladioli turned dark. I walked a circle sprinkling blood as I went, tracing a circle of steel with a bloody machete. Carla shut her eyes as the blood rained upon her.

I smeared blood on myself and placed the still-twitching body upon the flower mound. Then I stood once again at the foot of the grave. We were cut off now inside the blood circle, alone with the night, and our thoughts. Carla's eyes flashed white at me as I began the chant.

"Hear me, Arthur Fiske. I call you from the grave. By blood, magic, and steel, I call you. Arise, Arthur, come to us, come to me, Arthur Fiske." Carla joined me as she was supposed to. "Come to us, Arthur, come to us, Arthur. Arthur, arise." We called his name in ever-rising voices.

The flowers shuddered. The mound heaved upward, and the chicken slid to the side. A hand clawed free, ghostly pale. A second hand and Carla's voice failed her. She began moving round the gravestone to kneel to the left of the heaving mound. There was such wonder, even awe, in her face, as I called Arthur Fiske from the grave.

The arms were free. The top of a dark-haired head was in sight, but the top was almost all there was. The mortician had done his best, but Arthur's had been a closed-casket funeral.

The right side of his face was gone, blasted away. Clean white bone shone at jaw and skull, and silver bits of wire where the bone had been strung together. It still wasn't a face. The nose was empty holes, bare and white. The skin was shredded and snipped short to look neater. The left eye rolled wildly in the bare socket. I could see the tongue moving between the broken teeth. Arthur Fiske struggled from the grave.

I tried to remain calm. It could be a mistake. "Is that Arthur?"

Her hoarse whisper came to me. "Yes."

"That is not a heart attack."

"No." Her voice was calm now, incredibly normal. "No, I shot him at close range."

"You killed him, and had me bring him back."

Arthur was having some trouble freeing his legs, and I ran to Carla. I tried to help her to her feet but she wouldn't move.

"Get up, get up, damn it, he'll kill you!"

Her next words were very quiet. "If that's what he wants."

"God help me, a suicide."

I forced her to look at me instead of the thing in the grave. "Carla, a murdered zombie always kills his murderer first, always. No forgiveness, that is a rule. I can't control him until after he has killed you. You have to run, now."

She saw me, understood, I think, but said, "This is the only way to be free of guilt. If he forgives me, I'll be free."

"You'll be dead!"

Arthur freed himself and was sitting on the crushed, earth-strewn flowers. It would take him a little while to organize, but not too long.

"Carla, he will kill you. There will be no forgiveness." Her eyes had wandered back to the zombie, and I slapped her twice, very hard. "Carla, you will die out here, and for what? Arthur is dead, really dead. You don't want to die."

Arthur slid off the flowers and stood uncertainly. His eye rolling around in its socket finally spotted us. Though he didn't have much to show expression with, I could see joy on his shattered face. There was a twitch of a smile as he shambled toward us, and I began dragging her away. She didn't fight me, but she was a dead, awkward weight. It is very hard to drag someone away if they don't want to go.

I let her sink back to the ground. I looked at the clumsy but determined zombie and decided to try. I stood in front of him, blocking him from Carla. I called upon whatever power I possessed and talked to him. "Arthur Fiske, hear me, listen only to me."

He stopped moving and stared down at me. It was working, against all the rules, it was working.

It was Carla who spoiled it. Her voice saying, "Arthur, Arthur, forgive me."

He was distracted and tried to move toward her voice. I stopped him with a hand on his chest. "Arthur, I command you, do not move. I who raised you command you."

She called one more time. That was all he needed. He flung me away absentmindedly. My head hit the tombstone. It wasn't much of a blow, no blood like on television, but it took everything out of me for a minute. I lay in the flowers, and it seemed very important to hear myself breathe.

Arthur reached down for her, slowly. His face twitched, and his tongue made small sounds that might have been "Carla."

The clumsy hands stroked her hair. He half-fell, half-knelt by her. She drew back at that, afraid.

I started crawling over the flowers toward them. She was not going to commit suicide with my help.

The hands stroked her face, and she backed away, just a few inches. The thing crawled after her. She backpedaled faster, but he came on surprisingly quick. He pinned her under his body, and she started screaming.

I half-crawled, half-fell across the zombie's back.

The hands crept up her body, touching her shoulders.

Her eyes rolled back to me. "Help me!"

I tried. I tugged at him, trying to pull him off her. Zombies do not have supernatural strength, no matter what the media would like you to think, but Arthur had been a large, muscular man. If he could have felt pain, I might have pulled him off, but there was no real way to distract him.

"Anita, please!"

The hands settled on her neck and squeezed.

I found the machete where it had dropped to the ground. It was sharp, and did damage, but he couldn't feel it. I chopped at his head and back. He ignored me. Even decapitated, he would keep coming. His hands were the problem. I knelt and sighted at his lower arm. I didn't dare try it any closer to her face. The blade flashed silver. I brought it down with all the strength in my back and arms, but it took five blows to break the bone.

The separated hand kept squeezing as if it were still attached. I threw the machete down and began prying one finger at a time from her neck. It was time consuming.

Carla stopped struggling. I screamed my rage and helplessness at him and kept prying up the fingers. The strong hands squeezed until there was a cracking sound. Not a sharp pencil-break like a leg or an arm, but a crackling as the bones crushed together. Arthur seemed satisfied. He stood up from the body. All expression left him. He was empty, waiting for a command.

I fell back into the flowers, not sure whether to cry, or scream, or just run. I just sat there and shook. But I had to do something about the zombie. I couldn't just leave him to wander around.

I tried to tell him to stay, but my voice wouldn't come. His eye followed me as I stumbled to the car. I came back with a handful of salt. In the other hand I scooped the fresh grave dirt. Arthur watched me without expression. I stood at the outer edge of the circle. "I give you back to the earth from which you came."

I threw the dirt upon him. He turned to face me.

"With salt I bind you to your grave." The salt sounded like sleet on his suit. I made the sign of a cross with the machete. "With steel I give you back."

I realized that I had begun the ceremony without getting another chicken. I bent and retrieved the dead one and slit it open. I drew still-warm and bloody entrails free. They glistened in the moonlight. "With flesh and blood I command you, Arthur, return to your grave and walk no more."

He lay down upon the grave. It was as if he had lain in quicksand. It just swallowed him up. With a last shifting of flowers, the grave was as before, almost.

I threw the gutted chicken to the ground and knelt beside the woman's body. Her neck flopped at an angle just slightly wrong.

I got up and shut the trunk of my car. The sound seemed to echo, too loud. Wind seemed to roar in the tall trees. The leaves rustled and whispered. The trees all looked like flat black shadows, nothing had any depth to it. All noises were too loud. The world had become a one-dimensional cardboard thing. I was in shock. It would keep me numb and safe for a little while. Would I dream about Carla tonight? Would I try to save her again and again? I hoped not.

Somewhere up above, nighthawks flitted. Their cries came thin and eerie, echoing loud. I looked at the body by the grave. The whiteness of it stained now with dirt. So much for the other half of my fee.

I got in the car, smearing blood over the steering wheel and key. There were phone calls to make: to my boss, to the police, and to cancel the rest of my appointments. I would be raising no more dead tonight. There was a taxi to send away. I wondered how much the meter had run up.

My thoughts ran in dull, frightened circles. I began to shake, hands trembling. Tears came hot and violent. I sobbed and screamed in the privacy of my car. When I could breathe without choking, and my hand was steady, I put the car in gear. I would definitely be seeing Carla tonight and Arthur. What's one more nightmare?

I left Carla there alone, with Arthur's forgiveness, one leg lost in the flowers of his grave.

IN BEAUTY, LIKE THE NIGHT

by Norman Partridge

Norman Partridge is the author of the novels *Saguaro Riptide, The Ten Ounce Siesta, Slippin' into Darkness, Wildest Dreams,* and *Dark Harvest,* which was named one of the 100 Best Books of 2006 by *Publishers Weekly.* He also wrote a media-tie in novel *The Crow: Wicked Prayer,* which was later adapted into the fourth *Crow* film.

Partridge's short fiction—which has appeared in *Amazing Stories* and *Cemetery Dance* and in a number of anthologies, such as *Dark Voices 6, Love in Vein,* and *Retro Pulp Tales*—has been collected in three volumes: *Mr. Fox and Other Feral Tales, Bad Intentions,* and *The Man with the Barbed-Wire Fists.*

In the introduction to the latter collection, Partridge describes in detail his first experience seeing *Night of the Living Dead* at the local drive-in. "The drive-in in my hometown had not one… not two… but *three* cemeteries as neighbors," Partridge says. "Realizing that, a nasty little idea began to nibble at the corners of my imagination. I couldn't help but wonder what would happen if the dead folks in those cemeteries clawed their way out of their graves and came shuffling across the road to pay us a little visit."

Which sounds to me like the origin of many zombie tales if not this one in particular.

The beach was deserted.

Somehow, they knew enough to stay out of the sun.

Nathan Grimes rested his elbows on the balcony and peered through his binoculars. As he adjusted the focus knob, the smooth, feminine mounds that bordered the crescent-shaped beach became nets of purslane and morning glory, and the green blur that lay beyond sharpened to a crazy quilt of distinct colors—emerald, charcoal, glimpses of scarlet—a dark panorama of manchineel trees, sea grapes, and coconut palms.

Nathan scanned the shadows until he found the golden-bronze color of her skin. Naked, just out of reach of the sun's rays, she leaned against the gentle curve of a coconut palm, curling a strand of singed blonde hair around the single finger that remained on her left hand. Her fingertip was red—with nail polish, not blood—and she thrust it into her mouth and licked both finger and hair, finally releasing a spit curl that fought the humid Caribbean breeze for a moment and then drooped in defeat.

Kara North, Miss December.

Nathan remembered meeting Kara at the New Orleans Mansion the previous August. She'd posed in front of a bountifully trimmed Christmas tree for Teddy Ching's centerfold shot, and Nathan—fresh off a plane from the Los Angeles offices of *Grimesgirl* magazine—had walked in on the proceedings, joking that the holiday decorations made him feel like he'd done a Rip Van Winkle in the friendly skies.

Nathan smiled at the memory. There were several elegantly wrapped packages under the tree that August day, but each one was empty, just a prop for Teddy's photo shoot. Kara had discovered that sad fact almost immediately, and they'd all had a good laugh about her mercenary attitude while Teddy shot her with a little red Santa cap on her head and sassy red stockings on her feet and nothing but golden-bronze flesh in between.

Empty boxes. Nathan shook his head. He'd seen the hunger in Kara's eyes when the shoot was over. A quick study, that one. Right off she'd known that he alone could fill those boxes in a finger-snap.

And now she knew enough to stay out of the sun. They all did. Nathan had been watching them for two days, ever since the morning after the accident. He wasn't worried about them breaking into the house, for his Caribbean sanctuary was a Moorish palace surrounded by high, broken-bottle-encrusted walls that were intended to fend off everyone from prying *paparazzi* to anti-porn assassins. No, the thing that worried him about the dead Grimesgirls was that they didn't act at all like the zombies he'd seen on television.

Most of those miserable gut-buckets had crawled out of the grave and weren't very mobile. In fact, Nathan couldn't remember seeing any zombies on the tube that bore much of a resemblance to their living brethren, but that could simply be chalked up to the journalistic penchant for photographing the most grotesque members of any enemy group. It was an old trick. Just as they'd focused attention on the most outrageous members of the SDS and the Black Panthers in order to turn viewers against those groups way back when in the sixties, the media would now focus on the most bizarre specimens of this current uprising.

Uprising. It was an odd word to choose—once such a hopeful word for Nathan's generation—but it seemed somehow appropriate, now stirring images not of demonstration but of reanimation. Cemeteries pitted with open graves, shrouds blowing across empty boulevards… midnight glimpses of a shadow army driven by an insatiable hunger for human flesh.

Nathan wondered what the network anchors would make of Kara North. All theories about media manipulation aside, he doubted that there were many other suntanned zombies besides last year's Miss December. Stateside, the victims of an accident such as the one that had occurred on Grimes Island would have been devoured by predator zombies before reanimation could occur. That hadn't happened here, because there weren't any predator zombies on the island when Kara and the others had perished. So something different had happened here, maybe something that hadn't happened before, anywhere.

Kara raised her good hand in what might have been a feeble wave.

"Freaks," Nathan whispered, unable to fight off his signature wry smile. "Zombie freaks." He set down the binoculars—an expensive German product, for Nathan Grimes demanded the best in everything—and picked up his pistol, a Heckler & Koch P7M13, also German, also expensive.

The sun inched lower in the sky. The waves became silver mirrors, glinting in Nathan's eyes. He put on sunglasses and the glare flattened to a soft pearly glow. As the horizon melted electric blue and the shadows thickened beneath the coconut palms, Kara North, Miss December, shambled toward the glass-encrusted walls of Nathan's beachfront palace. Again, she curled a lock of blonde hair around her finger. Again, she sucked the burned strands wet.

Strange that she could focus on her hair and ignore her mutilated hand, Nathan thought as he loaded the Heckler. His gut told him that her behavior was more than simple instinct, and he wondered just how far her intelligence extended. Did she know that she was dead? Was she capable of posing such a question?

Could she think?

The curl drooped, uncoiled, and again Kara went to sucking it. Nathan remembered a Christmas that had come in August complete with the holiday smells of hot buttered rum and Monterey pine, the sounds of the air-conditioner running on HIGH COOL and seasoned oak crackling in the fireplace. He recalled Kara's dreams and the way she kissed and her red nails slashing through wrapping paper as she opened gifts he'd originally intended for Ronnie. And then, when he was fully ready to surrender to his memories, the shifting July winds brushed back across Grimes Island, carrying the very real stink of scorched metal and charred rubber.

The scent of destruction.

Nathan covered his nose and raised the pistol.

Two days ago, Nathan had the situation under control. Certainly, considering the circumstances, the arrangements for evacuating the Grimesgirls from the United States had been maddening. Certainly, such arrangements would have been completely impossible if Nathan hadn't had the luxury of satellite communications, but such perks went hand in hand with network ownership.

Two days ago, he was, in short, a completely satisfied man. After all, the foresight which some had dubbed paranoia was paying off, and his contingency plan to end all contingency plans was taking shape: he had his own island fortress, adequate provisions, and a plan to sit out the current difficulties in the company of twelve beautiful centerfold models.

So, two days ago, he didn't worry as the hands of his Rolex crossed past the appointed hour of the Grimesgirls' arrival, for the dangerous part of the evacuation operation had already been carried out with military precision. In rapid succession, a trio of Bell JetRanger choppers had touched down on the roof of the New Orleans Mansion, and the Grimesgirls had been transported without incident to a suburban airfield where a private security force was guarding Nathan's Gulfstream IV. Needless to say, takeoff had been immediate.

Of course, the operation was costly, but Nathan considered it a wise investment. He expected that there would be a real shortage of attractive female flesh by the time the government got things under control. The public, as always, would have an immediate need for his services, and he figured that the people he laughingly referred to as his "readers" wouldn't mind looking at last season's models, at least until the competition got into gear.

If there was any competition left. Nathan got himself a tequila—half listening for the Gulfstream, half watching the latest parade of gut-buckets on CNN—and soon he was imagining his chief competitors as walking corpses, one with gold chains circling his broken neck and an expensive toupee covering the gnaw marks on his skull, the other with his trademark pipe jammed between rotted lips, gasping, unable to fill his lungs with enough oxygen to kindle a blaze in the tar-stained brier.

Nathan grinned, certain that he'd never suffer such a humiliating end. He was a survivor. He had plans. And he would get started on them right now, while he waited.

He found a yellow legal pad and started brainstorming titles. GRIMESGIRLS: OUR ISLAND YEAR. No, too much fun in that one. GRIMESGIRLS: FROM HELL TO PARADISE. Better. He'd have to search for the right tone to stifle those who would accuse him of exploitation. And Teddy Ching's pictures would have to match. Hopefully, Teddy had shot lots of nice stuff during the evacuation—decaying faces mashed against the windows of the Mansion, the French Quarter streets clogged with zombies—shots that stank of danger. Pictures like that would make a perfect contrast to the spreads they'd do on the island.

GRIMESGIRLS: NATIONAL TREASURES SAVED. Nathan stared at what he'd written and smiled. Patriotic. Proud. Words as pretty as dollar signs.

Wind from the open door caught the paper, and Nathan trapped it against the table. For the first time he noticed the darkness, the suffocating gray shroud that had come long before sunset. The plane was horribly late. He'd been so caught up in planning the magazine that he'd lost track of time. Jesus. The Gulfstream could be trapped inside the storm, fighting it, low on fuel....

The storm rustled over the coconut palms with a sound like a giant broom sweeping the island clean. Rainwater guttered off the tile roof. It was only five o'clock, but the darkness seemed impenetrable. Nathan sent Buck and Pablo to the landing strip armed with flares. He put on a coat and paced on the balcony of his suite until the thrashing sounds of the approaching Gulfstream drove him inside. He stared into the darkness, imagining that it was as thick as pudding, and he was truly startled when the explosion bloomed in the distance. Ronnie (Miss October three years past) tried to embrace him, but he pushed her away and rushed from the room. It was much later, after the rain had diminished to a drizzling mist, that he stepped outside and smelled the wreck for the first time.

Buck and Pablo didn't return. The night passed, and then the morning. Nathan didn't go looking for the boys. He was afraid that they might be looking for him. He hid his pistol and the keys to his Jeep, and he slapped Ronnie when she called him a coward. After that she was quiet, and when she'd been quiet for a very long time he played at being magnanimous. He opened the wall safe and left her alone with a peace offering.

Downstairs, he hid the yellow legal pad in a desk drawer that he rarely opened. He closed the drawer carefully, slowly, without a sound.

That was how it began, two days ago, on Grimes Island. Since then, the living had moved quietly, listening for the footsteps of the dead.

The Heckler was warm, and as Nathan reloaded it he wished that his talents as a marksman were worthy of such a fine weapon. He set the pistol on his dresser and went downstairs, fighting the memory of the purple-gray mess that Kara North's forehead had become when one of his shots—the fifth or the sixth—finally found the mark.

That wasn't the way he wanted to remember her. He wanted to remember Miss December. No gunshots, only Teddy's camera clicking. No blood, only a red Santa cap. Sassy red socks. And nothing but golden-bronze flesh in between.

Nathan took a bottle of Cuervo Gold from beneath the bar. When it came to tequila he preferred Chinaco, but he'd finished the last bottle on the night of the crash and now the cheaper brand would have to do.

"I saw what you did." Ronnie confronted him the way a paperback detective would, sliding the Heckler across the mahogany bar, marring the wood with a long, ugly scratch. "You should have asked Kara in for a drink, made it a little easier on the poor girl. That was a damn rude way to say goodbye, Nate."

Nathan filled a glass with ice, refusing to meet Ronnie's patented withering stare, but that didn't stop her words. "She looked so cute, too, worshiping you from a distance with those big blue eyes of hers. Did you see the way she tried to curl her hair?" Ronnie clicked her tongue against her teeth. "It's a shame what a little humidity can do to a really nice *coiffure*."

Nathan said nothing, slicing a lime now, and Ronnie giggled. "Strong and silent, huh? C'mon, Nate, you're the one who blew off the top of her head. Tell me how it felt."

Nathan stared at the tip of Ronnie's nose, avoiding her eyes Once she'd been an autumnal vision with hair the color of fallen leaves. Miss October. She'd had the look of practiced ease, skin the color of brandy, and large chocolate eyes that made every man in America long for a cold night. But Nathan had learned all too well the October power of those eyes, the way they could chill a man with a single frosty glance.

He pocketed the Heckler. He'd have to be more careful about leaving the gun where she could get at it. Coke freaks could get crazy. He poured Cuervo Gold into his glass and then drank, pretending that the only thing bothering him was the quality of the tequila. Then he risked a quick glance at her eyes, still chocolate-brown but now sticky with a yellow sheen that even Teddy Ching couldn't airbrush away.

Ronnie picked up a cocktail napkin and shredded its corners. "Why her? Why'd you shoot Kara and not the others?"

"She was the first one that came into range." Nathan swirled his drink with a swizzle stick shaped like the cartoon Grimesgirl that ran on the last page of every issue. "It was weird. When I looked into Kara's eyes, I had the feeling that she was relieved to see me. Relieved! Then I raised the gun, and it was as if she suddenly realized...."

Ronnie tore the napkin in half, then quarters. "They don't realize, Nate. They don't think."

"They're not like those things on TV, Ronnie. You noticed the way she looked at me. Christ, she actually waved at me today. I'm not saying that they're geniuses, but there's something there... something I don't like."

Bits of purple paper dotted the mahogany bar. Ronnie fingered them one by one, lazily reassembling the napkin. Nathan sensed her disapproval. He knew that she wanted him to strap on his pistol and go gunning for the Grimesgirls as if he were Lee Van Cleef in some *outré* spaghetti western.

"Look, Ronnie, it's not like they're acting *normal*, beating down our walls like the things on TV do. We just have to be a little careful, is all. There are eleven of them now, and sooner or later they'll all wander close to the gate the same way that Kara did. Then I can nail them with no problem. And then we can go out again... it'll be safe."

"Don't be so sure." He made the mistake of sighing and her voice rose angrily. "They didn't fly in by themselves, you know. There was a pilot, a copilot... maybe even a few guards. And Teddy. That's at least five or six more people." Now it was her turn to sigh. "Not to mention Buck and Pablo."

"You might be right. But who knows, the others might be so crippled up that they can't get over to this side of the island fast, or at all. Or they could have been incinerated in the explosion. Maybe that's what happened to Buck and Pablo." Nathan looked at her, not wanting to say that the boys might have been someone's dinner, and she pursed her lips, which was a hard thing for her to do because they were full and pouty.

"Hell, maybe the boys got away," he said, realizing that he was grasping at straws. "Took a boat or something. I can't see the docks from here, so I can't be sure. It could be that they reasoned with the girls, tricked them somehow—"

"Are you really saying that zombies can think? That's crazy! If they're dead, they're hungry. That's it—that's what they say on TV. And Kara North sucking a little spit curl doesn't convince me otherwise."

Nathan cut another slice of lime and sucked it, appreciating the sharp tang. It was the last lime on the island, and he was determined to enjoy it. "Maybe the whole thing has something to do with the crash," he said, taking another tack. "I can't figure it. I saw the explosion, but all the girls seem to be in pretty good shape. Kara was missing a few fingers and her hair was singed, and a few of the others are kind of wracked up, but none of them is badly burned, like you'd expect."

"We could drive out to the plane and see what happened for ourselves," Ronnie offered. "They can't catch us in the Jeep." She touched his hand, lightly, tentatively. "We might be able to salvage some stuff from the wreck. Someone might have had a rifle, maybe even one with a scope, and that would be a much better weapon than your pistol."

Nathan considered her argument, then jerked his hand away as soon as he realized what lay behind it. "Who was bringing it in for you? C'mon, Ronnie… you know what I'm talking about. Who was your mule this trip?"

She tried to look hurt. Did a good job of it. "You think you're quite a detective, don't you? Well, round up the usual suspects. Ronnie's a coke freak waiting on a mule. Buck and Pablo pulled a Houdini, or maybe they had a powwow with Kara and her pals, the world's first intellectual gut-buckets. C'mon, Nate, put it together for me, but do it before those things out there turn nasty and come after us." She grabbed the remnants of the napkin and flung purple confetti at his face. "Wake up, boss. The party's over. Me, you've got figured, but them… they're dead, and they're hungry, and that's that."

She let the words hang there for a minute. Then she rose and walked to the stairs, gracefully, like brandy pouring from a bottle. *With fluid elegance,* he thought wryly. He watched her calves flex, enjoyed the way she swung her ass for him. Eagerly, he ran his thumb over the little plastic breasts on the cartoon-inspired swizzle stick.

"Me, you've got figured." She did the measured over-the-shoulder glance that she'd used three years ago in her Grimesgirl centerfold, then turned and ran long fingers over her naked breasts, along her narrow hips. Nathan's thumb traveled over the cute swizzle-stick ass; he pressed down without realizing it, and the plastic snapped in two.

Ronnie laughed, climbing the stairs, not looking back.

After he'd come, Nathan kicked off the satin sheets and opened the wall safe. He cut three lines on a vanity mirror and presented them to Ronnie, then hurried downstairs because he hated the sound of her snorting. In the kitchen, he popped open a Pepsi and took a box of Banquet fried chicken out of the freezer. He chose two breasts and three thighs, placed them on a sheet of Reynolds Wrap, and fired the oven.

While he waited for the chicken, he turned on the television and fiddled with the satellite controls until he found something besides snow. Immediately, he recognized the Capitol dome in the upper right-hand corner of the screen, just below the CNN logo. It was a favorite camera setup of Washington correspondents, but there was no reporter standing in frame. There wasn't a voiceover, either.

A gut-bucket in a hospital gown staggered into view, then lurched away from the light. Another followed, this one naked, fleshless. Nathan watched, fascinated. It was only a matter of time before one of the zombies knocked over the camera or smashed the lights. Why didn't the network cut away? He couldn't figure it out.

Unless he'd tuned in some kind of study. Unless the camera had been set up to record the zombies. Bolted down. Protected. That kind of thing.

But to send it out on the satellite? It didn't make any sense. Then Nathan remembered that all satellite broadcasts weren't intended for public consumption. He might be picking up a direct feed *to* CNN instead of a broadcast *from* CNN. In the past he'd enjoyed searching for just such feeds with his satellite dish—on a location to network feed, you could pick up all the nasty remarks that reporters made about the government gobbledygook they fed to the American public, and you could find out what really went on during the commercial breaks at any number of live events.

Nathan stared at the CNN logo superimposed in the corner of the screen. Was that added at the network, or would a technician in a mobile unit add it from location? He wished he knew enough about the technical end of broadcasting to decide. He switched channels, searching for another broadcast. When he was sure he'd exhausted all possibilities, he tried to return to the CNN transmission.

He couldn't find it.

It wasn't there anymore.

A blank hiss filled the room. Nathan hit the mute button on the remote control. A few minutes passed before he noticed the burning chicken, but he couldn't bring himself to do anything about it, didn't want to look at it. Images coiled like angry snakes in his mind, ready to strike, ready to poison him. The explosion, the fleshless zombie on TV, Kara North's mutilated hand.

The snakes struck, and Nathan lurched to the sink and vomited Pepsi.

First he heard her shouts, and he was up off the couch and almost to the stairs before he remembered that he'd left the gun on the kitchen sink. He pivoted too quickly at the foot of the stairway, lurched against the wall, and then ran to the gun, Ronnie's insistent cries still filling his ears.

He returned to the staircase just as she began her descent. "He was calling me," she said, her eyes wild, unfocused. "Outside. I heard him. I went out onto the balcony but I couldn't see…. But I talked to him, and he answered me! Christ, we've got to let him in!"

"You mean someone's alive out there?"

Ronnie nodded, naked, shivering, her hair a sweaty tangle. Nathan didn't like what he saw any better than what he'd heard. Maybe she was just strung out. Maybe she'd been dreaming. Sure.

One of the gut-buckets had pounded on the gate and she'd imagined the rest. Or maybe someone had indeed survived the crash.

"We're not opening up until I check things out," Nathan said. "Just stay here. Don't move." He squeezed her shoulders to reinforce the order.

Upstairs, he punched several buttons on the bedroom wall before stepping onto the balcony. Deadwhite light spilled across the compound, glittering eerily over the glass-encrusted walls and illuminating the beach. A man wearing a blue uniform stood near the gate. Either the pilot or the copilot. His complexion was sallow in the artificial light, and his chin was bruised a deep purple. He stared up at Nathan and his brow creased, as if he hadn't expected to see Nathan at all.

The pilot's mouth opened.

In the distance, a wave washed over the beach.

"Ronnie… I've come to see… Ronnie."

"Jesus!" Nathan lowered the Heckler. "What happened out there? The explosion… how did you—"

"Ronnie… Ronnie… I've come to see… Ron… *neeeee*. I've come…."

The muscles in Nathan's forearms quivered in revulsion. He forced himself to raise the Heckler and aim.

He fired. Missed.

Muddy gray eyes stared into the frosty light. Wide, frantic. The thing waved its hands, wildly signaling Nathan to stop. He fired again, but the shot whizzed over the zombie's shoulder. Hurriedly, it backed off, ripping at its coat and the sweat-stained shirt beneath.

Nathan's third shot clipped the thing's ear just as it ripped open its shirt.

"I'm expected," it screeched. "Expected and I've come to see…."

Nathan swore, stunned by the sight of a half-dozen plastic bags filled with cocaine secured to the zombie's chest with strips of medical tape.

Ronnie's mule. Two days dead and still trying to complete its deal.

The thing moved forward. It was smiling now, sure that Nathan finally understood.

Nathan took aim—*Nathan, stop!*—but black lights exploded in his head before he could squeeze off another shot. *"You're crazy, Nathan!"* He hit the balcony floor, cutting his left eyebrow on the uneven tile, and his mind had barely processed that information and recognized Ronnie's voice when he realized that the Heckler was being pried from his fingers. *"He's alive, and you tried to kill him!"* He tried to rise and this time he glimpsed the heavy German binoculars arcing towards him.

He had just managed to close his eyes when the binoculars smashed into his bloody brow.

Screaming. God, she was screaming.

She must have realized the truth.

Nathan struggled to his feet just as Ronnie's cries were punctuated by gun-shots. He leaned against the balcony and tried to focus on what was happening on the beach.

But they weren't on the beach. The big gate stood open, and the dead pilot was inside the compound, backing Ronnie across a patch of stunted grass. She fired the Heckler and cocaine puffed from one of the packets taped to the thing's chest. She got off three more shots that destroyed the zombie's left shoulder. Its left arm came loose, slithered through its shirtsleeve, and dropped silently to the grass. The thing stared down at its severed limb, confused by the sudden amputation.

Ronnie retreated under the jutting balcony.

The zombie followed her into the house.

Nathan stumbled through the bedroom doorway. Ronnie wasn't screaming anymore. That sound had been replaced by subtler but no less horrifying noises: the Heckler clicking, empty, the zombie whispering Ronnie's name. Dizzily, Nathan reached the top of the stairway just as Ronnie mounted the first stair. He tried to grab her but the pilot got hold of her first and tugged her away.

It stared at her for a moment, still pleading, as if it only wanted her to take delivery, but as it pulled her closer its expression changed.

Its nostrils flared.

It pushed her down onto the stairs and held her there.

Its mouth widened, but no words were left there.

Its eyes were wild, suddenly gleaming.

Hungry.

Dry teeth clamped Ronnie's left breast. She squealed and pulled away, but the thing punched its fingers through her left thigh, holding her down. An urge had been triggered, and suddenly the gut-bucket was insatiable. Its teeth ripped Ronnie's flesh; it swallowed without chewing; it was a shark in the grip of a feeding frenzy.

Nathan backed away, staring at the zombie, glancing at the empty pistol on the hallway floor. Another gut-bucket shambled forward from the shadowy bar. This one had something in its hand, a machete, and Nathan was suddenly glad that he was going to die because he didn't think he could bear living in a world where you couldn't tell the living from the dead, where fucking corpses could talk, could remember, could fool you right up to the moment when they started to bite and tear and swallow....

The rusty machete cleaved the pilot's head from his shoulders; the dead thing collapsed on top of Ronnie.

The holder of the machete stared up at him, and Nathan froze like a deer trapped by a pair of headlights.

"Christ, boss, don't worry. I'm alive," Buck Taylor said, and then he went to close the gate.

Buck said he couldn't eat or drink so soon after cleaning up the remains of

Ronnie and the gut-bucket pilot. Instead, he talked. Nathan tried not to drink too much Cuervo Gold, tried to listen, but his thoughts turned inexorably to the puzzle of the pilot's strange behavior.

"So the storm was coming down in buckets, splattering every damn inch of soil. Pablo was drinking coffee, and I'd had so much that I just had to take a piss, but it was really coming down—"

The rusty machete lay before Buck on the oak tabletop; his fingers danced over the blade as he spoke. He had once been a center for the Raiders—Good Old Number 66 had never missed a game in seven seasons of play—but Nathan couldn't imagine that he'd ever looked this bad, not even after the most desperate contest imaginable. His bald pate was knotted with bruises, and every time he touched them he looked wistful, like he was wishing he'd had a helmet.

"—so I hacked my way into the forest and got under a tree, that kind with leaves like big pancakes. And I started to piss. And just then I heard the engines. Holy Christ, I got zipped up quick and—"

The twin sixes on Buck's football jersey were smeared with slimy black stains. There was a primitive splint on his left arm, held in place with strips torn from a silver-and-black bandana. The massive biceps swelling between the damp strips of wood was an ugly color much worse than the blue-green of a natural bruise. It reminded Nathan of rotten cantaloupe, a sickly gray color. And the smell coming from the other side of the table was—

"—pissed all over my leg. I ain't ashamed to say it, because the left wing tore off just then and I thought I was dead for sure, with the plane heading straight for me. So I dived—"

Quickly. The pilot had been able to think quickly. He'd ripped off his shirt to show Nathan the cocaine. He'd gotten Ronnie to open the gate. And even though he'd lost an arm to Ronnie's gunfire, he'd acted as if he believed that he was still alive until he got close to her, the first live human he'd encountered since reanimating. That confrontation had triggered his horrible—

"—second thoughts, but there wasn't time. The broken wing flipped around in midair like a piece of balsa wood. No telling where it was gonna end up. Then the 'stream slammed sideways into a big stand of palm trees that bounced it right back onto the landing strip. It rolled and the other wing twisted off. And the wing that was still in the air—"

Came down on the machete. Buck's fingers did. Nathan watched them, and he slid away from the table, eased away from Number 66.

"I could see Pablo in the van. Even through the storm. I saw him trying to find a place to set his coffee. And then the wing hit the van, and the damn thing just exploded."

So the van had exploded. That was why the zombies hadn't been burned. The plane hadn't even caught fire—its fuel tanks were probably near empty after fighting the storm. But the van had had a full tank.

"I'm ashamed about that, but there was really nothing I could do. The fire was so intense. Even the zombies didn't go near it, and by the time it burned itself out there wasn't anything left of the van or Pablo."

Nathan's fingers closed around the pistol. He remembered the pilot ripping open his shirt. He remembered the pilot grabbing Ronnie, the momentary confusion in his muddy eyes, the excited gleam as he surrendered to the feeding frenzy. Buck was in control now, surely he was. But what would happen when he came close to his boss?

Nathan raised the Heckler. Buck grinned, like he didn't quite understand. Nathan looked at Buck's wounds, at the untouched glass of beer in front of him. Good Old Number 66 wasn't drinking, and he hadn't wanted any fried chicken. Maybe he didn't want fried chicken anymore. Maybe he didn't realize that yet, just like he didn't remember what had killed him.

"Buck, I want you to go back outside, back out with them," Nathan said, speaking as he would speak to a child. "You see, risking temptation is the dangerous part. It'll make you lose what's left of your mind."

"Boss, are you okay? Maybe you should get some sleep, stop thinking about Ronnie for a while. Maybe you should—"

Oh, they were smart. Getting smarter every minute. "You can't fool me, Buck. You can fool yourself, but you can't fool me."

Nathan aimed and Buck jolted backward, out of his chair, scrambling now. The first bullet exploded his left biceps, shattering the makeshift splint as it exited, but Buck didn't slow because football instincts die hard. He sprang to his feet, tucked his head, and charged across the kitchen.

His eyes shone with vitality, but Nathan was certain that it was the vitality of death, not life. Buck launched himself in a flying tackle and together they crashed to the floor. Nathan raised the Heckler, and Buck couldn't fight him off because the wound in his left arm was too severe, so he fought back the only way he could. He bit Nathan's shoulder, set his teeth, and tore.

Nathan screamed. White blotches of pain danced before his eyes.

Nathan's finger tightened on the trigger.

A bullet shattered the skull of Good Old Number 66.

Nathan saw it this way:

The crash had killed them instantly. All of them. And when they opened their eyes they found themselves on Grimes Island, just where they were supposed to be, and they imagined themselves survivors. They wandered through the lush forest, across the coral beaches, finding nothing to tempt them, nothing to trigger the horrible hunger.

Trapped in a transition period between death and rebirth they retained different levels of intelligence but were limited by overwhelming instincts. Instinctively, they knew enough to stay out of the sun. It was a simple matter of self-preservation, for the tropical sun could speed their decay. The instinct to devour the living was strong in them as well, but only when they were exposed to temptation. Nathan was sure of that after his experiences with Buck and the pilot. He was also certain that as long as temptation was absent up to the very point that the feeding frenzy took control, the dead of Grimes Island could still function at a level that separated them from the gut-buckets. Oh, they functioned at different sub-levels as he'd seen with Kara North, the pilot, and Buck, but in some cases, they functioned just as well as the living.

Perhaps something in human flesh, once devoured, triggered the change in behavior. Maybe something in the blood. Or perhaps it was the very act of cannibalism. Nathan didn't know the cause, didn't much care.

His wounded shoulder was scarlet-purple and swollen. Five days had passed since Buck had attacked him, and he couldn't decide if the bite was worse or better. Just to be safe, he'd injected himself with antibiotics, but he didn't know if his first aid made the slightest difference.

He didn't know if he was alive, or dead, or somewhere in between.

To clarify his thoughts, he noted his symptoms on the legal pad he'd hidden in his desk after the plane crash. Many were perplexing. He wished that he could consult with a scientist or a doctor, but his first attempt at stateside communications had proved fruitless, and soon he was afraid to communicate with anyone. He didn't relish the idea of ending up as a science project in some lab, and he didn't want an extermination squad invading Grimes Island, either.

The thing that bothered him most was that his heart was still beating. He couldn't understand how that was possible until he remembered that Buck's heart had been beating when he'd shot him—Nathan had felt it pounding against his own chest as they wrestled on the floor—and he was certain that Buck had been dead. Looking at his wounded shoulder, remembering the fire in Buck's eyes when he'd attacked, Nathan was positive of that. There were other symptoms, as well.

He couldn't eat. Every evening he cooked some fried chicken, even though the smell made him gag and the oily feel of it made him shiver. Last night he'd forced himself to eat two breasts and a thigh, and he'd spent the next five hours coiled in a cramped ball on the kitchen floor before finally surrendering to the urge to vomit. And he couldn't keep down Pepsi or Jose Cuervo either. The Cuervo Gold was especially bad; it burned his throat and made him miserable for hours. He did suck ice cubes, but only to keep his throat comfortable. And he'd started snorting the cocaine that Ronnie's mule had brought in, but only because he was afraid to sleep.

Cocaine. Maybe that was the problem. They said that cocaine killed the appetite, didn't they? And he'd started using the stuff at about the same time that he'd stopped eating. But five days without food... God, that was a long time. So it had to be more than just the cocaine. Didn't it?

He closed his eyes and thought about hunger, about food. He tried to picture the most appetizing banquet imaginable.

Nothing came to him for the longest time. Then he saw Kara North's mangled hand. The pilot's severed arm. Buck's ruined head.

His gut roiled.

He opened his eyes.

The facts seemed irrefutable, but somehow Nathan couldn't bring himself to leave the compound or, conversely, let the Grimesgirls enter. They were on the beach every night, enjoying themselves, tempting him. Miss November and Miss February sang love songs, serenading Nathan from the wrong side of the glass-encrusted walls. He watched them, smiling his wry smile on the outside, inside despising his cowardice.

He was bored, but he didn't risk watching television, either. If the networks had returned to the airwaves, he would certainly find himself looking straight into the eyes of living, breathing people, and while he seriously doubted that such a stimulus could trigger the feeding frenzy, he didn't want to expose himself, just to be on the safe side.

He didn't want to lose what he had.

So he snorted cocaine and wrote during the day. At night, he watched them. They all came to the beach now, even Teddy Ching. He had no legs; that's why he'd taken so long to cross the island. But Teddy didn't let that stop him. He dragged himself along, eagerly pursuing the Grimesgirls, his exposed spine wiggling as happily and uncontrollably as a puppy's tail. Three cameras were strung around his neck, and he often propped himself against the base of a manchineel tree and photographed the girls as they frolicked on the beach below.

More than anything, Nathan wished that he could develop those pictures. His Grimesgirls were still beautiful. Miss July, her stomach so firm, so empty above a perfect heart-shaped trim. Miss May, her skinless forehead camouflaged with a wreath of bougainvillea and orchids. The rounded breasts of Miss April, sunset bruised and shadowed, the nipples so swollen. The sunken yellow hollows beneath Miss August's eyes, hot dry circles, twin suns peering from her face with all the power of that wonderful month.

Twin suns in the middle of the night.

She walks in beauty, like the night... in beauty, like the night... of cloudless climes and... starry skies and all that's best of dark and bright...

And all that's best of dark and bright...

Nathan couldn't remember the rest of it. He wrote the words on his yellow pad, over and over, but he couldn't remember. He closed his eyes, and when he opened them the sea was hard with the flat light of morning.

He hurried inside long before the sunshine kissed the balcony.

The beach was deserted.

PRAIRIE

by Brian Evenson

Brian Evenson is the author of the books *Altmann's Tongue, Contagion, Dark Property*, and *Father of Lies*, among others. In 2005, his collection, *The Wavering Knife*, won the International Horror Guild Award. Two years later, his novel *The Open Curtain* was also a finalist, as well as for the Edgar Award. In addition to his own fiction, Evenson has translated the work of others into English, including the novel *Electric Flesh* by Claro (from the original French). A media tie-in novel, *Aliens: No Exit*, will be released around the same time as this volume, and Evenson has a new short story collection due out in 2009, called *Fugue State*.

This story, which originally appeared in the magazine *The Silver Web*, was inspired by Cabeza de Vaca's sixteenth century account of crossing North America after being shipwrecked, and Werner Herzog's movie *Aguirre, the Wrath of God* which, Evenson says, has a brilliant, mad ending. He says he was interested, too, in thinking about how certain places seem to have a dark but magical quality to them. How zombies entered into it is a mystery, however.

I.

Early evening, still distant from the prairie, we encountered a man with skin flayed half-free of his back. He allowed us to inspect that portion of him, and we saw the underskin, purpled and creased with folds that in their convolution resembled the human brain.

The runds off his back he had tanned and twisted into a belt, which he wore and which our captain tried, unsuccessfully, to purchase of him. When our physician inquired after the particulars of his persecutor, the man answered by unfurling from his rucksack a flapping sheet of skin with a large and hardened callous aswash at one end of it which, upon formal inspection, proved an empty, flavid face.

II.

Our paroch of late has taken to baptizing all we encounter, tallying their particulars on wound scrolls before they are slaughtered. As we walk, he counts the names, phrases aloud before us the petitions he will employ before the Church

225

as, spreading forth his lists of converts, he renders plea for sainthood.

III.

The air is fumid, choking. Near midday we were greeted by a man who made claim to raise the dead. Our captain bared his weapon and lopped the head from Rusk, with whom he has been at odds throughout the voyage, and then bade the man have at his task. The self-appointed Jesus sewed Rusk's head back onto the frame and then, with shaking fingers, uttered his shallow pronouncements. After ample wait, the captain ordered this fellow's head struck from his shoulders as well.

We carried the heads spikeshafted and passed onward. Nearing the prairie, they began to mumble, at which we sandsunk their shafts, abandoned them.

IV.

We have reached the prairie, the dead progressing in droves through shackle and quaking grass. We captured one and he was drawn forth with little struggle, falling nearly insensate once raised from the ground. His flesh was dark and stinking. We examined his armature, the way his mouth had been resewn and mandibled. Avelling the membrane lining the chest, we found the internal organs neatly removed, the lower orifices stoppered. With a sleight pressure of his palm, our physician sloughed away the skin that remnanted to the skull, then exposed the upper portion of the braincase by means of a racksaw. The brain had been removed, the emptied interior case showing in its blotchwork signs of siriasis or, as it is commonly called, sideration.

Our physician made severe notes and, when done, asked for the sake of experiment that the body be released. We lowered it to the earth and watched it come animate, stumble away.

V.

During the night, Latour harnessed a dead woman, for we have been long on the road. Devoid of resilience, she came too rapidly asunder beneath his hips. Even with eyes gritted shut he could gain no satisfaction. The paroch refused his confession.

VI.

At times one discovers the living hidden among the dead, the which can be discerned by the color manifest in their flesh, the sentience of their regard. They crouch to the center of a drove, allowing the dead to sweep them along.

One, we managed to capture. When he made pretense of death, the physician pierced him with his instruments until the man could not but grow bloody and roar.

We jointed his limbs, packed them in salt. His eyes shuttered and then opened again, his torso regaining a torpid motion. We watched his body struggle out and away from us. His boxed limbs thumped against the lid, grinding the salt.

VII.

We have consumed the remaining provisions. We eat the living when we ferret them out, and have eaten the horses as well. Still the prairie continues without cease.

The dead prove too festered and rizzared to consume. Instead, we encircle them and employ them as mounts. We tie them by twos front to back and lop free the heads. Sitting on the planed necks and shoulders, we goad them to motion by prodding the forward remnant of the brain's root.

VIII.

The prairie is subdued in dust and sand, footing given way. The dead are sparser and often balsamated, their armature careful and fresh. There is no sign of who has prepared them.

This morning we saw approaching at some distance a lone figure with a purposiveness that proved him still alive. When he came closer, he was seen to be slung with a large sack, groaning beneath its weight.

He attempted flight, but mounted athwart the dead we soon rode him down. Dropping the sack, he murdered Latour and Broch before being killed himself.

We struck a fire and ate what we could of the newly dead, then slit back the sack. Inside were two gray and curled women who stumbled away when released. We rode them down and coupled them severally. Later, we directed their movement by ropes slung about their necks. Later still, we ate their fleshly portions.

IX.

There is no water, no matter how deep we dig. All provision is gone, the dead here shot through with venom so that upon consuming them we die ourselves. Our paroch is mad and wandering. Our physician is dead, and all the others dead too but for five of us.

The physician pursues us with a sentience we have hitherto disallowed the dead. We awoke last morning to find him astraddle the captain, whom he had killed, consuming the fellow's face. We dragged the physician off, breaking his legs and plucking free his eyes to hinder further pursuit on his behalf. We broke the captain's legs as well.

There is some discouragement among the men who remain. Yet I have urged them to push forward, and for the instant they comply.

X.

This midday a glister at some distance and the movement of far figures like lice. We rode forward and found there what I must deem a templature for preparing the corpse, hastily abandoned, the heaped organs on its surface still spongy with blood.

I have examined the apparatus at length but can make nothing of it, nor of its functioning, though it has in my awkwardness contrived to lay bare my palm to the bone. The others, seeing my fate, destroyed the device before I could query it further.

XI.

My injured palm swells. I am without water, food. Save myself, the remainder of the party have returned, hoping to reach the edge of the prairie before dying. I have opted to continue, hoping to strive to the center and whatever is established there, if center there be.

There is no satisfaction anywhere. I wander among the dead, awaiting the moment when I shall pass imperceptibly from the stumbling of the living into the stumbling of the dead.

Avaunt.

EVERYTHING IS BETTER WITH ZOMBIES

by Hannah Wolf Bowen

Hannah Wolf Bowen's fiction has appeared in *Lady Churchill's Rosebud Wristlet*, *Polyphony 6*, *Fantasy Magazine*, *Strange Horizons*, *Abyss & Apex*, *Ideomancer*, *The Fortean Bureau*, and *Alchemy*. She is also currently one of the fiction editors of *Chiaroscuro*, a webzine devoted to dark fiction.

"Everything Is Better with Zombies" began as a joke. "I had a list of things that everything was better with," Bowen says. "Monkeys was on the list. Also, pirates. One day in the summer of 2004, I was in a chatroom with several writer friends and I said (for reasons not clear to me now), 'Everything is better with zombies,' and then thought, 'Hmm.' One of those writer friends, I believe, challenged me to make a story out of it, and so I did."

The story deals with the idea of loyalty, and with the question of what you do when what seems like the loyal, faithful thing conflicts with what's the right thing for you. But when it came to researching the story, Bowen just googled a bunch of zombie facts and played a lot of *Resident Evil*.

Everything would be better with zombies. Take my junior high school graduation. Everything would have been better if zombies had shuffled in to "Pomp and Circumstance." They would have lurched into the gym, devoured the principal's brains, and shuffled out again.

There were no zombies at graduation. We walked in line. We took our seats. Living dead.

I've long suspected that I might be a zombie. If I were a zombie, how would I know? I study scary and not-scary movies. I read books. I play the relevant video games until my thumbs ache and my eyes grow tired and dry.

My best friend Lionel says that he would know. "You'd walk," he says, and demonstrates, shambling gait and arms draped in the air. He lists left, which helps to make it work, but Lion's walked badly for a while now. He's not doing it for effect. "And you'd go 'Braaains!' and everyone would run away."

Lion scowls and sits down beside me on the crumbly step. He picks at the grass growing up through the cracks. He would be out of luck, if it came to running from the zombies.

Besides, he's described half the town. If I were a zombie, I don't believe Lion would know.

There are lots of ways to end up with a zombie. You can start with a dead person, or you can start with a live one, or you can start with a live one and turn him undead. That's part of what makes it so confusing. I know what a zombie is supposed to be like, but I could be wrong.

I spend my days reading up at the library instead of packing for the move. Late afternoon, I ride my bike past the stoplight to the hardware store where Lion works. He fetches his bike from the alley and we pedal, not talking, up the road, across the tracks, and out of town.

If we lived other than where we do, maybe we could explore. Turn left instead of right. Ride a little further than ever before. Or keep going through the cornfield that's grown up tall, bumpity-bump to the other side with the wind around us like the sea.

But we live where we live and we have all our lives up until now, and the other side of the cornfield looks a lot like this one. So we stand on the pedals and creak up Salt Hill, then over the spray-painted bridge to gravel-topped Strawberry Road, which curves sharp to the left and down and if you're not careful, you'll fly off into the air with the creek down below. I almost did, the first times that we came this way, and then some other times later when I thought I knew how to ride it, but was wrong.

I have it now. I lean and the bike swings left beneath me, and Lion yells but his words are shredded by the wind. I coast all the way down to the cemetery, and there I stop.

You can make a zombie with a disease. You can make a zombie with a potion. You can make a zombie with the right chants and voodoo charms. You may be able to make a zombie in other ways, too. It's hard to be sure.

What we can be sure of is that some of the graves in the cemetery aren't as neat as they ought to be. The town isn't all that big. You'd expect that we'd know everyone, and you'd be right. But sometimes we find headstones we haven't found before and Lion lingers to read them over and over aloud.

I head down to the creek because the cemetery is a lot like the town and barring unexpected headstones, I know every corner by heart. So I sit on the muddy bank on a rock or on a fallen log and listen to the creek go splish-splashity by.

I see the footprint there. I'm still studying it when Lion comes up, muttering, "Emily Fitzhugh, '87 to—what's that?"

He spots the footprint right away. It's hard to miss. The water is edged in mud, speckled with raccoon fingerprints. But this print is in a smooth empty spot and clear as if I'd stamped it there just now. One left footprint, deeper at the ball of the foot and the toes, like she stepped down from the grassy tree-shaded bank, dropped and sank, pushed off against the yielding muck and landed her right foot in the creek, or on a stepping stone.

"Not me," I say. "Do you think it's Emily?" But my name is Emily, too.

Lion gives me a hand up, long chilly fingers wrapping my wrist. I kick off my sneakers and pick my way through the mud to the stepping stones, cool and rough beneath my toes. I crouch down, teetering, to examine the others ahead. There's another print, imperfect, rubber stamp in need of ink. And on the far bank grass, a smudge of mud on a flattened dandelion. I stand and wave to Lion. "She went this way."

"You don't know that she's a zombie," Lion says as we walk our bikes back up Salt Hill. The side that sweeps down to the cemetery is steep and we've no momentum to carry us up. Instead, we'll trudge to the top of the hill and remount there. "She could be a ghoul or a ghost or a skeleton. We could've made her up."

"You saw the footprint," I remind him. "We didn't make her up." We'd followed the trail to the highway. We'd paced along the shoulder, searching for the spot where she'd stepped back off the road. We hadn't found anything. But even Lion had agreed that the print by the creek was beautifully clear. "And if she'd been a skeleton, it would have just been bone. And ghosts wouldn't leave any prints at all."

"They might," Lion says, "if they were acting out their deaths."

I shrug. "But a ghoul—"

"You don't know she's a zombie. You don't know she's dead at all."

I blink up at Lion and into the sun. It's sinking now behind the top of the hill, though it'll be above us still on the way down. Interrupting is an unLion-like thing to do and he's scowling, staring hard ahead, and so I'm thrown. "Yeah," I agree at last. "But what kind of freak goes barefoot in a cemetery?"

Lion slants a glance at my sneakers where they hang, laces bound to the handlebars. I shrug again, and he laughs.

Jokes may not be better with zombies. The problem about jokes with zombies is that they all have the same punch line. It all comes down to brains.

Sometimes I wish the rest of life was more like jokes about zombies. But maybe it is. Lion went up to see his doctors today and so I skip Amanda's end-of-the-summer party, sit out on the porch and count fireflies and pretend not to hear my dad saying we'll have to hit the road soon, to get me to my mom's new place before school starts up there. Later, there's bike tire whir on pavement. Lion coasts to a stop in the porchlight, panting hard. I offer him my lemonade and ask, "What do zombies want with brains?"

"Maybe they're jealous." But he says it like he's not quite paying attention and it's been, I guess, a not-so-good day. "When you're a zombie," he begins, "do you remember who you were?"

I take my lemonade glass back and set it with a thunk down on the porch steps. I fetch my bike and my pack from the side of the house. We ride slowly down the street and my pack lies close against my back and even coasting where I can, my shirt grows sticky with sweat. Over the tracks and out of town and up the hill. We don't have much momentum. Lion seems tired. We dismount and walk the bikes towards the top.

"You're quiet," he says.

"So are you."

"Yeah, but I'm always quiet."

"I think," I say, "that if I was a zombie, I wouldn't want to remember who I was. It's not like I could go back."

I sneak a glance at him through the gloom, but this is a new moon night and it's dark out here in the way that it never is in town. He plows on up the hill, throws back, "When I'm a zombie, will you want to see me?"

"Lion," I start, but we're at the top of the hill, climbing back onto our bikes, and I don't know what I'd meant to say.

Zombies will kill anyone. They'll eat anybody's brains. It doesn't matter if the brains belong to their dad, or their daughter, or their best friend. I don't know if this means that they don't remember, or that they do. And if we find the other Emily, it won't prove anything. But I've never seen a zombie before, however hard I've looked. Probably it's best to start with one that I don't know.

Lion beats me down the hill. He doesn't do that often, but tonight he's pushing hard and besides, I rode my brakes. I leave him alone when I get there, dropping my pack to the grass and digging for the flashlight, but Lion says, "Don't."

Dark pools like water at the base of the hill. The creek shivers by and a cricket chir-squeaks and I spook, drop the flashlight before I realize that it's only Lion who's caught my other hand. "Don't *do* that."

He's not listening. He's staring hard into the night, into the shadows under the trees. We could see every star if it wasn't cloudy, but this is Illinois and it's always cloudy here when you could use a little light. Night washes the color out of Lion's face, out of his bright hair and his red shirt. He could already be dead.

If Lion were a zombie, how would I know?

Someone locks the cemetery gates at night. I don't know who. It doesn't matter; the fence is barely waist-high and we hop it, iron slick under sweaty palms as we lift ourselves across. Lion steps deftly around headstones that I can't even see. I thump a knee twice into stone, fall back and follow instead.

The grass is on the long side of short: tended, but ambivalently, so it hides rocks and holes and things to trip me up. I keep one eye on Lion, one on the ground. I reach out as we skirt the headstone, where the grey of grass gives way to the grey of turned-over earth, and dip the tips of my fingers into the carven E.

"Lion," I say. "Do you think she's scared?"

He stops, abrupt, and we almost collide. I skip sideways, sinking my shoes into the soft heavy soil of Emily's grave. I imagine the shiver of bodies moving, the strong twiggy fingerbone grasp on my ankle. But this patch of ground is already disturbed and not only by worms. The zombies can't grab you if the zombies have already gone.

"When you're a zombie," Lion says, "you shouldn't have to be scared."

I don't think of Lion as scared. He's too steady, too serious, Lion, my friend. He's braver about dead things than anyone I know. I guess he'd have to be.

You don't have to run from zombies. You just have to walk at a brisk pace, and maybe zigzag once in a while. You don't have to run to catch them either. They're not that fast. But Lion isn't waiting, or even walking. I've never seen him like this.

This isn't the first time that we've chased a zombie. I keep a list in a notebook that lives in my backpack, and Lion keeps one in his head. We can't be sure that every disturbed grave has a zombie in it. Probably there are ghouls and ghosts and skeletons, like he said. Probably there are vampires. Possibly there are mummies, too. You'd have to go out of your way to mummify anyone, here, which isn't to say that it couldn't be done.

But most of them are zombies if they're anything at all. You can tell from the prints, from the shuffling gait. You can tell from the town. If we were mostly beset by vampires, I think we'd be paler, colder, lonelier. Instead we move slow and try not to think.

I never thought Lion cared. He's a smart kid, reads a lot, might have been skipped up a grade if he hadn't missed so much school. But he's never seemed to mind the town or to mind not leaving it. He thinks the zombies are kind of neat, but he's only ever chased them because I do.

But tonight I'm not so much chasing as stumbling along behind as he tracks like a hound. We splash through the creek, no time for stepping stones or for taking off shoes. The bank on the other side is steep. The hill above is steeper. I grab onto slender trees for balance and to pull myself up. I lunge and my right shoelace swings with my stride, sticks soggy to my ankle.

At the top it levels out and opens up. The ditch is filled with fireflies and there's the highway, empty except when the semis pass, swallowing the miles and spitting out exhaust. They say it runs clear to Colorado, two lanes each direction with reflectors in the stripes. I've ridden along it going into the city, or with Lion to see a movie or a band, or going to see my mom's new place in the city, by the new high school that's supposed to be mine. I've ridden along it, up until now, back again.

This is where we lost her trail before. Tonight he doesn't pause. He lopes across the highway, crashing into the cornfield and I lose him, hear stalks bending, breaking, but the wind is in the corn, and so am I.

I stop. I can see where the corn's been pushed down where Lion passed, or the zombie girl, or a deer. I can hear the rattle of the stalks and a weird no-cricket stillness and then the wind as it kicks up again. I step deeper into the field and flattened stalks crunch underfoot like so many bones. I'd left my backpack in the cemetery; I hadn't expected we'd just take off like this. What would I do, if I found the zombie or if the zombie found me? I could, I think, just walk slowly, carefully, back to town.

But I have to be sure that I don't get grabbed. In this field, in the dark, I can't know where she is, or if she's still here at all. Something moves, off to my left, heavier than the wind, and I whisper, "Lion?" because it didn't matter. If it's the zombie, she probably already knows that I'm here. I hold my breath.

And let it out, explosive yelp, as Lion yells, more like a scream, ragged and sharp. I turn blindly into the corn, plow through to the tractor path between fields and, "Lion!" I yell. Another creek ahead, path of least resistance and you can't see color in the dark, but movement, yes. I run. I stop at the top of the bank, Lion in a heap below and behind me a sound, a staggering heavy tread and a retreating break of corn. I gather myself to turn, to chase, and then I don't. I couldn't leave Lion behind.

Endings may not be better with zombies. You can't have a happy ending and zombies both. Even if the hero survives. Even if her friends do, and let's face it: they don't. I skid down the bank on stones and loose dirt, catching an old tree to halt my slide. It's cooler down here. Heat rises. Fog settles in low-slung spots. And Lion shivers, hands around a twisted ankle, dirty face streaked and smudged. Not that he'd admit to tears. Not that I want him to. But I know I can't ask, "Are you okay?" and so try, "Did you see her?" instead.

He doesn't answer. He doesn't seem to hear. Also, did she see him? She shambled away and left us here. I don't know what that means. Maybe he wasn't the only one who could follow a trail. Maybe the zombie girl could, too. Then things would change. There'd be riots. Martial law. Boarded-up doors and baseball bats. I'd have to stay. They'd need me here.

But that's the other problem about endings with zombies: you only win if you cheat. You can run away if there's only one. You can dodge around two or smash them with a bat. But there are never just one or two zombies. Instead there's three, or four, or lots, shambling in cornfields or down the street, and it never really works, holing up and hiding out. I wouldn't bet against a zombie. Not on my life.

Only, it's a long walk back and an ankle's a bad thing to hurt and so even if we get that far, Lion won't be able to bike. "Did she bite you?" I ask, and he shakes his head, "Not yet," without any more tears, just that sidekick's resolve in his eye. I swallow hard. I pull him to his feet and I hug him, fierce, say into his chest, "I'm going to *miss* you."

Zombies pretend to be about how there are worse things than death. It isn't true. Being one is an in-between state, and the way out is pretty much what you'd expect. Zombies are about how there are worse things than life.

Lion's taller than I am and heavier still, but he leans on my shoulder and limps, more than usual, until we're back by the highway again. We know where we're going, have purpose and brains. I think we beat the zombie girl there. I break a low branch from a tree at the edge of the fields and Lion takes it from my hands. It's the best that we can do. He tries a few practice swings, and maybe baseball players know about zombies, too: you don't drop the bat unless you're going to run.

But you do run, in the end. That's how you get away from zombies. You back away a couple of steps. You say goodbye. And then you turn. You run. You don't look over your shoulder. You don't zig, because one too many zags puts you back where you began.

You run because zombies are slow but inevitable, and also because they're right. There are worse things than life, and zombies are better with everything.

HOME DELIVERY

by Stephen King

Stephen King is the best-selling, award-winning author of innumerable classics, including *The Shining, Carrie, Cujo,* and *The Dead Zone*. Each of those books has been adapted to film, as have many of King's other novels and stories. Other projects include editing *Best American Short Stories 2007*, and his recent collaboration on a musical with rocker John Mellencamp called *Ghost Brothers of Darkland County*. King's latest novel, *Duma Key*, was published in early 2008. A new short fiction collection, *Just After Sunset*, is due out in November.

Although King is probably the world's foremost horror writer, he hasn't frequently explored the subject of zombies in his fiction. His recent novel *Cell*, however, *is* about zombies, and of course, there's this story. Also of possible zombie relevance is King's novel *Pet Sematary*; if not zombies per se, it certainly contains zombie-like things.

This story first appeared in *Book of the Dead*. As with much of King's fiction, it takes place in a small town in Maine, and using that point of view examines a menacing supernatural horror. And as with much of King's fiction, it manages to at once be both horrific and affecting.

Considering that it was probably the end of the world, Maddie Pace thought she was doing a good job. *Hell* of a good job. She thought, in fact, that she just might be coping with the End of Everything better than anyone else on earth. And she was *positive* she was coping better than any other *pregnant* woman on earth.

Coping.

Maddie Pace, of all people.

Maddie Pace, who sometimes couldn't sleep if, after a visit from Reverend Johnson, she spied a single speck of dust under the dining-room table. Maddie Pace, who, as Maddie Sullivan, used to drive her fiancé, Jack, crazy when she froze over a menu, debating entrees sometimes for as long as half an hour.

"Maddie, why don't you just flip a coin?" he'd asked her once after she had managed to narrow it down to a choice between the braised veal and the lamb chops, and then could get no further. "I've had five bottles of this goddam

German beer already, and if you don't make up y'mind pretty damn quick, there's gonna be a drunk lobsterman *under* the table before we ever get any food *on* it!"

So she had smiled nervously, ordered the braised veal, and spent most of the ride home wondering if the chops might not have been tastier, and therefore a better bargain despite their slightly higher price.

She'd had no trouble coping with Jack's proposal of marriage, however; she'd accepted it—and him—quickly, and with tremendous relief. Following the death of her father, Maddie and her mother had lived an aimless, cloudy sort of life on Little Tall Island, off the coast of Maine. "If I wasn't around to tell them women where to squat and lean against the wheel," George Sullivan had been fond of saying while in his cups and among his friends at Fudgy's Tavern or in the back room of Prout's Barber Shop, "I don't know what'n hell they'd do."

When her father died of a massive coronary, Maddie was nineteen and minding the town library weekday evenings at a salary of $41.50 a week. Her mother minded the house—or did, that was, when George reminded her (sometimes with a good hard shot to the ear) that she had a house which needed minding.

When the news of his death came, the two women had looked at each other with silent, panicky dismay, two pairs of eyes asking the same question: *What do we do now?*

Neither of them knew, but they both felt—felt strongly—that he had been right in his assessment of them: they needed him. They were just women, and they needed him to tell them not just what to do, but how to do it, as well. They didn't speak of it because it embarrassed them, but there it was—they hadn't the slightest clue as to what came next, and the idea that they were prisoners of George Sullivan's narrow ideas and expectations did not so much as cross their minds. They were not stupid women, either of them, but they *were* island women.

Money wasn't the problem; George had believed passionately in insurance, and when he dropped down dead during the tiebreaker frame of the League Bowl-Offs at Big Duke's Big Ten in Machias, his wife had come into better than a hundred thousand dollars. And island life was cheap, if you owned your place and kept your garden tended and knew how to put by your own vegetables come fall. The *problem* was having nothing to focus on. The *problem* was how the center seemed to have dropped out of their lives when George went facedown in his Island Amoco bowling shirt just over the foul line of lane nineteen (and goddam if he hadn't picked up the spare his team had needed to win, too). With George gone their lives had become an eerie sort of blur.

It's like being lost in a heavy fog, Maddie thought sometimes. *Only instead of looking for the road, or a house, or the village, or just some landmark like that lightning-struck pine out on the point, I am looking for the wheel. If I can ever find it, maybe I can tell* myself *to squat and lean my shoulder to it.*

At last she found her wheel: it turned out to be Jack Pace. Women marry their fathers and men their mothers, some say, and while such a broad statement can hardly be true all of the time, it was close enough for government work in Maddie's case. Her father had been looked upon by his peers with fear and admiration—"Don't fool with George Sullivan, dear," they'd say. "He'll knock the nose off your face if you so much as look at him wrong."

It was true at home, too. He'd been domineering and sometimes physically abusive, but he'd also known things to want and work for, like the Ford pick-up, the chainsaw, or those two acres that bounded their place to the south. Pop Cook's land. George Sullivan had been known to refer to Pop Cook as one armpit-stinky old bastid, but the old man's aroma didn't change the fact that there was quite a lot of good hardwood left on those two acres. Pop didn't know it because he had gone to living across the reach in 1987, when his arthritis really went to town on him, and George let it be known on Little Tall that what that bastid Pop Cook didn't know wouldn't hurt him none, and furthermore, he would disjoint the man or woman that let light into the darkness of Pop's ignorance. No one did, and eventually the Sullivans got the land, and the hardwood on it. Of course the good wood was all logged off inside of three years, but George said that didn't matter a tinker's damn; land always paid for itself in the end. That was what George said and they believed him, believed *in* him, and they worked, all three of them. He said: You got to put your shoulder to this wheel and *push* the bitch, you got to push ha'ad because she don't move easy. So that was what they did.

In those days Maddie's mother had kept a produce stand on the road from East Head, and there were always plenty of tourists who bought the vegetables she grew (which were the ones George *told* her to grow, of course), and even though they were never exactly what her mother called "the Gotrocks family," they made out. Even in years when lobstering was bad and they had to stretch their finances even further in order to keep paying off what they owed the bank on Pop Cook's two acres, they made out.

Jack Pace was a sweeter-tempered man than George Sullivan had ever thought of being, but his sweet temper only stretched so far, even so. Maddie suspected that he might get around to what was sometimes called home correction—the twisted arm when supper was cold, the occasional slap or downright pad-dling—in time; when the bloom was off the rose, so as to speak. There was even a part of her that seemed to expect and look forward to that. The women's magazines said marriages where the man ruled the roost were a thing of the past, and that a man who put a hard hand on a woman should be arrested for assault, even if the man in question was the woman in question's lawful wedded husband. Maddie sometimes read articles of this sort down at the beauty shop, but doubted if the women who wrote them had the slightest idea that places like the outer islands even existed. Little Tall *had* produced one writer, as a matter of fact—Selena St. George—but she wrote mostly about politics and hadn't been back to the island, except for a single Thanksgiving dinner, in years.

"I'm not going to be a lobsterman all my life, Maddie," Jack told her the week before they were married, and she believed him. A year before, when he had asked her out for the first time (she'd said yes almost before all the words could get out of his mouth, and she had blushed to the roots of her hair at the sound of her own naked eagerness), he would have said, "I *ain't* going to be a lobsterman all my life." A small change... but all the difference in the world. He had been going to night school three evenings a week, taking the old *Island Princess* over and back. He would be dog-tired after a day of pulling pots, but off he'd go just the same, pausing only long enough to shower off the powerful smells of lobster and brine and to gulp two No Dōz with hot coffee. After a while, when she saw he really meant to stick to it, Maddie began putting up hot soup for him to drink on the ferry-ride over. Otherwise he would have had nothing but one of those nasty red hot-dogs they sold in the *Princess*'s snack-bar.

She remembered agonizing over the canned soups in the store—there were so *many!* Would he want tomato? Some people didn't like tomato soup. In fact, some people *hated* tomato soup, even if you made it with milk instead of water. Vegetable soup? Turkey? Cream of chicken? Her helpless eyes roved the shelf display for nearly ten minutes before Charlene Nedeau asked if she could help her with something—only Charlene said it in a sarcastic way, and Maddie guessed she would tell all her friends at high school tomorrow, and they would giggle about it in the girls' room, knowing exactly what was wrong with her—poor mousy little Maddie Sullivan, unable to make up her mind over so simple a thing as a can of *soup*. How she had ever been able to decide to accept Jack Pace's proposal was a wonder and a marvel to all of them... but of course they didn't know about the wheel you had to find, and about how, once you found it, you had to have someone to tell you when to stoop and where exactly to push the damned thing.

Maddie had left the store with no soup and a throbbing headache.

When she worked up nerve enough to ask Jack what his favorite soup was, he had said: "Chicken noodle. Kind that comes in the can."

Were there any others he specially liked?

The answer was no, just chicken noodle—the kind that came in the can. That was all the soup Jack Pace needed in his life, and all the answer (on that particular subject, at least) that Maddie needed in hers. Light of step and cheerful of heart, Maddie climbed the warped wooden steps of the store the next day and bought the four cans of chicken noodle soup that were on the shelf. When she asked Bob Nedeau if he had any more, he said he had a whole damn *case* of the stuff out back.

She bought the entire case and left him so flabbergasted that he actually carried the carton out to the truck for her and forgot all about asking why she wanted so *much*—a lapse for which his long-nosed wife and daughter took him sharply to task that evening.

"You just better believe it and never forget," Jack had said that time not long before they tied the knot (she *had* believed it, and had never forgotten). "More than a lobsterman. My dad says I'm full of shit. He says if draggin pots was good enough for his old man, and his old man's old man and all the way back to the friggin Garden of Eden to hear *him* tell it, it ought to be good enough for me. But it ain't—*isn't,* I mean—and I'm going to do better." His eye fell on her, and it was a stern eye, full of resolve, but it was a loving eye, full of hope and confidence, too. "More than a lobsterman is what I mean to be, and more than a lobsterman's wife is what I intend for you to be. You're going to have a house on the mainland."

"Yes, Jack."

"And I'm not going to have any friggin Chevrolet." He drew in a deep breath and took her hands in his. "I'm going to have an *Oldsmobile.*"

He looked her dead in the eye, as if daring her to scoff at this wildly upscale ambition. She did no such thing, of course; she said yes, Jack, for the third or fourth time that evening. She had said it to him thousands of times over the year they had spent courting, and she confidently expected to say it a million times before death ended their marriage by taking one of them—or, better, both of them together. *Yes, Jack;* had there ever in the history of the world been two words which made such beautiful music when laid side by side?

"More than a friggin lobsterman, no matter what my old man thinks or how much he laughs." He pronounced this last word in the deeply downeast way: *loffs.* "I'm going to do it, and do you know who's going to help me?"

"Yes," Maddie had responded calmly. "*I* am."

He had laughed and swept her into his arms. "You're damned tooting, my little sweetheart," he'd told her.

And so they were wed, as the fairytales usually put it, and for Maddie those first few months—months when they were greeted almost everywhere with jovial cries of "Here's the newlyweds!"—*were* a fairytale. She had Jack to lean on, Jack to help her make decisions, and that was the best of it. The most difficult household choice thrust upon her that first year was which curtains would look best in the living room—there were so *many* in the catalogue to choose from, and her mother was certainly no help. Maddie's mother had a hard time deciding between different brands of toilet paper.

Otherwise, that year consisted mostly of joy and security— the joy of loving Jack in their deep bed while the winter wind scraped over the island like the blade of a knife across a breadboard, the security of having Jack to tell her what it was they wanted, and how they were going to get it. The loving was good—so good that sometimes when she thought of him during the days her knees would feel weak and her stomach fluttery— but his way of knowing things and her growing trust in his instincts were even better. So for awhile it *was* a fairytale, yes.

Then Jack died and things started getting weird. Not just for Maddie, either. For everybody.

Just before the world slid into its incomprehensible nightmare, Maddie discovered she was what her mother had always called "preg," a curt word that was like the sound you made when you had to rasp up a throatful of snot (that, at least, was how it had always sounded to Maddie). By then she and Jack had moved next to the Pulsifers on Gennesault Island, which was known simply as Jenny by its residents and those of nearby Little Tall.

She'd had one of her agonizing interior debates when she missed her second period, and after four sleepless nights she made an appointment with Dr. McElwain on the mainland. Looking back, she was glad. If she'd waited to see if she was going to miss a third period, Jack would not have had even one month of joy and she would have missed the concerns and little kindnesses he had showered upon her.

Looking back—now that she was *coping*—her indecision seemed ludicrous, but her deeper heart knew that going to have the test had taken tremendous courage. She had wanted to be more convincingly sick in the mornings so she could be surer; she had longed for nausea to drag her from her dreams. She made the appointment when Jack was out at work, and she went while he was out, but there was no such thing as *sneaking* over to the mainland on the ferry; too many people from both islands saw you. Someone would mention casually to Jack that he or she had seen his wife on the *Princess* t'other day, and then Jack would want to know what it was all about, and if she'd made a mistake, he would look at her like she was a goose.

But it hadn't been a mistake; she was with child (and never mind that word that sounded like someone with a bad cold trying to clear his throat), and Jack Pace had had exactly twenty-seven days to look forward to his first child before a bad swell had caught him and knocked him over the side of *My Lady-Love*, the lobster boat he had inherited from his Uncle Mike. Jack could swim, and he had popped to the surface like a cork, Dave Eamons had told her miserably, but just as he did, another heavy swell came, slewing the boat directly into him, and although Dave would say no more, Maddie had been born and brought up an island girl, and she knew: could, in fact, *hear* the hollow thud as the boat with its treacherous name smashed its way into her husband's head, letting out blood and hair and bone and perhaps the part of his brain that had made him say her name over and over again in the dark of night, when he came into her.

Dressed in a heavy hooded parka and down-filled pants and boots, Jack Pace had sunk like a stone. They had buried an empty casket in the little cemetery at the north end of Jenny Island, and the Reverend Johnson (on Jenny and Little Tall you had your choice when it came to religion: you could be a Methodist, or if that didn't suit you, you could be a lapsed Methodist) had presided over this empty coffin as he had so many others. The service ended, and at the age of twenty-two Maddie had found herself a widow with a bun in the oven and no one to tell her where the wheel was, let alone when to put her shoulder to it or how far to push it.

She thought at first she'd go back to Little Tall, back to her mother, to wait her time, but a year with Jack had given her a little perspective and she knew her mother was as lost—maybe even *more* lost—than she was herself, and that made her wonder if going back would be the right thing to do.

"Maddie," Jack told her again and again (he was dead in the world but not, it seemed, inside her head; inside her head he was as lively as any dead man could possibly get… or so she had thought *then*), "the only thing you can ever decide on is not to decide."

Nor was her mother any better. They talked on the phone and Maddie waited and hoped for her mother to just *tell* her to come back home, but Mrs. Sullivan could tell no one over the age of ten anything. "Maybe you ought to come on back over here," she had said once in a tentative way, and Maddie couldn't tell if that meant *please come home* or *please don't take me up on an offer which was really just made for form's sake.* She spent long, sleepless nights trying to decide which it had been and succeeded only in confusing herself more.

Then the weirdness started, and the greatest mercy was that there was only the one small graveyard on Jenny (and so many of the graves filled with those empty coffins—a thing which had once seemed pitiful to her now seemed another blessing, a grace). There were two on Little Tall, both fairly large, and so it began to seem so much safer to stay on Jenny and wait.

She would wait and see if the world lived or died.

If it lived, she would wait for the baby.

And now she was, after a life of passive obedience and vague resolves that usually passed like dreams an hour or two after she got out of bed, finally *coping.* She knew that part of this was nothing more than the effect of being slammed with one massive shock after another, beginning with the death of her husband and ending with one of the last broadcasts the Pulsifers' high-tech satellite dish had picked up: a horrified young boy who had been pressed into service as a CNN reporter saying that it seemed certain that the President of the United States, the first lady, the Secretary of State, the honorable senior senator from Oregon, and the emir of Kuwait had been eaten alive in the White House East Room by zombies.

"I want to repeat this," the accidental reporter had said, the firespots of his acne standing out on his forehead and chin like stigmata. His mouth and cheeks had begun to twitch; his hands shook spastically. "I want to repeat that a bunch of corpses have just lunched up on the President and his wife and a whole lot of other political hotshots who were at the White House to eat poached salmon and cherries jubilee." Then the kid had begun to laugh maniacally and to scream *Go, Yale! Boola-boola!* at the top of his voice. At last he bolted out of the frame, leaving a CNN news-desk untenanted for the first time in Maddie's memory. She and the Pulsifers sat in dismayed silence as the news-desk disappeared and an ad for Boxcar Willie records—not available in any store, you could get this amazing collection only by dialing the 800 number currently appearing on the bottom of your screen—came on. One of little Cheyne Pulsifer's crayons was on the end table beside the chair Maddie was sitting in, and for some crazy reason she picked it up and wrote the number down on a sheet of scrap paper before Mr. Pulsifer got up and turned off the TV without a single word.

Maddie told them good night and thanked them for sharing their TV and their Jiffy Pop.

"Are you sure you're all right, Maddie dear?" Candi Pulsifer asked her for the fifth time that night, and Maddie said she was fine for the fifth time that night, that she was *coping,* and Candi said she *knew* she was, but she was welcome to the upstairs bedroom that used to be Brian's anytime she wanted. Maddie hugged Candi, kissed her cheek, declined with the most graceful thanks she could find, and was at last allowed to escape. She had walked the windy half mile back to her own house and was in her own kitchen before she realized that she still had the scrap of paper on which she had jotted the 800 number. She had dialed it, and there was nothing. No recorded voice telling her all circuits were currently busy or that the number was out of service; no wailing siren sound that indicated a line interruption; no boops or beeps or clicks or clacks. Just smooth silence. That was when Maddie knew for sure that the end had either come or was coming. When you could no longer call the 800 number and order the Boxcar Willie records that were not available in any store, when there were for the first time in her living memory no Operators Standing By, the end of the world was a foregone conclusion.

She felt her rounding stomach as she stood there by the phone on the wall in the kitchen and said it out loud for the first time, unaware that she had spoken: "It will have to be a home delivery. But that's all right, as long as you get ready and stay ready, kiddo. You have to remember that there just isn't any other way. It *has* to be a home delivery."

She waited for fear and none came.

"I can cope with this just fine," she said, and this time she heard herself and was comforted by the sureness of her own words.

A baby.

When the baby came, the end of the world would itself end.

"Eden," she said, and smiled. Her smile was sweet, the smile of a madonna. It didn't matter how many rotting dead people (maybe Boxcar Willie among them, for all she knew) were shambling around the face of the earth.

She would have a baby, she would accomplish her home delivery, and the possibility of Eden would remain.

The first reports came from an Australian hamlet on the edge of the outback, a place with the memorable name of Fiddle Dee. The name of the first American town where the walking dead were reported was perhaps even more memorable: Thumper, Florida. The first story appeared in America's favorite supermarket tabloid, *Inside View.*

DEAD COME TO LIFE IN SMALL FLORIDA TOWN! the headline screamed. The story began with a recap of a film called *Night of the Living Dead,* which

Maddie had never seen, and went on to mention another—*Macumba Love*—which she had also never seen. The article was accompanied by three photos. One was a still from *Night of the Living Dead,* showing what appeared to be a bunch of escapees from a loonybin standing outside an isolated farmhouse at night. One was from *Macumba Love,* showing a blonde whose bikini top appeared to be holding breasts the size of prize-winning gourds. The blonde was holding up her hands and screaming in horror at what could have been a black man in a mask. The third purported to be a picture taken in Thumper, Florida. It was a blurred, grainy shot of a person of indeterminate sex standing in front of a video arcade. The article described the figure as being "wrapped in the cerements of the grave," but it could have been someone in a dirty sheet.

No big deal. BIGFOOT RAPES CHOIR BOY last week, dead people coming back to life this week, the dwarf mass murderer next week.

No big deal, at least, until they started to come out in other places, as well. No big deal until the first news film ("You may want to ask your children to leave the room," Tom Brokaw introduced gravely) showed up on network TV, decayed monsters with naked bone showing through their dried skin, traffic accident victims, the morticians' concealing make-up sloughed away so that the ripped faces and bashed-in skulls showed, women with their hair teased into dirt-clogged beehives where worms and beetles still squirmed and crawled, their faces alternately vacuous and informed with a kind of calculating, idiotic intelligence. No big deal until the first horrible stills in an issue of *People* magazine that had been sealed in shrink-wrap and sold with an orange sticker that read NOT FOR SALE TO MINORS!

Then it was a big deal.

When you saw a decaying man still dressed in the mud-streaked remnants of the Brooks Brothers suit in which he had been buried tearing at the throat of a screaming woman in a tee-shirt that read PROPERTY OF THE HOUSTON OILERS, you suddenly realized it might be a very big deal indeed.

That was when the accusations and saber rattling had started, and for three weeks the entire world had been diverted from the creatures escaping their graves like grotesque moths escaping diseased cocoons by the spectacle of the two great nuclear powers on what appeared to be an undivertible collision course.

There were no zombies in the United States, Communist Chinese television commentators declared; this was a self-serving lie to camouflage an unforgivable act of chemical warfare against the People's Republic of China, a more horrible (and deliberate) version of what had happened in Bhopal, India. Reprisals would follow if the dead comrades coming out of their graves did not fall down decently dead within ten days. All U.S. diplomatic people were expelled from the mother country and there were several incidents of American tourists being beaten to death.

The President (who would not long after become a Zombie Blue Plate Special himself) responded by becoming a pot (which he had come to resemble, having put on at least fifty pounds since his second-term election) calling a kettle black. The U.S. government, he told the American people, had incontrovertible evidence that the only walking-dead people in China had been set loose deliberately, and while the Head Panda might stand there with his slanty-eyed face hanging out, claiming there were over eight thousand lively corpses striding around in search of the ultimate collectivism, *we* had definite proof that there were less than forty. It was the *Chinese* who had committed an act—a *heinous* act—of chemical warfare, bringing loyal Americans back to life with no urge to consume anything but other loyal Americans, and if these Americans— some of whom had been good Democrats—did not lie down decently dead within the next *five* days, Red China was going to be one large slag pit.

NORAD was at DEFCON-2 when a British astronomer named Humphrey Dagbolt spotted the satellite. Or the spaceship. Or the creature. Or whatever in hell's name it was. Dagbolt was not even a professional astronomer but only an amateur star-gazer from the west of England—no one in particular, you would have said—and yet he almost certainly saved the world from some sort of thermonuclear exchange, if not flat-out atomic war. All in all not a bad week's work for a man with a deviated septum and a bad case of psoriasis.

At first it seemed that the two nose-to-nose political systems did not *want* to believe in what Dagbolt had found, even after the Royal Observatory in London had pronounced his photographs and data authentic. Finally, however, the missile silos closed and telescopes all over the world homed in, almost grudgingly, on Star Wormwood.

The joint American/Chinese space mission to investigate the unwelcome newcomer lifted off from the Lanzhou Heights less than three weeks after the first photographs had appeared in the *Guardian,* and everyone's favorite amateur astronomer was aboard, deviated septum and all. In truth, it would have been hard to have kept Dagbolt off the mission—he had become a worldwide hero, the most renowned Briton since Winston Churchill. When asked by a reporter on the day before lift-off if he was frightened, Dagbolt had brayed his oddly endearing Robert Morley laugh, rubbed the side of his truly enormous nose, and exclaimed, "Petrified, dear boy! Utterly pet-trified!"

As it turned out, he had every reason to be petrified.

They all did.

The final sixty-one seconds of received transmission from the *Xiaoping/Truman* were considered too horrible for release by all three governments involved, and so no formal communiqué was ever issued. It didn't matter, of course; nearly twenty thousand ham operators had been monitoring the craft, and it seemed that at least nineteen thousand of them had been rolling tape when the craft had been—well, was there really any other word for it?—invaded.

Chinese voice: Worms! It appears to be a massive ball of—

American voice: Christ! Look out! It's coming for us!

Dagbolt: Some sort of extrusion is occurring. The portside window is—

Chinese voice: Breach! Breach! To your suits, my friends! (Indecipherable gabble.)

American voice: —and appears to be eating its way in—

Female Chinese voice (Ching-Ling Soong): Oh stop it stop the eyes—

(Sound of an explosion.)

Dagbolt: Explosive decompression has occurred. I see three—er, four—dead, and there are worms... everywhere there are worms—

American voice: Faceplate! Faceplate! *Faceplate!*

(Screaming.)

Chinese voice: Where is my mamma? Oh dear, where is my mamma?

(Screams. Sounds like a toothless old man sucking up mashed potatoes.)

Dagbolt: The cabin is full of worms—what appear to be worms, at any rate— which is to say that they really *are* worms, one realizes—that have apparently extruded themselves from the main satellite—what we took to be—which is to say one means—the cabin is full of floating body parts. These space-worms apparently excrete some sort of acid—

(Booster rockets fired at this point; duration of the burn is 7.2 seconds. This may have been an attempt to escape or possibly to ram the central object. In either case, the maneuver did not work. It seems likely that the blast-chambers themselves were clogged with worms and Captain Lin Yang—or whichever officer was then in charge—believed an explosion of the fuel tanks themselves to be imminent as a result of the clog. Hence the shutdown.)

American voice: Oh my Christ they're in my head, *they're eating my fuckin br—*

(Static.)

Dagbolt: I believe that prudence dictates a strategic retreat to the aft storage compartment; the rest of the crew is dead. No question about that. Pity. Brave bunch. Even that fat American who kept rooting around in his nose. But in another sense I don't think—

(Static.)

Dagbolt: —dead after all because Ching-Ling Soong—or rather, Ching-Ling Soong's severed head, one means to say— just floated past me, and her eyes were open and blinking. She appeared to recognize me, and to—

(Static.)

Dagbolt: —keep you—

(Explosion. Static.)

Dagbolt: —around me. I repeat, all around me. Squirming things. They—I say, does anyone know if—

(Dagbolt, screaming and cursing, then just screaming. Sounds of toothless old man again.)

(Transmission ends.)

The *Xiaoping/Truman* exploded three seconds later. The extrusion from the rough ball nicknamed Star Wormwood had been observed from better than three hundred telescopes earth-side during the short and rather pitiful conflict. As the final sixty-one seconds of transmission began, the craft began to be obscured by something that certainly *looked* like worms. By the end of the final transmission, the craft itself could not be seen at all—only the squirming mass of things that had attached themselves to it. Moments after the final explosion, a weather satellite snapped a single picture of floating debris, some of which was almost certainly chunks of the worm-things. A severed human leg clad in a Chinese space suit floating among them was a good deal easier to identify.

And in a way, none of it even mattered. The scientists and political leaders of both countries knew exactly where Star Wormwood was located: above the expanding hole in earth's ozone layer. It was sending something down from there, and it was not Flowers by Wire.

Missiles came next. Star Wormwood jigged easily out of their way and then returned to its place over the hole.

On the Pulsifers' satellite-assisted TV, more dead people got up and walked, but now there was a crucial change. In the beginning the zombies had only bitten living people who got too close, but in the weeks before the Pulsifers' high-tech Sony started showing only broad bands of snow, the dead folks started *trying* to get close to the living folks.

They had, it seemed, decided they *liked* what they were biting.

The final effort to destroy the thing was made by the United States. The President approved an attempt to destroy Star Wormwood with a number of orbiting nukes, stalwartly ignoring his previous statements that America had never put atomic SDI weapons in orbit and never would. Everyone else ignored them, as well. Perhaps they were too busy praying for success.

It was a good idea, but not, unfortunately, a workable one. Not a single missile from a single SDI orbiter fired. This was a total of twenty-four flat-out failures.

So much for modern technology.

And then, after all these shocks on earth and in heaven, there was the business of the one little graveyard right here on Jenny. But even that didn't seem to count much for Maddie because, after all, she had not been there. With the end of civilization now clearly at hand and the island cut off—*thankfully* cut off, in the opinion of the residents—from the rest of the world, old ways had reasserted themselves with unspoken but inarguable force. By then they all knew what was going to happen; it was only a question of when. That, and being ready when it did.

Women were excluded.

It was Bob Daggett, of course, who drew up the watch roster. That was only right, since Bob had been head selectman on Jenny for about a thousand years. The day after the death of the President (the thought of him and the first lady wandering witlessly through the streets of Washington, D.C., gnawing on human arms and legs like people eating chicken legs at a picnic was not mentioned; it was a little much to bear, even if the bastid and his blonde wife *were* Democrats), Bob Daggett called the first men-only Town Meeting on Jenny since sometime before the Civil War. Maddie wasn't there, but she heard. Dave Eamons told her all she needed to know.

"You men all know the situation," Bob said. He looked as yellow as a man with jaundice, and people remembered his daughter, the one still living at home on the island, was only one of four. The other three were other places... which was to say, on the mainland.

But hell, if it came down to that, they *all* had folks on the mainland.

"We got one boneyard here on Jenny," Bob continued, "and nothin ain't happened there yet, but that don't mean nothin *will*. Nothin ain't happened yet lots of places... but it seems like once it starts, nothin turns to somethin pretty goddam quick."

There was a rumble of assent from the men gathered in the grammar-school gymnasium, which was the only place big enough to hold them. There were about seventy of them in all, ranging in age from Johnny Crane, who had just turned eighteen, to Bob's great-uncle Frank, who was eighty, had a glass eye, and chewed tobacco. There was no spittoon in the gym, of course, so Frank Daggett had brought an empty mayonnaise jar to spit his juice into. He did so now.

"Git down to where the cheese binds, Bobby," he said. "You ain't got no office to run for, and time's a-wastin."

There was another rumble of agreement, and Bob Daggett flushed. Somehow his great-uncle always managed to make him look like an ineffectual fool, and if there was anything in the world he hated worse than looking like an ineffectual fool, it was being called Bobby. He owned property, for Chrissake! And he *supported* the old fart—bought him his goddam chew!

But these were not things he could say; old Frank's eyes were like pieces of flint.

"Okay," Bob said curtly. "Here it is. We want twelve men to a watch. I'm gonna set a roster in just a couple minutes. Four-hour shifts."

"I can stand watch a helluva lot longer'n four hours!" Matt Arsenault spoke up, and Davey told Maddie that Bob said after the meeting that no welfare-slacker like Matt Arsenault would have had the nerve to speak up like that in a meeting of his betters if that old man hadn't called him Bobby, like he was a kid instead of a man three months shy of his fiftieth birthday, in front of all the island men.

"Maybe you can n maybe you can't," Bob said, "but we got plenty of warm bodies, and nobody's gonna fall asleep on sentry duty."

"I ain't gonna—"

"I didn't say *you*," Bob said, but the way his eyes rested on Matt Arsenault suggested that he might have *meant* him. "This is no kid's game. Sit down and shut up."

Matt Arsenault opened his mouth to say something more, then looked around at the other men—including old Frank Daggett—and wisely held his peace.

"If you got a rifle, bring it when it's your trick," Bob continued. He felt a little better with Arsenault more or less back in his place. "Unless it's a twenty-two, that is. If you ain't got somethin bigger'n that, come n get one here."

"I didn't know the school kep a supply of em handy," Cal Partridge said, and there was a ripple of laughter.

"It don't now, but it will," Bob said, "because every man jack of you with more than one rifle bigger than a twenty-two is gonna bring it here." He looked at John Wirley, the school principal. "Okay if we keep em in your office, John?"

Wirley nodded. Beside him, Reverend Johnson was dry-washing his hands in a distraught way.

"Shit on that," Orrin Campbell said. "I got a wife and two kids at home. Am I s'posed to leave em with nothin to defend themselves with if a bunch of cawpses come for an early Thanksgiving dinner while I'm on watch?"

"If we do our job at the boneyard, none will," Bob replied stonily. "Some of you got handguns. We don't want none of those. Figure out which women can shoot and which can't and give em the pistols. We'll put em together in bunches."

"They can play Beano," old Frank cackled, and Bob smiled, too. That was more like it, by the Christ.

"Nights, we're gonna want trucks posted around so we got plenty of light." He looked over at Sonny Dotson, who ran Island Amoco, the only gas station on Jenny. Sonny's main business wasn't gassing cars and trucks—shit, there was no place much on the island to drive, and you could get your go ten cents cheaper on the mainland—but filling up lobster boats and the motorboats he ran out of his jackleg marina in the summer. "You gonna supply the gas, Sonny?"

"Am I gonna get cash slips?"

"You're gonna get your ass saved," Bob said. "When things get back to normal—if they ever do—I guess you'll get what you got coming."

Sonny looked around, saw only hard eyes, and shrugged. He looked a bit sullen, but in truth he looked more confused than anything, Davey told Maddie the next day.

"Ain't got n'more'n four hunnert gallons of gas," he said. "Mostly diesel."

"There's five generators on the island," Burt Dorfman said (when Burt spoke everyone listened; as the only Jew on the island, he was regarded as a creature both quixotic and fearsome, like an oracle that works about half the time). "They all run on diesel. I can rig lights if I have to."

Low murmurs. If Burt said he could do it, he could. He was a Jewish electrician, and there was a feeling on the outer islands, unarticulated but powerful, that that was the best kind.

"We're gonna light that graveyard up like a friggin stage," Bob said.

Andy Kingsbury stood up. "I heard on the news that sometimes you can shoot one of them things in the head and it'll stay down, and sometimes it won't."

"We've got chainsaws," Bob said stonily, "and what won't stay dead... why, we can make sure it won't move too far alive."

And, except for making out the duty roster, that was pretty much that.

Six days and nights passed and the sentries posted around the little graveyard on Jenny were starting to feel a wee bit silly ("I dunno if I'm standin guard or pullin my pud," Orrin Campbell said one afternoon as a dozen men stood around the cemetery gate, playing Liars' Poker) when it happened... and when it happened, it happened fast.

Dave told Maddie that he heard a sound like the wind wailing in the chimney on a gusty night, and then the gravestone marking the final resting place of Mr. and Mrs. Fournier's boy Michael, who had died of leukemia at seventeen (bad go, that had been, him being their only child and them being such nice people and all), fell over. A moment later a shredded hand with a moss-caked Yarmouth Academy class ring on one finger rose out of the ground, shoving through the tough grass. The third finger had been torn off in the process.

The ground heaved like (like the belly of a pregnant woman getting ready to drop her load, Dave almost said, and hastily reconsidered) a big wave rolling into a close cove, and then the boy himself sat up, only he wasn't anything you could really recognize, not after almost two years in the ground. There were little splinters of wood sticking out of what was left of his face, Davey said, and pieces of shiny blue cloth in the draggles of his hair. "That was coffin-linin," Davey told her, looking down at his restlessly twining hands. "I know that as well's I know m'own name." He paused, then added: "Thank Christ Mike's dad dint have that trick."

Maddie had nodded.

The men on guard, bullshit-scared as well as revolted, opened fire on the reanimated corpse of the former high-school chess champion and All-Star second baseman, tearing him to shreds. Other shots, fired in wild panic, blew chips off his marble gravestone, and it was just luck that the armed men had been loosely grouped together when the festivities commenced; if they had been divided up into two wings, as Bob Daggett had originally intended, they would very likely have slaughtered each other. As it was, not a single islander was hurt, although Bud Meechum found a rather suspicious-looking hole torn in the sleeve of his shirt the next day.

"Prob'ly wa'ant nothin but a blackberry thorn, just the same," he said. "There's an almighty lot of em out at that end of the island, you know." No one would dispute that, but the black smudges around the hole made his frightened wife think that his shirt had been torn by a thorn with a pretty large caliber.

The Fournier kid fell back, most of him lying still, other parts of him still twitching... but by then the whole graveyard seemed to be rippling, as if an earthquake were going on there—but *only* there, noplace else.

Just about an hour before dusk, this had happened.

Burt Dorfman had rigged up a siren to a tractor battery, and Bob Daggett flipped the switch. Within twenty minutes, most of the men in town were at the island cemetery.

Goddam good thing, too, Dave Eamons said, because a few of the deaders almost got away. Old Frank Daggett, still two hours from the heart attack that would carry him off just as the excitement was dying down, organized the new men so they wouldn't shoot each other, either, and for the final ten minutes the Jenny boneyard sounded like Bull Run. By the end of the festivities, the powder smoke was so thick that some men choked on it. The sour smell of vomit was almost heavier than the smell of gunsmoke… it was sharper, too, and lingered longer.

And still some of them wriggled and squirmed like snakes with broken backs—the fresher ones, for the most part.

"Burt," Frank Daggett said. "You got them chainsaws?"

"I got em," Burt said, and then a long, buzzing sound came out of his mouth, a sound like a cicada burrowing its way into tree bark, as he dry-heaved. He could not take his eyes from the squirming corpses, the overturned gravestones, the yawning pits from which the dead had come. "In the truck."

"Gassed up?" Blue veins stood out on Frank's ancient, hairless skull.

"Yeah." Burt's hand was over his mouth. "I'm sorry."

"Work y'fuckin gut all you want," Frank said briskly, "but toddle off n get them saws while you do. And you… you… you… you…"

The last "you" was his grandnephew Bob.

"I can't, Uncle Frank," Bob said sickly. He looked around and saw five or six of his friends and neighbors lying crumpled in the tall grass. They had not died; they had swooned. Most of them had seen their own relatives rise out of the ground. Buck Harkness over there lying by an aspen tree had been part of the crossfire that had cut his late wife to ribbons; he had fainted after observing her decayed, worm-riddled brains exploding from the back of her head in a grisly gray splash. "I can't. I c—"

Frank's hand, twisted with arthritis but as hard as stone, cracked across his face.

"You can and you will, chummy," he said.

Bob went with the rest of the men.

Frank Daggett watched them grimly and rubbed his chest, which had begun to send cramped throbs of pain all the way down his left arm to the elbow. He was old but he wasn't stupid, and he had a pretty good idea what those pains were, and what they meant.

"He told me he thought he was gonna have a blow-out, and he tapped his chest when he said it," Dave went on, and placed his hand on the swell of muscle over his own left nipple to demonstrate.

Maddie nodded to show she understood.

"He said, 'If anything happens to me before this mess is cleaned up, Davey, you and Burt and Orrin take over. Bobby's a good boy, but I think he may have lost his guts for at least a little while... and you know, sometimes when a man loses his guts, they don't come back.'"

Maddie nodded again, thinking how grateful she was—how very, very grateful—that she was not a man.

"So then we did it," Dave said. "We cleaned up the mess."

Maddie nodded a third time, but this time she must have made some sound, because Dave told her he would stop if she couldn't bear it; he would gladly stop.

"I can bear it," she said quietly. "You might be surprised how much I can bear, Davey." He looked at her quickly, curiously, when she said that, but Maddie had averted her eyes before he could see the secret in them.

Dave didn't know the secret because no one on Jenny knew. That was the way Maddie wanted it, and the way she intended to keep it. There had been a time when she had, perhaps, in the blue darkness of her shock, pretended to be coping. And then something happened that *made* her cope. Four days before the island cemetery vomited up its corpses, Maddie Pace was faced with a simple choice: cope or die.

She had been sitting in the living room, drinking a glass of the blueberry wine she and Jack had put up during August of the previous year—a time that now seemed impossibly distant—and doing something so trite it was laughable. She was Knitting Little Things. Booties, in fact. But what else *was* there to do? It seemed that no one would be going across the reach to the Wee Folks store at the Ellsworth Mall for quite some time.

Something had thumped against the window.

A bat, she thought, looking up. Her needles paused in her hands, though. It seemed that something bigger had moved jerkily out there in the windy dark. The oil lamp was turned up high and kicking too much reflection off the panes for her to be sure. She reached to turn it down and the thump came again. The panes shivered. She heard a little pattering of dried putty falling on the sash. Jack had been planning to reglaze all the windows this fall, she remembered, and then thought, *Maybe that's what he came back for.* That was crazy, he was on the bottom of the ocean, but...

She sat with her head cocked to one side, her knitting now motionless in her hands. A little pink bootie. She had already made a blue set. All of a sudden it seemed she could hear so *much.* The wind. The faint thunder of surf on Cricket Ledge. The house making little groaning sounds, like an elderly woman making herself comfortable in bed. The tick of the clock in the hallway.

"Jack?" she asked the silent night that was now no longer silent. "Is it you, dear?" Then the living-room window burst inward and what came through was not really Jack but a skeleton with a few mouldering strings of flesh hanging from it.

His compass was still around his neck. It had grown a beard of moss.

The wind flapped the curtains in a cloud above him as he sprawled, then

LESS THAN ZOMBIE

by Douglas E. Winter

Douglas E. Winter is the author of the novel *Run* and the editor of the anthologies *Prime Evil* and *Revelations*. He's a critic as well, reviewing for publications as diverse as *The Magazine of Fantasy & Science Fiction*, *Harper's Bazaar*, *Video Watchdog*, and the *Washington Post*. He's written the critical biographies *Stephen King: The Art of Darkness* and *Clive Barker: The Dark Fantastic*, as well as *Faces of Fear: Encounters with the Creators of Modern Horror*. When not writing horror and suspense fiction, Winter works as an attorney for one of the most prestigious law firms in the world.

Winter is the author of three sure-fire zombie classics: "Less Than Zombie," "Bright Lights, Big Zombie," and "The Zombies of Madison County." As you might guess from the titles, the stories riff on the literary works of Bret Easton Ellis, Jay McInerney, and Robert James Waller. It went without saying that one of them had to appear in this volume. Each succeeds so brilliantly that choosing between them was like trying to decide which family member to save from the zombie hordes. Luckily for you, all three stories will appear in Winter's story collection *American Zombie*, not deep in the gullet of your undead neighbor. (Tough luck, Mom and little Suzie.)

People are afraid to live on the streets of Los Angeles. This is the last thing I say before I get back into the car. I don't know why I keep saying this thing. It's something I started and now I can't stop. Nothing else seems to matter. Not the fact that I'm no longer eighteen and the summer is gone and it's raining and the windshield wipers go back and forth, back and forth, and that Skip and DJ and Deb will soon be sitting with me again. Not the blood that splattered the legs of my jeans, which felt kind of hot and tight, as I stood in the alley and watched. Not the stain on the arm of the wrinkled, damp sweater I wear, a sweater that had looked fresh and clean last night. All of this seems meaningless next to that one sentence. It seems easier to hear that people are afraid to live rather than Skip say "This is real" or that song they keep playing on the radio. Nothing else seems to matter but those ten, no, eleven words. Not the rain or the cold wind, which seemed to propel the car down the street and into the alley, or the faded smells of marijuana and sex that still flow through the car. All it comes down to is that the living are dying and the dying are living but that people, whether alive or dead, are still fucking afraid.

It's actually the weekend, a Saturday night, and the party by this guy named Schuyler or Wyler was nothing and no one seems to know just where Lana is having her party and there's nothing much else to do except go to a club, go to a movie, go to the Beverly Center, but there aren't any good bands playing and everyone's seen all the movies and we went to the Beverly Center last night so I've been driving around and around in the hills overlooking Sunset and Skip is telling me that we've got to score some crystal meth. DJ does another line and he's running his finger over his teeth and gums and he asks Skip whatever happened to his friend Michael and Skip says "Really?" and DJ laughs and Skip pushes in my Birthday Party tape and twists up the volume and Nick Cave starts to scream.

I light a cigarette and remember something, a dream maybe, about running down the streets of Los Angeles, and I pass the cigarette to Skip and he takes a drag and passes it back to Jane and Jane takes a drag and passes it back to Skip. DJ lights a cigarette of his own and just ahead a billboard reads Your Message Here and beneath it is an empty space. A car is stopped at the next light, a silver Ferrari, and when I pull up next to it, I turn my head to see two guys inside wearing sunglasses and one of them looks at me and I look back at him and he starts to roll down his window and I drive fast out of the hills and back into the city. The rain is pouring harder and the sidewalks are empty and the streets shine like black mirrors and I start thinking about last summer and I make a couple of wrong turns and end up back on Sunset.

Summer. There is nothing much to remember about last summer. Nights at clubs like Darklands, Sleepless, Cloud Zero, The End. Waking up at noon and watching MTV. A white Lamborghini parked in front of Tower Records. The Swans concert, DJ pissing in the aisle at the Roxy in the middle of "Children of God." A prostitute with a broken arm, waving me over on Santa Monica and asking me if I'd like to have a good time. Breakfast at Gaylords, Mimosas with Perrier-Jouët. Lunch with my mother at the Beverly Wilshire and then driving her to LAX for the redeye back to Boston. Dinner with Deb and her parents at R.T.'s, blackened mahimahi, Cobb salad, Evian water, and feeling Deb up under the table while her father talked about the Dodgers. The new S.P.K. album. Going to Palm Springs with Skip over Labor Day weekend and getting fucked up and watching a lizard crawl along a palm tree for about an afternoon. Jane's abortion. Monster billboards of Mick Jagger grinning down on Hollywood Boulevard like the skull of a rotting corpse. Clive getting busted, DWI and possession, and his father getting him off and buying him a new 380SL. Hearing the Legendary Pink Dots on AM radio. And, oh yeah, got up on his hands and knees and looked at her from black sockets in which barnacles had grown.

He made grunting sounds. His fleshless mouth opened and the teeth chomped down. He was hungry… but this time chicken noodle soup would not serve. Not even the kind that came in the can.

Gray stuff hung and swung beyond those dark barnacle-encrusted holes, and she realized she was looking at whatever remained of Jack's brain. She sat where she was, frozen, as he got up and came toward her, leaving black kelpy tracks on the carpet, fingers reaching. He stank of salt and fathoms. His hands stretched. His teeth chomped mechanically up and down. Maddie saw he was wearing the remains of the black-and-red-checked shirt she had bought him at L. L. Bean's last Christmas. It had cost the earth, but he had said again and again how warm it was, and look how well it had lasted, how much of it was left even after being under water all this time.

The cold cobwebs of bone which were all that remained of his fingers touched her throat before the baby kicked in her stomach—for the first time—and her shocked horror, which she had believed to be calmness, fled, and she drove one of the knitting needles into the thing's eye.

Making horrid thick choking noises that sounded like the suck of a swill pump, he staggered backward, clawing at the needle, while the half-made pink bootie swung in front of the cavity where his nose had been. She watched as a sea slug squirmed from that nasal cavity and onto the bootie, leaving a trail of slime behind it.

Jack fell over the end table she'd gotten at a yard sale just after they had been married—she hadn't been able to make her mind up about it, had been in agonies about it, until Jack finally said either she was going to buy it for their living room or he was going to give the biddy running the sale twice what she was asking for the goddam thing and then bust it up into firewood with—

—with the—

He struck the floor and there was a brittle, cracking sound as his febrile, fragile form broke in two. The right hand tore the knitting needle, slimed with decaying brain tissue, from his eye-socket and tossed it aside. His top half crawled toward her. His teeth gnashed steadily together.

She thought he was trying to grin, and then the baby kicked again and she remembered how uncharacteristically tired and out of sorts he'd sounded at Mabel Hanratty's yard-sale that day: *Buy it, Maddie, for Chrissake! I'm tired! Want to go home and get m'dinner! If you don't get a move on, I'll give the old bat twice what she wants and bust it up for firewood with my—*

Cold, dank hand clutching her ankle; polluted teeth poised to bite. To kill her and kill the baby. She tore loose, leaving him with only her slipper, which he chewed on and then spat out.

When she came back from the entry, he was crawling mindlessly into the kitchen—at least the top half of him was—with the compass dragging on the tiles. He looked up at the sound of her, and there seemed to be some idiot question in those black eye-sockets before she brought the ax whistling down, cleaving his skull as he had threatened to cleave the end table.

His head fell in two pieces, brains dribbling across the tile like spoiled oatmeal, brains that squirmed with slugs and gelatinous sea worms, brains that smelled like a woodchuck exploded with gassy decay in a high-summer meadow.

Still his hands clashed and clittered on the kitchen tiles, making a sound like beetles.

She chopped… chopped… chopped.

At last there was no more movement.

A sharp pain rippled across her midsection and for a moment she was gripped by terrible panic: *Is it a miscarriage? Am I going to have a miscarriage?* But the pain left and the baby kicked again, more strongly than before.

She went back into the living room, carrying an ax that now smelled like tripe.

His legs had somehow managed to stand.

"Jack, I loved you so much," she said, "but this isn't you." She brought the ax down in a whistling arc that split him at the pelvis, sliced the carpet, and drove deep into the solid oak floor beneath.

The legs separated, trembled wildly for almost five minutes, and then began to grow quiet. At last even the toes stopped twitching.

She carried him down to the cellar piece by piece, wearing her oven gloves and wrapping each piece with the insulating blankets Jack had kept in the shed and which she had never thrown away—he and the crew threw them over the pots on cold days so the lobsters wouldn't freeze.

Once a severed hand closed upon her wrist. She stood still and waited, her heart drumming heavily in her chest, and at last it loosened again. And that was the end of it. The end of *him*.

There was an unused cistern, polluted, below the house—Jack had been meaning to fill it in. Maddie slid the heavy concrete cover aside so that its shadow lay on the earthen floor like a partial eclipse and then threw the pieces of him down, listening to the splashes. When everything was gone, she worked the heavy cover back into place.

"Rest in peace," she whispered, and an interior voice whispered back that her husband was resting in *pieces,* and then she began to cry, and her cries turned to hysterical shrieks, and she pulled at her hair and tore at her breasts until they were bloody, and she thought, *I am insane, this is what it's like to be insa—*

But before the thought could be completed, she had fallen down in a faint, and the faint became a deep sleep, and the next morning she felt all right.

She would never tell, though.

Never.

"I can bear it," she told Dave Eamons again, thrusting aside the image of the knitting needle with the bootie swinging from the end of it jutting out of the kelp-slimed eye-socket of the thing which had once been her husband, and co-creator of the child in her womb. "Really."

So he told her, perhaps because he had to tell someone or go mad, but he glossed over the worst parts. He told her that they had chainsawed the corpses that absolutely refused to return to the land of the dead, but he did not tell her that some parts had continued to squirm—hands with no arms attached to them clutching mindlessly, feet divorced from their legs digging at the bullet-chewed earth of the graveyard as if trying to run away—and that these parts had been doused with diesel fuel and set afire. Maddie did not have to be told this part. She had seen the pyre from the house.

Later, Gennesault Island's one firetruck had turned its hose on the dying blaze, although there wasn't much chance of the fire spreading, with a brisk easterly blowing the sparks off Jenny's seaward edge. When there was nothing left but a stinking, tallowy lump (and still there were occasional bulges in this mass, like twitches in a tired muscle), Matt Arsenault fired up his old D-9 Caterpillar—above the nicked steel blade and under his faded pillowtick engineer's cap, Matt's face had been as white as cottage cheese—and plowed the whole hellacious mess under.

The moon was coming up when Frank took Bob Daggett, Dave Eamons, and Cal Partridge aside. It was Dave he spoke to.

"I knew it was coming, and here it is," he said.

"What are you talking about, Unc?" Bob asked.

"My heart," Frank said. "Goddam thing has thrown a rod."

"Now, Uncle Frank—"

"Never mind Uncle Frank this n Uncle Frank that," the old man said. "I ain't got time to listen to you play fiddlyfuck on the mouth-organ. Seen half my friends go the same way. It ain't no day at the races, but it could be worse; beats hell out of getting whacked with the cancer-stick.

"But now there's this other sorry business to mind, and all I got to say on that subject is, when I go down I intend to *stay* down. Cal, stick that rifle of yours in my left ear. Dave, when I raise my left arm, you sock yours into my armpit. And Bobby, you put yours right over my heart. I'm gonna say the Lord's Prayer, and when I hit amen, you three fellows are gonna pull your triggers at the same time."

"Uncle Frank—" Bob managed. He was reeling on his heels.

"I told you not to start in on that," Frank said. "And don't you *dare* faint on me, you friggin pantywaist. Now get your country butt over here."

Bob did.

Frank looked around at the three men, their faces as white as Matt Arsenault's had been when he drove the 'dozer over men and women he had known since he was a kid in short pants and Buster Browns.

"Don't you boys frig this up," Frank said. He was speaking to all of them, but his eye might have been particularly trained on his grandnephew. "If you feel like maybe you're gonna backslide, just remember I'd'a done the same for any of you."

"Quit with the speech," Bob said hoarsely. "I love you, Uncle Frank."

"You ain't the man your father was, Bobby Daggett, but I love you, too," Frank said calmly, and then, with a cry of pain, he threw his left hand up over his head like a guy in New York who has to have a cab in a rip of a hurry, and started in with his last prayer. "Our Father who art in heaven—*Christ,* that hurts!—hallow'd be Thy name—oh, son of a *gun!*—Thy kingdom come, Thy will be done, on earth as it… as it…"

Frank's upraised left arm was wavering wildly now. Dave Eamons, with his rifle socked into the old geezer's armpit, watched it as carefully as a logger would watch a big tree that looked like it meant to do evil and fall the wrong way. Every man on the island was watching now. Big beads of sweat had formed on the old man's pallid face. His lips had pulled back from the even, yellowy-white of his Roebuckers, and Dave had been able to smell the Polident on his breath.

"…as it is in heaven!" the old man jerked out. "Lead us not into temptation butdeliverusfromevilohshitonitforeverandeverAMEN!"

All three of them fired, and both Cal Partridge and Bob Daggett fainted, but Frank never did try to get up and walk.

Frank Daggett had meant to *stay* dead, and that was just what he did.

Once Dave started that story he had to go on with it, and so he cursed himself for ever starting. He'd been right the first time; it was no story for a pregnant woman.

But Maddie had kissed him and told him she thought he had done wonderfully, and that Frank Daggett had done wonderfully, too. Dave went out feeling a little dazed, as if he had just been kissed on the cheek by a woman he had never met before.

In a very real sense, that was true.

She watched him go down the path to the dirt track that was one of Jenny's two roads and turn left. He was weaving a little in the moonlight, weaving with tiredness, she thought, but reeling with shock, as well. Her heart went out to him… to all of them. She had wanted to tell Dave she loved him and kiss him squarely on the mouth instead of just skimming his cheek with her lips, but he might have taken the wrong meaning from something like that, even though he was bone-weary and she was almost five months pregnant.

But she *did* love him, loved *all* of them, because they had gone through hell in order to make this little lick of land forty miles out in the Atlantic safe for her.

And safe for her baby.

"It will be a home delivery," she said softly as Dave went out of sight behind the dark hulk of the Pulsifers' satellite dish. Her eyes rose to the moon. "It will be a home delivery… and it will be fine."

LESS THAN ZOMBIE

by Douglas E. Winter

Douglas E. Winter is the author of the novel *Run* and the editor of the anthologies *Prime Evil* and *Revelations*. He's a critic as well, reviewing for publications as diverse as *The Magazine of Fantasy & Science Fiction, Harper's Bazaar, Video Watchdog*, and the *Washington Post*. He's written the critical biographies *Stephen King: The Art of Darkness* and *Clive Barker: The Dark Fantastic*, as well as *Faces of Fear: Encounters with the Creators of Modern Horror*. When not writing horror and suspense fiction, Winter works as an attorney for one of the most prestigious law firms in the world.

Winter is the author of three sure-fire zombie classics: "Less Than Zombie," "Bright Lights, Big Zombie," and "The Zombies of Madison County." As you might guess from the titles, the stories riff on the literary works of Bret Easton Ellis, Jay McInerney, and Robert James Waller. It went without saying that one of them had to appear in this volume. Each succeeds so brilliantly that choosing between them was like trying to decide which family member to save from the zombie hordes. Luckily for you, all three stories will appear in Winter's story collection *American Zombie*, not deep in the gullet of your undead neighbor. (Tough luck, Mom and little Suzie.)

People are afraid to live on the streets of Los Angeles. This is the last thing I say before I get back into the car. I don't know why I keep saying this thing. It's something I started and now I can't stop. Nothing else seems to matter. Not the fact that I'm no longer eighteen and the summer is gone and it's raining and the windshield wipers go back and forth, back and forth, and that Skip and DJ and Deb will soon be sitting with me again. Not the blood that splattered the legs of my jeans, which felt kind of hot and tight, as I stood in the alley and watched. Not the stain on the arm of the wrinkled, damp sweater I wear, a sweater that had looked fresh and clean last night. All of this seems meaningless next to that one sentence. It seems easier to hear that people are afraid to live rather than Skip say "This is real" or that song they keep playing on the radio. Nothing else seems to matter but those ten, no, eleven words. Not the rain or the cold wind, which seemed to propel the car down the street and into the alley, or the faded smells of marijuana and sex that still flow through the car. All it comes down to is that the living are dying and the dying are living but that people, whether alive or dead, are still fucking afraid.

It's actually the weekend, a Saturday night, and the party by this guy named Schuyler or Wyler was nothing and no one seems to know just where Lana is having her party and there's nothing much else to do except go to a club, go to a movie, go to the Beverly Center, but there aren't any good bands playing and everyone's seen all the movies and we went to the Beverly Center last night so I've been driving around and around in the hills overlooking Sunset and Skip is telling me that we've got to score some crystal meth. DJ does another line and he's running his finger over his teeth and gums and he asks Skip whatever happened to his friend Michael and Skip says "Really?" and DJ laughs and Skip pushes in my Birthday Party tape and twists up the volume and Nick Cave starts to scream.

I light a cigarette and remember something, a dream maybe, about running down the streets of Los Angeles, and I pass the cigarette to Skip and he takes a drag and passes it back to Jane and Jane takes a drag and passes it back to Skip. DJ lights a cigarette of his own and just ahead a billboard reads Your Message Here and beneath it is an empty space. A car is stopped at the next light, a silver Ferrari, and when I pull up next to it, I turn my head to see two guys inside wearing sunglasses and one of them looks at me and I look back at him and he starts to roll down his window and I drive fast out of the hills and back into the city. The rain is pouring harder and the sidewalks are empty and the streets shine like black mirrors and I start thinking about last summer and I make a couple of wrong turns and end up back on Sunset.

Summer. There is nothing much to remember about last summer. Nights at clubs like Darklands, Sleepless, Cloud Zero, The End. Waking up at noon and watching MTV. A white Lamborghini parked in front of Tower Records. The Swans concert, DJ pissing in the aisle at the Roxy in the middle of "Children of God." A prostitute with a broken arm, waving me over on Santa Monica and asking me if I'd like to have a good time. Breakfast at Gaylords, Mimosas with Perrier-Jouët. Lunch with my mother at the Beverly Wilshire and then driving her to LAX for the redeye back to Boston. Dinner with Deb and her parents at R.T.'s, blackened mahimahi, Cobb salad, Evian water, and feeling Deb up under the table while her father talked about the Dodgers. The new S.P.K. album. Going to Palm Springs with Skip over Labor Day weekend and getting fucked up and watching a lizard crawl along a palm tree for about an afternoon. Jane's abortion. Monster billboards of Mick Jagger grinning down on Hollywood Boulevard like the skull of a rotting corpse. Clive getting busted, DWI and possession, and his father getting him off and buying him a new 380SL. Hearing the Legendary Pink Dots on AM radio. And, oh yeah, the thing with the zombies.

It's ten P.M. and I'm sitting at the bar in Citrus with Skip and DJ and Jane and the television down at the end is turned to MTV but the sound is off. I order a Stoli straight up and DJ orders a Rolling Rock and Jane orders a Kir and Skip orders a champagne cocktail and Jane changes her mind and orders a champagne cocktail. We look at the menus for a while but we're not very hungry since we did a half a gram at this guy Schuyler's or Wyler's party so we sit at the bar and we talk about new videos and this girl I don't know comes up to me and thanks me for the ride to Bel Air. Jane digs in her purse and I think she takes some Quaaludes and I look down the bar and out the window and I see nothing at all. "What are we going to do?" I ask no one in particular. "What are we going to do?" Skip asks back and he gives me a matchbook and shows me the handwritten address on the back, some place in the Valley, and he tells the bartender that we'll take the check.

I drive to Jane's house. Nobody's home. Jane forgets the security code and Skip is telling her to try typing the year, it's always the year, and she types one nine eight nine into the little box and the red light goes green and the front door's open and we're inside. We walk through the darkness of the hall to get to the kitchen and there's a note on the table with the telephone number of the hotel where her mother and father, or her mother and her mother's lover, are spending the holidays. There's a stack of unread newspapers and a can of Diet Coke and an empty box of Wheat Thins and then the three videotapes.

"Deal with it" Skip says and he picks up the videotapes and he walks into the living room and he starts on the vodka and tries to turn on the television. I sit on the floor with DJ and Jane, and her parents have one of these big-screen TVs, forty-five inches maybe, with a pair of videotape machines on top, and Skip finds the right buttons and the first tape is rolling. I think that maybe DJ got the tapes or probably Jane, she was at Claremont for a while and had a friend who knew some guy whose brother worked one time at a video store, a film student, and this guy stuck them away when the lists came out, and Jane maybe balled him and got the tapes, so we're watching them, all in a row, three of them, lying on the floor of this high-ceilinged living room with this antique furniture and this print by Lucian Freud and Jane keeps telling us that she's seen all these movies before even though she hasn't. Skip is sitting with the remote control in his hand and he doesn't say a word, he keeps flicking the fast forward, jumping ahead to the best scenes, and the first one is called *Dawn of the Dead* and right away this zombie's head gets blown apart by a shotgun blast and this other zombie gets its head chopped off and the next one is just called *Zombie* and the last one I can't remember much about except the part where this doctor blew away this little girl, she was a zombie, and he put the pistol almost right to her head and the pieces of head and brains and blood went spraying away across the inside of an elevator and just for a moment you could see right through the space where her brain used to be and I look at Jane right after this happens but she isn't looking at me, she's looking at Skip and DJ, and I guess she knows what she wants, don't we all?

An hour later, there's no more vodka and there's no more beer and the television is turned to MTV and Jane just lays there on the floor of her parents' living room, staring at the ceiling, while DJ fucks her for about the third time. Skip is on the telephone in Jane's bedroom, trying to score some meth from a dealer in the city, and after a while I'm in there with him, looking at the poster of The Doors and the poster of The Smiths and listening to him say "Deal with it" over and over before he slams the telephone back onto the cradle and rolls his eyes at me and looks at the posters and says "Strange days and strange ways" and then he starts to smile and I think I get it.

The telephone rings and Skip answers and it's Deb. Skip sighs and waves me to the phone and I say hello and she says hello and asks me what I want for Christmas and can she talk to Jane. I tell her I don't know and that Jane can't talk right now and she says that's okay, she's coming over, don't go, she'll be right there and I say okay and good-bye and she says good-bye. I watch Skip go through the drawers of Jane's desk. He stuffs a pack of cigarettes and a lighter into his pocket and hands me a Polaroid picture and it's Jane when she was a little girl and she's standing in front of a fat birthday cake with eight blue-and-white candles and she is smiling a big smile and I don't tell him that that's me standing next to her, the little blond kid with the burry haircut and the thick black glasses. He isn't looking at the photograph anyway, he's looking at me, and all he says is "You faggot" and then he has his hands on the buckle of my jeans and he's pulling me onto the bed on top of him.

Afterward, we smoke a couple of cigarettes and I follow Skip back downstairs. DJ has found another bottle of beer somewhere and he's sitting on the couch watching MTV. Jane is still lying on the carpet, staring at the ceiling, and the fingers of her right hand are moving, clutching into a fist, flattening, then clutching into a fist again. Skip walks over to her and unzips his jeans and says that Deb is on her way and doesn't anybody know how we can score some meth. Jane's right hand flattens, then curls into another fist, then flattens again, and she looks up at Skip and says "Well?" and DJ looks up from the television and says "Well what?"

Another video flashes by. Another. Then another. Love and Rockets has no new tale to tell by the time Deb shows up. She's wearing a silk blouse and a brown leather miniskirt that she bought at Magnin's in Century City. "Love you" she says to no one at all. She kisses DJ on the cheek and sticks out her tongue at Skip and Skip acts like he doesn't notice and keeps on fucking Jane. She says hello to me and I say hello back and she tries on my sunglasses. She walks across the room and starts searching through a stack of CDs. She holds up an old album by Bryan Ferry, puts it down, and picks up one by This Mortal Coil. She says "Can I play this?" and when nobody answers, she slides it into the player and punches a few buttons and cranks the stereo up loud. DJ is watching MTV and Skip is watching MTV while he's fucking Jane and Jane is still looking at the ceiling and I'm trying not to look at Deb. She is singing along with Elizabeth Fraser, swaying back and forth in a kind of dance. I dreamed, she is singing, you dreamed about me. Then she sits down in front of the fireplace and slips a joint out of the pocket of her skirt and she takes off my sunglasses and squints her eyes and she looks a long time at the joint before lighting it. "Song for the Siren" winds down and there's a moment of silence and Skip is pulling himself off Jane with a sound that is hot and wet.

"Next" he says, and he looks first at Deb, then at me.

I dream, but I dream about me. I see myself walking through the streets of downtown Los Angeles and the day is cloudy and the sun goes out and it starts to rain and I start to run and I see myself start to run. In my dream I am chasing myself, running past the Sheraton Grande, past the Bonaventure, past the Arco Tower, and for a minute I think I am going to catch up but the streets are slippery with rain and I fall once, twice, and when I stand again I can't see anyone but this teenager at the opposite corner of the intersection and when I look again it's me, a younger me, and he's fifteen years old and he turns away and starts to run and I start chasing him and now he's thirteen years old and he runs and I run and now he is eleven years old and he is getting younger with each step, younger and smaller, and now he's nine years old and he's eight years old and he's seven years old and I've almost caught him and he's six years old and he turns into this alley and I'm right behind him and he's four years old and it's a dead-end street and he's three years old and he can just barely run and I catch him and he's two years old and I pull him up into my arms and I'm at the end of the alley and he's one year old and I'm standing on the porch of our house, the house where I grew up in Riverside, and he's six months old and I'm knocking on the door and I can hear footsteps inside and he's three months old and my mother is coming to the door and I can't wait for her to see me and he's just a baby and he's getting smaller and he's disappearing and the door is opening and my mother is looking out and he's gone and I'm gone and then there's nothing. Nothing at all.

It's midnight. Still raining. Jane's parents live in the Flatlands, next door to the French actor in that new CBS sitcom, and his dog is barking as we get in the car and Skip shows me the matchbook and the handwritten address and gives me some directions. I drive toward Westwood and take a right onto Beverly Glen and somewhere in the hills I stop at a liquor store for some cigarettes and a bottle of Freixenet and then I'm back at the wheel and I'm driving onto Mulholland and into the Valley and onto the Ventura Freeway and I look at Skip and he acts like he's smiling, his left hand keeping beat on his leg and it's right on target, one two three four, one two three four, but I don't know the song on the radio, I've never heard it before. I look into the rearview mirror and I see that Deb is all over Jane and I see that DJ is watching them and I see that Deb's tongue is in Jane's mouth and I look at Skip and I see that he is watching me while I'm watching DJ who is watching Deb and Jane and I still don't know the name of that song.

Skip taps me on the shoulder and we're coming up on the exit and he has just popped something into his mouth and he downs it with the last of the Freixenet. He drops the black bottle onto the floor and opens his palm to me as if to say "Want some?" and I look at the little yellow pill and I wonder if I could use some Valium. The music is loud with guitars, it sounds like the Cult, and Skip is pounding out the big electric beat on the window, harder and harder, and spiderwebs are running across the glass and he hits the window one more time and it shatters and he shows me his hand. Little cuts run along his knuckles but he hasn't started bleeding and the song ends and the commercial begins and he turns the volume back down. We go to the Lone Star Chili Parlor in Hidden Hills and sit there drinking coffee and wait awhile because we're early and then we go back to the car.

The Valley at two A.M. Van Nuys Boulevard out farther than I thought it went. The moon is curled and shiny and I pull into the parking lot and for some reason Skip seems nervous and we pass the empty theater twice and I keep asking him why and he keeps asking me if I really want to go through with this and I keep telling him that I do. Jane is digging around for something in her purse and Deb is saying "I want to see" and DJ is trying to laugh and as soon as I step out of the car and I look at the line in the shadows, I tell him again.

The mall is no Galleria, not even a mall, just a hollow horseshoe, a curve of little shops, the theater, a drugstore, a pizza place, a karate club, and lots of empty windows lined with whitewash and old newspapers and printed signs that say Commercial Space. There's a chubby kid sitting in a lounge chair in front of the theater, wearing Vuarnets and reading *The Face* and taking ten dollars from each person who wants to go inside. He doesn't even look up as we walk by. DJ pays him and Deb takes my hand and we're inside and the hallway is lined with torn movie posters and shattered glass and spray paint and Skip nods at me and points to the handwritten sign that reads Club Dead.

The lobby looks something like an attic and it's dark and crammed with furniture. Some guy at the back, the manager maybe, is dealing dollar bills to a pair of policemen. He nods at Skip and he nods at me and he lets us through and this girl in the corner winks at me and tries to smile, pale white lipstick and her tongue licking out, and she knows Skip and she says something that I can't hear and Skip gives her the finger.

Inside the lights are bright and it takes my eyes a while to adjust. The place is crowded but we find a table and five chairs and DJ orders a round, four Coronas and a Jack Daniels, straight up, for Deb. "Black Light Trap" is playing over the sound system and the bar is lined with boys trying to look interested in anything but what's about to go down. No one is looking at Jane, plain Jane. Some are looking at Deb and some are looking at these other girls smoking clove cigarettes and standing or sitting in little groups. Skip points out his friend Philip, standing in the back and wearing sunglasses and a black Bauhaus T-shirt.

I get up from the table and go to the bar and then outside with Philip and it's raining and I can hear Shriekback from inside singing that we make our own mistakes and I score from Philip and then I go to the bathroom and lock the door and stare at myself in the mirror. Somebody knocks on the door and I put my foot back against it and say "Deal with it" and lay out three lines and do them and take a drink from the faucet and decide I need a haircut.

It's hot back in the theater and I hold my Corona up to my face, my forehead. There's a man sitting at a table next to us whose eyes are closed so tight that he is crying. The girl he's sitting with is tugging at the crotch of her Guess jeans and drinking a California Cooler and she's fourteen if she's a day. When the man opens his eyes, he looks at his Rolex and he looks at the stage and he looks at the girl and for some reason I'm relieved.

That's when the music goes down and the lights dim and there's some applause, scattered, and the music revs up again, something by Skinny Puppy, and at long last it's showtime. There are video screens set in a line over the stage and I look up and they shoot on one by one and it's a clip, just a short sixty seconds or so, from one of the films we saw, a grainy bootleg copy of a copy of a copy with subtitles in some foreign language, Spanish I think, and the zombies are loose inside a shopping mall and Skinny Puppy is pounding on and the singer's voice is barking deep down trauma hounds and the film clip jumps and now it's from some place back east, you can tell by the trees, and this is from television, from the news last summer, before they stopped talking, before the lists came out, and these soldiers are sweeping through a little town and the buildings are burning and the air is filled with smoke and they're moving house to house and they're blasting the doors and firing inside and now there's a pile of bodies and it's on fire and now it's that commercial, that public service announcement, whatever, and the Surgeon General is saying that the dead are alive, they're coming back to life, but we're killing them again, it's okay, it's all right, and somebody told me he's dead, all those guys are dead, and now the film clip jumps again and the colors roll over and over and the picture steadies and there's a test pattern. Skip says "This is it" and a new picture fades in and then this real tinny music, more like muzak, and it's a video, a home video, something shot with a Handycam maybe, and the picture is a basement or a garage, just bare walls, grey concrete, and after about a minute shadows start walking across the walls and then the first one's out on stage.

The music is gone and there's nothing but silence and a kind of hum, the tape is hissing, and the camera goes out of focus and the picture breaks up and then it's back in focus and she is looking at the camera. She's recent, blond and tall and sort of cute, and she's wearing a Benetton sweatshirt and acid-wash 501 jeans and it's hard to believe she's dead.

"This is real" Skip says to me and he turns to DJ and Deb and Jane and he says "For real." It's quiet in the club, quiet except for the hissing tape, and on the tape the girl is staring at the camera for a long time and nothing else happens. The floor behind her is covered with plastic trash bags and what looks like newspaper and there's a thin wooden cot and there's a worktable in the corner and I wonder why there's a power saw on the table and it does seem warm and I reach for my Corona and the bottle is empty and I look around for the waitress and everybody is watching the screen so I do too. This guy comes into the picture with a coil of rope and he's wearing this black hood and she sees him or hears him and she starts to turn his way and she stumbles and her legs are caught, there are chains on her ankles, and now there's another guy and he's wearing a ski mask and he's coming up behind her and he's carrying a chain and something like a harness, a leather harness, and I look at Deb and Deb looks at me and now they're hitting the girl with the chain and she falls to the ground and they're hitting her some more and now the rope is around her and the harness is over her face and I look at Deb and Deb is touching herself and I look back at the video and they're cutting her clothes and now they're cutting her and I look at Deb and Deb looks at me and she reaches to touch me and now they loop the rope around her neck and Deb's hand is moving up my leg and now the first guy is gone and Deb's hand is moving and now he's back and Deb is squeezing me and he's got a hammer and he swings it once and he swings it twice and Deb is squeezing me harder and now the rope is fastened overhead and someone in the audience says "Yeah" and Skip's arm circles Jane and he pulls her close and says "For real" and now they are yanking the rope and the noose is tightening and her feet are off the floor and Deb's hand is moving and squeezing and I tell her to slow down and she stops and says to hold on a minute and I try and I look back at the screen and now they have a set of hooks and Deb's hand is moving again and the hooks connect to chains and her hand is moving faster and the chains go taut and faster and there's a sound like a scream and faster and her head is bent back and faster and now they have a dildo and faster and they're fitting it with nails and faster and faster and faster now they have a boy, faster a little naked boy, and faster now they have a blowtorch and faster now they have a power drill and faster now they have and now they have and now they and now they and now and now and now the picture is gone and my crotch is wet and Deb reaches over and hands me a napkin.

It's four A.M. and it's getting cold and we're still sitting in the club and Skip is picking lint from my sweater and telling me that he wants to leave. The Clan of Xymox fades to Black and it's a wonderful life, the singer is singing, it's a wonderful, wonderful life. Jane is vomiting in the corner and the lights are dark and red and for a moment I think it looks like blood. DJ is turned away, watching two boys wet-kissing in the shadows beyond the stage and taking deep pulls on another Corona. Deb is out back fucking this guy from U.S.C., bleach-blond and tan and wearing a white Armani sweater. Skip is telling me that we ought to leave real soon now. The music clicks off and it's smoke and laughter and broken glass and the sound of Jane spitting up and then the live band saunters onto the stage and the band is called 3 but there are four of them. The bass player has a broken right hand and Skip says "The bass player has a broken right hand" and slides a clove cigarette from his shirt pocket. The four-man band called 3 starts playing a speed metal version of "I Am the Walrus" and Deb is standing in front of me and she kisses me and tells Skip she's ready and Skip is saying that we have to leave and DJ is pulling Jane by the arm and Jane is still bent over and I wonder if I should ask if she's okay and my eyes meet Skip's and he cuts them to the exit and the next thing you know, we're gone.

Skip says Jimmy has a camera and I drive over to Jimmy's house, but Jimmy, somebody remembers, is either dead or in Bermuda, so I drive to Toby's place and this black kid answers the door wearing white underwear and a hard-on. A lava lamp bubbles red in the living room behind him. "Toby's busy" the black kid says and shuts the door. I take the Hollywood Freeway to Western Avenue but it's not right and I take the Hollywood Freeway to Alvarado but it's not right and I drive downtown and I take an exit, any exit, and I see the Sheraton Grande and I see the Bonaventure and I see the Arco Tower and I think it's time to run. Skip says to stop but it's still not right and I turn the corner and now it's right and so I stop and Skip tosses Jane out the door and she's facedown in the gravel and it sounds like she's going to vomit again.

"You didn't have to do that" somebody says but I don't know who. DJ is sitting up in the backseat and he pulls his arm from around Deb and shrugs and looks down at Jane. Skip starts to laugh and it sounds like choking and he turns up the radio and it's the New Order single and Jane is crawling away from the car. Skip is pulling something from under his jacket and his door slams and I check the rearview mirror. I look at the reflection of Deb's eyes for a moment and I don't say anything more.

The car is stopped in the middle of the street, at the mouth of an alley, and I see now that it's the alley from my dream, a hidden place, a perfect place, and Jane is crawling away from the car and Skip is walking toward her and he's taking his time and there's something in his hand, something long and sharp, and it glows in the glare of the headlights and his shadow is streaking across the brick walls of the alley and I think I've just seen this. Skip is standing over her and I see Jane start to say something and Skip is shaking his head as if he's saying no and then he's bending down toward her and she just watches as he cuts her once, then again, and she rolls onto her back and he flicks the knife past her face and she doesn't blink, doesn't move, and now the back door slams and DJ and Deb are out of the car and walking down the alley and now I'm walking down the alley and when we get there Skip shows us the knife, a thick military job, and Jane is bleeding on her arms and hands and a little on her neck and DJ says "Make it like the movie" and Skip says "This is the movie." He looks at DJ and he looks at Deb and he looks at me and he looks at Jane and he slides the knife into her stomach and the sound is soft and she barely moves and there isn't much blood at all, so he slides the knife into her stomach again, then into her shoulder, and this time she shudders and her back arches up and she seems to moan and the blood bubbles up but it isn't very red, it isn't very red at all. Deb says "Oh" and Skip tosses the knife aside and Jane rolls onto her stomach and I think she's starting to cry, just a little, and he looks around the alley but there's nothing there, garbage cans and crumpled papers and the burned-out hulk of an RX-7, and he finds a brick and he throws it at her and she curls up like a baby and DJ picks up the brick and throws it and Deb picks up the brick and throws it and then it's my turn and I pick up the brick and throw it and hit her in the head.

We kick her for a while and then she starts to crawl and there still isn't much blood and it's the wrong color, almost black I guess, and it isn't very shiny and it's just like dripping, not spraying around or anything, and she is almost to the end of the alley and the street ends and there's a curb and there's a sidewalk and there's a wall and there's a light from somewhere beaming down and she crawls some more. Her head is in the gutter and Skip looks at DJ and he is saying "This is real" and he pulls at Jane's hair and her head is bent back and her mouth is open and he's dragging her forward and then he's pressing her face against the curb and her upper teeth are across the top of the curb, her lips are pulled back into a smile and it looks like the smile in the Polaroid, Jane is eight years old, and her head is hanging there by those upper teeth and I look at Skip and I look at DJ and I look at Deb and Deb is looking down and she's smiling too and Skip is saying "Real" and he puts his boot on the back of Jane's head and he presses once, twice, and that smile widens into a kiss, a full mouth kiss on the angle of concrete, and then he stomps downward and the sound is like nothing I have ever heard.

The sound is on the radio. I'm listening to the radio and it echoes along the alley and it plays song after song after song. I'm sitting on the curb with Skip and DJ and Deb, and DJ is smoking another cigarette and the stubs are collecting at his feet and there are seven or eight of them and we've been here an hour and it's nearly light and we've been waiting but now it's time to go.

"Okay, Jane" Deb says and she is standing and she is jabbing Jane with her foot and she is saying "We gotta go." Skip is standing and DJ is standing and Deb is looking at her Swatch and she says "Get up" and then she says "You can get up now." She is jabbing Jane with her foot and Jane isn't moving and Skip is wiping his knife and looking at Jane and DJ is smoking his cigarette and looking at Jane and I'm just looking at Jane and then I think I know. No, I do know. I'm sure I know.

"She's coming back, right?" Deb is saying and she's looking at Skip and she's looking at DJ and then she's looking at me. "Bret?" she is asking me and she is crossing her arms and she isn't smiling now. "She's coming back, isn't she?" Deb is saying "I mean, we're all coming back, right?" Skip is putting the knife in his pocket and DJ is finishing his cigarette and I am standing and she is saying "Right?"

People are afraid to live on the streets of Los Angeles. This is the last thing I say as I walk away from Skip and DJ and Deb and get back into the car. I don't know why I keep saying this thing. It's something I started and now I can't stop. Nothing else seems to matter.

I sit behind the wheel of the car and I watch the windshield wipers go back and forth, back and forth, back and forth, and the city blurs, out of focus, beneath the thin black lines. I want to say that people are afraid. I want to say that people are afraid of something and I can't remember what and maybe it's nothing, maybe it's a dream and I am running, I am running after something and I can't remember what, I can't remember the dream, and the windshield wipers go back and forth, back and forth. People are afraid of something and in my dream I am running and the radio is playing and I try to listen but it is playing the song I do not know. The windshield wipers go back and forth. The doors open and close and then I drive away.

SPARKS FLY UPWARD

by Lisa Morton

Lisa Morton is a horror author and screenwriter. Her short fiction has appeared in a number of anthologies, including *Mondo Zombie*, *Dark Delicacies*, *Dark Terrors 6*, *The Museum of Horrors*, and *Horrors! 365 Scary Stories*, among others. Her work has also appeared in magazines such as *Cemetery Dance*, including her story "Tested," which won the Bram Stoker Award. In addition to her fiction writing, Morton has also authored two books of non-fiction—*The Halloween Encyclopedia* and *The Cinema of Tsui Hark*—and edited the recently released *A Hallowe'en Anthology: Literary and Historical Writings Over the Centuries*.

Morton feels that many writers who have tackled the theme of zombies have fallen into a trap trying to "out-taboo" each other with extreme sex. So when it came time to write a zombie story of her own, she asked herself what taboos were left that could be dealt with in a zombie tale. "My answer was political ones," Morton said. "It's hard to imagine a more heated political topic than abortion, and when I thought of combining that with a tale of survivors carefully rationing out their resources, it all fell into place."

My breath is corrupt, my days are extinct,
the graves are ready for me.

Job 17:1

Blessed and holy is he that hath part in
the first resurrection…

Revelations 20:6

June 16

Tomorrow marks one year ago that the Colony was begun here, and I think just about everyone is busy preparing for a big celebration. We just had our first real harvest two weeks ago, so there'll be plenty of good things to eat, and as for drink—well, the product of George's still is a little extreme for most tastes, so Tom and a few of the boys made a foray outside yesterday for some real liquor.

Of course I was worried when Tom told me he was going (and not even for something really vital, just booze), but he said it wasn't so bad. The road was almost totally clear for the first five miles after they left the safety of the Colony, and even most of Philipsville, the pint-sized town where they raided a liquor store, was deserted. Tom said he shot one in the liquor store cellar when he went down there to check on the good wines; it was an old woman, probably the one-time shopkeeper's wife locked away. Unfortunately, she'd clawed most of the good bottles off to smash on the floor. Tom took what was left, and an unopened case of good burgundy he found untouched in a corner. There are 131 adults in the Colony, and he figured he'd have a bottle for every two on Anniversary Day.

It's been two weeks since any of the deadheads have been spotted near the Colony walls, and Pedro Quintero, our top marksman, picked that one off with one shot straight through the head from the east tower. It would be easy to fool ourselves into thinking the situation is finally mending... easy and dangerous, because it's not. The lack of deadheads seen around here lately proves only one thing: That Doc Freeman was right in picking this location, away from the cities and highways.

Of course Doc Freeman was right—he's right about everything. He said we should go this far north because the south would only keep getting hotter, and sure enough it's been in the 80s here for over a week now. I don't want to think what it is down in L.A. now—probably 120, and that's in the shade.

Tomorrow will be a tribute to Doc Freeman as much as an anniversary celebration. If it hadn't been for him... well, I suppose Tom and little Jessie and I would be wandering around out there with the rest of them right now, dead for a year but still hungry. Always hungry.

It's funny, but before all the shit came down, Doc Freeman was just an eccentric old college professor teaching agricultural sciences and preaching survival. Tom always believed Freeman had been thinking about cutting out anyway, even before the whole zombie thing, because of the rising temperatures. He told his students that agriculture in most parts of the U.S. was already a thing of the past, and it would all be moving up to Canada soon.

When the deadheads came (Doc Freeman argued, as did a lot of other environmentalists, that they were caused by the holes in the ozone layer, too), it was the most natural thing in the world, I guess, for him to assemble a band of followers and head north. He'd chosen the site for the Colony, set up policy and government, designed the layout of fields, houses and fences, and even assigned each of us a job, according to what we were best at. It had all been scary at first, of course —especially with 3-year-old Jessie—but we all kind of fell into place. I even discovered I was a talented horticulturist—Doc says the best after him—and in some ways this new life is better than the old one.

Of course there are a lot of things we all miss—ice cream, uncalloused hands, t.v. Del still scans the shortwave radio, hoping he'll pick something up on it. In a year, he has only once, and that transmission ended with the sound of gunshots.

So we accept our place in the world—and the fact that it may be the last place. Tomorrow we do more than accept it, we celebrate it.

I wish I knew exactly how to feel.

June 17

Well, the big day has come and gone.

Tom is beside me, snoring in a blissful alcoholic oblivion. Tomorrow he'll be in the fields again, so he's earned this.

Jessie is in her room next door, exhausted from all the games she played and sweets she ate. Tom actually let me use a precious hour of videotape to record her today.

And yet I wasn't the only one crying when Doc Freeman got up and made his speech about how his projections show that if we continue at our present excellent rate, we'll be able to expand the colony in three years. Expand it carefully, he added. Meaning that in three years there'll be probably forty or fifty couples—like Tom and I—begging for the precious right to increase our family.

I know Doc is right, that we must remember the lessons of the old world and not outgrow our capacity to produce, to sustain that new growth... but somehow it seems wrong to deny new life when we're surrounded by so much death.

Especially when the new life is in me.

June 24

I've missed two now, and so I felt certain enough to go see Dale Oldfield. He examined me as best he could (he's an excellent G.P., but his equipment is still limited), and he concluded I'd guessed right.

I am pregnant.

Between the two of us we figured it at about six weeks along. Dale thanked me for not trying to hide it, then told me he would have to report it to Doc Freeman. I asked only that Tom and I be allowed to be there when he did. He agreed, and we decided on tomorrow afternoon.

I went home and told Tom. At first he was thrilled—and then he remembered where we were.

I told Tom we'd be seeing Doc Freeman tomorrow about it, and he became obsessed with the idea that he'd somehow convince Doc to let us have the baby.

I couldn't stand to hear him torture himself that way, so I read stories to Jessie and held her until we both fell asleep in her narrow child-sized bed.

June 25

We saw Doc Freeman today. Dale Oldfield confirmed the situation, then gracefully excused himself, saying he'd be in his little shack-cum-office when we needed him.

Doc Freeman poured all three of us a shot of his private stock of Jim Beam, then he began the apologies. Tom tried to argue him out of it, saying a birth would be good for morale, and we could certainly handle just one more in the Colony… but Doc told him quietly that, unlike many of the young couples, we already had a child and couldn't expect special treatment. Tom finally gave in, admitting Doc was right—and I'd never loved him more than I did then, seeing his pain and regret.

He went with me to tell Dale we'd be needing his services next week, and Dale just nodded, his head hung low, not meeting our eyes.

Afterwards, in our own bungalow, Tom and I argued for hours. We both got crazy, talking about leaving the Colony, building our own little fortress somewhere, even overthrowing Doc Freeman… but I think we both knew it was all fantasy. Doc Freeman had been right again—we did have Jessie, and maybe in a few more years the time would be right for another child.

But not now.

July 2

Tomorrow is the day set for us to do it.

God, I wish there was another way. Unfortunately, even after performing a D&C three times in the last year, Dale still has never had the clinic's equipment moved to the Colony. It's ironic that we can send out an expedition for booze, but not one for medical equipment. Doc Freeman says that's because the equipment is a lot bigger than the booze, and the Colony's only truck has been down basically since we got here.

So tomorrow Tom, Dale and I will make the 18-mile drive to Silver Creek, the nearest town big enough to have had a family planning clinic. Dale, who has keys to the clinic, assures me the only dangerous part will be getting from the car to the doors of the clinic. They can't get inside, he tells me, so we'll be safe—until we have to leave again, that is.

Funny… when he's telling me about danger, he only talks about dead-heads.

He never mentions the abortion.

July 3

I didn't sleep much last night. Tom held me but even he dozed off for a while. It's morning as I write this, and I hear Jessie starting to awaken. After I get her up, I'll try to tell her mommy and daddy have to leave for a while, and nice Mrs. Oldfield will watch her. She'll cry, but hopefully not because she understands what's really going on.

It's later now—Jessie's taken care of, and Dale's got the jeep ready to go. Tom and I check our supplies again: An automatic .38 with full magazine, an Uzi with extra clips, a hunting rifle with scope and plenty of ammo, three machetes and the little wooden box. Dale's also got his shotgun and a Walther PPK that he says makes him feel like James Bond. Everyone teases him about it, telling him things like the difference is that Bond's villains were all alive to begin with. Dale always glowers and shuts up.

It's time to go.

We climbed into the jeep. Tom asked why I was bringing you (diary) along, and I told him it was my security blanket and rabbit's foot. He shut up and Dale gunned the engine. We had to stop three times on the way out to exchange hugs and good luck wishes with people who ran up from the fields when we went by.

We're about 15 miles out now, and it's been the way Tom said—quiet. After the gates swung open and we pulled onto the dusty road, it must've been 10 minutes before we saw the first deadhead. It was lumbering slowly across a sere field, still fifty yards from the road as we whipped by.

A few miles later there was a small pack of three in the road, but they were spaced wide apart. Dale drove around two of them; they clawed in vain at the jeep, but we were doing 60 and they just scraped their fingers. The third one was harder to drive around—there were car wrecks on either side of the road—so Dale just whomped into him. He flew over the welded cage at the front of the jeep and landed somewhere off to the side of the road. We barely felt it.

We'd just reached the outskirts of Silver Creek when Dale slowed down and cleared his throat. Then he said, Listen, Sarah, there's something you ought to know about the clinic. He asked me if I'd talked to any of the others he'd already escorted out here.

Of course I had, but they had only assured me of Dale's skilled, painless technique, and that they'd be there if I needed to talk. None of them had said much about the clinic itself.

I said this to Dale, and he asked me something strange.

He asked if I was religious.

Tom and I looked at each other, then Tom asked Dale what he was getting at.

Dale stammered through something about how the deadheads tend to go back to places that were important to them, like their homes or shopping malls or schools.

We nodded—everyone knew that—and Dale asked if we'd ever heard of Operation SoulSave.

I swear I literally tasted something bad in my mouth. How could I forget? The fundamentalists who used to stand around outside abortion clinics and shout insults and threats at people who went in. I was with a friend once—a very young friend—when it happened to her.

Then I realized what he was saying. I couldn't believe it. I tried to ask him, but my words just tripped all over each other. He nodded and told us.

They're still here.

Most of Silver Creek was empty. We saw some of them inside dusty old storefronts, gazing at us stupidly as we drove by, but they probably hadn't fed in well over a year and were pretty sluggish. Either that, or they'd just been that way in life—staring slack-jawed as it passed them by.

That wasn't the case, however, with the group before the clinic.

There must have been 20 of them, massed solidly before the locked doors. As we drove towards them, I saw their clothes, once prim and starched, now stained will all those fluids they'd long ago feared or detested. One still held up a sign (I realized a few seconds later he had taped it to his wrist as he died) which read OPERATION SOULSAVE—SAVE A SOUL FOR CHRIST! Several sported the obligatory ABORTION IS MURDER t-shirts, now tattered and discolored.

Their leader was the Priest. I remembered him from before, when he'd been on all the news programs, spouting his vicious rhetoric while his flock chanted behind him. Of course, he looked different now—somebody had snacked on his trapezius, so his Roman Collar was covered in dried gore and hung askew, and his head (he was also missing a considerable patch of scalp on that same side) canted strangely at an odd angle.

I saw Dale eyeing them and muttering something under his breath. I asked him what it was so I could write it down: *Yet man is born unto trouble, as the sparks fly upward.* He said it was from the Bible. I was surprised; I didn't know Dale read the Bible.

Tom responded with a quote from one of the more contemporary prophets: *I used to be disgusted, now I try to be amused.* Then he asked Dale what we were going to do. Dale, who was practiced in this, said he'd drive around the building once, which would draw most of them away from the front long enough for us to get in. They wouldn't bother the jeep when we weren't in it.

Dale headed for the next corner. Tom pulled the .38 and held it, and I remembered.

I was thinking about the time I had to go to a different clinic with my friend Julie. It was before I started you, diary; in fact, I started you about the time Julie disappeared with most of the rest of the world. So I've never written any of this down before.

Julie had gotten pregnant from her boyfriend Sean, who split when she told him. Abortions were legal then (this was a long time ago), but could be costly, and Julie, who was still going to college (as I was), had no money. She went to her parents, but they threw her out of the house. She thought about having the baby and putting it up for adoption, but she had no health insurance, wouldn't be able to afford the actual birth, and regarded overpopulation as the end of the world. This, obviously, was before the deadheads arrived and clarified *that* issue.

So I'd lent her the money, and agreed to go with her to the clinic. She made the appointment, worried about it so much she didn't sleep the night before, almost backed out twice on the drive there—and all so she could be confronted by the fine Christian citizens of Operation SoulSave.

They had seated themselves on either side of the walkway leading into the clinic. Even though it was in another state and time, they wore the same t-shirts and held the same signs. They were mainly male, or women in clothes so tight they seemed life-threatening. They all had vacuous smiles on their faces, that gave way to cruel snarls of contempt whenever anyone went into or out of the clinic doors.

Julie took one look at them and didn't want to leave the car. I told her we'd be late, and she said it didn't matter.

We'd talked about the morality of abortion already, and had agreed that it was obvious that the unformed, early fetus was only an extension of the mother's body, and as such each woman had the right to make her own decision. I reminded Julie of this as she sat shivering in the car, and she'd said that wasn't why she didn't want to go past them.

She was afraid of *them*. She said they seemed like a mindless horde, capable of any violence they were directed to commit.

She'd had no idea how right she was.

We drove slowly around one corner. Sure enough, they stumbled after us. Then Dale threw it into fourth, and we screeched the rest of the way around the block.

When we got back to the main entrance, there were only five or six still there, not including one that dragged itself around on two partially eaten legs. Tom handed me the Uzi, while he took the .38 and cradled the box. Dale opted for a machete (I didn't want to have to see him use it minutes before he operated on *me*).

We sprinted from car to door. Tom shot two right between the eyes. I raised the Uzi, forgetting its rapid-fire design, and ripped one of them completely apart. I felt my stomach turn over as I saw some stale gray stuff splatter the doors. Dale just kept running, shouldering the last two aside. One rebounded and grabbed his left arm. he whirled and brought the machete down, severing the thing's hand, then kicking it away. He pried the dead hand from his arm, threw it aside, and told us to cover him while he unlocked the door.

As he fiddled with the keys, Tom shot the two Dale had barreled through. Then the .38 jammed. He began to fieldstrip it, and I looked nervously down the street, where the ones we'd tricked were shambling back, led by the gruesome Priest. Suddenly I felt something on my ankle. I looked down to see the legless one had dragged itself up the steps, and was bringing its gaping maw to bear on my lower calf. I freaked out and grabbed the Walther from Dale's holster; I think I was screaming as I fired into the zombie's peeling head. It died and let go, thick brown liquid draining onto its SAVE A SOUL—CLOSE A CLINIC t-shirt.

Then Dale had the doors open and we were in.

Later, Tom told me he had to pry the pistol from my fingers while Dale started up the generator and got things ready.

Then before I knew it Dale was there, in gloves and mask, saying he was ready.

I don't remember much of the actual operation, except that I asked Tom to wait outside—and the sound. The horrible sound the whole time we were in there:

Them, pounding on the doors, slow heavy thuds, relentless, unmerciful.

Dale was, as I've said before, an excellent doctor, and it was over soon. He made sure I didn't see what he put into the tiny wooden box Tom had carried in, and I didn't ask. The box, which had been beautifully crafted by Rudy V., would be taken back to the Colony and buried there.

There was one thing I had to ask, though, as morbid a thought as it was. I had to know if—I had to be sure Dale had—God, I can't even write it.

But he knew what I was asking, and as he stripped off the gloves he told me I didn't have to worry. None of the ones aborted had ever come back. The rest of us had to be cremated or have the brain destroyed upon death, or we'd resurrect.

How ironic, I thought, that this was how we would finally lay to rest the Great Debate. They weren't human enough to come back. Abortion isn't murder.

Getting out would be harder than getting in, but Dale had it all down. Tom would crawl out a side window, drawing them away from Dale and me. Dale would lock the front door while Tom and I covered him, then we'd all head for the jeep. I was, of course, still weak, and Tom didn't want to leave my side, but Dale told him it was the safest way, and he'd be sure I was okay. Tom reluctantly agreed.

It went down without mishap. They were slow and easily confused, and by the time they saw two of us on the stoop and one by the jeep, they didn't know which way to turn. Tom shot a couple who were in our way. Once Dale had the doors locked, he pocketed the keys, took the Uzi from me, and I carried the little coffin as we ran for the jeep.

Once we were inside, Dale started it up and pulled away. They were already hammering on the sides, clawing the welded cage, drooling a yellowish bile. One wouldn't let go as we drove off, and it got dragged fifty feet before its fingers tore off. Tom actually shouted something at it.

Dale was ready to speed out of town when I asked him to stop the jeep and go back. He stopped, then both he and Tom turned to stare at me, as open-mouthed as any deadhead. They asked why, and I just handed Tom our box, took the rifle, got out and started walking back.

They ran up on either side of me, Tom saying I was still delirious from the operation, Dale arguing I could start hemorrhaging seriously. I ignored them both as I saw the deadheads at the end of the street staggering forward now.

I had to wipe tears out of my eyes—I didn't even know I was crying—as I raised the rifle and sighted on the first one. I fired, and saw it flung backwards to lie unmoving in the street, truly finally dead. Tom and Dale both tried to take the rifle from me, but I shrugged them off and fired again. Tom argued we were done here, and there was no point in wasting ammo on these fuckers, but I told him I had to. Then I told him—told them both—why.

After that they left me alone until all the deadheads were gone but one—the Priest. My arms were shaking so bad I almost couldn't hold the gun steady, but he was close—thirty feet away now—and hard to miss. My first shot blew part of his neck—and whatever was left of the Collar—away, but the last one brought him down.

I dropped the gun, and Tom and Dale had to carry me back to the jeep.

But now I'm at home in bed, and Dale says I'm physically okay. I miss the child I'll never know, a pain which far outweighs the physical discomfort, but Jessie is here, and she hugs me a long time before Tom sends her to bed.

Now I'm smiling as I think of that street, and write this. Because I know that none of the women who come after me will have to endure more than the horror of giving up part of themselves.

MEATHOUSE MAN
by George R. R. Martin

George R. R. Martin is the best-selling author of the Song of Ice and Fire epic fantasy series and a range of other novels including *Fevre Dream*, *The Armageddon Rag*, *Dying of the Light*, and *Hunter's Run* (with Daniel Abraham and Gardner Dozois). He is a prolific author of short stories, which have garnered numerous nominations and wins for the field's major awards, including the Hugo, Nebula, Stoker, and World Fantasy awards.

His short work was recently collected in the mammoth, two-volume *Dreamsongs*, in which Martin relates the story of how "Meathouse Man" came to be published. It first appeared in Damon Knight's *Orbit 18*, but was originally intended for Harlan Ellison's *The Last Dangerous Visions*. Ellison, however, rejected it and challenged Martin to "tear the guts out of the story and rewrite the whole thing from page one."

So Martin did that, and "opened a vein as well." While writing the story, Martin was emotionally in a lot of pain, so he poured all of it into "Meathouse Man." And even now, almost thirty years later, he finds it a painful one to reread.

I
IN THE MEATHOUSE

They came straight from the ore-fields that first time, Trager with the others, the older boys, the almost-men who worked their corpses next to his. Cox was the oldest of the group, and he'd been around the most, and he said that Trager had to come even if he didn't want to. Then one of the others laughed and said that Trager wouldn't even know what to do, but Cox the kind-of leader shoved him until he was quiet. And when payday came, Trager trailed the rest to the meathouse, scared but somehow eager, and he paid his money to a man downstairs and got a room key.

He came into the dim room trembling, nervous. The others had gone to other rooms, had left him alone with her (no, *it*, not her but *it*, he reminded himself, and promptly forgot again). In a shabby gray cubicle with a single smoky light.

He stank of sweat and sulfur, like all who walked the streets of Skrakky, but there was no help for that. It would be better if he could bathe first, but the room did not have a bath. Just a sink, double bed with sheets that looked dirty even in the dimness, a corpse.

She lay there naked, staring at nothing, breathing shallow breaths. Her legs were spread; ready. Was she always that way, Trager wondered, or had the man before him arranged her like that? He didn't know. He knew how to do it (he did, he *did*, he'd read the books Cox gave him, and there were films you could see, and all sorts of things), but he didn't know much of anything else. Except maybe how to handle corpses. That he was good at, the youngest handler on Skrakky, but he had to be. They had forced him into the handlers' school when his mother died, and they made him learn, so that was the thing he did. This, this he had never done (but he knew how, yes, yes, he *did*); it was his first time.

He came to the bed slowly and sat to a chorus of creaking springs. He touched her and the flesh was warm. Of course. She was not a corpse, not really, no; the body was alive enough, a heartbeat under the heavy white breasts, she breathed. Only the brain was gone, ripped from her, replaced with a deadman's synthabrain. She was meat now, an extra body for a corpsehandler to control, just like the crew he worked each day under sulfur skies. She was not a woman. So it did not matter that Trager was just a boy, a jowly frog-faced boy who smelled of Skrakky. She (no *it*, remember?) would not care, could not care.

Emboldened, aroused and hard, the boy stripped off his corpse-handler's clothing and climbed in bed with the female meat. He was very excited; his hands shook as he stroked her, studied her. Her skin was very white, her hair dark and long, but even the boy could not call her pretty. Her face was too flat and wide, her mouth hung open, and her limbs were loose and sagging with fat.

On her huge breasts, all around the fat dark nipples, the last customer had left tooth-marks where he'd chewed her. Trager touched the marks tentatively, traced them with a finger. Then, sheepish about his hesitations, he grabbed one breast, squeezed it hard, pinched the nipple until he imagined a real girl would squeal with pain. The corpse did not move. Still squeezing, he rolled over on her and took the other breast into his mouth.

And the corpse responded.

She thrust up at him, hard, and meaty arms wrapped around his pimpled back to pull him to her. Trager groaned and reached down between her legs. She was hot, wet, excited. He trembled. How did they do that? Could she really get excited without a mind, or did they have lubricating tubes stuck into her, or what?

Then he stopped caring. He fumbled, found his penis, put it into her, thrust. The corpse hooked her legs around him and thrust back. It felt good, real good, better than anything he'd ever done to himself, and in some obscure way he felt proud that she was so wet and excited.

It only took a few strokes; he was too new, too young, too eager to last long.

A few strokes was all he needed—but it was all she needed too. They came together, a red flush washing over her skin as she arched against him and shook soundlessly.

Afterwards she lay again like a corpse.

Trager was drained and satisfied, but he had more time left, and he was determined to get his money's worth. He explored her thoroughly, sticking his fingers everywhere they would go, touching her everywhere, rolling it over, looking at everything. The corpse moved like dead meat.

He left her as he'd found her, lying face up on the bed with her legs apart. Meathouse courtesy.

The horizon was a wall of factories, all factories, vast belching factories that sent red shadows to flick against the sulfur-dark skies. The boy saw but hardly noticed. He was strapped in place high atop his automill, two stories up on a monster machine of corroding yellow-painted metal with savage teeth of diamond and duralloy, and his eyes were blurred with triple images. Clear and strong and hard he saw the control panel before him, the wheel, the fuel-feed, the bright handle of the ore-scoops, the banks of light that would tell of trouble in the refinery under his feet, the brake and emergency brake. But that was not all he saw. Dimly, faintly, there were echoes; overlaid images of two other control cabs, almost identical to his, where corpse hands moved clumsily over the instruments.

Trager moved those hands, slow and careful, while another part of his mind held his own hands, his real hands, very still. The corpse controller hummed thinly on his belt.

On either side of him, the other two automills moved into flanking positions. The corpse hands squeezed the brakes; the machines rumbled to a halt. On the edge of the great sloping pit, they stood in a row, shabby pitted juggernauts ready to descend into the gloom. The pit was growing steadily larger; each day new layers of rock and ore were stripped away.

Once a mountain range had stood here, but Trager did not remember that.

The rest was easy. The automills were aligned now. To move the crew in unison was a cinch, any decent handler could do *that*. It was only when you had to keep several corpses busy at several different tasks that things got tricky. But a good corpsehandler could do that too. Eight-crews were not unknown to veterans; eight bodies linked to a single corpse controller moved by a single mind and eight synthabrains. The deadmen were each tuned to one controller, and only one; the handler who wore that controller and thought corpse-thoughts in its proximity field could move those deadmen like secondary bodies. Or like his own body. If he was good enough.

Trager checked his filtermask and earplugs quickly, then touched the fuel-feed, engaged, flicked on the laser-knives and the drills. His corpses echoed his moves, and pulses of light spit through the twilight of Skrakky. Even through his plugs he could hear the awful whine as the ore-scoops revved up and lowered. The rock-eating maw of an automill was even wider than the machine was tall.

Rumbling and screeching, in perfect formation, Trager and his corpse crew descended into the pit. Before they reached the factories on the far side of the plain, tons of metal would have been torn from the earth, melted and refined and processed, while the worthless rock was reduced to powder and blown out into the already unbreathable air. He would deliver finished steel at dusk, on the horizon.

He was a good handler, Trager thought as the automills started down. But the handler in the meathouse—now, she must be an artist. He imagined her down in the cellar somewhere, watching each of her corpses through holos and psi circuits, humping them all to please her patrons. Was it just a fluke, then, that his fuck had been so perfect? Or was she always that good? But how, *how*, to move a dozen corpses without even being near them, to have them doing different things, to keep them all excited, to match the needs and rhythm of each customer so exactly?

The air behind him was black and choked by rock-dust, his ears were full of screams, and the far horizon was a glowering red wall beneath which yellow ants crawled and ate rock. But Trager kept his hard-on all across the plain as the automill shook beneath him.

The corpses were company-owned; they stayed in the company deadman depot. But Trager had a room, a slice of the space that was his own in a steel-and-concrete warehouse with a thousand other slices. He only knew a handful of his neighbors, but he knew all of them too; they were corpsehandlers. It was a world of silent shadowed corridors and endless closed doors. The lobby-lounge, all air and plastic, was a dusty deserted place where none of the tenants ever gathered.

The evenings were long there, the nights eternal. Trager had bought extra light-panels for his particular cube, and when all of them were on they burned so bright that his infrequent visitors blinked and complained about the glare. But always there came a time when he could read no more, and then he had to turn them out, and the darkness returned once more.

His father, long gone and barely remembered, had left a wealth of books and tapes, and Trager kept them still. The room was lined with them, and others stood in great piles against the foot of the bed and on either side of the bathroom door. Infrequently he went on with Cox and the others, to drink and joke and prowl for real women. He imitated them as best he could, but he always felt out of place. So most of his nights were spent at home, reading and listening to the music, remembering and thinking.

That week he thought long after he'd faded his light panels into black, and his thoughts were a frightened jumble. Payday was coming again, and Cox would be after him to return to the meathouse, and yes, yes, he wanted to. It had been good, exciting; for once he had felt confident and virile. But it was so easy, cheap, *dirty*. There had to be more, didn't there? Love, whatever that was? It had to be better with a real woman, had to, and he wouldn't find one of those in a meathouse. He'd never found one outside, either, but then he'd never really had the courage to try. But he had to try, *had* to, or what sort of life would he ever have?

Beneath the covers he masturbated, hardly thinking of it, while he resolved not to return to the meathouse.

But a few days later, Cox laughed at him and he had to go along. Somehow he felt it would prove something.

A different room this time, a different corpse. Fat and black, with bright orange hair, less attractive than his first, if that was possible. But Trager came to her ready and eager, and this time he lasted longer. Again, the performance was superb. Her rhythm matched his stroke for stroke, she came with him, she seemed to know exactly what he wanted.

Other visits; two of them, four, six. He was a regular now at the meathouse, along with the others, and he had stopped worrying about it. Cox and the others accepted him in a strange half-hearted way, but his dislike of them had grown, if anything. He was better than they were, he thought. He could hold his own in a meathouse, he could run his corpses and his automills as good as any of them, and he still thought and dreamed. In time he'd leave them all behind, leave Skrakky, be something. They would be meathouse men as long as they would live, but Trager knew he could do better. He believed. He would find love.

He found none in the meathouse, but the sex got better and better, though it was perfect to begin with. In bed with the corpses, Trager was never dissatisfied; he did everything he'd ever read about, heard about, dreamt about. The corpses knew his needs before he did. When he needed it slow, they were slow. When he wanted to have it hard and quick and brutal, then they gave it to him that way, perfectly. He used every orifice they had; they always knew which one to present to him.

His admiration of the meathouse handler grew steadily for months, until it was almost worship. Perhaps somehow he could meet her, he thought at last. Still a boy, still hopelessly naive, he was sure he would love her. Then he would take her away from the meathouse to a clean, corpseless world where they could be happy together.

One day, in a moment of weakness, he told Cox and the others. Cox looked at him, shook his head, grinned. Somebody else snickered. Then they all began to laugh. "What an *ass* you are, Trager," Cox said at last. "There is no fucking *handler!* Don't tell me you never heard of a feedback circuit?"

He explained it all, to laughter; explained how each corpse was tuned to a controller built into its bed, explained how each customer handled his own meat, explained why non-handlers found meathouse women dead and still.

And the boy realized suddenly why the sex was always perfect. He was a better handler than even he had thought.

That night, alone in his room with all the lights burning white and hot, Trager faced himself. And turned away, sickened. He was good at his job, he was proud of that, but the rest. . .

It was the meathouse, he decided. There was a trap there in the meathouse, a trap that could ruin him, destroy life and dream and hope. He would not go back; it was too easy. He would show Cox, show all of them. He could take the hard way, take the risks, feel the pain if he had to. And maybe the joy, maybe the love. He'd gone the other way too long.

Trager did not go back to the meathouse. Feeling strong and decisive and superior, he went back to his room. There, as years passed, he read and dreamed and waited for life to begin.

1

WHEN I WAS ONE-AND-TWENTY

Josie was the first.

She was beautiful, had always been beautiful, knew she was beautiful; all that had shaped her, made her what she was. She was a free spirit. She was aggressive, confident, conquering. Like Trager, she was only twenty when they met, but she had lived more than he had, and she seemed to have the answers. He loved her from the first.

And Trager? Trager before Josie, but years beyond the meathouse? He was taller now, broad and heavy with both muscle and fat, often moody, silent and self-contained. He ran a full five-crew in the ore fields, more than Cox, more than any of them. At night, he read books; sometimes in his room, sometimes in the lobby. He had long since forgotten that he went there to meet someone. Stable, solid, unemotional; that was Trager. He touched no one, and no one touched him. Even the tortures had stopped, though the scars remained *inside*. Trager hardly knew they were there; he never looked at them.

He fit in well now. With his corpses.

Yet—not completely. Inside, the dream. Something believed, something hungered, something yearned. It was strong enough to keep him away from the meathouse, from the vegetable life the others had all chosen. And sometimes, on bleak lonely nights, it would grow stronger still. Then Trager would rise from his empty bed, dress, and walk the corridors for hours with his hands shoved deep into his pockets while something twisted, clawed, and whimpered in his gut. Always, before his walks were over, he would resolve to do something, to change his life tomorrow.

But when tomorrow came, the silent gray corridors were half-forgotten, the demons had faded, and he had six roaring, shaking automills to drive across the pit. He would lose himself in routine, and it would be long months before the feelings came again.

Then Josie. They met like this:

It was a new field, rich and unmined, a vast expanse of broken rock and rubble that filled the plain. Low hills a few weeks ago, but the company skimmers had leveled the area with systematic nuclear blast mining, and now the automills were moving in. Trager's five-crew had been one of the first, and the change had been exhilarating at first. The old pit had been just about worked out; here there was a new terrain to contend with, boulders and jagged rock fragments, baseball-sized fists of stone that came shrieking at you on the dusty wind. It all seemed exciting, dangerous. Trager, wearing a leather jacket and filter-mask and goggles and earplugs, drove his six machines and six bodies with a fierce pride, reducing boulders to powder, clearing a path for the later machines, fighting his way yard by yard to get whatever ore he could.

And one day, suddenly, one of the eye echoes suddenly caught his attention. A light flashed red on a corpse-driven automill. Trager reached, with his hands, with his mind, with five sets of corpse-hands. Six machines stopped, but still another light went red. Then another, and another. Then the whole board, all twelve. One of his automills was out. Cursing, he looked across the rock field towards the machine in question, used his corpse to give it a kick. The lights stayed red. He beamed out for a tech.

By the time she got there—in a one-man skimmer that looked like a teardrop of pitted black metal—Trager had unstrapped, climbed down the metal rings on the side of the automill, walked across the rocks to where the dead machine stopped. He was just starting to climb up when Josie arrived; they met at the foot of the yellow-metal mountain, in the shadow of its treads.

She was field-wise, he knew at once. She wore a handler's coverall, earplugs, heavy goggles, and her face was smeared with grease to prevent dust abrasions. But still she was beautiful. Her hair was short, light brown, cut in a shag that was jumbled by the wind; her eyes, when she lifted the goggles, were bright green. She took charge immediately.

All business, she introduced herself, asked him a few questions, then opened a repair bay and crawled inside, into the guts of the drive and the ore-smelt and the refinery. It didn't take her long; ten minutes, maybe, and she was back outside.

"Don't go in there," she said, tossing her hair from in front of her goggles with a flick of her head. "You've got a damper failure. The nukes are running away."

"Oh," said Trager. His mind was hardly on the automill, but he had to make an impression, made to say something intelligent. "Is it going to blow up?" he asked, and as soon as he said it he knew that *that* hadn't been intelligent at all. Of course it wasn't going to blow up; runaway nuclear reactors didn't work that way, he knew that.

But Josie seemed amused. She smiled—the first time he saw her distinctive flashing grin—and seemed to see him, *him*, Trager, not just a corpsehandler. "No," she said. "It will just melt itself down. Won't even get hot out here, since you've got shields built into the walls. Just don't go in there."

"All right." Pause. What could he say now? "What do I do?"

"Work the rest of your crew, I guess. This machine'll have to be scrapped.

It should have been overhauled a long time ago. From the looks of it, there's been a lot of patching done in the past. Stupid. It breaks down, it breaks down, it breaks down, and they keep sending it out. Should realize that something is wrong. After that many failures, it's sheer self-delusion to think the thing's going to work right next time out."

"I guess," Trager said. Josie smiled at him again, sealed up the panel, and started to turn.

"Wait," he said. It came out before he could stop it, almost in spite of him. Josie turned, cocked her head, looked at him questioningly. And Trager drew a sudden strength from the steel and the stone and the wind; under sulfur skies, his dreams seemed less impossible. Maybe, he thought. Maybe.

"Uh. I'm Greg Trager. Will I see you again?"

Josie grinned. "Sure. Come tonight." She gave him the address.

He climbed back into his automill after she had left, exulting in his six strong bodies, all fire and life, and he chewed up rock with something near to joy. The dark red glow in the distance looked almost like a sunrise.

When he got to Josie's, he found four other people there, friends of hers. It was a party of sorts. Josie threw a lot of parties and Trager—from that night on—went to all of them. Josie talked to him, laughed with him, *liked* him, and suddenly his life was no longer the same.

With Josie, he saw parts of Skrakky he had never seen before, did things he had never done:

—he stood with her in the crowds that gathered on the streets at night, stood in the dusty wind and sickly yellow light between the windowless concrete buildings, stood and bet and cheered himself hoarse while grease-stained mechs raced yellow rumbly tractor-trucks up and down and down and up.

—he walked with her through the strangely silent and white and clean underground Offices, and sealed air-conditioned corridors where off-worlders and paper-shufflers and company executives lived and worked.

—he prowled the rec-malls with her, those huge low buildings so like a warehouse from the outside, but full of colored lights and game rooms and cafeterias and tape shops and endless bars where handlers made their rounds.

—he went with her to dormitory gyms, where they watched handlers less skillful than himself send their corpses against each other with clumsy fists.

—he sat with her and her friends, and they woke dark quiet taverns with their talk and with their laughter, and once Trager saw someone looking much like Cox staring at him from across the room, and he smiled and leaned a bit closer to Josie.

He hardly noticed the other people, the crowds that Josie surrounded herself with; when they went out on one of her wild jaunts, six of them or eight or ten, Trager would tell himself that he and Josie were going out, and that some others had come along with them.

Once in a great while, things would work out so they were alone together, at her place, or his. Then they would talk. Of distant worlds, of politics, of corpses and life on Skrakky, of the books they both consumed, of sports or games or friends they had in common. They shared a good deal. Trager talked a lot with Josie. And never said a word.

He loved her, of course. He suspected it the first month, and soon he was convinced of it. He loved her. This was the real thing, the thing he had been waiting for, and it had happened just as he knew it would.

But with his love: agony. He could not tell her. A dozen times he tried; the words would never come. What if she did not love him back?

His nights were still alone, in the small room with the white lights and the books and the pain. He was more alone than ever now; the peace of his routine, of his half-life with his corpses, was gone, stripped from him. By day he rode the great automills, moved his corpses, smashed rock and melted ore, and in his head rehearsed the words he'd say to Josie. And dreamed of those that she'd speak back. She was trapped too, he thought. She'd had men, of course, but she didn't love them, she loved him. But she couldn't tell him, any more than he could tell her. When he broke through, when he found the words and the courage, then everything would be all right. Each day he said that to himself, and dug swift and deep into the earth.

But back home, the sureness faded. Then, with awful despair, he knew that he was kidding himself. He was a friend to her, nothing more, never would be more. Why did he lie to himself? He'd had hints enough. They had never been lovers, never would be; on the few times he'd worked up the courage to touch her, she would smile, move away on some pretext, so he was never quite sure that he was being rejected. But he got the idea, and in the dark it tore at him. He walked the corridors weekly now, sullen, desperate, wanting to talk to someone without knowing how. And all the old scars woke up to bleed again.

Until the next day. When he would return to his machines, and believe again. He must believe in himself, he knew that, he shouted it out loud. He must stop feeling sorry for himself. He must do something. He must tell Josie. He would.

And she would love him, cried the day.

And she would laugh, the nights replied.

Trager chased her for a year, a year of pain and promise, the first year that he had ever *lived*. On that the night-fears and the day-voice agreed; he was alive now. He would never return to the emptiness of his time before Josie; he would never go back to the meathouse. That far, at least, he had come. He could change, and someday he would be strong enough to tell her.

Josie and two friends dropped by his room that night, but the friends had to leave early. For an hour or so they were alone, talking about nothing. Finally she had to go. Trager said he'd walk her home.

He kept his arm around her down the long corridors, and he watched her face, watched the play of light and shadow on her cheeks as they walked from light to darkness. "Josie," he started. He felt so fine, so good, so warm, and it came out. "I love you."

And she stopped, pulled away from him, stepped back. Her mouth opened, just a little, and something flickered in her eyes. "Oh, Greg," she said. Softly. Sadly. "No, Greg, no, don't, don't." And she shook her head.

Trembling slightly, mouthing silent words, Trager held out his hand. Josie did not take it. He touched her cheek, gently, and wordless she spun away from him.

Then, for the first time ever, Trager shook. And the tears came.

Josie took him to her room. There, sitting across from each other on the floor, never touching, they talked.

J: ... *known it for a long time... tried to discourage you, Greg, but I didn't just want to come right out and... I never wanted to hurt you... a good person... don't worry....*

T: ... *knew it all along... that it would never... lied to myself. . . wanted to believe, even if it wasn't true... I'm sorry, Josie, I'm sorry, I'm sorry, I'm sorry-imsorryimsorry....*

J: ... *afraid you would go back to what you were... don't Greg, promise me... can't give up... have to believe....*

T: *why?*

J: ... *stop believing, then you have nothing... dead... you can do better... a good handler... get off Skrakky find something... no life here... someone... you will, you will, just believe, keep on believing....*

T: ... *you... love you forever, Josie... forever... how can I find someone... never anyone like you, never... special...*

J: ... *oh, Greg... lots of people... just look... open...*

T: (laughter)... *open?...first time I ever talked to anyone...*

J: ... *talk to me again, if you have to ... I can talk to you... had enough lovers, everyone wants to get to bed with me, better just to be friends....*

T: ...*friends...* (laughter)... (tears)...

II
PROMISES OF SOMEDAY

The fire had burned out long ago, and Stevens and the forester had retired, but Trager and Donelly still sat around the ashes on the edges of the clear zone.

They talked softly, so as not to wake the others, yet their words hung long in the restless night air. The uncut forest, standing dark behind them, was dead still; the wildlife of Vendalia had all fled the noise that the fleet of buzztrucks made during the day.

"...a full six-crew, running buzztrucks, I know enough to know that's not easy," Donelly was saying. He was a pale, timid youth, likeable but self-conscious about everything he did. Trager heard echoes of himself in Donelly's stiff words. "You'd do well in the arena."

Trager nodded, thoughtful, his eyes on the ashes as he moved them with a stick. "I came to Vendalia with that in mind. Went to the gladiatorial once, only once. That was enough to change my mind. I could take them, I guess, but the whole idea made me sick. Out here, well, the money doesn't even match what I was getting on Skrakky, but the work is, well, clean. You know?"

"Sort of," said Donelly. "Still, you know, it isn't like they were real people out there in the arena. Only meat. All you can do is make the bodies as dead as the minds. That's the logical way to look at it."

Trager chuckled. "You're too logical, Don. You ought to *feel* more. Listen, next time you're in Gidyon, go to the gladiatorials and take a look. It's ugly, *ugly*. Corpses stumbling around with axes and swords and morningstars, hacking and hewing at each other. Butchery, that's all it is. And the audience, the way they cheer at each blow. And *laugh*. They *laugh*, Don! No." He shook his head, sharply. "No."

Donelly never abandoned an argument. "But why not? I don't understand, Greg. You'd be good at it, the best. I've seen the way you work your crew."

Trager looked up, studied Donelly briefly while the youth sat quietly, waiting. Josie's words came back; open, be open. The old Trager, the Trager who lived friendless and alone and closed inside a Skrakky handlers' dorm, was gone. He had grown, changed.

"There was a girl," he said, slowly, with measured words. Opening. "Back on Skrakky, Don, there was a girl I loved. It, well, it didn't work out. That's why I'm here, I guess. I'm looking for someone else, for something better. That's all part of it, you see." He stopped, paused, tried to think his words out. "This girl, Josie, I wanted her to love me. You know." The words came hard. "Admire me, all that stuff. Now, yeah, sure, I could do good running corpses in the arena. But Josie could never love someone who had a job like *that*. She's gone now, of course, but still. . . the kind of person I'm looking for, I couldn't find them as an arena corpse-master." He stood up, abruptly. "I don't know. That's what's important, though, to me. Josie, somebody like her, someday. Soon, I hope."

Donelly sat quiet in the moonlight, chewing his lip, not looking at Trager, his logic suddenly useless. While Trager, his corridors long gone, walked off alone into the woods.

They had a tight-knit group; three handlers, a forester, thirteen corpses. Each day they drove the forest back, with Trager in the forefront. Against the

Vendalian wilderness, against the blackbriars and the hard gray ironspike trees and the bulbous rubbery snaplimbs, against the tangled hostile forest, he would throw his six-crew and their buzztrucks. Smaller than the automills he'd run on Skrakky, fast and airborne, complex and demanding, those were buzztrucks. Trager ran six of them with corpse hands, a seventh with his own. Before his screaming blades and laser knives, the wall of wilderness fell each day. Donelly came behind him, pushing three of the mountain-sized rolling mills, to turn the fallen trees into lumber for Gidyon and other cities of Vendalia. Then Stevens, the third handler, with a flame-cannon to burn down stumps and melt rocks, and the soilpumps that would ready the fresh clear land for farming. The forester was their foreman. The procedure was a science.

Clean, hard, demanding work; Trager thrived on it by day. He grew lean, almost athletic; the lines of his face tightened and tanned, he grew steadily browner under Vendalia's hot bright sun. His corpses were almost part of him, so easily did he move them, fly their buzztrucks. As an ordinary man might move a hand, a foot. Sometimes his control grew so firm, the echoes so clear and strong, that Trager felt he was not a handler working a crew at all, but rather a man with seven bodies. Seven strong bodies that rode the sultry forest winds. He exulted in their sweat.

And the evenings, after work ceased, they were good too. Trager found a sort of peace there, a sense of belonging he had never known on Skrakky. The Vendalian foresters, rotated back and forth from Gidyon, were decent enough, and friendly. Stevens was a hearty slab of a man who seldom stopped joking long enough to talk about anything serious. Trager always found him amusing. And Donelly, the self-conscious youth, the quiet logical voice, he became a friend. He was a good listener, empathetic, compassionate, and the new open Trager was a good talker. Something close to envy shone in Donelly's eyes when Trager spoke of Josie and exorcised his soul. And Trager knew, or thought he knew, that Donelly was himself, the old Trager, the one before Josie who could not find the words.

In time, though, after days and weeks of talking, Donelly found his words. Then Trager listened, and shared another's pain. And he felt good about it. He was helping; he was lending strength; he was needed.

Each night around the ashes, the two men traded dreams. And wove a hopeful tapestry of promises and lies.

Yet still the nights would come.

Those were the worst times, as always; those were the hours of Trager's long lonely walks. If Josie had given Trager much, she had taken something too; she had taken the curious deadness he had once had, the trick of not-thinking, the pain-blotter of his mind. On Skrakky, he had walked the corridors infrequently; the forest knew him far more often.

After the talking all had stopped, after Donelly had gone to bed, that was when it would happen, when Josie would come to him in the loneliness of his tent. A thousand nights he lay there with his hands hooked behind his head, staring at the plastic tent film while he relived the night he'd told her. A thousand times he touched her cheek, and saw her spin away.

He would think of it, and fight it, and lose. Then, restless, he would rise and go outside. He would walk across the clear area, into the silent looming forest, brushing aside low branches and tripping on the underbrush; he would walk until he found water. Then he would sit down, by a scum-choked lake or a gurgling stream that ran swift and oily in the moonlight. He would fling rocks into the water, hurl them hard and flat into the night to hear them when they splashed.

He would sit for hours, throwing rocks and thinking, till finally he could convince himself the sun would rise.

Gidyon; the city; the heart of Vendalia, and through it of Slagg and Skrakky and New Pittsburg and all the other corpseworlds, the harsh ugly places where men would not work and corpses had to. Great towers of black and silver metal, floating aerial sculpture that flashed in the sunlight and shone softly at night, the vast bustling spaceport where freighters rose and fell on invisible firewands, malls where the pavement was polished, ironspike wood that gleamed a gentle gray; Gidyon.

The city with the rot. The corpse city. The meatmart.

For the freighters carried cargoes of men, criminals and derelicts and troublemakers from a dozen worlds bought with hard Vendalian cash (and there were darker rumors, of liners that had vanished mysteriously on routine tourist hops). And the soaring towers were hospitals and corpseyards, where men and women died and deadmen were born to walk anew. And all along the ironspike boardwalks were corpse-seller's shops and meathouses.

The meathouses of Vendalia were far-famed. The corpses were guaranteed beautiful.

Trager sat across from one, on the other side of the wide gray avenue, under the umbrella of an outdoor cafe. He sipped a bittersweet wine, thought about how his leave had evaporated too quickly, and tried to keep his eyes from wandering across the street. The wine was warm on his tongue, and his eyes were very restless.

Up and down the avenue, between him and the meathouse, strangers moved. Dark-faced corpsehandlers from Vendalia, Skrakky, Slagg; pudgy merchants, gawking tourists from the Clean Worlds like Old Earth and Zephyr, and dozens of question marks whose names and occupations and errands Trager would never know. Sitting there, drinking his wine and watching, Trager felt utterly cut off. He could not touch these people, could not reach them; he didn't know how, it wasn't possible, it wouldn't work. He could rise and walk out into the street and grab one, and still they would not touch. The stranger would only pull free and run. All his leave like that, all of it; he'd run through all the bars of Gidyon, forced a thousand contacts, and nothing had clicked.

His wine was gone. Trager looked at the glass dully, turning it in his hands, blinking. Then, abruptly, he stood up and paid his bill. His hands trembled.

It had been so many years, he thought as he started across the street. Josie, he thought, forgive me.

Trager returned to the wilderness camp, and his corpses flew their buzztrucks like men gone wild. But he was strangely silent around the campfire, and he did not talk to Donelly at night. Until finally, hurt and puzzled, Donelly followed him into the forest. And found him by a languid death-dark stream, sitting on the bank with a pile of throwing stones at his feet.

T:... *went in... after all I said, all I promised... still I went in....*

D:... *nothing to worry... remember what you told me... keep on believing....*

T:... *did believe, DID... no difficulties... Josie...*

D:... *you say I shouldn't give up, you better not... repeat everything you told me, everything Josie told you... everybody finds someone... if they keep looking... give up, dead... all you need... openness... courage to look... stop feeling sorry for yourself... told me that a hundred times....*

T:... *fucking lot easier to tell you than do it myself. . .*

D:... *Greg... not a meathouse man... a dreamer... better than they are...*

T: *(sighing)... yeah... hard, though... why do I do this to myself?...*

D:... *rather be like you were?... not hurting, not living?... like me?...*

T:... *no... no... you're right....*

2

THE PILGRIM, UP AND DOWN

Her name was Laurel. She was nothing like Josie, save in one thing alone. Trager loved her.

Pretty? Trager didn't think so, not at first. She was too tall, a half-foot taller than he was, and she was a bit on the heavy side, and more than a bit on the awkward side. Her hair was her best feature, her hair that was red-brown in winter and glowing blond in summer, that fell long and straight down past her shoulders and did wild beautiful things in the wind. But she was not beautiful, not the way Josie had been beautiful. Although, oddly, she grew more beautiful with time, and maybe that was because she was losing weight, and maybe that was because Trager was falling in love with her and seeing her through kinder eyes, and maybe that was because he *told* her she was pretty and the very telling made it so. Just as Laurel told him he was wise, and her belief gave him wisdom. Whatever the reason, Laurel was very beautiful indeed after he had known her for a time.

She was five years younger than he, clean-scrubbed and innocent, shy where Josie had been assertive. She was intelligent, romantic, a dreamer; she was wondrously fresh and eager; she was painfully insecure, and full of hungry need.

She was new to Gidyon, fresh from the Vendalian outback, a student forester. Trager, on leave again, was visiting the forestry college to say hello to a teacher who'd once worked with his crew. They met in the teacher's office. Trager had two weeks free in a city of strangers and meathouses; Laurel was alone. He showed her the glittering decadence of Gidyon, feeling smooth and sophisticated, and she was suitably impressed.

Two weeks went quickly. They came to the last night. Trager, suddenly afraid, took her to the park by the river that ran through Gidyon and they sat together on the low stone wall by the water's edge. Close, not touching.

"Time runs too fast," he said. He had a stone in his hand. He flicked it out over the water, flat and hard. Thoughtfully, he watched it splash and sink. Then he looked at her. "I'm nervous," he said, laughing. "I—Laurel. I don't want to leave."

Her face was unreadable (wary?). "The city is nice," she agreed.

Trager shook his head violently. "No. *No!* Not the city, you. Laurel, I think I… well…"

Laurel smiled for him. Her eyes were bright, very happy. "I know," she said.

Trager could hardly believe it. He reached out, touched her cheek. She turned her head and kissed his hand. They smiled at each other.

He flew back to the forest camp to quit. "Don, Don, you've got to meet her," he shouted. "See, you can do it, *I did* it, just keep believing, keep trying. I feel so goddamn good it's obscene."

Donelly, stiff and logical, smiled for him, at a loss as how to handle such a flood of happiness. "What will you do?" he asked, a little awkwardly. "The arena?"

Trager laughed. "Hardly, you know how I feel. But something like that. There's a theatre near the spaceport, puts on pantomime with corpse actors. I've got a job there. The pay is rotten, but I'll be near Laurel. That's all that matters."

They hardly slept at night. Instead they talked and cuddled and made love. The lovemaking was a joy, a game, a glorious discovery; never as good technically as the meathouse, but Trager hardly cared. He taught her to be open. He told her every secret he had, and wished he had more secrets.

"Poor Josie," Laurel would often say at night, her body warm against his. "She doesn't know what she missed. I'm lucky. There couldn't be anyone else like you."

"No," said Trager, "*I'm* lucky."

They would argue about it, laughing.

Donelly came to Gidyon and joined the theatre. Without Trager, the forest work had been no fun, he said. The three of them spent a lot of time together, and Trager glowed. He wanted to share his friends with Laurel, and he'd already mentioned Donelly a lot. And he wanted Donelly to see how happy he'd become, to see what belief could accomplish.

"I like her," Donelly said, smiling, the first night after Laurel had left.

"Good," Trager replied, nodding.

"No," said Donelly. "Greg, I *really* like her."

They spent a *lot* of time together.

"Greg," Laurel said one night in bed, "I think that Don is … well, after me. You know."

Trager rolled over and propped his head up on his elbow. "God," he said. He sounded concerned.

"I don't know how to handle it."

"Carefully," Trager said. "He's very vulnerable. You're probably the first woman he's ever been interested in. Don't be too hard on him. He shouldn't have to go through the stuff I went through, you know?"

***

The sex was never as good as a meathouse. And, after a while, Laurel began to close. More and more nights now she went to sleep after they made love; the days when they talked till dawn were gone. Perhaps they had nothing left to say. Trager had noticed that she had a tendency to finish his stories for him. It was nearly impossible to come up with one he hadn't already told her.

"He said *that?*" Trager got out of bed, turned on a light, and sat down frowning. Laurel pulled the covers up to her chin.

"Well, what did *you* say?"

She hesitated. "I can't tell you. It's between Don and me. He said it wasn't fair, the way I turn around and tell you everything that goes on between us, and he's right."

"*Right!* But I tell you everything. Don't you remember what we…"

"I know, but…"

Trager shook his head. His voice lost some of its anger. "What's going on, Laurel, huh? I'm scared, all of a sudden. I love you, remember? How can everything change so fast?"

Her face softened. She sat up, and held out her arms, and the covers fell back from full soft breasts. "Oh, Greg," she said. "Don't worry. I love you, I always will, but it's just that I love him too, I guess. You know?"

Trager, mollified, came into her arms, and kissed her with fervor. Then, suddenly, he broke off. "Hey," he said, with mock sternness to hide the trembling in his voice, "who do you love *more?*"

"You, of course, always you."

Smiling, he returned to the kiss.

"I know you know," Donelly said. "I guess we have to talk about it."

Trager nodded. They were backstage in the theatre. Three of his corpses walked up behind him, and stood arms crossed, like a guard. "All right." He looked straight at Donelly, and his face—smiling until the other's words—was suddenly stern. "Laurel asked me to pretend I didn't know anything. She said you felt guilty. But pretending was quite a strain, Don. I guess it's time we got everything out in the open."

Donelly's pale blue eyes shifted to the floor, and he stuck his hands into his pockets. "I don't want to hurt you," he said.

"Then don't."

"But I'm not going to pretend I'm dead, either. I'm not. I love her too."

"You're supposed to be my friend, Don. Love someone else. You're just going to get yourself hurt this way."

"I have more in common with her than you do."

Trager just stared.

Donelly looked up at him. Then, abashed, back down again. "I don't know. Oh, Greg. She loves you more anyway, she said so. I never should have expected anything else. I feel like I've stabbed you in the back. I…"

Trager watched him. Finally, he laughed softly. "Oh, shit, I can't take this. Look, Don, you haven't stabbed me, c'mon, don't talk like that. I guess, if you love her, this is the way it's got to be, you know. I just hope everything comes out all right."

Later that night, in bed with Laurel; "I'm worried about him," he told her.

His face, once tanned, now ashen. "Laurel?" he said. Not believing.

"I don't love you anymore. I'm sorry. I don't. It seemed real at the time, but now it's almost like a dream. I don't even know if I ever loved you, really."

"Don," he said woodenly.

Laurel flushed. "Don't say anything bad about Don. I'm tired of hearing you run him down. He never says anything except good about you."

"Oh, Laurel. Don't you *remember?* The things we said, the way we felt? I'm the same person you said those words to."

"But I've grown," Laurel said, hard and tearless, tossing her red-gold hair. "I remember perfectly well, but I just don't feel that way anymore."

"Don't," he said. He reached for her.

She stepped back. "Keep your hands off me. I told you, Greg, it's *over.* You have to leave now. Don is coming by."

It was worse than Josie. A thousand times worse.

III

WANDERINGS

He tried to keep on at the theatre; he enjoyed the work, he had friends there. But it was impossible. Donelly was there every day, smiling and being friendly, and sometimes Laurel came to meet him after the day's show and they went off together, arm in arm. Trager would stand and watch, try not to notice. While the twisted thing inside him shrieked and clawed.

He quit. He would not see them again. He would keep his pride.

The sky was bright with the lights of Gidyon and full of laughter, but it was dark and quiet in the park.

Trager stood stiff against a tree, his eyes on the river, his hands folded tightly against his chest. He was a statue. He hardly seemed to breathe. Not even his eyes moved.

Kneeling near the low wall, the corpse pounded until the stone was slick with blood and its hands were mangled clots of torn meat. The sounds of the blows were dull and wet, but for the infrequent scraping of bone against rock.

They made him pay first, before he could even enter the booth. Then he sat there for an hour while they found her and punched through. Finally, though, finally; "Josie."

"Greg," she said, grinning her distinctive grin. "I should have known. Who else would call all the way from Vendalia? How are you?"

He told her.

Her grin vanished. "Oh, Greg," she said. "I'm sorry. But don't let it get to you. Keep going. The next one will work out better. They always do."

Her words didn't satisfy him. "Josie," he said, "How are things back there? You miss me?"

"Oh, sure. Things are pretty good. It's still Skrakky, though. Stay where you are, you're better off." She looked offscreen, then back. "I should go, before your bill gets enormous. Glad you called, love."

"*Josie*," Trager started. But the screen was already dark.

Sometimes, at night, he couldn't help himself. He would move to his home screen and ring Laurel. Invariably her eyes would narrow when she saw who it was. Then she would hang up.

And Trager would sit in a dark room and recall how once the sound of his voice made her so very, very happy.

The streets of Gidyon are not the best of places for lonely midnight walks. They are brightly lit, even in the darkest hours, and jammed with men and deadmen. And there are meathouses, all up and down the boulevards and the ironspike boardwalks.

Josie's words had lost their power. In the meathouses, Trager abandoned dreams and found cheap solace. The sensuous evenings with Laurel and the fumbling sex of his boyhood were things of yesterday; Trager took his meat-mates hard and quick, almost brutally, fucked them with a wordless savage power to the inevitable perfect orgasm. Sometimes, remembering the theatre, he would have them act out short erotic playlets to get him in the mood.

In the night. Agony.

He was in the corridors again, the low dim corridors of the corpsehandlers' dorm on Skrakky, but now the corridors were twisted and torturous and Trager had long since lost his way. The air was thick with a rotting gray haze, and growing thicker. Soon, he feared, he would be all but blind.

Around and around he walked, up and down, but always there was more corridor, and all of them led nowhere. The doors were grim black rectangles, knobless, locked to him forever; he passed them by without thinking, most of them. Once or twice, though, he paused, before doors where light leaked around the frame. He would listen, and inside there were sounds, and then he would begin to knock wildly. But no one ever answered.

So he would move on, through the haze that got darker and thicker and seemed to burn his skin, past door after door after door, until he was weeping and his feet were tired and bloody. And then, off a ways, down a long, long corridor that loomed straight before him, he would see an open door. From it came light so hot and white it hurt the eyes, and music bright and joyful, and the sounds of people laughing. Then Trager would run, though his feet were raw bundles of pain and his lungs burned with the haze he was breathing. He would run and run until he reached the room with the open door.

Only when he got there, it was his room, and it was empty.

Once, in the middle of their brief time together, they'd gone out into the wilderness and made love under the stars. Afterwards she had snuggled hard against him, and he stroked her gently. "What are you thinking?" he asked.

"About us," Laurel said. She shivered. The wind was brisk and cold. "Some-times I get scared, Greg. I'm so afraid something will happen to us, something that will ruin it. I don't ever want you to leave me."

"Don't worry," he told her. "I won't."

Now, each night before sleep came, he tortured himself with her words. The good memories left him with ashes and tears; the bad ones with a wordless rage.

He slept with a ghost beside him, a supernaturally beautiful ghost, the husk of a dead dream. He woke to her each morning.

He hated them. He hated himself for hating.

3
DUVALIER'S DREAM

Her name does not matter. Her looks are not important. All that counts is that she *was*, that Trager tried again, that he forced himself on and made himself believe and didn't give up. He *tried*.

But something was missing. Magic?

The words were the same.

How many times can you speak them, Trager wondered, *speak them and believe them, like you believed them the first time you said them? Once? Twice? Three times, maybe? Or a hundred? And the people who say it a hundred times, are they really so much better at loving? Or only at fooling themselves? Aren't they really people who long ago abandoned the dream, who use its name for something else?*

He said the words, holding her, cradling her, and kissing her. He said the words, with a knowledge that was surer and heavier and more dead than any belief. He said the words and *tried*, but no longer could he mean them.

And she said the words back, and Trager realized that they meant nothing to him. Over and over again they said the things each wanted to hear, and both of them knew they were pretending.

They tried *hard*. But when he reached out, like an actor caught in his role, doomed to play out the same part over and over again, when he reached out his hand and touched her cheek—the skin was smooth and soft and lovely. And wet with tears.

IV
ECHOES

"I don't want to hurt you," said Donelly, shuffling and looking guilty, until Trager felt ashamed for having hurt a friend.

He touched her cheek, and she spun away from him.

"I never wanted to hurt you," Josie said, and Trager was sad. She had given him so much; he'd only made her guilty. Yes, he was hurt, but a stronger man would never have let her know.

He touched her cheek, and she kissed his hand.

"I'm sorry, I don't," Laurel said. And Trager was lost. What had he done, where was his fault, how had he ruined it? She had been so sure. They had had so much.

He touched her cheek, and she wept.

How many times can you speak them, his voice echoed, *speak them and believe them, like you believed them the first time you said them?*

The wind was dark and dust heavy, the sky throbbed painfully with flickering scarlet flame. In the pit, in the darkness, stood a young woman with goggles and a filtermask and short brown hair and answers. "It breaks down, it breaks down, it breaks down, and they keep sending it out," she said. "Should realize that something is wrong. After that many failures, it's sheer self-delusion to think the thing's going to work right next time out."

The enemy corpse is huge and black, its torso rippling with muscle, a product of months of exercise, the biggest thing that Trager has ever faced. It advances across the sawdust in a slow, clumsy crouch, holding the gleaming broadsword in one hand. Trager watches it come from his chair atop one end of the fighting arena. The other corpsemaster is careful, cautious.

His own deadman, a wiry blond, stands and waits, a morningstar trailing down in the blood-soaked arena dust. Trager will move him fast enough and well enough when the time is right. The enemy knows it, and the crowd.

The black corpse suddenly lifts its broadsword and scrambles forward in a run, hoping to use reach and speed to get its kill. But Trager's corpse is no longer there when the enemy's measured blow cuts the air where he had been.

Sitting comfortably above the fighting pit/down in the arena, his feet grimy with blood and sawdust—Trager/the corpse—snaps the command/swings the morningstar—and the great studded ball drifts up and around, almost lazily, almost gracefully. Into the back of the enemy's head, as he tries to recover and turn. A flower of blood and brain blooms swift and sudden, and the crowd cheers.

Trager walks his corpse from the arena, then stands to receive applause. It is his tenth kill. Soon the championship will be his. He is building such a record that they can no longer deny him a match.

She is beautiful, his lady, his love. Her hair is short and blond, her body very slim, graceful, almost athletic, with trim legs and small hard breasts. Her eyes are bright green, and they always welcome him. And there is a strange erotic innocence in her smile.

She waits for him in bed, waits for his return from the arena, waits for him eager and playful and loving. When he enters, she is sitting up, smiling for him, the covers bunched around her waist. From the door he admires her nipples.

Aware of his eyes, shy, she covers her breasts and blushes. Trager knows it is all false modesty, all playing. He moves to the bedside, sits, reaches out to stroke her cheek. Her skin is very soft; she nuzzles against his hand as it brushes her. Then Trager draws her hands aside, plants one gentle kiss on each breast, and a not-so-gentle kiss on her mouth. She kisses back, with ardor; their tongues dance.

They make love, he and she, slow and sensuous, locked together in a loving embrace that goes on and on. Two bodies move flawlessly in perfect rhythm, each knowing the other's needs. Trager thrusts, and his other body meets the thrusts. He reaches, and her hand is there. They come together (always, *always*, both orgasms triggered by the handler's brain), and a bright red flush burns on her breasts and earlobes. They kiss.

Afterwards, he talks to her, his love, his lady. You should always talk afterwards; he learned that long ago.

"You're lucky," he tells her sometimes, and she snuggles up to him and plants tiny kisses all across his chest. "Very lucky. They lie to you out there, love. They teach you a silly shining dream and they tell you to believe and chase it and they tell you that for you, for everyone, there is someone. But it's all wrong. The universe isn't fair, it never has been, so why do they tell you so? You run after the phantom, and lose, and they tell you next time, but it's all rot, all empty rot. Nobody ever finds the dream at all, they just kid themselves, trick themselves so they can go on believing. It's just a clutching lie that desperate people tell each other, hoping to convince themselves."

But then he can't talk anymore, for her kisses have gone lower and lower, and now she takes him in her mouth. And Trager smiles at his love and gently strokes her hair.

Of all the bright cruel lies they tell you, the cruelest is the one called love.

DEADMAN'S ROAD

by Joe R. Lansdale

Joe R. Lansdale writes in many different genres—mysteries, westerns, horror—and in many different formats—novels, short stories, teleplays, comic books. Notable work in television includes writing for *Batman: The Animated Series*; in comics, the western series *Jonah Hex*. His novels include *Mucho Mojo* and *The Bottoms*, among many others. A new novel, *Leather Maiden,* was recently published, and he's currently working on a novel in his Hap and Leonard series called *Vanilla Ride*. Lansdale is also an accomplished editor, with a number of anthologies published, such as *Razored Saddles* and the award-winning *Retro Pulp Tales*. He's a seven-time winner of the Bram Stoker Award, and has been named a Grand Master by the World Horror Society.

Aside from "Deadman's Road," Lansdale has authored other important works of zombie fiction, including his Stoker Award-winning story "On the Far Side of the Cadillac Desert with Dead Folks," and his cult-classic novel *Dead in the West*. Lansdale says that this story features lots of flashing teeth and blazing six guns, and boy, is he right. The story—which features the gun-toting reverend from *Dead in the West*—jumped into his head full-blown when he encountered a sign while traveling that read, simply: DEAD MAN'S ROAD.

The evening sun had rolled down and blown out in a bloody wad, and the white, full moon had rolled up like an enormous ball of tightly wrapped twine. As he rode, the Reverend Jebidiah Rains watched it glow above the tall pines. All about it stars were sprinkled white-hot in the dead-black heavens.

The trail he rode on was a thin one, and the trees on either side of it crept toward the path as if they might block the way, and close up behind him. The weary horse on which he was riding moved forward with its head down, and Jebidiah, too weak to fight it, let his mount droop and take its lead. Jebidiah was too tired to know much at that moment, but he knew one thing. He was a man of the Lord and he hated God, hated the sonofabitch with all his heart.

And he knew God knew and didn't care, because he knew Jebidiah was his messenger. Not one of the New Testament, but one of the Old Testament, harsh and mean and certain, vengeful and without compromise; a man who would have shot a leg out from under Moses and spat in the face of the Holy Ghost and scalped him, tossing his celestial hair to the wild four winds.

It was not a legacy Jebidiah would have preferred, being the bad man messenger of God, but it was his, and he had earned it through sin, and no matter how hard he tried to lay it down and leave it be, he could not. He knew that to give in and abandon his God-given curse, was to burn in hell forever, and to continue was to do as the Lord prescribed, no matter what his feelings toward his mean master might be. His Lord was not a forgiving Lord, nor was he one who cared for your love. All he cared for was obedience, servitude and humiliation. It was why God had invented the human race. Amusement.

As he thought on these matters, the trail turned and widened, and off to one side, amongst tree stumps, was a fairly large clearing, and in its center was a small log house, and out to the side a somewhat larger log barn. In the curtained window of the cabin was a light that burned orange behind the flour-sack curtains. Jebidiah, feeling tired and hungry and thirsty and weary of soul, made for it.

Stopping a short distance from the cabin, Jebidiah leaned forward on his horse and called out, "Hello, the cabin."

He waited for a time, called again, and was halfway through calling when the door opened, and a man about five-foot two with a large droopy hat, holding a rifle, stuck himself part of the way out of the cabin, said, "Who is it calling? You got a voice like a bullfrog."

"Reverend Jebidiah Rains."

"You ain't come to preach none, have you?"

"No, sir. I find it does no good. I'm here to beg for a place in your barn, a night under its roof. Something for my horse, something for myself if it's available. Most anything, as long as water is involved."

"Well," said the man, "this seems to be the gathering place tonight. Done got two others, and we just sat asses down to eat. I got enough you want it, some hot beans and some old bread."

"I would be most obliged, sir," Jebidiah said.

"Oblige all you want. In the meantime, climb down from that nag, put it in the barn and come in and chow. They call me Old Timer, but I ain't that old. It's cause most of my teeth are gone and I'm crippled in a foot a horse stepped on. There's a lantern just inside the barn door. Light that up, and put it out when you finish, come on back to the house."

When Jebidiah finished grooming and feeding his horse with grain in the barn, watering him, he came into the cabin, made a show of pushing his long black coat back so that it revealed his ivory-handled .44 cartridge-converted revolvers. They were set so that they leaned forward in their holsters, strapped close to the hips, not draped low like punks wore them. Jebidiah liked to wear them close to the natural swing of his hands. When he pulled them it was a movement quick as the flick of a hummingbird's wings, the hammers clicking from the cock of his thumb, the guns barking, spewing lead with amazing accuracy. He had practiced enough to drive a cork into a bottle at about a hundred paces, and he could do it in bad light. He chose to reveal his guns that way to show he was ready for any attempted ambush. He reached up and pushed his wide-brimmed black hat back on his head, showing black hair gone gray-tipped. He thought having his hat tipped made him look casual. It did not. His eyes always seemed aflame in an angry face.

Inside, the cabin was bright with kerosene lamp light, and the kerosene smelled, and there were curls of black smoke twisting about, mixing with gray smoke from the pipe of Old Timer, and the cigarette of a young man with a badge pinned to his shirt. Beside him, sitting on a chopping log by the fireplace, which was too hot for the time of year, but was being used to heat up a pot of beans, was a middle-aged man with a slight paunch and a face that looked like it attracted thrown objects. He had his hat pushed up a bit, and a shock of wheat-colored, sweaty hair hung on his forehead. There was a cigarette in his mouth, half of it ash. He twisted on the chopping log, and Jebidiah saw that his hands were manacled together.

"I heard you say you was a preacher," said the manacled man, as he tossed the last of his smoke into the fireplace. "This here sure ain't God's country."

"Worse thing is," said Jebidiah, "it's exactly God's country."

The manacled man gave out with a snort, and grinned.

"Preacher," said the younger man, "my name is Jim Taylor. I'm a deputy for Sheriff Spradley, out of Nacogdoches. I'm taking this man there for a trial, and most likely a hanging. He killed a fella for a rifle and a horse. I see you tote guns, old style guns, but good ones. Way you tote them, I'm suspecting you know how to use them."

"I've been known to hit what I aim at," Jebidiah said, and sat in a rickety chair at an equally rickety table. Old Timer put some tin plates on the table, scratched his ass with a long wooden spoon, then grabbed a rag and used it as a pot holder, lifted the hot bean pot to the table. He popped the lid off the pot, used the ass-scratching spoon to scoop a heap of beans onto plates. He brought over some wooden cups and poured them full from a pitcher of water.

"Thing is," the deputy said, "I could use some help. I don't know I can get back safe with this fella, havin' not slept good in a day or two. Was wondering, you and Old Timer here could watch my back till morning? Wouldn't even mind if you rode along with me tomorrow, as sort of a backup. I could use a gun hand. Sheriff might even give you a dollar for it."

Old Timer, as if this conversation had not been going on, brought over a bowl with some moldy biscuits in it, placed them on the table. "Made them a week ago. They've gotten a bit ripe, but you can scratch around the mold. I'll warn you though, they're tough enough you could toss one hard and kill a chicken on the run. So mind your teeth."

"That how you lost yours, Old Timer?" the manacled man said.

"Probably part of them," Old Timer said.

"What you say, preacher?" the deputy said. "You let me get some sleep?"

"My problem lies in the fact that I need sleep," Jebidiah said. "I've been busy, and I'm what could be referred to as tuckered."

"Guess I'm the only one that feels spry," said the manacled man.

"No," said Old Timer. "I feel right fresh myself."

"Then it's you and me, Old Timer," the manacled man said, and grinned, as if this meant something.

"You give me cause, fella, I'll blow a hole in you and tell God you got in a nest of termites."

The manacled man gave his snort of a laugh again. He seemed to be having a good old time.

"Me and Old Timer can work shifts," Jebidiah said. "That okay with you, Old Timer?"

"Peachy," Old Timer said, and took another plate from the table and filled it with beans. He gave this one to the manacled man, who said, lifting his bound hands to take it, "What do I eat it with?"

"Your mouth. Ain't got no extra spoons. And I ain't giving you a knife."

The manacled man thought on this for a moment, grinned, lifted the plate and put his face close to the edge of it, sort of poured the beans toward his mouth. He lowered the plate and chewed. "Reckon they taste scorched with or without a spoon."

Jebidiah reached inside his coat, took out and opened up a pocket knife, used it to spear one of the biscuits, and to scrape the beans toward him.

"You come to the table, young fella," Old Timer said to the deputy. "I'll get my shotgun, he makes a move that ain't eatin', I'll blast him and the beans inside him into that fireplace there."

Old Timer sat with a double barrel shotgun resting on his leg, pointed in the general direction of the manacled man. The deputy told all that his prisoner had done while he ate. Murdered women and children, shot a dog and a horse, and just for the hell of it, shot a cat off a fence, and set fire to an outhouse with a woman in it. He had also raped women, stuck a stick up a sheriff's ass, and killed him, and most likely shot other animals that might have been some good to somebody. Overall, he was tough on human beings, and equally as tough on livestock.

"I never did like animals," the manacled man said. "Carry fleas. And that woman in the outhouse stunk to high heaven. She ought to eat better. She needed burning."

"Shut up," the deputy said. "This fella," and he nodded toward the prisoner, "his name is Bill Barrett, and he's the worst of the worst. Thing is, well, I'm not just tired, I'm a little wounded. He and I had a tussle. I hadn't surprised him, wouldn't be here today. I got a bullet graze in my hip. We had quite a dust up. I finally got him down by putting a gun barrel to his noggin' half a dozen times or so. I'm not hurt so bad, but I lost blood for a couple days. Weakened me. You'd ride along with me, Reverend, I'd appreciate it."

"I'll consider it," Jebidiah said. "But I'm about my business."

"Who you gonna preach to along here, 'sides us?" the deputy said.

"Don't even think about it," Old Timer said. "Just thinking about that Jesus foolishness makes my ass tired. Preaching makes me want to kill the preacher and cut my own throat. Being at a preachin' is like being tied down in a nest red bitin' ants."

"At this point in my life," Jebidiah said. "I agree."

There was a moment of silence in response to Jebidiah, then the deputy turned his attention to Old Timer. "What's the fastest route to Nacogdoches?"

"Well now," Old Timer said, "you can keep going like you been going, following the road out front. And in time you'll run into a road, say thirty miles from here, and it goes left. That should take you right near Nacogdoches, which is another ten miles, though you'll have to make a turn somewhere up in there near the end of the trip. Ain't exactly sure where unless I'm looking at it. Whole trip, traveling at an even pace ought to take you two day."

"You could go with us," the deputy said. "Make sure I find that road."

"Could," said Old Timer, "but I won't. I don't ride so good anymore. My balls ache I ride a horse for too long. Last time I rode a pretty good piece, I had to squat over a pan of warm water and salt, soak my taters for an hour or so just so they'd fit back in my pants. "

"My balls ache just listening to you," the prisoner said. "Thing is, though, them swollen up like that, was probably the first time in your life you had man-sized balls, you old fart. You should have left them swollen."

Old Timer cocked back the hammers on the double barrel. "This here could go off."

Bill just grinned, leaned his back against the fireplace, then jumped forward. For a moment, it looked as if Old Timer might cut him in half, but he realized what had happened.

"Oh yeah," Old Timer said. "That there's hot, stupid. Why they call it a fire place."

Bill readjusted himself, so that his back wasn't against the stones. He said, "I'm gonna cut this deputy's pecker off, come back here, make you fry it up and eat it."

"You're gonna shit and fall back in it," Old Timer said. "That's all you're gonna do."

When things had calmed down again, the deputy said to Old Timer, "There's no faster route?"

Old timer thought for a moment. "None you'd want to take."

"What's that mean?" the deputy said.

Old Timer slowly lowered the hammers on the shotgun, smiling at Bill all the while. When he had them lowered, he turned his head, looked at the deputy. "Well, there's Deadman's Road."

"What's wrong with that?" the deputy asked.

"All manner of things. Used to be called Cemetery Road. Couple years back

304 · JOE R. LANSDALE

that changed."

Jebidiah's interest was aroused. "Tell us about it, Old Timer."

"Now I ain't one to believe in hogwash, but there's a story about the road, and I got it from someone you might say was the horse's mouth."

"A ghost story, that's choice," said Bill.

"How much time would the road cut off going to Nacogdoches?" the deputy asked.

"Near a day," Old Timer said.

"Damn. Then that's the way I got to go," the deputy said.

"Turn off for it ain't far from here, but I wouldn't recommend it," Old Timer said. "I ain't much for Jesus, but I believe in haints, things like that. Living out here in this thicket, you see some strange things. There's gods ain't got nothing to do with Jesus or Moses, or any of that bunch. There's older gods than that. Indians talk about them."

"I'm not afraid of any Indian gods," the deputy said.

"Maybe not," Old Timer said, "but these gods, even the Indians ain't fond of them. They ain't their gods. These gods are older than the Indian folk their ownselfs. Indians try not to stir them up. They worship their own."

"And why would this road be different than any other?" Jebidiah asked. "What does it have to do with ancient gods?"

Old Timer grinned. "You're just wanting to challenge it, ain't you, Reverend? Prove how strong your god is. You weren't no preacher, you'd be a gunfighter, I reckon. Or, maybe you are just that. A gunfighter preacher."

"I'm not that fond of my god," Jebidiah said, "but I have been given a duty. Drive out evil. Evil as my god sees it. If these gods are evil, and they're in my path, then I have to confront them."

"They're evil, all right," Old Timer said.

"Tell us about them," Jebidiah said.

"Gil Gimet was a bee keeper," Old timer said. "He raised honey, and lived off of Deadman's Road. Known then as Cemetery Road. That's 'cause there was a graveyard down there. It had some old Spanish graves in it, some said Conquistadores who tromped through here but didn't tromp out. I know there was some Indians buried there, early Christian Indians, I reckon. Certainly there were stones and crosses up and Indian names on the crosses. Maybe mixed breeds. Lots of intermarrying around here. Anyway, there were all manner people buried up there. The dead ground don't care what color you are when you go in, 'cause in the end, we're all gonna be the color of dirt."

"Hell, " Bill said. "You're already the color of dirt. And you smell like some pretty old dirt at that."

"You gonna keep on, mister," Old Timer said, "and you're gonna wind up having the undertaker wipe your ass." Old Timer cocked back the hammers on the shotgun again. "This here gun could go off accidently. Could happen, and who here is gonna argue it didn't?"

"Not me," the deputy said. "It would be easier on me you were dead, Bill."

Bill looked at the Reverend. "Yeah, but that wouldn't set right with the Reverend, would it, Reverend?"

"Actually, I wouldn't care one way or another. I'm not a man of peace, and I'm not a forgiver, even if what you did wasn't done to me. I think we're all rich and deep in sin. Maybe none of us are worthy of forgiveness."

Bill sunk a little at his seat. No one was even remotely on his side. Old Timer continued with his story.

"This here bee keeper, Gimet, he wasn't known as much of a man. Mean-hearted is how he was thunk of. I knowed him, and I didn't like him. I seen him snatch up a little dog once and cut the tail off of it with his knife, just cause he thought it was funny. Boy who owned the dog tried to fight back, and Gimet, he cut the boy on the arm. No one did nothin' about it. Ain't no real law in these parts, you see, and wasn't nobody brave enough to do nothin'. Me included. And he did lots of other mean things, even killed a couple of men, and claimed self-defense. Might have been, but Gimet was always into something, and whatever he was into always turned out with someone dead, or hurt, or humiliated."

"Bill here sounds like he could be Gimet's brother," the deputy said.

"Oh, no," Old Timer said, shaking his head. "This here scum-licker ain't a bump on the mean old ass of Gimet. Gimet lived in a little shack off Cemetery Road. He raised bees, and brought in honey to sell at the community up the road. Guess you could even call it a town. Schow is the way the place is known, on account of a fella used to live up there was named Schow. He died and got ate up by pigs. Right there in his own pen, just keeled over slopping the hogs, and then they slopped him, all over that place. A store got built on top of where Schow got et up, and that's how the place come by the name. Gimet took his honey in there to the store and sold it, and even though he was a turd, he had some of the best honey you ever smacked your mouth around. Wish I had me some now. It was dark and rich, and sweeter than any sugar. Think that's one reason he got away with things. People don't like killing and such, but they damn sure like their honey."

"This story got a point?" Bill said.

"You don't like way I'm telling it," Old Timer said, "why don't you think about how that rope's gonna fit around your neck. That ought to keep your thoughts occupied, right smart."

Bill made a grunting noise, turned on his block of wood, as if to show he wasn't interested.

"Well, now, honey or not, sweet tooth, or not, everything has an end to it. And thing was he took to a little gal, Mary Lynn Twoshoe. She was a part Indian gal, a real looker, hair black as the bottom of a well, eyes the same color, and she was just as fine in the features as them pictures you see of them stage actresses. She wasn't five feet tall, and that hair of hers went all the way down her back. Her daddy was dead. The pox got him. And her mama wasn't too well off, being sickly, and all. She made brooms out of straw and branches she trimmed down. Sold a few of them, raised a little garden and a hog. When all this happened, Mary Lynn was probably thirteen, maybe fourteen. Wasn't no older than that."

"If you're gonna tell a tale," Bill said, "least don't wander all over the place."

"So, you're interested?" Old Timer said.

"What else I got to do?" Bill said.

"Go on," Jebidiah said. "Tell us about Mary Lynn."

Old Timer nodded. "Gimet took to her. Seen her around, bringing the brooms her mama made into the store. He waited on her, grabbed her, and just threw her across his saddle kickin' and screamin', like he'd bought a sack of flour and was ridin' it to the house. Mack Collins, store owner came out and tried to stop him. Well, he said something to him. About how he shouldn't do it, least that's the way I heard it. He didn't push much, and I can't blame him. Didn't do good to cross Gimet. Anyway, Gimet just said back to Mack, 'Give her mama a big jar of honey. Tell her that's for her daughter. I'll even make her another jar or two, if the meat here's as sweet as I'm expecting.'

"With that, he slapped Mary Lynn on the ass and rode off with her."

"Sounds like my kind of guy," Bill said.

"I have become irritated with you now," Jebidiah said. "Might I suggest you shut your mouth before I pistol whip you."

Bill glared at Jebidiah, but the Reverend's gaze was as dead and menacing as the barrels of Old Timer's shotgun.

"Rest of the story is kind of grim," Old Timer said. "Gimet took her off to his house, and had his way with her. So many times he damn near killed her, and then he turned her loose, or got so drunk she was able to get loose. Time she walked down Cemetery Road, made it back to town, well, she was bleeding so bad from having been used so rough, she collapsed. She lived a day and died from loss of blood. Her mother, out of her sick bed, rode a mule out there to the cemetery on Cemetery Road. I told you she was Indian, and she knew some Indian ways, and she knew about them old gods that wasn't none of the gods of her people, but she still knew about them.

"She knew some signs to draw in cemetery dirt. I don't know the whole of it, but she did some things, and she did it on some old grave out there, and the last thing she did was she cut her own throat, died right there, her blood running on top of that grave and them pictures she drawed in the dirt."

"Don't see how that done her no good," the deputy said.

"Maybe it didn't, but folks think it did," Old Timer said. "Community that had been pushed around by Gimet, finally had enough, went out there in mass to hang his ass, shoot him, whatever it took. Got to his cabin they found Gimet dead outside his shack. His eyes had been torn out, or blown out is how they looked. Skin was peeled off his head, just leaving the skull and a few hairs. His chest was ripped open, and his insides was gone, exceptin' the bones in there.

And them bees of his had nested in the hole in his chest, had done gone about making honey. Was buzzing out of that hole, his mouth, empty eyes, nose, or where his nose used to be. I figure they'd rolled him over, tore off his pants, they'd have been coming out of his asshole."

"How come you weren't out there with them?" Bill said. "How come this is all stuff you heard?"

"Because I was a coward when it come to Gimet," Old Timer said. "That's why. Told myself wouldn't never be a coward again, no matter what. I should have been with them. Didn't matter no how. He was done good and dead, them bees all in him. What was done then is the crowd got kind of loco, tore off his clothes, hooked his feet up to a horse and dragged him through a blackberry patch, them bees just burstin' out and hummin' all around him. All that ain't right, but I think I'd been with them, knowing who he was and all the things he'd done, I might have been loco too. They dumped him out on the cemetery to let him rot, took that girl's mother home to be buried some place better. Wasn't no more than a few nights later that folks started seeing Gimet. They said he walked at night, when the moon was at least half, or full, like it is now. Number of folks seen him, said he loped alongside the road, following their horses, grabbing hold of the tail if he could, trying to pull horse and rider down, or pull himself up on the back of their mounts. Said them bees was still in him. Bees black as flies, and angry whirling all about him, and coming from inside him. Worse, there was a larger number of folks took that road that wasn't never seen again. It was figured Gimet got them."

"Horse shit," the deputy said. "No disrespect, Old Timer. You've treated me all right, that's for sure. But a ghost chasing folks down. I don't buy that."

"Don't have to buy it," Old Timer said. "I ain't trying to sell it to you none. Don't have to believe it. And I don't think it's no ghost anyway. I think that girl's mother, she done something to let them old gods out for a while, sicked them on that bastard, used her own life as a sacrifice, that's what I think. And them gods, them things from somewhere else, they ripped him up like that. Them bees is part of that too. They ain't no regular honey bee. They're some other kind of bees. Some kind of fitting death for a bee raiser, is my guess."

"That's silly," the deputy said.

"I don't know," Jebidiah said. "The Indian woman may only have succeeded in killing him in this life. She may not have understood all that she did. Didn't know she was giving him an opportunity to live again… Or maybe that is the curse. Though there are plenty others have to suffer for it."

"Like the folks didn't do nothing when Gimet was alive," Old Timer said. "Folks like me that let what went on go on."

Jebidiah nodded. "Maybe."

The deputy looked at Jebidiah. "Not you too, Reverend. You should know better than that. There ain't but one true god, and ain't none of that hoodoo business got a drop of truth to it."

"If there's one god," Jebidiah said, "there can be many. They are at war with one another, that's how it works, or so I think. I've seen some things that have shook my faith in the one true god, the one I'm servant to. And what is our god but hoodoo? It's all hoodoo, my friend."

"Okay. What things have you seen, Reverend?" the deputy asked.

"No use describing it to you, young man," Jebidiah said. "You wouldn't believe me. But I've recently come from Mud Creek. It had an infestation of a sort. That town burned down, and I had a hand in it."

"Mud Creek," Old Timer said. "I been there."

"Only thing there now," Jebidiah said, "is some charred wood."

"Ain't the first time it's burned down," Old Timer said. "Some fool always rebuilds it, and with it always comes some kind of ugliness. I'll tell you straight. I don't doubt your word at all, Reverend."

"Thing is," the deputy said, "I don't believe in no haints. That's the shortest road, and it's the road I'm gonna take."

"I wouldn't," Old Timer said.

"Thanks for the advice. But no one goes with me or does, that's the road I'm taking, provided it cuts a day off my trip."

"I'm going with you," Jebidiah said. "My job is striking at evil. Not to walk around it."

"I'd go during the day," Old Timer said. "Ain't no one seen Gimet in the day, or when the moon is thin or not at all. But way it is now, it's full, and will be again tomorrow night. I'd ride hard tomorrow, you're determined to go. Get there as soon as you can, before dark."

"I'm for getting there," the deputy said. "I'm for getting back to Nacogdoches, and getting this bastard in a cell."

"I'll go with you," Jebidiah said. "But I want to be there at night. I want to take Deadman's Road at that time. I want to see if Gimet is there. And if he is, send him to his final death. Defy those dark gods the girl's mother called up. Defy them and loose my god on him. What I'd suggest is you get some rest, deputy. Old Timer here can watch a bit, then I'll take over. That way we all get some rest. We can chain this fellow to a tree outside, we have to. We should both get slept up to the gills, then leave here mid-day, after a good dinner, head out for Deadman's Road. Long as we're there by nightfall."

"That ought to bring you right on it," Old Timer said. "You take Deadman's Road. When you get to the fork, where the road ends, you go right. Ain't no one ever seen Gimet beyond that spot, or in front of where the road begins. He's tied to that stretch, way I heard it."

"Good enough," the deputy said. "I find this all foolish, but if I can get some rest, and have you ride along with me, Reverend, then I'm game. And I'll be fine with getting there at night."

Next morning they slept late, and had an early lunch. Beans and hard biscuits again, a bit of stewed squirrel. Old Timer had shot the rodent that morning while Jebidiah watched Bill sit on his ass, his hands chained around a tree in the front yard. Inside the cabin, the deputy had continued to sleep.

But now they all sat outside eating, except for Bill.

"What about me?" Bill asked, tugging at his chained hands.

"When we finish," Old Timer said. "Don't know if any of the squirrel will be left, but we got them biscuits for you. I can promise you some of them. I might even let you rub one of them around in my plate, sop up some squirrel gravy."

"Those biscuits are awful," Bill said.

"Ain't they," Old Timer said.

Bill turned his attention to Jebidiah. "Preacher, you ought to just go on and leave me and the boy here alone. Ain't smart for you to ride along, cause I get loose, ain't just the deputy that's gonna pay. I'll put you on the list."

"After what I've seen in this life," Jebidiah said, "you are nothing to me. An insect… So, add me to your list."

"Let's feed him," the deputy said, nodding at Bill, "and get to moving. I'm feeling rested and want to get this ball started."

The moon had begun to rise when they rode in sight of Deadman's Road. The white cross road sign was sticking up beside the road. Trees and brush had grown up around it, and between the limbs and the shadows, the crudely painted words on the sign were halfway readable in the waning light. The wind had picked up and was grabbing at leaves, plucking them from the ground, tumbling them about, tearing them from trees and tossing them across the narrow, clay road with a sound like mice scuttling in straw.

"Fall always depresses me," the deputy said, halting his horse, taking a swig from his canteen.

"Life is a cycle," Jebidiah said. "You're born, you suffer, then you're punished."

The deputy turned in his saddle to look at Jebidiah. "You ain't much on that resurrection and reward, are you?"

"No, I'm not."

"I don't know about you," the deputy said, "but I wish we hadn't gotten here so late. I'd rather have gone through in the day."

"Thought you weren't a believer in spooks?" Bill said, and made with his now familiar snort. "You said it didn't matter to you."

The deputy didn't look at Bill when he spoke. "I wasn't here then. Place has a look I don't like. And I don't enjoy temptin' things. Even if I don't believe in them."

"That's the silliest thing I ever heard," Bill said.

"Wanted me with you," Jebidiah said. "You had to wait."

"You mean to see something, don't you, preacher?" Bill said.

"If there is something to see," Jebidiah said.

"You believe Old Timer's story?" the deputy said. "I mean, really?"

"Perhaps."

Jebidiah clucked to his horse and took the lead.

When they turned onto Deadman's Road, Jebidiah paused and removed a small, fat bible from his saddlebag.

The deputy paused too, forcing Bill to pause as well. "You ain't as ornery as I thought," the deputy said. "You want the peace of the bible just like anyone else."

"There is no peace in this book," Jebidiah said. "That's a real confusion. Bible isn't anything but a book of terror, and that's how God is: Terrible. But the book has power. And we might need it."

"I don't know what to think about you, Reverend," the deputy said.

"Ain't nothin' you can think about a man that's gone loco," Bill said. "I don't want to stay with no man that's loco."

"You get an idea to run, Bill, I can shoot you off your horse," the deputy said. "Close range with my revolver, far range with my rifle. You don't want to try it."

"It's still a long way to Nacogdoches," Bill said.

The road was narrow and of red clay. It stretched far ahead like a band of blood, turned sharply to the right around a wooded curve where it was as dark as the bottom of Jonah's whale. The blowing leaves seemed especially intense on the road, scrapping dryly about, winding in the air like giant hornets. The trees, which grew thick, bent in the wind, from right to left. This naturally led the trio to take to the left side of the road.

The farther they went down the road, the darker it became. By the time they got to the curve, the woods were so thick, and the thunderous skies had grown so dark, the moon was barely visible; its light was as weak as a sick baby's grip.

When they had traveled for some time, the deputy said, obviously feeling good about it, "There ain't nothing out here 'sides what you would expect. A possum maybe. The wind."

"Good for you, then," Jebidiah said. "Good for us all."

"You sound disappointed to me," the deputy said.

"My line of work isn't far from yours, Deputy. I look for bad guys of a sort, and try and send them to hell… Or in some cases, back to hell."

And then, almost simultaneous with a flash of lightning, something crossed the road not far in front of them.

"What the hell was that?" Bill said, coming out of what had been a near stupor.

"It looked like a man," the deputy said.

"Could have been," Jebidiah said. "Could have been."

"What do you think it was?"

"You don't want to know."

"I do."

"Gimet," Jebidiah said.

The sky let the moon loose for a moment, and its light spread through the trees and across the road. In the light there were insects, a large wad of them, buzzing about in the air.

"Bees," Bill said. "Damn if them ain't bees. And at night. That ain't right."

"You an expert on bees?" the deputy asked.

"He's right," Jebidiah said. "And look, they're gone now."

"Flew off," the deputy said.

"No… no they didn't," Bill said. "I was watching, and they didn't fly nowhere. They're just gone. One moment they were there, then they was gone, and that's all there is to it. They're like ghosts."

"You done gone crazy," the deputy said.

"They are not insects of this earth," Jebidiah said. "They are familiars."

"What?" Bill said.

"They assist evil, or evil beings," Jebidiah said. "In this case, Gimet. They're like a witch's black cat familiar. Familiars take on animal shapes, insects, that sort of thing."

"That's ridiculous," the deputy said. "That don't make no kind of sense at all."

"Whatever you say," Jebidiah said, "but I would keep my eyes alert, and my senses raw. Wouldn't hurt to keep your revolvers loose in their holsters. You could well need them. Though, come to think of it, your revolvers won't be much use."

"What the hell does that mean?" Bill said.

Jebidiah didn't answer. He continued to urge his horse on, something that was becoming a bit more difficult as they went. All of the horses snorted and turned their heads left and right, tugged at their bits; their ears went back and their eyes went wide.

"Holy hell," Bill said, "what's that?"

Jebidiah and the deputy turned to look at him. Bill was turned in the saddle, looking back. They looked too, just in time to see something that looked pale blue in the moonlight, dive into the brush on the other side of the road. Black dots followed, swarmed in the moonlight, then darted into the bushes behind the pale, blue thing like a load of buckshot.

"What was that?" the deputy said. His voice sounded as if it had been pistol whipped.

"Already told you," Jebidiah said.

"That couldn't have been nothing human," the deputy said.

"Don't you get it," Bill said, "that's what the preacher is trying to tell you. It's Gimet, and he ain't nowhere alive. His skin was blue. And he's all messed up. I seen more than you did. I got a good look. And them bees. We ought to break out and ride hard."

"Do as you choose," the Reverend said. "I don't intend to."

"And why not?" Bill said.

"That isn't my job."

"Well, I ain't got no job. Deputy, ain't you supposed to make sure I get to Nac-ogdoches to get hung? Ain't that your job?"

"It is."

"Then we ought to ride on, not bother with this fool. He wants to fight some grave crawler, then let him. Ain't nothing we ought to get into."

"We made a pact to ride together," the deputy said. "So we will."

"I didn't make no pact," Bill said.

"Your word, your needs, they're nothing to me," the deputy said.

At that moment, something began to move through the woods on their left. Something moving quick and heavy, not bothering with stealth. Jebidiah looked in the direction of the sounds, saw someone, or something, moving through the underbrush, snapping limbs aside like they were rotten sticks. He could hear the buzz of the bees, loud and angry. Without really meaning to, he urged the horse to a trot. The deputy and Bill joined in with their own mounts, keeping pace with the Reverend's horse.

They came to a place off the side of the road where the brush thinned, and out in the distance they could see what looked like bursting white waves, frozen against the dark. But they soon realized it was tombstones. And there were crosses. A graveyard. The graveyard Old Timer had told them about. The sky had cleared now, the wind had ceased to blow hard. They had a fine view of the cemetery, and as they watched, the thing that had been in the brush moved out of it and went up the little rise where the graves were, climbed up on one of the stones and sat. A black cloud formed around its head, and the sound of buzzing could be heard all the way out to the road. The thing sat there like a king on a throne. Even from that distance it was easy to see it was nude, and male, and his skin was gray—blue in the moonlight—and the head looked misshapen. Moon glow slipped through cracks in the back of the horror's head and poked out of fresh cracks at the front of its skull and speared out of the empty eye sockets. The bee's nest, visible through the wound in its chest, was nestled between the ribs. It pulsed with a yellow-honey glow. From time to time, little black dots moved around the glow and flew up and were temporarily pinned in the moonlight above the creature's head.

"Jesus," said the deputy.

"Jesus won't help a bit," Jebidiah said.

"It's Gimet, ain't it? He… it… really is dead," the deputy said.

"Undead," Jebidiah said. "I believe he's toying with us. Waiting for when he plans to strike."

"Strike?" Bill said. "Why?"

"Because that is his purpose," Jebidiah said, "as it is mine to strike back. Gird your loins, men, you will soon be fighting for your life."

"How about we just ride like hell?" Bill said.

In that moment, Jebidiah's words became prophetic. The thing was gone from the grave stone. Shadows had gathered at the edge of the woods, balled up, become solid, and when the shadows leaped from the even darker shadows of the trees, it was the shape of the thing they had seen on the stone, cool blue in the moonlight, a disaster of a face, and the teeth… They were long and sharp. Gimet leaped in such a way that his back foot hit the rear of Jebidiah's animal, allowing him to spring over the deputy's horse, to land hard and heavy on Bill. Bill let out a howl and was knocked off his mount. When he hit the road, his hat flying, Gimet grabbed him by his bushy head of straw-colored hair and dragged him off as easily as if he were a kitten. Gimet went into the trees, tugging Bill after him. Gimet blended with the darkness there. The last of Bill was a scream, the raising of his cuffed hands, the cuffs catching the moonlight for a quick blink of silver, then there was a rustle of leaves and a slapping of branches, and Bill was gone.

"My God," the deputy said. "My God. Did you see that thing?"

Jebidiah dismounted, moved to the edge of the road, leading his horse, his gun drawn. The deputy did not dismount. He pulled his pistol and held it, his hands trembling. "Did you see that?" he said again, and again.

"My eyes are as good as your own," Jebidiah said. "I saw it. We'll have to go in and get him."

"Get him?" the deputy said. "Why in the name of everything that's holy would we do that? Why would we want to be near that thing? He's probably done what he's done already… Damn, Reverend. Bill, he's a killer. This is just as good as I might want. I say while the old boy is doing whatever he's doing to that bastard, we ride like the goddamn wind, get on out on the far end of this road where it forks. Gimet is supposed to be only able to go on this stretch, ain't he?"

"That's what Old Timer said. You do as you want. I'm going in after him."

"Why? You don't even know him."

"It's not about him," Jebidiah said.

"Ah, hell. I ain't gonna be shamed." The deputy swung down from his horse, pointed at the place where Gimet had disappeared with Bill. "Can we get the horses through there?"

"Think we will have to go around a bit. I discern a path over there."

"Discern?"

"Recognize. Come on, time is wasting."

They went back up the road a pace, found a trail that led through the trees. The moon was strong now as all the clouds that had covered it had rolled away like wind blown pollen. The air smelled fresh, but as they moved forward, that changed. There was a stench in the air, a putrid smell both sweet and sour, and it floated up and spoiled the freshness.

"Something dead," the deputy said.

"Something long dead," Jebidiah said.

Finally the brush grew so thick they had to tie the horses, leave them. They pushed their way through briars and limbs.

"There ain't no path," the deputy said. "You don't know he come through this way."

Jebidiah reached out and plucked a piece of cloth from a limb, held it up so that the moon dropped rays on it. "This is part of Bill's shirt. Am I right?"

The deputy nodded. "But how could Gimet get through here? How could he get Bill through here?"

"What we pursue has little interest in the things that bother man. Limbs, briars. It's nothing to the living dead."

They went on for a while. Vines got in their way. The vines were wet. They were long thick vines, and sticky, and finally they realized they were not vines at all, but guts, strewn about and draped like decorations.

"Fresh," the deputy said. "Bill, I reckon."

"You reckon right," Jebidiah said.

They pushed on a little farther, and the trail widened, making the going easier. They found more pieces of Bill as they went along. The stomach. Fingers. Pants with one leg in them. A heart, which looked as if it has been bitten into and sucked on. Jebidiah was curious enough to pick it up and examine it. Finished, he tossed it in the dirt, wiped his hands on Bill's pants, the one with the leg still in it, said, "Gimet just saved you a lot of bother and the State of Texas the trouble of a hanging."

"Heavens," the deputy said, watching Jebidiah wipe blood on the leg-filled pants.

Jebidiah looked up at the deputy. "He won't mind I get blood on his pants," Jebidiah said. "He's got more important things to worry about, like dancing in the fires of hell. And by the way, yonder sports his head."

Jebidiah pointed. The deputy looked. Bill's head had been pushed onto a broken limb of a tree, the sharp end of the limb being forced through the rear of the skull and out the left eye. The spinal cord dangled from the back of the head like a bell rope.

The deputy puked in the bushes. "Oh, God. I don't want no more of this."

"Go back. I won't think the less of you, cause I don't think that much of you to begin with. Take his head for evidence and ride on, just leave me my horse."

The deputy adjusted his hat. "Don't need the head… And if it comes to it, you'll be glad I'm here. I ain't no weak sister."

"Don't talk me to death on the matter. Show me what you got, boy."

The trail was slick with Bill's blood. They went along it and up a rise, guns drawn. At the top of the hill they saw a field, grown up, and not far away, a sagging shack with a fallen down chimney.

They went that direction, came to the shack's door. Jebidiah kicked it with the toe of his boot and it sagged open. Once inside, Jebidiah struck a match and waved it about. Nothing but cobwebs and dust.

"Must have been Gimet's place," Jebidiah said. Jebidiah moved the match before him until he found a lantern full of coal oil. He lit it and placed the lantern on the table.

"Should we do that?" the deputy asked. "Have a light. Won't he find us?"

"In case you have forgotten, that's the idea."

Out the back window, which had long lost its grease paper covering, they could see tombstones and wooden crosses in the distance. "Another view of the graveyard," Jebidiah said. "That would be where the girl's mother killed herself."

No sooner had Jebidiah said that, then he saw a shadowy shape move on the hill, flitting between stones and crosses. The shape moved quickly and awkwardly.

"Move to the center of the room," Jebidiah said.

The deputy did as he was told, and Jebidiah moved the lamp there as well. He sat it in the center of the floor, found a bench and dragged it next to the lantern. Then he reached in his coat pocket and took out the bible. He dropped to one knee and held the bible close to the lantern light and tore out certain pages. He wadded them up, and began placing them all around the bench on the floor, placing the crumpled pages about six feet out from the bench and in a circle with each wad two feet apart.

The deputy said nothing. He sat on the bench and watched Jebidiah's curious work. Jebidiah sat on the bench beside the deputy, rested one of his pistols on his knee. "You got a .44, don't you?"

"Yeah. I got a converted cartridge pistol, just like you."

"Give me your revolver."

The deputy complied.

Jebidiah opened the cylinders and let the bullets fall out on the floor.

"What in hell are you doing?"

Jebidiah didn't answer. He dug into his gun belt and came up with six silver-tipped bullets, loaded the weapon and gave it back to the deputy.

"Silver," Jebidiah said. "Sometimes it wards off evil."

"Sometimes?"

"Be quiet now. And wait."

"I feel like a staked goat," the deputy said.

After a while, Jebidiah rose from the bench and looked out the window. Then he sat down promptly and blew out the lantern.

Somewhere in the distance a night bird called. Crickets sawed and a large frog bleated. They sat there on the bench, near each other, facing in opposite directions, their silver-loaded pistols on their knees. Neither spoke.

Suddenly the bird ceased to call and the crickets went silent, and no more was heard from the frog. Jebidiah whispered to the deputy.

"He comes."

The deputy shivered slightly, took a deep breath. Jebidiah realized he too was breathing deeply.

"Be silent, and be alert," Jebidiah said.

"All right," said the deputy, and he locked his eyes on the open window at the back of the shack. Jebidiah faced the door, which stood halfway open and sagging on its rusty hinges.

For a long time there was nothing. Not a sound. Then Jebidiah saw a shadow move at the doorway and heard the door creak slightly as it moved. He could see a hand on what appeared to be an impossibly long arm, reaching out to grab at the edge of the door. The hand clutched there for a long time, not moving. Then, it was gone, taking its shadow with it.

Time crawled by.

"It's at the window," the deputy said, and his voice was so soft it took Jebidiah a moment to decipher the words. Jebidiah turned carefully for a look.

It sat on the window sill, crouched there like a bird of prey, a halo of bees circling around its head. The hive pulsed and glowed in its chest, and in that glow they could see more bees, so thick they appeared to be a sort of humming smoke. Gimet's head sprouted a few springs of hair, like withering grass fighting its way through stone. A slight turn of its head allowed the moon to flow through the back of its cracked skull and out of its empty eyes. Then the head turned and the face was full of shadows again. The room was silent except for the sound of buzzing bees.

"Courage," Jebidiah said, his mouth close to the deputy's ear. "Keep your place."

The thing climbed into the room quickly, like a spider dropping from a limb, and when it hit the floor, it stayed low, allowing the darkness to lay over it like a cloak.

Jebidiah had turned completely on the bench now, facing the window. He heard a scratching sound against the floor. He narrowed his eyes, saw what looked like a shadow, but was in fact the thing coming out from under the table.

Jebidiah felt the deputy move, perhaps to bolt. He grabbed his arm and held him.

"Courage," he said.

The thing kept crawling. It came within three feet of the circle made by the crumpled bible pages.

The way the moonlight spilled through the window and onto the floor near the circle Jebidiah had made, it gave Gimet a kind of eerie glow, his satellite bees circling his head. In that moment, every aspect of the thing locked itself in Jebidiah's mind. The empty eyes, the sharp, wet teeth, the long, cracked nails, blackened from grime, clacking against the wooden floor. As it moved to cross between two wads of scripture, the pages burst into flames and a line of crackling blue fulmination moved between the wadded pages and made the circle light up fully, all the way around, like Ezekiel's wheel.

Gimet gave out with a hoarse cry, scuttled back, clacking nails and knees against the floor. When he moved, he moved so quickly there seemed to be missing spaces between one moment and the next. The buzzing of Gimet's bees was ferocious.

Jebidiah grabbed the lantern, struck a match and lit it. Gimet was scuttling along the wall like a cockroach, racing to the edge of the window.

Jebidiah leaped forward, tossed the lit lantern, hit the beast full in the back as it fled through the window. The lantern burst into flames and soaked Gimlet's back, causing a wave of fire to climb from the thing's waist to the top of its head, scorching a horde of bees, dropping them from the sky like exhausted meteors.

Jebidiah drew his revolver, snapped off a shot. There was a howl of agony, and then the thing was gone.

Jebidiah raced out of the protective circle and the deputy followed. They stood at the open window, watched as Gimet, flame-wrapped, streaked through the night in the direction of the graveyard.

"I panicked a little," Jebidiah said. "I should have been more resolute. Now he's escaped."

"I never even got off a shot," the deputy said. "God, but you're fast. What a draw."

"Look, you stay here if you like. I'm going after him. But I tell you now, the circle of power has played out."

The deputy glanced back at it. The pages had burned out and there was nothing now but a black ring on the floor.

"What in hell caused them to catch fire in the first place?"

"Evil," Jebidiah said. "When he got close, the pages broke into flames. Gave us the protection of God. Unfortunately, as with most of God's blessings, it doesn't last long."

"I stay here, you'd have to put down more pages."

"I'll be taking the bible with me. I might need it."

"Then I guess I'll be sticking."

They climbed out the window and moved up the hill. They could smell the odor of fire and rotted flesh in the air. The night was as cool and silent as the graves on the hill.

Moments later they moved amongst the stones and wooden crosses, until they came to a long wide hole in the earth. Jebidiah could see that there was a burrow at one end of the grave that dipped down deeper into the ground.

Jebidiah paused there. "He's made this old grave his den. Dug it out and dug deeper."

"How do you know?" the deputy asked.

"Experience… And it smells of smoke and burned skin. He crawled down there to hide. I think we surprised him a little."

Jebidiah looked up at the sky. There was the faintest streak of pink on the horizon. "He's running out of daylight, and soon he'll be out of moon. For a while."

"He damn sure surprised me. Why don't we let him hide? You could come back when the moon isn't full, or even half full. Back in the daylight, get him then."

"I'm here now. And it's my job."

"That's one hell of a job you got, mister."

"I'm going to climb down for a better look."

"Help yourself."

Jebidiah struck a match and dropped himself into the grave, moved the match around at the mouth of the burrow, got down on his knees and stuck the match and his head into the opening.

"Very large," he said, pulling his head out. "I can smell him. I'm going to have to go in."

"What about me?"

"You keep guard at the lip of the grave," Jebidiah said, standing. "He may have another hole somewhere, he could come out behind you for all I know. He could come out of that hole even as we speak."

"That's wonderful."

Jebidiah dropped the now dead match on the ground. "I will tell you this. I can't guarantee success. I lose, he'll come for you, you can bet on that, and you better shoot those silvers as straight as William Tell's arrows."

"I'm not really that good a shot."

"I'm sorry," Jebidiah said, and struck another match along the length of his pants seam, then with his free hand, drew one of his revolvers. He got down on his hands and knees again, stuck the match in the hole and looked around. When the match was near done, he blew it out.

"Ain't you gonna need some light?" the deputy said. "A match ain't noth-in'."

"I'll have it." Jebidiah removed the remains of the bible from his pocket, tore it in half along the spine, pushed one half in his coat, pushed the other half before him, into the darkness of the burrow. The moment it entered the hole, it flamed.

"Ain't your pocket gonna catch inside that hole?" the deputy asked.

"As long as I hold it or it's on my person, it won't harm me. But the minute I let go of it, and the aura of evil touches it, it'll blaze. I got to hurry, boy."

With that, Jebidiah wiggled inside the burrow.

In the burrow, Jebidiah used the tip of his pistol to push the bible pages forward. They glowed brightly, but Jebidiah knew the light would be brief. It would burn longer than writing paper, but still, it would not last long.

After a goodly distance, Jebidiah discovered the burrow dropped off. He found himself inside a fairly large cavern. He could hear the sound of bats, and smell bat guano, which in fact, greased his path as he slid along on his elbows until he could stand inside the higher cavern and look about. The last flames of the bible burned itself out with a puff of blue light and a sound like an old man breathing his last.

Jebidiah listened in the dark for a long moment. He could hear the bats squeaking, moving about. The fact that they had given up the night sky, let Jebidiah know daylight was not far off.

Jebidiah's ears caught a sound, rocks shifting against the cave floor. Something was moving in the darkness, and he didn't think it was the bats. It scuttled, and Jebidiah felt certain it was close to the floor, and by the sound of it, moving his way at a creeping pace. The hair on the back of Jebidiah's neck bristled like porcupine quills. He felt his flesh bump up and crawl. The air became stiffer with the stench of burnt and rotting flesh. Jebidiah's knees trembled. He reached cautiously inside his coat pocket, produced a match, struck it on his pants leg, held it up.

At that very moment, the thing stood up and was brightly lit in the glow of the match, the bees circling its skin-stripped skull. It snarled and darted forward. Jebidiah felt its rotten claws on his shirt front as he fired the revolver. The blaze from the bullet gave a brief, bright flare and was gone. At the same time, the match was knocked out of his hand and Jebidiah was knocked backwards, onto his back, the thing's claws at his throat. The monster's bees stung him. The stings felt like red-hot pokers entering his flesh. He stuck the revolver into the creature's body and fired. Once. Twice. Three times. A fourth.

Then the hammer clicked empty. He realized he had already fired two other shots. Six dead silver soldiers were in his cylinders, and the thing still had hold of him.

He tried to draw his other gun, but before he could, the thing released him, and Jebidiah could hear it crawling away in the dark. The bats fluttered and screeched.

Confused, Jebidiah drew the pistol, managed to get to his feet. He waited, listening, his fresh revolver pointing into the darkness.

Jebidiah found another match, struck it.

The thing lay with its back draped over a rise of rock. Jebidiah eased toward it. The silver loads had torn into the hive. It oozed a dark, odiferous trail of death and decaying honey. Bees began to drop to the cavern floor. The hive in Gimet's chest sizzled and pulsed like a large, black knot. Gimet opened his mouth, snarled, but otherwise didn't move.

Couldn't move.

Jebidiah, guided by the last wisps of his match, raised the pistol, stuck it against the black knot, and pulled the trigger. The knot exploded. Gimet let out with a shriek so sharp and loud it startled the bats to flight, drove them out of the cave, through the burrow, out into the remains of the night.

Gimet's claw-like hands dug hard at the stones around him, then he was still and Jebidiah's match went out.

Jebidiah found the remains of the bible in his pocket, and as he removed it, tossed it on the ground, it burst into flames. Using the two pistol barrels like large tweezers, he lifted the burning pages and dropped them into Gimet's open chest. The body caught on fire immediately, crackled and popped dryly, and was soon nothing more than a blaze. It lit the cavern up bright as day.

Jebidiah watched the corpse being consumed by the biblical fire for a moment, then headed toward the burrow, bent down, squirmed through it, came up in the grave.

He looked for the deputy and didn't see him. He climbed out of the grave and looked around. Jebidiah smiled. If the deputy had lasted until the bats charged out, that was most likely the last straw, and he had bolted.

Jebidiah looked back at the open grave. Smoke wisped out of the hole and out of the grave and climbed up to the sky. The moon was fading and the pink on the horizon was widening.

Gimet was truly dead now. The road was safe. His job was done.

At least for one brief moment.

Jebidiah walked down the hill, found his horse tied in the brush near the road where he had left it. The deputy's horse was gone, of course, the deputy most likely having already finished out Deadman's Road at a high gallop, on his way to Nacogdoches, perhaps to have a long drink of whisky and turn in his badge.

THE SKULL-FACED BOY

by David Barr Kirtley

David Barr Kirtley is the author of dozens of short stories. His work frequently appears in *Realms of Fantasy*, and he has also sold fiction to the magazines *Weird Tales* and *Intergalactic Medicine Show*, the podcasts *Escape Pod* and *Pseudopod*, and the anthologies *New Voices in Science Fiction* and *The Dragon Done It*. His story "Save Me Plz" was selected for inclusion in *Fantasy: The Best of the Year, 2008 Edition*.

Kirtley wrote this story during the summer of 2000, when he was on a horror-writing kick and wanted to try a zombie story. "I tend to identify with individuals who are looked down on and mistreated because they're different," he says, "so it was natural for me to start thinking about telling my story from the point of view of a zombie."

The other inspiration was a falling out Kirtley had with one of his best friends a few months before he wrote the story. "I felt he was really mistreating his girl-friend and was just generally acting like a complete jerk," Kirtley says. "And all of our friends were mindlessly going along with whatever he did and repeating whatever he said."

Like the zombies in this story.

It was past midnight, and Jack and Dustin were driving along a twisted path through the woods. Jack was at the wheel. He was arguing with Dustin over Ashley.

Jack had always thought she had a pretty face—thin, arching eyebrows, a slightly upturned nose, a delicate chin. She'd dated Dustin in college for six months, until he got possessive and she got restless. Now, Jack thought, maybe she was interested in him.

But Dustin insisted, "She'll give me another chance. Someday."

"Not according to her," Jack said, with a pointed look.

He turned his eyes back to the road, and in the light of the high beams he saw a man stumble into the path of the car. Without thinking, Jack swerved.

The car bounced violently, and then its left front side smashed into a tree.

The steering column surged forward, like an ocean wave, and crushed Jack's stomach. Dustin wasn't wearing a seatbelt. He flew face-first through the windshield, rolled across the hood, and tumbled off onto the ground.

Jack awoke, disoriented.

A man was pounding on the side of the car, just beyond the driver's side window, which was cracked and foggy and opaque. Jack pushed at the door, which creaked open just enough for him to make out the man's face. The man stared at Jack, then turned and started to walk off.

Jack shouted, "Call for help."

But the man didn't respond. He wandered toward the woods.

"Hey!" Jack screamed. He brushed aside a blanket of shattered glass and released his seatbelt. He pushed his seat backward, slowly extricating his bleeding stomach from the steering column, then dragged himself out the door and onto the ground, and he crawled after the man, who continued to walk away.

Finally Jack found the strength to stand. He lurched to his feet, grabbed the man by the shirtfront, shoved him back against a tree, and demanded, "What's wrong with you? Get help." Jack glanced about desperately and added, "I have to find my friend."

The man gave a long and wordless moan. Jack stared at him. The man was very pale, with disheveled hair. His face was encrusted with dirt, and his teeth were twisted and rotten. His eyes were… oozing.

Suddenly Dustin's voice burst out, "He's dead."

Jack turned. Dustin stood there, his nose and cheeks torn away. Two giant white eyeballs filled the sockets of his freakishly visible skull. Scraps of flesh hung from his jaw. Jack screamed.

Dustin stumbled over to the wrecked car, to where one of its side-view mirrors hung loosely. He tore off the mirror and stared into it. For a long time, he neither moved nor spoke.

Finally he called out, "That man has come back from the dead. Look at him, Jack. He's dead, and so am I."

Jack shuddered and backed away from the man.

Dustin's eyeballs fixed on Jack's stomach.

Apprehensive, Jack looked down. He lifted his blood-drenched shirt to expose the mangled mess beneath.

"And so are you," Dustin said.

Jack and Dustin set out on foot. They climbed to the top of a high bluff and watched the bodies of dead men stumble through the grassy fields below. Dustin sat with his back turned, so that his ruined face was lost in shadows. He said, "It's everyone. Everyone who died is coming back."

The dead man who had caused the accident was following them. He stumbled from the trees and regarded Jack vacantly.

Jack approached the man and said, "Can you talk?"

The man paused a moment, as if trying to focus, then gave another inarticulate groan. He wandered away.

Jack said to Dustin, "Why is he like that, and we aren't?"

Dustin said, "He dug himself out of the ground. He's been dead a long time—rotted flesh, rotted brains."

"Are there others like us?" Jack said.

"I don't know." Dustin leapt to his feet and called out to the valley below, "Hey! Can you hear me? Can you understand what I'm saying?"

The warm and fetid air carried back only wails. Dustin shrugged.

He and Jack followed the road until they came to a small house with its lights on.

Jack suggested, "We can call for help."

"What help?" Dustin said. "We're past that."

But he followed Jack toward the house, whose front door was open wide. They paused on the porch. They could see into the kitchen, where a woman stood clenching a baseball bat. A dead boy had backed her into a corner, and he shambled across the yellow linoleum toward her. Dry dirt tumbled from his sleeves and fell in a winding trail behind him.

He spoke, in a faint and quavering way: "Mom… help me."

"Stay back," she warned, her voice cracking. "Stay away from me. You're dead. I know you're dead."

Jack started forward, but Dustin held out an arm to stop him.

"Mom," the boy said. "What's wrong? Don't hurt me…"

"Stop it!" the woman shrieked, but her arms shuddered and she collapsed, sobbing. The boy fell upon her. He clawed at her hair, and she thrashed. He tore at her scalp with his teeth.

Jack cringed and turned away. The woman screamed, then gurgled, then was silent. When Jack looked again, he saw that Dustin was regarding the gruesome scene with fascination.

Jack growled, "What's wrong with you? We could've stopped it."

"We're dead now," Dustin said. "We help the dead, not them." He gestured at the woman.

"You're crazy," Jack said.

Dustin ignored him. "I want to see this."

"You—" Jack stopped as the woman rose, her head a cracked and bloody mess. She stepped clumsily forward.

She moaned.

"You'd be like her," Dustin whispered. "Mindless… hungry. If that first one had gotten into the car, chewed up your head, before you rose."

Jack strode into the kitchen, eased around the woman, the boy, and the blood-splattered floor, and stepped toward the phone.

"I'm calling home," Jack said, lifting the receiver. "I have to call my dad. Tell him I'm—"

"What?" Dustin said darkly. "All right?"

Jack hesitated.

Dustin said, "Jack, you're dead. You're lost to him. He'll never take you in."

Jack paused a moment, then began to dial. Dustin turned and stepped out into the night. The phone rang once, and instantly someone answered.

"Jack?" It was his father's voice.

"I'm coming home," Jack said. "I… can't stay on the line." He hung up.

He snatched some keys off the counter and slipped from the house. He spotted Dustin, who had walked out into the fields among the great crowds of the dead and was shouting to them, "Can you understand me? If you can hear me, step forward. If you understand just that much."

Jack circled the house, to where a car was parked. He took the car, and drove north for an hour, along Interstate 95, toward Waterville. He stared at his reflection in the rearview mirror. His face was jaundiced, discolored and sickly, but if he covered his gaping stomach then in dim light he might pass for living.

He pulled up in front of his house and got out of the car. In the front yard lay a dead man whose forehead had a bullet through it. Jack shuddered, and circled around back. The old wood steps creaked as he stepped onto the back porch and knocked. He hung back in the shadows. A curtain was drawn aside, and faces peered out.

From inside the house someone called: "Jack! It's Jack."

The door opened, and Jack's father stood there, clutching a rifle. He stared, then gasped and dropped back, raising the gun.

Jack cowered and said quickly, "Dad. Listen. Please. I'm not like the others." The rifle was now aimed straight at Jack's forehead, and Jack stared into the depths of its barrel. Then the barrel slowly sank, as his father lowered the gun.

Finally his father said, "Come inside, son."

Jack stepped into the house.

His father chained him to the rusty pipe that ran out of the side of the garage and into the ground, and said, "I'm sorry. It's only for the night. It's the only way they'll let you stay here." Nine people were holed up in the house—Jack's father had taken in some vacationers.

Jack whispered sadly, "I understand."

His father went back inside.

The moon was bright, and the garage cast a thick black shadow over Jack. All across the neighborhood, dogs were barking. The night seemed to go on forever, and Jack never slept. He supposed that he would never sleep again.

Days passed.

Several large groups arrived. Jack stayed out of sight, and most of the visitors departed, headed south. Those who stayed would sometimes let Jack inside, but they kept their distance from him, and always had weapons ready.

During the day the men went out, scavenging for food and ammunition, and at night they told stories of the dead men they'd destroyed. Then they would glance at Jack and fall silent.

He was chained up each night, weeks of that.

One day at dusk, Jack was sitting on a sofa in the living room when gunshots crackled outside. The residents brandished their weapons and took up positions by the windows.

Someone pounded on the front door. A gruff voice outside hollered, "Let us in! For God's sake, let us in. They're coming."

Jack's father, rifle at the ready, leapt forward and threw open the door. Two tall men in hunting gear rushed into the house, each of them carrying several guns. Jack's father slammed the door behind them.

One of the newcomers gasped, "We heard about this house. They said you'd take us in. We've got almost no bullets left."

Jack's father said, "It's my house, and you're—"

Then the newcomer spotted Jack and lurched wildly, falling back against the front wall and violently cocking a shotgun. The man screamed, "They're in the house!," and raised his weapon.

Jack's father leapt in front of the gun and yelled, "Don't shoot! That's my son. He won't hurt you."

The gun's barrel wove in tight circles as the newcomer sought a clear shot.

Jack called out, "Please! It's all right."

The newcomer glanced at his companion, who was now hunched in the corner and moaning, "Oh shit. Oh shit, it's in here with us."

Jack's father said firmly, "You can leave if you want."

There was a long, tense silence. Finally, the newcomer lowered his gun and said, "All right. We'll let it alone." He glared at Jack, and added, "But you stay the hell away from me."

The newcomer was named Sam, and his companion was Todd. Sam was bigger and louder, and leader of the two.

After things had settled down, Todd explained, "We joined up with a militia to hold Portland. But the dead, they…" He stopped and stared at the floor.

Sam said flatly, "It's not good down there. Not good at all."

Jack's father said, "Where did you hear about this house?"

"In Freeport," Todd said. "Some people had stayed here. There was a girl too. She had a note for your son." Todd fished an envelope out of his vest pocket. He glanced uneasily at Jack and said, "I guess that's him."

Sam grumbled, "Maybe that's not such a good idea."

Jack's father scowled and said, "Let him have it."

Todd shrugged and tossed the note out onto the table. Jack scooped up the note and opened it.

It was from Ashley, letting him know that she was all right and that he should join her if he wasn't safe. She gave the address where she was. Jack stuck the note into his pocket.

Sam's voice was shaky: "South of here there's this dead kid with no face.

People call him the skull-faced boy. He's smart, he can talk, like that one there." Sam nodded at Jack.

Jack murmured, "Dustin."

Todd said sharply, "What?"

Jack said, "He hurt his face like that. I saw it."

Sam stared, horrified. "You know him?"

Jack realized that he'd said something wrong.

"Dustin was a friend from school," Jack's father explained. "He was with Jack the night this... all started."

Todd's voice was almost hysterical: "Sam! This is crazy. He's one of them. One of the skull-faced boy's—"

"Shut up!" Sam growled. "Just shut up."

There was a long silence.

Jack's father said, "Come on, son. Let's go outside."

Jack was chained up again. Then he crouched there in the shadow of the garage and listened to the voices that drifted out through the bright cracks in the boarded-up windows.

First came Jack's father's voice: "What's this all about?"

Todd replied anxiously, "We lost Portland because of the skull-faced boy. He's organized the dead down south into some sort of army."

Sam broke in, "He's trained them. They go after people they know—family, friends. The dead act like they have feelings. People hesitate, won't fight, then it's too late."

Jack's father said, "What's that got to do with us?"

"Don't you get it?" It was Todd again. "Jack is part of this. He's friends with the skull-faced boy. He's pretending to be nice, just waiting for his chance to strike."

"He's dangerous," Sam added. "He knows about this house, and now the one in Freeport too. What else does he know? He's got to be destroyed."

"No," Jack's father said.

Todd pressed him, "He's not your son anymore. Your son is dead and gone. Now it's just a thing, a thing in your son's body. Using your own love against you."

Sam added, "People have a right to protect themselves. If one of these folks here went out one night and shot that thing you keep in the backyard, I wouldn't blame them."

One of the other residents hissed, "Keep your voice down. He might hear."

After that the voices fell to a low, incomprehensible murmur.

Jack waited for hours. Then he watched as the back door swung open. A shadowy figure with a gun crept across the yard toward him.

Was it Sam? Or Todd? Or one of the others? In the darkness, Jack couldn't tell.

It was his father, who stepped from the shadows, then bent to unlock the chains and said, "It's not safe for you here anymore. I'm sorry."

"I'm sorry too," Jack whispered, rising to his feet. He hugged his father, then escaped into the night.

Jack found Dustin's army standing in a great field north of Portland. The thousands of dead milled about in loose formations and watched Jack with their empty eyes. Their groans filled the night.

Jack moved among them and shouted, "Dustin! I'm looking for Dustin. Dustin, can you hear me?"

Finally a voice responded, "Hey! Hey you. What do you want?"

Jack stopped and turned. A balding dead man in olive fatigues was approaching.

Jack said, "I'm looking for the skull-faced boy."

"The Commander, you mean," the man replied. "He'll want to see you too. We can use someone like you."

The man led Jack through the crowds, up to a low hill where a small crowd of dead men conversed in hushed tones. Dustin stood at the peak of the hill, and his back was turned. Standing like that he seemed normal, familiar.

Jack called out, "Dustin."

Dustin glanced backward, so that one white eye showed in his eerie skeletal profile. He wore a ratty army jacket. He said, "You've come back." Then he turned away, so that again all that was visible was the back of his head, and said, "Where have you been?"

"Up north," Jack said.

Dustin asked, "Did you encounter any of the living? Any armed groups?"

"No," Jack lied.

"We'll be headed that way," Dustin continued. "North. Along 95, toward Waterville… Your hometown." He waited for a reaction.

Jack said nothing.

Finally Dustin added, "Anyway, it's time for training." He walked out to the edge of the hill and regarded the hordes below, then shouted, "Don't shoot!"

They moaned back, "Don't… shoot…"

"It's me!" Dustin yelled. "You know me!"

The voices of the dead drifted up toward the sky: "It's me… You know me…"

"Please help me," Dustin shouted.

"Please… help me…" they wailed.

Dustin nodded with satisfaction and turned away from the crowds. "That's our strategy, Jack. My soldiers possess determination, but not much else. A resemblance to loved ones is one of our few assets."

Jack said, "What are you doing? What do you think you're going to accomplish?"

"Peace," Dustin said, then added, "The living want to destroy us. All of us. Our only chance is to convert them, to make them like us."

Jack stared at the lines of moaning dead. They stretched as far as he could see.

Dustin added, "And we're winning, thanks to my plan. I got the idea from that boy, who converted his mother. You remember, that first night, we saw him."

"To hell with your plan," Jack said angrily. "I lost my home because of your plan."

Instantly Dustin turned to face Jack and said, "So you did go home." That menacing skull-face leaned in close. "Are people hiding there?"

Jack turned away.

"At your house?" Dustin pressed. "Is that where they are? My army's fragile, Jack. They're slow and clumsy and stupid. A nest of armed resistance, even a small one, can wreak havoc. I have to know about it."

Jack said, "Leave them alone. Leave my father alone."

"We're headed north, Jack," Dustin said. "The plan is already in motion."

"Don't," Jack insisted, then added, "Just for now. They won't bother you. Push east. Toward Freeport."

"Freeport?" Dustin was dismissive. "What's there?"

Jack reached into his pocket and pulled out the note. He answered in a low voice, "Ashley."

Later that night, Dustin said to Jack, "She'll have to be converted. It's the only way."

Jack said, "Killed, you mean."

"I want her with us," Dustin said. "She's in danger now. Any random dead person might get to her, damage her mind—destroy what makes her special. She'll be safer this way."

Jack wondered: Why did I do it? Why betray Ashley? To protect his father, yes, but… the truth—he wanted to see her again. Would she accept him, if they were the same? If she were dead too?

Jack said, "It won't be easy."

"No," Dustin agreed. "That's why I need you with me. My soldiers follow orders, mostly. I tell them where to march, who to attack, what to say. But I can't stop them from feeding, Jack, which means that most of my new recruits arrive as damaged goods. There's not much officer material around here."

Jack was skeptical. "You want to make me an officer?"

Dustin answered, "I can't use regular troops for this. There's too much risk to Ashley. I have to use officers—men I can trust not to damage her—and I've got few enough of those."

Some of the dumb, moaning ones wandered past, and Jack imagined them ripping at Ashley's soft forehead with their teeth.

"I'll go," Jack said then. "For Ashley. To make sure nothing happens to her."

"For Ashley," Dustin agreed.

Dustin called a meeting of his officers, and held up a photograph that showed him and Ashley standing beside a campfire and embracing. Dustin said, "This is her. Make sure she's not damaged."

The army marched east, thousands of groaning dead shambling along the interstate. Dustin moved among them, shouting orders: "When we reach the town, seek out places you know, people you know. Remember what to say: 'Don't shoot! You know me! Help me!'"

The mumbled replies echoed through the trees: "Don't shoot... you know me... help me..."

Dustin had a dozen officers—dead men armed with rifles and pistols—who stayed close by his side. Dustin himself carried a shotgun, and kept a combat knife tucked in his boot. Jack followed along behind them, and held his rifle limply, and stared down at the damp pine needles that passed beneath his feet. He was full of foreboding.

Dustin lowered his voice and said to his officers, "They've probably never fought dead men like us before—fast, smart, armed. That surprise will be our biggest advantage."

One of the officers grumbled, "They've spent weeks boarding up this house. How are we going to get in?"

Jack called out, "I can get us in."

Dustin turned and studied him, then nodded.

The house was a sprawling Victorian that sat in the middle of a grove of white cedars. Dustin led the squad forward. They all crouched low and scurried across the lawn in a tight column, their weapons held ready. Jack and Dustin hurried up the front steps while the others ducked behind the porch railing or dropped into the long grass.

Jack hammered on the door and shouted, "Let us in! It's Sam! For God's sake, let us in, they're coming!"

After a few moments, he heard the bolt snap out of place. The door opened a crack. Dustin rammed the barrel of his shotgun into the opening and pulled the trigger. Blood exploded through the gap, splattering crimson across the porch, then Dustin kicked open the door.

The officers sprang up, firearms bristling, and charged into the house. Gunfire rang out all around. Jack was swept along into the foyer, which was already littered with bodies. A staircase led up to the second floor.

"Cover the stairs," Dustin ordered Jack. "Make sure no one comes down."

Jack aimed his gun up toward the second floor landing. The other officers poured off into the side rooms, and sounds of violence shook the house.

Suddenly a doorway under the stairs flew open. Jack swung his rifle to cover it, but then a muzzle flashed and a bullet caught him in the chest, and he stumbled back against a small table and knocked over a lamp, which shattered on the floor.

Dustin shouted, "The basement! They're in the basement."

Three of the officers stormed down the basement steps. Beneath Jack's feet the floorboards rattled, and horrible screams filtered up from below. Jack stuck a finger into his chest and rooted out the bullet.

Another officer jogged up to stand at Dustin's side and said, "Sir, we've got your girl. She's in the study. Bleeding."

Dustin nodded. "I want to be with her when she rises. Finish this."

"Yes, sir." The officer walked to the open front door and called out, "Come here. Come on. Now."

Jack watched, horrified, as crowds of moaning dead men stumbled in through the door and began to gorge on the newly fallen corpses.

Jack grabbed Dustin's arm and said, "What are you doing? We can use these people."

Dustin said, "They'll try to shoot us as soon as they rise. It's better this way."

Jack cast one last grim look at the feeding dead, then followed Dustin through several doorways and into a study.

Ashley lay in an overstuffed chair, flanked by officers. Her pretty face was still. A trickle of blood flowed from a single bullet hole in the center of her chest.

One of the officers said, "She's not breathing. It won't be long."

Dustin ordered, "I want to be alone with her."

The officers herded Jack from the room. He paced down a long, lonely hallway, then out the front door and into the yard, where he sat, leaning back against a tall white cedar and waiting for Ashley to appear.

Finally she did, framed in the light of the doorway. Her figure was slender, her hair long and lustrous. But her beautiful face had been carved away, until there was nothing left but eyeballs and bone.

Dustin came and stood beside her, and their twin skull faces regarded each other.

Later that night, as Jack and Dustin stood together in the yard, Jack said bitterly, "I can't believe you did that. She was beautiful."

To which Dustin replied, "Ashley will always be beautiful. To me. You loved her face. I love her. Who deserves her more?"

"I want to talk to her," Jack said.

"No, you'll stay away." Dustin's voice held a nasty edge. "Or I'll tell her that you led us here. That you betrayed her."

Jack flinched, and Dustin strode away, calling over his shoulder, "I'm the only one who understands her now, understands what she's going through."

For hours Jack wandered aimlessly among the dead, among the masses of rotting flesh. Their awfulness, their stupidity, was overwhelming, and made him want to gag.

Then, through the clusters of corpses, he caught a glimpse of white skull. He walked away.

He wound a path through the dead, and sneaked an occasional backward glance. The skull was there. It gained on him.

Finally, it caught him.

Ashley said, "Jack. It is you." She leaned her horrible skull-face toward him, and her exposed eyeballs studied him. She said, "Dustin didn't tell me you were here. Say something. Do you recognize me, Jack? Do you understand?"

He didn't answer.

Then she was suspicious. "Did you have anything to do with this? Did you help him do this?

Jack turned away and stumbled off into the hordes. In that moment he envied them—their lack of thought, of remorse. He couldn't bear to confront Ashley. Now there was only one thing he could do, that might deceive her, that might make her leave him alone.

"Don't hurt me…" he groaned loudly, desperately. "Please… help me."

THE AGE OF SORROW

by Nancy Kilpatrick

Nancy Kilpatrick is the author the Power of the Blood vampire series, which includes the novels *Child of the Night, Near Death, Reborn, Bloodlover*, and a fifth volume which is currently in progress. She is also the author of the non-fiction book *The Goth Bible*, and with Nancy Holder, she edited her eighth horror anthology, *Outsiders*. She's a prolific author of short fiction as well, with recent sales to the anthologies *Blood Lite, Monsters Noir*, and *Moonstone Monsters: Vampires* and *Moonstone Monsters: Zombies*. Her work has been a finalist for several awards, and she won the Arthur Ellis Award for best short story in 1992. Nancy was a guest of honor at the 2007 World Horror Convention. She lives in Montréal, Québec.

This story came about as a result of Kilpatrick asking herself how a woman would deal with being the only human survivor in a world overrun by zombies. "Would she do anything differently than a man would? Would she be blasting zombies right, left and center 24/7?" Kilpatrick asks. "I've never been a proponent of the helpless female standing and shrieking as the zombies come for her. I don't know any women like that."

Grief had taken hold of her long ago. Long before the cataclysm. Long before everything had disintegrated: the planet; its people; her life. Hope for the future.

She crouched at the top of the hill, turning her head slowly from side to side, seeing only what the UV aviator goggles allowed her to view, scanning 180 degrees of verdant landscape, watching. Always watching. This valley had once been prime farmland, teeming with crops, and quietly nestled in it twin villages alive with quaint houses, one school that catered to the children of the entire population, a church each for the two big branches of Christianity, a synagogue, and a mosque. The two church steeples poked above the foliage, their crosses glinting in the afternoon sun, and she remembered reading what Joseph Campbell had said: you can tell what a culture values by its tallest buildings. She wondered if that applied to the beings who now dwelled in the villages.

There must still be fields for soccer and softball, the hospital, the shops that the populace had supported, although she hadn't visited the villages in months and couldn't be certain. Here and there a house was partially visible—she could just make out the pastel clapboard walls, splotches of color on this oh-so-green canvas of life that now flowed down the hills like lava. Over the last few years the plants had grown at an unnatural pace, devouring everything in their wake: the homes, the fields, the people. No, not the people. They had managed anyway. For a while.

Despite it all, she could not view this land so far from the place of her birth as anything but lush, the green vibrant shades ranging from yellow-tinged to near black. The sun, despite the thick layer of ozone which trapped its rays, managed to give the plants what they needed. They weren't suffering from any "greenhouse effect" but seemed to flourish and propagate. It was just humanity that had fared badly in all this.

She knew she should head back. Even if a freak storm didn't crop up, sunset wasn't far off. And there was plenty to do. Always. The crops she tended religiously that provided her only fresh food needed watering. She should examine that weakness in the fence, figure out the strongest repair possible with the materials she had on hand so that she didn't need to go to either of the villages. There were fruits and vegetables to harvest, cook and put up, which meant gathering wood that had to be gotten out here, where it wasn't safe when darkness set in. Her life had become all work, everything geared towards survival. "Of the fittest," she said aloud for some reason, her voice sounding odd, the words ringing strangely in her ears. It had been so long since she'd heard herself speak.

But inertia had hold of her. She knew she was about mid-cycle, her most fertile time, halfway between periods—scant though they were now. Energy was not especially low during ovulation, just not high, and she felt a lack of focus. That would change within two weeks, when the flow began. But that would be later. Today she just wanted to sit and stare into the infinity of the horizon. "Slouching towards menopause," she had written in her journal. Now, slouching, lounging, slacking off, literally or figuratively, all of that was a rarity in her life. There was too much to do, all the time, every day, and in the night the never-ending battle with loneliness and despair. And terror.

She pulled the glasses down for a second, hoping the hat brim could protect her eyes, but she could not help a quick glance at the sun, a brilliant orange, heading down the hazy sky, and tried to recall its precise color when it had been yellow. She could not. It was as if the sun had always been the color of a pumpkin. As if everything in nature had always been this way. She fixed the glasses back over her eyes and willed herself to stand, to get moving, but her body refused to be pushed. Just a few more minutes. I've got a few minutes to spare, she assured herself.

Suddenly the bells at one of the churches began to ring, just as they did automatically every Sunday morning, afternoon and evening. Then the bells of the other church answered, the two playing back and forth. The sound reverberated around the valley, through her, washing away worries and fear, leaving her mellow, and remembering.

Church bells had rung the morning she and Gary married. A happy sound, full of the promise of a history yet to be lived. I was so young, she thought. So naïve. Now, it seemed as if she had always been her current age, forty. But then, on that day, at twenty, and Gary twenty-one, she had trusted him with her future; had trusted him to not betray her; to not betray them.

The house, the bills, a pregnancy that ended in an abortion because they were too young, he said, and she had agreed, yes, they were too young, with plenty of time ahead. A job that held her interest while she finished law school, then clerking at a prestigious firm until they hired her and she moved up the ranks of corporate law. A job she ultimately detested, now that she was honest with herself on a full-time basis. But back then, she tolerated it all, even the loss of the child she had not birthed. She tolerated it because of Gary, in the name of their love.

A lot of good that did her now. Gary. Her profession. Her childless life, and now it was too late for children. Not chronologically, although forty pushed it, but in all the other ways that made conceiving impossible, especially the circumstances of her life.

The choices we make, she thought grimly, as the last bell tolled. Those roads not taken. One road leads to another and that to another and eventually those choices have moved you down a path of no return. Why hadn't someone told her? Why hadn't her mother said this is how it is before she died? *Decide here, now, and go this way or that; some choices are irreversible.* But her mother was a liberal thinker, an early feminist. Someone who believed possibilities defined life and allowed it to constantly evolve. And her father? She had never gotten a fix on him. And after her parents divorced, he became a ghost. The man whose sperm had helped form her was friendly enough. He bought her things. Paid for her education. Walked her down the aisle. But if she went blind she couldn't pick him out of a crowd. Not his voice, his scent, his touch.

All the wrong choices, she thought. Me. Gary. My parents. Everybody on the planet. The earth reeked with wrong choices. And now there were just two choices: Live or Die.

Her gloomy reverie broke when she caught movement in the distance. She pulled the goggles down to her neck; the sun had set. The sky had grayed fast, without her noticing. Startled, she jumped to her feet, staring to the west, watching the figure that looked male coming through the trees quickly. She spun in a circle and saw movement in most directions. Nearly surrounded, she had to hurry.

She raced down the mound, tearing through the high green towards the compound, a bootlace untying en route. She ripped off her gloves and threw them aside so she could get to the key hanging around her neck and pulled the rope over her head as she ran.

Tonight they were moving swiftly and she had just reached the gate when she heard rustling behind her. She didn't dare take the time to look. Her hand trembled as she forced the large key into the huge padlock, yanked it open, pulled it from the bar and got herself inside and the door locked just as the first of them reached the gate.

The stench of rot forced her back. The solar yard light that increased illumination with the darkness allowed her to see this one all too clearly. A face no longer recognizable, living decay. His bloated blue fingers pushed their way through the chain links, reaching out for her.

All around the compound they gathered, aligning their dull eyes, the light of life missing, with the openings of the links. Her stomach lurched and her heart hammered. Three years and she had not gotten used to the sight of them and imagined she never would.

What flesh had not thoroughly corrupted or fallen away was bilious and left her gagging. They made sounds, low, moany noises that reminded her of sick or hurt animals. At one time, when it all began, she had felt sorry for them, imagining they were in pain. But that was early on. Back when she did not, could not believe that they wanted her dead. But now she believed.

She forced herself to turn, commanded herself to not look at any of them. The fence needing repair filled her thoughts, but she knew it could not be breached. Not tonight, not next week. It was just her constant worrying, something to focus on. How she had to be, always alert, never able to rest, the price of survival.

Despite the sounds that filled the air with their groans and shufflings and the squishy noises of flesh no longer alive pressing against other dead flesh or metal or grass underfoot, she managed to walk to the well and with trembling hands began lowering the metal bucket. It dropped down into the water with a splash and although it was too dark now to see to the bottom, through the rope she held she could feel the bucket submerge. She turned the crank to hoist it up. When the pail reached the top she grabbed it to the ledge, untied it, locked the carbon filter on top and hauled it, water sloshed over the sides, to the vegetable garden where she moistened one row of plants. Above her the sky had turned slate and no stars shown through the thick cloud cover. *The moon goddess is not making her presence known tonight,* she thought. *Artemis the huntress. Nothing worth hunting anymore.*

The numbers of them had grown until they were two and three deep around the fence in places. Every day she thanked whatever deities still cared about this poor planet for the fact that this disease first rotted the brain of the inflicted, otherwise they would long ago have taken to using tools and breeching her barrier. Tonight their presence seemed to turn the air from warm to hot, or at least *she* felt hot.

A flash memory, the day one of them touched her. Putrid flesh clamping onto her shoulder, cool puffy fingers curling around her, grabbing on, trying to hold her back, trying to absorb her warm life through her T-shirt. Panicked, she broke free and ran as fast as she could, snagging a shovel for protection as she went, racing until the breath burned her lungs and her vision blurred. And still it pursued her until she found safety in an abandoned store, bolting the door, watching it pawing the glass to get at her, unable to think clearly enough to shatter the glass, which told her a lot.

The news had declared this outbreak another super bug, spread by physical contact. Unresponsive to antibiotics. Not to worry, the man on Channel 7 said, a serum was being developed. All would be well. But she had felt its touch through thin fabric, watched its face close up all through the night until the first rays of the sun forced it to take refuge from the impending light which must hurt its rotting skin. By morning she knew that all would not be well. Things would never be right again. After that experience, she had changed.

Fueled by mounting terror, she booked a flight, just wanting to get as far away from the horrors as possible. An article had identified a few spots on the planet as trouble free; the more isolated, the scientist said, the better. He named New Zealand as the safest place on Earth. He was wrong.

Muscles trembling, she hefted another pail of water to the garden. The lettuce looked wilty, so she gave each plant extra liquid, hoping they would perk up. The growing season here extended all year, although last summer the heat had been almost unbearable and much of her crop burned. She lost forty pounds over four months and had been forced to go into the villages and raid gardens, and cupboards for tinned food, and stock up on all the vitamins she could get her hands on. Now she took a handful of those plus the brown seaweed extract she'd been swallowing for the last half decade to detoxify her body of radiation fallout. One good thing about no more humans on the planet: no more politicians dropping bombs on one another.

The garden had been, like so much in the last few years, a learning experience. Come this summer she planned to add a UV filter to the shade over the plants for the hottest part of the day. Thank god the well was artesian and would, theoretically, last forever. Not that she would. And there were no heirs to take her place. Fortunately.

The things outside the gate continued to moan and groan and produce squishy sounds. Sometimes she thought she heard her name, but that couldn't be. They were no longer living beings, not living in the way she was. Flesh and organs and bone decomposing, they moved by instinct, and the instinct the nearly dead seemed to possess directed them towards the living of which she was, to her knowledge, the last in this region. Perhaps in this country. The world. She had no way of knowing.

She finished the watering, sprayed organic pesticide on the plants, and then did a final visual check of the compound. Everything in order. An acre was not too much to manage, and from the front yard she could see every inch of the property but for what lay behind the mound. She had macheted the vines and scrub that grew wildly and regularly mowed the grass with an old hand mower she'd found on one of the farms, flattening everything but the garden. Facing the mound, she walked to her right, stopping two feet from the fence and at her approach the sounds from the cool bodies increased in volume like insects swarming. She could see one side of the back fence. None of them were at that corner, where repairs were needed. She reminded herself that the damage wasn't urgent. Still, knowing that a weakness existed made her nervous. Not nervous enough to go there, in the darkness of night, which would draw attention to that area. And to her. She couldn't do anything to fix it now, and a sudden pain as her ovary struggled to expel an egg into her fallopian tubes turned her away from the yard and towards the house.

On the way she plucked four lettuce leaves, picked a ripe tomato, a yellow pepper, and with the Army knife she always carried in a sheath around her belt she sliced off one small head of a broccoli, all of it going into a basket which she carried in one hand. With the other hand she hefted the last pail of water. Carefully she headed down the two steps and inside, closing and locking the door after her, which drowned out most of the din that unnerved her still, and stood, back resting for a moment against the wooden barrier, happy for contact with even the inanimate.

Finally she pushed herself away, dropped the basket on the table and set the pail by the sink, took off the goggles and her hat and began to roll up her shirt sleeves. As an afterthought she removed her shirt but left the cotton tank top on. Immediately her body temperature lowered.

She crossed the room to the wall under the one window and checked the bank of batteries charged by eight 75 Watt solar panels on the roof. A flip of a switch cranked up the air filtering system from low—where she kept it when she went out—to high. The fully charged batteries meant she could waste a few amps to enjoy a bit of music as she ate. Something soothing. She flipped through the CDs and found Pachelbel's *Canon*, then changed her mind—too gloomy. Maybe Delibes' *Lakme*. Something lighter, that spoke of hope. Of springtime. Springtime.

As the music played, she scrubbed all of the vegetables thoroughly in the carbon-filtered water. Likely it did nothing much for the pollutants in the air still circling the earth, but then she wasn't certain what to do about them. She pulled a chopping knife from the rack and started on the pepper, gutting it, setting the seeds aside to dry, her mind wandering to a springtime only five years ago. The last one where she had seen Gary alive.

How could life have seemed so ordinary? she wondered. She rinsed and sliced into the tomato, the pungent smell reaching her nostrils, and added it and the pepper to the lettuce she washed and tore into bite-size pieces.

Spring, the weather beautifully mild, the scent of lilac in the air, the scent of hope. She and Gary met for lunch at a small café downtown, near the campus where he taught. She told the receptionist she'd be gone for an hour and a half but when she was seated Gary said he had to get back to the college and could only stay thirty minutes.

They sat on the terrace and ordered—both had salads and café lattes—and she remembered gazing at the young people, semi-stripped for the mild temperature. They all looked so healthy and happy. Nothing like a twenty-year-old body, she thought, although at thirty-five she wasn't in bad shape at all, thanks to a daily jog before work.

She recalled looking over Gary's shoulder as he munched on Caesar salad and seeing her reflection in the restaurant's window: chestnut hair, large dark eyes, an oval face with few signs of wrinkles, nothing that tri-monthly derma-abrasions and a bit of Botox couldn't fix.

She glanced at Gary and saw him not watching her but staring at those same bodies. It was only a fragment of time, and yet in that split second she knew he had been unfaithful.

He felt her look and his handsome face closed around the emotion. "How's your day?" he asked.

She put down her fork. "Who is she?"

"She?" He looked uncomfortable. "You'll have to be more precise than that or—"

"The one you're fucking. What's her name?"

He opened his mouth, his expression guarded, his eyes haughty, but she locked onto him, a human laser, and said, "Don't bother lying. Just tell me." Her voice, remarkably calm to her own ears, must have put him at ease.

"Her name is Eileen."

"A student?"

"First year."

"I suppose she came to discuss a paper or project."

"A project. Not a very good one. I gave her direction."

They could have been talking about the city's plans for revamping the waterfront, or a new movie to be seen. Suddenly, she couldn't bear it, the strain of the last fifteen years. Without a word, she picked up her bag and stood.

"Wait, look—"

But before he could say more she was out of earshot. My life is a facade, she thought. Years and years of ignoring truth. In those moments of that perfect spring day she knew that she had barely loved him when she was twenty and now did not love him at all. At least in the way that mattered between a woman and a man. The most hurtful part was that she knew it was mutual.

She ran for an hour, but she could not have said what streets, or even what district. Her ringtone—nineteen notes of *The Flower Duet*—played again and again until she pulled the cellphone from her purse and tossed it into a trash can, then, when the shoulder bag grew annoying, she pitched it as well.

Sometime later she showed up at the front door, without keys. Darkness had set in. The trees and grass and the other homes on the street looked stunned. And she saw everything as if for the first time.

She rang the bell and he let her in, moving away from the door as she passed him, not wanting a fight, but neither did she. Apparently the relationship was not worth fighting for. She climbed the stairs, suddenly exhausted, and entered their bedroom to find his matching suitcases on the bed, both three-quarters packed.

Slowly she removed her clothes and let them drop to the floor then ran a bath and sank into a hot tub, a glass of Beaujolais in her hand, and fell asleep. When she woke, the water was cold, tinted with the undrunk wine as if it had been blood that spilled. The house was tomb silent. His suitcases were gone. She found a note on the dresser: something about being sorry, and wishing her a nice life. She had ripped it into tiny pieces and flushed it down the toilet.

She cut up the broccoli raw and added it to the salad. A small bottle of olive oil sat on the floor in the coolest part of the kitchen area and she opened it to add a few drops to the vegetables, then pushed the cork back in. For a moment she stood looking at the salad, then covered the bowl with an elasticized net to keep insects out, turned and walked to the couch that doubled as a bed in this one-room house and fell onto it, exhausted. Always exhausted. Always unable to sleep.

Why was all this coming back to her now? It felt like the disease of memory crept through her mind and heart, hiding, surging to the fore when she least expected it and did not want it.

She glanced around the room helplessly. She had positioned the couch so that from here she could see every corner, and the door. One room. Convenient. Life condensed. Half buried in the earth like a grave, the design geared to keeping the heat down. And a small *Alice Through the Looking Glass* door behind the couch, but it only locked from the other side. The tunnel led through the dirt mound and would bring her 100 feet outside the compound should this house be invaded.

One high-pitched, sharp laugh erupted from her. The idea was absurdity itself. If the compound was invaded, she would have no home. Outside the compound, where could she escape to? She had watched the villagers succumb until none were left uninfected. And if any were whole she had not come across them in the last year. But she had been making fewer and fewer trips into the villages because seeing these creatures cowering from the light became too much. Besides, most of the supplies she needed she already had, stored in a small shed just outside the door—canned goods, ammunition for the one rifle stationed next to the couch, and the handgun she carried in a holster around her waist—weapons she had only fired in practice and was not sure she could actually use on these formerly living humans.

While there was still gas in the pumps and a couple of functioning vehicles left in the villages, she had already brought up many bottles of water, in case the well ran dry. Clothing, shoes, sheets and towels and kitchen equipment. Propane tanks, although she rarely cooked meals anymore. Over time she had learned through books how to use the solar panels. Getting them from the hardware store to the compound had been one thing, hauling them to the roof had been another. And the heavy batteries had tested her physical strength and ingenuity even more. Batteries to store the raw energy, a converter to turn it into something useful which then powered what had become a decreasing need for energy. With no TV broadcasts, no radio, no phones, no Internet, no contact with the outside world but for a CB radio that she left on but had stopped sending out messages from months ago, she only needed lighting and music to get by. Get by. That's what she was doing, getting by. Barely. "Everything the female survivalist needs," she said aloud, hearing her voice, the sound in the stillness so alien to her ears it brought tears to her eyes.

Why was she alive when others were not? How had this nightmarish existence come upon her? Maybe she really had died and gone to hell and this was it. The Dante book she had read in her youth with the lovely Doré etchings described hell but she knew there were many more than nine levels.

When the bacterial infections began, they rampaged through chronic care facilities, then hospitals in general, schools, workplaces, anywhere and everywhere human beings had physical contact with one another. At the same time, the ozone layer altered sufficiently that the icebergs at the North Pole melted, raising the sea level, turning what had been frozen tundra into almost pastoral terrain. Then the Antarctic ice began breaking off in large chunks and microorganisms trapped in the ice at both poles were released. Scientists learned that some lifeforms could lie in wait for millennia.

Wars became the norm, day to day reality on the news, thousands killed here and there, weaponry of all types deployed and the "limited nuclear war" became reality. Suddenly the air was not just polluted with smog but radioactive dust circled with the altered jet streams. Soil and water turned toxic, and multinationals focused their resources on cleaning out the poisons so that food could still be grown and water drunk, but only by citizens wealthy enough to pay for purification. The masses could not. Brand new immune-system diseases soared.

With enormous loss of life, human society began to disintegrate: garbage piled up; transportation came to a halt; medication ran out; electrical and cellular services died and depending on the season, people froze or burned to death, unless they were preyed upon by other human beings.

Her mind scanned the hellish reality she had witnessed over five short years, descending circle by circle. And all the while humanity tried to adapt. Her heart felt heavy: the naivety, the stupidity, the complacency. The men in power said it would all be alright in the end. But it wasn't alright. It would never be alright again. And just when things couldn't get worse, they did: the new plague spread rapidly, and suddenly the dying could not die.

But by then she was in New Zealand, traveling aimlessly. Nowhere to go. Nothing to do but sit back and watch the apocalypse unfold. *Wait your turn*, she told herself, but her turn had not come.

In truth, New Zealand, and some of the other isolated islands in this region were the last to go. Although this country was not spared the nuclear fallout, they did manage to stem the flow of visitors and immigrants and eventually movement by their own citizens—nobody went in or out. But by then it was too late. For humanity, for Gary's plea with her to come home to him in that last phone call. Everything was always too late.

She picked up the journal she had been keeping, the latest one, atop a pile of five large books, one per year since she had arrived here, chronicling the deterioration and her own existence. Writing helped keep her sane, even though some days took up barely half a page, filled with mundane details of gardening, eating, defecating. Other entries analyzed the politics, or the science as she understood it—and with all the time in the world and all the books and magazines and newspapers in the library she had learned quite a bit. But the worst entries, the ones that made her cringe, were those where she saw her emotions sprayed on the page as if they were her blood. Tortured by loneliness and despair, she could barely re-read those. Because despite all that she had learned, and all that she understood, as far as she knew, she was the last person alive on the planet. Every attempt with the CB had met with dead air.

"Dante had no idea!" she mumbled, her voice almost an echo in her ears. The circles of hell were infinite.

Suicidal thoughts nearly overwhelmed her more times than she could count, and she did not yet know why she still lived, unscathed by the new plague, unaltered by the deadly air. But answers, like everything else, were in short supply, and she'd long ago stopped her obsessive reading and wondering about why she seemed immune to what affected others. Diseases that should have killed everyone, if only the others could die.

But they could not die. They hid from daylight and wandered aimlessly at night. No, not aimlessly. They always found their way to her compound. She wondered if they sought her out for a connection to life when they possessed little resembling that. The walking dead, her only companions. And the worst part was, some were not as decayed. Some she recognized still: Joe who used to run the butcher shop; Lucy from the pharmacy; Ned and his wife Sarah who farmed just outside the villages and ran a fruit and vegetable stand... The memory of their faces as they had been overlapped with how they were now moved a wave of hysteria up from her gut that caught in her throat and suddenly she found herself sobbing uncontrollably.

This fit lasted only seconds. Her last eruption had been about six months ago.

She picked up the pen and began writing, trying to convey in words the feelings that washed through her like waves in a storm. She could never get over how quickly the illnesses overtook the living. One day she had gone into the chemist's and Lucy had been fine. The next day she had dark circles beneath her eyes and sneezed uncontrollably. The third day Bill, the owner, said she was "Out with a sniffle." The next night Lucy was spotted walking the streets at midnight, her skin mottled, her eyes bearing an opaque sheen. People tried to talk with her, to help her, but she seemed incapable of speech, only incoherent mutterings and soft moans. And those that she touched came down with the sickness.

Lucy was the first local to go. As the numbers of the undead increased, people packed up their families and fled the villages, as many as could get away. She had no idea where they went, where they *could* go.

She found this house and when the grocery store and the hardware shop were abandoned she began stocking up, building the fence, securing her world. And then they came. Those who were left. Dozens from villages that once had claimed a combined population of 10,000. Every night they swarmed from their homes and headed to hers. A macabre ritual. *Maybe they're as lonely as I am*, she wrote. *I'm half dead in a different way. Maybe it's a strange, symbiotic curse and we need each other. If I cease to survive, will they? If they disappear tomorrow, will I still exist? How Zen*, she wrote. *How perfectly, horribly Zen.*

Suddenly she felt heavy, tired, and her eyes would not stay open. She sank down to a full recline, telling herself that if she fell asleep now she would be up in the middle of the night, but not heeding the warning.

In a dream that she knows to be a dream she walks over fields covered with wildflowers under a yellow sun crossing a blue sky with few clouds. The cool earth beneath her feet, the sweet scent of lilac in the air, a mild and warm breeze blows her skirt and her hair… She closes her eyes and feels heat penetrate to her bones, warming her, even as she thinks: the sun is too strong!

A sound jolts her and she spins around to see a man coming towards her. He is dressed in blue jeans, a t-shirt and his body is muscular. With hair the color of the sun and eyes that she can see as he nears are blue as the sky, he is as alive as the day. As real as nature that heals and cleanses itself, over time.

Suddenly the man is Gary, and he stops before her and reaches out to cup her chin. His touch is electric. It is as if her body is nothing but electrical current as sparks explode throughout her, sending signals to her brain, her heart, her genitals. She quivers, hungry for this, fearful of it at the same time. Without opening his mouth he says to her "Don't worry! This was meant to be."

How? she wonders. "Are you dead?" she asks.

He smiles and pulls her to him, kissing her full on the lips, and she tastes his familiar tongue inside her mouth, moving, probing. An image flashes through her of dark unwholesomeness. An invasion.

She jerked awake, her body covered with sweat. She sat up abruptly and felt chilly, as if the temperature had plummeted. She grabbed the blanket from the foot of the couch and wrapped it around her shoulders, still shivering.

Disoriented, she looked around the darkened room, lit only by one 15 Watt coiled florescent that she kept lit over the kitchen table to stave off the demons of darkness. But the demons had gotten through, again.

She stood on shaky legs, feeling her cool forehead, and then headed to a cupboard where she kept a first aid bag. She placed the thermometer under her tongue and walked to the one window while she waited, moving the bar that held the thick wooden shutters so she could open them and look out.

Darkness filled the night. And silence. Nothing. Once her eyes adjusted, she scanned the periphery of the fence to the gate, as far as the window would let her see. They had gone, at least from the area within her view.

A full moon hung in the sky as if pasted there on top of the blackness. She squinted at the orb, struggling to see the face that she had seen as a child, but the thickened atmosphere blurred details.

When she pulled out the thermometer and read it under the lamp she saw that her temperature was normal. She did not feel sick. A glance in the mirror by the door showed a too-thin face, haggard, but she had accepted that. She looked weary but bright-eyed. Absently she smoothed back her short hair, running fingers through it like a comb. I'm alright, she thought, feeling both relief and despair that she was not sick. "You're ovulating," she told her image. The serious image looked back at her with an expression that said: So? What does it matter? "Soon you'll get old and die," she said. The image did not reply. Old and die. Would she, *could* she die? Or was her destiny that of the undead, the ones who were sick but unable to get well, unable to die, caught in a balance of the battle of microorganisms that kept them in a terrible, stasis. That kept them walking endlessly, feebly, helplessly, unable to give themselves wholeheartedly to entropy. Weak, mindless, incapable of using tools—"Isn't that what defines us as human?" she challenged her image. But the image, as always, did not long to respond.

Suddenly, in anger, she threw off the blanket, stalked to the couch, grabbed the rifle, and unbolted the door. The night air felt cooler, and the cold wind of a storm snapped at her. Tonight she wanted change. Something would die. One of them. Or her. It didn't matter. This couldn't go on!

Aware of the insanity of her thinking, she would not stop herself. She stormed to the fence and strode along the periphery. Soon she was passing the side of the vegetable garden, the side of the mound then reached the back of the dirt mound that enclosed her house, her prison. Nothing. No one. Where were they? Had they fled in despair? Had an alien ship come down and taken them all away? Did the balance of power finally fall to one side and the life-destroying organisms win and they at long last died? Tonight of all nights she wanted to find out. She wanted to stare into one of those hideous faces, to confront this half-being, to find a way to send it to oblivion. Maybe that was the way to go. Get over her aversion and shoot them in the head, one by one, until there were no more. Then she could walk free! What would it matter if that left her alone? She was alone now, totally. Thoroughly. The world she remembered had receded like a long-ago dream barely recalled.

She passed the weakness in the fence and saw that it had not been breeched. Nothing had been breeched, just her psyche.

Her quick strides brought her around to the other side of the mound, then back into what she deemed the front yard. Not one of the not-quite-dead. Frustrated, she stepped outside of the glow of the yard light and glared up at the impassive moon. Suddenly she gave in to an impulse of a different sort: snapping her head further back, letting the glow of the other-worldly light freeze her face, she howled like an animal. Wailed over and over into the impending storm until the sounds turned to shrieking. She dropped the rifle. Out of her control, her body staggered around the yard, arms protecting her solar plexus, screaming, sobbing, blind with the impossibleness of despair. She only stopped when she slammed against the fence and crumpled to the ground, her back braced against the chain link, her body curled into a fetal position.

Out of her mind with grief, it took time to realize that something was different. She felt a burning at the back of her neck. The hotness moved along her flesh from side to side and at first she did not know what caused it. But then she did. Cold, so intense it felt hot, comforting, caressing her skin. Behind her, close, she heard breathing. Wet breathing. And while her mind warned her that she should be frightened, at the closeness, the touch, another part of her ached for more. She sat up, pressing her back against the fence. More fingers touched her, caressing her as a lover would, as Gary had. Their foul odor entered her nostrils as flowers. Lilacs. She reached back over her shoulder; flesh met flesh. And as the rain blew from every direction, for the first time in a long time her sorrow evaporated into the wind.

BITTER GROUNDS

by Neil Gaiman

Neil Gaiman is the best-selling author of *American Gods, Coraline*, and *Anansi Boys*, among many other novels. He's also the writer of the popular *Sandman* comic book series, and has done work in television and film. His television projects include the BBC miniseries *Neverwhere*, which he later adapted into a novel, and a script for *Babylon 5*; in the realm of film, he co-wrote the screenplays for the films *MirrorMask* and *Beowulf*, and wrote the English-language screenplay of Hayao Miyazaki's anime film *Princess Mononoke*. His novel *Stardust* was made into a film in 2007.

Gaiman has won most if not all of the major awards the SF, fantasy, and horror genres have to offer, including 3 Hugos, 2 Nebulas, the World Fantasy Award, 4 Bram Stoker Awards, and 11 Locus Awards.

"Bitter Grounds" originally appeared in the Caribbean fantasy anthology *Mojo: Conjure Stories*. On his blog, which can be found at journal.neilgaiman.com, Gaiman says that he suspects that the ideal reader of this story "reads it once, goes 'hmph…' and then, a week or so later, with the story sort of itching in the back of her head, goes back to read it again, and finds that it's topographically reconfigured into a completely different story."

1
"Come back early or never come"

In every way that counted, I was dead. Inside somewhere maybe I was screaming and weeping and howling like an animal, but that was another person deep inside, another person who had no access to the face and lips and mouth and head, so on the surface I just shrugged and smiled and kept moving. If I could have physically passed away, just let it all go, like that, without doing anything, stepped out of life as easily as walking through a door, I would have. But I was going to sleep at night and waking in the morning, disappointed to be there and resigned to existence.

Sometimes I telephoned her. I let the phone ring once, maybe even twice, before I hung up.

The me who was screaming was so far inside nobody knew he was even there at all. Even I forgot that he was there, until one day I got into the car—I had to go to the store, I had decided, to bring back some apples—and I went past the store that sold apples and I kept driving, and driving. I was going south, and west, because if I went north or east I would run out of world too soon.

A couple of hours down the highway my cell phone started to ring. I wound down the window and threw the cell phone out. I wondered who would find it, whether they would answer the phone and find themselves gifted with my life.

When I stopped for gas I took all the cash I could on every card I had. I did the same for the next couple of days, ATM by ATM, until the cards stopped working.

The first two nights I slept in the car.

I was halfway through Tennessee when I realized I needed a bath badly enough to pay for it. I checked into a motel, stretched out in the bath, and slept in it until the water got cold and woke me. I shaved with a motel courtesy kit plastic razor and a sachet of foam. Then I stumbled to the bed, and I slept.

Awoke at 4:00 a.m., and knew it was time to get back on the road.

I went down to the lobby.

There was a man standing at the front desk when I got there: silver-gray hair although I guessed he was still in his thirties, if only just, thin lips, good suit rumpled, saying, "I *ordered* that cab an *hour* ago. One *hour* ago." He tapped the desk with his wallet as he spoke, the beats emphasizing his words.

The night manager shrugged. "I'll call again," he said. "But if they don't have the car, they can't send it." He dialed a phone number, said, "This is the Night's Out Inn front desk…. Yeah, I told him…. Yeah, I told him."

"Hey," I said. "I'm not a cab, but I'm in no hurry. You need a ride somewhere?"

For a moment the man looked at me like I was crazy, and for a moment there was fear in his eyes. Then he looked at me like I'd been sent from Heaven. "You know, by God, I do," he said.

"You tell me where to go," I said. "I'll take you there. Like I said, I'm in no hurry."

"Give me that phone," said the silver-gray man to the night clerk. He took the handset and said, "You can *cancel* your cab, because God just sent me a Good Samaritan. People come into your life for a reason. That's right. And I want you to think about that."

He picked up his briefcase—like me he had no luggage—and together we went out to the parking lot.

We drove through the dark. He'd check a hand-drawn map on his lap, with a flashlight attached to his key ring; then he'd say, "Left here," or "This way."

"It's good of you," he said.

"No problem. I have time."

"I appreciate it. You know, this has that pristine urban-legend quality, driving down country roads with a mysterious Samaritan. A Phantom Hitchhiker story. After I get to my destination, I'll describe you to a friend, and they'll tell me you died ten years ago, and still go round giving people rides."

"Be a good way to meet people."

He chuckled. "What do you do?"

"Guess you could say I'm between jobs," I said. "You?"

"I'm an anthropology professor." Pause. "I guess I should have introduced myself. Teach at a Christian college. People don't believe we teach anthropology at Christian colleges, but we do. Some of us."

"I believe you."

Another pause. "My car broke down. I got a ride to the motel from the highway patrol, as they said there was no tow truck going to be there until morning. Got two hours of sleep. Then the highway patrol called my hotel room. Tow truck's on the way. I got to be there when they arrive. Can you believe that? I'm not there, they won't touch it. Just drive away. Called a cab. Never came. Hope we get there before the tow truck."

"I'll do my best."

"I guess I should have taken a plane. It's not that I'm scared of flying. But I cashed in the ticket; I'm on my way to New Orleans. Hour's flight, four hundred and forty dollars. Day's drive, thirty dollars. That's four hundred and ten dollars spending money, and I don't have to account for it to anybody. Spent fifty dollars on the motel room, but that's just the way these things go. Academic conference. My first. Faculty doesn't believe in them. But things change. I'm looking forward to it. Anthropologists from all over the world." He named several, names that meant nothing to me. "I'm presenting a paper on the Haitian coffee girls."

"They grow it, or drink it?"

"Neither. They sold it, door to door in Port-au-Prince, early in the morning, in the early years of the century."

It was starting to get light, now.

"People thought they were zombies," he said. "You know. The walking dead. I think it's a right turn here."

"Were they? Zombies?"

He seemed very pleased to have been asked. "Well, anthropologically, there are several schools of thought about zombies. It's not as cut-and-dried as popularist works like *The Serpent and the Rainbow* would make it appear. First we have to define our terms: are we talking folk belief, or zombie dust, or the walking dead?"

"I don't know," I said. I was pretty sure *The Serpent and the Rainbow* was a horror movie.

"They were children, little girls, five to ten years old, who went door-to-door through Port-au-Prince selling the chicory coffee mixture. Just about this time of day, before the sun was up. They belonged to one old woman. Hang a left just before we go into the next turn. When she died, the girls vanished. That's what the books tell you."

"And what do you believe?" I asked.

"That's my car," he said, with relief in his voice. It was a red Honda Accord, on the side of the road. There was a tow truck beside it, lights flashing, a man beside the tow truck smoking a cigarette. We pulled up behind the tow truck.

The anthropologist had the door of the car opened before I'd stopped; he grabbed his briefcase and was out of the car.

"Was giving you another five minutes, then I was going to take off," said the tow-truck driver. He dropped his cigarette into a puddle on the tarmac. "Okay, I'll need your triple-A card, and a credit card."

The man reached for his wallet. He looked puzzled. He put his hands in his pockets. He said, "My wallet." He came back to my car, opened the passenger-side door and leaned back inside. I turned on the light. He patted the empty seat. "My wallet," he said again. His voice was plaintive and hurt.

"You had it back in the motel," I reminded him. "You were holding it. It was in your hand."

He said, "God *damn it*. God fucking *damn* it to hell."

"Everything okay there?" called the tow-truck driver.

"Okay," said the anthropologist to me, urgently. "This is what we'll do. You drive back to the motel. I must have left the wallet on the desk. Bring it back here. I'll keep him happy until then. Five minutes, it'll take you five minutes." He must have seen the expression on my face. He said, "Remember. People come into your life for a reason."

I shrugged, irritated to have been sucked into someone else's story.

Then he shut the car door and gave me a thumbs-up.

I wished I could just have driven away and abandoned him, but it was too late, I was driving to the hotel. The night clerk gave me the wallet, which he had noticed on the counter, he told me, moments after we left.

I opened the wallet. The credit cards were all in the name of Jackson Anderton.

It took me half an hour to find my way back, as the sky grayed into full dawn. The tow truck was gone. The rear window of the red Honda Accord was broken, and the driver's-side door hung open. I wondered if it was a different car, if I had driven the wrong way to the wrong place; but there were the tow-truck driver's cigarette stubs, crushed on the road, and in the ditch nearby I found a gaping briefcase, empty, and beside it, a manila folder containing a fifteen-page typescript, a prepaid hotel reservation at a Marriott in New Orleans in the name of Jackson Anderton, and a packet of three condoms, ribbed for extra pleasure.

On the title page of the typescript was printed:

This was the way Zombies are spoken of: They are the bodies without souls. The living dead. Once they were dead, and after that they were called back to life again.

Hurston, *Tell My Horse*

I took the manila folder, but left the briefcase where it was. I drove south under a pearl-colored sky.

People come into your life for a reason. Right.

I could not find a radio station that would hold its signal. Eventually I pressed the scan button on the radio and just left it on, left it scanning from channel to channel in a relentless quest for signal, scurrying from gospel to oldies to Bible talk to sex talk to country, three seconds a station with plenty of white noise in between.

…Lazarus, who was dead, you make no mistake about that, he was dead, and Jesus brought him back to show us—I say to show us…

…what I call a Chinese dragon. Can I say this on the air? Just as you, y'know, get your rocks off, you whomp her round the backatha head, it all spurts outta her nose. I damn near laugh my ass off…

…If you come home tonight I'll be waiting in the darkness for my woman with my bottle and my gun…

…When Jesus says will you be there, will you be there? No man knows the day or the hour, so will you be there…

…president unveiled an initiative today…

… fresh-brewed in the morning. For you, for me. For every day. Because every day is freshly ground…

Over and over. It washed over me, driving through the day, on the back roads. Just driving and driving.

They become more personable as you head south, the people. You sit in a diner, and along with your coffee and your food, they bring you comments, questions, smiles, and nods.

It was evening, and I was eating fried chicken and collard greens and hush puppies, and a waitress smiled at me. The food seemed tasteless, but I guessed that might have been my problem, not theirs.

I nodded at her politely, which she took as an invitation to come over and refill my coffee cup. The coffee was bitter, which I liked. At least it tasted of something.

"Looking at you," she said, "I would guess that you are a professional man. May I enquire as to your profession?" That was what she said, word for word.

"Indeed you may," I said, feeling almost possessed by something, and affably pompous, like W. C. Fields or the Nutty Professor (the fat one, not the Jerry

Lewis one, although I am actually within pounds of the optimum weight for my height). "I happen to be… an anthropologist, on my way to a conference in New Orleans, where I shall confer, consult, and otherwise hobnob with my fellow anthropologists."

"I knew it," she said. "Just looking at you. I had you figured for a professor. Or a dentist, maybe."

She smiled at me one more time. I thought about stopping forever in that little town, eating in that diner every morning and every night. Drinking their bitter coffee and having her smile at me until I ran out of coffee and money and days.

Then I left her a good tip, and went south and west.

2

"Tongue brought me here"

There were no hotel rooms in New Orleans, or anywhere in the New Orleans sprawl. A jazz festival had eaten them, every one. It was too hot to sleep in my car, and even if I'd cranked a window and been prepared to suffer the heat, I felt unsafe. New Orleans is a real place, which is more than I can say about most of the cities I've lived in, but it's not a safe place, not a friendly one.

I stank, and itched. I wanted to bathe, and to sleep, and for the world to stop moving past me.

I drove from fleabag motel to fleabag motel, and then, at the last, as I had always known I would, I drove into the parking lot of the downtown Marriott on Canal Street. At least I knew they had one free room. I had a voucher for it in the manila folder.

"I need a room," I said to one of the women behind the counter.

She barely looked at me. "All rooms are taken," she said. "We won't have anything until Tuesday."

I needed to shave, and to shower, and to rest. *What's the worst she can say?* I thought. *I'm sorry, you've already checked in?*

"I have a room, prepaid by my university. The name's Anderton."

She nodded, tapped a keyboard, said "Jackson?" then gave me a key to my room, and I initialed the room rate. She pointed me to the elevators.

A short man with a ponytail, and a dark, hawkish face dusted with white stubble, cleared his throat as we stood beside the elevators. "You're the Anderton from Hopewell," he said. "We were neighbors in the *Journal of Anthropological Heresies*." He wore a white T-shirt that said "Anthropologists Do It While Being Lied To."

"We were?"

"We were. I'm Campbell Lakh. University of Norwood and Streatham. Formerly North Croydon Polytechnic. England. I wrote the paper about Icelandic spirit walkers and fetches."

"Good to meet you," I said, and shook his hand. "You don't have a London accent."

"I'm a Brummie," he said. "From Birmingham," he added. "Never seen you at one of these things before."

"It's my first conference," I told him.

"Then you stick with me," he said. "I'll see you're all right. I remember my first one of these conferences, I was scared shitless I'd do something stupid the entire time. We'll stop on the mezzanine, get our stuff, then get cleaned up. There must have been a hundred babies on my plane over, IsweartoGod. They took it in shifts to scream, shit, and puke, though. Never fewer than ten of them screaming at a time."

We stopped on the mezzanine, collected our badges and programs. "Don't forget to sign up for the ghost walk," said the smiling woman behind the table. "Ghost walks of Old New Orleans each night, limited to fifteen people in each party, so sign up fast."

I bathed, and washed my clothes out in the basin, then hung them up in the bathroom to dry.

I sat naked on the bed, and examined the papers that had been in Anderton's briefcase. I skimmed through the paper he had intended to present, without taking in the content.

On the clean back of page five he had written, in a tight, mostly legible scrawl, *In a perfect perfect world you could fuck people without giving them a piece of your heart. And every glittering kiss and every touch of flesh is another shard of heart you'll never see again. Until walking (waking? calling?) on your own is unsupportable.*

When my clothes were pretty much dry I put them back on and went down to the lobby bar. Campbell was already there. He was drinking a gin and tonic, with a gin and tonic on the side.

He had out a copy of the conference program, and had circled each of the talks and papers he wanted to see. ("Rule one, if it's before midday, fuck it unless you're the one doing it," he explained.) He showed me my talk, circled in pencil.

"I've never done this before," I told him. "Presented a paper at a conference."

"It's a piece of piss, Jackson," he said. "Piece of piss. You know what I do?"

"No," I said.

"I just get up and read the paper. Then people ask questions, and I just bullshit," he said. "Actively bullshit, as opposed to passively. That's the best bit. Just bullshitting. Piece of utter piss."

"I'm not really good at, um, bullshitting," I said. "Too honest."

"Then nod, and tell them that that's a really perceptive question, and that it's addressed at length in the longer version of the paper, of which the one you are reading is an edited abstract. If you get some nut job giving you a really difficult time about something you got wrong, just get huffy and say that it's not about what's fashionable to believe, it's about the truth."

"Does that work?"

"Christ yes. I gave a paper a few years back about the origins of the Thuggee sects in Persian military troops. It's why you could get Hindus and Muslims equally becoming Thuggee, you see—the Kali worship was tacked on later. It would have begun as some sort of Manichaean secret society—"

"Still spouting that nonsense?" She was a tall, pale woman with a shock of white hair, wearing clothes that looked both aggressively, studiedly Bohemian and far too warm for the climate. I could imagine her riding a bicycle, the kind with a wicker basket in the front.

"Spouting it? I'm writing a fucking book about it," said the Englishman. "So, what I want to know is, who's coming with me to the French Quarter to taste all that New Orleans can offer?"

"I'll pass," said the woman, unsmiling. "Who's your friend?"

"This is Jackson Anderton, from Hopewell College."

"The Zombie Coffee Girls paper?" She smiled. "I saw it in the program. Quite fascinating. Yet another thing we owe Zora, eh?"

"Along with *The Great Gatsby*" I said.

"Hurston knew F. Scott Fitzgerald?" said the bicycle woman. "I did not know that. We forget how small the New York literary world was back then, and how the color bar was often lifted for a genius."

The Englishman snorted. "Lifted? Only under sufferance. The woman died in penury as a cleaner in Florida. Nobody knew she'd written any of the stuff she wrote, let alone that she'd worked with Fitzgerald on *The Great Gatsby*. It's pathetic, Margaret."

"Posterity has a way of taking these things into account," said the tall woman. She walked away.

Campbell stared after her. "When I grow up," he said, "I want to be her."

"Why?"

He looked at me. "Yeah, that's the attitude. You're right. Some of us write the best-sellers; some of us read them. Some of us get the prizes; some of us don't. What's important is being human, isn't it? It's how good a person you are. Being alive."

He patted me on the arm.

"Come on. Interesting anthropological phenomenon I've read about on the Internet I shall point out to you tonight, of the kind you probably don't see back in Dead Rat, Kentucky. Id est, women who would, under normal circumstances, not show their tits for a hundred quid, who will be only too pleased to get 'em out for the crowd for some cheap plastic beads."

"Universal trading medium," I said. "Beads."

"Fuck," he said. "There's a paper in that. Come on. You ever had a Jell-O shot, Jackson?"

"No."

"Me neither. Bet they'll be disgusting. Let's go and see."

We paid for our drinks. I had to remind him to tip.

"By the way," I said. "F. Scott Fitzgerald. What was his wife's name?"

"Zelda? What about her?"

"Nothing," I said.

Zelda. Zora. Whatever. We went out.

3
"Nothing, like something, happens anywhere"

Midnight, give or take. We were in a bar on Bourbon Street, me and the English anthropology prof, and he started buying drinks—real drinks, this place didn't do Jell-O shots—for a couple of dark-haired women at the bar. They looked so similar they might have been sisters. One wore a red ribbon in her hair; the other wore a white ribbon. Gauguin might have painted them, only he would have painted them bare-breasted, and without the silver mouse-skull earrings. They laughed a lot.

We had seen a small party of academics walk past the bar at one point, being led by a guide with a black umbrella. I pointed them out to Campbell.

The woman with the red ribbon raised an eyebrow. "They go on the Haunted History tours, looking for ghosts. You want to say, 'Dude, this is where the ghosts come; this is where the dead stay.' Easier to go looking for the living."

"You saying the tourists are *alive?*" said the other, mock concern on her face.

"When they *get* here," said the first, and they both laughed at that.

They laughed a lot.

The one with the white ribbon laughed at everything Campbell said. She would tell him, "Say 'fuck' again," and he would say it, and she would say "Fook! Fook!" trying to copy him. And he'd say, "It's not *fook,* it's *fuck,*" and she couldn't hear the difference, and would laugh some more.

After two drinks, maybe three, he took her by the hand and walked her into the back of the bar, where music was playing, and it was dark, and there were a couple of people already, if not dancing, then moving against each other.

I stayed where I was, beside the woman with the red ribbon in her hair.

She said, "So you're in the record company too?"

I nodded. It was what Campbell had told them we did. "I hate telling people I'm a fucking academic," he had said reasonably, when they were in the ladies' room. Instead he had told them that he had discovered Oasis.

"How about you? What do you do in the world?"

She said, "I'm a priestess of Santeria. Me, I got it all in my blood; my papa was Brazilian, my momma was Irish-Cherokee. In Brazil, everybody makes love with everybody and they have the best little brown babies. Everybody got black slave blood; everybody got Indian blood; my poppa even got some Japanese blood. His brother, my uncle, he looks Japanese. My poppa, he just a good-looking man. People think it was my poppa I got the Santeria from, but no, it was my grandmomma—said she was Cherokee, but I had her figgered for mostly high yaller when I saw the old photographs. When I was three I was talking to dead folks. When I was five I watched a huge black dog, size of a

Harley-Davidson, walking behind a man in the street; no one could see it but me. When I told my mom, she told my grandmomma, they said, 'She's got to know; she's got to learn.' There was people to teach me, even as a little girl.

"I was never afraid of dead folk. You know that? They never hurt you. So many things in this town can hurt you, but the dead don't hurt you. Living people hurt you. They hurt you so bad."

I shrugged.

"This is a town where people sleep with each other, you know. We make love to each other. It's something we do to show we're still alive."

I wondered if this was a come-on. It did not seem to be.

She said, "You hungry?"

"A little," I said.

She said, "I know a place near here they got the best bowl of gumbo in New Orleans. Come on."

I said, "I hear it's a town where you're best off not walking on your own at night."

"That's right," she said. "But you'll have me with you. You're safe, with me with you."

Out on the street, college girls were flashing their breasts to the crowds on the balconies. For every glimpse of nipple the onlookers would cheer and throw plastic beads. I had known the red-ribbon woman's name earlier in the evening, but now it had evaporated.

"Used to be they only did this shit at Mardi Gras," she said. "Now the tourists expect it, so it's just tourists doing it for the tourists. The locals don't care. When you need to piss," she added, "you tell me."

"Okay. Why?"

"Because most tourists who get rolled, get rolled when they go into the alleys to relieve themselves. Wake up an hour later in Pirates' Alley with a sore head and an empty wallet."

"I'll bear that in mind."

She pointed to an alley as we passed it, foggy and deserted. "Don't go there," she said.

The place we wound up in was a bar with tables. A TV on above the bar showed *The Tonight Show* with the sound off and subtitles on, although the subtitles kept scrambling into numbers and fractions. We ordered the gumbo, a bowl each.

I was expecting more from the best gumbo in New Orleans. It was almost tasteless. Still, I spooned it down, knowing that I needed food, that I had had nothing to eat that day.

Three men came into the bar. One sidled; one strutted; one shambled. The sidler was dressed like a Victorian undertaker, high top hat and all. His skin was fish-belly pale; his hair was long and stringy; his beard was long and threaded with silver beads. The strutter was dressed in a long black leather coat, dark clothes underneath. His skin was very black. The last one, the shambler, hung back, waiting by the door. I could not see much of his face, nor decode his race: what I could see of his skin was a dirty gray. His lank hair hung over his face. He made my skin crawl.

The first two men made straight to our table, and I was, momentarily, scared for my skin, but they paid no attention to me. They looked at the woman with the red ribbon, and both of the men kissed her on the cheek. They asked about friends they had not seen, about who did what to whom in which bar and why. They reminded me of the fox and the cat from *Pinocchio*.

"What happened to your pretty girlfriend?" the woman asked the black man.

He smiled, without humor. "She put a squirrel tail on my family tomb."

She pursed her lips. "Then you better off without her."

"That's what I say."

I glanced over at the one who gave me the creeps. He was a filthy thing, junkie thin, gray-lipped. His eyes were downcast. He barely moved. I wondered what the three men were doing together: the fox and the cat and the ghost.

Then the white man took the woman's hand and pressed it to his lips, bowed to her, raised a hand to me in a mock salute, and the three of them were gone.

"Friends of yours?"

"Bad people," she said. "Macumba. Not friends of anybody."

"What was up with the guy by the door? Is he sick?"

She hesitated; then she shook her head. "Not really. I'll tell you when you're ready."

"Tell me now."

On the TV, Jay Leno was talking to a thin blond woman, IT&S NOT .UST T½E MOVIE, said the caption. SO H.VE SS YOU SE¾N THE AC ION F!GURE? He picked up a small toy from his desk, pretended to check under its skirt to make sure it was anatomically correct, [LAUGHTER], said the caption.

She finished her bowl of gumbo, licked the spoon with a red, red tongue, and put it down in the bowl. "A lot of kids they come to New Orleans. Some of them read Anne Rice books and figure they learn about being vampires here. Some of them have abusive parents; some are just bored. Like stray kittens living in drains, they come here. They found a whole new breed of cat living in a drain in New Orleans, you know that?"

"No."

SLAUGHTER S] said the caption, but Jay was still grinning, and *The Tonight Show* went to a car commercial.

"He was one of the street kids, only he had a place to crash at night. Good kid. Hitchhiked from LA to New Orleans. Wanted to be left alone to smoke a little weed, listen to his Doors cassettes, study up on chaos magick and read the complete works of Aleister Crowley. Also get his dick sucked. He wasn't particular about who did it. Bright eyes and bushy tail."

"Hey," I said. "That was Campbell. Going past. Out there."

"Campbell?"

"My friend."

"The record producer?" She smiled as she said it, and I thought, *She knows. She knows he was lying. She knows what he is.*

I put down a twenty and a ten on the table, and we went out onto the street, to find him, but he was already gone. "I thought he was with your sister," I told her.

"No sister," she said. "No sister. Only me. Only me."

We turned a comer and were engulfed by a crowd of noisy tourists, like a sudden breaker crashing onto the shore. Then, as fast as they had come, they were gone, leaving only a handful of people behind them. A teenaged girl was throwing up in a gutter, a young man nervously standing near her, holding her purse and a plastic cup half-full of booze.

The woman with the red ribbon in her hair was gone. I wished I had made a note of her name, or the name of the bar in which I'd met her.

I had intended to leave that night, to take the interstate west to Houston and from there to Mexico, but I was tired and two-thirds drunk, and instead I went back to my room. When the morning came I was still in the Marriott. Everything I had worn the night before smelled of perfume and rot.

I put on my T-shirt and pants, went down to the hotel gift shop, picked out a couple more T-shirts and a pair of shorts. The tall woman, the one without the bicycle, was in there, buying some Alka-Seltzer.

She said, "They've moved your presentation. It's now in the Audubon Room, in about twenty minutes. You might want to clean your teeth first. Your best friends won't tell you, but I hardly know you, Mister Anderton, so I don't mind telling you at all."

I added a traveling toothbrush and toothpaste to the stuff I was buying. Adding to my possessions, though, troubled me. I felt I should be shedding them. I needed to be transparent, to have nothing.

I went up to the room, cleaned my teeth, put on the jazz festival T-shirt. And then, because I had no choice in the matter; or because I was doomed to confer, consult, and otherwise hobnob; or because I was pretty certain Campbell would be in the audience and I wanted to say good-bye to him before I drove away, I picked up the typescript and went down to the Audubon Room, where fifteen people were waiting. Campbell was not one of them.

I was not scared. I said hello, and I looked at the top of page one.

It began with another quote from Zora Neale Hurston:

Big Zombies who come in the night to do malice are talked about. Also the little girl Zombies who are sent out by their owners in the dark dawn to sell little packets of roasted coffee. Before sun-up their cries of "Café grillé" can be heard from dark places in the streets and one can only see them if one calls out for the seller to come with the goods. Then the little dead one makes herself visible and mounts the steps.

Anderton continued on from there, with quotations from Hurston's contemporaries and several extracts from old interviews with older Haitians, the man's paper leaping, as far as I was able to tell, from conclusion to conclusion, spinning fancies into guesses and suppositions and weaving those into facts.

Halfway through, Margaret, the tall woman without the bicycle, came in and simply stared at me. I thought, *She knows I'm not him. She knows.* I kept reading though. What else could I do? At the end, I asked for questions.

Somebody asked me about Zora Neale Hurston's research practices. I said that was a very good question, which was addressed at greater length in the finished paper, of which what I had read was essentially an edited abstract.

Someone else—a short, plump woman—stood up and announced that the zombie girls could not have existed: zombie drugs and powders numbed you, induced deathlike trances, but still worked fundamentally on belief—the belief that you were now one of the dead, and had no will of your own. How, she asked, could a child of four or five be induced to believe such a thing? No. The coffee girls were, she said, one with the Indian rope trick, just another of the urban legends of the past.

Personally I agreed with her, but I nodded and said that her points were well made and well taken, and that from my perspective—which was, I hoped, a genuinely anthropological perspective—what mattered was not whether it was easy to believe, but, much more importantly, if it was the truth.

They applauded, and afterward a man with a beard asked me whether he might be able to get a copy of the paper for a journal he edited. It occurred to me that it was a good thing that I had come to New Orleans, that Anderton's career would not be harmed by his absence from the conference.

The plump woman, whose badge said her name was Shanelle Gravely-King, was waiting for me at the door. She said, "I really enjoyed that. I don't want you to think that I didn't."

Campbell didn't turn up for his presentation. Nobody ever saw him again.

Margaret introduced me to someone from New York and mentioned that Zora Neale Hurston had worked on *The Great Gatsby.* The man said yes, that was pretty common knowledge these days. I wondered if she had called the police, but she seemed friendly enough. I was starting to stress, I realized. I wished I had not thrown away my cell phone.

Shanelle Gravely-King and I had an early dinner in the hotel, at the beginning of which I said, "Oh, let's not talk shop." And she agreed that only the very dull talked shop at the table, so we talked about rock bands we had seen live, fictional methods of slowing the decomposition of a human body, and about her partner, who was a woman older than she was and who owned a restaurant, and then we went up to my room. She smelled of baby powder and jasmine, and her naked skin was clammy against mine.

Over the next couple of hours I used two of the three condoms. She was sleeping by the time I returned from the bathroom, and I climbed into the bed next to her. I thought about the words Anderton had written, hand-scrawled on the back of a page of the typescript, and I wanted to check them, but I fell asleep, a soft-fleshed jasmine-scented woman pressing close to me.

After midnight, I woke from a dream, and a woman's voice was whispering in the darkness.

She said, "So he came into town, with his Doors cassettes and his Crowley books, and his handwritten list of the secret URLs for chaos magick on the Web, and everything was good. He even got a few disciples, runaways like him, and he got his dick sucked whenever he wanted, and the world was good.

"And then he started to believe his own press. He thought he was the real thing. That he was the dude. He thought he was a big mean tiger-cat, not a little kitten. So he dug up… something… someone else wanted.

"He thought the something he dug up would look after him. Silly boy. And that night, he's sitting in Jackson Square, talking to the Tarot readers, telling them about Jim Morrison and the cabala, and someone taps him on the shoulder, and he turns, and someone blows powder into his face, and he breathes it in.

"Not all of it. And he is going to do something about it, when he realizes there's nothing to be done, because he's all paralyzed. There's fugu fish and toad skin and ground bone and everything else in that powder, and he's breathed it in.

"They take him down to emergency, where they don't do much for him, figuring him for a street rat with a drug problem, and by the next day he can move again, although it's two, three days until he can speak.

"Trouble is, he needs it. He wants it. He knows there's some big secret in the zombie powder, and he was almost there. Some people say they mixed heroin with it, some shit like that, but they didn't even need to do that. He wants it.

"And they told him they wouldn't sell it to him. But if he did jobs for them, they'd give him a little zombie powder, to smoke, to sniff, to rub on his gums, to swallow. Sometimes they'd give him nasty jobs to do no one else wanted. Sometimes they'd just humiliate him because they could—make him eat dog shit from the gutter, maybe. Kill for them, maybe. Anything but die. All skin and bones. He'd do anything for his zombie powder.

"And he still thinks, in the little bit of his head that's still him, that he's not a zombie. That he's not dead, that there's a threshold he hasn't stepped over. But he crossed it long time ago."

I reached out a hand, and touched her. Her body was hard, and slim, and lithe, and her breasts felt like breasts that Gauguin might have painted. Her mouth, in the darkness, was soft and warm against mine.

People come into your life for a reason.

4
"Those people ought to know who we are and tell that we are here"

When I woke, it was still almost dark, and the room was silent. I turned on the light, looked on the pillow for a ribbon, white or red, or for a mouse-skull earring, but there was nothing to show that there had ever been anyone in the bed that night but me.

I got out of bed and pulled open the drapes, looked out of the window. The sky was graying in the east.

I thought about moving south, about continuing to run, continuing to pretend I was alive. But it was, I knew now, much too late for that. There are doors, after all, between the living and the dead, and they swing in both directions.

I had come as far as I could.

There was a faint *tap-tapping* on the hotel-room door. I pulled on my pants and the T-shirt I had set out in, and barefoot, I pulled the door open.

The coffee girl was waiting for me.

Everything beyond the door was touched with light, an open, wonderful predawn light, and I heard the sound of birds calling on the morning air. The street was on a hill, and the houses facing me were little more than shanties. There was mist in the air, low to the ground, curling like something from an old black-and-white film, but it would be gone by noon.

The girl was thin and small; she did not appear to be more than six years old. Her eyes were cobwebbed with what might have been cataracts; her skin was as gray as it had once been brown. She was holding a white hotel cup out to me, holding it carefully, with one small hand on the handle, one hand beneath the saucer. It was half filled with a steaming mud-colored liquid.

I bent to take it from her, and I sipped it. It was a very bitter drink, and it was hot, and it woke me the rest of the way.

I said, "Thank you."

Someone, somewhere, was calling my name. The girl waited, patiently, while I finished the coffee. I put the cup down on the carpet; then I put out my hand and touched her shoulder. She reached up her hand, spread her small gray fingers, and took hold of mine. She knew I was with her. Wherever we were headed now, we were going there together.

I remembered something somebody had once said to me. "It's okay. Every day is freshly ground," I told her.

The coffee girl's expression did not change, but she nodded, as if she had heard me, and gave my arm an impatient tug. She held my hand tight with her cold, cold fingers, and we walked, finally, side by side into the misty dawn.

SHE'S TAKING HER TITS TO THE GRAVE

by Catherine Cheek

Catherine Cheek has sold fiction to magazines such as *Ideomancer*, *Susurrus*, and *Cat Tales*. She also has stories forthcoming in anthologies such as *The Leonardo Variations*—an anthology to benefit the Clarion Writers' Workshop, of which Cheek is a graduate—and *Last Drink Bird Head*, a charity anthology whose proceeds will go toward promoting literacy. When not writing, Cheek plays with molten glass and takes care of her two children (and nine pets).

The idea for this story came from the theme of the 2007 World Fantasy Convention which was "ghosts and revenants." Cheek didn't know what a revenant was, so she looked it up and discovered it was a person who came back from the dead and caused great trouble for the living. "It's that last part that intrigued me," she says. "What kind of trouble could they cause?"

Cheek could relate to the character in the story—a trophy wife who returns from the dead to find her body is not what it used to be. "My body is getting older every day, and I suspect that it will one day actually stop working," she says. "Life is a fatal epidemic."

Melanie hitchhiked for the first time ever after she climbed out of her grave. A week later, and she wouldn't have been able to flirt her way into the trunk of a late model sedan, much less shotgun with full access to the radio. But she had had a stellar figure, a southern California tan, and bleach-blonde hair that could pass for natural. Maintaining a beautiful body had landed her a rich husband, and she'd kept the position of wife long past the time when a less successful trophy would have been replaced.

That nice face and body still served her, for the embalmers had done a great job preserving her not-inconsequential looks. The middle-aged chiropractor who drove her from the cemetery would happily have driven her all the way across town to the house she shared with Brandon, her husband, but she decided to go to Larry's condo first.

More than anything else, she needed to find the man who had raised her from the dead.

A few people noticed as she walked from the parking lot to Larry's door, and she got some second looks, but she paid them no mind. People often mistook her for an actress or a model here in Los Angeles, the land of the Barbie.

The steps up to Larry's condo seemed endless when you were wearing four-inch heels. She smoothed her hair, cleared her throat before knocking on Larry's door, and felt a thrill of anticipation. Wasn't he going to be happy to see she was alive again!

But Larry's mouth gaped, closed partially, then reopened. His eyes bugged out, like a fish flopping on a shore gasping for air.

"What are *you* doing here?" Larry finally said. "I thought you were dead."

"I am." She pushed her way into the condo, irritated. For that, she didn't slip her pumps off and line them up next to his five pairs of shoes on the tile, but tracked grave dirt across his white carpet. "And I don't appreciate you raising me from the grave if this is the kind of welcome I'm going to get."

Larry had slipped on his loafers to walk two feet from the carpet to the door, and now he took them off. His linen pants were cuffed, but not wrinkled, and he smoothed the fabric out as he settled at the far edge of the couch. "Why are you here?"

"Because you raised me." Melanie looked at her fingers. The grave had not yet been filled in with dirt, a small blessing, but her manicure looked terrible. "Why are you being such a prick? Come on, it's me, baby."

"Did someone murder you?" Larry asked. He perched on the edge of the cushion, hands resting on knees, leaning away from her. "Is that why you're haunting the living?"

"No one killed me, Larry, I just went in for a routine tummy tuck. Must have been some kind of complication."

"So if no one murdered you, why are you haunting me?"

Melanie frowned. She'd been excited to see him, flattered that he loved her enough to raise her from the dead, but now it was apparent that he didn't. All those times he swore he couldn't get enough of her, and now he was tapping nicotine-stained fingers (and she had always hated how his condo stank like cigarettes), his gaze flicking towards the door. Why had she ever slept with this man?

Back when she was alive, a strong chest and blue eyes must have outweighed his other faults. "Aren't you going to offer me a drink?"

"You want a drink?" he spluttered, as though pouring a glass of wine for the woman he'd been carrying on an affair with for four months was the last thing on his mind. "You want a *drink?*"

"I want *something.*"

"I, uh, I've got some orange juice."

He got the drink from the fridge, still sidling around her as though she were a crazy bag lady instead of a rich, young (young-looking, anyway) and beautiful woman who, now that she was thinking about it, was probably too good for him. After he handed her the glass, he watched her drink it, not sitting, but standing expectantly, as though she were an auditor, or an in-law: someone distasteful he couldn't wait to get rid of. After she drank the orange juice, she realized the discomfort was mutual.

Funny, when she'd first met him, she had thought he might be the kind of lover who'd keep her amused for years, a secret pleasure for when Brandon was working late again, a not-so-secret one for when Brandon went out of town. And yet by the time she finished the orange juice, she realized that what had started as a very promising affair was over.

As suddenly as, well, as death.

"Gotta go," she said, setting the half-finished glass of orange juice on the coffee table, next to the coaster. "I'm late."

Larry didn't laugh or offer her a ride home, and she had already walked down all the stairs when she remembered she didn't have her car.

It was easier to go without a soul than a car in this town. She felt her skirt for keys which weren't there, since they don't bury you with car keys, and muttered some unladylike words. They don't bury you with a purse, either, no matter if it was Prada and went very well with the shoes. And they don't bury you with money, or even a bus pass, that mythology about the river Styx notwithstanding.

Nor had she ever walked so far in her life. No one had ever told her how awkward it would be to find her way home when she was used to having a car, and now she had to navigate around freeway overpasses and alley walls behind shopping complexes, which would have been no fun to traverse even if she were alive and wearing sensible footwear.

She thought about hitchhiking again, but decided she didn't really want to talk. She'd just ended an affair, after all. She needed some alone time.

But it was warm for May, and the horizon held a brown layer of smog. No one left their cars, no one walked the streets if they could help it, and the air had a grimy feel to it that would have burned her lungs if she were still breathing. She walked for several hours, until she wanted someone to give her a ride, her husband maybe, or a girlfriend. Then she wanted someone to talk to. And maybe a glass of merlot.

By the time she staggered up the pavement in front of their house, the lacquered layer of hairspray on her professionally dyed hair was starting to flake off, she was getting a little squishy around the eyes, and the flies kept landing on her, especially her eyes and mouth. She tried to wave them off, but her coordination wasn't what it should have been, so she kept smacking her boobs. Those were still as plump as ever, which was only fitting seeing as how she had paid more for them than she had for her first car. Her sister Jessica had mocked her for the waste of money, but Jessica had the same flat chest Melanie had been cursed with and hadn't even managed to get married.

She undid another button, displaying more of the cleavage she had bought. Men loved her breasts. Someone had raised her from the dead just so they could see them again.

Probably Brandon. Her husband was the kind of guy who could make anything happen with enough money. She'd have to thank him when she saw him again, but right now she was tired, she was irritable, and she needed a drink.

Melanie pounded at the door, even though Brandon wouldn't be home. Maybe the housekeeper would let her in.

A woman screamed.

Melanie turned. The petite blonde wore a camel-colored suit that might have been Chanel until someone let out the seams beyond what its lines were ever meant to bear. She kept screaming, her hands in the air (holding a set of car keys that looked suspiciously familiar), and screaming, and screaming, until it became obvious to the both of them that no Dudley Do-Right was going to sweep out of the bushes and save her.

Brandon's secretary, Cindy. She better be there just to drop something off, Melanie thought. Just because she was dead didn't mean Brandon could cheat. Melanie waited until the buxom waif grew hoarse.

Cindy tapered off to fluttering hands near her throat, and finally, when nothing else seemed to work, the girl spoke.

"You… you're dead!"

"Is Brandon home?"

"You're dead!"

Cindy began to scream again, which was really irritating, because one, Melanie still wanted a decent drink, and two, she needed to see Brandon to figure out what to do about this whole "rising from the grave" nuisance. Cindy kept screaming, so Melanie finally plucked the keychain directly from her fingers. Sure enough, there was a house key. Melanie unwound it from the ring.

"You can't do that!" Cindy had regained some spunk, even if it was just the pique of a woman whose sorority sister had just puked on her new blouse. "Those are *mine*."

She tried to take them back, and might have succeeded (death does terrible things to your muscle tone) except at that point, the orange juice that Melanie had drunk poured down her leg, embarrassing them both. It wasn't pee, she wanted to explain, it was just orange juice and maybe a little embalming fluid, but there was no way to gracefully recover from such an event, no matter what finishing school you had attended, so neither tried. They just stared at each other for a long uncomfortable moment. Melanie dropped the key ring.

With an exaggerated shudder, Cindy scooped up the keys and drove off. In Melanie's Mercedes. In her Mercedes!

"You bitch!" Melanie screamed at the car as it squealed away. Only dead a few days and Brandon was letting his secretary drive *her* Mercedes? He'd better offer her several karats of apology for that.

Melanie let herself in the house and went straight to the bar. She poured herself a drink, and then another. She accidentally spilled some vermouth on her blouse, so she decided to change out of her grave outfit and have a shower. She had a really beautiful shower, she decided. The whole house was beautiful, really, and her clothing had been tastefully selected. She'd taken it for granted while she was alive, but now that she was dead, the luxury of organic cotton towels and travertine underfoot actually meant something to her. Maybe it wasn't a living-dead thing, maybe it was just relief that she was finally home, where she was supposed to be.

She did her Pilates video workout and her nightly skin care regimen, then went to bed, only to find that she couldn't sleep.

She turned on the television.

The next day, she skipped the Pilates workout.

Melanie found the remote and sat on the leather couch, putting her feet on a stack of magazines that she'd finally have time to read. The TiVo had four solid days' worth of programming on it, which for once sounded encouraging rather than daunting. She'd hardly had time for it before—she'd had too many hair and manicure and personal trainer appointments—but now that she was dead, there seemed little point.

Besides, after all she'd been through, she deserved a little "me" time.

The calendar on the fridge said her husband would be home in three days, but it was closer to five. By that time, she'd grown decidedly squishy, and not just around the eyes. Her fingers shrank at the tips, giving her a claw-like appearance that begged for an acrylic fill. The flesh on her thighs sagged, detaching from the bones. She thought about the liposuction she'd gotten, and tsked silently.

Melanie watched QVC, drank everything in the liquor cabinet, and felt her body decompose. Really, Brandon was being insensitive; he could have at least called. She emailed him, then emailed her mom and her sister, just to say hi, back from the dead, what's up with you?

She was lonely. She wanted comfort and companionship so desperately that she'd already decided not to be bitchy, to let the appearance of the blonde bimbo (who looked like a younger version of herself, she decided) just pass over. She could always argue about it later, and anyway, she'd always suspected that Brandon led a double life. She had had her lovers; why should he be any different?

The key rattled, and Brandon opened the kitchen door.

"Dear God," Brandon said, garment bag dangling off his shoulder and laptop case in his hand. "What's that horrible smell?"

"That's not very nice," said Melanie, feeling hurt. She had endured a lot in the past few days, and while she considered herself thick-skinned, Brandon's complete lack of empathy pissed her off. "Here I am, risen from the grave, even if not exactly fresh any more, and all you can do is complain that I'm a corpse? What did you expect?"

"Melanie?" Brandon said, his voice half wonderment and half horror. The garment bag slipped from his hands. He turned and vomited in the sink.

If Melanie's tear ducts had been still functional, she probably would have cried. Really, why did he have to be so dramatic?

She stood, leaving a puddle of formaldehyde-tainted liquor and various body fluids on the couch. (She didn't feel guilty; it was only from IKEA.) She meant to seductively slink into the kitchen, one hand coquettishly outlining her cleavage, but she couldn't manage more than a shuffle. It was a wonder her tongue still worked, when you came to think about it.

"What were you doing, planning a business trip right after you raised me from the dead? Didn't you think you might need to be here for me?"

Brandon made strangled gurgling noises. He pressed himself against the granite-topped island, hands splayed out as though he were Vanna White and the under-counter wine case a lovely vowel.

It was an awkward pose, Melanie decided. Actually this whole situation was awkward. "Brandon…"

"God, no, please no…"

She gave him her best pout. That pout had gotten her emeralds before, but now it seemed broken. She sighed. "So, what now? Why did you raise me from the dead?"

"No, no, no…" he moaned.

She snapped her fingers in front of his face. "Hello!" *She* was the one who had died, what right did he have to act like his life was turned upside down? He had always been a firm, take-charge kind of guy. An alpha male, he called himself. He dominated in tennis, took no prisoners when he negotiated a deal, and drove like an asshole on the freeway. And yet here he was, bawling like a scared little boy.

"Brandon!" she tried again, and when that didn't work, she slapped him.

It wasn't much of a slap, but as soon as her flesh touched his face, Brandon's eyes rolled up in his head and he passed out, smacking his head against the counter and then the floor, his hands squeaking uselessly down the front of the dishwasher.

She sighed, and put her hands on her hips. Useless. Completely useless. And he obviously wasn't the person who had raised her. She nudged him with her foot, but he wasn't faking.

Melanie found her purse and her cell phone. She took his keys out of his pocket. She was going to take the z4, but she felt a little bad about slapping him, so she took the Audi instead. And even though he'd never liked the upholstery color, she put a plastic bag over the driver's seat, because the half case of Rémy she'd drunk wasn't preserving her as alcohol was supposed to. It seemed to be turning her insides into a slurry of decay.

At this rate, she'd be nothing but a skeleton before the month was out.

Melanie got behind the wheel of the Audi and took off, hoping that some innate psychic sense would take her to the person that brought her back from the grave.

It didn't. She took out her cell phone and dialed 411.

"Hello, can you give me the name of a necromancer?" she asked the operator.

"I'm sorry, we don't have that listing."

"Try surrounding cities, anything in Los Angeles County," Melanie said. She'd never heard of someone looking up necromancers in the yellow pages, but there were apparently a lot of things she'd never heard of which existed.

"Sorry, ma'am. Nothing."

"How about 'witch-doctor'?" she asked.

"I'm sorry, we don't have that—" The phone flew out of her hand and her already damaged face smacked the steering wheel.

Melanie touched her face, and her hand came away sticky. Steam rose from the front of her car, the hood crumpled into an M. Great, that was just what she needed, to rear-end someone. The little Geo Metro ahead of her had also been crumpled, its frame bent around the base of the tire.

Well, at least it wasn't an expensive car.

And it was her fault. She used to make calls while driving all the time, but now that she was decomposing, her reflexes had slipped.

She pulled her car to a gas station on the other side of the intersection.

"My baby! You hurt my baby!" The other driver had neglected her car in the intersection and walked towards Melanie, despite the fact that traffic whizzed by them.

Melanie didn't see a car seat in the other vehicle, but a bat-eared Chihuahua's head peered out of the woman's arms, and she realized the woman was talking about her dog.

How ridiculous. The woman had been in a car accident, just *survived* it, and she was worried about her stupid pet?

"I'm going to sue! My baby has whiplash!" The woman shook the dog at Melanie's side window to demonstrate. "Do you hear me? Whiplash!"

Melanie turned the engine off and fumbled on the floorboards for her cell phone. She'd hoped she'd be able to get out of this without calling the cops, but that didn't look like it was going to happen. She put on her sunglasses, unbuckled her seat belt, and opened the door.

"Eww!" the woman said audibly, as if Melanie stunk like old garbage. She put her hands to her nose, except she was still holding the dog, so it went too.

Melanie decided she didn't like the Chihuahua woman. True, she hadn't had a shower in a few days, but the woman was rude. "Get your car out of the road, so you don't block traffic."

"Oh, my God," the woman said, in a horrified gasp. "Your face!"

"What?" Melanie wrenched the rear view mirror to inspect herself. The steering wheel had torn flesh away from her forehead, exposing bone. She almost cried. Her beautiful face, gashed open. Make-up wouldn't fix that.

Her lip started to quiver, and her throat closed up as if she were about to sob. She had *known* this would happen someday—she was finally losing her looks.

The Chihuahua wriggled out of its owner's grasp and scampered forward, its bark like the bark of a real dog played at 78rpm. When it reached Melanie's leg, it chomped into her lower calf, shaking its head back and forth until it tore off a chunk. The rat-dog sank its teeth in, gnawing as though it had found a delectable morsel.

"Bitsy! Bitsy, stop it!" The woman picked up her Chihuahua and pulled the piece of flesh out of its mouth. "That's dirty, don't eat that."

"Dirty!" Melanie wailed. That was it. She wasn't going to deal with this bitch's problems. Rat-dog woman would have to deal with the mess herself. "Screw you!"

She stormed off, crossing the street without even bothering to look for traffic. Cars screeched and honked, one missing her by inches, but she didn't care. Peace and quiet, though…

Oh, and to find whoever had raised her from the dead, but since there weren't any warlocks in her social circle, there was the horrifying possibility that it was an old boyfriend from high school or someone she barely even knew, but whoever it was, he could find her on his own.

She was done with living people. The living were so rude, so… judgmental about the least bit of decay.

She looked around, getting her bearings. She'd started driving without any goal in mind, and realized she'd driven north of Van Nuys, not too far from where she'd lived as a child. Hills rose ahead of her. She and her sister used to climb to the top of those hills to see the sunset when they were younger.

She took the crow's path, cutting across lawns and parking lots and once over a chain-link fence despite a "No Trespassing" sign. What was the point of following city ordinances when you weren't even obeying the laws of nature?

Flesh was falling off faster now. She'd been buried more than a week earlier, after all, and the temperatures had to be in the nineties. Flies clustered around her wound, each carrying off a small mouthful. She thought of them as lightening her load.

The tendons in her legs weren't working as well as they had, and her gait slowed to a weary shuffle, but since she didn't have to sleep or rest or eat (though she wouldn't have minded a glass of wine) she was able to travel all afternoon and through the night. She didn't mind.

By dawn she'd reached far enough up the hill that she could see pinkish light creep over the town. She carefully sat down, her back against the concrete support of a power line, and watched the sun rise.

Time ceased to have meaning. The sun rose and set, animals carried on their daily business, and the trees got older. Her flesh rotted away, her skin and eyes dried and shrunk, and her lips pulled back. Her hair stayed blonde, her teeth were still white and straight, and her breasts still defied gravity (those silicone implants would last forever) but she didn't care much about that any more.

She'd grown lazy and peaceful, now that she didn't have anyone to impress. Whatever magic animated her left her able to think and see, even without eyes and a brain. On the day her sister hiked up the hill, she was still able to wave.

Jessica was boyishly thin and dirty, hair hanging around her face in walnut-colored dreadlocks. She had loose cargo pants, a tiny tank top, and a haversack made of Guatemalan fabric with *Peace Corp* written on it. Her neck was hung with bone and shell beads strung on thongs, and she had lines on her face even though she was only in her mid-thirties. She was more beautiful than anything.

Jessica sat down next to her gracefully, not winded from the climb up the hill.

"Oh, my God," Jess whispered. "I am so, so sorry."

"It's okay."

"No, I mean it. When I came back for the funeral, I had no idea. I mean, it was such a shock for me that you died in the first place, what with you being so young, and I completely forgot about the shaman. I'm sorry."

"Really, Jessica, it's okay."

"You can yell, it's okay, I deserve it. You must be so mad at me."

"No. I'm not mad. I'm happy." Jess was the only one who had been nice to Melanie since she died. How could she yell at someone who apologized to a corpse? "What happened?"

"It was this shaman, see, at least, he said he was a shaman, and he asked me if I wanted to live forever." Jess sat cross-legged with her elbows on her knees, as though she were used to sitting on the ground. "I said no, but my sister would, because you once said you were more afraid of getting old than anything else. It was kind of a joke."

Melanie waited for the rest of the story, but Jess stopped and leaned back. Melanie belatedly realized she'd been too silent. "Go on."

"I thought he was kidding. He was kind of drunk, you know? And then as soon as I got home from the funeral, I got an email from you, and then from Brandon, saying that you'd been wandering around scaring people, and I realized I'd really screwed things up. It took a month or so before I could get my visa sorted out and come back to the States again, or I would have been here earlier." Jess sighed. "I'm so sorry. It must have been horrible for you."

"No, not bad." Melanie said. It was getting harder to talk now that she didn't have lips. "Happens to everyone."

Jess pulled one of the bead and bone necklaces off. She laid it on the ground beside Melanie's bony hand. "I got him to give me this. This will let you die the second time, when you're ready." She kissed Melanie on the skull.

"Thanks," Melanie said. She didn't reach for the necklace yet, since she had all the time in the world. "But I'm going to enjoy the view for a while."

DEAD LIKE ME

by Adam-Troy Castro

Adam-Troy Castro is the author of the novel *Emissaries from the Dead*—an interstellar murder mystery, not a zombie novel, despite the title. He's also written three *Spider-Man* novels and a pop culture book called *My Ox is Broken!* about the television show *The Amazing Race*. His short fiction has appeared in such magazines as *The Magazine of Fantasy & Science Fiction*, *Science Fiction Age*, *Analog*, *Cemetery Dance*, and in a number of anthologies. His work has been nominated for several awards, including the Hugo, Nebula, and Stoker.

"Dead Like Me" is a set of instructions, to a hapless protagonist, about how to survive the zombie plague by joining it. The question that prompted it was: Zombies don't breathe, so how do they track their victims? "Certainly not by scent," Castro says. "If not by scent, how? If we know the method, can we fool them? And from there I got to: What will it cost?"

So. Let's summarize. You held out for longer than anybody would have ever dreamed possible. You fought with strength you never knew you had. But in the end it did you no damned good. There were just too many of the bastards. The civilization you believed in crumbled; the help you waited for never arrived; the hiding places you cowered in were all discovered; the fortresses you built were all overrun; the weapons you scrounged were all useless; the people you counted on were all either killed or corrupted; and what remained of your faith was torn raw and bleeding from the shell of the soft complacent man you once were. You lost. Period. End of story. No use whining about it. Now there's absolutely nothing left between you and the ravenous, hollow-eyed forms of the Living Dead.

Here's your Essay Question: How low are you willing to sink to survive?

Answer:

First, wake up in a dark, cramped space that smells of rotten meat. Don't wonder what time it is. It doesn't matter what time it is. There's no such thing as time anymore. It's enough that you've slept, and once again managed to avoid dreaming.

That's important. Dreaming is a form of thinking. And thinking is dangerous. Thinking is something the Living do, something the Dead can't abide. The
Dead can sense where it's coming from, which is why they were always able to
find you, back when you used to dream. Now that you've trained yourself to
shuffle through the days and nights of your existence as dully and mindlessly
as they do, there's no reason to hide from them anymore. Oh, they may curl
up against you as you sleep (two in particular, a man and woman handcuffed
together for some reason you'll never know, have crawled into this little alcove
with you), but that's different: that's just heat tropism. As long as you don't
actually think, they won't eat you.

Leave the alcove, which is an abandoned storage space in some kind of large
office complex. Papers litter the floor of the larger room outside; furniture
is piled up against some of the doors, meaning that sometime in the distant
past Living must have made their last stands here. There are no bones. There
are three other zombies, all men in the ragged remains of three-piece suits,
lurching randomly from one wall to the other, changing direction only when
they hit those walls, as if they're blind and deaf and this is the only way they
know how to look for an exit.

If you reach the door quickly they won't be able to react in time to follow
you.

Don't Remember.

Don't Remember your name. Only the Living have names.

Don't Remember you had a wife named Nina, and two children named Mark
and Kathy, who didn't survive your flight from the slaughterhouse Manhattan had become. Don't Remember them; any of them. Only the Living have
families.

Don't Remember that as events herded you south you wasted precious weeks
combing the increasing chaos of rural Pennsylvania for your big brother Ben,
who lived in Pittsburgh and had always been so much stronger and braver
than you. Don't Remember your childish, shellshocked hope that Ben would
be able to make everything all right, the way he had when you were both growing up with nothing. Don't Remember gradually losing even that hope, as the
enclaves of Living grew harder and harder to find.

The memories are part of you, and as long as you're still breathing, they'll
always be there if you ever decide you need them. It will always be easy to call
them up in all their gory detail. But you shouldn't want to. As long as you
remember enough to eat when you're hungry, sleep when you're tired, and
find warm places when you're cold, you know all you need to know, or ever
will need to know. It's much simpler that way.

Anything else is just an open invitation to the Dead.

Walk the way they walk: dragging your right foot, to simulate tendons that
have rotted away; hanging your head, to give the impression of a neck no longer

strong enough to hold it erect; recognizing obstructions only when you're in imminent danger of colliding with them. And though the sights before you comprise an entire catalogue of horrors, don't ever react.

Only the Living react.

This was the hardest rule for you to get down pat, because part of you, buried deep in the places that still belong to you and you alone, has been screaming continuously since the night you first saw a walking corpse rip the entrails from the flesh of the Living. That part wants to make itself heard. But that's the part which will get you killed. Don't let it have its voice.

Don't be surprised if you turn a corner, and almost trip over a limbless zombie inching its way up the street on its belly. Don't be horrified if you see a Living person trapped by a mob of them, about to be torn to pieces by them. Don't gag if one of the Dead brushes up against you, pressing its maggot-infested face up close against your own.

Remember: Zombies don't react to things like that. Zombies *are* things like that.

Now find a supermarket that still has stuff on the shelves. You can if you look hard enough; the Dead arrived too quickly for the Living to loot everything there was. Pick three or four cans off the shelves, cut them open, and eat whatever you find inside. Don't care whether they're soup, meat, vegetables, or dog food. Eat robotically, tasting nothing, registering nothing but the moment when you're full. Someday, picking a can at random, you may drink some drain cleaner or eat some rat poison. Chance alone will decide when that happens. But it won't matter when it does. Your existence won't change a bit. You'll just convulse, fall over, lie still a while, and then get up, magically transformed into one of the zombies you've pretended to be for so long. No fuss, no muss. You won't even have any reason to notice it when it happens. Maybe it's already happened.

After lunch, spot one of the town's few other Living people shuffling listlessly down the center of the street.

You know this one well. When you were still thinking in words you called her Suzie. She's dressed in clothes so old they're rotting off her back. Her hair is the color of dirty straw, and hideously matted from weeks, maybe months of neglect. Her most striking features are her sunken cheekbones and the dark circles under her gray unseeing eyes. Even so, you've always been able to tell that she must have been remarkably pretty, once.

Back when you were still trying to fight The Bastards—they were never "zombies" to you, back then; to you they were always The Bastards—you came very close to shooting Suzie's brains out before you realized that she was warm, and breathing, and alive. You saw that though she was just barely aware enough to scrounge the food and shelter that *kept* her warm and breathing, she was otherwise almost completely catatonic.

She taught you it was possible to pass for Dead.

She's never spoken a word to you, never smiled at you, never once greeted you with anything that even remotely resembled human feeling. But in the new world she's the closest thing you have to a lover. And as you instinctively cross the street to catch her, you should take some dim, distant form of comfort in the way she's also changed direction to meet you.

Remember, though: she's not really a lover. Not in the proper emotional sense of the word. The Dead hate love even more than they hate Thought. Only the Living love. But it's quite safe to fuck, and as long as you're here the two of you can fuck quite openly. Just like the Dead themselves do.

Of course, it's different with them. The necessary equipment is the first thing that rots away. But instinct keeps prodding them to try. Whenever some random cue rekindles the urge, they pick partners, and rub against each other in a clumsy, listless parody of sex that sometimes continues until both partners have been scraped into piles of carrion powder. The ultimate dry hump.

So feel no fear. It doesn't attract their attention when you and Suzie grab each other and go for a quickie in the middle of the street: to knead your hands against the novelty of warm skin, to smell stale sweat instead of the open grave, to take a rest from the horror that the world has become. Especially since, though you both do what you have to do, following all the mechanics of the act, neither one of you feels a damn thing. No affection, no pleasure, and certainly no joy.

That would be too dangerous.

Do what you have to do. Do it quickly. And then take your leave of each other. Exchange no kisses, no goodbyes, no cute terms of endearment, no acknowledgement that your tryst was anything but a collision between two strangers walking in opposite directions. Just stagger away without looking back. Maybe you'll see each other again. Maybe not. It really doesn't matter either way.

Spend the next few hours wandering from place to place, seeing nothing, hearing nothing, accomplishing nothing. But still drawing breath. Never forget that. Let the part of you still capable of caring about such things count that as a major victory.

At mid-afternoon pass the place where a school bus lies burned and blackened on one side. A small group of Living had trusted it to carry them to safety somewhere outside the city; but it didn't even get five blocks through the obstacle course of other crashed vehicles before hundreds of Dead had imprisoned them in a cage of groping flesh. You were a block and a half away, watching the siege, and when the people in the bus eventually blew themselves up, to avoid a more horrific end, the heat of the fireball singed the eyebrows from your face. At the time, you'd felt it served you right for not helping. These days, if you were capable of forming an opinion on anything, you'd feel that the Living were silly bastards.

It's stupid to resist. Only the Living resist. Resistance implies will, and if there's one thing the Dead don't have it's will. Exist the way they do, dully accepting everything that happens to you, and you stand a chance.

That's the one major reason your brother Ben is dead. Oh, you can't know what happened to him. You know what happened to your wife and kids—you know because you were watching, trapped behind a chain-link fence, as a lurching mob of what had once been elementary school children reduced them to shredded beef—but you'll never ever find out what happened to Ben. Still, if you ever did find out what happened to him, you would not be surprised. Because he'd always been a leader. A fighter. He'd always taken charge of every crisis that confronted him, and inspired others with his ability to carry them through. He was always special, that way. And when the Dead rose, he brought a whole bunch of naive trusting people down into his grave with him.

You, on the other hand, were never anything special. You were always a follower, a yes-man, an Oreo. You were always quick to kiss ass, and agree with anybody who raised his voice loudly enough. You never wanted to be anything but just another face in the crowd. And though this profited you well, in a society that was merely going to hell, it's been your single most important asset in the post-plague world that's already arrived there. It's the reason you're still breathing when all the brave, heroic, defiant, mythic ones like your brother Ben and the people in the school bus are just gnawed bones and Rorschach stains on the pavement.

Take pride in that. Don't pass too close to the sooty remains of the school bus, because you might remember how you stood downwind of their funeral pyre, letting it bathe your skin and fill your lungs with the ashes of their empty defiance. You might remember the cooked-meat, burnt rubber stench… the way the clouds billowed over you, and through you, as if you were far more insubstantial than they.

Don't let that happen. You'll attract Dead from blocks away. Force it back. Expunge it. Pretend it's not there. Turn your mind blank, your heart empty, and your soul, for lack of a better word, Dead.

There. That's better.

Still later that afternoon, while rummaging through the wreckage of a clothing store for something that will keep you warm during the rapidly approaching winter, you find yourself cornered and brutally beaten by the Living.

This is nothing to concern yourself with.

It's just the price you have to pay, for living in safety the way you do. They're just half-mad from spending their lives fleeing one feeding frenzy or another, and they have to let off some steam. It's not like they'll actually kill you, or hurt you so bad you'll sicken and die. At least not deliberately. They may go too far and kill you accidentally, but they won't kill you deliberately. There are already more than enough Dead people running around, giving them trouble. But they hate you. They consider people like you and Suzie traitors. And they wouldn't be able to respect themselves if they didn't let you know it.

There are four of them, this time: all pale, all in their late teens, all wearing the snottily evil grins of bullies whose chosen victim has detected their approach too late. The closest one is letting out slack from a coil of chain at his side. The chain ends in a padlock about the size of a fist. And though you try to summon your long-forgotten powers of speech, as their blows rain against your ribs, it really doesn't matter. They already know what you would say.

Don't beg.

Don't fight back.

Don't see yourself through their eyes.

Just remember: the Living might be dangerous, but the Dead are the real bastards.

It's later. You're in too much pain to move. That's all right. It'll go away, eventually. One way or the other. Alive or dead, you'll be up on your feet in no time.

Meanwhile, just lie there, in your own stink, in the wreckage of what used to be a clothing store, and for Christ's sake be quiet. Because only the Living scream.

Remember that time, not long after the Dead rose, when there were always screams? No matter how far you ran, how high you climbed or how deep you dug, there were always the screams, somewhere nearby, reminding you that though you might have temporarily found a safe haven for the night, there were always others who had found their backs against brick walls. Remember how you grew inured to those screams, after a while, and even found yourself able to sleep through them. And as the weeks turned to months, you found your tolerance rewarded—because the closer the number of survivors approached zero, the more that constant backdrop of screaming faded away to a long oppressive silence broken only by the low moans and random shuffling noises of the Dead.

It's a quiet world, now. And if you're to remain part of it, you're going to have to be quiet too. Even if your throat catches fire and your breath turns as ragged as sandpaper and your sweat pools in a puddle beneath you and your ribs scrape together every time you draw a breath and the naked mannequins sharing this refuge with you take on the look of Nina and Mark and Kathy and Ben and everybody else who ever mattered to you and the look on their faces becomes one of utter disgust and you start to hear their voices saying that you're nothing and that you were always nothing but that they'd never known you were as much a nothing as you've turned out to be. Shut up. Even if you want to tell them, these people who once meant everything to you, that you held on as long as any normal man could be expected to hold on, but there are limits, and you exceeded those limits, you really did, but there was just another set of limits beyond them, and another beyond those, and the new world kept making all these impossible demands on you and there were only so many impossible things you could bear. Be silent. Even if you hear Nina shrieking your name and Mark telling you he's afraid and Kathy screaming for you to save her. Even if you hear Ben demanding that you stand up like a man, for once.

Endure the pain. Ignore the fever. Don't listen to what your family is trying to tell you.

Why should you listen to *their* advice? It didn't help them.

No, this is what you should keep in mind, while you're waiting to see if you'll live or die:

On the off-chance you are still alive when you stumble to your feet tomorrow, don't look at the fitting mirror on the wall behind you. It's the first intact mirror you've encountered in months. Nothing unusual about that, of course: there just isn't much unshattered glass left in the world these days. But the looters and the rioters and the armies and the Living Dead have left this particular mirror untouched, and though it's horrendously discolored by dust, it still works well enough to destroy you.

If you don't look at it you'll be okay.

If you do look at it you'll see the matted blood in your tangled shoulder-length hair and the flies crawling in your long scraggly beard and the prominent ribs and the clothes so worn they exist only as strips of rags and the dirt and the sores and the broken nose and the swollen mouth and the closed slit that was until recently your left eye and you'll realize that this is as close to being Dead as you can get without actually being there, and that it sucks, and you'll be just in the right frame of mind, after your long night of delirium, to want to do something about it.

And you'll stagger out into the street, where the Dead will be milling about doing nothing the way they always do and you'll be in the center of them and you'll be overcome with a sudden uncontrollable anger and you'll open your mouth as wide as you can and you'll scream: *"Hey!"*

And the Dead will freeze in something very much resembling a double-take and slowly swivel in your direction and if you really wanted to you could bury everything burning you up inside down where it was only a minute ago and you won't want to and you'll scream *"Hey!"* again, in a voice that carries surprisingly far for something that hasn't been used in so long, and the Dead will start coming for you, and you won't care because you'll be screaming *"You hear me, you stinking bastards? I'm alive! I think and I feel and I care and I'm better than you because you'll never have that again!"*

And you'll die in agony screaming the names of everybody you used to love.

This may be what you want.

And granted, you will go out convinced you've just won a moral victory.

But remember, only the Living bother with such things; the Dead won't even be impressed. They'll just be hungry.

And if you let yourself die, then within minutes what's left of you will wake up hungry too, with only one fact still burning in its poor rotting skull: that Suzie's faking.

ZORA AND THE ZOMBIE

by Andy Duncan

Andy Duncan's fiction has appeared in magazines such as *Asimov's Science Fiction*, *Realms of Fantasy*, *Conjunctions*, *Weird Tales*, and *SCI FICTION*, and in anthologies such as *Starlight 1*, *Eclipse One*, *Mojo: Conjure Stories*, and *Wizards*. Much of his short fiction has been collected in *Beluthahatchie and Other Stories*, which won the World Fantasy Award. Duncan won the World Fantasy Award, again, for his story "The Pottawatomie Giant" and won the Theodore Sturgeon Memorial Award for "The Chief Designer." He also co-edited (with F. Brett Cox) the anthology *Crossroads: Tales of the Southern Literary Fantastic*. When not writing, Duncan teaches in the Honors College of the University of Alabama and works as a senior editor at a business-to-business magazine.

This story was a finalist for both the Stoker and Nebula awards. It was also reprinted in *The Year's Best Fantasy and Horror*, and in that volume, Duncan is quoted as saying that he'd been inspired by the work of Zora Neale Hurston for years, but that this story was the first time he'd attempted to write about her. "I marvel that many readers, judging from their comments, never heard of Hurston," he says. "Had I realized beforehand that this story would be many readers' introduction to her I wouldn't have dared write it."

"What is the truth?" the houngan shouted over the drums. The mambo, in response, flung open her white dress. She was naked beneath. The drummers quickened their tempo as the mambo danced among the columns in a frenzy. Her loose clothing could not keep pace with her kicks, swings and swivels. Her belt, shawl, kerchief, dress floated free. The mambo flung herself writhing onto the ground. The first man in line shuffled forward on his knees to kiss the truth that glistened between the mambo's thighs.

Zora's pencil point snapped. Ah, shit. Sweat-damp and jostled on all sides by the crowd, she fumbled for her penknife and burned with futility. Zora had learned just that morning that the Broadway hoofer and self-proclaimed anthropologist Katherine Dunham, on her Rosenwald fellowship to Haiti—the one that rightfully should have been Zora's—not only witnessed this very truth ceremony a year ago, for good measure underwent the three-day initiation to become Mama Katherine, bride of the serpent god Damballa—the heifer!

Three nights later, another houngan knelt at another altar with a platter full of chicken. People in the back began to scream. A man with a terrible face flung himself through the crowd, careened against people, spread chaos. His eyes rolled. The tongue between his teeth drooled blood. "He is mounted!" the people cried. "A loa has made him his horse." The houngan began to turn. The horse crashed into him. The houngan and the horse fell together, limbs entwined. The chicken was mashed into the dirt. The people moaned and sobbed. Zora sighed. She had read this in Herskovitz, and in Johnson too. Still, maybe poor fictional Tea Cake, rabid, would act like this. In the pandemonium she silently leafed to the novel section of her notebook. "Somethin' got after me in mah sleep, Janie," she had written. "Tried tuh choke me tuh death."

Another night, another compound, another pencil. The dead man sat up, head nodding forward, jaw slack, eyes bulging. Women and men shrieked. The dead man lay back down and was still. The mambo pulled the blanket back over him, tucked it in. Perhaps tomorrow, Zora thought, I will go to Pont Beudet, or to Ville Bonheur. Perhaps something new is happening there.

"Miss Hurston," a woman whispered, her heavy necklace clanking into Zora's shoulder. "Miss Hurston. Have they shared with you what was found a month ago? Walking by daylight in the Ennery road?"

Doctor Legros, chief of staff at the hospital at Gonaives, was a good-looking mulatto of middle years with pomaded hair and a thin mustache. His three-piece suit was all sharp creases and jutting angles, like that of a paper doll, and his handshake left Zora's palm powder dry. He poured her a belt of raw white clairin, minus the nutmeg and peppers that would make it palatable to Guede, the prancing black-clad loa of derision, but breathtaking nonetheless, and as they took dutiful medicinal sips his small talk was all big, all politics—whether Mr. Roosevelt would be true to his word that the Marines would never be back; whether Haiti's good friend Senator King of Utah had larger ambitions; whether America would support President Vincent if the grateful Haitians were to seek to extend his second term beyond the arbitrary date technically mandated by the Constitution—but his eyes, to Zora who was older than she looked and much older than she claimed, posed an entirely different set of questions. He seemed to view Zora as a sort of plenipotentiary from Washington, and only reluctantly allowed her to steer the conversation to the delicate subject of his unusual patient.

"It is important for your countrymen and your sponsors to understand, Miss Hurston, that the beliefs of which you speak are not the beliefs of civilized men, in Haiti or elsewhere. These are Negro beliefs, embarrassing to the rest of us, and confined to the canaille—to the, what is the phrase, the backwater areas, such as your American South. These beliefs belong to Haiti's past, not her future."

Zora mentally placed the good doctor waistcoat-deep in a backwater area of Eatonville, Florida, and set gators upon him. "I understand, Doctor Legros, but I assure you I'm here for the full picture of your country, not just the Broadway version, the tomtoms and the shouting. But in every ministry, veranda and salon I visit, why, even in the office of the director-general of the Health Service, what is all educated Haiti talking about but your patient, this unfortunate woman Felicia Felix-Mentor? Would you stuff my ears, shelter me from the topic of the day?"

He laughed, his teeth white and perfect and artificial. Zora, self-conscious of her own teeth, smiled with her lips closed, chin down. This often passed for flirtation. Zora wondered what the bright-eyed Doctor Legros thought of the seductive man-eater Erzulie, the most "uncivilized" loa of all. As she slowly crossed her legs, she thought: Huh! What's Erzulie got on Zora, got on me?

"Well, you are right to be interested in the poor creature," the doctor said, pinching a fresh cigarette into his holder while looking neither at it nor at Zora's eyes. "I plan to write a monograph on the subject myself, when the press of duty allows me. Perhaps I should apply for my own Guggenheim, eh? Clement!" He clapped his hands. "Clement! More clairin for our guest, if you please, and mangoes when we return from the yard."

As the doctor led her down the central corridor of the gingerbread Victorian hospital, he steered her around patients in creeping wicker wheelchairs, spat volleys of French at cowed black women in white, and told her the story she already knew, raising his voice whenever passing a doorway through which moans were unusually loud.

"In 1907, a young wife and mother in Ennery town died after a brief illness. She had a Christian burial. Her widower and son grieved for a time, then moved on with their lives, as men must do. *Empty this basin immediately! Do you hear me, woman? This is a hospital, not a chickenhouse!* My pardon. Now we come to a month ago. The Haitian Guard received reports of a madwoman accosting travelers near Ennery. She made her way to a farm and refused to leave, became violently agitated by all attempts to dislodge her. The owner of this family farm was summoned. He took one look at this poor creature and said, 'My God, it is my sister, dead and buried nearly thirty years.' Watch your step, please."

He held open a French door and ushered her onto a flagstone veranda, out of the hot, close, blood-smelling hospital into the hot, close outdoors, scented with hibiscus, goats, charcoal and tobacco in bloom. "And all the other family members, too, including her husband and son, have identified her. And so one mystery was solved, and in the process, another took its place."

In the far corner of the dusty, enclosed yard, in the sallow shade of an hourglass grove, a sexless figure in a white hospital gown stood huddled against the wall, shoulders hunched and back turned, like a child chosen It and counting.

"That's her," said the doctor.

As they approached, one of the hourglass fruits dropped onto the stony ground and burst with a report like a pistol firing, not three feet behind the huddled figure. She didn't budge.

"It is best not to surprise her," the doctor murmured, hot clairin breath in Zora's ear, hand in the small of her back. "Her movements are… unpredictable." As yours are not, Zora thought, stepping away.

The doctor began to hum a tune that sounded like

> Mama don't want no peas no rice
> She don't want no coconut oil
> All she wants is brandy
> Handy all the time

but wasn't. At the sound of his humming, the woman—for woman she was; Zora would resist labeling her as all Haiti had done—sprang forward into the wall with a fleshy smack, as if trying to fling herself face first through the stones, then sprang backward with a half-turn that set her arms to swinging without volition, like pendulums. Her eyes were beads of clouded glass. The broad lumpish face around them might have been attractive had its muscles displayed any of the tension common to animal life.

In her first brush with theater, years before, Zora had spent months scrubbing bustles and darning epaulets during a tour of that damned *Mikado*, may Gilbert and Sullivan both lose their heads, and there she learned that putty cheeks and false noses slide into grotesquerie by the final act. This woman's face likewise seemed to have been sweated beneath too long.

All this Zora registered in a second, as she would a face from an elevated train. The woman immediately turned away again, snatched down a slim hourglass branch and slashed the ground, back and forth, as a machete slashes through cane. The three attached fruits blew up, *bang bang bang*, seeds clouding outward, as she flailed the branch in the dirt.

"What is she doing?"

"She sweeps," the doctor said. "She fears being caught idle, for idle servants are beaten. In some quarters." He tried to reach around the suddenly nimble woman and take the branch.

"Nnnnn," she said, twisting away, still slashing the dirt.

"Behave yourself, Felicia. This visitor wants to speak with you."

"Please leave her be," Zora said, ashamed because the name Felicia jarred when applied to this wretch. "I didn't mean to disturb her."

Ignoring this, the doctor, eyes shining, stopped the slashing movements by seizing the woman's skinny wrist and holding it aloft. The patient froze, knees bent in a half-crouch, head averted as if awaiting a blow. With his free hand, the doctor, still humming, still watching the woman's face, pried her fingers from the branch one by one, then flung it aside, nearly swatting Zora. The patient continued saying, "Nnnnn, nnnnn, nnnnn," at metronomic intervals. The sound lacked any note of panic or protest, any communicative tonality whatsoever, was instead a simple emission, like the whistle of a turpentine cooker.

"Felicia?" Zora asked.

"Nnnnn, nnnnn, nnnnn."

"My name is Zora, and I come from Florida, in the United States."

"Nnnnn, nnnnn, nnnnn."

"I have heard her make one other noise only," said the doctor, still holding up her arm as if she were Joe Louis, "and that is when she is bathed or touched with water—a sound like a mouse that is trod upon. I will demonstrate. Where is that hose?"

"No need for that!" Zora cried. "Release her, please."

The doctor did so. Felicia scuttled away, clutched and lifted the hem of her gown until her face was covered and her buttocks bared. Zora thought of her mother's wake, where her aunts and cousins had greeted each fresh burst of tears by flipping their aprons over their heads and rushing into the kitchen to mewl together like nestlings. Thank God for aprons, Zora thought. Felicia's legs, to Zora's surprise, were ropy with muscle.

"Such strength," the doctor murmured, "and so untamed. You realize, Miss Hurston, that when she was found squatting in the road, she was as naked as all mankind."

A horsefly droned past.

The doctor cleared his throat, clasped his hands behind his back, and began to orate, as if addressing a medical society at Columbia. "It is interesting to speculate on the drugs used to rob a sentient being of her reason, of her will. The ingredients, even the means of administration, are most jealously guarded secrets."

He paced toward the hospital, not looking at Zora, and did not raise his voice as he spoke of herbs and powders, salves and cucumbers, as if certain she walked alongside him, unbidden. Instead she stooped and hefted the branch Felicia had wielded. It was much heavier than she had assumed, so lightly had Felicia snatched it down. Zora tugged at one of its twigs and found the dense, rubbery wood quite resistant. Lucky for the doctor that anger seemed to be among the emotions cooked away. What emotions were left? Fear remained, certainly. And what else?

Zora dropped the branch next to a gouge in the dirt that, as she glanced at it, seemed to resolve itself into the letter M.

"Miss Hurston?" called the doctor from halfway across the yard. "I beg your pardon. You have seen enough, have you not?"

Zora knelt, her hands outstretched as if to encompass, to contain, the scratches that Felicia Felix-Mentor had slashed with the branch. Yes, that was definitely an M, and that vertical slash could be an I, and that next one—

MI HAUT MI BAS
Half high, half low?

Doctor Boas at Barnard liked to say that one began to understand a people only when one began to think in their language. Now, as she knelt in the hospital yard, staring at the words Felicia Felix-Mentor had left in the dirt, a phrase welled from her lips that she had heard often in Haiti but never felt before, a Creole phrase used to mean "So be it," to mean "Amen," to mean "There you have it," to mean whatever one chose it to mean but always conveying a more or less resigned acquiescence to the world and all its marvels.

"Ah bo bo," Zora said.

"Miss Hurston?" The doctor's dusty wingtips entered her vision, stood on the delicate pattern Zora had teased from the dirt, a pattern that began to disintegrate outward from the shoes, as if they produced a breeze or tidal eddy. "Are you suffering perhaps the digestion? Often the peasant spices can disrupt refined systems. Might I have Clement bring you a soda? Or"—and here his voice took on new excitement—"could this be perhaps a feminine complaint?"

"No, thank you, Doctor," Zora said as she stood, ignoring his outstretched hand. "May I please, do you think, return tomorrow with my camera?"

She intended the request to sound casual but failed. Not in *Damballa Calls*, not in *The White King of La Gonave*, not in *The Magic Island*, not in any best-seller ever served up to the Haiti-loving American public had anyone ever included a photograph of a Zombie.

As she held her breath, the doctor squinted and glanced from Zora to the patient and back, as if suspecting the two women of collusion. He loudly sucked a tooth. "It is impossible, madame," he said. "Tomorrow I must away to Port-de-Paix, leaving at dawn and not returning for—"

"It must be tomorrow!" Zora blurted, hastily adding, "because the next day I have an appointment in… Petionville." To obscure that slightest of pauses, she gushed, "Oh, Doctor Legros," and dimpled his tailored shoulder with her forefinger. "Until we have the pleasure of meeting again, surely you won't deny me this one small token of your regard?"

Since she was a sprat of thirteen sashaying around the gatepost in Eaton-ville, slowing Yankees aboil for Winter Park or Sunken Gardens or the Weeki Wachee with a wink and a wave, Zora had viewed sexuality, like other talents, as a bank of backstage switches to be flipped separately or together to achieve specific effects—a spotlight glare, a thunderstorm, the slow, seeping warmth of dawn. Few switches were needed for everyday use, and certainly not for Doctor Legros, who was the most everyday of men.

"But of course," the doctor said, his body ready and still. "Doctor Belfong will expect you, and I will ensure that he extend you every courtesy. And then, Miss Hurston, we will compare travel notes on another day, n'est-ce pas?"

As she stepped onto the veranda, Zora looked back. Felicia Felix-Mentor stood in the middle of the yard, arms wrapped across her torso as if chilled, rocking on the balls of her calloused feet. She was looking at Zora, if at anything. Behind her, a dusty flamingo high-stepped across the yard.

Zora found signboards in Haiti fairly easy to understand in French, but the English ones were a different story. As she wedged herself into a seat in the crowded tap-tap that rattled twice a day between Gonaives and Port-au-Prince, Felicia Felix-Mentor an hour planted and taking root in her mind, she found herself facing a stern injunction above the grimy, cracked windshield: "Passengers Are Not Permitted To Stand Forward While the Bus Is Either at a Standstill or Approaching in Motion."

As the bus lurched forward, tires spinning, gears grinding, the driver loudly recited: "Dear clients, let us pray to the Good God and to all the most merciful martyrs in heaven that we may be delivered safely unto our chosen destination. Amen."

Amen, Zora thought despite herself, already jotting in her notebook. The beautiful woman in the window seat beside her shifted sideways to give Zora's elbow more room, and Zora absently flashed her a smile. At the top of the page she wrote, "Felicia Felix-Mentor," the hyphen jagging upward from a pothole. Then she added a question mark and tapped the pencil against her teeth.

Who had Felicia been, and what life had she led? Where was her family? Of these matters, Doctor Legros refused to speak. Maybe the family had abandoned its feeble relative, or worse. The poor woman may have been brutalized into her present state. Such things happened at the hands of family members, Zora knew.

Zora found herself doodling a shambling figure, arms outstretched. Nothing like Felicia, she conceded. More like Mr. Karloff's monster. Several years before, in New York to put together a Broadway production that came to nothing, Zora had wandered, depressed and whimsical, into a Times Square movie theater to see a foolish horror movie titled *White Zombie.* The swaying sugar cane on the poster ("She was not dead… She was not alive… WHAT WAS SHE?") suggested, however spuriously, Haiti, which even then Zora hoped to visit one day. Bela Lugosi in Mephistophelean whiskers proved about as Haitian as Fannie Hurst, and his Zombies, stalking bug-eyed and stiff-legged around the tatty sets, *all* looked white to Zora, so she couldn't grasp the urgency of the title, whatever Lugosi's designs on the heroine. Raising Zombies just to staff a sugar mill, moreover, struck her as wasted effort, since many a live Haitian (or Floridian) would work a full Depression day for as little pay as any Zombie and do a better job too. Still, she admired how the movie Zombies walked mindlessly to their doom off the parapet of Lugosi's castle, just as the fanatic soldiers of the mad Haitian King Henri Christophe were supposed to have done from the heights of the Citadel Laferriere.

But suppose Felicia *were* a Zombie—in Haitian terms, anyway? Not a supernaturally revived corpse, but a sort of combined kidnap and poisoning victim, released or abandoned by her captor, her bocor, after three decades.

Supposedly, the bocor stole a victim's soul by mounting a horse backward, facing the tail, and riding by night to her house. There he knelt on the doorstep, pressed his face against the crack beneath the door, bared his teeth, and *sssssssst!* He inhaled the soul of the sleeping woman, breathed her right into his lungs. And then the bocor would have marched Felicia (so the tales went) past her house the next night, her first night as a Zombie, to prevent her ever recognizing it or seeking it again.

Yet Felicia *had* sought out the family farm, however late. Maybe something had gone wrong with the spell. Maybe someone had fed her salt—the hair-of-the-dog remedy for years-long zombie hangovers. Where, then, was Felicia's bocor? Why hold her prisoner all this time, but no longer? Had he died, setting his charge free to wander? Had he other charges, other Zombies? How had Felicia become both victim and escapee?

"And how do you like your Zombie, Miss Hurston?"

Zora started. The beautiful passenger beside her had spoken.

"I beg your pardon!" Zora instinctively shut her notebook. "I do not believe we have met, Miss…?"

The wide-mouthed stranger laughed merrily, her opalescent earrings shimmering on her high cheekbones. One ringlet of brown hair spilled onto her forehead from beneath her kerchief, which like her tight-fitting, high-necked dress was an ever-swirling riot of color. Her heavy gold necklace was nearly lost in it. Her skin was two parts cream to one part coffee. Antebellum New Orleans would have been at this woman's feet, once the shutters were latched.

"Ah, I knew you did not recognize me, Miss Hurston." Her accent made the first syllable of "Hurston" a prolonged purr. "We met in Arcahaie, in the hounfort of Dieu Donnez St. Leger, during the rite of the fishhook of the dead." She bulged her eyes and sat forward slack-jawed, then fell back, clapping her hands with delight, ruby ring flashing, at her passable imitation of a dead man.

"You may call me Freida. It is I, Miss Hurston, who first told you of the Zombie Felix-Mentor."

Their exchange in the sweltering crowd had been brief and confused, but Zora could have sworn that her informant that night had been an older, plainer woman. Still, Zora probably hadn't looked her best, either. The deacons and mothers back home would deny it, but many a worshipper looked better outside church than in.

Zora apologized for her absent-mindedness, thanked this, Freida? for her tip, and told her some of her hospital visit. She left out the message in the dirt, if message it was, but mused aloud:

"Today we lock the poor woman away, but who knows? Once she may have had a place of honor, as a messenger touched by the gods."

"No, no, no, no, no, no, no," said Freida in a forceful singsong. "No! The gods did not take her powers away." She leaned in, became conspiratorial. "Some *man*, and only a man, did that. You saw. You know."

Zora, teasing, said, "Ah, so you have experience with men."

"None more," Freida stated. Then she smiled. "Ah bo bo. That is night talk. Let us speak instead of daylight things."

The two women chatted happily for a bouncing half-hour, Freida questioning and Zora answering—talking about her Haiti book, turpentine camps, the sights of New York. It was good to be questioned herself for a change, after collecting from others all the time. The tap-tap jolted along, ladling dust equally onto all who shared the road: mounted columns of Haitian Guards, shelf-hipped laundresses, half-dead donkeys laden with guinea-grass. The day's shadows lengthened.

"This is my stop," said Freida at length, though the tap-tap showed no signs of slowing, and no stop was visible through the windows, just dense palm groves to either side. Where a less graceful creature would merely have stood, Freida rose, then turned and edged toward the aisle, facing not the front but, oddly, the back of the bus. Zora swiveled in her seat to give her more room, but Freida pressed against her anyway, thrust her pelvis forward against the older woman's bosom. Zora felt Freida's heat through the thin material. Above, Freida flashed a smile, nipped her own lower lip, and chuckled as the pluck of skin fell back into place.

"I look forward to our next visit, Miss Hurston."

"And where might I call on you?" Zora asked, determined to follow the conventions.

Freida edged past and swayed down the aisle, not reaching for the handgrips. "You'll find me," she said, over her shoulder.

Zora opened her mouth to say something but forgot what. Directly in front of the bus, visible through the windshield past Freida's shoulder, a charcoal truck roared into the roadway at right angles. Zora braced herself for the crash. The tap-tap driver screamed with everyone else, stamped the brakes and spun the wheel. With a hellish screech, the bus slewed about in a cloud of dirt and dust that darkened the sunlight, crusted Zora's tongue, and hid the charcoal truck from view. For one long, delirious, nearly sexual moment the bus tipped sideways. Then it righted itself with a tooth-loosening *slam* that shattered the windshield. In the silence, Zora heard someone sobbing, heard the engine's last faltering cough, heard the front door slide open with its usual clatter. She righted her hat in order to see. The tap-tap and the charcoal truck had come to rest a foot away from one another, side by side and facing opposite directions. Freida, smiling, unscathed, kerchief still angled just so, sauntered down the aisle between the vehicles, one finger trailing along the side of the truck, tracking the dust like a child. She passed Zora's window without looking up, and was gone.

"She pulled in her horizon like a great fish-net. Pulled it from around the waist of the world and draped it over her shoulder. So much of life in its meshes! She called in her soul to come and see."

Mouth dry, head aching from the heat and from the effort of reading her own chicken-scratch, Zora turned the last page of the manuscript, squared the stack and looked up at her audience. Felicia sat on an hourglass root, a baked yam in each hand, gnawing first one, then the other.

"That's the end," Zora said, in the same soft, non-threatening voice with which she had read her novel thus far. "I'm still unsure of the middle," she continued, setting down the manuscript and picking up the Brownie camera, "but I know this is the end, all right, and that's something."

As yam after yam disappeared, skins and all, Felicia's eyes registered nothing. No matter. Zora always liked to read her work aloud as she was writing, and Felicia was as good an audience as anybody. She was, in fact, the first audience this particular book had had.

While Zora had no concerns whatsoever about sharing her novel with Felicia, she was uncomfortably aware of the narrow Victorian casements above, and felt the attentive eyes of the dying and the mad. On the veranda, a bent old man in a wheelchair mumbled to himself, half-watched by a nurse with a magazine.

In a spasm of experiment, Zora had salted the yams, to no visible effect. This Zombie took salt like an editor took whiskey.

"I'm not in your country to write a novel," Zora told her chewing companion. "Not officially. I'm being paid just to do folklore on this trip. Why, this novel isn't even set in Haiti, ha! So I can't tell the foundation about this quite yet. It's our secret, right, Felicia?"

The hospital matron had refused Zora any of her good china, grudgingly piling bribe-yams onto a scarred gourd-plate instead. Now, only two were left. The plate sat on the ground, just inside Felicia's reach. Chapter by chapter, yam by yam, Zora had been reaching out and dragging the plate just a bit nearer herself, a bit farther away from Felicia. So far, Felicia had not seemed to mind.

Now Zora moved the plate again, just as Felicia was licking the previous two yams off her fingers. Felicia reached for the plate, then froze, when she registered that it was out of reach. She sat there, arm suspended in the air.

"Nnnnn, nnnnn, nnnnn," she said.

Zora sat motionless, cradling her Brownie camera in her lap.

Felicia slid forward on her buttocks and snatched up two yams—choosing to eat them where she now sat, as Zora had hoped, rather than slide backward into the shade once more. Zora took several pictures in the sunlight, though none of them, she later realized, managed to penetrate the shadows beneath Felicia's furrowed brow, where the patient's sightless eyes lurked.

"Zombies!" came an unearthly cry. The old man on the veranda was having a spasm, legs kicking, arms flailing. The nurse moved quickly, propelled his wheelchair toward the hospital door. "I made them all Zombies! Zombies!"

"Observe my powers," said the mad Zombie-maker King Henri Christophe, twirling his stage mustache and leering down at the beautiful young(ish) anthropologist who squirmed against her snakeskin bonds. The mad king's broad white face and syrupy accent suggested Budapest. At his languid gesture, black-and-white legions of Zombies both black and white shuffled into view around the papier-mâché cliff and marched single file up the steps of the balsa parapet, and over. None cried out as he fell. Flipping through his captive's notebook, the king laughed maniacally and said, "I never knew you wrote this! Why, this is *good!*" As Zombies toppled behind him like ninepins, their German Expressionist shadows scudding across his face, the mad king began hammily to read aloud the opening passage of *Imitation of Life*.

Zora woke in a sweat.

The rain still sheeted down, a ceremonial drumming on the slate roof. Her manuscript, a white blob in the darkness, was moving sideways along the desktop. She watched as it went over the edge and dashed itself across the floor with a sound like a gust of wind. So the iguana had gotten in again. It loved messing with her manuscript. She should take the iguana to New York, get it a job at Lippincott's. She isolated the iguana's crouching, bowlegged shape in the drumming darkness and lay still, never sure whether iguanas jumped and how far and why.

Gradually she became aware of another sound nearer than the rain: someone crying.

Zora switched on the bedside lamp, found her slippers with her feet and reached for her robe. The top of her writing desk was empty. The manuscript must have been top-heavy, that's all. Shaking her head at her night fancies, cinching her belt, yawning, Zora walked into the corridor and nearly stepped on the damned iguana as it scuttled just ahead of her, claws clack-clack-clacking on the hardwood. Zora tugged off her left slipper and gripped it by the toe as an unlikely weapon as she followed the iguana into the great room. Her housekeeper, Lucille, lay on the sofa, crying two-handed into a handkerchief. The window above her was open, curtains billowing, and the iguana escaped as it had arrived, scrambling up the back of the sofa and out into the hissing rain. Lucille was oblivious until Zora closed the sash, when she sat up with a start.

"Oh, Miss! You frightened me! I thought the Sect Rouge had come."

Ah, yes, the Sect Rouge. That secret, invisible mountain-dwelling cannibal cult, their distant nocturnal drums audible only to the doomed, whose blood thirst made the Klan look like the Bethune-Cookman board of visitors, was Lucille's most cherished night terror. Zora had never had a housekeeper before, never wanted one, but Lucille "came with the house," as the agent had put it. It was all a package: mountainside view, Sect Rouge paranoia, hot and cold running iguanas.

"Lucille, darling, whatever is the matter? Why are you crying?"

A fresh burst of tears. "It is my faithless husband, madame! My Etienne. He has forsaken me... for Erzulie!" She fairly spat the name, as a wronged woman in Eatonville would have spat the infamous name of Miss Delpheeny.

Zora had laid eyes on Etienne only once, when he came flushed and hatless to the back door to show off his prize catch, grinning as widely as the dead caiman he held up by the tail. For his giggling wife's benefit, he had tied a pink ribbon around the creature's neck, and Zora had decided then that Lucille was as lucky a woman as any.

"There, there. Come to Zora. Here, blow your nose. That's better. You needn't tell me any more, if you don't want to. Who is this Erzulie?"

Zora had heard much about Erzulie in Haiti, always from other women, in tones of resentment and admiration, but she was keen for more.

"Oh, madame, she is a terrible woman! She has every man she wants, all the men, and… and some of the women, too!" This last said in a hush of reverence. "No home in Haiti is safe from her. First she came to my Etienne in his dreams, teasing and tormenting his sleep until he cried out and spent himself in the sheets. Then she troubled his waking life, too, with frets and ill fortune, so that he was angry with himself and with me all the time. Finally I sent him to the houngan, and the houngan said, 'Why do you ask me what this is? Any child could say to you the truth: You have been chosen as a consort of Erzulie.' And then he embraced my Etienne, and said: 'My son, your bed above all beds is now the one for all men to envy.' Ah, madame, religion is a hard thing for women!"

Even as she tried to console the weeping woman, Zora felt a pang of writerly conscience. On the one hand, she genuinely wanted to help; on the other hand, everything was material.

"Whenever Erzulie pleases, she takes the form that a man most desires, to ride him as dry as a bean husk, and to rob his woman of comfort. Oh, madame! My Etienne has not come to my bed in… in… *twelve days!*" She collapsed into the sofa in a fresh spasm of grief, buried her head beneath a cushion and began to hiccup. Twelve whole days, Zora thought, my my, as she did dispiriting math, but she said nothing, only patted Lucille's shoulder and cooed.

Later, while frying an egg for her dejected, red-eyed housekeeper, Zora sought to change the subject. "Lucille. Didn't I hear you say the other day, when the postman ran over the rooster, something like, 'Ah, the Zombies eat well tonight!'"

"Yes, madame, I think I did say this thing."

"And last week, when you spotted that big spider web just after putting the ladder away, you said, 'Ah bo bo, the Zombies make extra work for me today.' When you say such things, Lucille, what do you mean? To what Zombies do you refer?"

"Oh, madame, it is just a thing to say when small things go wrong. Oh, the milk is sour, the Zombies have put their feet in it, and so on. My mother always says it, and her mother too."

Soon Lucille was chatting merrily away about the little coffee girls and the ritual baths at Saut d'Eau, and Zora took notes and drank coffee, and all was well. Ah bo bo!

The sun was still hours from rising when Lucille's chatter shut off mid-sentence. Zora looked up to see Lucille frozen in terror, eyes wide, face ashen.

"Madame... Listen!"

"Lucille, I hear nothing but the rain on the roof."

"Madame," Lucille whispered, "the rain has stopped."

Zora set down her pencil and went to the window. Only a few drops pattered from the eaves and the trees. In the distance, far up the mountain, someone was beating the drums—ten drums, a hundred, who could say? The sound was like thunder sustained, never coming closer but never fading either.

Zora closed and latched the shutters and turned back to Lucille with a smile. "Honey, that's just man-noise in the night, like the big-mouthing on the porch at Joe Clarke's store. You mean I never told you about all the lying that men do back home? Break us another egg, Cille honey, and I'll tell *you* some things."

> Box 128-B
> Port-au-Prince, Haiti
> November 20, 1936
>
> Dr. Henry Allen Moe, Sec.
> John Simon Guggenheim Memorial Foundation
> 551 Fifth Avenue
> New York City, New York
>
> Dear Dr. Moe,

I regret to report that for all my knocking and ringing and dust-raising, I have found no relatives of this unfortunate Felix-Mentor woman. She is both famous and unknown. All have heard of her and know, or think they know, the two-sentence outline of her "story," and have their own fantasies about her, but can go no further. She is the Garbo of Haiti. I would think her a made-up character had I not seen her myself, and taken her picture as... evidence? A photograph of the Empire State Building is evidence too, but of what? That is for the viewer to say.

I am amused of course, as you were, to hear from some of our friends and colleagues on the Haiti beat their concerns that poor Zora has "gone native," has thrown away the WPA and Jesse Owens and the travel trailer and all the other achievements of the motherland to break chickens and become an initiate in the mysteries of the Sect Rouge. Lord knows, Dr. Moe, I spent twenty-plus years in the Southern U.S., beneath the constant gaze of every First Abyssinian Macedonian African Methodist Episcopal Presbyterian Pentecostal Free Will Baptist Assembly of God of Christ of Jesus with Signs Following minister mother and deacon, all so full of the spirit they look like death eating crackers, and in all that time I never once came down with even a mild case of Christianity. I certainly won't catch the local disease from only six months in Haiti....

Obligations, travel and illness—"suffering perhaps the digestion," thank you, Doctor Legros—kept Zora away from the hospital at Gonaives for some weeks. When she finally did return, she walked onto the veranda to see Felicia, as before, standing all alone in the quiet yard, her face toward the high wall. Today Felicia had chosen to stand on the sole visible spot of green grass, a plot of soft imprisoned turf about the diameter of an Easter hat. Zora felt a deep satisfaction upon seeing her, this self-contained, fixed point in her traveler's life.

To reach the steps, she had to walk past the mad old man in the wheelchair, whose nurse was not in sight today. Despite his sunken cheeks, his matted eyelashes, his patchy tufts of white hair, Zora could see he must have been handsome in his day. She smiled as she approached.

He blinked and spoke in a thoughtful voice. "I will be a Zombie soon," he said.

That stopped her. "Excuse me?"

"Death came for me many years ago," said the old man, eyes bright, "and I said, No, not me, take my wife instead. And so I gave her up as a Zombie. That gained me five years, you see. A good bargain. And then, five years later, I gave our oldest son. Then our daughter. Then our youngest. And more loved ones, too, now all Zombies, all. There is no one left. No one but me." His hands plucked at the coverlet that draped his legs. He peered all around the yard. "I will be a Zombie soon," he said, and wept.

Shaking her head, Zora descended the steps. Approaching Felicia from behind, as Doctor Legros had said that first day, was always a delicate maneuver. One had to be loud enough to be heard but quiet enough not to panic her.

"Hello, Felicia," Zora said.

The huddled figure didn't turn, didn't budge, and Zora, emboldened by long absence, repeated the name, reached out, touched Felicia's shoulder with her fingertips. As she made contact, a tingling shiver ran up her arm and down her spine to her feet. Without turning, Felicia emerged from her crouch. She stood up straight, flexed her shoulders, stretched her neck, and spoke.

"Zora, my friend!"

Felicia turned and was not Felicia at all, but a tall, beautiful woman in a brief white gown. Freida registered the look on Zora's face and laughed.

"Did I not tell you that you would find me? Do you not even know your friend Freida?"

Zora's breath returned. "I know you," she retorted, "and I know that was a cruel trick. Where is Felicia? What have you done with her?"

"Whatever do you mean? Felicia was not mine to give you, and she is not mine to take away. No one is owned by anyone."

"Why is Felicia not in the yard? Is she ill? And why are you here? Are you ill as well?"

Freida sighed. "So many questions. Is this how a book gets written? If Felicia were not ill, silly, she would not have been here in the first place. Besides." She squared her shoulders. "Why do you care so about this… powerless woman? This woman who let some man lead her soul astray, like a starving cat behind an eel-barrel?" She stepped close, the heat of the day coalescing around. "Tell a woman of power your book. Tell *me* your book," she murmured. "Tell *me* of the mule's funeral, and the rising waters, and the buzzing pear-tree, and young Janie's secret sigh."

Zora had two simultaneous thoughts, like a moan and a breath interlaced: *Get out of my book!* and *My God, she's jealous!*

"Why bother?" Zora bit off, flush with anger. "You think you know it by heart already. And besides," Zora continued, stepping forward, nose to nose, "there are powers other than yours."

Freida hissed, stepped back as if pattered with stove-grease.

Zora put her nose in the air and said, airily, "I'll have you know that Felicia is a writer, too."

Her mouth a thin line, Freida turned and strode toward the hospital, thighs long and taut beneath her gown. Without thought, Zora walked, too, and kept pace.

"If you must know," Freida said, "your writer friend is now in the care of her family. Her son came for her. Do you find this so remarkable? Perhaps the son should have notified you, hmm?" She winked at Zora. "He is quite a muscular young man, with a taste for older women. Much, *much* older women. I could show you where he lives. I have been there often. I have been there more than he knows."

"How dependent you are," Zora said, "on men."

As Freida stepped onto the veranda, the old man in the wheelchair cringed and moaned. "Hush, child," Freida said. She pulled a nurse's cap from her pocket and tugged it on over her chestnut hair.

"Don't let her take me!" the old man howled. "She'll make me a Zombie! She will! A Zombie!"

"Oh, pish," Freida said. She raised one bare foot and used it to push the wheelchair forward a foot or so, revealing a sensible pair of white shoes on the flagstones beneath. These she stepped into as she wheeled the chair around. "Here is your bocor, Miss Hurston. What use have I for a Zombie's cold hands? Au revoir, Miss Hurston. Zora. I hope you find much to write about in my country… however you limit your experiences."

Zora stood at the foot of the steps, watched her wheel the old man away over the uneven flagstones.

"Erzulie," Zora said.

The woman stopped. Without turning, she asked, "What name did you call me?"

"I called you a true name, and I'm telling you that if you don't leave Lucille's Etienne alone, so the two of them can go to hell in their own way, then I... well, then I will forget all about you, and you will never be in my book."

Freida pealed with laughter. The old man slumped in his chair. The laughter cut off like a radio, and Freida, suddenly grave, looked down. "They do not last any time, do they?" she murmured. With a forefinger, she poked the back of his head. "Poor pretty things." With a sigh, she faced Zora, gave her a look of frank appraisal, up and down. Then she shrugged. "You are mad," she said, "but you are fair." She backed into the door, shoved it open with her behind, and hauled the dead man in after her.

The tap-tap was running late as usual, so Zora, restless, started out on foot. As long as the road kept going downhill and the sun stayed over yonder, she reasoned, she was unlikely to get lost. As she walked through the countryside she sang and picked flowers and worked on her book in the best way she knew to work on a book, in her own head, with no paper and indeed no words, not yet. She enjoyed the caution signs on each curve—"La Route Tue et Blesse," or, literally, "The Road Kills And Injures."

She wondered how it felt, to walk naked along a roadside like Felicia Felix-Mentor. She considered trying the experiment when she realized that night had fallen. (And where was the tap-tap, and all the other traffic, and why was the road so narrow?) But once shed, her dress, her shift, her shoes would be a terrible armful. The only efficient way to carry clothes, really, was to wear them. So thinking, she plodded, footsore, around a sharp curve and nearly ran into several dozen hooded figures in red, proceeding in the opposite direction. Several carried torches, all carried drums, and one had a large, mean-looking dog on a rope.

"Who comes?" asked a deep male voice. Zora couldn't tell which of the hooded figures had spoken, if any.

"Who wants to know?" she asked.

The hoods looked at one another. Without speaking, several reached into their robes. One drew a sword. One drew a machete. The one with the dog drew a pistol, then knelt to murmur into the dog's ear. With one hand he scratched the dog between the shoulder blades, and with the other he gently stroked its head with the moon-gleaming barrel of the pistol. Zora could hear the thump and rustle of the dog's tail wagging in the leaves.

"Give us the words of passage," said the voice, presumably the sword-wielder's, as he was the one who pointed at Zora for emphasis. "Give them to us, woman, or you will die, and we will feast upon you."

"She cannot know the words," said a woman's voice, "unless she too has spoken with the dead. Let us eat her."

Suddenly, as well as she knew anything on the round old world, Zora knew exactly what the words of passage were. Felicia Felix-Mentor had given them to her. *Mi haut, mi bas.* Half high, half low. She could say them now. But she would not say them. She would believe in Zombies, a little, and in Erzulie, perhaps, a little more. But she would not believe in the Sect Rouge, in blood-oathed societies of men. She walked forward again, of her own free will, and the red-robed figures stood motionless as she passed among them. The dog whimpered. She walked down the hill, hearing nothing behind but a growing chorus of frogs. Around the next bend she saw the distant lights of Port-au-Prince and, much nearer, a tap-tap idling in front of a store. Zora laughed and hung her hat on a caution sign. Between her and the bus, the moonlit road was flecked with tiny frogs, distinguished from bits of gravel and bark only by their leaping, their errands of life. Ah bo bo! She called in her soul to come and see.

CALCUTTA, LORD OF NERVES

by Poppy Z. Brite

Poppy Z. Brite is the author of many novels, including *Lost Souls*, *Exquisite Corpse*, *Liquor*, and *Soul Kitchen*, among others. Her short fiction has appeared in a number of anthologies, such as *Borderlands*, *Dark Terrors 3*, *Shadows Over Baker Street*, *McSweeney's Enchanted Chamber of Astonishing Stories*, and *Outsiders*. A new short fiction collection, *Antediluvian Tales*, was released in 2007. She is also co-editor (with Martin H. Greenberg) of the vampire erotica anthologies *Love in Vein* and *Love in Vein 2*.

This story was nominated for the World Fantasy Award, losing out to another story in this volume: "This Year's Class Picture" by Dan Simmons. Which is ironic, because "Calcutta, Lord of Nerves" was inspired by Simmons's novel *Song of Kali*. "I approached Calcutta and the goddess Kali from a very different point of view," Brite says, "but my story would never have been written without Dan's novel." (Incidentally, in his acceptance speech, Simmons said the award should have gone to "Calcutta.")

This story is a sort of travelogue through the zombie-ravaged city of Calcutta, more picaresque than plot-driven. "It basically consists of a guy walking around and looking at things," Brite says. "What makes the story interesting (I hope) is that the sights he sees are extremely unusual and vivid."

I was born in a North Calcutta hospital in the heart of an Indian midnight just before the beginning of the monsoon season. The air hung heavy as wet velvet over the Hooghly River, offshoot of the holy Ganga, and the stumps of banyan trees on the Upper Chitpur Road were flecked with dots of phosphorus like the ghosts of flames. I was as dark as the new moon in the sky, and I cried very little. I feel as if I remember this, because this is the way it must have been.

My mother died in labor, and later that night the hospital burned to the ground. (I have no reason to connect the two incidents; then again, I have no reason not to. Perhaps a desire to live burned on in my mother's heart. Perhaps the flames were fanned by her hatred for me, the insignificant mewling infant that had killed her.) A nurse carried me out of the roaring husk of the building and laid me in my father's arms. He cradled me, numb with grief.

My father was American. He had come to Calcutta five years earlier, on business. There he had fallen in love with my mother and, like a man who will not pluck a flower from its garden, he could not bear to see her removed from the hot, lush, squalid city that had spawned her. It was part of her exotica. So my father stayed in Calcutta. Now his flower was gone. He pressed his thin chapped lips to the satin of my hair. I remember opening my eyes—they felt tight and shiny, parched by the flames—and looking up at the column of smoke that roiled into the sky, a night sky blasted cloudy pink like a sky full of blood and milk.

There would be no milk for me, only chemical-tasting drops of formula from a plastic nipple. The morgue was in the basement of the hospital and did not burn. My mother lay on a metal table, a hospital gown stiff with her dying sweat pulled up over her red-smeared crotch and thighs. Her eyes stared up through the blackened skeleton of the hospital, up to the milky bloody sky, and ash filtered down to mask her pupils.

My father and I left for America before the monsoon came. Without my mother Calcutta was a pestilential hellhole, a vast cremation grounds, or so my father thought. In America he could send me to school and movies, ball games and Boy Scouts, secure in the knowledge that someone else would take care of me or I would take care of myself. There were no *thuggees* to rob me and cut my throat, no *goondas* who would snatch me and sell my bones for fertilizer. There were no cows to infect the streets with their steaming sacred piss. My father could give me over to the comparative wholesomeness of American life, leaving himself free to sit in his darkened bedroom and drink whiskey until his long sensitive nose floated hazily in front of his face and the sabre edge of his grief began to dull. He was the sort of man who has only one love in his lifetime, and knows with the sick fervor of a fatalist that this love will be taken from him someday, and is hardly surprised when it happens.

When he was drunk he would talk about Calcutta. My little American mind rejected the place—I was in love with air conditioning, hamburgers and pizza, the free and indiscriminating love that was lavished upon me every time I twisted the TV dial—but somewhere in my Indian heart I longed for it. When I turned eighteen and my father finally failed to wake up from one of his drunken stupors, I returned to the city of my bloody birth as soon as I had the plane fare in my hand.

Calcutta, you will say. What a place to have been when the dead began to walk.

And I reply, what better place to be? What better place than a city where five million people look as if they are already dead—might as well be dead—and another five million wish they were?

I have a friend named Devi, a prostitute who began her work at the age of fifteen from a tarpaper shack on Sudder Street. Sudder is the Bourbon Street of Calcutta, but there is far less of the carnival there, and no one wears a mask on Sudder Street because disguises are useless when shame is irrelevant. Devi works the big hotels now, selling American tourists or British expatriates or

German businessmen a taste of exotic Bengal spice. She is gaunt and beautiful and hard as nails. Devi says the world is a whore, too, and Calcutta is the pussy of the world. The world squats and spreads its legs, and Calcutta is the dank sex you see revealed there, wet and fragrant with a thousand odors both delicious and foul. A source of lushest pleasure, a breeding ground for every conceivable disease.

The pussy of the world. It is all right with me. I like pussy, and I love my squalid city.

The dead like pussy too. If they are able to catch a woman and disable her enough so that she cannot resist, you will see the lucky ones burrowing in between her legs as happily as the most avid lover. They do not have to come up for air. I have seen them eat all the way up into the body cavity. The internal female organs seem to be a great delicacy, and why not? They are the caviar of the human body. It is a sobering thing to come across a woman sprawled in the gutter with her intestines sliding from the shredded ruin of her womb, but you do not react. You do not distract the dead from their repast. They are slow and stupid, but that is all the more reason for you to be smart and quick and quiet. They will do the same thing to a man—chew off the soft penis and scrotal sac like choice morsels of squid, leaving only a red raw hole. But you can sidle by while they are feeding and they will not notice you. I do not try to hide from them. I walk the streets and look; that is all I do anymore. I am fascinated. This is not horror, this is simply more of Calcutta.

First I would sleep late, through the sultry morning into the heat of the afternoon. I had a room in one of the decrepit marble palaces of the old city. Devi visited me here often, but on a typical morning I woke alone, clad only in twisted bedsheets and a luxurious patina of sweat. Sun came through the window and fell in bright bars across the floor. I felt safe in my second-story room as long as I kept the door locked. The dead were seldom able to navigate stairs, and they could not manage the sustained cooperative effort to break down a locked door. They were no threat to me. They fed upon those who had given up, those too traumatized to keep running: the senile, abandoned old, the catatonic young women who sat in gutters cradling babies that had died during the night. These were easy prey.

The walls of my room were painted a bright coral and the sills and door were aqua. The colors caught the sun and made the day seem cheerful despite the heat that shimmered outside. I went downstairs, crossed the empty courtyard with its dry marble fountain, and went out into the street. This area was barren in the heat, painfully bright, with parched weeds lining the road and an occasional smear of cow dung decorating the gutter. By nightfall both weeds and dung might be gone. Children collected cow shit and patted it into cakes held together with straw, which could be sold as fuel for cooking fires.

I headed toward Chowringhee Road, the broad main thoroughfare of the city. Halfway up my street, hunched under the awning of a mattress factory, I saw one of the catatonic young mothers. The dead had found her too. They had already taken the baby from her arms and eaten though the soft part at the top of the skull. Vacuous bloody faces rose and dipped. Curds of tender brain fell from slack mouths. The mother sat on the curb nearby, her arms cradling nothing. She wore a filthy green sari that was ripped across the chest. The woman's breasts protruded heavily, swollen with milk. When the dead finished with her baby they would start on her, and she would make no resistance. I had seen it before. I knew how the milk would spurt and then gush as they tore into her breasts. I knew how hungrily they would lap up the twin rivers of blood and milk.

Above their bobbing heads, the tin awning dripped long ropy strands of cotton. Cotton hung from the roof in dirty clumps, caught in the corners of the doorway like spiderweb. Someone's radio blared faintly in another part of the building, tuned to an English-language Christian broadcast. A gospel hymn assured Calcutta that its dead in Christ would rise. I moved on toward Chowringhee.

Most of the streets in the city are positively cluttered with buildings. Buildings are packed in cheek-by-jowl, helter-skelter, like books of different sizes jammed into a rickety bookcase. Buildings even sag over the street so that all you see overhead is a narrow strip of sky crisscrossed by miles of clotheslines. The flapping silks and cottons are very bright against the sodden, dirty sky. But there are certain vantage points where the city opens up and all at once you have a panoramic view of Calcutta. You see a long muddy hillside that has become home to a *bustee,* thousands and thousands of slum dwellings where tiny fires are tended through the night. The dead come often to these slums of tin and cardboard, but the people do not leave the *bustee*—where would they go? Or you see a wasteland of disused factories, empty warehouses, blackened smokestacks jutting into a rust-colored sky. Or a flash of the Hooghly River, steel-gray in its shroud of mist, spanned by the intricate girder-and-wirescape of the Howrah Bridge.

Just now I was walking opposite the river. The waterfront was not considered a safe place because of the danger from drowning victims. Thousands each year took the long plunge off the bridge, and thousands more simply waded into the water. It is easy to commit suicide at a riverfront because despair collects in the water vapor. This is part of the reason for the tangible cloud of despair that hangs over Calcutta along with its veil of humidity.

Now the suicides and the drowned street children were coming out of the river. At any moment the water might regurgitate one, and you would hear him scrabbling up the bank. If he had been in the water long enough he might tear himself to spongy gobbets on the stones and broken bricks that littered the waterfront; all that remained would be a trace of foul brown odor, like the smell of mud from the deep part of the river.

Police—especially the Sikhs, who are said to be more violent than Hindus—had been taking the dead up on the bridge to shoot them. Even from far away I could see spray-patterns of red on the drab girders. Alternately they set the dead alight with gasoline and threw them over the railing into the river. At night it was not uncommon to see several writhing shapes caught in the downstream current, the fiery symmetry of their heads and arms and legs making them into five-pointed human stars.

I stopped at a spice vendor's stand to buy a bunch of red chrysanthemums and a handful of saffron. The saffron I had him wrap in a twist of scarlet silk. "It is a beautiful day," I said to him in Bengali. He stared at me, half amused, half appalled. "A beautiful day for what?"

True Hindu faith calls upon the believer to view all things as equally sacred. There is nothing profane—no dirty dog picking through the ash bin at a cremation ground, no stinking gangrenous stump thrust into your face by a beggar who seems to hold you personally responsible for all his woes. These things are as sacred as feasting day at the holiest temple. But even for the most devout Hindus it has been difficult to see these walking dead as sacred. They are empty humans. That is the truly horrifying thing about them, more than their vacuous hunger for living flesh, more than the blood caked under their nails or the shreds of flesh caught between their teeth. They are soulless; there is nothing in their eyes; the sounds they make—their farts, their grunts and mewls of hunger—are purely reflexive. The Hindu, who has been taught to believe in the soul of everything, has a particular horror of these drained human vessels. But in Calcutta life goes on. The shops are still open. The confusion of traffic still inches its way up Chowringhee. No one sees any alternatives.

Soon I arrived at what was almost invariably my day's first stop. I would often walk twenty or thirty miles in a day—I had strong shoes and nothing to occupy my time except walking and looking. But I always began at the Kalighat, temple of the Goddess.

There are a million names for her, a million vivid descriptions: Kali the Terrible, Kali the Ferocious, skull-necklace, destroyer of men, eater of souls. But to me she was Mother Kali, the only one of the vast and colorful pantheon of Hindu gods that stirred my imagination and lifted my heart. She was the Destroyer, but all final refuge was found in her. She was the goddess of the age. She could bleed and burn and still rise again, very awake, beautifully terrible.

I ducked under the garlands of marigolds and strands of temple bells strung across the door, and I entered the temple of Kali. After the constant clamor of the street, the silence inside the temple was deafening. I fancied I could hear the small noises of my body echoing back to me from the ceiling far above. The sweet opium glaze of incense curled around my head. I approached the idol of Kali, the *jagrata*. Her gimlet eyes watched me as I came closer.

She was tall, gaunter and more brazenly naked than my friend Devi even at her best moments. Her breasts were tipped with blood— at least I always imagined them so—and her two sharp fangs and the long streamer of a tongue that uncurled from her open mouth were the color of blood too. Her hair whipped about her head and her eyes were wild, but the third crescent eye in the center of her forehead was merciful; it saw and accepted all. The necklace of skulls circled the graceful stem of her neck, adorned the sculpted hollow of her throat. Her four arms were so sinuous that if you looked away even for an instant, they seemed to sway. In her four hands she held a noose of rope, a skull-staff, a shining sword, and a gaping, very dead-looking severed head. A silver bowl sat at the foot of the statue just beneath the head, where the blood from the neck would drip. Sometimes this was filled with goat's or sheep's blood as an offering. The bowl was full today. In these times the blood might well be human, though there was no putrid smell to indicate it had come from one of the dead.

I laid my chrysanthemums and saffron at Kali's feet. Among the other offerings, mostly sweets and bundles of spice, I saw a few strange objects. A fingerbone. A shriveled mushroom of flesh that turned out upon closer inspection to be an ear. These were offerings for special protection, mostly wrested from the dead. But who was to say that a few devotees had not lopped off their own ears or finger joints to coax a boon from Kali? Sometimes when I had forgotten to bring an offering, I cut my wrist with a razor blade and let a few drops of my blood fall at the idol's feet.

I heard a shout from outside and turned my head for a moment. When I looked back, the four arms seemed to have woven themselves into a new pattern, the long tongue seemed to loll farther from the scarlet mouth. And—this was a frequent fantasy of mine—the wide hips now seemed to tilt forward, affording me a glimpse of the sweet and terrible petalled cleft between the thighs of the goddess.

I smiled up at the lovely sly face. "If only I had a tongue as long as yours, Mother," I murmured, "I would kneel before you and lick the folds of your holy pussy until you screamed with joy." The toothy grin seemed to grow wider, more lascivious. I imagined much in the presence of Kali.

Outside in the temple yard I saw the source of the shout I had heard. There is a stone block upon which the animals brought to Kali, mostly baby goats, are beheaded by the priests. A gang of roughly dressed men had captured a dead girl and were bashing her head in on the sacrificial block. Their arms rose and fell, ropy muscles flexing. They clutched sharp stones and bits of brick in their scrawny hands. The girl's half-pulped head still lashed back and forth. The lower jaw still snapped, though the teeth and bone were splintered. Foul thin blood coursed down and mingled with the rich animal blood in the earth beneath the block. The girl was nude, filthy with her own gore and waste. The flaccid breasts hung as if sucked dry of meat. The belly was burst open with gases. One of the men thrust a stick into the ruined gouge between the girl's legs and leaned on it with all his weight.

Only in extensive stages of decay can the dead be told from the lepers. The dead are greater in number now, and even the lepers look human when compared to the dead. But that is only if you get close enough to look into the eyes. The faces in various stages of wet and dry rot, the raw ends of bones rubbing through skin like moldy cheesecloth, the cancerous domes of the skulls are the same. After a certain point lepers could no longer stay alive begging in the streets, for most people would now flee in terror at the sight of a rotting face. As a result the lepers were dying, then coming back, and the two races mingled like some obscene parody of incest. Perhaps they actually could breed. The dead could obviously eat and digest, and seemed to excrete at random like everyone else in Calcutta, but I supposed no one knew whether they could ejaculate or conceive.

A stupid idea, really. A dead womb would rot to pieces around a fetus before it could come halfway to term; a dead scrotal sac would be far too cold a cradle for living seed. But no one seemed to know anything about the biology of the dead. The newspapers were hysterical, printing picture upon picture of random slaughter by dead and living alike. Radio stations had either gone off the air or were broadcasting endless religious exhortations that ran together in one long keening whine, the edges of Muslim, Hindu, Christian doctrine beginning to fray and blur.

No one in India could say for sure what made the dead walk. The latest theory I had heard was something about a genetically engineered microbe that had been designed to feed on plastic: a microbe that would save the world from its own waste. But the microbe had mutated and was now eating and "replicating" human cells, causing basic bodily functions to reactivate. It did not much matter whether this was true. Calcutta was a city relatively unsurprised to see its dead rise and walk and feed upon it. It had seen them doing so for a hundred years.

All the rest of the lengthening day I walked through the city. I saw no more dead except a cluster far away at the end of a blocked street, in the last rags of bloody light, fighting each other over the bloated carcass of a sacred cow.

My favorite place at sunset is by the river where I can see the Howrah Bridge. The Hooghly is painfully beautiful in the light of the setting sun. The last rays melt onto the water like hot *ghee,* turning the river from steel to khaki to nearly golden, a blazing ribbon of light. The bridge rises black and skeletal into the fading orange sky. Tonight an occasional skirl of bright flowers and still-glowing greasy embers floated by, the last earthly traces of bodies cremated farther up the river. Above the bridge were the burning *ghats* where families lined up to incinerate their dead and cast the ashes into the holy river. Cremation is done more efficiently these days, or at least more hurriedly. People can reconcile in their hearts their fear of strangers' dead, but they do not want to see their own dead rise.

I walked along the river for a while. The wind off the water carried the scent of burning meat. When I was well away from the bridge, I wandered back into the maze of narrow streets and alleyways that lead toward the docks in the far southern end of the city. People were already beginning to settle in for the night, though here a bedroom might mean your own packing crate or your own square of sidewalk. Fires glowed in nooks and corners. A warm breeze still blew off the river and sighed its way through the winding streets. It seemed very late now. As I made my way from corner to corner, through intermittent pools of light and much longer patches of darkness, I heard small bells jingling to the rhythm of my footsteps. The brass bells of rickshaw men, ringing to tell me they were there in case I wished for a ride. But I could see none of the men. The effect was eerie, as if I were walking alone down an empty nighttime street being serenaded by ghostly bells. The feeling soon passed. You are never truly alone in Calcutta.

A thin hand slid out of the darkness as I passed. Looking into the doorway it came from, I could barely make out five gaunt faces, five forms huddled against the night. I dropped several coins into the hand and it slid out of sight again. I am seldom begged from. I look neither rich nor poor, but I have a talent for making myself all but invisible. People look past me, sometimes right through me. I don't mind; I see more things that way. But when I am begged from I always give. With my handful of coins, all five of them might have a bowl of rice and lentils tomorrow.

A bowl of rice and lentils in the morning, a drink of water from a broken standpipe at night.

It seemed to me that the dead were among the best-fed citizens of Calcutta.

Now I crossed a series of narrow streets and was surprised to find myself coming up behind the Kalighat. The side streets are so haphazardly arranged that you are constantly finding yourself in places you had no idea you were even near. I had been to the Kalighat hundreds of times, but I had never approached it from this direction. The temple was dark and still. I had not been here at this hour before, did not even know whether the priests were still here or if one could enter so late. But as I walked closer I saw a little door standing open at the back. The entrance used by the priests, perhaps. Something flickered from within: a candle, a tiny mirror sewn on a robe, the smoldering end of a stick of incense.

I slipped around the side of the temple and stood at the door for a moment. A flight of stone steps led up into the darkness of the temple. The Kalighat at night, deserted, might have been an unpleasant prospect to some. The thought of facing the fierce idol alone in the gloom might have made some turn away from those steps. I began to climb them.

The smell reached me before I ascended halfway. To spend a day walking through Calcutta is to be assailed by thousands of odors both pleasant and foul: the savor of spices frying in *ghee*, the stink of shit and urine and garbage, the sick-sweet scent of the little white flowers called *mogra* that are sold in garlands and that make me think of the gardenia perfume American undertakers use to mask the smell of their corpses.

Almost everyone in Calcutta is scrupulously clean in person, even the very poor. They will leave their trash and their spit everywhere, but many of them wash their bodies twice a day. Still, everyone sweats under the sodden veil of heat, and at midday any public place will be redolent with the smell of human perspiration, a delicate tang like the mingled juices of lemons and onions. But lingering in the stairwell was an odor stronger and more foul than any I had encountered today. It was deep and brown and moist; it curled at the edges like a mushroom beginning to dry. It was the perfume of mortal corruption. It was the smell of rotting flesh.

Then I came up into the temple, and I saw them.

The large central room was lit only with candles that flickered in a restless draft, first this way, then that. In the dimness the worshippers looked no different from any other supplicants at the feet of Kali. But as my eyes grew accustomed to the candlelight, details resolved themselves. The withered hands, the ruined faces. The burst body cavities where ropy organs could be seen trailing down behind the cagework of ribs.

The offerings they had brought.

By day Kali grinned down upon an array of blossoms and sweetmeats lovingly arranged at the foot of her pedestal. The array spread there now seemed more suited to the goddess. I saw human heads balanced on raw stumps of necks, eyes turned up to crescents of silver-white. I saw gobbets of meat that might have been torn from a belly or a thigh. I saw severed hands like pale lotus flowers, the fingers like petals opening silently in the night.

Most of all, piled on every side of the altar, I saw bones. Bones picked so clean that they gleamed in the candlelight. Bones with smears of meat and long snotty runners of fat still attached. Skinny arm-bones, clubby leg-bones, the pretzel of a pelvis, the beadwork of a spine. The delicate bones of children. The crumbling ivory bones of the old. The bones of those who could not run.

These things the dead brought to their goddess. She had been their goddess all along, and they her acolytes.

Kali's smile was hungrier than ever. The tongue lolled like a wet red streamer from the open mouth. The eyes were blazing black holes in the gaunt and terrible face. If she had stepped down from her pedestal and approached me now, if she had reached for me with those sinuous arms, I might not have been able to fall to my knees before her. I might have run. There are beauties too terrible to be borne.

Slowly the dead began to turn toward me. Their faces lifted and the rotting cavities of their nostrils caught my scent. Their eyes shone iridescent. Faint starry light shimmered in the empty spaces of their bodies. They were like cutouts in the fabric of reality, like conduits to a blank universe. The void where Kali ruled and the only comfort was in death.

They did not approach me. They stood holding their precious offerings and they looked at me—those of them that still had eyes—or they looked through me. At that moment I felt more than invisible. I felt empty enough to belong among these human shells.

A ripple seemed to pass through them. Then—in the uncertain candlelight, in the light that shimmered from the bodies of the dead—Kali did move.

The twitch of a finger, the deft turn of a wrist—at first it was so slight as to be nearly imperceptible. But then her lips split into an impossibly wide, toothy grin and the tip of her long tongue curled. She rotated her hips and swung her left leg high into the air. The foot that had trod on millions of corpses made a *pointe* as delicate as a prima ballerina's. The movement spread her sex wide open.

But it was not the petalled mandala-like cleft I had imagined kissing earlier. The pussy of the goddess was an enormous deep red hole that seemed to lead down to the center of the world. It was a gash in the universe, it was rimmed in blood and ash. Two of her four hands beckoned toward it, inviting me in. I could have thrust my head into it, then my shoulders. I could have crawled all the way into that wet crimson eternity, and kept crawling forever.

Then I did run. Before I had even decided to flee I found myself falling down the stone staircase, cracking my head and my knee on the risers. At the bottom I was up and running before I could register the pain. I told myself that I thought the dead would come after me. I do not know what I truly feared was at my back. At times I thought I was running not away from something, but toward it.

I ran all night. When my legs grew too tired to carry me I would board a bus. Once I crossed the bridge and found myself in Howrah, the even poorer suburb on the other side of the Hooghly. I stumbled through desolate streets for an hour or more before doubling back and crossing over into Calcutta again. Once I stopped to ask for a drink of water from a man who carried two cans of it slung on a long stick across his shoulders. He would not let me drink from his tin cup, but poured a little water into my cupped hands. In his face I saw the mingled pity and disgust with which one might look upon a drunk or a beggar. I was a well-dressed beggar, to be sure, but he saw the fear in my eyes.

In the last hour of the night I found myself wandering through a wasteland of factories and warehouses, of smokestacks and rusty corrugated tin gates, of broken windows. There seemed to be thousands of broken windows. After a while I realized I was on the Upper Chitpur Road. I walked for a while in the watery light that fills the sky before dawn. Eventually I left the road and staggered through the wasteland. Not until I saw its girders rising around me like the charred bones of a prehistoric animal did I realize I was in the ruins of the hospital where I had been born.

The hole of the basement had filled up with broken glass and crumbling metal, twenty years' worth of cinders and weeds, all washed innocent in the light of the breaking dawn. Where the building had stood there was only a vast depression in the ground, five or six feet deep. I slid down the shallow embankment, rolled, and came to rest in the ashes. They were infinitely soft; they cradled me. I felt as safe as an embryo. I let the sunrise bathe me. Perhaps I had climbed into the gory chasm between Kali's legs after all, and found my way out again.

Calcutta is cleansed each morning by the dawn. If only the sun rose a thousand times a day, the city would always be clean.

Ashes drifted over me, smudged my hands gray, flecked my lips. I lay safe in the womb of my city, called by its poets Lord of Nerves, city of joy, the pussy of the world. I felt as if I lay among the dead. I was that safe from them: I knew their goddess, I shared their many homes. As the sun came up over the mud and glory of Calcutta, the sky was so full of smoky clouds and pale pink light that it seemed, to my eyes, to burn.

FOLLOWED

by Will McIntosh

Will McIntosh's fiction has been published in *Strange Horizons*, *Asimov's Science Fiction*, *Postscripts*, *Interzone*, and *Futurismic*. His story "Perfect Violet" was selected to appear in *Science Fiction: Best of the Year, 2008 Edition*. McIntosh is currently working on his first novel, *Soft Apocalypse*, based on the story of the same name published in *Interzone*.

McIntosh says that zombies are a way to face the existential terror we feel at the awareness of our own mortality. "I think people love zombie fiction because it explores that terror so directly—the dead are right there, in your face, and they're not 'undead' beings with supernatural powers and sexy lives, they're corpses," he says. "Corpses scare the shit out of us."

"Followed" is the result of a discussion McIntosh initiated in a graduate social psychology class he was teaching, in which he posed the question: If you knew you could save lives for $100 each, how many would you save? "I pointed out that we probably can save lives for $100 or less, and we don't," McIntosh says, "and each of us has to live with that knowledge, or rationalize it away, or sell our cars."

She came wandering down the sidewalk like any other corpse, her herky-jerky walk unmistakable among the fluid strides of the living. She was six or seven, Southeast Asian, maybe Indian, her ragged clothes caked in dried mud. Pedestrians cut a wide berth around her without noticing her at all.

I thought nothing of her, figured the person she followed had ditched her in a car, and she was catching up in that relentless way that corpses do. I was downtown, sitting outside Jittery Joe's Coffee Shop on a summer afternoon. There were still a few weeks before fall semester, so I was relaxed, in no hurry to get anywhere.

I returned to the manuscript I was reading, and didn't think another thing of the corpse until I noticed her in my peripheral vision, standing right in front of my table. I glanced up at her, turned, looked over my shoulder, then back at her. Then I realized. She was looking at *me* with that unfocused stare, with those big, lifeless brown eyes. As if she was claiming me. But that couldn't be. I waited for her to move on, but she just stood. I lifted my coffee halfway to my mouth, set it back down shakily.

The woman at the next table, dressed in a green hemp dress, her foot propped on an empty chair, looked at me over the top of her paperback with thinly veiled disdain. When I caught her eye she looked back down at the paperback.

I lurched to my feet, the metal chair screeching on the brick pavement, my barely touched coffee sloshing onto the table, and retreated down the sidewalk.

I ducked into the anonymity of my parked car and lingered there, tracking the corpse in my rear-view mirror as she lurched toward me. Maybe it was a mistake, a misunderstanding—maybe she'd walk right past me. My Volvo Green was a fuel-cell vehicle, dammit, the most efficient I could afford, not an energy pig like most corpse-magnets drove. How could I have hooked a corpse? I cracked my window, waited to see if she would pass.

I heard her little feet scuffing the pebbly pavement as she drew close. She stopped three feet from my door, turned and faced me. Her face was round and babyish, her chin a tiny knot under her slack, open mouth. She was so tiny.

I started the car and pulled out, almost hitting another car. As I drove off I saw my corpse in the side mirror, lurching down the sidewalk, patiently following whatever homing device the dead used to track those they had claimed.

Every few minutes I pulled back the curtain to see if she was coming. And then there she was, walking along the side of the road with her head down. She turned up my driveway, stubbed her toe on the thin lip of asphalt, stumbled, regained her tenuous balance. She struggled stiffly up the three steps to my front door and stopped. I dropped the curtain, got up and locked the dead bolt.

I phoned Jenna.

"I have a corpse," I said as soon as she answered.

"Oh my God, Peter," Jenna said. There was a long pause. "Are you sure?"

"Well Christ," I wailed, "she's standing on my fucking doorstep. I'm pretty sure she's mine."

"I don't understand. You don't deserve a corpse."

"I know. Jesus, I can't believe it. I just can't believe it."

Jenna consoled me by ticking off the evidence, all the ways I was not like other corpse-owners. Then she changed the subject. I wasn't in the mood to talk about university politics or how-was-your-day minutiae, so I got off the phone after making plans to have dinner with her.

I tried to distract myself by turning on the TV. I checked the stock market. The Dow was up almost three percent, the NASDAQ two. I switched to the news. The president was conducting a press conference in a field of newly constructed windmills, on her decision to pull out of the Kyoto III accord. "We're doing everything we can to curb global warming," she said to the cameras, "but we will not bow to foreign pressure. The American way of life is not negotiable." Blah, blah, blah. Even with the news cameras picking the best angles a few hundred of her corpses were visible, cordoned from her by a phalanx of blue-suited secret service agents. The corpse of an emaciated four- or five-year-old black boy, his distended belly bulging as if a kickball was hidden under his skin, wandered through a breach and headed toward the president. He was swept up by an agent and returned to the crowd. But gently—the administration didn't want to give Amnesty International any more ammunition.

I tried to take solace in the president's corpses. She had eighty or ninety thousand, piled twenty deep around the White House gates, more arriving daily. I only had one.

I flipped through the channels. Strange how most TV shows depicted the world as corpseless. Nary a corpse to be seen on the sitcoms, cop shows, interactives—all those people, walking the streets, working, cutting up with friends, and not one of them followed by a corpse. Had there really been a time when there were no corpses? I could hardly imagine it anymore.

I pulled back the curtain, looked at her standing motionless in front of my door. I couldn't help myself. I wondered if there were clues on her to tell me who she was, or how she died. Some sort of evidence that the cosmic actuarial table that sent her to me had made an error.

I went to the door and opened it. She came in, her bare feet tracking dirt onto the hardwood floor.

"Look around," I said with a sweep of my hand, "I don't have that much stuff." I gave her a tour. "Solar power, fluorescent bulbs." I pointed out that all my furniture was used. She didn't look, only stared up at me. "I try to buy locally grown food. I voted for the One World party." Nothing. I scanned the room for more evidence.

"What did I do?" I asked her empty face. "Tell me what I did!"

She'd been a cute kid. I pictured her laughing, running, playing hop-scotch on the sidewalk like my sister used to. I pictured her drinking brown water out of a dirty metal cup, lying in bed, dying of typhoid or dysentery. Maybe her family couldn't afford a bed—maybe she'd died on a straw mat on the floor in the corner of a dirt hut. I let a familiar indignant anger rise in me at the injustice of it.

She was so completely silent standing there. Unmoving, not breathing. She's going to be with me for the rest of my life, I thought. How could I possibly stand that?

I sat in my recliner in the living room. She stood in front of me, at arm's length, and stared. I took a good look at her. Skinny legs with bony knees. Very brown feet. Long black hair littered with leaves and twigs. Her red, mud-caked shorts had a single front pocket. I reached over and, flinching at the stiff, cold feel of her flesh, felt around in her pocket with two fingers. There was something in it—I fished it out. It was a button, a shiny new button. Gunmetal grey with veins of teal snaking through it. I turned it over; it was cool and smooth, unmarked— the kind of thing a little girl might carry around if she didn't have any Barbies to play with.

I lifted her dirty hand by the wrist, turned it palm-up, put the button in her hand, closed her cold fingers over it, and gently lowered her hand back to her side. The button clattered to the hardwood floor.

"Is she there?" Jenna asked. I nodded. My corpse stood outside the restaurant door, staring in at me through the plate glass. I should have picked a restaurant farther from my house so I could eat before she reached me. "Just ignore her," Jenna whispered.

An elderly couple opened the door to leave, and my corpse came in, ignored. As much unseen as ignored—not like a lost dog but like a block of wood, or a wisp of autumn wind. She came and stood in front of me, staring, a pretty button tucked in her pocket. Jenna kept eating as if nothing had changed, though she examined my corpse out of the corner of her eye. I forked a half-spear of asparagus in lemon butter into my mouth, chewed and swallowed, felt it lodge in my throat.

Mine was not the only corpse in the establishment. There were about ten, actually. Two stood by the bar, their eyes in shadow under the dim light of stained-glass lamps, their filthy rags out of place among pressed pants, white shirts, polished wood and chrome. An attractive, well-dressed thirty-something couple had three of them hovering around their table, like their own personal wait-staff. One was an old, stooped Asian man, another a twelve-year-old black girl, the third a five-year-old who could have been my corpse's long-lost sister. Jesus, they must be living like complete pigs to rack up so many corpses.

The door opened as another couple left. An infant corpse crawled in, her back foot just clearing the door as it closed. She was nude; her jerky crawl reminded me of a turtle's. She made a grunting sound as she labored across the floor, stopped in front of the already well-attended couple, plopped onto her butt, stared up at the woman. The woman kept eating her paella, one of the restaurant's specialties. The man said something and she laughed, covering her mouth.

Out of the corner of my eye I thought I saw my corpse glance down at my plate. I jerked my head around and looked at her intently. Her eyes were glazed and fixed on my face.

"What's the matter?" Jenna said. "Don't stare at her," she hissed, as if I had picked my nose. "What? What is it?"

"I'd swear she just looked down at my plate," I said.

"Do you want to split a dessert?" She asked.

I wondered if I had imagined that quick, furtive glance. Probably. "You go ahead and get one, I'm pretty full." I put my fork down, my blackened salmon hardly touched.

When I got home I sat at the kitchen table and wrote a $3000 check to the World Hunger Fund. I usually sent them $50 or so. Three grand hurt, but I could afford it. Looking up, I was startled by a face staring in through the kitchen window. Her face. Until now she'd stood facing the windowless front door. Evidently she could learn. She stared, unblinking. She never blinked—I guess I'd noticed, but it hadn't fully registered till now.

As I worked the check into an envelope I found myself holding it so my corpse could see it. I wondered, was the little girl still in there, aware of where she was and what was happening, or was she just an empty shell?

I tore up the check and wrote another, for $10,000. That much I could not easily afford. I walked it to the mailbox. It was a beautiful night; the moon was full, the crickets and cicadas deafening. Two houses down and across the street, the corpse of a tall, scrawny black man squatted, peering with one eye through the lighted crack of a drawn shade. My corpse came around the house, pushing through the waist-high grass and native weeds (another testament to my green sensitivities, another reason why this corpse was a mistake), and met me on the way back. She followed me to the front door. I closed it in her face.

I got up early the next morning after a mostly sleepless night. I pulled up the shade, and there was her little round face. She was just tall enough for her nose to be above the bottom of the window frame.

"Shit." I thumped my forehead on the molding, fought back a hitching sob. I had really hoped I could buy her off.

"Get the hell away from me!" I shouted through the closed window before yanking the shade back down.

While I showered I pictured my corpse waiting patiently outside the window. Why couldn't it have been a man—an old man with no teeth? Fall semester loomed. My first class was in five days. I couldn't imagine teaching with a corpse staring at me.

None of the students had corpses, so mine was the only one in my 10 a.m. class. The students politely avoided looking at her, even though she stood barely three feet in front of me, her head craned to stare up at my face as I went over the syllabus.

My hands shook from exhaustion and nerves as I held the syllabus. I'd been a wreck the night before, had four or five drinks to staunch my anxiety, took forever to figure out what I would wear. I debated whether to dress down—a t-shirt and jeans—to demonstrate that I was just a regular guy, that I lived simply and didn't really deserve a corpse. But would the students see through me, think I was being pretentious? I'd finally pulled out a pair of black jeans and my white shirt, the shirt I'd been wearing the day my corpse had shown up, actually. Smart casual, the sort of outfit I usually wore.

Things got worse as I started to lecture. I tend to pace back and forth as I talk, and as I did she shadowed me, taking two small, lurching steps for every one of mine. The scuff of her little feet on the linoleum floor set my teeth on edge. Bare feet scuffing on dirty floors made me nuts, the way some people go nuts at the sound of fingernails on a chalkboard, or the feel of cotton balls. I stopped pacing.

I kept losing my train of thought, stumbling over words. I made eye contact with one of my new students; she quickly looked down, pretending to take notes, though I hadn't said anything important. I was barely saying anything coherent, let alone important.

Without realizing it I found myself looking right at my corpse, as if I were lecturing to her. She stared back. I forced myself to look away, at the blank white wall in the back of the room, realized I was pacing again, and she was pacing with me—scuff-*scuff*, scuff-*scuff*, jerking along like… like what? Like a dead child.

I let the class out early and headed to my office in a fog—exhausted, hung over, wondering how I could possibly make it through my one o'clock class. She did her best to keep up—I could hear the scuffing behind me.

A surge of anger tore through me and I wheeled, pointed at her, opened my mouth to speak. Her gaze flickered to my chest for a split second, then back up. This time I'd seen it, there was no doubt. Her eyes had dropped and almost—not quite, but *almost*—focused.

"I saw that!" I said, stabbing my finger at her. I was in the hall outside my office, confronting a corpse. Jack popped his bald head out of his office, took in the scene, pulled his head back inside.

Embarrassed, I wheeled and headed into my office, leaving the door ajar, allowing her to follow. I stared down at her.

"Tell me what I did!" I shouted, leaning down and pushing my face close to hers. "I'm a good person! I don't deserve this!" I wanted her to focus, to look at me, to listen to what I was saying. I saw the little pinkish-grey dollop dangling from the back of her throat. Below that, darkness.

I yanked the onyx Buddha statue off my desk and hurled it over her head. It crashed into a bookshelf, shattering a framed picture of Yankee Stadium, scattering a half-dozen textbooks.

"Jesus! sYou okay?" Jack called. I hefted my computer monitor over my head and slammed it to the floor at her feet. It split partway, popping and sparking. Then Jack was on me; I hadn't seen him come in, but he was behind me and had his arms wrapped around my chest.

"Calm down, calm down!" he shouted.

I struggled, tried to yank free. I'm not sure what I would have done if I'd gotten free. I truly hope I wouldn't have brought the computer console down on her head. I gave a final, violent tug. My shirt ripped loudly.

"Shhhh, shhhh," Jack said into my ear. "You're okay, it's okay, shhhh." I started to cry. Jack held on until he felt me relax, then loosened his grip, kept his arms around me for a moment longer, let me go.

Jack and I didn't know each other very well; it added to the surreal feel as I stood in my demolished office, crying. Through a blur of tears I saw a button lying on the floor by my corpse's foot. In a daze I knelt and picked it up. It was her button—grey, with veins of teal. Unmistakable. How had it gotten out of her pocket?

"I think the shirt's a total loss," Jack said behind me a little sheepishly. I looked down at my shirt. There was a long tear along the seam under the arm, and the front was flapped open—three or four buttons had popped off.

I guess you never look at the buttons on a shirt, even if you button them a thousand times. The buttons on my white shirt were gunmetal grey, with veins of teal. Quite unique. They weren't as bright and new as my corpse's button, because they'd taken a few turns in the dryer.

Gently I lifted her hand and turned it over, ran my finger over her tiny palm, over the pads of her baby fingers. Rough. Not the fingers of a child who spent much time playing hopscotch.

"Is everyone all right?" Maggie, from down at the end of the hall, stood in my doorway. Behind her two more of my colleagues craned their necks, trying to see what was happening. There was rarely excitement in our department; maybe an irate student once in a while, but never shattered glass or exploding computer monitors.

"Everything's fine," Jack said. He was a good guy, I realized. I was still down on my knees, staring at the button, my eyes red and tear-stained. The crowd dispersed, trailed by two corpses.

Jack squatted, put his arm around my shoulder. "You okay now?"

I nodded.

"I'm not gonna say I understand how you feel, but it must be awful."

I nodded.

"If you ever want to talk, just knock."

I nodded a third time. He patted my back and left.

It was nearly time for my one o'clock class. I kept a sweater in the bottom drawer of my desk for days when the a/c was cranked too high. I pulled the sweater over the ruined shirt, and, as my head popped through, I thought I caught my corpse glancing down at the button lying at her feet.

I stooped and retrieved the button, slipped it into her pocket, next to the other, shinier one.

I went around the corner to the bathroom, held the door open for my corpse when it started to swing shut on her. I washed my face and combed my hair, her watchful eyes reflected in the mirror.

I yanked a couple of paper towels from the dispenser, wet them under the faucet, knelt and wiped the worst of the dirt from my corpse's chubby cheeks and forehead. I tried to comb some of the debris out of her hair, but it was hopelessly tangled. I shoved the comb into my back pocket and plucked the biggest chips out by hand. I glanced at my watch. Time for class.

After retrieving a stack of syllabi and the class roll from my office I headed into the airy central lobby, up the double flight of stairs, steadying myself with the silver metal handrail. Halfway up I turned and looked back. My corpse was struggling up the second step, her legs too small, and too stiff, to make the climb easily. I went back down, wrapped my arms around my corpse, and carried her up the stairs.

THE SONG THE ZOMBIE SANG

by Harlan Ellison® and Robert Silverberg

Between them, Harlan Ellison and Robert Silverberg have won pretty much every award the science fiction and fantasy field has to offer; heck, *individually* they've each won pretty much every award the field has to offer. Both have been named Grand Masters by the Science Fiction and Fantasy Writers of America (the organization's life-time achievement award), and between them they have 12 Hugos, 8 Nebulas, and 27 Locus awards, among a slew of other awards. They are, quite simply, living legends. To include a story by either would be an honor; to have one written by both of them is transcendent.

In his collaborative collection, *Partners in Wonder*, Ellison said that this story was inspired by a writer he encountered while teaching at a college writing workshop. The man was "smashed drunk from morning to night" but still managed to put himself in front of the typewriter every morning to bang out a few words. "It was as though he was a zombie," Ellison said, "that he continued writing only as a reflex, the way a frog's leg jumps when it receives a galvanic shock, that he might as well be dead and stored in a vault except when he had to write."

From the fourth balcony of the Los Angeles Music Center the stage was little more than a brilliant blur of constantly changing chromatics—stabs of bright green, looping whorls of crimson. But Rhoda preferred to sit up there. She had no use for the Golden Horseshoe seats, buoyed on their grab-grav plates, bobbling loosely just beyond the fluted lip of the stage. Down there the sound flew off, flew up and away, carried by the remarkable acoustics of the Center's Takamuri dome. The colors were important, but it was the sound that really mattered, the patterns of resonance bursting from the hundred quivering outputs of the ultracembalo.

And if you sat below, you had the vibrations of the people down there—

She was hardly naive enough to think that the poverty that sent students up to the top was more ennobling than the wealth that permitted access to a Horseshoe; yet even though she had never actually sat through an entire concert down there, she could not deny that music heard from the fourth balcony was purer, more affecting, lasted longer in the memory. Perhaps it *was* the vibrations of the rich.

Arms folded on the railing of the balcony, she stared down at the rippling play of colors that washed the sprawling proscenium. Dimly she was aware that the man at her side was saying something. Somehow responding didn't seem important. Finally he nudged her, and she turned to him. A faint, mechanical smile crossed her face. "What is it, Laddy?"

Ladislas Jirasek mournfully extended a chocolate bar. Its end was ragged from having been nibbled. "Man cannot live by Bekh alone," he said.

"No, thanks, Laddy." She touched his hand lightly.

"What do you see down there?"

"Colors. That's all."

"No music of the spheres? No insight into the truths of your art?"

"You promised not to make fun of me."

He slumped back in his seat. "I'm sorry. I forget sometimes."

"Please, Laddy. If it's the liaison thing that's bothering you, I—"

"I didn't say a word about liaison, did I?"

"It was in your tone. You were starting to feel sorry for yourself. Please don't. You know I hate it when you start dumping guilt on me."

He had sought an official liaison with her for months, almost since the day they had met in Contrapuntal 301. He had been fascinated by her, amused by her, and finally had fallen quite hopelessly in love with her. Still she kept just beyond his reach. He had had her, but had never possessed her. Because he did feel sorry for himself, and she knew it, and the knowledge put him, for her, forever in the category of men who were simply not for long-term liaison.

She stared down past the railing. Waiting. Taut. A slim girl, honey-colored hair, eyes the lightest gray, almost the shade of aluminum. Her fingers lightly curved as if about to pounce on a keyboard. Music uncoiling eternally in her head.

"They say Bekh was brilliant in Stuttgart last week," Jirasek said hopefully.

"He did the Kreutzer?"

"And Timijian's Sixth and *The Knife* and some Scarlatti."

"Which?"

"I don't know. I don't remember what they said. But he got a ten-minute standing ovation, and *Der Musikant* said they hadn't heard such precise ornamentation since—"

The houselights dimmed.

"He's coming," Rhoda said, leaning forward. Jirasek slumped back and gnawed the chocolate bar down to its wrapper.

Coming out of it was always gray. The color of aluminum. He knew the charging was over, knew he'd been unpacked, knew when he opened his eyes that he would be at stage right, and there would be a grip ready to roll the ultracembalo's input console onstage, and the filament gloves would be in his right-hand jacket pocket. And the taste of sand on his tongue, and the gray fog of resurrection in his mind.

Nils Bekh put off opening his eyes.

Stuttgart had been a disaster. Only he knew how much of a disaster. Timi would have known, he thought. He would have come up out of the audience during the scherzo, and he would have ripped the gloves off my hands, and he would have cursed me for killing his vision. And later they would have gone to drink the dark, nutty beer together. But Timijian was dead. Died in '20, Bekh told himself. Five years before me.

I'll keep my eyes closed, I'll dampen the breathing. Will the lungs to suck more shallowly, the bellows to vibrate rather than howl with winds. And they'll think I'm malfunctioning, that the zombianic response wasn't triggered this time. That I'm still dead, really dead, not—

"Mr. Bekh."

He opened his eyes.

The stage manager was a thug. He recognized the type. Stippling of unshaved beard. Crumpled cuffs. Latent homosexuality. Tyrant to everyone backstage except, perhaps, the chorus boys in the revivals of Romberg and Friml confections.

"I've known men to develop diabetes just catching a matinee," Bekh said.

"What's that? I don't understand."

Bekh waved it away. "Nothing. Forget it. How's the house?"

"Very nice, Mr. Bekh. The houselights are down. We're ready."

Bekh reached into his right-hand jacket pocket and removed the thin electronic gloves, sparkling with their rows of minisensors and pressors. He pulled the right glove tight, smoothing all wrinkles. The material clung like a second skin. "If you please," he said. The grip rolled the console onstage, positioned it, locked it down with the dogging pedals, and hurried offstage left through the curtains.

Now Bekh strolled out slowly. Moving with great care: tubes of glittering fluids ran through his calves and thighs, and if he walked too fast the hydrostatic balance was disturbed and the nutrients didn't get to his brain. The fragility of the perambulating dead was a nuisance, one among many. When he reached the grab-grav plate, he signalled the stage manager. The thug gave the sign to the panel-man, who passed his fingers over the color-coded keys, and the grab-grav plate rose slowly, majestically. Up through the floor of the stage went Nils Bekh. As he emerged, the chromatics keyed sympathetic vibrations in the audience, and they began to applaud.

He stood silently, head slightly bowed, accepting their greeting. A bubble of gas ran painfully through his back and burst near his spine. His lower lip twitched slightly. He suppressed the movement. Then he stepped off the plate, walked to the console, and began pulling on the other glove.

He was a tall, elegant man, very pale, with harsh brooding cheekbones and a craggy, massive nose that dominated the flower-gentle eyes, the thin mouth. He looked properly romantic. An important artistic asset, they told him when he was starting out, a million years ago.

As he pulled and smoothed the other glove, he heard the whispering. When one has died, one's hearing becomes terribly acute. It made listening to one's own performances that much more painful. But he knew what the whispers were all about. Out there someone was saying to his wife:

"Of course he doesn't *look* like a zombie. They kept him in cold till they had the techniques. *Then* they wired him and juiced him and brought him back."

And the wife would say, "How does it work, how does he keep coming back to life, what is it?"

And the husband would lean far over on the arm of his chair, resting his elbow, placing the palm of his hand in front of his mouth and looking warily around to be certain that no one would overhear the blurred inaccuracies he was about to utter. And he would try to tell his wife about the residual electric charge of the brain cells, the persistence of the motor responses after death, the lingering mechanical vitality on which they had seized. In vague and rambling terms he would speak of the built-in life-support system that keeps the brain flushed with necessary fluids. The surrogate hormones, the chemicals that take the place of blood. "You know how they stick an electric wire up a frog's leg, when they cut it off? Okay. Well, when the leg jerks, they call that a galvanic response. Now, if you can get a whole *man* to jerk when you put a current through him—not really jerking, I mean that he walks around, he can play his instrument—"

"Can he think too?"

"I suppose. I don't know. The brain's intact. They don't let it decay. What they do, they use every part of the body for its mechanical function—the heart's a pump, the lungs are bellows—and they wire in a bunch of contacts and leads, and then there's a kind of twitch, an artificial burst of life—of course, they can keep it going only five, six hours, then the fatigue-poisons start to pile up and clog the lines—but that's long enough for a concert, anyway—"

"So what they're really doing is, they take a man's brain, and they keep it alive by using his own body as the life-support machine," the wife says brightly. "Is that it? Instead of putting him into some kind of box, they keep him in his own skull, and do all the machinery inside his body—"

"That's it. That's it exactly, more or less. More or less."

Bekh ignored the whispers. He had heard them all hundreds of times before. In New York and Beirut, in Hanoi and Knossos, in Kenyatta and Paris. How fascinated they were. Did they come for the music, or to see the dead man walk around?

He sat down on the player's ledge in front of the console, and laid his hands along the metal fibers. A deep breath: old habit, superfluous, inescapable. The fingers already twitching. The pressors seeking the keys. Under the close-cropped gray hair, the synapses clicking like relays. Here, now. Timijian's Ninth Sonata. Let it soar. Bekh closed his eyes and put his shoulders into his work, and from the ring of outputs overhead came the proper roaring tones. There.

It has begun. Easily, lightly, Bekh rang in the harmonics, got the sympathetic pipes vibrating, built up the texture of sound. He had not played the Ninth for two years. Vienna. How long is two years? It seemed hours ago. He still heard the reverberations. And duplicated them exactly; this performance differed from the last one no more than one playing of a recording differs from another. An image sprang into his mind: a glistening sonic cube sitting at the console in place of a man. Why do they need me, when they could put a cube in the slot and have the same thing at less expense? And I could rest. And I could rest. There. Keying in the subsonics. This wonderful instrument! What if Bach had known it? Beethoven? To hold a whole world in your fingertips. The entire spectrum of sound, and the colors, too, and more: hitting the audience in a dozen senses at once. Of course, the music is what matters. The frozen, unchanging music. The pattern of sounds emerging now as always, now as he had played it at the premiere in '19. Timijian's last work. Decibel by decibel, a reconstruction of my own performance. And look at them out there. Awed. Loving. Bekh felt tremors in his elbows; too tense, the nerves betraying him. He made the necessary compensations. Hearing the thunder reverberating from the fourth balcony. What is this music all about? Do I in fact understand any of it? Does the sonic cube comprehend the B Minor Mass that is recorded within itself? Does the amplifier understand the symphony it amplifies? Bekh smiled. Closed his eyes. The shoulders surging, the wrists supple. Two hours to go. Then they let me sleep again. Is it fifteen years, now? Awaken, perform, sleep. And the adoring public cooing at me. The women who would love to give themselves to me. Necrophiliacs? How could they even want to touch me? The dryness of the tomb on my skin. Once there were women, yes, Lord, yes! Once. Once there was life, too. Bekh leaned back and swept forward. The old virtuoso swoop; brings down the house. The chill in their spines. Now the sound builds toward the end of the first movement. Yes, yes, so. Bekh opened the topmost bank of outputs and heard the audience respond, everyone sitting up suddenly as the new smash of sound cracked across the air. Good old Timi: a wonderful sense of the theatrical. Up. Up. Knock them back in their seats. He smiled with satisfaction at his own effects. And then the sense of emptiness. Sound for its own sake. Is this what music means? Is this a masterpiece? I know nothing any more. How tired I am of playing for them. Will they applaud? Yes, and stamp their feet and congratulate one another on having been lucky enough to hear me tonight. And what do they know? What do I know? I am dead. I am nothing. I am nothing. With a demonic two-handed plunge he hammered out the final fugal screams of the first movement.

Weatherex had programmed mist, and somehow it fit Rhoda's mood. They stood on the glass landscape that swept down from the Music Center, and Jirasek offered her the pipe. She shook her head absently, thinking of other things. "I have a pastille," she said.

"What do you say we look up Inez and Treat, see if they want to get something to eat?"

She didn't answer.

"Rhoda?"

"Will you excuse me, Laddy? I think I want to be all by myself for a while."

He slipped the pipe into his pocket and turned to her. She was looking through him as if he were no less glass than the scene surrounding them. Taking her hands in his own, he said, "Rhoda, I just don't understand. You won't even give me time to find the words."

"Laddy—"

"No. This time I'll have my say. Don't pull away. Don't retreat into that little world of yours, with your half-smiles and your faraway looks."

"I want to think about the music."

"There's more to life than music, Rhoda. There has to be. I've spent as many years as you working inside my head, working to create something. You're better than I am, you're maybe better than anyone I've ever heard, maybe even better than Bekh someday. Fine: you're a great artist. But is that all? There's something more. It's idiocy to make your art your religion, your whole existence."

"Why are you doing this to me?"

"Because I love you."

"That's an explanation, not an excuse. Let me go, Laddy. Please."

"Rhoda, art doesn't mean a damn thing if it's just craft, if it's just rote and technique and formulas. It doesn't mean anything if there isn't love behind it, and caring, and commitment to life. You deny all that. You split yourself and smother the part that fires the art…"

He stopped abruptly. It was not the sort of speech a man could deliver without realizing, quickly, crushingly, how sententious and treacly it sounded. He dropped her hands. "I'll be at Treat's, if you want to see me later." He turned and walked away into the shivering reflective night.

Rhoda watched him go. She suspected there were things she should have said. But she hadn't said them. He disappeared. Turning, she stared up at the overwhelming bulk of the Music Center, and began slowly to walk toward it.

"Maestro, you were exquisite tonight," the pekinese woman said in the Green Room. "Golden," added the bullfrog sycophant. "A joy. I cried, really cried," trilled the birds. Nutrients bubbled in his chest. He could feel valves flapping. He dipped his head, moved his hands, whispered thankyous. Staleness settled grittily behind his forehead. "Superb." "Unforgettable." "Incredible." Then they went away and he was left, as always, with the keepers. The man from the corporation that owned him, the stage manager, the packers, the electrician. "Perhaps it's time," said the corporation man, smoothing his mustache lightly. He had learned to be delicate with the zombie.

Bekh sighed and nodded. They turned him off.

"Want to get something to eat first?" the electrician said. He yawned. It had been a long tour, late nights, meals in jetports, steep angles of ascent and rapid re-entries.

The corporation man nodded. "All right. We can leave him here for a while. I'll put him on standby." He touched a switch.

The lights went off in banks, one by one. Only the nightlights remained for the corporation man and the electrician, for their return, for their final packing.

The Music Center shut down.

In the bowels of the self-contained system the dust-eaters and a dozen other species of cleanup machines began stirring, humming softly.

In the fourth balcony, a shadow moved. Rhoda worked her way toward the downslide, emerging in the center aisle of the orchestra, into the Horseshoe, around the pit, and onto the stage. She went to the console and let her hands rest an inch above the keys. Closing her eyes, catching her breath. I will begin my concert with the Timijian Ninth Sonata for Unaccompanied Ultracembalo. A light patter of applause, gathering force, now tempestuous. Waiting. The fingers descending. The world alive with her music. Fire and tears, joy, radiance. All of them caught in the spell. How miraculous. How wonderfully she plays. Looking out into the darkness, hearing in her tingling mind the terrible echoes of the silence. Thank you. Thank you all so much. Her eyes moist. Moving away from the console. The flow of fantasy ebbing.

She went on into the dressing room and stood just within the doorway, staring across the room at the corpse of Nils Bekh in the sustaining chamber, his eyes closed, his chest still, his hands relaxed at his sides. She could see the faintest bulge in his right jacket pocket where the thin gloves lay, fingers folded together.

Then she moved close to him, looked down into his face, and touched his cheek. His beard never grew. His skin was cool and satiny, a peculiarly feminine texture. Strangely, through the silence, she remembered the sinuous melody of the *Liebestod,* that greatest of all laments, and rather than the great sadness the passage always brought to her, she felt herself taken by anger. Gripped by frustration and disappointment, choked by betrayal, caught in a seizure of violence. She wanted to rake the pudding-smooth skin of his face with her nails. She wanted to pummel him. Deafen him with screams. Destroy him. For the lie. For the lies, the many lies, the unending flow of lying notes, the lies of his life after death.

Her trembling hand hovered by the side of the chamber. Is this the switch? She turned him on.

He came out of it. Eyes closed. Rising through a universe the color of aluminum. Again, then. Again. He thought he would stand there a moment with eyes closed, collecting himself, before going onstage. It got harder and harder. The last time had been so bad. In Los Angeles, in that vast building, balcony upon balcony, thousands of blank faces, the ultracembalo such a masterpiece of construction. He had opened the concert with Timi's Ninth. So dreadful. A sluggish performance, note-perfect, the tempi flawless, and yet sluggish, empty, shallow. And tonight it would happen again. Shamble out on stage, don the gloves, go through the dreary routine of re-creating the greatness of Nils Bekh.

His audience, his adoring followers. How he hated them! How he longed to turn on them and denounce them for what they had done to him. Schnabel rested. Horowitz rested. Joachim rested. But for Bekh there was no rest. They had not allowed him to go. Oh, he could have refused to let them sustain him. But he had never been that strong. He had had strength for the loveless, light-less years of living with his music, yes. For that there had never been enough time. Strong was what he had had to be. To come from where he had been, to learn what had to be learned, to keep his skills once they were his. Yes. But in dealing with people, in speaking out, in asserting himself… in short, having courage… no, there had been very little of that. He had lost Dorothea, he had acceded to Wizmer's plans, he had borne the insults Lisbeth and Neil and Cosh—ah, gee, Cosh, was he still alive?—the insults they had used to keep him tied to them, for better or worse, always worse. So he had gone with them, done their bidding, never availed himself of his strength—if in fact there was strength of that sort buried somewhere in him—and in the end even Sharon had despised him.

So how could he go to the edge of the stage, stand there in the full glare of the lights and tell them what they were? Ghouls. Selfish ghouls. As dead as he was, but in a different way. Unfeeling, hollow.

But if he could! If he could just once outwit the corporation man, he would throw himself forward and he would shout—

Pain. A stinging pain in his cheek. His head jolted back; the tiny pipes in his neck protested. The sound of flesh on flesh echoed in his mind. Startled, he opened his eyes. A girl before him. The color of aluminum, her eyes. A young face. Fierce. Thin lips tightly clamped. Nostrils flaring. Why is she so angry? She was raising her hand to slap him again. He threw his hands up, wrists crossed, palms forward, to protect his eyes. The second blow landed more heavily than the first. Were delicate things shattering within his reconstructed body?

The look on her face! She hated him.

She slapped him a third time. He peered out between his fingers, astonished by the vehemence of her eyes. And felt the flooding pain, and felt the hate, and felt a terribly wonderful sense of life for just that one moment. Then he remembered too much, and he stopped her.

He could see as he grabbed her swinging hand that she found his strength improbable. Fifteen years a zombie, moving and living for only seven hundred four days of that time. Still, he was fully operable, fully conditioned, fully muscled.

The girl winced. He released her and shoved her away. She was rubbing her wrist and staring at him silently, sullenly.

"If you don't like me," he asked, "why did you turn me on?"

"So I could tell you I know what a fraud you are. These others, the ones who applaud and grovel and suck up to you, they don't know, they have no idea, but *I* know. How can you do it? How can you have made such a disgusting spectacle of yourself?" She was shaking. "I heard you when I was a child," she said. "You changed my whole life. I'll never forget it. But I've heard you lately. Slick formulas, no real insight. Like a machine sitting at the console. A player piano. You know what player pianos were, Bekh. That's what you are."

He shrugged. Walking past her, he sat down and glanced in the dressing-room mirror. He looked old and weary, the changeless face changing now. There was a flatness to his eyes. They were without sheen, without depths. An empty sky.

"Who are you?" he asked quietly. "How did you get in here?"

"Report me, go ahead. I don't care if I'm arrested. Someone had to say it. You're shameful! Walking around, pretending to make music—don't you see how awful it is? A performer is an interpretative artist, not just a machine for playing the notes. I shouldn't have to tell you that. An interpretative artist. Artist. Where's your art now? Do you see beyond the score? Do you grow from performance to performance?"

Suddenly he liked her very much. Despite her plainness, despite her hatred, despite himself. "You're a musician."

She let that pass.

"What do you play?" Then he smiled. "The ultracembalo, of course. And you must be very good."

"Better than you. Clearer, cleaner, deeper. Oh, God, what am I doing here? You *disgust* me."

"How can I keep on growing?" Bekh asked gently. "The dead don't grow."

Her tirade swept on, as if she hadn't heard. Telling him over and over how despicable he was, what a counterfeit of greatness. And then she halted in midsentence. Blinking, reddening, putting hands to lips. "Oh," she murmured, abashed, starting to weep. "Oh. *Oh!*"

She went silent.

It lasted a long time. She looked away, studied the walls, the mirror, her hands, her shoes. He watched her. Then, finally, she said, "What an arrogant little snot I am. What a cruel foolish bitch. I never stopped to think that you—that maybe—I just didn't think—" He thought she would run from him. "And you won't forgive me, will you? Why should you? I break in, I turn you on, I scream a lot of cruel nonsense at you—"

"It wasn't nonsense. It was all quite true, you know. Absolutely true." Then, softly, he said, "Break the machinery."

"Don't worry. I won't cause any more trouble for you. I'll go, now. I can't tell you how foolish I feel, haranguing you like that. A dumb little puritan, puffed up with pride in her own art. Telling *you* that you don't measure up to my ideals. When I—"

"You didn't hear me. I asked you to break the machinery."

She looked at him in a new way, slightly out of focus. "What are you talking about?"

"To stop me. I want to be gone. Is that so hard to understand? You, of all people, should understand that. What you say is true, very very true. Can you put yourself where I am? A thing, not alive, not dead, just a thing, a tool, an implement that, unfortunately, thinks and remembers and wishes for release. Yes, a player piano. My life stopped and my art stopped, and I have nothing to belong to now, not even the art. For it's always the same. Always the same tones, the same reaches, the same heights. Pretending to make music, as you say. Pretending."

"But I can't—"

"Of course you can. Come, sit down, we'll discuss it. And you'll play for me."

"Play for you?"

He reached out his hand and she started to take it, then drew her hand back. "You'll have to play for me," he said quietly. "I can't let just anyone end me. That's a big, important thing, you see. Not just anyone. So you'll play for me." He got heavily to his feet. Thinking of Lisbeth, Sharon, Dorothea. Gone, all gone now. Only he, Bekh, left behind, some of him left behind, old bones, dried meat. Breath as stale as Egypt. Blood the color of pumice. Sounds devoid of tears and laughter. Just sounds.

He led the way, and she followed him, out onto the stage, where the console still stood uncrated. He gave her his gloves, saying, "I know they aren't yours. I'll take that into account. Do the best you can." She drew them on slowly, smoothing them.

She sat down at the console. He saw the fear in her face, and the ecstasy, also. Her fingers hovering over the keys. Pouncing. God, Timi's Ninth! The tones swelling and rising, and the fear going from her face. Yes. Yes. He would not have played it that way, but yes, just so. Timi's notes filtered through *her* soul. A striking interpretation. Perhaps she falters a little, but why not? The wrong gloves, no preparation, strange circumstances. And how beautifully she plays. The hall fills with sound. He ceases to listen as a critic might; he becomes part of the music. His own fingers moving, his muscles quivering, reaching for pedals and stops, activating the pressors. As if he plays through her. She goes on, soaring higher, losing the last of her nervousness. In full command. Not yet a finished artist, but so good, so wonderfully good! Making the mighty instrument sing. Draining its full resources. Underscoring this, making that more lean. Oh, yes! He is in the music. It engulfs him. Can he cry? Do the tearducts still function? He can hardly bear it, it is so beautiful. He has forgotten, in all these years. He has not heard anyone else play for so long. Seven hundred four days. Out of the tomb. Bound up in his own meaningless performances. And now this. The rebirth of music. It was once like this all the time, the union of composer and instrument and performer, soul-wrenching, all-encompassing.

For him. No longer. Eyes closed, he plays the movement through to its close by way of her body, her hands, her soul. When the sound dies away, he feels the good exhaustion that comes from total submission to the art.

"That's fine," he said, when the last silence was gone. "That was very lovely." A catch in his voice. His hands were still trembling; he was afraid to applaud.

He reached for her, and this time she took his hand. For a moment he held her cool fingers. Then he tugged gently, and she followed him back into the dressing room, and he laid down on the sofa, and he told her which mechanisms to break, after she turned him off, so he would feel no pain. Then he closed his eyes and waited.

"You'll just—go?" she asked.

"Quickly. Peacefully."

"I'm afraid. It's like murder."

"I'm dead," he said. "But not dead enough. You won't be killing anything. Do you remember how my playing sounded to you? Do you remember why I came here? Is there life in me?"

"I'm still afraid."

"I've earned my rest," he said. He opened his eyes and smiled. "It's all right. I like you." And, as she moved toward him, he said, "Thank you."

Then he closed his eyes again.

She turned him off. Then she did as he had instructed her.

Picking her way past the wreckage of the sustaining chamber, she left the dressing room. She found her way out of the Music Center—out onto the glass landscape, under the singing stars, and she was crying for him.

Laddy. She wanted very much to find Laddy now. To talk to him. To tell him he was almost right about what he'd told her. Not entirely, but more than she had believed… before. She went away from there. Smoothly, with songs yet to be sung.

And behind her, a great peace had settled. Unfinished, at last the symphony had wrung its last measure of strength and sorrow.

It did not matter what Weatherex said was the proper time for mist or rain or fog. Night, the stars, the songs were forever.

PASSION PLAY

by Nancy Holder

Nancy Holder is the author of more than eighty novels, including *Pretty Little Devils*, *Daughter of the Flames*, and *Dead in the Water*, which won the Bram Stoker Award for best novel. She's also written a number of media tie-in novels, for properties such as *Buffy the Vampire Slayer*, *Highlander*, and *Smallville*. Writing as Chris P. Flesh, Holder is the author of the Pretty Freekin Scary series of books for children. A new paranormal romance novel, *Son of the Shadows,* was released in August. Holder's short fiction—which has appeared in anthologies such as *Borderlands*, *Confederacy of the Dead*, *Love in Vein*, and *The Mammoth Book of Dracula*—has won her the Stoker Award three times.

Holder says this story was inspired by the Oberammergau Passion Play, which originated in 1634, during the Thirty Years' War. "Bubonic plague had spread all over Bavaria. The citizens of Oberammergau begged God to spare them," she says. "In return, they would put on a play about the crucifixion and resurrection of Jesus every ten years. The ravages of the plague ceased, and the Oberammergauers kept their vow. They still perform the play, most recently in 2000."

It was a chilly May morning, and Cardinal Schonbrun's knees cracked as he took his seat beside Father Meyer in the Passionspielhaus. Father Meyer heard the noise very clearly; he was acutely aware of every sound, smell, and sight around him: of the splinters in the planks of the large, open-air stage before them, the smell of dew, the dampness of his palms. The murmurs of anticipation of the assembling crowd, and those of speculation—and derision—when his own people, scattered among the thousands, caught sight of him. He was aware that he looked like a prisoner, wedged between his friend Hans Ahrenkiel, the bishop of Munich, and his nemesis, the cardinal. He was aware that his life as a priest would be over that day.

The cardinal scowled at Father Meyer and said, "Is it true what I've just heard?"

Father Meyer licked his lips. How had he hoped to keep it a secret? "That depends on what it is, Eminence."

"Did you give absolution to the wandelnder Leichnam this morning?

Though his heart sank—someone had betrayed him—Father Meyer regarded the cardinal steadily. "Ja. Does that surprise you?"

Cardinal Schonbrun made a shocked noise. On Father Meyer's left, the bishop shook his head mournfully.

"Did it partake of the Holy Eucharist?"

The cardinal was a much younger man than Father Meyer could ever remember being. Blond and blue-eyed, vigorous and vital. Filled with New Ideas for the New Church. The kind of man Rome wanted to lead her flocks into the twenty-first century.

The kind of man Father Meyer, gray and aged, was not.

Father Meyer raised his chin. "The Church has always offered her mercy to the condemned. Ja. I did it."

The cardinal's face mottled with anger. He opened his mouth, glanced at the swelling audience, and spoke in a harsh, tense whisper. "Think what you've done, man! Polluted the body of Christ. You've made a mockery of the Sacraments, of your own vows—"

Father Meyer spread open his hands. "All I know, Your Eminence, is that Oberammergau, my village and that of my ancestors… that this village made a vow to God. And that now, four hundred years later, we're shaming that vow with what we are doing today."

Bishop Ahrenkiel touched Father Meyer's arm. They had sat in the rectory together, drinking ancient Benedictine brandy and discussing the New Ideas. In companionable silence, they'd listened to Father Meyer's collections of Gregorian chants, gone through scrapbooks of Passion Plays through the centuries. Father Meyer had hoped that Bishop Ahrenkiel, at least, would understand. But he, alas, was a New Bishop.

"I thought we had gone through all that, Johannes," he said now, for the obvious benefit of the cardinal. "These are not living creatures. They have no souls. The Vatican has spoken on the matter and—"

"The Vatican is wrong." Father Meyer turned anguished eyes toward the young cardinal. "Everyone is wrong. Your Eminence, I've spent time among these Leichname. I—I feel they are my ministry. They aren't merely corpses, as science would have us believe. I hear their hearts, though they cannot speak. They seek the Father, as we all do. They hope for love, and mercy, and justice."

"Father Meyer," the cardinal began, but at that moment, the single voice of the Prologue, a man dressed in a simple white robe with a band of gold around his forehead, called them to order:

"Bend low, bend low…"

Those same words had rung through the Passion Meadow for centuries, as once again the Bavarian village of Oberammergau renewed its covenant with God: the townspeople would perform a play glorifying the suffering and resurrection of Christ—the Passion—if the Lord would spare them from the ravages of the Plague. In 1633, it had worked: no more fevers that shook the body; no more pustules that burst and ran; no more deaths. After the vow, grace.

Oberammergau was not unique in this bargaining: in the 1600s, many villages, towns, and cities promised to put on Passion Plays in return for survival. But in all the world, Oberammergau was the only village that still honored its pledge. The villagers pointed to this fidelity as the reason the town had also been spared the horrors of the more recent plague, the one that turned men and women, even tiny babies, into hellish monsters—the walking dead, rotting, slathering, mindless. What terror had run throughout the world.

Now, of course, the zombies were contained, and could even be controlled—as they would be today, on the Passion stage. Such a gift from God, such a miracle.

And as through the centuries, people from all over the world came to see God's miracles. Nearly half a million souls flocked to Oberammergau in the course of each decade's one hundred summer performances. But this year, the numbers were doubling—tripling—because of the introduction of the new element—a Newer way to glorify the agony and suffering of Our Lord Jesus Christ.

"Death from the sinner I release" sang the Prologue figure. And the crowd stirred—in eagerness, Father Meyer thought bitterly, at what was to come. But if his plan worked, they would leave this place with their bloodlust unsated.

"Sir," Father Meyer began, but a stalwart hausfrau behind him tapped him on the shoulder and said, "Hsst!"

The Prologue soloist sang on. It was Anton Veck, whom Father Meyer knew well. Anton had been an altar boy, was still busy in the parish church of St. Peter and St. Paul in a thousand helpful little ways. Anton, Anton, he thought, was it you who told them? Anton had been there. And he had not approved.

And, most damning of all, he was a cousin of Kaspar Mueller.

With a sigh, Father Meyer bowed his head and pulled his rosary from his pocket. He would not watch the play, though he, like every other Oberammergauer, counted his life not in years but in how many Passion Plays he had either performed in or seen. At sixty-five, this was his sixth cycle.

And though until this year, he had held the position of second-in-command on the Council of Six and Twelve, the committee that oversaw every aspect of the play, including the most important one: choosing the actors who were to play out the Passion of Christ.

He'd known the rules; they had to be Oberammergauers, or to have lived among the native-born for at least twenty years. In the case of the women, they had to be virgins, and young—cast-off restrictions reimposed during the cycle of the zombie plague, in the hope of pleasing God more fully.

He'd known the rules: the most prominent families must be represented.

And he hadn't disregarded the rules. He'd simply answered to a higher law; and that was why, after today, he knew he would be defrocked. No matter. He would continue in the work without the blessing of his Church.

Without the blessing. His throat tightened. Thumb and forefinger slipped over the worn wooden beads of the rosary his father had carved for him.

"Put that away," the cardinal whispered angrily. Rosaries were not appreci-ated in the New Church.

Father Meyer covered the rosary with both his hands. His lips moved as he mentally counted the beads. Carved with love, in rosette shapes to honor the Virgin. It was a beautiful thing, and should be in a museum. Like the Old Church, he thought, with Her compassion and Her love.

His thoughts drifted back to the choosing of the roles. It had been a foregone conclusion, at least to the others, that Kaspar Mueller would play Christ. He had done so for three cycles, and no family in Oberammergau was more prominent, nor more powerful, than his. But to play Christ for a fourth Play? Thirty years older than when he began? Father Meyer had pointed out, correctly enough, that women over the age of thirty-five weren't even allowed in the play. Should a sixty-three-year-old man portray a man almost half his age?

"That doesn't matter. It's his spiritual qualities that matter most," Adolph Mueller, who was on the Council—and another of Kaspar's cousins—had asserted.

But the fact of his health remained. He was older, frailer. The part of Christ was grueling—each Passion Play lasted eight hours, with only a break for lunch; and then there was the matter of hanging on the Cross—

—and then there was the matter of Kaspar's falling from his front porch and breaking his ribs.

Father Meyer had assumed that would end the discussion; they would have to choose another, younger man. But Kaspar let it be known that he wouldn't hear of it, wouldn't share the stage with anyone else. Nor would he allow his understudy to take over the role.

The priest was concerned, and let that fact be known to the Council. And in deference to his office, the discussion continued. But Father Meyer should have realized the weakness of his position: the Muellers were one of the founding families of Oberammergau, and they owned the largest hotel, two restaurants, and four taverns. They also donated generously each year to the village's State Woodcarving School. Father Meyer's family hadn't arrived until near the end of the nineteenth century. To most Oberammergauers, the Meyers were little better than interlopers. And of what benefit would it be to please the parish priest over the largest employer in town?

Yet finally, after much deliberation, Kaspar announced he would allow the placement of a double of himself upon the Cross during the crucifixion scene: one of the zombies, the wandelndere Leichname—changing corpses—as they were called in German, changed yet again, to look like him.

"Think of it," Adolph Mueller had exhorted the Council. "At last we can depict the true Passion of Christ. We can drive nails through its palms, and pierce its—"

"Father, really, you must watch or people will talk," Cardinal Schonbrun said as he stood.

Father Meyer shook himself. The sun was high in the sky. The stage was empty, the curtains closed. It was the lunch interval. Four hours had passed.

It was time. He called upon the Virgin for courage.

"People already talk, Eminence," he said. "The talk hasn't stopped since I stepped down from the Council."

"Which is why we're here," the cardinal cut in, gesturing to the bishop and the many priests assembled around them. "To prove that the Church approves of these proceedings, even if you do not."

Bishop Ahrenkiel put his arm around Father Meyer. "Come. Let's go have some sausage and a beer. The cardinal would surely not object?"

Father Meyer's heart jumped in his chest. Now was the moment. Goodbye, his soul whispered to Holy Mother Church. Forgive me.

"I'm—I'm not hungry," he stammered, his fear showing. "If I may be excused to go to my house for the interval?"

The cardinal regarded him. "I think not. I think you should eat with us, Father."

He forced himself not to panic. "But I'm not feeling—"

"Nein. You must come with us, Father Meyer."

Father Meyer sagged. The cardinal must have guessed his plan to slip backstage and free the ten Leichname the village had purchased. Why had he dreamed it would be possible? He was a fool. A cursed old fool.

"Father Meyer?" Cardinal Schonbrun pressed, gesturing for him to walk beside him.

Father Meyer forced back tears. Perhaps he could find another way. He could not believe that in four hours they would actually crucify the pitiful thing.

"It's done in movies and things all the time," Bishop Ahrenkiel murmured as Father Meyer plodded slightly behind the cardinal. "It has been approved by the various humane organizations, the unions, the—"

"Don't speak to me." Father Meyer turned his head away from his old friend.

"But, Johannes—"

"Don't."

They sat in the crowded rooms of the Mueller Hotel, among the tourists, who were titillated by the presence of live zombies in their midst. Though long ago the contagion had been stopped, still people held the old fears.

Maria Mueller, Kaspar's daughter, brought the priests large mugs of beer and plates of pork ribs and sauerkraut. Though in her forties, she curtsied daintily to the bishop and the cardinal, but pointedly turned her back on Father Meyer. No one in the village had spoken to him since he'd resigned from the Council.

"It goes well, does it not?" Bishop Ahrenkiel asked her. "Everyone must be so proud."

She frowned. "This is our holy obligation, Your Eminence. We don't do it out of pride."

Father Meyer pursed his lips. One of the Lord's own creatures would be made to suffer horribly this afternoon, for another's sin of pride.

They had told him the zombies had no nerve endings.

Father Meyer sat hunched in his seat with tears running down his cheeks. He clutched his rosary while he watched the creature writhe in agony as they stretched open its palm and slammed the nail through.

"The movements are being directed with a remote control device, Johannes," the bishop reminded him, with a hint of pride in his voice. "It really doesn't feel anything. It's only made to look that way."

The other palm. The sound of the hammer on the nail echoed against the baffles on the walls. Blood spurted in the air and streamed over the end of the cross and onto the stage.

Chang, whang whang whang!

The creature struggled. Its mouth opened, closed, opened.

The hausfrau behind them moaned.

"Do you see?" Cardinal Schonbrun said to Father Meyer. "This reminds everyone of the suffering of Our Lord. It brings them nearer to God. I've never felt such emotion during a Passion Play. The scourging... that was excellent, Bishop Ahrenkiel, was it not?"

The bishop grunted, neither assent nor dissent.

Father Meyer brought his rosary to his heart as they hoisted the cross upward. The zombie swayed, then fell forward, pinioned in place by the spikes in its hands and feet. Blood flowed in rivulets from the crown of thorns, some into its mouth. The blue contact lenses gleamed as its—his—eyes gazed toward heaven. Such monumental pain. Father Meyer doubled his fists, feeling upon his own flesh the whip marks, the holes in his hands, the thorns digging into his scalp.

Unable to suppress a sob, he remembered what he had done that morning:

Dawn had been hours away. In the high Alps, in his beloved, unheated church, it was freezing.

He looked at the unmoving figure in the darkened confessional, closed the curtain, and rested his hand against the side of the booth. The swell of an ancient chant, *Rorate caeli*, masked the thundering of his heart. He inhaled the bittersweet odor of incense and gazed at the crucifix above the altar, at the gentle face carved five, six hundred years before by one of the Oberammergau faithful. The wounds, as fresh and red as at Calvary; the agony, the love.

"Most wondrous Savior," Father Meyer whispered, "if I'm doing wrong, forgive me. Please understand, oh Lord, that I believe this to be a child of Thine, and if it—if he—is not, and I do pollute Thy body, as the Church charges... if I offend Thee, I am heartily sorry."

He stepped into his side of the confessional and drew the curtain. He sat, took a deep breath, and, crossing himself, began.

"Bless me, Father, for I have sinned. It has been..." He hesitated. Who could say, how long it had been, for the one who sat in silence on the other side of the screen?"

"…it has been some time since my last confession. These are my sins." He swallowed hard and thought for a moment. How to proceed? It had been so clear last night, when he'd resolved to do this. So obviously a divine inspiration. But now, now when he was doing it, really risking it, he felt alone, untried.

But thus had our Savior felt, he thought, and was comforted in his fear.

"I have had… thoughts, Father. I have had thoughts that were other than those Our Lord would have us think. I have wished for things…"

He leaned his damp forehead against the screen. Such monumental pride, to speak for another! To dare to dream what was in another's heart. A heart that didn't even beat, not really. A mind that didn't think.

Nein, he didn't believe that.

"Listen," he whispered to the silhouette he could see through the screen. "I absolve you and forgive you of any sinful thought or deed, in the Name of the Father, and the Son, and the Holy Ghost, amen." He squinted through the crosshatches. "Do you understand? Go in peace. God has forgiven—"

"Father," came a voice, and Father Meyer started violently. It had spoken! Praise be to God! He knew, he had always believed, he had prayed—

"It's Anton," the voice went on, and he realized it was the Veck boy, standing just outside the curtain. "The cardinal and the bishop are at my cousin's hotel. They're asking for you."

Father Meyer looked now at the figure on the cross. The figure he had dared to forgive. The stage was set for the climax of the Play, the Passion and the suffering of the Lord. The three crosses had been raised—on the other two, the actors playing the Thieves hung supported by belts beneath their loincloths, as Kaspar Mueller would have been. The Holy Women in their veils and robes clasped their hands and wept. The Roman Centurion stood to one side, pondering. The players gazed up at the wandelnder Leichnam, nailed to Kaspar Mueller's cross while the old man hid behind a pile of rocks, which would be used later in the Resurrection scene. They spoke to the zombie, and it was Kaspar who answered, in his quavering, old man's voice.

Behind the cross, Kaspar cried out, "Eli, Eli, lama sabachthani!" and the Pharisees reviled him for calling out to the prophet Elias.

And the figure on the cross, pale and slight, panted and looked up, then down. Reanimated corpse, Father Meyer's head insisted.

His heart replied, An innocent man, doomed to suffer like this ten times. For each zombie was to be used for ten performances: they had devised ways to fill the holes in its—his—hands with wax, to stitch up and conceal the wound in his side. Ten times they would do this to it. For the glory of God.

And the glory of Oberammergau.

The soldier offered the sponge of vinegar to the creature when Kaspar Mueller cried out, "I thirst." And it tasted the bile. Father Meyer was certain of it.

"Mother, behold thy son," Kaspar Mueller gasped.

The zombie looked down at Krista Veck.

Father Meyer gripped his rosary. He could not let this continue. His holy office required he speak the truth of God as he knew it. As long as he was a priest, he was compelled to act on behalf of the Shepherd's lambs—

"It is over," said Kaspar. The ribcage of the zombie worked furiously. "Into Thy hands I commend my spirit." Its head drooped forward.

"Ah," murmured the cardinal.

A low, ominous rumbling filled the theater. It was the time in the Play for the earthquake and the rending of the Temple. The crosses jittered on the stage. The zombie's palms began to bleed again.

"It is God's hand on us!" cried the actor who played Enan.

Blood streamed from its side and hands. Its—his—head bobbed. Father Meyer could abide no more. He rose to his feet and cried, "Ja! It is!"

"Father!" the cardinal said, grabbing his hand.

Father Meyer shook him off and crawled over him. He ran down the stairs to the front of the stage. Before anyone could stop him, he leaped on it and grabbed the wrist of the startled Centurion.

"You cannot do this! As a priest of God, I order you to stop!"

"What? What?" Kaspar demanded, appearing from behind the rocks. He was dressed as the risen Christ, in pure white robes.

"Blasphemer!" Father Meyer shouted at him. He thrust himself away from the Centurion, pushed Krista Veck and the other Holy Women out of his way, and scrabbled onto the rocks. "Help me get him down! For the love of God, help me!"

"Get down from there!" The cardinal's voice rang over the rising voices of the crowd and the actors. "Get Father Meyer off the stage."

"Father, please." Rudi Mangasser, the Centurion, grasped Father Meyer's ankle. The priest yanked his leg free.

"For God's sake, Rudi! I baptized you. Help me!" Father Meyer pulled at the spike in the middle of the Leichnam's palm. It was hammered in all the way to the bone; blood pooled around it, smearing Father Meyer's fingers.

"Help me. Help me." He stared at the audience, which had leapt to its feet. Angry faces. Looks of horror. Some were backing away, others rushing forward. Others were crying.

"He is a being! We cannot do this!" He reached across the limp body and yanked off the crown of thorns, bringing skin with it.

A sudden, piercing chorus of screams erupted from the onlookers. Startled, Father Meyer froze and looked at them. Fingers pointed toward the stage—at him, he supposed. He dug his fingers into the zombie's palm, straining to pull out the nail.

The head slowly lifted. Who had the remote control device? Father Meyer wondered vaguely. But the screams grew louder. People turned to run from the theater. The cardinal and the bishop crossed themselves and sank to their knees.

The head wobbled. Father Meyer took hold of it beneath the jaw to support it. The flesh was hot.

Hot—

The head turned. It was covered with large, red sores from which pus flowed like blood.

"The Pest!" someone shrieked. "It has the Plague!"

Shaking, Father Meyer stared into the sightless eyes. New sores exploded over the zombie's body even as Father Meyer watched. They ruptured in a jagged line along the would in its side; they traveled over its chest, its stomach.

The heavens filled with a rumbling. The earth—not just the stage—began to shake.

"It's a trick!" someone shouted. "The priest has the control box!"

There were cries of outrage now. Krista Veck tore off her veil and shook her fist at Father Meyer while Rudi Mangasser scrambled onto the rocks and pulled him down.

"Idiot!" Rudi shouted, slapping Father Meyer across the face as they both fell to the stage floor. "What are you doing, you crazy old man?"

"I? I?" Father Meyer pushed Rudi aside and knelt in front of the zombie. He made the sign of the cross and folded his hands. Two red sores bubbled from his own palms.

Stigmata. But stigmata of a different sort. Of the New Church. And a New sickness, he supposed, which would cripple the world, as the Old sickness had four hundred years before.

He burst into tears and opened his arms. "The covenant is broken. God has spoken through one of His children, to tell us of His great displeasure.

His wounds dropped onto the boards. "A changing corpse? My beloved, my brethren, we are all changing corpses! All!"

"Get him off the stage!" Cardinal Schonbrun shouted again.

"No, don't touch me! I have it already!" Father Meyer warned, but he knew it was too late.

Then, as one being, the throng roared and flew at him. A hundred hands grabbed him, hitting, punching, crushing. They kicked his shins and aching knees. Someone slammed a fist into his side. A woman he had never seen before wrapped her fingers around his clerical collar and choked him, choked hard until he couldn't breathe, couldn't see.

Then the face of the woman swelled with boils. He watched, horrified, as they burst and a thick, oozing pus ran down her face.

"She's got it, too!" shouted a man beside her.

She grabbed her face and wailed. Sores rose on the backs of her hands, exploded, splattering the man's face; and everywhere the infection touched him, pustules rose, crusted, split. The man fell to his knees, shrieking.

The contagion engulfed the crowd like a flood of forty days and forty nights. Cries of terror shattered Father Meyer's ears. The sky pounded with thunder, the hoof beats of four horsemen; timbers and scenery fractured and crashed.

The stage split open, and the ground beneath it, and people screamed and flailed wildly as they tumbled into the pit. All, all tore asunder.

A jag of lightning slammed into the cross on the stage, igniting it at the base, bonfire-hot. Hellfire-hot. The zombie opened its mouth once, twice. Its head lolled to the side, and its sightless gaze moved, moved.

It fixed on Father Meyer. Seemed to look at him... yes! Froze there, staring at the priest of the Old Church, the Old love.

Behold thy son. Behold him.

Father Meyer raised his hand and blessed him. The zombie bowed his head. The flames engulfed him, and he was gone.

"He did this to us!" Cardinal Schonbrun cried, and three men grabbed Father Meyer, pulling at him, beating him, weeping with rage.

Father Meyer stared at the fire as his arms were wrenched from their sockets, as blows and burning splinters rained down on his head. New sores erupted, burst, ran over his other wounds. No pain could be worse; no agony—

No. No pain could surpass that in his heart.

No fear could be greater than the fear in his soul.

He raised his gaze to heaven. "Father, forgive us," he whispered, with the last breath of his body. "We didn't know. We really didn't."

ALMOST THE LAST STORY BY ALMOST THE LAST MAN

by Scott Edelman

Scott Edelman's fiction has appeared in a variety of anthologies and magazines, such as *Crossroads: Tales of the Southern Literary Fantastic, Postscripts, Forbidden Planets, Summer Chills,* and *The Mammoth Book of Monsters.* When not writing, Edelman edits *Science Fiction Weekly* and *SCI FI Magazine,* and in the past edited the fiction magazine *Science Fiction Age.*

Edelman is something of a zombie genius. He's had stories appear in each of James Lowder's Eden Studios zombie anthologies: *The Book of All Flesh, The Book of More Flesh,* and *The Book of Final Flesh,* and he's been nominated for the Bram Stoker Award three times for his zombie fiction. As I read each of his zombie stories I thought for sure I'd found one to include in the book—that there'd be no way he'd top himself after *that* story, only to discover that each was better than the last. And that's without even mentioning his brilliant "A Plague on Both Your Houses," a five-act Shakespearean play that he describes as a cross between *Romeo and Juliet* and *Night of the Living Dead.*

This story, which is one of his Stoker Award nominees, is not in any way Shakespearean, but one reviewer compared it to the work of another literary legend: W. H. Auden.

Maybe it would be best to begin this way.

Let's start, in fact, on the day that it *all* started, with Laura already at work in the county library. But here's the thing—as the day goes by, maybe she won't even come to realize yet that the dead are suddenly refusing to stay dead, because life happens that way, with momentous things occurring across town while we, in our homes, in our ignorance, clip our fingernails or floss our teeth. Earthquakes roar, floods rise, towers fall… and somewhere on the other side of the globe a man who may not hear of these things for many months, if at all, scrapes with his stick in a small patch of dusty earth and prays for rain. If he ever grows perturbed on that day, it will only be because the rain fails to come, and not due to dark happenings on continents far away.

For our purposes, let it begin that way for Laura, who did not notice her world tilting on its axis. She noticed little that first day of the change because little affected her personally, save that fewer patrons than normal wandered into her branch of the library. The ripples had not yet reached her.

But still, that small alteration to her routine puzzled her a bit, as over the years she had grown accustomed to the predictable rhythms of her week, but she let that feeling drop, and on the whole, it turned out to be an unusually good workday for her. She was able to spend less of her time that shift reshelving books that had been left on tables, and more of it catching up on paperwork, so she ended the day pleased.

As she headed back to her apartment that night, she treated herself to Chinese take-out. Maybe when she unpacks her dinner special, she should even find an extra fortune cookie at the bottom of the bag. Now *that* would cause her to smile. Because there's something else that you should know about Laura. She's been using the vocabulary words printed on the back of each fortune to teach herself Chinese, not the best method, perhaps, but still, hers, and the surprise cookie put her one word closer to her goal. See, she was planning to visit China someday. Adding that information just about now should help add poignancy to her tale, considering what we already know is inevitably to come and what she does not.

And so, later that night, after the additional reward of a very special episode of one of her favorite television shows, during which two estranged sisters are reunited, plus the rush she got from the way she'd been able to avoid a phone call from her mother thanks to caller ID, she would tuck into bed pleased with herself and with the world and ready to fall into a peaceful sleep, knowing nothing of the chaos elsewhere and suspecting less, much as our man working his field with a stick might finally set aside that stick and stretch out on his straw mat to drift away while looking up at the stars, never knowing that he had just lived through a December 7, or an August 6, or a September 11.

It was only the next day, when Laura slid that morning's newspapers onto the rods that kept them from getting tattered as they were being read, that she learned there had been anything special about the day before. She wasn't sure that she believed it, though. The facts of the miraculous resurrection seemed to her as if they should instead be shelved under fiction. She grew angry with herself, and angry with her former ignorance as well, believing that had such a grand difference been born in the universe, she should have been able to feel it. That the rules of life and death should change without her knowledge and permission didn't seem right.

She overheard much talk at her branch (all in whispers, of course) as to what it meant, and how one should proceed to walk through such an unexpected world, but she knew of no other way to live, and believed that one should accept the directions in which fate pushes us. She had never been able to see a different way for herself before, thanks in part (or so she felt) to the mother whose call she had avoided the night before, and saw no reason that she should try to see a different way for herself now. And so, in the face of the death of death, which would likely cause most people to abandon their routines, she still returned each day to carry out her duties.

Each successive day, however, will bring fewer of the living and more of the dead to browse in her department, until her regular clientele is completely replaced. At first, perhaps, she'll hardly notice that the undead *are* undead, for there'll be no slavering over her flesh the way she would have assumed. They'll just be shuffling slowly along, extracting books from the shelves, and sitting at the tables much the same way the regulars had. They won't behave so differently from the living, and so she won't notice that they're *not* living.

But then something will happen that will finally cause her to see and believe the great change that has occurred. Perhaps she'll notice that these new visitors are more intense at their tasks than those who had come before. Maybe it will be the fact that there is no whispering and no cause for her to shush. Or perhaps it's that she finally notices that no one is taking any bathroom breaks. Whatever the catalyst, she will eventually *see*. They'll seem more serious than those she was used to, and though more and more of them will drift in each day, so that some will finally have to stand, they'll be even better behaved than those who over her long years of service she'd grown used to, who by that time will have been entirely replaced, so that she is the only living creature who shows up there each day. But still, even that, even noting that only the dead surround her, will not cause her to change her routine.

She'll come to understand that the men, women, and children (though they really have to be understood as *former* men, women and children) are actually looking for something in the pages of those books, something that matters to them a great deal. They're not just going through the rote motions that had obsessed them in life. But what exactly are they seeking?

She watches them eagerly, intently, knowing that if she could only figure out what they sought, that she would find something meaningful there for herself as well, something that had waited just one step ahead of her her entire life.

Somehow it would all start to make sense. *All* of it.

No, forget that. Forget about Laura and her mother and the stale taste of fortune cookies. That's no way to begin this. It doesn't seem right at all. There's got to be a better way.

I'm going to start over, which is something that's a lot easier to do here on this page than from where I'm standing.

How about this for an opening, then?

The day the zombies came, Emily was dropping by the library (yes, there's that library again; it's important; you'll see) to visit her friend Rachel, which also means that it was the day that Rachel died. But as Emily arrived to take her friend to lunch, she doesn't know that yet. She knew that there was something odd about the day though. In fact, as she parked her car and fumbled for change for the meter, she wondered, what with the strange news reports that had been coming over her car radio during her drive, whether the two old friends should postpone their outing for another day.

Maybe I'll even have her pause for a moment and think it a hoax. She'll wonder whether this was just like that old-time Martian invasion that drove everybody mad when it was first broadcast on the radio, or man's supposed landing on the moon. (Which will have *you* wondering for a moment which of us didn't believe man ever made it to the moon, Emily or me. It's Emily. At least, most of the time, it's Emily.) And then she'll think, whether the broadcasts were a ratings trick or not, did it really matter? Regardless of the dangers of this world, life had to go on. She knew that. Life happened, and you had to happen, too. There would always be disruptions worthy of locking the doors and pulling down the shades, if you wanted to find them.

As you can tell, Emily is the sort of person who lives in two worlds, both this one, the one we all agree upon as reality, and another one, one slightly askew, to keep that first one at arm's length. She always felt that though a person had to live *in* the world, it did not mean she had to be *of* it. One should be able to keep the world at a distance so that it did not disrupt one's plans, and live as if all life's problems were on the other side of the world, as if she lived in a hut somewhere, her husband out most of the day poking at yams in the soil. Together they would be happy, less because of any affinity they had for each other than because of their separateness from society and its ills. They would live in ignorance of headlines and be bound together by that simplicity. The beating drums of the world would appear muffled and distant.

Emily survived many tragedies that way. Compared to her divorce, dealing with the resurrection of the dead would be a snap.

As she walked up the steps of the library, approaching the intricate wrought-iron gates at the entrance, wondering whether she and Rachel should do Chinese or Italian, a man ran toward her and then past her, screaming as he headed for the street. Blood spurted from one shoulder. In Emily's shock, it took her a moment to edit that initial thought to, no, not from his shoulder, but from the place where his arm used to be. She was ashamed to admit to herself that she felt relieved when he passed by her without spattering blood on her new blouse, which she had bought just for this occasion.

As she stood frozen, halfway between the street and the library entrance, one of the undead stumbled out the gates above her after its escaping prey. Its skin was grey, and its clothing still spilled clods of earth from its disinterment. Blood dripped from its mouth. Emily will do her best to force her legs to move before the dead thing shifts its focus to her, but her internal struggle proves unnecessary, as the shell of a man totters as it tries to move from one step to the next, loses its balance, and then rolls past her, tumbling down the length of the stairs.

After it finally struck the pavement, it lay motionless for a moment, and Emily thought it could be taken for a pile of cloth and bones, but then, as she watched, it slowly rose to its feet and looked up at her, really *looked* at her, she thought. She'd heard the radio hosts surmise that these undead things were beyond thought, but it certainly seemed to her to be thinking, almost considering for a moment whether it could make its way back up those steps to her.

Before it turned from her and shuffled down the street, in search, apparently, of an easier target, Emily would have sworn that it shrugged.

Emily rushed inside, calling out her friend's name. There'll be some personal detail seeded into the text before this so that you'll know that even with what Emily has been handed in life, she is still an optimistic sort, one who even in the face of what she has just seen expected to find her friend alive. (Maybe you'll learn of a lost dog who made its way home, or a parent whose cancer scare passed. Let's make it the dog. I'll have her see one on the street earlier as she parks her car so that there'll be a reason for her to wistfully remember a few details. People are often taught more lasting lessons by pets than by parents.)

From across the room, Emily could make out that Rachel stood where Emily had always found her, behind the counter where she checked out books, but by then, Rachel was no longer Emily's friend. A bite that had been taken out of Rachel's neck had allowed blood to spill down the front of her blouse. Her skin was not yet grey; it was deathly pale, but not yet the color of the creature who had fallen past Emily on its hunt, so perhaps it had happened not so long ago. Emily will think that if only she had arrived a half an hour earlier, perhaps she would have found her friend alive. It does not occur to her to think that if she had arrived a half an hour earlier, maybe they would both be dead. But that's just the kind of person Emily is.

(Thank the dog.)

Emily did not enter the vast room to approach her friend. She hung back in the hallway and noted that no one else remained there, neither human nor zombie. That was a good thing. Emily took that to mean that perhaps she could be safe there, in a building at the top of stairs which seemed untenable to the dead. It all depended what her friend had turned into. It did not seem to Emily as if Rachel had become a predator. Her friend had always been gentle. Could she ever become anything but, whatever the circumstance? Emily did not think that death necessarily had to be a life-altering experience.

Emily noticed that the whole time she watched, Rachel stayed by her station, her fingers on her keyboard, her dull eyes looking straight ahead, waiting... but for what? Did some spark that still glowed somewhere inside her still expect customers to come? Maybe she was merely doing what had always been expected of her in life, out of a habit that transcended death. Or was she waiting for Emily, only for a different reason than she would have been waiting earlier, cannily hoping to entice her close, too close, with a feigned calmness that was truly no longer hers? If only Emily could figure it out, unravel the suddenly mysterious why of her friend, she felt that somehow everything would then make sense, and she'd know, with or without a dog, with or without a husband who poked at the earth with a stick, how she was meant to live her life from that day forward.

No… that's all wrong, too.

This is getting frustrating. I usually don't vacillate like this, at least not when it comes to putting words on the page. Give me a few moments…

I've got it. Let's begin this way instead.

Walter was at the main branch of the library researching his next novel the day the zombies came. (I know, I know. What's with these libraries, you're thinking. Surely there's a more exciting place to go with this. But no, for me, there isn't. And you'll soon see why.) When the screaming began, echoing down the narrow hallways and filling the cavernous room in which he sat, there were so many books stacked about him that he needed to stand to see what was happening. The first thing he saw was that the librarian, who had been so kind to him over the years, but whose name he had never bothered to learn (later, he would berate himself for that), was beating her fists against the back of a man who was no longer a man. The thing was biting chunks out of her neck and spitting gristle as it growled. They soon both fell behind the counter so that Walter was no longer able to see them, but he could still hear the unsettling sounds of feasting.

Walter ducked back down below the wall of books that he had built around him (and I will have to think later about whether to stress the metaphor of this, with examples of how he had shielded himself with books during all other aspects of his life) and crawled from the room, unashamed (well, only slightly ashamed), for he had learned long ago that he was a writer, not a fighter. He did not lift his head, thinking unrealistically that if he couldn't see zombies, they could not see him, until he bumped up against tiny chairs, and realized that he had reached the children's section.

Craning his neck to look up, he saw one of the undead holding a young girl up to its mouth and chewing its way through her organs. Perhaps flecks of her blood will splash onto his face. Perhaps he will only imagine it, as the reality might be too much for you. Or perhaps it will be both, that flecks of blood will splash onto his face but he will only *think* that he imagined it, because it won't be too much for you; it will be too much for *him*. The girl wriggled erratically as she died, and Walter, noting that the zombie was too lost in the frenzy of its feast to notice him, leapt to his feet and ran past.

Walter knew the layout of the library intimately, as it had become his second home (well, actually, more like his first home, as his apartment had never become a true home to him), and made his way to the vault in which he knew the rare holdings were stored. At night, it was kept locked, but during the day the staff left it open for easier access. He had a hunch that he could be protected in there. He would lock himself in, and no zombie would be able to figure out how to get in after him. Surely, zombies couldn't calculate combinations. Numbers were too complex for them. All they knew was one body, another body, another body…

Getting out again once things had calmed down again, when he would be seen once more as a person, and not just a body, not just a snack, would be easy, because safes were designed to prevent people from breaking in, not *out*. Right?

He hoped he was right. He was sure he was right. At least that's what he kept telling himself as the air inside the vault grew moist and stuffy, and he struggled, mostly in vain, to hear whether the screaming outside had stopped.

Sigh.

No… no… no.

I'm afraid that last try didn't hold together any better than the first two. It didn't bring alive what it's like to live among the dead.

But… unfortunately… that third account is really the best narrative I have to work with. Because that one's my life. Because that one's the truth as I have lived it.

And because now, especially now, metaphor has to go. From now on, I should only write what actually happened.

I should only write the truth.

On the other hand, my old tools seem so reassuring at a time like this, and my old coping mechanisms so tempting. I keep thinking that there must be a reason for that. With so few other comforts left in the world, I hope I can be forgiven for backsliding. (Come to think of it, are there *any* other comforts left in the world, not counting the mere fact of just being alive itself?) Or maybe it's more than just backsliding. Maybe, like a cigarette smoker teetering on the verge of quitting, I just need one more dose of my drug before giving it up for good.

So let me try once more to explain. I hope that this time it will work out better for you. For both of us.

Here we go…

I once knew a woman who loved her husband so much that she could not bear to let him go. When Marilyn swore that she would be true to him in sickness and health, she meant it. But that isn't always such a good thing. For when her husband grew ill, she kept him pinned to life in the hospital when he would have been much happier in the grave. Perhaps in a different story she would have kept him from the grave as a form of punishment, but not in this story, because that would be ironic, and Marilyn loved him without irony. As he lay there while some machines breathed for him, others circulated his blood, and still others carried away his wastes, she would look at him, at the forest of tubes binding him to an unfulfillable promise, and weep.

"Don't go," she would whisper, repeating it like a mantra, though one with infinite variation. "You can't go. Not yet. You mustn't go."

But eventually, he went.

Luckily for her, his death came on a day when the dead were no longer dying. When all life signs ceased, the nurses scurried in to the alarms and buzzers they had expected long before. There was nothing more that they could do, and they, at least, having long since lost patience with Marilyn anyway, were glad of it. The most important lesson to be learned in this place was letting go, and they wished that she had not been such a slow student. As a doctor came in to verify what the nurses already knew, and murmured the sympathetic words he had been trained to utter about her loss (so how sympathetic could they have been anyway?), the woman's husband reached out suddenly, grabbed a nurse by the wrist, and ripped her arm out of its socket. The blood splattered the wife across her folded arms, sore from hugging herself as she wept. She screamed, not taking her eyes from her husband as the remaining nurses joined the doctor in wrapping restraints about the man. Once they were done and he was attached to the bed, they all fled the room, carrying the injured nurse with them, leaving Marilyn alone.

As the man (or what was once a man; I have no true word for him, as our terminology has not yet advanced as much as our species; "zombie" seems so fraught with baggage) struggled impotently and snapped at flesh that was out of reach, Marilyn thought that she heard her husband call her name. Buried in his grunts, or so she thought, were sounds she knew so well, murmurs, endearments, the echoes of living words past, and so she stepped closer, stunned to find herself in such a bizarre situation. She had heard from the small TV bolted to one corner of the ceiling that they listened to as she waited for him to wake, that scenes like this were playing themselves out all across the country. Across the world. (Well, not in every corner of the world, as we have already discussed. Somewhere, there will always be that man, happily oblivious, and that stick.) But she never expected to have someone she knew drawn into such a predicament, and especially not herself. Death is what happened to other people. Careless people.

She tilted her head and closed her eyes to listen more intently, and something she heard made her certain. She swore that she *could* make out her name. And so she moved even closer to him, erasing that final space between them, and let his teeth rip into her flesh, so that she, too, could join him in the only afterlife that people from then on would ever know.

No, that's not right. No one likes reading about people who voluntarily turn themselves into victims. We want to see people who take action, who make choices, who triumph over adversity instead of surrendering to it. So. How about this…

I once knew a woman who *hated* her husband so much that she could not bear to let him go. He was rich, and so tried his best to pay Catherine to leave, but he could never seem to name her price, as she had no price. (Something he found hard to believe, since as I said, he was rich.) And so he turned instead to trying to simply leave her, but none of his escape plans worked. She kept reeling him back in, with the orchestrated disapproval of their friends, the withholding of time with his children, or, at its most drastic, with threats of libels plausible enough that she knew they would stick. Many were the times he flew to the opposite coast in the morning only to be persuaded to return in the evening. She stayed on the grounds of their estate and made sure that he stayed there with her.

Once the zombies came (because, yes, I give up, what else am I supposed to call them?), her job became that much easier. He no longer wanted to travel into the city (which had quickly descended into chaos), and so did his job from his home office, ordering about with phone calls, e-mails and faxes others who did not have the luxury of his monied sort of refuge. As he worked, he would keep an eye on the perimeter of their estate via security cameras, making sure that the outside world did not invade. Catherine had her own security cameras, ones her husband did not know about, and she would check on him often during the day to make sure he had not fled.

This went on until the weight of the outside world and the weight of her husband's inner world grew so great that he could take it no longer. One day, she came upon him slumped in the bath in a room devoid of both his cameras and hers. The water was tinged with red, the cuts on his wrists were lengthwise. In that moment, as he hesitated between life and new life, she hugged him and wrenched him from the water. Not caring that he was covering her with both suds and blood, she dragged him to their safe room. It had been installed to protect them from those who would take their wealth and their lives by force, and now it would protect her from the invisible force that would dare to take her husband.

She knew what was going to happen next, and so she moved quickly.

She set him folded on the far side of the safe room, his legs stretched out on the floor, his back against one of the reinforced walls. She did not know why she took such care as she laid him there. She could have tossed him the length of the room and not caused him any damage. What was to come would come regardless.

She retreated outside, watching him, waiting for him to reanimate. When she saw her husband begin to twitch, she slammed shut the door to the safe room and locked it. She was glad that her husband was back, little caring in what state he was back.

She sat on the king-sized bed, and listened to him slam against the walls of his prison. He would try to break free, continuously, never tiring, and so at last, she would know forever where he was.

That was a bit closer, perhaps, but still…

No, that one wasn't right, either. So far, with each of these stories, I'm making it all sound too pat.

I really should stop trying to make sense of it. After all, part of the truth of zombies (and by zombies I mean more than just the raw reality of each individual one of them, I mean the concept, the very fact that they exist) is that there is no sense to them. No one expects a hurricane to make sense, or an earthquake to have a point. And I've learned that about zombies by now, too. But it turns out to be just like the way people look up at the passing clouds and without even trying find a seahorse, a cow, or even Abe Lincoln. I can't seem to stop. That is what I do. It just happens.

It's a compulsion, I guess. I look at life, messy, chaotic, preposterous life, dismantle its unanswered mysteries and incongruous facts, rearrange them until there is a beauty not supplied by random events, and put them back together again so that all the pieces fit. I transform nonsense into serendipity. That's a man up there in that moon, damn it, no matter what I'm told about an accidental pattern of asteroids. And I'm supposed to behave differently in response to *this* latest upheaval?

So I find myself telling myself these stories, not consciously choosing to start them and seemingly not able to consciously choose to stop. Maybe that's my way of going into shock. But what I saw when I first stepped from the safety of the vault told me that this pretense of attempting to make sense of how I live now, how we all live now, is in itself senseless.

When I finally opened the vault door, the first thing I noticed was the silence. I was amazed by how quiet it had become. No more guttural raging from the undead; no further death throes from the living. As I moved slowly down the hallways, though, I found evidence of each. Red splashes darkened the walls; stray bones littered the floors. But there were no zombies, and no humans. I could easily put together the story of what had happened during my hermitage from the disgusting detritus alone, but I struggled not to. What I had seen with my own eyes had been horrible enough; I didn't want to add my imagination to the mix. And besides, I was too hungry to do so. That and only that was what had overcome my fear enough to bring me out of the vault. I would not have moved had not my body's command been, "Move or die."

I made my way as slowly as my hunger would allow to the machines I had so often eaten from while researching my previous books. I knew the taste of stale moon pies far too well. My honesty made me put money in the machine rather than break open the glass case, but I felt silly for it. Was there still a world out there that cared?

After I had eaten two bags of pretzels and a box of Raisinets, and downed two cans of orange soda, I could think straight again. Only then did it come to me that I should secure the library's front door, because based on the signs around which I had tiptoed, there had been no one left alive with the luck to have done it before. Except for me, everyone who had been in the library when the attack began had died.

I moved slowly and silently toward the front of the building, and strangely, a part of me felt just as badly for the fallen books that had been knocked to the floor in struggles as another part of me did when gazing at what must have been the sites of fallen people. Each time, I was embarrassed for feeling that way, but… I'm a writer. That's just one more action I can't control.

I passed the bank of computers at which I had often sat to check my e-mail, and saw that the screensavers still danced. I couldn't resist. I slapped the space-bar and punched in my password. Amid the spam was a note from my agent, wondering if I still lived. I replied to him that I did, and since three days had passed since he'd sent his message, I asked him the same question. I started browsing through my favorite blogs, discovering that no part of the world had escaped this plague, when I suddenly remembered—the front gate. There'd be enough time for exploration on the Internet later.

As I swung shut the wrought-iron gates at the library's main entrance, I worried that I was being premature by not yet having checked every inch of the building. Was I alone in here?

Was I locking death out? Or locking it inside, the better for it to catch me?

I had to take that chance, unless I wanted to spend my days living inside a locked vault until those outside sorted this all out and we all got back to normal.

As I looked down at the base of the steps on the milling undead, it was as if they could sense me, as if they felt that by merely continuing to live that I was taunting them. They careened off each other as they gathered into clumps. It was unnerving to study them that way, knowing that they were studying me. I moved back from the gates in the hope that I would be less noticeable. It seemed to work. They wandered off again, listless zombies once more; from this height, they might as well have been commuters on their way to work. Only their job was eating the actual commuters, not that this city had any left. There were none of the living left, at least not on the streets that surrounded the library, that much was clear. All of the action was past.

I could not escape, though, the signs of actions past. I had tried before to avoid the implications of such signs, but would the world ever be rid of them? Dark stains everywhere, as random as oil slicks, told me what had happened out there, what I had thankfully missed while inside the vault. Automobiles appeared to have been flung randomly across the landscape outside, one flipped onto its back on the bottom steps of the library, others piled up against each other as far into the distance as I could see. An armored car lay on its side amid the chaos. I could picture the drivers dodging both living and dead, each terrified that he or she would migrate from being one to being the other, losing control first of their vehicles and finally their lives.

I didn't want to keep reliving that, so I looked again at the armored car. It was filled with money, I imagined, which my last royalty statements told me I needed more of. I could probably go out there if I was crazy enough to risk it and grab all the cash I could carry. But what good would that do me now? We had evolved overnight into a world beyond money. A new economy ruled the world, and it was one based on meat. As I stared at the armored car and thought wistfully of a past and future no longer within my reach, I thought I could see something move through a small, narrow window in the vehicle's side. I studied that slot, and though there was no more movement, I could tell that, yes, as I was looking, someone was looking back. I risked stepping closer to the gates again, but unfortunately, at that distance I could not read any expression there. I could barely make out any features at all, an eye, a nose; just enough to tell me that I was not alone.

Then I saw a hand, its curled fingers beckoning me forward.

I was not the last man in the world after all, not some Robinson Crusoe stranded after the rise of the zombies.

Or maybe, come to think of it, I was, and as the tale promised, I'd just found my Friday.

The stories come more slowly now. I know, I know, I promised you that they wouldn't come at all any longer. But if you out there were in here with me, were at my side, you'd see that there is good reason for them to continue.

And besides, maybe *this* will be the story worth telling.

(Or maybe, just maybe, I will tell them until I finally admit that there might no longer be any stories worth telling.)

So...

There once was a woman—I won't give her a name, I won't bother giving any of them names any longer, for after all, aren't they all just archetypes? Aren't they really just you and me?—who had tried and tried (and tried and tried) to have a child, but no matter what she and her husband and the doctors and the insurance companies and the midwives (and the potential grandmothers) did, she kept miscarrying. But somehow, even as her husband suggested, at first gently and then more insistently, that they consider adoption, she avoided the choice he was pushing upon her, and she also avoided despair. She knew that she would eventually have a child, a child of her own, and so she was able to shut out all the voices that yammered around her. And she almost proved those voices wrong, too, by carrying a fetus nearly to term.

So close...

But then it died, too, just like all of the others. She could sense the motionlessness inside, the potential that had become merely a weight. She felt the absence in a way she had never known before one could feel an absence. She had always been honest with her husband before. As a couple, they prided themselves on their honesty. But this time she could not bear to tell him the truth. She knew what would happen next, what the doctors would insist, and she didn't want to endure again what she'd endured so many times already. So she prayed, just as, for the first time in her life since she had been a child, she had been praying for a child of her own. And then, just before the next day's already scheduled prenatal appointment, which she had thought she would have to break so as not to reveal what had occurred, she felt movement within.

But the movement felt more violent than any kicking the baby had done before, prior to what she convinced herself was only a brief nap. She could feel things ripping and tearing inside, and her spotting became bleeding, enough to frighten her. She went alone to the doctor, not wanting to have to be forced to tell her husband what was going on, and when the doctor gave her a sonogram, he saw no heartbeat. He was baffled, and did not know what to tell her. Nothing had prepared him for this. How could there be movement with no heartbeat?

And then, perhaps in response to the sonogram's invasion, the movements increased.

The woman clutched her stomach and screamed, and as the doctor rushed to his wall of supplies to find a way to relieve her agony, the baby chewed its way out of its mother's womb and poked its head through the skin of her stomach. The doctor, even in the midst of the insanity of the event, reacted reflexively, reaching for the child, instinctively wanting to see that, whatever else was incomprehensible about this moment, it was healthy, not able to see the dead skin hidden by the blanket of blood. The child snapped at him as it wriggled free from its dying mother, and the doctor backed away hurriedly, tripping over his own feet, and then fled the room.

Or perhaps he should only attempt to flee. Perhaps after he loses his balance, instead of righting himself and continuing on, he should fall to the floor, and the child, the thing, should fall from the mother, now dead atop the examining table, and begin to feast upon the doctor. Perhaps that would make more dramatic sense.

However the scene ends, we should keep in mind that it is a scene which with many variations played itself out around the world that day, as the fruits of failed pregnancies suddenly resulted not in dead babies, but in undead ones. But neither this mother nor this doctor could know that. But even if they had known, what other choices would they have made? There was barely escape from the plague without; how could there be escape from the plague within?

So let's just say that this particular baby struggled its way free from its mother's guts, and slid off the examining table, whether onto the warm doctor or onto the cold linoleum to be decided later. What will happen next would remain the same regardless.

It crawled out of the examining room into an office which by then had been emptied by the (bloodied or unbloodied) doctor's screaming. It pulled and wriggled its way down the street, unable to move in any way other than that of a real baby. Perhaps someday, if it survived, it would learn to walk, though physically it would never have more than a newborn's form, but for now, it crawled, making slow progress. People on the street gave it a wide berth, the trail of blood that it left behind itself clear warning of its intent, and though it grew frustrated, that frustration could not propel it quickly enough to overtake any of them.

But then a dog came over, sniffing, curious, unafraid, and close enough for the zombie child to grab hold of its front paws. It yanked at them roughly, breaking the dog's front legs. As the animal squealed and struggled vainly to retreat, the baby pulled itself forward along the length of the dog's trembling body to reach and snap the back legs as well. The baby had no teeth as yet, and so could not chew its way into the animal's belly as its tiny brain desired, so it had to punch its way in with small but strong fists and suck on the red, raw meat it had exposed.

As the child feasted, it felt itself pulled away from its orgy of blood, and before it could react to this affront, tossed through the air. It bounced off the back wall of a small cage, and as it attempted to reorient itself and go on the attack once more, the door slammed shut.

The woman whose dog had just been killed had a cage in which she would transport her dog to the park each day in the back of her van, and the zombie baby found itself trapped within. It beat blindly at the sides of the cage, but the metal was too strong for it to bend.

The woman smiled as she drove it back to her home. The reason she had a dog, she always knew, was because she could not have a child, and now, most unexpectedly, she *had* a child. She saw it as a gift from God. She did not care that it was dead, or that she would obviously have to be very, very careful or she would end up dead herself. She would love it for the rest of her life, even after the world came through the other side of this plague. She would tell no one of it, so that when all the other zombies were rounded up and destroyed, her baby would remain safe. She would love it and care for it as long as she lived.

But she would never let it out of its cage.

Well… maybe that *won't* turn out to be one of the stories worth telling. Right now, in the midst of it all, it seems somewhat pointless to even bother creating stories, but I know that someday the world will want to make sense of what we went through together, and someone will have to step forward to do that. That someone might as well be me. So I at least have to try.

One thing I've been realizing, as my subconscious mind weaves life into art (well, let others decide later if there's any art there) is that all zombie stories are true. Also, no zombie stories are true. Because, you see, there are no zombie *stories* until I write them. The universe has no opinion of us. No matter how much we want to pretend, real life does not contain the quality of story. No arcs, no morals, no meaning. Life is what we make of it.

And I was finally, after a lifetime of typing, in a position to make something of it.

It had been a week since I had taken refuge in this place. Undoubtedly, whoever was inside the armored car had to have been there nearly as long, or he would not still be alive. However long the person had been trapped, he—or she, I shouldn't forget there was a chance that it could be a she—surely needed food by now. And it was up to me to help.

I rushed back to the candy machine that I had long since cracked open, having abandoned the comforting illusion of order that dropping change in the slot had earlier brought me, and filled my pockets with pretzels, beef jerky, soda, and whatever else could fit. The cans, cold through the cloth of my jacket, reminded me that the city's electricity still worked, which had to be a good sign, right? Somewhere out there the wheels of industry kept turning, and human beings had to be the ones turning them. Or so I hoped. I'm afraid I didn't understand enough about technology to know for sure. I'm not that kind of writer. I'd research that after what I told myself I had to do, if there was an after.

I ran down to the ground floor and paused at the far end of the hallway that led to the main entrance, back enough from the gates so that though I could make out the foot traffic, I could not be easily seen. I watched as the zombies moved in their random patterns and waited for the street ahead to clear. There would come a moment, I was sure, in which nothing stood between me and the armored car, and no one hovered close enough to catch me even if I was noticed.

And then, trying not to think too much about it, I ran. It was not a pretty thing, as I am a writer, not a runner. Those two roles cohabit rarely, and certainly not in me. I am ashamed to say that it was not courage that propelled me clumsily on. It was loneliness that had overcome my fear, not altruism.

When I was closer to the armored car than I was to the library's front door, I suddenly thought—what if that hadn't been a living person I had seen staring back at me through that narrow window? What if the guard had died in the crash and was now himself a zombie, and the face was that of something struggling to get out and unable to figure out how... and hungry?

It was too late to dwell on that for more than an instant, because out of the corner of an eye, I could see a shuffling form. As I ran more quickly, soda sloshing, the thick back door of the armored car was raised in front of me, and I dove in. The door slammed shut behind me and I turned my head quickly to see that, yes, thankfully, I was visiting someone still alive. The man in the stained guard uniform locking the door looked far the worse for wear than I did, but he was still a man. The air hung heavy with sweat, but after someone has lived in the back of a small truck for a week, I guess I was lucky I could stand it at all.

I lay there, breathing heavily, feeling drained as much from the tension as the exertion, and did not protest as the guard patted me down. I knew what he was looking for, and was just thankful at this juncture that he was eating my food instead of attempting to eat me. He snapped a huge chocolate chip cookie in half and shoved both pieces in his mouth, then popped a soda, which exploded across his face thanks to my mad dash. But he wasn't angry, as he surely would have been back in the old days of only a week before. He just laughed, and took a long pull from the can.

"Thanks," he said, wiping the crumbs and foam from his face. "I don't think a soda has ever tasted this good. And as you might guess, I haven't had many reasons to laugh in a while."

I nodded and forced a smile. I was glad to see him, to know that I wasn't alone, but I wasn't happy about the fact that I'd had to come to him, rather than the reverse, to do it.

"Why are you still here?" I said, a little too terse, considering what should be joyful circumstances. "Once you knew I was inside, why didn't you make a break for the library? That place is like a fortress."

He swiveled clumsily about and showed me his right foot, the ankle of which twisted at an ugly angle.

"I'd never have made it with this," he said. "Once we flipped, and I felt the snap, I knew that it was all over for me."

"But you have to try, Barry," I said. He started when I called him by name, so I pointed at his ID badge, still hanging from his chest pocket. "I didn't want to feel responsible for you starving out here, so I brought food, but it's too risky to do more than once. You can't expect me to continue supplying you. And you can't last forever in here alone."

"I didn't plan on lasting forever." He shrugged. The bags under his eyes shrugged with him. "Would have been nice, though. But better starved to death than eaten to death. I'll admit I expected to end up with a bigger coffin. But this one will have to do."

"No," I said suddenly and firmly, surprised at myself even as I blurted it out. "I'm not going to let that happen. We ought to be able to get you up those steps and into the library if we work together. I can distract them. They don't move that fast."

"Faster than me," he said wearily.

His expression was a defeated one, but I knew better than to accept it as irreversible. If there's one thing I've learned over the years, it's that people want to live.

"We've got to try," I said. "You don't want me to have come this far for nothing. I ought to at least get a chance to save your life."

He laughed, which I considered progress. I peered out the small window in the rear door, back up the steps of the library to safety. The front gates looked infinitely far away. I was stunned that I had survived the first leg of the journey. But I knew that regardless of how treacherous it seemed, I was going back. If I was going to die, it was going to be in that library, or at the very least trying to get back to that library, and not in the rear of an armored car. Barry might have been willing to settle for a coffin of that size, but mine had to be a little larger.

And contain the complete works of Shakespeare besides.

Barry had not answered, but it was as if we had made a silent decision. We watched and waited, too weary for small talk (which we both hoped and pretended that there would be time for later), too weary for anything but studying the street, praying for a moment when it would be completely clear, and allow Barry time to hobble to safety. But unlike earlier that day, no such moment came. Each time the random patterns of the shuffling undead had the streets almost emptied, there would always be one lone zombie lingering under a stop light as if waiting for it to change. I didn't really think it could be doing that, responding to the world that used to be, no, not in real life, only in stories maybe, but still, there it was. The lights did not function, and so it stared up at the pole.

Until I grew tired of waiting.

"I'm going to distract him," I whispered.

The guard ordered me not to in one of those voices guards have and grabbed at my arm, but I leapt through the door anyway, and was back on the street before he could do anything about it. Instead of running immediately toward the steps leading up to the door of the library as any sane person would have done, I ran at the light-distracted zombie, prayed for it to notice me before I got too close, then veered away at the last possible instant I knew I could still outrun it. It was pulled along in my wake by its undead desire.

"Now," I shouted back at Barry over my shoulder. "This is your chance. Take it!"

I watched as he tumbled out from the safety of his truck and began hopping, but I could not spare him any more of my attention after that. A second zombie, perhaps sensing my presence on that street as I imagined only a zombie could (or was that truly only a power of my imagination?), had come around a corner, and now I had to distract two of them. Luckily, even though my lack of anything resembling an athletic past slowed me down, death kept the zombies even slower. As I ran, it seemed to me that they must only catch their prey by surprise, and with persistence, for they did not have speed on their side. I lured them away from the path Barry had to be taking, but when I saw a third zombie appear, I knew that I could tempt fate no longer. There were getting to be too many trajectories for me to calculate to stay alive. I swooped down on the struggling guard, who had just reached the bottom of the steps, and grabbed him by the shoulders, nearly knocking him down.

As I shouted at him to move, I don't think I used any actual words.

We ran a desperate three-legged race together, dodging the undead who slowly began to follow us as I pulled him up step by step, agonizingly slow ourselves. As we neared the door, I could hear the snapping of teeth behind us, and knew that Barry had slowed me down too much. I dove in, pushing him ahead of me, and from my knees slammed the gates shut behind us. Gasping, I stood, looking in awe at the dead flesh that obscured my vision of anything beyond. They glared at us, but we were protected from them. Once we moved more deeply inside the building, they would forget about us, as they had forgotten about all else, and drift away.

We were safe.

We laughed, and there was a hysterical tinge to our laughter, as I imagined there would always be in circumstances where death seemed so close, and yet was repulsed.

And then a zombie who must have snuck through the door while I'd been outside rescuing and doing my supposedly distracting dance reached out from within the library and, with a sickening groan, completely ripped off Barry's injured leg.

Now here's a story that I think I still deserve to tell. I don't know that there are many more like that, stories that I have actually earned. And besides, I'm doing a pretty good job of proving that there isn't much else that I'm good for.

A writer (again, no names please), no longer having access to a human audience, and unable to stop writing, begins to write stories suitable only for the undead. He cannot write the love stories he was used to writing, because the zombies know nothing of love. He can no longer write stories in which the motivations are based on greed, because zombies know nothing of money. All that is left to him is to write stories of action and adventure (well, boring and repetitive action and adventure), because zombies know of that, in their own special but limited way. Since the zombies know of only one thing, all the stories sound the same, but this writer, he figures that it doesn't matter, because if zombies have one trait, it is patience.

My agent, on the other hand, tells me that my readers do *not* have patience, and certainly have no desire to read of writers. The only people who want to read of writers, or so he tells me, are other writers. But what does he know? Anyway, at this time, I probably have no agent. And I say this not the way a beginning writer in search of an agent does. I say this because my agent has probably been eaten.

Which some might say isn't a bad end for an agent.

But since he is dead and my fictional writer's readers are also dead, we might as well just move on.

The stories this writer writes all follow the same pattern, as zombies are easily entertained. They begin with the sense that there is walking meat nearby. And then it is spotted. And then it is chased.

And then the walking meat is no longer walking, for the living is inside the dead.

The writer types out many variations of this outline, because that is all that he knows how to do, and when there are no more stories to tell, he's going to continue to tell them anyway. Some of his tales are set on city streets. Some are on country roads. Still others take place in zoos, in shopping malls and schools and airplanes. But whatever the setting, at their heart, they are all the same.

Shuffle.

Shamble.

Shuffle a little more quickly.

Run. (Well, as zombies run anyway.)

Run, run, run.

Eat!

Eventually, this writer, who is obviously not very self-aware, or he would have given up long ago—or if not long ago, at least once his audience had deserted him—realizes that he has written hundreds of such stories. But now that the reams of paper are stacked high next to his manual typewriter (because he refused to let the fall of civilization keep him from his appointed rounds), he had no idea what to do with them. There were no zombie magazines in which to publish them, no zombie bookstores in which they could be sold.

At least, not yet, he thinks.

And so he decides he must go out into the street, the street which he had avoided for so long, and declaim his stories. He expected that this would be the end of him, and he was ready for it. After all, a lion tamer may stick his head into a lion's mouth for a brief moment, but let him attempt to read *Hamlet* while so inserted and all will be lost. But he had been too alone for too long, and without an audience even longer. Whatever was to happen had to be better than what had happened so far.

But when he actually begins his readings, out in the middle of an intersection that hadn't known a car for years, he was pleasantly surprised. Zombies gathered and approached him, but they only came to a certain point, and then came no further. As he read, they stood about him in a circle and seemed to listen. (Well, he could pretend that about those that had ears, at least.) So he did not stop reading, even as he grew hoarse. He felt fulfilled. He believed that he had at last found the one, true audience he had been seeking his entire life.

But then he realizes that he is getting to the end of the stories that he has brought along with him, and encased in a circle of the dead, as it were, there was no opening in the crowd for him to get back to the additional manuscripts that remained in his hiding place back inside. So when he gets to the end of the last story in his hands, he begins all over again.

The zombies begin to growl. They may like the repetitiveness of theme, but they do not like the repetition of actual stories. He tries to back away, but there is nothing behind him but more of the undead. They move forward, and their circle closes tightly around him until it is difficult for him to breathe from the weight of them. And as they start to tear him to quivering shreds, he has just enough time to think, "Everyone's a critic—"

—before he has no more time in which to think.

But no. That's not right either.

Because even though the ending is horrifying, and the writer's fate undeserved (though I can think of a few publishers who might wish that all writers ended up that way), there's still a moral to the telling of the tale. Zombies are a force of nature, and forces of nature do not come equipped with morals. Forces of nature do not come packaged with a purpose, a message, or a reason. They just *are*. Which is why the guard was suddenly dead, destroyed just when we thought we'd gotten back to safety.

Or maybe... maybe the one thing that forces of nature can share with fiction is that they often bring along with them a sense of *irony*.

We would have heard the zombie that had slipped in during my trip outside coming toward us if we had not been laughing so loudly after our return to the supposed protection of the library. Perhaps a force of nature cannot allow such joy to continue without a response. We were hysterical with relief, slapping each other on our backs as we extricated ourselves from our heap on the floor, and so I didn't even realize that anything unplanned was happening until the guard's laughter turned to a howl of pain.

I sprung away from him to see that Barry's right leg was no longer his. It was in the zombie's hands, dripping blood. The guard kept screaming while clawing at his spurting leg, which spilled more blood than a body should be able to lose and still have the screaming continue. There was nothing I could do for him, no way to save him. Even if I was able to tie off the leg, to stop the bleeding, he would be one of them soon, and after *my* leg. I knew what I had to do. I hoped that he was too dazed from loss of blood to realize what was coming.

I helped him stand on his remaining foot. His moaning was by then barely audible, and he was nearly unconscious, which made what I was about to do easier.

I opened the gate that protected us from the few zombies still milling about at the top of the stairs, and pushed him into the midst of them. For a brief moment, he surged with more energy. He mustered a scream, but then the undead began to tear him apart, and the screaming stopped.

While they were distracted in their feeding, I was able to step back from the door without fear that any of them would enter. But still, I kept my eye on them at all times as I circled around the zombie inside that had stolen our rescue from us. It was intent on its snack, chewing on the leg that had broken in the first place to start the chain of events that led us to this horrible event. So it didn't notice me at all as I rushed at it from behind and shoved it out to join his fellows. As I slammed the gate again, this time hopefully not to be opened again until the Earth shifted on its axis once more, I could see that it showed no sign of even having noticed that anything had happened. He just continued attacking the leg of the man I had gotten killed.

See, in a story, this would never have turned out that way. In a story, which has to make sense, which has to provide rewards for its journey, or else we wouldn't call it "story," Barry would have lived, but life does not often promise such rewards, and when it does, rarely delivers. In a story, the two of us could have struggled to make a life for ourselves here until the world woke from this zombie dream and brought rescue, or until we found a way to make contact with the enclave of civilization that I'd know—well, at least in a story that I'd know and hope—would be out there. Fiction would have given us both a better end.

Unfortunately, I am a better writer than God chooses to be.

For it does not seem as if either rescue or solace will be found. I no longer even think it possible.

No one answers the e-mails I send out on the intermittent days I am even able to send them. No one posts updates to the Web sites I used to visit. In fact, day by day, sites that I had previously been able to visit are gone. I have grown so used to error messages that life itself seems an error message.

With each part of the Web that vanishes, I imagine that a part of the real world has gone as well. When it all goes, I will be alone.

Well, not entirely alone. I will still have my friends. Shakespeare is here. And Frost. And Faulkner and Austen and Carver and Proust. All telling me of the worlds in which they lived. Worlds that continued to exist only because I am still here to read about them. I've always known that fact, and the lesson it taught me is that *my* world will not continue to exist unless someone is there to read about it.

That is why I have been creating these stories. That's why I've always created stories. But I can't do it any longer. I see that I have lived too long, have lived through the time of my usefulness out to the time beyond stories. I could keep trying to tell them, but what would be the point of that? It's not worth remaining in a world without readers, and I doubt that you still exist.

My world can survive *my* death. But it cannot survive *yours*.

Art for art's sake was never what I was about. Art alone was never enough.

So I'm going to stop writing.

And I'm going to start praying.

Prayer.

I've tried it.

And it just isn't working for me.

But it does plant the seed for one last story.

I give you my word. And this time, you can *believe* my promise.

After the world went to Hell, a priest who had been traveling hurried back to his flock so that they could still make it into Heaven.

He didn't make it home alive, the same way most of the world didn't make it home alive as the disease began to spread. But he made it home.

Newly dead (the reason does not matter), he walked through the night, a stranger to exhaustion, shuffling along the highway toward his church as cars sped by (speeding more quickly when they saw him) filled with passengers in search of a freedom they would never find. By the time he entered his small town, having been on the move for the better part of a week, it was Sunday, and the members of his congregation had made their way uncertainly to their church. They knew what had been going on in the world, that it was the stuff of Revelations come at last, and since they knew that their priest had headed to New York for a conference, they assumed he was dead, and they did not expect to see him again. But they also knew that it was Sunday, and this was where they should be.

They were all sitting quietly in their pews, wondering whether one of them should step forward and stumble through the service, when the priest himself stumbled in. No one spoke. No one fled as he assumed his usual place, even though it was clear what he had become. Because they had faith.

(Something which I do not have.)

He tried to lead them in prayer, though perhaps "tried" is not the best word, as it implies volition, and he was operating on habit and tropism and half-forgotten dream, but regardless, the words would not come, as neither his mouth nor his brain were suitable for speech any longer. So the parishioners prayed on their own, standing and sitting and singing and speaking and remaining silent as they had always done, for they knew well what God expected of them.

Their priest growled before them, a deep rumble that some of them felt was not all that much different than what they had already been hearing for so many years.

When it became the proper time for the congregation to receive Communion, the priest stretched out his hands, and with the fingers that remained to him, gestured them all forward. They did not hesitate. They filed toward him, not frightened by his yellow eyes, or the pallor of his skin, or the fact that beneath his shredded clothing his flesh was shredded as well. They felt themselves in the presence of a miracle, and one does not argue with a miracle. They only knew that it was the usual time of the week to be made one with God.

When his flock was lined up before him, the priest seemed to freeze. The momentum of his faith had gotten him this far, but that did not mean that he was capable of much in the way of independent action and thought. As he paused, he was vaguely aware that something more active was expected of him, but the fog refused to lift so that he could see what that something was. After death, if one goes through the motions of life, it can only be by traversing the ruts one had chosen in life. He sensed somehow that he was expected to feed them, but he had not prepared. He had no consecrated wafers with which to proceed, no consecrated wine with which to wash away sins.

So he fed them of his flesh and quenched them with his blood.

He pulled open the tatters of his shirt and tore mouth-sized gobbets from his chest. One by one, he dropped them on waiting tongues, mumbling incoherently each time he did so. Then each of his congregants went back to his or her life, and as they had been promised, knew life eternal.

And as for the priest, he remained in his sanctuary, and fed the dwindling members of his flock each Sunday, until no flesh remained with which he could do so. But by that time, it didn't matter, as there were none left who required salvation.

And there you have it—the last tale I'm ever going to tell.

The last story…

I never thought I'd ever consider a story and judge it to be the last. I thought I'd die in the middle of telling a tale. But now… why bother? The telling of tales is through. And I, too, am almost through. Let it be the last story, and let it be told by the last man.

The candy machines are empty now, and I've resorted to licking the empty wrappings that I'd previously abandoned. All that's left in the soda machine are a few cans of grape. I've long ago gone through the desks of the missing (why can't I think dead?) workers and found every last candy bar and cracker. Electricity is random, and water has slowed to a trickle, which means that the world beyond this one is sending signals to me that it is running down. Entropy is rising. Soon I will be out of both food and water, and my only choices will be…

Do I die because I no longer have anything left to eat?

Or because I let myself be eaten?

There seems to be little difference between the two. Whether I choose death by action or death by inaction, I will have still chosen death. I have been backed into a corner. I guess I should consider that is a good thing, because it means that I will not be a victim in my own death. I will be a participant.

When I go (which will not be long, or else my choice will be taken from me), will I be the last? Isolated as I am, I can't tell. I'll never know. I guess that each of us, wherever we are, will appear to be the last to ourselves. And if we appear to be the last, then we are the last.

But if by some miracle, I am not the last man telling the last story, if there are others who someday read these words, who have managed to restore a civilization to this planet currently hovering between life and death, think of me from time to time as you go about your day. Think of us. I lived in a time of no hope, feeling there was no life outside my own, and with no new life to follow.

I wish that you could know this time, as I have known the times before my own. I wish that I could trust that you would be there to someday read these words, even if you are not human, even if you must be a visitor who travels to our world a million years from now to discover what exists on the third planet from the sun, and all you find is the shuffling undead, the same ones I have known, still hunting, still searching, much like we were, only eternal. Will you be able to figure out who we once were, or will you merely sit in awe and wonder at how such shambling creatures could have built this world and then seemingly forgotten how they brought it into existence. If you come here, to this building, to this vault, to these pages, you will know. It is important that you know.

In any case, I do not think you will be coming, not from this world or any other. I may be imaginative, I may be a dreamer, but I am unable to live in either imagination or dream.

And so I will be gone soon. With my strength fading, and with your future existence to read these words in doubt, I do not know why I struggle to write them.

Well… maybe I do.

I *can't* stop writing.

Well… I can.

It will be when I stop living.

And with strength finally fading… it is time for me to do both.

I cannot write. I can barely think. I can only choose.

So goodbye.

In case you surprise me, and come to read these words, let's leave it like this:

Did I starve? Was I eaten? As long as I do not write the words, I did neither, and continue to exist, in the eternal present, forever alive, as immortal as the undead. I can be with you still.

Whoever you are, whenever you are, as long as you are, *if* you are… keep me alive.

So perhaps I was wrong.

Perhaps art alone, art for art's sake, *can* be enough. It feels enough now, as I make my choice.

Meanwhile, our man with a stick and plot of land, who toiled on the other side of the globe and slept under different stars (remember him, the one who knew nothing of our roaring earthquakes, rising floods, or falling towers?), wakes before dawn from troubling dreams.

While he'd slept, the strange visions had made sense to him, but once he was awake, it all slipped away. When he rose from his straw mat and woke his son and tried to tell the boy what he had seen, because dreams were meaningful to his people, he remembered nothing of libraries or zombies or the taste of grape soda. All that came to him was the uncomfortable feeling of having been in the heart of a big city, which to him was frightening enough.

He had heard of such places, but knew of no one who had ever visited one, and he was glad that he instead had been born here, with his patch of earth and the mountains that surrounded it, with his stick and a son whom he needed to teach how to survive with little more than that.

But that was enough. Why would anyone require more? A wife for him and a mother for the boy, perhaps… but more? Those would be riches he did not need.

Tomorrow, in fact, if asked to remember his dream of the previous morning, *this* morning, he would answer, "What dream? I remember no dream." And, though some might choose to judge him and his way of life, he is at peace with the universe as he knew it, and he will go on as before, content, fulfilled, and utterly and happily oblivious to the fact that half a world away, almost the last man on Earth believed that he had finished telling almost the last stories.

HOW THE DAY RUNS DOWN

by John Langan

John Langan is the author of several stories, including "Episode Seven: Last Stand Against the Pack in the Kingdom of the Purple Flowers," which appeared in my anthology *Wastelands: Stories of the Apocalypse*. That story, and all of his other fiction to date, was originally published in *The Magazine of Fantasy & Science Fiction*. By the time this anthology sees print, these will have been collected in *Mr. Gaunt and Other Uneasy Encounters*, along with a previously unpublished novella. Other forthcoming work includes a story in Ellen Datlow's anthology, *Poe*.

"How the Day Runs Down," which is original to this volume, resulted from Langan's notion to write a monologue from the point of view of the Stage Manager in Thornton Wilder's play, *Our Town*, in which "our town" was infested with zombies. "I'm not sure what prompted me to combine those two things," Langan said. "There was a certain mordant humor in the juxtaposition of the Stage Manager's homespun wisdom with zombie horror that appealed to me."

(The stage dark with the almost-blue light of the late, late night, when you've been up well past the third ranks of late-night talk shows, into the land of the infomercial, the late show movies whose soundtrack is out of sync with its characters' mouths and which may break for commercial without regard for the action on the screen, the rebroadcast of the news you couldn't bear to watch the first time. It is possible—just—to discern rows of smallish, rectangular shapes running across the stage, as well as the bulk of a more substantial, though irregular, shape to the rear. The sky is dark: no moon, no stars.

(When the STAGE MANAGER snaps on his flashlight—a large one whose bright beam he sweeps back and forth over the audience once, twice, three times—the effect of the sudden light, the twirl of shadows around the theater, is emphasized by brushes rushing over drums, which give the sound of leaves, and a rainstick, which conjures the image of bones clicking against one another more than it does rain.

(Having surveyed the audience to his apparent satisfaction, the Stage Manager trains his light closer to home. This allows the audience to see the rows of tombstones that stretch the width of the stage, two deep in most places, three in a couple. Even from his quick inspection of them, it is clear that these are old tombstones, most of them chipped and worn almost smooth. The Stage Manager spares a moment for the gnarled shape behind the tombstones, a squat willow, before positioning the flashlight on the ground to his left, bottom down, so that its white light draws a cone in the air. He settles himself down beside it, his back leaning for and finding a tombstone, his legs gradually crossing in front of him.

(It has to be said, even with the light shining right beside him, the Stage Manager is not easy to see. A reasonable guess would locate him somewhere in his late forties, but estimates a decade to either side would not be unreasonable. His eyes are deep set, sheltered under heavy brows and the bill of the worn baseball cap on his head. His nose is thick and may have been broken in some distant confrontation; the shadows from the light spilling across his face make it difficult to decide if his broad upper lip sports a mustache; although his solid chin is clear of any hair. His ethnicity is uncertain; he could put in an appearance at most audience members' family reunions as a cousin twice-removed and not look out of place. He is dressed warmly, for late fall, in a bomber jacket, flannel shirt, jeans, and heavy boots.)

Stage Manager: Zombies. As with most things in life, the reality, when compared to the high-tech, Hollywood-gloss of the movies, comes as something of a surprise. For one thing, there's the smell, a stench that combines all the worst elements of raw sewage and rotted meat, together with the faint tang of formaldehyde. Folks used to think that last was from the funeral homes—whatever they'd used to pickle dear Aunt Myrtle—but as it turned out, this wasn't the case. It's just part of the smell they bring with them. Some people—scientists, doctors—have speculated that it's the particular odor of whatever is causing the dead to rise up and stagger around; although I gather other scientists and doctors have disagreed with that theory. But you don't have to understand the chemistry of it to know that it's theirs.

For another thing, when it comes to zombies, no one anticipated how persistent the damned things would be. You shoot them in the chest, they keep on coming. You shoot them in the leg—hell, you blow their leg clean off with your shotgun at point-blank range, they fall on their side, flop around for a minute or two, then figure out how to get themselves on their front so they can pull themselves forward with their hands, while they push with their remaining leg. And all the time, the leg you shot off is twitching like mad, as if, if it had a few more nerve cells at its disposal, it would find a way to continue after you itself. There is shooting in the head—it's true, that works, destroy enough brain matter and they drop—but do you have any idea what it's like to try to hit a moving target, even a slow-moving one, in the head at any kind of distance? Especially if you aren't using a state-of-the-art sniper rifle, but the snub-nosed thirty-eight you bought ten years ago when the house next door was burglarized and haven't given a thought to since—and the face you're aiming at belongs to your pastor, who just last Saturday was exhorting the members of your diminished congregation not to lose hope, the Lord was testing you.

(From high over the Stage Manager's head, a spotlight snaps on, illuminating OWEN TREZZA standing in the center aisle about three-quarters of the way to the stage. He's facing the back of the theater. At a guess, he's in his mid-thirties, his brown hair standing out in odd directions the way it does when you've slept on it and not washed it for several days running, his glasses duct-taped on the right side, his cheeks and chin full of stubble going to beard. The denim jacket he's wearing is stained with dirt, grass, and what it would be nice to think of as oil, as are his jeans. The green sweatshirt under his jacket is, if not clean, at least not marred by any obvious discolorations; although whatever logo it boasted has flaked away to a few scattered flecks of white. In his outstretched right hand, he holds a revolver with an abbreviated barrel that wavers noticeably as he points it at something outside the spotlight's reach.)

Owen: Oh, Jesus. Oh, sweet Jesus. Stop. Stop right there! Pastor Parks? Please—don't come any closer. Pastor? It's Owen, Owen Trezza. Please—can you please stay where you are? I don't want to—you really need to stay there. We just have to make sure—Jesus. Please. Owen Trezza—I attend the ten o'clock service. With my wife, Kathy. We sit on the left side of the church—our left, a couple pews from the front. Pastor Parks? Can you please stop? I know you're probably in shock, but—please, if you don't stop, I'm going to have to shoot. It's Owen. My wife's expecting our first child. She has red hair. Will you stop? Will you just stop? Goddamnit, Pastor, I will shoot! I don't want to, but you're giving me no choice. Please! I don't want to have to pull this trigger, but if you don't stay where you are, I'll have to. Don't make me do this. For Christ's sake, won't you stop? I have a child on the way. I don't want to have to shoot you.

(From outside the range of the spotlight, the sound of inexpensive loafers dragging across the carpet.)

Owen: Pastor Parks—Michael—Michael Parks, this is your final warning. Stop right there. Stop. Right. There.

(The shoes continue their scrape over the carpet. From the rear of the theater, a terrible odor rolls forward, like the cloud that hangs around the carcass of a deer two days dead and burst open on a hot summer afternoon. Owen's hand is shaking badly. He grabs his right wrist with his left hand, which steadies it enough for him to pull the trigger. The gun cracks like an especially loud firecracker and jerks up and away. Owen brings it back to aim.)

Owen: Okay—that was a warning shot. Now please stay where you are.

(The rough noise of the steps is joined by the outline of a figure at the edge of the spotlight's glow. Owen shoots a second time; again, the gun cracks and leaps back. He swings it around and pulls the trigger four times, straining to keep the pistol pointed ahead. Now the air is heavy with the sharp smell of gunsmoke. Hands at its sides, back stiff, swaying like a metronome as it walks, the figure advances into the light. It is a man perhaps ten years Owen's senior, dressed in a pair of khaki slacks and a black short-sleeved shirt whose round white collar is crusted with dried blood. Except for a spot over his collar, which is open in a dull, ragged wound the color of old liver, his skin is gray. Although it is difficult to see his face well, it is slack, his mouth hanging open, his eyes vacant. The hammer clacks as Owen attempts to fire his empty gun.)

Owen: Come on, Pastor Parks. I'm sorry I called you Michael. Come on—I know you can hear me. Stop. Please. Stop. Will you stop? Will you just stop? For the love of Christ, will you just fucking STOP!

(PASTOR MICHAEL PARKS—or, the zombie formerly known by that name—does not respond to Owen's latest command any more than he has those preceding it. Owen's hands drop. A look passes over his face—the momentary stun of someone recognizing his imminent mortality—only to be chased off by a surge of denial. He starts to speak.

(Whatever he was about to say, whether plea or threat or defiance, is drowned out by a BOOM that staggers the ears. Simultaneously, the back of Pastor Parks's head blows out in a spray of stale blood and congealed brains and splinters of bone that spatters those sitting to either side of the aisle. The minister drops to the floor.

(The Stage Manager has risen to his feet. In his right hand, he holds out a long-barreled pistol trailing a wisp of smoke. For what is probably not more than five seconds, he keeps the gun trained on the pastor's unmoving body, then raises the revolver and returns it to a shoulder holster under his left arm. Owen Trezza continues staring at the corpse as the spotlight snaps off. The Stage Manager resumes his seat.)

Stage Manager: No, there are some marksmen and -women about, that's for sure, but it's equally sure they're in the minority. Most folks have to rely on other methods. A few would-be he-men have tried to play Conan the Barbarian, rushed the zombies with a hatchet in one hand, a butcher knife in the other. One particularly inspired specimen, a heavyset guy named Gary Floss, rip-started the chainsaw he'd bought to take down the line of pines in front of his house. (This was a mistake: then everyone saw what lousy shape Gary kept his house in.) The problem is, that hatchet you have in your right hand isn't a weapon; it's a tool you've used splitting wood for the fireplace, and while it's probably sharp enough for another winter's worth of logs, it's not going to separate someone's head from their shoulders with a single blow from your mighty arm. The same thing's true for the knife sweating up your left hand: it's cutlery, and if you recall the effort it takes to slice a roast with it—a roast that is not trying to find its way inside your skull with its persistent fingers—you might want to reconsider your chances of removing limbs with ease. Even if you have a razor-sharp ax and an honest-to-God machete, these things are actually rather difficult to use well. The movies—again—aside, no one picks up this kind of weapon and is instantly skilled with it; you need training. In the meantime, you're likely to leave your hatchet lodged in a collar bone, the pride of your assorted knives protruding above a hip.

As for Gary Floss and his chainsaw—you want to be careful swinging one of those around. A man could take off an arm.

(To the right and left of the theater, the snarl of a chainsaw starting. It revs once, twice, a third time, changes pitch as it catches on something. It blends with a man's voice shrieking—then silence.)

Stage Manager: What works is fire. Zombies move away from fire faster than they move towards a fresh kill. The problem is, they're not especially flammable—no more than you or I are—so you have to find a way to make the fire stick. For a time, this meant Billy Joe Royale's homemade napalm. A lingering sense of civic responsibility precludes me from disclosing the formula for Billy Joe's incendiary weapon, which he modified from suggestions in—was it *The Anarchist Cookbook*? or an old issue of *Soldier of Fortune*? or something he'd watched on the Discovery Channel, back before it stopped broadcasting? (It's the damnedest thing: do you know, the History Channel's still on the air? Just about every other channel's gone blue. Once in a while, one of the stations out of the City will manage a broadcast; the last was a week and a half ago, when the ABC affiliate showed a truncated news report that didn't tell anyone much they hadn't already heard or guessed, and a rerun of an episode of *General Hospital* from sometime in the late nineties. But wherever the History Channel is located, someone programmed in twenty-four hours' worth of old World War II documentaries that have been playing on continuous loop ever since. You go from D-Day to Pearl Harbor to Anzio, all of it in black and white, interrupted by colorful ads for restaurant chains that haven't served a meal in a month, cars that no one's seen on the road for as long, movies that never made it to the theater. Truth to tell, I think the folks who bother to waste their generator's power on the TV do so more for the commercials than any nostalgia for a supposed Greatest Generation. These days, a Big Mac seems an almost fabulous extravagance, a Cadillac opulent decadence, a new movie an impossible indulgence.)

That's all a bit off-topic, though. We were talking about Billy Joe and his bathtub napalm. By the time he perfected the mixture, the situation here had slid down the firepole from not-too-bad to disastrous, all within the matter of a couple of days. Where we are—

Son of a gun. I never told you the name of this place, did I? I apologize. It's—the zombies have become so much the center of existence that they're the default topic of conversation, what we have now instead of the weather. This is the town of Goodhope Crossing, specifically, the municipal cemetery out behind the Dutch Reformed Church. Where I'm sitting is the oldest part of the place; the newer graves are...

(The Stage Manager points out at the audience.)

Stage Manager: Relax, relax. While there's nowhere that's completely safe anymore, the cemetery's no worse a danger than anyplace else. For the better part of—I reckon it must be going on four decades, local regulations have decreed that every body must be buried in a properly sealed coffin, and that coffin must be buried within a vault. To prevent contamination of groundwater and the like. The zombies have demonstrated their ability to claw their way out of all sorts of coffins time and again, but I have yet to hear of any of them escaping a vault. Rumors to the contrary, they're not any stronger than you or me; in fact, as a rule, they tend to be weaker. And the longer they go without feeding, the weaker they become. Muscle decay, you know. Hunger doesn't exactly kill them—it more slows them down to the point they're basically motionless. Dormant, you might say. So the chances are good that anyone who might've been squirming around down there in the dirt has long since run out of gas. Granted, not that I'm in any rush to make absolutely sure.

It is true, those who passed on before the requirement for a vault were able to make their way to the surface. A lot of them weren't exactly in the best of shape to begin with, though, and the ordeal of breaking out of their coffins and fighting up through six feet of earth—the soil in these parts is dense, thick with clay and studded with rocks—it didn't do anything to help their condition, that's for sure. Some of the very old ones didn't arrive in one piece, and there were some who either couldn't complete the trip or weren't coherent enough even to start it.

(Stage right, a stage light pops on, throwing a dim yellow glow over one of the tombstones and JENNIFER and JACKSON HOWLAND, her standing behind the headstone, him seated on the ground in front of and to its right. They are sister and brother, what their parents' friends secretly call Catholic or Irish twins: Jennifer is ten months her brother's senior, which currently translates to seventeen to his sixteen. They are siblings as much in their build—tall yet heavy—as they are in their angular faces, their brown eyes, their curly brown hair. Both are dressed in orange hunting caps and orange hunting vests over white cable-knit sweaters, jeans, and construction boots. Jennifer props a shotgun against her right hip and snaps a piece of bubblegum. Jackson has placed his shotgun on the ground behind him; chin on his fists, he stares at the ground.)

Jennifer: I still say you're sitting too close.

Jackson: It's fine, Jenn.

Jennifer: Yeah, well, see how fine it is when I have to shoot you in the head to keep you from making me your Happy Meal.

(Jackson sighs extravagantly, pushes himself backwards, over and behind his gun.)

Jackson: There. Is that better?

Jennifer: As long as the person whose grave you're sitting on now doesn't decide your ass would make a tasty treat.

(Jackson glares at her and climbs to his feet.)

Jennifer: Aren't you forgetting something?

(She nods at the shotgun lying on the ground. Jackson thrusts his hands in the pockets of his vest.)

Jackson: I'm sure there'll be plenty of time for me to arm myself if anything shows up.

Jennifer: Don't be so sure. Christine Compton said her family was attacked by a pair of eaters who ran like track stars.

Jackson: Uh-huh.

Jennifer: Why would she make that up?

Jackson: She—did Mr. Compton kill them?

Jennifer: It was Mrs. Compton, actually. Christine's dad can't shoot worth shit.

Jackson: Regardless—they're both dead, these sprinting zombies. Again. So we don't have to worry about them.

Jennifer: There could be others. You never know.

Jackson: I'll take my chances. (Pauses.) Besides, it's not as if we need to be here in the first place.

Jennifer: Oh?

Jackson: Don't you think, if Great-grandma Rose were going to return, she would have already? I mean, it's been like, what? ten days? two weeks? since the last ones dug themselves out. And it took them a while to do that.

Jennifer: Right, which means there could be others who'll need even longer.

Jackson: Do you really believe that?

Jennifer: Look—it's what Dad wants, okay?

Jackson: And we all know he's the poster-child for mental health these days.

Jennifer: What do you expect? After what happened to Mom and Lisa—

Jackson: What he says happened.

Jennifer: Not this shit again.

Jackson: All I'm saying is, the three of them were in the car—in a Hummer, for Christ's sake. They had guns. How does that situation turn against you? That's an honest question. I'd love to know how you go from that to—

Jennifer: Just shut up.

Jackson: Whatever.

(The siblings look away from one another. Jackson wanders the graves to the right, almost off-stage, then slowly turns and walks back to their great-grandmother's grave. While he does, Jennifer checks her gun, aims it at the ground in front of the tombstone, and returns it to its perch on her hip. Jackson steps over his shotgun and squats beside the grave.)

Jackson: Did Dad even know her?

Jennifer: His grandmother? I don't think so. Didn't she die before he was born? Like, years before, when Grandpa Jack was a kid?

Jackson: I guess. I don't remember. Dad and I never talked about that kind of stuff—family history.

Jennifer: I'm pretty sure he never met her.

Jackson: Great.

(Another pause.)

Jennifer: You want to know what I keep thinking about?

Jackson: Do I have a choice?

Jennifer: Hey, fuck you. If that's the way you're going to be, fuck you.

Jackson: I'm sorry. Sorry, geez.

Jennifer: Forget it.

Jackson: Seriously. Come on. I'm sorry.

Jennifer: I was going to say that, for like the last week, I haven't been able to get that Thanksgiving we went to Grandpa Jack's out of my head. That cranberry sauce Dad made—

Jackson: Oh yeah, yeah! Man, that was awful. What was it he put in it…

Jennifer: Jalapeño peppers.

Jackson: Yes! Yes! Remember, Grandpa started coughing so hard—

Jennifer: His teeth shot out onto Mom's plate!

Jackson: Yeah… (He wipes his eyes.) Hey. (He stands, stares down at the grave.) Is that—what is that?

Jennifer: What?

Jackson: (Pointing.) There. In the middle. See how the ground's…

(Jennifer positions her gun, setting the stock against her shoulder, lowering the barrel, and steps around the headstone.)

Jennifer: Show me.

(Jackson kneels, brings his right hand to within an inch of the ground.)

Jennifer: Not so close.

Jackson: You see it, right?

(Jennifer nods. Jackson rises and steps back onto his gun, almost tripping over it.)

Jennifer: You might want to cover your ears.

(Jennifer fires five times into the earth. Jackson slaps his hands to either side of his head as dirt jumps up from the grave. The noise of the shotgun is considerable, a roar that chases its echoes around the inside of the theater. There's a fair amount of gunsmoke, too, so that when Jennifer steps back and raises her gun, Jackson coughs and waves his arms to clear the air.)

Jackson: Holy shit.

Jennifer: No sense in doing a half-assed job.

Jackson: Was it her?

Jennifer: I think so. Something was right at the surface.

Jackson: Let's hope it wasn't a woodchuck.

Jennifer: Do you see any woodchuck guts?

Jackson: I don't see much of anything. (He stoops, retrieves his shotgun.) Does this mean we can go home?

Jennifer: We should probably wait a couple more minutes, just to be sure.

Jackson: Wonderful.

(The two of them stare down at the grave. The stage light pops off.)

Stage Manager: Siblings.

Right—what else can I tell you about the town? I don't imagine latitude and longitude are much use; I'm guessing it'll be more helpful for me to say that New York City's about an hour and a half south of here, Hartford an hour and a half east, and the Hudson River twenty minutes west. In an average year, it's hot in the summer, cold in the winter. There's enough snow to give the kids their fair share of snow days; you can have thunderstorms so fierce they spin off tornadoes like tops. At one time, this was IBM country; that, and people who commuted to blue collar jobs in the City at places like Con Ed. That changed twice, the first time in the early nineties, when IBM collapsed and sent a host of middle-aged men and women scrambling for work. The second time was after 9/11, when all the affluent folks who'd suddenly decided Manhattan was no longer their preferred address realized that, for the same amount of money you were spending on your glorified walk-in closet, you could be the owner of a substantial home on a reasonable piece of property in place that was still close enough to the City for you to have a manageable commute.

Coming after the long slowdown in new home construction that had followed IBM's constriction, this sent real estate prices up like a Fourth of July rocket. Gentrification, I guess you'd call it. What it meant was that your house significantly appreciated in value in what seemed like no more than a month—it wasn't overnight, no, not that fast, but fast enough, I reckon. We're talking thirty, forty, fifty percent climbs, sometimes higher, depending on how close you were to a Metro-North station, or the Taconic Parkway. It also meant a boom in the construction of new homes—luxury models, mostly. They didn't quite achieve the status of McMansions, but they were too big on the outside with too few rooms on the inside and crowded too close to their neighbors, with a front yard that was just about big enough to be worth the effort it was going to cost you to yank the lawnmower to life every other Saturday. If you owned any significant amount of property, the temptation to cash in on all the contractors making up for lost time was nigh irresistible. That farm that hadn't ever been what you'd call a profit-machine, and that had been siphoning off more money that it gave back for more years than you were comfortable admitting, became a dozen, fifteen parcels of land, a new little community with a name, something like Orchard Hills, that you could tell yourself was an acknowledgement of its former occupant.

What this expansion of houses meant was that, when the zombies started showing up in significant numbers, they found family after family waiting for them in what must have seemed like enormous lunchboxes.

(From the balcony, another spotlight snaps on, its tightly focused beam picking out MARY PHILLIPS standing in front of the orchestra pit. Although she faces the audience, her gaze is unfocused. She cannot be thirty. Her red hair has been cut recently—poorly, practically hacked off in places, where it traces the contours of her skull, and only partially touched in others, where it sprouts in tufts and a couple of long strands that suggest its previous style. The light freckles on her face are disturbed by the remnants of what must have been an enormous black eye, which has faded to a motley of green and yellow, and a couple of darker spots, radiating out from her right eye. She is wearing a white dress shirt whose brownish polka dots appear to have been applied irregularly, even haphazardly, a pair of almost-new dark jeans, and white sneakers clumped with mud. She keeps her hands at her sides in tight fists.)

Mary: I was in the kitchen, boiling water for pasta. We'd had a gas delivery a couple of weeks before—it's funny: everything's falling to pieces—this was after the first outbreak had been contained, and all the politicians and pundits were saying yes, we'd had a close call, but the worst was past—what had happened in India, Asia, what was happening in South America—none of that was going to happen here. No matter that there were reports the things—what we were calling the eaters, because zombies sounded too ridiculous—the eaters had been sighted in a dozen different places from Maine to California, none of them previously affected. You heard stories—my next-door neighbor, Barbara Odenkirk—she was the HR director for an ad agency in Manhattan, and she commuted to the City every day, took the train from Beacon. The last time we talked, she told me that there were more of them, the eaters, along the sides of the tracks every trip. She said none of the guys on the train acted particularly concerned—if an eater came too close to a moving train, it didn't end well for them. I asked her about the places alongside the tracks, what about them, the towns and cities and houses—I'd taken that same ride I don't know how many times, when Ted and I first started seeing one another, and I remembered all the houses you saw sitting off in the woods. Oh, Barbara said, she was sure the local police were on top of the situation. They weren't, of course, not like Barbara thought. I don't know why. When that soccer game in Cold Spring was attacked—we were so surprised, so shocked, so outraged. We should have been packing our cars, cramming everything we could fit into our Volvos and BMWs and heading out of town, tires screaming. Where, I'm not sure. Maybe north, up to the Adirondacks—I heard the situation isn't as bad there. Even the Catskills might have been better.

But the gas truck pulled into the driveway the way it did every six months, and the power was on more than it was out, and we could drive to Shop Rite—where, if the shelves were stocked thinner than we'd ever seen them, and the butcher case was empty, not to mention the deli and fish counters, we could fill our baskets with enough of the foods we were used to for us to tell ourselves that the President was right, we were through the roughest part of this, and almost believe it. Ted had bought a portable generator when the first outbreak was at its height, and it looked as if Orlando would be overrun; everyone else was buying whatever guns they could lay their hands on, and here's my husband asking me to help him unload this heavy box from the back of the car. He was uptight—I think he was expecting me to rake him over the coals for not having returned from Wal-Mart with an armful of rifles. I wasn't angry; if anything, I was impressed with his foresight. I wasn't especially concerned about being armed—at that point, I still believed the police and National Guard were capable of dealing with the eaters, and if they weren't,

I was surrounded by neighbors who were two steps away from forming their own militia. The blackouts, though—we were lucky: the big one only lasted here until later that same night. According to NPR, there were places where the lights were out for a week, ten days. But there were shorter outages every few days, most no more than five or ten seconds, a few a solid couple of hours. Having the generator—not to mention the big red containers of gas I had no idea how Ted had obtained: rationing was already in effect, and most gas stations were pretty serious about it—that generator gave me a feeling of security no machine gun could have matched. To tell the truth, I was more worried by Ted's insistence that he could hook it up himself. Being in IT does not give you the magical ability to master any and all electrical devices—how many times had I said that to him? Especially when Sean Reynolds two houses over is an electrician who loves helping out with this kind of stuff. But no, he's fully capable of doing this, which is what he'd said about the home entertainment system he tripped half the circuit breakers in the house setting up. What was I supposed to do? I made sure to unplug the computers, though, as well as the entertainment center.

Somehow—with a lot more cursing than I was happy with the kids hearing from their father—he succeeded, which is why, on that particular afternoon, I was standing at the kitchen stove waiting for a pot of water to boil. Robbie had asked for mac and cheese again, and I wasn't inclined to argue with her, since Brian would eat it, too, and we had more than enough boxes of it stacked in the pantry. It was the organic kind that only needed a little bit of milk added to make the sauce, which I thought was more economical; although the stuff had cost more to begin with, so where's the sense in that? The power had gone out an hour earlier, and while we tried to use the generator prudently, starting it up now didn't seem especially extravagant. I waited until I was ready to start dinner, then ran out onto the back porch, down the stairs, and under the porch to where Ted had installed the generator. When Ted was home, the moment he heard that lock click, he dropped whatever he was doing to dash into the kitchen and asked if I'd made sure it was safe to go outside. No matter what I replied, he'd insist on checking, himself—as if he could see better through his glasses than I could with 20/20 vision. I got that it was a guy thing, and in its own way, I suppose it was kind of sweet. Really, though—unless there was an eater standing outside the door, I didn't think I had anything to worry about. They weren't much for running—most of them had trouble walking. Okay, high school track was ten years and two kids in my past, but I was still in good enough shape from chasing after those kids to leave Ted eating my dust. Granted, my husband's idea of exercise was putting away the dishes; the point is, I wasn't concerned about being caught by an eater. From what I'd heard on the radio, they were most dangerous in large numbers, when they could trap you. Sure, there were woods at the edge of the backyard that could've hidden a decent-sized group of them, but I was fairly confident my well-armed neighbors would mow the lot of them down the second they staggered into the open.

We were pretty anal about checking the tree line; I tried to do it at least once an hour, usually on the hour when the hall clock played its electronic version of the Westminster Chimes, but some of the neighbors were at their windows every fifteen or twenty minutes. Matt Odenkirk had a pair of high-powered binoculars—they looked like they cost a bundle—and he would stand on his back porch staring into the woods for minutes at a time. It was as if he was certain the eaters were out there, doing their best to blend in with the foliage, and all he needed was to catch one of them moving to reach for the equally-expensive-looking rifle balanced against the railing and be the hero of the neighborhood. Which never happened. I don't think he fired that gun once—I don't think it was in his hands when—when they—when he—

The generator started no problem; I was out and in the house almost before the kids realized. I turned on the stove light and filled a pot with water from the cooler—which always drove Ted crazy. "That's for drinking-only," he'd say. "Use the water from the filter jugs for cooking." But our water tasted funny; I'm sorry, it did, and no matter how many times you passed it through those jugs, it was like drinking from a sulfur spring. "What do you mean?" Ted would—he'd insist. "It tastes fine." Okay, I'd say, then you can drink it, which he would, of course, to prove his point. When he wasn't home, though—on a day like today, when he'd driven in to IBM because they were open—I can't imagine what they could have been doing, what business they could have been conducting, with everything the way it was—on a day like today, we used the bottled water for cooking.

I lit the burner, set the pot on it, and switched on the transistor radio. Usually, I kept the radio quiet, because who knew what the news was going to be today? Granted, NPR wasn't as bad as any of the TV channels, which, as things had deteriorated in Florida and Alabama, had taken to broadcasting their raw footage, so that when Mobile was overrun, you saw all the carnage in color and up close and personal. But NPR had sent a reporter to Mobile, and when the National Guard lines collapsed, she was caught on the wrong side—trapped inside a car. The eaters got her, and you heard pretty much everything. First, she's saying "Oh no, oh please," as they pound on the car windows. Then the windows shatter, she screams, and you can hear the eaters, the slap of their hands on the upholstery as they grab at her and miss, the rip of the reporter's clothes where they catch her, and their voices—I know there's a lot of debate about the sounds they make, whether they're expressions of coherent thought or just some kind of muscle spasm, but I swear, I listened to that broadcast all the way through, and those were voices, they were saying something. I couldn't make out what, because now the reporter was shrieking, emptying her lungs in panic and pain. I thought that was as bad as it would get—as it could get—but I was wrong. There was a sound—it was the sound a drumstick makes when you twist it off the Thanksgiving turkey, a long tearing followed by a pop—only, it was… wet. The reporter's voice went from high to low, from scream to moan, and that moan—it was awful, it was what comes out of you the moment you set one foot into death and feel it tugging the rest of you after. The rest—one of the eaters figured out how to open one of the car doors. Whatever the reporter was wearing rasped on the seat as she was dragged out, her moan rising a little as she realized this was it, and then there was a noise like the rest of that Thanksgiving bird being torn apart in all directions, this succession of ripping and snapping, and then you hear the eaters feeding, stuffing pieces of the reporter into their mouths, grunting with pleasure at the taste. It—

Robbie was old enough to understand what was on the radio, and even Brian picked up on more than you expected. I didn't want to expose them to something like that. As it was, they heard too much from the other kids in the neighborhood, especially the McDonald girls. Alice, their mother, was one of those parents who likes to pretend they're treating their kids with what they call respect, when really, all they're doing is exposing them to all kinds of things they're too young to handle. A parent—a mother isn't supposed to—that's not your job. Your job—your duty, your sacred duty—it is your sacred duty to protect those children, to keep them safe no matter what—you have to protect them, no matter—

Well, I was. With the generator running, I could let them watch a DVD, which had gone from a daily occurrence—sometimes twice-daily—to a treat like going to the movies had been when I was their age. They were so thrilled Robbie was willing to sit down to *The Incredibles*, which Brian adored but didn't do anything for her. So with the two of them safely seated in front of the TV, I was safe to turn on the radio, low, and try to catch up with what news I could as the water came to a boil.

And you know, the news wasn't bad. I wouldn't call it good, exactly, but the National Guard seemed to be making progress. They'd held onto Orlando; although apparently Disney World was the worse for it; and had caught a significant number of the eaters on one of the major highways—I can't remember the number; it may have been Highway 1—where they'd brought in the air power, let the planes drop bombs on the eaters until they were in so many microscopic pieces. Given what we learned about them in the weeks after, this was about the worst thing that could have happened, since it spread bits of them and their infection to the four winds, but at the time, it sounded like a step forward. There was talk of retaking Mobile; a team of Navy SEALs had rescued a group of survivors holed up in City Hall, and a squad of Special Forces had made an exploratory journey into the city that had brought them to within sight of the harbor. Of course, the powers-that-be are going to tell you that things are better than they are, but I was willing to believe them.

I heard the truck pull up outside, heard the slow rumble of its engine, the squeal and hiss of its air brakes. I noticed it, but I wasn't especially concerned. The Rosses had sold their house across the street to a couple from the City who supposedly had paid them almost a million dollars for it. The news made our eyes goggle; Ted and I spent a giddy couple of hours imagining how we might spend our million. Once we went online to check housing prices in the Adirondacks, though, all our fantasies came crashing down. Up north, a million was the least you'd pay for a place not even half the size of ours. We knew Canada had closed the border, but we looked anyway. With the state of the U.S. dollar, it was more like 1.5 million for the same undersized house. It appeared we would be staying where we were. And we'd have new neighbors, whose moving truck had arrived.

Sometimes, I think about that driver. I don't know anything about him—or her, it could have been a woman; although, for some reason, I always picture a man. Not a kid: someone in his fifties, maybe, kind of heavyset, with a crew cut that doesn't hide the gray in his hair. He's been around long enough to have seen all kinds of crises, which is why he doesn't panic, keeps working through this one. No one else at the delivery company wants to make the drive upstate with him, risk the wilds to the north, but he's happy to leave the City for a day. Everybody's on edge. There are soldiers and heavily armed police clustered at all the docks, the airports, the train stations, the bus terminals. Everyone who arrives in the City is supposed to be examined by a doctor flanked by a pair of men who keep the laser-sights of their pistols centered on the traveler's forehead for the duration of the exam. The slightest cause for concern—fever, swollen and tender glands, discolored tongue—is grounds for immediate quarantine. Protest, and those men to either side of the doctor are expressly authorized to put a pair of bullets in your head. What's worse is, with the police largely off the streets, groups of ordinary citizens have taken it on themselves to patrol the City for eaters. They've given themselves license to stop and question anyone they consider suspicious, and if you ask what gives them the right, they'll be only too happy to show you the business ends of their assorted pistols and rifles. There's been at least one major shootout between two of these patrols, each of whom claimed they thought the other were eaters. Cops had to be pulled off port duty to bring it under control, which they did by shooting most of the participants.

I can't imagine anything happened to the driver while he was in the City. My guess is, he passed through the checkpoints and was on his way without a hitch. It was a nice, early fall morning, the air cool but not cold, the leaves on the verge of losing their green, the sun bright but not oppressive. Maybe he had the radio on, was listening to one of the AM stations out of the City. He heard the news out of Florida and thought, *I knew it*. He decided to take the next exit, stop at a Dunkin' Donuts for a celebratory coffee and a Boston Cream.

As he steered into the parking lot, maybe he noticed the absence of any other cars. Or maybe he saw the lights on in the donut shop and assumed he'd arrived during a lull in business. He parked the truck, climbed down from the cab, and walked toward the glass door. There are times I see him striding up to the counter, his eyes on the racks of donuts on the wall opposite him, not aware of anything unusual until he sees that all the racks are empty. In what feels to him like slow-motion, he turns to the tables to his right and takes in the floor slick with blood, the remains of the last patrons scattered across the tables. Then I think, *That's ridiculous—there's no way he would not have seen all of that right away*. The second he swung open the door, he would have smelled it. Chances are, he wouldn't have had to go that far—he would have seen the blood splashed across the windows and immediately turned around. Either way—whether he bolts out of the place or walks away without going in—he would be distracted, shocked by what he's (almost) seen. Maybe the closest he's been to something like this has been an image on the TV. It's the reason he doesn't pick up on the feet dragging across the tarmac until the eater is out from around the front of the truck and practically on him. The driver's eyes bulge; if he's never been this close to such carnage, you can be sure he's never had an eater lurching towards him, either. His feet catch on one another and he trips, which causes the eater to trip and fall on top of him. For one horrifying moment, he's under the thing, under that stink, the teeth clacking in his ear as it tries to take a bite out of him, those hands pawing at him. He drives his right elbow back and up into its face. Fireworks of pain burst in his arm but the eater rolls off him. He scrambles to his feet, kicking at the eater's hands as they try to drag him down again, and climbs up and into the truck's cab. Maybe he jumps when the eater slaps the door, almost drops the keys his fingers can't fit into the ignition. The eater pounds the door, throws itself against it, actually makes the truck rock ever-so-slightly. The key slides into place, the engine turns over, and the driver grinds the gears putting the truck into first. He speeds out of that parking lot so fast the rear end of the truck bashes a telephone pole, throwing open one of the rear doors and tumbling a couple of plastic crates out onto the road. His foot doesn't leave the gas pedal. Let them take it out of his pay. His heart is hammering, his hands trembling on the wheel. If he smokes, he's desperate for a cigarette; if he quit, he wishes he hadn't; if he never has, he wishes he'd started.

It wouldn't have been until that Dunkin' Donuts was a good thirty, forty minutes in his rearview mirror that the driver would have felt his right elbow throbbing. When he glanced down, he saw blood on the seat and floor. He turned his arm over. His stomach squeezed at the torn skin bright with blood, the pair of broken teeth protruding just above the joint. His foot relaxed on the gas; the truck slowed to the point it was barely moving. His vision constricted to a tunnel; he wondered if he was about to faint. He took the wheel with his right hand, reached around with his left, and felt for the jagged edges of the eater's teeth. The blood made them slippery, hard to keep hold of. He dug his fingers into his skin, seeking purchase, but that only squeezed out more blood. There was no choice; he had to stop. He clicked on the hazards, steered to the shoulder, and set the brake. He did not turn off the engine. He leaned over and slid the First Aid box out from under his seat. His fingers slipped on the catch. Once he had it open, he found the bottle of sterile saline and the stack of gauze bandages. He sprayed half the bottle over his elbow, unwrapped a couple of bandages, and wiped his skin. There was a pair of tweezers in the box; despite his shaking hand, he succeeded in tugging one, and then the other, tooth from his arm. Their extraction caused more bleeding. He dropped the tweezers on the floor, next to the teeth, and emptied the remainder of the saline on his elbow. There were enough gauze pads left for him to wipe his elbow off and improvise a bandage using the roll of surgical tape.

No one really understood what brought the eaters out of the ground, up off their tables in the morgues and funeral homes, in the first place. There was all kinds of speculation, some of it ridiculous—Hell was full: Ted and I had a good laugh over that one—some of it more plausible but still theoretical—NPR had on a scientist from the CDC who talked about a kind of super-bacteria, like a nasty staph infection that could colonize a human host in order to gain more flesh to consume; although that seemed like a lot for a single microorganism to accomplish. Besides, none of the eaters the government had captured showed the slightest response to any of the antibiotics they were injected with. I wondered if it was a combination of causes, several bacteria working together, but Ted swore that was impossible. Because the IT thing made him an expert in bacteriology, too.

What we did know was that, if an eater got its teeth in you, even if you escaped becoming its next meal, you were finished all the same. It just took longer—between thirty minutes and forty-eight hours. The initial symptoms were a raging fever, swollen and tender glands, and a tongue the color of old meat; in short order, these were followed by hallucinations, convulsions, and death. Anywhere from five minutes to two hours after your heart had ceased beating, your body—reanimated was the technical term. It was incurable, and if you presented to your doctor or a hospital ER with the telltale signs, you were taken as fast as possible to a hospital room, hooked up to monitors for your heart rate and blood pressure, and strapped onto a bed. If there was an experimental cure making the rounds that day, it would be tested on you. When it didn't work, you would be offered the services of the clergy, and left for the inevitable. An armed guard was stationed outside your door; after the monitors had confirmed your death, he would enter the room, unholster his pistol, and make sure you didn't return. At first, the guards were given silencers, but people complained, said they felt better hearing the gunshot, knowing they were safe.

I don't know how much of this the driver knew, but I'm guessing he'd heard most of it, which is why he didn't take himself to the nearest hospital as soon as he realized what had happened to him. Instead, he switched off the hazards, released the brake, and headed back out onto the road. It could be he was thinking he had to make this last delivery while he could, but I doubt it. He was already dead; his body simply needed to catch up to that fact. His mind, though—his mind was not having any of this. As far as his mind was concerned, he'd scraped his arm, that was all, hardly enough to have turned him into one of those things, and if he went on with this day the way he'd intended, everything would be fine. If he had to roll down his window, because the cab had grown so hot he checked to be sure he hadn't turned the heater on high, he must be fighting off the cold that was making the rounds at work. That same cold must be what was causing the skin under his jaw to feel so sore. The temptation to tilt the rearview mirror so he could inspect his tongue must have been almost too much to resist.

If the driver heard anything moving in the back of the truck, he probably assumed it was more of the plastic crates come loose, maybe a piece of furniture that had broken the straps securing it. Of course, by then his fever would have ignited, so the eaters could have banged around the inside of that container for the hours it took him to complete what should have been a sixty-minute trip and I doubt he would have noticed. Or, the sounds might have registered, but—you know how it is when you're that sick: you're aware of what's going on around you, but there's a disconnect—it fails to mean what it should. How else do you explain what led this guy to drive a large moving truck full of eaters into the middle of a neighborhood—into the middle of our neighborhood—my neighborhood, the place where I lived with my husband and my kids, my girl and my boy—how else do you explain someone fucking up so completely, so enormously?

That's right—the truck that came to a stop outside the house (as I watched bubbles forming at the bottom of the pot of water I was heating) was full—it was packed with eaters. Don't ask me how many. And no, I don't know how they got in there. I'd never heard of anything like that before. Maybe the things were chasing someone who climbed into the back of the truck thinking the eaters wouldn't be able to follow them and was wrong. Maybe the eaters started as a group of infected who were in the same state of denial as the driver and wanted to hide themselves until they recovered—which, of course, they didn't. Maybe they didn't jump into the truck all at the same time: maybe a few were in pursuit of a meal, a few more were looking to hide, and a few others thought they'd found a cool place to escape the sun. As the fever soared within him, his neck ached so bad swallowing became agony, his tongue swelled in his mouth, the driver must have let the truck slow to a stop over and over again, leaning his head on the steering wheel for whatever comfort its lukewarm plastic could provide. There would have been plenty of opportunities for eaters to hitch a ride with him.

I don't know what that man's fate was, whether he died the moment he set the parking brake, or opened the door and stepped down from the cab to let his customers know their furniture had arrived, or if the eaters figured out the door handle and dragged him from his seat. But I hope they got to him first; I hope he found himself in the middle of a group of eaters and had consciousness left to understand what was about to happen to him. I hope—I pray; I get down on my knees and plead with God Almighty that those things ripped him apart while his heart was still beating. I hope they stripped the flesh from his arms and legs. I hope they jammed their fingers into him and rooted around for his organs. I hope they bit through his ears the way you do a tough piece of steak. I hope he suffered. I hope he felt pain like no one ever felt before. That's why I spend so much time imagining him, so that his death can be as real—as vivid—to me as possible. I—

The first bubbles had lifted themselves off the bottom of the pot and drifted up through the water to burst at the surface. On the radio, the report about the Special Forces in Mobile had ended, and the anchor was talking about sightings of eaters in places like Bangor, Carbondale, and Santa Cruz, which the local authorities were writing off as hysteria but at least some of which, the anchor said, there was disturbing evidence were true; in which case, they represented a new phase in what he called the Reanimation Crisis. From the living room, Brian yelped and said, "Scary!" which he did when something on the screen was too much for him; Robbie said, "It's okay—Vi's gonna get them out. Watch," one of those grace notes your kids sound that makes you catch your breath, it's so unexpected, so pure. There was a knock at the front door.

It sounded like a knock. When I rewind it and play it again in my mind, it still sounds like a knock, no matter how I try to hear it otherwise. None of the descriptions of the eaters mentioned anything about knocking. Besides, I hadn't heard anyone's gun going off, which I fully expected would announce the arrival of eaters in our neck of the woods. Of course, this was because everyone was watching the treeline behind the houses; I realize how ridiculous it sounds, how unforgivably stupid, but it never occurred to any of us that the eaters might walk right up to our front doors and knock on them. Or—I don't know—maybe we were aware of the possibility, but assumed there was no way a single eater, let alone a truckload of them, could appear in the middle of the street without someone noticing.

I left the pot with the wisps of steam starting to curl off the water and walked down the front stairs to the door. At the top of the stairs, I thought it might be Ted home from work, but on the way down I decided it couldn't be him, because he wouldn't have bothered knocking, would he? It had to be a neighbor, probably the McDonald girls come to ask if Robbie wanted to go out and play with them. They were forever doing things like that, showing up five minutes before dinner and asking Robbie to play with them—which, the second she heard their voices, Robbie naturally was desperate to do. I tried to compromise, told Robbie she could go out for a little while after she was done with her food, or invited the McDonald girls to join us for dinner, but Robbie would insist she wasn't hungry, or the McDonald girls would say they had already eaten, or were going to have pizza later, when their father brought it home. At which, Robbie would ask why we couldn't have pizza, which Brian would hear and start chanting, "Piz-za! Piz-za! Piz-za!" Sometimes I let Robbie run out and kept a plate warm for her, let her eat with Ted and me when he got home, which she loved, being at the table with Mommy and Daddy and no little brother. Sometimes, though, I told the McDonald girls to return in half an hour, Roberta was sitting down to her dinner—and prepared myself for the inevitable storm of protests. I hadn't made up my mind what my decision this time would be, but my stomach was clenching. I turned the lock, twisted the doorknob, and pulled the door open.

They say that time slows down in moments of crisis; for some people, maybe it does. For me, swinging that door in was like hitting the fast-forward button on the DVD player, when the images on the screen advance so fast they appear as separate pictures. One moment, I'm standing with the door in my hand and a trio of eaters on the front step. They're women, about my age. I think—the one nearest me is missing most of her face. Except for her right eye, which is cloudy and blue and looks as if it's a glass eye that's been scuffed, I'm staring at bare bone adorned with tatters and shreds of muscle and skin. Her mouth—her teeth part, and I have the absurd impression she's about to speak to me.

The next moment, I'm scrambling up the stairs backwards. I could leap them three at a time—I have in the past—but there's no way I'm turning my back on the figures who have entered the house. The pair behind the faceless one don't appear nearly as desiccated: their skin is blue-gray, and their faces show no expression, but compared to what's raising her right foot to climb the stairs after me, they're practically normal.

The moment after that, I'm in the kitchen, one hand reaching for the handle of the pot of water, which hasn't come to full boil yet. Behind me, I can hear the stairs shifting under the eaters' weight. I can smell them—God, everything I've heard about the way the things smell is true. I want to call to the kids, tell them to get in here with me, but it's all I can do not to vomit.

That second, the second my fingers are closing around the handle—that's the one I return to. When I replay the three minutes it took my life to disintegrate, I focus on me in the kitchen. I can't remember how I got there. I mean, I know how I went from the stairs to the kitchen, I don't know why. Once I reached the top of the stairs, it would have been easy enough to haul myself to my feet and run into the living room, to Robbie and Brian. We could have—I could have shoved the couch out from the wall, used it to delay the eaters while we ran for the back door—or even around them, back down the stairs and out the front door, or into the downstairs rec room. We could have barricaded ourselves in the garage. We—instead, I ran for the kitchen. I realize I must have been thinking about a weapon; I must have been searching for something to defend myself—us with, and the pot on the stove must have been the first thing that occurred to me. This has to be what made me choose the kitchen, but I can't remember it. All I have is me on the stairs, and then my fingers curling around that piece of metal.

Which isn't in my hand anymore; it's lying on the kitchen floor, and Miss Skull-Face's right eye has sagged downwards because the pot has collapsed her cheek where it struck it. The hot water doesn't appear to have had any affect on her; although a couple of the pieces of flesh dangling from her face have fallen onto her blouse. She's moving towards me fast, her hands outstretched, and I see that she's missing two of the fingers on her left hand, the ring and pinkie, and I wonder if she lost them trying to prevent whoever it was from tearing off her face.

The next thing, I'm on the floor, on my back, which is numb. My head is swimming. Across the kitchen tiles from me, Miss Skull-Face struggles to raise herself from her back. At the time, I don't know what's happened, but I realize now the eater's rush carried us into the wall, stunning us both. The other eaters are nowhere to be seen.

And then I'm on the other side of the kitchen island, which I've scooted around on my butt. I'm driving the heel of my left foot straight into the eater's face, the shock of the impact traveling through the sole of my sneaker up my leg. I feel as much as hear the crunch of bone splintering. I'm as scared as I've ever been, but the sensation of the eater's face breaking under my foot sends a rush of animal satisfaction through me. Although I'm intent on the web of cracks spreading out from the sudden depression where Miss Skull-Face's nose and cheeks used to be, I'm aware that her companions are not in the kitchen.

I must—if I haven't before, I must understand that the other eaters have left Miss Skull-Face to deal with me and turned in search of easier—of the—I know I pull myself off the floor, and I'm pretty sure I kick the same spot on the eater's face with the toe of my sneaker, because afterwards, it's smeared with what I think are her brains. What I remember next is—

(To the front, rear, left, and right of the theater, the air is full of screaming. At first, the sound is so loud, so piercing, that it's difficult for anyone in the audience to do anything more than cover her or his ears. Mary raises her hands to either side of her head; it does not appear that the Stage Manager does, even as the screams climb the register from terror to pain. Muffled by skin and bone, the screams resolve themselves into a pair of voices. It is hard to believe that such noises could issue from the throats of anything human; they seem more like the shrieks of an animal being vivisected. As they continue for four, five, six seconds—an amount of time that, under other circumstances, would pass almost without notice but that, with the air vibrating like a plucked guitar string, stretches into hours—it becomes possible to distinguish the screams as a single word tortured to the edge of intelligibility, made the vessel for unbearable pain: "Mommy.")

(The screaming stops—cut off. Mary removes her hands from her ears hesitantly, as if afraid her children's screams might start again.)

Mary: That's—there are—they—there are some—I don't—there are some things a mother shouldn't have to see, all right? My parents—I—when I was growing up, our next door neighbors' oldest son died of leukemia, and my mother said, "No parent should outlive their children." Which is true. I used to think it was the worst thing that could happen to you as a parent, especially of small children. But I was wrong—I was—they—oh, they had them in their teeth—

(Now Mary screams; head thrown back, eyes closed, hands clutching her shirt, she opens her mouth and pours forth a wail of utter loss. When her scream subsides to a low moan, her head drops forward. She brings her hands to her head, runs one over it while the other winds one of the long strands of her hair around itself.

(From the front of the theater, Mary's voice speaks, but from the echoey quality of the words, it's clear this is a recording.)

Mary's Voice: That second, the second my fingers are closing around the handle—that's the one I return to. When I replay the three minutes it took my life to disintegrate, I focus on me in the kitchen. I can't remember how I got there. I mean, I know how I went from the stairs to the kitchen, I don't know why. Once I reached the top of the stairs, it would have been easy enough to haul myself to my feet and run into the living room, to Robbie and Brian. We could have—Robbie and Brian. I didn't want to expose them to something like that. A parent—a mother isn't supposed to—that's not your job. Your job—your duty, your sacred duty, is to protect those children, to keep them safe no matter what—we—instead, I ran for the kitchen. I realize I must have been thinking about a weapon; I must have been searching for something to defend myself—us with, and the pot on the stove must have been the first thing that occurred to me. This has to be what made me choose the kitchen, but I can't remember it. You have to protect them, no matter—

(The recording stops. The spotlight snaps off, and Mary is gone, lost to the darkness.

(Slowly, the Stage Manager comes to his feet. Once he is up, he looks away from the audience, towards the willow behind him. He takes a deep breath before turning towards the audience again.)

Stage Manager: Here's the problem. When you sign up for this job—when you're cast in the part, if you like—you're told your duties will be simple and few. Keep an eye on things. Not that there's much you can do—not that there's anything you can do, really—but there isn't much that needs doing, truth to tell. Most of the business of day-to-day existence takes care of itself, runs ahead on the same tracks its used for as long as there've been people. Good things occur—too few, I suppose most would say—and bad things, as well—which those same folks would count too numerous, I know—but even the very worst things happen now as I'm afraid they always have. Oh, sure, could be you can give a little nudge here or there, try to make sure this person won't be at work on a June morning that'll be full of gunfire, or steer the cop in the direction of that house she's had a nagging suspicion about, but mostly, you're there to watch it all take place.

Then something like this—then this, these zombies, folk getting up who should be lying down—it overtakes you, sweeps across the world and your part of it like—like I don't know what, something I don't have words for. You do the best you can—what you can, which mostly consists of putting on a brave face and not turning your eyes away from whatever horror's in front of you; although there may be opportunities for more direct action.

(Through his jacket, the Stage Manager pats his gun.)

Stage Manager: You try to maintain some semblance of a sense of humor, which is not always as hard as maybe it should be. There's something to the old saw about horror and humor being flip sides of the same coin. An idiot takes his arm off with his chainsaw trying to play hero—I grant you it's pretty grim fodder for laughs, but you make do with what's to hand—so to speak.

A situation like this, though, like this poor woman and her children—those children—I know what she saw when she ran into that living room. I know what that is on her shirt, and how it got there. I can't—I don't have the faintest idea what I'm supposed to do with that knowledge. I could tell you, I suppose, but to what end? You know what those things—those eaters, that's not a bad word, is it?—you know what they did to that little girl and that little boy. There's no need for the specifics. Maybe you'd rather hear about the scene that greeted Mary when she fled her house in horror, or maybe you've guessed that, too: her neighbors' houses overrun, pretty much without a single shot being fired.

This is the beginning of the second phase of the zombie trouble—what did that newscaster call it? The Reanimation Crisis? From something people were watching on their TVs, or seeing outside the windows of their trains, zombies become something that's waiting for you when you go to get in your car, that clatters around your garage, that thumps on your door. Situation like this, where folks have known the world's going to hell and been preparing themselves for it—which mostly means emptying their bank accounts accumulating as many guns as Wal-Mart'll sell them—you'd expect that all that planning would count for something, that those zombies never would have made it up Mary's front walk, that one or the other of her neighbors would have noticed what was tumbling out the back of that delivery truck and started shooting. There'd be a lot of noise, a lot of mess, possibly a close call or two, but everything would turn out well in the end. Mary would be home with her kids, her neighbors would be patting themselves on the backs with a certain amount of justifiable pride, and at least one zombie outbreak would have been contained. Instead, Mary's the only one to escape alive, which she accomplishes by running screaming out of her house, up the street and out onto Route 376, where she's struck by a red pickup truck driven by an eighteen-year-old girl who received it as a birthday present from her parents last month.

Mary avoids being hit head-on, which would've killed her, but she's tossed to the side of the road. To her credit, the girl stops, reverses, and leaves the truck to see to the woman who collided with it. Actually it's a risky move—for all the girl knows, she could've knocked down a zombie. Mary's pretty seriously concussed, but it's clear to the girl she hails from one of the big houses on the side street—the houses from which a few zombies are emerging, doused with blood. The girl doesn't waste any time: she hustles Mary into her truck and literally burns rubber racing away. The girl—who deserves a name: she's Beth Driscoll—Beth takes Mary into the center of Goodhope Crossing, to the new walk-in emergency-care place, and stays with her as the doctor examines her with an openly worried expression on his face. Mary's in what he's going to call a fugue state—like being part of the way into a coma—and she's never going to surface from it. The doctor—Dr. Bartram, for the record—tries to arrange for an ambulance to transfer her to one of the local hospitals, but all at once, the ambulances are very busy. By the time he considers driving her himself, the police will have told everyone to stay off the roads. When those same police start stumbling through the front doors with wounds of their own for the doc to treat, Mary will be placed on a cot in one of the hallways and left there. Beth will check on her as she's able, which won't be much, because she'll be busy helping the doc and his staff with the injured. After the medical facilities are transferred to St. Pat's church hall, Mary's installed there, given a futon-bed and a molded plastic chair and a garbage bag full of assorted sweatpants, t-shirts, underwear, and socks. Beth tends to her as she can.

Ted doesn't show up looking for his wife. In fairness to him, that's due to his having parked in front of his house about two minutes after Beth sped off with Mary. Once he realized what was taking place, he bolted his car for the house, whose front door he'd noticed open and which had him dreading the worst. The worst met him at the door, in the form of the pair who'd devoured his children, one of whom was holding Brian's stuffed frog, which was dark with blood. You may consider it a kindness that Ted died without seeing what was left of his beloved daughter and son upstairs.

Mary can eat and drink, use the toilet if you take her to it. Speak to her, and she'll bob her head in your direction. There are times, after Beth's sat with her for an hour, maybe read to her from the Bible (which Beth secretly hopes might produce a miraculous cure), the girl looks at Mary half-slumped in her chair, or reclining on her bed, and wonders if Mary isn't lucky to be like this, safe from the chaos that's descended on the world. She has no idea—she can have no idea that deep within Mary's psyche, she's standing at that stove for the ten-thousandth time, watching a pot full of water begin to boil, waiting for her children to start screaming.

(The Stage Manager sighs, looks up, looks down, rubs his hands together half-heartedly, sighs again.)

Stage Manager: I never finished telling you about the town, did I? Not that it makes much difference at this point, but maybe one or two of you are curious.

(Once more, the Stage Manager settles himself on the ground, against the headstone; although he appears to have more trouble finding a comfortable position than previously.)

Stage Manager: All right. What more is there to say about Goodhope Crossing? The longer-term history of the town isn't that much different from any other in this neck of the woods. There were farms around these parts as far back as the Dutch, but Goodhope Crossing, as the name suggests, owes itself to the railroads. In the years after the Civil War, when track was stitching up the country everywhere you looked, three north-south lines and one east-west line met one another right here.

(From the orchestra pit, a quartet of wooden train whistles sound softly.)

Stage Manager: There was a long, low hill to the east of the junction, a stream and some flatter land to the west. The town was plotted on that axis, the poorer folk crowding their small houses together on the hill, the better off setting up Main Street and its larger dwellings on the other side of the stream. From those two locations, the town spread outward, most of the commercial establishments opening on the other side of the hill; while the majority of new homes went up on and just off Main Street. Lot of Irish settled here; Poles and Italians, too. Big Catholic population: the local church, St. Patrick's, started on Main Street and by the turn of the century had moved across the stream to the top of another hill just south of the one most of its parish lived on. St. Pat's was part of the Archdiocese of New York; right before everything fell apart, they were the third or fourth largest congregation in the fold.

Interestingly—you might even say, ironically—enough, pretty much the entire surviving population has relocated to the hill, which remained a location of more… affordable housing. Control the high ground: it's what a military strategist will tell you, and it's a good plan, for zombies as much as anything. Once the half-dozen or so who'd staggered up Concord Street were dealt with, and all the dwellings had been checked and double-checked to be sure they were clear, folks started putting up the best barrier they could as fast as they could around the foot of the hill, tipping over cars; running barbed wire; propping up old boxsprings, mattresses; piling whatever looked as if it might hold a walking corpse at bay long enough for you to have a clear shot at it: sofas, bureaus, bookcases, china cabinets.

(From either side of the theater, the sounds of men and women grunting, furniture creaking atop other furniture.)

Stage Manager: Hillary Schwabel, who used to manage the local True Value hardware, strung some wires all the way around what people already had christened the Wall and hooked them to several of her louder alarms; she also hung a dozen motion-detector lights from trees and houses next to the Wall. Things are so sensitive a cat'll trip them, but it beats the alternative. As a rule, zombies travel in numbers; when you see one of them, you see ten, twenty, sometimes as many as fifty, a hundred. A significant percentage of that group is going to be limber enough to make a try at getting past the Wall—and all it takes is for one of them to succeed, grab someone and start biting, for you to want to know they're moving in your direction while they're still a safe distance away. It's another myth that they only, or mostly, move at night. Their eyesight's poor-to-nonexistent—apparently, the ravages death inflicts on the eyes are exacerbated by the process of reanimation. Although they never stop moving completely, if you should have the misfortune to come across them after dark, they're likely to be shuffling their feet, practically standing in place. No, they prefer the light; the dawn pouring through the trees sets them going. A bright day is practically a guarantee you're going to see some of them.

All of that said, a few of them have been known to travel by night, especially if the moon is full. And even inching forward a little bit at a time will bring you somewhere, eventually. Better safe than sorry, right?

Have you noticed how disasters bring out the clichés in droves? Why is that? Is the trite and overused that consoling? Or is it that, even though the brain is short-circuiting, it still wants to grasp what's going on, so it reaches for whatever tools are at hand, no matter how worn and rusted? Or is the language breaking down along with everything else? I've never been what you'd call a poet, but I have always prided myself on my phrasing, on a knack for finding a fit and even memorable form for whatever sentiment I'm attempting to convey. Lately, though—lately, I swear I sound more and more like a parody of a Good Ole Boy, your folksy uncle with his bucket of country wisdom.

Nor is that the worst. Before everything went down the crapper, one of my—you might say duties; although I considered it more a responsibility, if that distinction means anything to you—anyway, one of the things I did was to help those who'd shuffled off their mortal coils come to grips with their new condition. Mostly, this meant talking with them, taking them for a last look at their loved ones, about what you'd expect. In a few cases, I let them have one of their days over again, which, knowing what they knew now, tended to be a more unhappy experience than they'd anticipated. Even after I'd spoken to them, showed them what I could, there were a few who refused to walk down the long dark hall to join the ranks of those who'd gone before, who insisted on remaining in their house, or at the spot they'd ceased breathing, which was a shame, but was allowed for.

Once the dead started to rise, though—for the one thing, death no longer separated what lasted from what didn't; instead, the two remained bound together as the one began its new existence. For another thing, the destruction of that second life—or un-life—didn't allow matters to proceed on their natural course. Instead... well, maybe you want to see for yourselves.

(The theater's lights come on. Their harsh brightness reveals the center aisle, side aisles, front, and rear of the theater crowded with figures—with zombies, it appears, since the men, women, and children surrounding the audience bear the familiar signs of decay. Whatever shock and fear the appearance of so many of them in such proximity engenders, however, is gradually tempered by their complete lack of movement. Indeed, with the exception of one figure shuffling its way from the very back of the theater up the center aisle, the apparent zombies might as well be mannequins.)

Stage Manager: Being chained to that body as it stumbles along in the single-minded pursuit of flesh, as it finds and kills and consumes that flesh—it isn't good for the other part, for what I call the spark—it twists it, warps it, so that when it's cut loose, this is how it appears. Mostly. A few—I haven't worked out the exact numbers, but it's something on the order of one in a thousand, fifteen hundred—they show up hostile, violent, as if what they last were in life has followed them across its borders. There's no talking to them, let alone reasoning with them. I'm not certain what they could do to me—there've been rumors through the grapevine, but you know how that it is—but I'm not inclined to find out.

(The Stage Manager rises to his feet, withdrawing his revolver from its shoulder holster on the way. In a continuous motion, he extends his arm, sights along the long barrel of the gun, and squeezes the trigger. The gun's BOOM stuns the air; the young man in the brown three-piece suit who is approximately halfway to the stage jerks as the back of his head detonates in a surprisingly solid clump. The young man falls against one of the motionless forms in the aisle, an old woman wearing a blue dress and a knitted white pullover, who barely moves as he slides down her to the floor. The Stage Manager maintains his aim at the young man for five seconds, then levels the gun and sweeps it across the theater. It is difficult to ascertain whether his eye is on the figures in the aisle, the audience in their seats, or both. Unable to locate any further threats, he re-holsters the pistol. He remains standing.)

Stage Manager: That's—there's nothing else I can do. It means—I don't like thinking about what it means. It's a step up from what a fellow like that was, but—it's not a part of the job I relish. Could be, it would be a service to the rest of these folks, but I haven't got the stomach for it.

(The Stage Manager lowers himself to the ground. The lights dim but not all the way. The forms in the aisles remain where they are.)

Stage Manager: Once in a while—it's less and less, but it still happens—a regular person finds their way here. That was how I had the chance to talk with Billy Joe Royale, he-of-the-famous-homemade-napalm. I'd witnessed his handiwork in action—must have been the day after the day after that truckload of zombies parked in the middle of Mary Phillips's neighborhood. The number of zombies had increased exponentially; the cops had been overrun in most places; the National Guard who were supposed to be on their way remained an unfulfilled promise. Those who could had retreated to the parking lot of St. Pat's, which, since the hill hadn't yet been fortified, looked to be the most defensible position. I reckon it was, at that. There wasn't time for much in the way of barriers or booby-traps, but those men and women—there were forty-six of them—did what they could.

(From the right and left of the theater comes a cacophony of gunfire; of voices shouting defiance, instructions, obscenity, encouragement; of screams. It is underscored by a frenzied, atonal sawing of the violins. It subsides as the Stage Manager continues to speak, but remains faintly audible.)

Stage Manager: In the end, though, no matter how much ammunition you have, if the zombies have sufficient numbers, there's little you can hope for aside from escaping to fight another day. These folks couldn't expect that much: they'd backed themselves against the church's north wall, and the zombies were crowding the remaining three sides.

Exactly how Billy Joe succeeded in evading the zombies, finding his way inside St. Pat's, climbing up the bell-tower, and shimming out onto the roof—all the while carrying a large cloth laundry-bag of three-liter soda bottles full of an extremely volatile mixture—I'd like to take credit for it, but I was down below, all my attention focused on the by-now forty-two defenders staging what I was sure was their updated Alamo. They were aiming to die bravely, and I was not about to look away from that. When the first of Billy Joe's soda-bottle-bombs landed, no one, myself included, knew what had just taken place. About twenty feet back into the zombies' ranks, there was a flash and a clap and an eruption of heavy black smoke. Something had exploded, but none of the men and women could say what or why. When the second, third, fourth, and fifth bombs struck in an arc to either side of the first, and smoke was churning up into the air, and the smell of dead skin and muscle barbecuing was suddenly in everyone's nostrils, it was clear the cavalry had arrived. A couple of guys looked around, expecting a Humvee with a grenade-launcher on top, or an attack helicopter whose approach had been masked by the noise of the fighting. The rest were busy taking advantage of the wall of fire the bombs had created, which separated the zombies on this side of it from those on the other, reducing their numbers from who-could-count-how-many to a more manageable thirty or forty. While they worked on clearing the zombies closest to them, Billy Joe continued to lob bottle after bottle of his fiery concoction, dropping some of them into the thick of the zombies, holding onto others almost too long, so that they detonated over the zombies, literally raining fire down on their heads. He'd stuffed twenty-three bottles into that laundry bag, and he threw all but one of them.

(The din of the battle rises again, accompanied by the pops of a drumstick tapping on a drum, and the lower thrum of viols being plucked. The pops increase, the thrums increase, then the violins scream an interruption and all noise stops.)

Stage Manager: That last bomb was what killed him, a single-serve Coke bottle that remained in his hand past the point of safety. It blew off his right arm to the elbow and hurled him flaming from the roof. He didn't survive the fall, which was just as well, since his burning corpse was shot by roughly half the people he'd saved. Stupid, but understandable, I guess.

He took longer to show up than I'd anticipated, the better part of a day, during which his identity and his actions had been discovered, along with the two hundred additional bottles of napalm standing row after row in his parents' basement. Unfortunately, he hadn't seen fit to leave the formula, but those bombs were a big downpayment on buying those among the living sufficient time to move to the hill and begin the process of securing it. There've been a couple of tries at duplicating his secret mix, neither of which ended well.

(From the rear of the theater, the faint *crump* of explosions.)

Stage Manager: As for Billy Joe…

(Stage left, a stage light pops on, throwing a dim yellow glow over one of the tombstones and BILLY JOE ROYALE, who is a very young sixteen, his face struggling with its acne, a few longish hairs trying to play a goatee on his chin. He is dressed in an oversized blue New York Giants shirt, baggy jeans, and white sneakers. A backwards baseball cap lifts the blond hair from his forehead, which emphasizes the surprise smoothing his features. He hooks his thumbs in the pockets of his jeans in what must be an effort at appearing calm, cool. He sees the Stage Manager and nods at him. The bill of the Stage Manager's hat tilts in reply.)

Billy Joe: So are you, like, him?

Stage Manager: Who is that?

Billy Joe: You know—God.

Stage Manager: I'm afraid not.

Billy Joe: Oh. *Oh*. You aren't—

Stage Manager: I'm more of a minor functionary.

Billy Joe: What, is that some kinda angel or something?

Stage Manager: No. I'm—I meet people when they show up here, help them find their bearings. Then I send them on their way.

Billy Joe: Like a tour guide, one of those hospitality guys.

Stage Manager: Close enough.

Billy Joe: Where am I headed?

(The Stage Manager points stage right.)

Stage Manager: You see that hall over there?

Billy Joe: That looks pretty dark. I thought it was supposed to be all bright and shit.

Stage Manager: No, that's just an effect produced by the cells in your eyes dying.

Billy Joe: Oh. Where does it go?

Stage Manager: Where everyone else has gone.

(Billy Joe notices the figures in the aisles. He nods at them.)

Billy Joe: What about them? Are they—

Stage Manager: Yes.

Billy Joe: Shouldn't they be moving down that hall, too?

Stage Manager: They should.

Billy Joe: So why aren't they?

Stage Manager: I'm not sure. It's got something to do with what's going on—where you came from.

Billy Joe: These guys were like, the living dead?

Stage Manager: That's right.

Billy Joe: Wild. Any of them try to eat you?

Stage Manager: A couple.

Billy Joe: What'd you do?

Stage Manager: I shot them in the head.

Billy Joe: Huh. That work, here?

Stage Manager: It seemed to do the trick.

Billy Joe: It's just, I thought, you know, being where we are and all—

Stage Manager: Some things aren't all that much different. You'd be surprised.

Billy Joe: I guess so. Do you know, like, what caused all this shit—I mean, what brought all those guys back from the dead? Because Rob—he's this friend of mine—he was—anyway, Rob was like, It's all a big government conspiracy, and I was like, That's ridiculous: if it's a government conspiracy, why did it start in like, fucking India? And Rob—

Stage Manager: I don't know. I don't know what started it; I don't know what it is.

Billy Joe: Really?

Stage Manager: Really.

Billy Joe: Shit.

Stage Manager: Sorry.

Billy Joe: Does anyone?

Stage Manager: What do you mean?

Billy Joe: Does anyone know what's going on?

Stage Manager: Not that I've heard.

Billy Joe: Oh.

Stage Manager: Look—maybe there's someplace you'd like to see, someplace you'd like to go…

Billy Joe: Nah, I'm good.

Stage Manager: Are you sure there's nowhere? Your house, school—

Billy Joe: No, no—I mean, thanks and all, but—it's cool.

Stage Manager: All right; if you're sure.

Billy Joe: So… that's it?

Stage Manager: What else would you like?

Billy Joe: I don't know. Isn't there supposed to be some kinda book, you know, like a record of all the shit I've done?

Stage Manager: That's Santa Claus. Sorry—no, there's nothing like that. All the record you have of what you've done is what you can say about it.

Billy Joe: Huh. So what's it like?

Stage Manager: What's what like?

Billy Joe: Wherever that hall leads.

Stage Manager: Quiet.

Billy Joe: Oh.

(Billy Joe crosses the stage slowly, passing behind the Stage Manager, until he stands as far stage right as he can without leaving the stage.)

Billy Joe: That's it.

Stage Manager: It is.

Billy Joe: Well, no point in delaying the inevitable, right?

Stage Manager: I suppose not.

Billy Joe: Can you tell me one thing—before I go, can you answer one question?

Stage Manager: I can try.

Billy Joe: We're fucked, aren't we?

(The Stage Manager pauses, as if weighing his words.)

Stage Manager: There's always a chance—I realize how that sounds, but there's just enough truth left in it to make it worth saying. Things could turn around. Someone could discover a cure. Whatever's driving the zombies could die out—hell, it isn't even winter yet. A couple weeks of freezing temperatures could thin their numbers significantly. Or someone could be resistant to their bite, to the infection. With six-plus billion people on the planet, you figure there has to be one person it doesn't affect...

Billy Joe: Do you believe any of that shit?

Stage Manager: No.

Billy Joe: Yeah.

(He exits, stage right.)

Stage Manager: Understand, it's not that I don't want to believe any of it. I want to believe all of it. All of that shit, as my young friend would say. But doing so has traveled past the point of hard to the point of no return. No, this—this, I fear is how the day runs down for the human race. It's how *Homo sapiens sapiens* departs the scene, carried off a bite at a time in the teeth of the undead. If there weren't so much pain, so much suffering in the process, you could almost see the humor in it. This is the way the world ends, not with a bang, and not with a whimper, but with the bleak gusto of a low-budget horror movie.

(The Stage Manager reaches for his flashlight, which he shuts off and takes with him as he rises from his seat and walks to the back of the stage. He is visible against the bulk of the willow, and then the shadows have him. The theater lights come up, revealing the aisles still full of the dead. Men, women, old, young, most wearing their causes of their several demises, they encompass the audience, and do not move.)

For Fiona, and with thanks to John Joseph Adams.

ACKNOWLEDGMENTS

Many thanks to the following:

Jeremy Lassen and Jason Williams at Night Shade Books, for giving me another shot at this anthology racket, and for taking a chance on me in the first place. Also, to Ross Lockhart at Night Shade, who probably never gets enough credit, and to Marty Halpern for making us all look better by catching all the pesky errors that crept into the manuscript.

David Palumbo, for quite possibly the best zombie cover art ever.

Gordon Van Gelder: I'll probably be thanking him in every anthology I edit from here until eternity. I've said it before, but I'll say it again: He gave me my start in this field and taught me everything I know. Thanks again, boss.

My agent Jenny Rappaport, who is helping me take over the world, one anthology at a time.

Kris Dikeman, for helping me sort through the vast hordes of zombie fiction and for providing me a highly valuable second opinion when needed. On the brainoriffic scale, she gets five-out-of-five brains.

My friends Jack Kincaid and Jeremy Tolbert, who both listened to me blather on about zombies and served as beta-readers for my writing contributions to the book. And, of course, for our continuing years of friendship. If I ever turn into a zombie, I'll eat you guys last.

My mom, for being my biggest cheerleader.

All of the other kindly folks who assisted me in some way during the editorial process: Mickey Choate, Douglas Cohen, Richard Curtis, Ellen Datlow, Paula Guran, Andy Hine, Betty Russo, Bill Schafer, Claire Sclater, Nancy Stauffer, Kari Torson, Jeff VanderMeer, Renee Zuckerbrot, everyone who dropped suggestions into my zombie fiction database, and any others I may have forgotten.

The readers and reviewers who loved my first anthology, *Wastelands: Stories of the Apocalypse*, making it possible for me to do another.

And last, but certainly not least: a big thanks to all of the authors who appear in this anthology.

Night Shade Books Is an Independent Publisher of Quality SF, Fantasy and Horror

WASTELANDS

STORIES OF
THE APOCALYPSE

FEATURING

OCTAVIA E. BUTLER   GEORGE R.R. MARTIN
ORSON SCOTT CARD   STEPHEN KING
JONATHAN LETHEM   GENE WOLFE
AND MANY OTHERS

Edited by John Joseph Adams

ISBN 978-1-59780-105-8, Trade Paperback; $15.95

Famine, Death, War, and Pestilence: The Four Horsemen of the Apocalypse, the harbingers of Armageddon - these are our guides through the Wastelands.

Gathering together the best post-apocalyptic literature of the last two decades from many of today's most renowned authors of speculative fiction, including George R.R. Martin, Gene Wolfe, Orson Scott Card, Carol Emshwiller, Jonathan Lethem, Octavia E. Butler, and Stephen King, Wastelands explores the scientific, psychological, and philosophical questions of what it means to remain human in the wake of Armageddon. Whether the end of the world comes through nuclear war, ecological disaster, or cosmological cataclysm, these are tales of survivors, in some cases struggling to rebuild the society that was, in others, merely surviving, scrounging for food in depopulated ruins and defending themselves against monsters, mutants, and marauders.

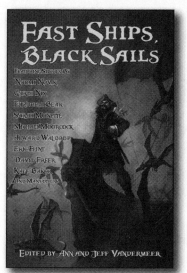
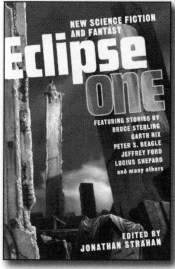

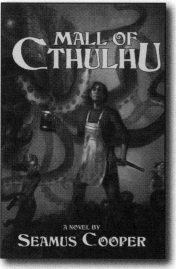

Night Shade Books Is an Independent Publisher of Quality SF, Fantasy and Horror

ISBN 978-1-892389-35-0 , Trade Paperback; $19.95

Lurker in the Lobby: The Guide to Lovecraftian Cinema by John Strysik and Andrew Milgore is the definitive guide to the movies and television inspired by the H. P. Lovecraft, cataloging over 150 feature films, short films, and television programs. It contains extensive stills, pre-production art, and promotional materials, and also features a full index breaking down the works by story, and production year.

In addition to extensive write-ups of individual works, *Lurker in the Lobby* also contains over a twenty interviews with writers, directors, actors and artists, from Roger Corman, John Carpenter, Jeffrey Combs, Guillermo Del Toro Del Toro, Stuart Gordon, Bernie Wrightson, and many others. *Lurker in the Lobby* is the last word on Lovecraftian Cinema. Andrew Milgore is the founder and curator of the annual Lovecraft International Film Festival.

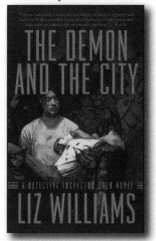

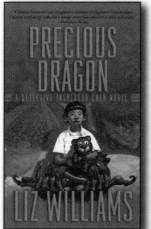

Follow the Continuing Adventures of Inspector Chen, Singapore Three's Premier Supernatural Investigator

John Constantine meets Chow Yun-Fat in this near-future occult thriller. Detective Inspector Chen is the Singapore Three police department's snake agent – that is – the detective in charge of supernatural and mystical investigations.

Chen has several problems: In addition to colleagues who don't trust him and his mystical ways, a patron goddess whom he has offended, and a demonic wife who's tired of staying home alone, he's been paired with one of Hell's own vice officers, Seneschal Zhu Irzh, to investigate the illegal trade in souls.

In *The Demon and the City*, Detective Inspector Chen leaves Singapore Three on long-deserved vacation, Hell's vice-deceive-on-loan, Zhu Irzh finds himself restless and bored. An investigating into the brutal, and seemingly-demonic murder of a beautiful young woman promises to be an interesting distraction.

Inspector Chen returns to Singapore Three to find Zhu Irzh's erratic behavior has placed the demon under suspicion. Tensions flair and the entire city find's itself under siege from otherworldly forces both Heavenly and Hellish in nature.

In *Precious Dragon*, Chen and Zhu are given a major assignment to escort an emissary from heaven on a diplomatic mission to hell. Zhu tries to dodge his demonic family's overtures, but ends up embroiled in hell's political intrigues. At the same time, a young boy born to ghostly parents in Hell is sent to live with his grandmother in Singapore Three. The boy, Precious Dragon, is being chased by Hell's most dangerous creatures and ends up being the key to unlock the mystery that is quickly spiraling out of control. Chen and Zhu find themselves in the middle of a struggle much bigger then they can fully comprehend, and when the dust finally settles, neither heaven nor hell will be the same.

Learn More About These and Other Titles From Night Shade Books At http://www.nightshadebooks.com

JOHN JOSEPH ADAMS is the assistant editor at *The Magazine of Fantasy & Science Fiction*, and has edited the anthologies *Wastelands* and *Seeds of Change*. He has written reviews for *Kirkus Reviews, Publishers Weekly,* and *Orson Scott Card's Intergalactic Medicine Show* and is the print news correspondent for *SCI FI Wire* (the news service of the SCI FI Channel). His non-fiction has also appeared in: *Amazing Stories, The Internet Review of Science Fiction, Locus Magazine, Novel & Short Story Writers Market, Science Fiction Weekly, Shimmer, Strange Horizons, Subterranean Magazine,* and *Writer's Digest.* He received his Bachelor of Arts degree in English from The University of Central Florida in December 2000. He currently lives in New Jersey, and is working on several new anthology projects.